NEW
TOEIC

# 決勝
# 新制多益

## 閱讀6回模擬試題 解析版

作者 ◎ Kim dae Kyun　　譯者 ◎ 林育珊／關亭薇

READING

# 作者序

筆者潛心著筆，將本書出版成冊。為了撰寫出貼近實際測驗的試題，筆者曾多次赴日參加多益測驗，持續致力於新制多益的解題分析。歷經這些過程後，終於完成這套直擊最新命題趨勢的著作。與舊制多益相比，新制多益的整體難度相對提升不少，考生在考前務必要精準掌握出題方向，並勤於練習仿真試題。

根據筆者的透徹分析，新制多益的改制內容與應考對策如下：

**PART 1** 請務必優先熟記高難度單字。在照片題型中，比起人物，將重點擺在事物上更有利於解題。

**PART 2** 切勿在聽完題目的當下，立即選填答案。通常需要經過一番思索，才能找出正確答案。

**PART 3** 為掌握聽力分數的關鍵，請務必充分練習。

**PART 4** 雖與舊制多益的難易度相當，但聽力的語速加快，這一點請特別留意。

筆者親自監聽錄音檔，精選配音員錄製本書。依照多益聽力測驗語速，完成最貼近實際考試的錄音。

**PART 5** 與舊制多益的難易度相當。

**PART 6** 短文填空題的難度提升，請善用本書勤加練習！

**PART 7** 為掌握閱讀分數的關鍵，充分練習本書的仿真試題，方能取得好成績。

筆者報考過230餘次的多益測驗，自詡是擁有最多滿分經驗的最強權威，至今仍持續參加測驗。這14年來在韓國EBS電台《金大鈞TOEIC KING》擔任內容策劃與主講人，節目不僅獲得大眾的認可，更讓我獲得專業主題類別最佳BJ（註：線上節目主持人）的殊榮。除此之外，就讀金大鈞英語學院的學生，也頻頻獲得滿分的佳績。多益滿分不再遙不可及，相信大家也能做到。我保證在本書的幫助下，大家勢必能快速提升多益成績！

歷史，由你來創造。
身為多益界的不敗傳奇，筆者亦將不負眾望，跨出更大的步伐向前邁進。

向上蒼與讀者致上謝意

金大鈞

# 目錄

# 新制多益題型更新重點

## PART 1

|  | 新制多益 | 舊制多益 |
|---|---|---|
| 題型 | 照片描述 | 照片描述 |
| 題數 | 總題數6題 | 總題數10題 |

題型不變，照片描述仍為四個選項。

 題數減少

## PART 2

|  | 新制多益 | 舊制多益 |
|---|---|---|
| 題型 | 應答問題 | 應答問題 |
| 題數 | 總題數25題 | 總題數30題 |

題型不變，應答問題仍為選出適當的選項。

 題數減少

## PART 3

|  | 新制多益 | 舊制多益 |
|---|---|---|
| 題型 | 簡短對話 | 簡短對話 |
| 題數 | 13組對話（每組3題）<br>總題數39題 | 10組對話（每組3題）<br>總題數30題 |

 新增三人對話與圖表題型　 對話和題數增加

## PART 4

|  | 新制多益 | 舊制多益 |
|---|---|---|
| 題型 | 簡短獨白 | 簡短獨白 |
| 題數 | 10組簡短獨白（每組3題）<br>總題數30題 | 10組簡短獨白（每組3題）<br>總題數30題 |

 新增圖表作答題型

# PART 5

|  | 新制多益 | 舊制多益 |
|---|---|---|
| 題型 | 句子填空 | 句子填空 |
| 題數 | 總題數30題 | 總題數40題 |

題型不變，選出適合填入句子中的單字或片語。

 題數減少

# PART 6

|  | 新制多益 | 舊制多益 |
|---|---|---|
| 題型 | 段落填空 | 段落填空 |
| 題數 | 總題數16題 | 總題數12題 |

 新增選一完整句子填入空格　 題數增加

# PART 7

|  | 新制多益 | 舊制多益 |
|---|---|---|
| 題型 | 單篇閱讀 | 單篇閱讀 |
| 題數 | 10篇單篇閱讀<br>每篇2–4題<br>總題數29題 | 9篇單篇閱讀<br>每篇2–5題<br>總題數28題 |
| 題型 | 雙篇閱讀 | 雙篇閱讀 |
| 題數 | 兩組雙篇閱讀<br>每組5題<br>總題數10題 | 四組雙篇閱讀<br>每組5題<br>總題數20題 |
| 題型 | 多篇閱讀 |  |
| 題數 | 三組多篇閱讀<br>每組5題<br>總題數15題 |  |
| 題數 | 總題數54題 | 總題數48題 |

 新增多篇閱讀題型　 題數增加

# 各大考題最新命題趨勢

新制多益的整體難度相對提升，唯有接受這個事實，認真準備才能取得佳績。本書準確分析出題趨勢，完全比照實際測驗，只要充分練習本書的試題，定能勇奪高分！

# PART 1 照片描述 核心攻略

通常只要聽懂**動詞關鍵字**，就能答出大部分的題目，但是仍有不少題目以**高難度單字**和**特殊描寫**命題。在新制多益 PART 1 中，只要聽到 holding、display、casting a shadow（蒙上陰影）、lead to、occupied、unoccupied 這些關鍵字，就是正確選項。然而值得注意的是，你可能會同時聽到**兩個以上**的高難度單字。

**1.**

(A) A woman is holding an oar. 女子拿著一支槳。
(B) A woman is tying a boat to a pier. 女子把小船繫在碼頭邊。
(C) A woman is getting out of the boat. 女子正從小船上下來。
(D) A woman is swimming across a lake. 女子正泳渡一座湖。

**解答** A

第一大題中，只要聽到 holding，就是正確的選項。若同時聽到高難度單字 oar（槳），就能更加肯定它就是正解。雖然 PART 1 中的單字相對容易，但千萬不可小覷，請務必注意單字的發音。vase 通常會唸成 [ves]，但在多益測驗中，若為英國腔，聽起來則像是 [vɑz]。

**2.**

(A) A knife has been placed on the chair. 刀子放在椅子上。

　　➜ 照片中並未出現刀和椅子。

(B) Flowers have been put in vases. 花插在花瓶裡。

　　➜ 這裡的 vases 發音為 [vɑzɪz]（英國腔）。雖然有時會將 vase 唸成 [ves]，但英式唸法
　　　　[vɑz] 通常才是正解，請務必熟記！

(C) A woman is watering some flowers. 一名女子正在澆花。

　　➜ 照片中並未出現人物和動作。

(D) A woman is buying some flowers. 一名女子正在買花。

　　➜ 照片裡看不到人物。

**解答** B

**3.**

(A) People are gathered at the entryway. 人們聚集在入口處。

(B) A door is beneath a staircase. 樓梯下方有一扇門。

(C) A man is repairing the stairs. 一名男子正在整修樓梯。

(D) Some pictures are propped against a wall. 牆邊靠著一些畫。

**解答** B

不同於過往題型，題目當中會出現針對事物的特殊描寫。將特殊描寫設為正解，
已成為一種出題趨勢。

請特別注意 PART 1 的第五、六題，雖然照片中有出現人物，但答案可能是單純
針對事物描寫的選項。

# PART 2 應答問題 核心攻略

眾多考生為 PART 2 苦惱不已。值得注意的是，PART 2 可不只是少了五題這麼簡單而已，命題方式反而變得更加巧妙、難度也隨之提升。所謂的「Read between the lines.」，即「**言外之意**」，將大量出現在考題中，考生必須要聽出背後的含義才能找出答案。碰到此類題型時，在聽完題目後，需要經過一番**思考**，才能挑出正確的答案。只要稍不留神，很容易就錯失下一題的解題機會。請務必勤加練習，熟悉此類題型的模式。

7. **Sales of the newly published books are higher than we expected.**
   新出版的書的銷量比我們預期的還要高。

   (A) We want to hire her. 我們想僱用她。

   → hire 僅與 higher 的發音相近，為錯誤選項。

   (B) I know they are very popular. 我知道它們很暢銷。

   → 為最適當的答案，表示「很暢銷」。

   (C) What is the bottom line? 主要重點是什麼？

   解答 B

8. **How will the new members be selected?**
   新成員會怎麼選出來？

   (A) They've already been chosen. 已經選出來了。

   → selected 可替換成 chosen，為正確答案。

   (B) Jane has a monthly membership. 珍持有月會員資格。

   (C) Is it on the third floor? 它在三樓嗎？

   → 不符合單複數一致性（members 為複數，it 為單數），為錯誤選項。

   解答 A

9. **Why don't you sign up for the TOEIC workshop with us?**
   你何不和我們一起報名多益工作坊？

   (A) I don't have time to go. 我沒空去。

   → 極為明確的回答，為正確答案。

   (B) There is a shop around the corner. 有一間店在轉角處。

   → shop 僅與 workshop 的發音相近，為錯誤選項。

   (C) At the auditorium. 在禮堂。

   解答 A

10. **Have you made any progress on the merger and acquisition meeting?**

併購會議，你們有任何進展嗎？

(A) The company's office. 公司的辦公室。

(B) We're getting together again next Monday. 我們下週一要再聚一次。

→ 表示「之後將繼續進行」的意思，為需要稍微思考一下的選項。

(C) Acquired immune deficiency syndrome. 後天免疫缺乏症候群。

→ acquired 僅與 acquisition 的發音相近，為錯誤選項。

解答 B

11. **What restaurant did you choose to host the retirement party?**

你選擇在哪間餐廳主辦退休歡送會？

(A) He said he will retire next year. 他說他明年退休。

(B) Mark is the host of the show. 馬克是活動的主持人。

(C) I'm still waiting for some price quotes. 我還在等一些報價。

→ 請熟記 quote 除了有「引用」的意思之外，作為名詞也有「報價」的意思。
quote = estimate

解答 C

12. **Didn't Susan already fill an order for this?**

蘇珊沒有填這個的訂單嗎？

(A) That was for December. 那是12月的事了。

→ 需要歷經一番思考才能解出的高難度題目。當出現像(A)這類的選項時，請先標記三角形符號，之後回過頭再聽一次。

(B) Fill her up with unleaded, please. 無鉛加滿，麻煩你。

→ 當出現和題目相同的單字 fill 時，不是答案的可能性極高。

(C) In chronological order. 照時間順序排列。

→ order 也是重複出現的單字，不是答案的可能性極高。

解答 A

# PART 3 簡短對話 核心攻略

PART 3 不僅對話的**篇幅較長**，特別要注意的是對話**語速也加快了**。從第32題開始，你將聽到語速極快的澳洲口音，而實際測驗中的語速也非常地快，請務必集中精神仔細聆聽。**詢問句意**為何的題目，大多屬於高難度命題，請利用本教材勤加練習！例如：對話中出現「Well, that's a good question.」且題目詢問本句句意為何時，這句話的意思並非是指「這真是個好問題。」，而是「He cannot provide the answer. (不太清楚，無法回答。)」的意思。

圖表類題型的難度則不如想像中困難。

PART 3 為**掌握聽力分數的關鍵**，同時也是題數最多 (39題)、難度較高的大題，請務必好好準備。

# PART 4 簡短獨白 核心攻略

PART 4 的難易度與舊制多益相當。在 PART 3 和 PART 4 的命題部分，解題線索不會只放在一個句子裡面，而是要聽懂兩三個句子後，才能找出答案。PART 4 的圖表類題型也是相對容易的部分。

經分析 PART 3 和 PART 4 的答案後，發現**不太會連續出現三次相同的答案**，也就是幾乎不太可能出現像是 AAA、BBB、CCC、DDD 這樣的答案。因此當你沒聽清楚題目時，不要重複選擇和前一題相同的答案，而是改選其他選項，如此一來猜中答案的機率相對較高，請務必牢記這個小訣竅。

# PART 5 句子填空 核心攻略

與舊制多益相比，PART 5 的總題數減少了 10 題，難易度不變，因此只要依照過往的準備方式來解題即可。不過偶爾也會出現一些容易誤答的題目。例如：片語 be selective about，正確答案應為 selective（挑剔的、有選擇性的），但選項中會出現 rigorous（嚴格的）作為出題陷阱來誤導你。碰到這類題目時，請務必好好**觀察放入句中的單字是否適當**。

PART 5 會因為每個月考試的難易度而有所差異，讓我們一起挑出難度偏高的題型吧！

**101.** Tina is one of the most popular musical artists in the world, ------- only Mozart in record sales.

(A) except
(B) into
(C) from
(D) behind

解答 D

本題必須先釐清句意後，才能正確解答。緹娜是位國際級的音樂家，專輯銷量排名第二，僅次於莫札特。這是很多考生都會答錯的題型，請仔細檢視一遍。

中譯 緹娜是位國際知名的音樂家，專輯銷量僅次於莫札特。

**102.** This year's Kinglish Conference will be held in Seoul, though it has ------- alternated between Tokyo and San Francisco.

(A) traditionally
(B) abruptly
(C) exactly
(D) necessarily

解答 A

本題要從選項中選出最適當的副詞。每次考試都會出現這類題型，難度不亞於上方的範例，請務必多加留意。

中譯 雖然金英大會歷來都是在東京和舊金山輪流舉行，但今年將在首爾舉辦。

**103.** As they had with the first, organizers of Kinglish Conference ------- managed to find an alternative speaker for the second canceled seminar.

(A) much
(B) excessively
(C) concurrently
(D) likewise

解答 D

本題要從選項中選出最適當的副詞。

中譯 如同上一個場次那般，金英大會主辦方比照辦理，設法為先前取消的第二場研討會找了另一位講師替代。

**104.** We should know that the terms are subject to change ------- when oil prices rise or fall.

(A) heavily
(B) quarterly
(C) still
(D) nearby

解答 B

請先掌握文意，才能找出正確答案。本句的文意為：「條款會隨著季度改變」。

中譯 我們都應該知道，每當油價漲跌時，每季的條款也應隨之調整。

**105.** ------- the world's tallest building was completed, HaJin and Tina Ltd. had already begun designing a taller one.

(A) By the time
(B) Whenever
(C) If
(D) Because

解答 A

屬於過去完成式的考題。經常以過去完成式和未來完成式來命題。

By the time＋主詞＋過去式, 主詞＋had p.p.

By the time＋主詞＋現在式, 主詞＋will have p.p.

中譯 當世界最高的建築完工時，哈金與緹娜公司已經在著手設計更高的建築了。

# PART 6 段落填空 核心攻略

PART 6 最難的地方在於要從選項（四個句子）中選出適當的句子填入空格中。這部分為新增加的題型，不僅要花費較多時間解題，平時也應在如何**掌握前後文意**上，下一番功夫。請利用本書徹底釐清觀念，並好好練習本大題的題型！

PART 6 會因每個月考試的難易度而有所差異，難易度較不固定，請務必勤加演練。

# PART 7 單／雙／多篇閱讀 核心攻略

最近總是聽到許多人談論 PART 7 的難度很高。PART 7 的總題數增加為 54 題,除了要花費很多時間解題之外,就連題目本身也不太容易理解。如果說 PART 3 是掌握聽力分數的關鍵,那麼 PART 7 就是**掌握閱讀分數的關鍵**。在舊制多益測驗中,原本可以輕鬆解題過關的短文閱讀,難度也大幅提升。而雙篇閱讀和多篇閱讀,也有逐漸變難的趨勢,建議大家可以利用本書精選的試題反覆演練。

另外,考生在寫到第 196–200 題時,常因解題時間不夠,隨便亂猜答案。當各位遇到這種狀況時,請特別留意 ABCD 答案的分配比例都是相同的!從開始實行新制多益測驗,一直到最近本書準備出版之際,我分析了這段期間內 PART 7 中 196–200 題的正確選項後發現:答案為 A 的次數為 18 次;答案為 B 的次數為 18 次;答案為 C 的次數為18次;答案為 D 的次數為 17 次,**ABCD 選項為答案的比例幾乎均等**。因此考生若碰上 PART 7 的作答時間不足,必須猜答案時,請務必分散風險作答。在此提醒,此技巧僅作為解題的輔助手段,希望大家還是以全力以赴解題為優先。

在 PART 7 中,同義詞替換的難度也逐漸提升。例如 retain 這個字最常用的意思為「留存 (to keep possession of)」或是「保持」。

例:**They insisted on retaining old customs.**
　　他們堅持沿用舊制。

但是你知道 retain 其實也有依合約「聘僱」某人從事有酬工作的意思嗎?
舉例而言:retain a lawyer 意思就是「聘請法律顧問」。

例1:**The team failed to retain him, and he became a free agent.**
　　那支球隊無法和他續約,於是他成為自由球員。

例2:**They have decided to retain a firm to conduct a survey.**
　　他們決定僱用一間公司來執行調查。

例3:**You may need to retain an attorney.**
　　你可能需要聘請律師。

最近在多益閱讀題中,改以 contract「依合約聘僱」的近義詞 retain 出題,讓眾多考生驚慌失措。這個用法甚至是英英字典裡的最後一個意思。因此當你在複習已經熟悉的單字時,請務必確認這個單字是否還有其他意思,並透過例句來學習,最重要的就是保持學習態度!

做完本書所有試題後,請反覆練習,重點在於**充分理解**所有例句,並維持**做筆記**的習慣。

七大攻略讀熟後,請翻開第一回擬真試題,實際測驗看看吧!

# 多益權威完美重現實戰考題

**101.** All employees will receive ------- letters and severance pay upon termination of employment.
(A) recommends
(B) recommendation
(C) recommended
(D) recommending

**102.** Mr. Stevens picked up some new supplies for the office ------- Stationery and Paper World.
(A) but
(B) as
(C) at
(D) after

**103.** ------- needs to come and repair the photocopier as soon as possible.
(A) Someone
(B) Us
(C) They
(D) Any

**104.** The company's new software is designed to update to the most recent version -------.
(A) automate
(B) automatic
(C) automated
(D) automatically

### 百分百擬真試題

試題完全比照新制多益出題趨勢；寫完全書共六回題本並讀懂解析，必能輕鬆掌握新制多益答題技巧！

# 多益權威完美解析

---

史蒂文斯先生在「文具與紙
的世界」為公司挑了一些新
用品。

**字彙**
supplies 用品
stationery 文具

102　Mr. Stevens picked up some new supplies for the office _____ Stationery and Paper World.
　(A) but　　　　　　　(B) as
　(C) at*　　　　　　　(D) after

本題要找出適當的介系詞。空格後方為購買用品的地點：文具與紙的世界 (Stationery and Paper World)，因此答案選 (C) at，意思為「在……」，才符合句意。在多益測驗中，常常出現以「We + at + 公司名稱」作為主詞的句子。

## 1. 題目原文加詳盡解析，解題重點一網打盡

題目與中譯左右對照，並附詳解，確實理解每題關鍵線索與陷阱！

---

130　The marketing department arranged to have weekly meetings to ensure a _____ effort is made on the new project.
　(A) mundane　　　　(B) transitional
　(C) reduced　　　　(D) concentrated*

行銷部門安排了週會的舉行，以確保大家在新專案上全力以赴。

**字彙**
arrange 安排
weekly 每週的
ensure 確保；保證
effort 努力

「每週都要開會的原因」應為「確保在新專案上全力以赴」語意上較為完整，因此答案為 (D)。(A) 中的 mundane 為高難度單字，幾乎未曾出現在以往的多益測驗中，但在最近的考題中，卻出現了這樣的單字。

* mundane 世俗的、平凡的　transitional 轉變的，過渡的
　reduced 減少的　　concentrated 全力以赴的

* 名詞 effort 的相關用法：
make an effort 努力
in an effort to 為……而努力去
a joint/group effort 共同合作
a concerted effort 齊心協力

## 2. 完美解題，瞄準最新出題方向

詳細解說新制多益命題趨勢以及與舊制多益之間的細微差異。

---

156　What is mentioned about fingerprint scanning technology?
　(A) It is purchased on a weekly basis.
　(B) It is one of Aspire's unique services.
　(C) It can be purchased for an extra fee.*
　(D) It can be added to an account by phone.

文中提到何者與指紋掃描技
術有關？
(A) 以每週支付方式購買。
(B) 需佩公司獨特的服務之一。
(C) 可以額外費用購買。
(D) 可以電話告知方式加入帳戶中。

**字彙**
unique 獨特的
extra 額外的
account 帳戶

閱讀題目時，請特別留意關鍵字 fingerprint scanning technology。第二段第四項中寫道：「fingerprint scanning technology for all entrances (additional charges will apply)」，表示要另外付費購買，因此答案為 (C)。在 Part 7 中，線索常出現在括號 ()、星號 * 或是 Note 當中。

* 答案改寫：additional → extra
　　　　　　charge → fee

221

## 3. 單字替換用法一手掌握

提供例題內重點單字「答案改寫」的用法，學會「換句話說」之答題邏輯的同時，還能同步擴充同義字彙量，一舉數得！

---

**字彙**
policy 保險單
account 帳戶
access 取得；進入
insurance 保險
familiarize 使熟悉
feature 特點
additional 更多的；額外的
payment 付款；款項
method 方式
receipt 收據
security 安全
timed 定時的
sensitive 機密的

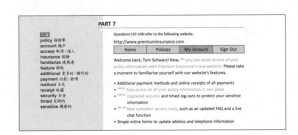

**PART 7**

Questions 147-148 refer to the following website.

http://www.premiuminsurance.com

| Home | Policies | My Account | Sign Out |

Welcome back, Tom Schwarz! Now, [147] you can easily access all your policy information with Premium Insurance's new website. **Please take a moment to familiarize yourself with our website's features.**

* Additional payment methods and online receipts of all payments
* [148] Easy access to all your policy information in one place
* [148] Upgraded security and timed log-outs to protect your sensitive information
* [148] New customer service tools, such as an updated FAQ and a live chat function
* Simple online forms to update address and telephone information

## 4. 相關詞彙補充，學習效率再加乘

補充與題目相關的字詞，學會一題等於背完5-10個單字，考前衝刺事半功倍！

---

105　The new policies are designed to curb lateness and _____ employee accountability.
　(A) promote*　　　　(B) declare
　(C) obtain　　　　　(D) benefit

新政策訂定的目的是要通
止遲到及提升員工責任感。

ACTUAL TEST　1

**字彙**
policy 政策
curb 遏止，控制
lateness 遲到
accountability 負有責任

PART 5

根據句意，訂定政策的目的在於「遏止遲到」和「提升員工責任感」，因此答案為 (A)。

* promote 提升；促進　declare 聲明　obtain 獲得　benefit 有益於

## 5. 字彙標示說明

**字彙** 表題目字彙
* 表 Parts 5、6 選項字彙

ACTUAL TEST

1

## READING TEST

In the Reading Test, you will read a variety of texts and answer several different types of reading comprehension questions. The entire Reading test will last 75 minutes. There are three parts, and directions are given for each part. You are encouraged to answer as many questions as possible within the time allowed.

You must mark your answers on the separate answer sheet. Do not write your answers in your test book.

## PART 5

**Directions:** A word or phrase is missing in each of the sentences below. Four answer choices are given below each sentence. Select the best answer to complete the sentence. Then mark the letter (A), (B), (C), or (D) on your answer sheet.

**101.** All employees will receive ------- letters and severance pay upon termination of employment.

(A) recommends
(B) recommendation
(C) recommended
(D) recommending

**102.** Mr. Stevens picked up some new supplies for the office ------- Stationery and Paper World.

(A) but
(B) as
(C) at
(D) after

**103.** ------- needs to come and repair the photocopier as soon as possible.

(A) Someone
(B) Us
(C) They
(D) Any

**104.** The company's new software is designed to update to the most recent version -------.

(A) automate
(B) automatic
(C) automated
(D) automatically

105. The new policies are designed to curb lateness and ------- employee accountability.

(A) promote
(B) declare
(C) obtain
(D) benefit

106. Most employees have cited the positive work ------- as the reason they have remained with the company.

(A) reconstruction
(B) environment
(C) employment
(D) position

107. Martin's Coffee ------- over 300 shops across Canada by next summer.

(A) will have
(B) has
(C) is having
(D) has had

108. This law was passed to protect citizens ------- own and operate small businesses.

(A) for
(B) who
(C) those
(D) as

109. The meeting with our new supplier has been rescheduled for an ------- time on Wednesday.

(A) hardly
(B) comfortably
(C) early
(D) eagerly

110. Haverstock Telephone & Cable has built a ------- as a provider of prompt customer service.

(A) privilege
(B) character
(C) reputation
(D) consequence

111. The employee handbook ------- the proper procedure for handling customer complaints.

(A) outlining
(B) outlines
(C) to outline
(D) is outlined

112. Mr. Randal has decided to install new vending machines in the lounge ------- everyone to use.

(A) if
(B) to
(C) for
(D) until

113. Smith International Trading's department managers ------- conduct employee satisfaction surveys.

(A) lively
(B) harshly
(C) routinely
(D) vastly

114. The consulting firm ------- several procedural changes that would improve the shipping company's efficiency.

(A) proposing
(B) proposed
(C) proposal
(D) proposals

**115.** The main responsibility of the volunteers is to help visitors ------- their way around the exhibition hall.

(A) do
(B) find
(C) put
(D) ask

**116.** Please retain this e-mail as ------- that your payment information has been entered into our system.

(A) confirm
(B) confirmed
(C) confirmable
(D) confirmation

**117.** Ms. Derlago started working at this bank almost a decade ago and has --------- assumed the role of assistant manager.

(A) ever
(B) yet
(C) so
(D) since

**118.** Mr. Barns is attempting to collect several references ------- for gaining employment at the hospital.

(A) required
(B) requiring
(C) requires
(D) will require

**119.** The -------- for building within the city limits are all listed on the city's permit website.

(A) probabilities
(B) allowances
(C) regulations
(D) varieties

**120.** ------- at Austin Tech University is considered the most advanced in the country.

(A) Research
(B) Researchers
(C) Researched
(D) Researches

**121.** Covington Ice Cream attributes its recent surge in sales to the addition of its newest flavor ------- its advertising campaigns.

(A) as for
(B) even so
(C) rather than
(D) after all

**122.** The service at Wallace Limos improved ------- after the customer surveys were conducted.

(A) tightly
(B) markedly
(C) manageably
(D) separately

**123.** These computers are reserved for people searching ------- employment opportunities in downtown London.

(A) for
(B) up
(C) as
(D) to

**124.** Please ensure that you have written all your information -------, as an error could result in a long delay in the process.

(A) affordably
(B) precisely
(C) unitedly
(D) decisively

**125.** June Austin's article on THP Power's expansion plans was very unique due to her ------- as a former employee.

(A) detail
(B) prospect
(C) investment
(D) perspective

**126.** Human resources employees were able to solve the problem among ------- without intervention from the department manager.

(A) themselves
(B) theirs
(C) their
(D) they

**127.** Mr. Brown is ------- when it comes to international company policies, so we had better ask him.

(A) appropriate
(B) knowledgeable
(C) undeveloped
(D) triumphant

**128.** Car insurance claims must be made ------- policy owners receive bills for damages.

(A) as well as
(B) as soon as
(C) in regard to
(D) in addition to

**129.** With such a beautiful beach and huge assortment of art galleries, Adelaine Town is quite a ------- tourist spot.

(A) offering
(B) proposing
(C) promising
(D) identifying

**130.** The marketing department arranged to have weekly meetings to ensure a ------- effort is made on the new project.

(A) mundane
(B) transitional
(C) reduced
(D) concentrated

GO ON TO THE NEXT PAGE

## PART 6

**Directions:** Read the texts that follow. A word, phrase, or sentence is missing in parts of each text. Four answer choices for each question are given below the text. Select the best answer to complete the text. Then mark the letter (A), (B), (C), or (D) on your answer sheet.

**Questions 131-134** refer to the following information.

**Extended Vacations**

Employees who have been with Star Packaging for at least two years may be ____131.____ to receive an additional five days of summer vacation. ____132.____. Department managers will be responsible for reviewing the applications and those ____133.____ who qualify will have their names entered into a lottery system. Those who have been at the company for five years or longer will be given ____134.____, and up to fifteen names will be drawn from the lottery.

131. (A) prominent
 (B) cooperative
 (C) exclusive
 (D) eligible

132. (A) Employees can fill out an application
 and return it to their manager.
 (B) For example, all long-term employees
 will receive additional benefits packages.
 (C) However, competitive salary raises will
 be given to a few deserving employees.
 (D) Management is pleased to announce
 that new employees have been hired.

133. (A) candidates
 (B) awardees
 (C) suppliers
 (D) occupants

134. (A) prefer
 (B) preferred
 (C) preference
 (D) preferential

Questions 135-138 refer to the following notice.

---

**Channel 8 News Turns 60!**

On March 15, Channel 8 News, the city's number one news source, celebrates its sixtieth anniversary. That's six decades of studio and live ___135.___. For well over half a century, we at Channel 8 News ___136.___ our viewers breaking news coverage, insightful commentaries, and wonderful human-interest stories from across the city and region. We would like to invite you, our loyal viewers, to our celebration. On March 15, we will hold an open house from 4:30 P.M. to 6:00 P.M. at our studio on Kingsley Street. Take part in a studio tour and see first-hand what goes on behind the scenes and watch a demonstration of our state-of-the-art broadcasting equipment. ___137.___. There is no charge to attend this event, but you do have to register. We hope to see you all at this ___138.___ occasion.

---

135. (A) concerts
 (B) discussions
 (C) programming
 (D) teaching

136. (A) offers
 (B) offering
 (C) will offer
 (D) have offered

137. (A) The station will remain a vital part of this city for years to come.
 (B) You will even have the chance to meet and talk with our news anchors.
 (C) This celebration will be the third one to take place in March.
 (D) Channel 8 News will be acquired by a national news network in a few months.

138. (A) special
 (B) specialize
 (C) especially
 (D) specialization

Questions 139-142 refer to the following information.

This is just a reminder that residents of Archer Court are required to obtain a permit for any exterior home-improvement projects. Interior changes do not currently need a permit. __139.__, all external jobs, large and small, must be authorized in advance.

In the past, some residents have assumed that their contractors are responsible for arranging permits. __140.__. In truth, property owners must obtain the necessary permits themselves. Building inspectors may visit a site at any time, and if the property owner does not have a permit, fines may be issued.

__141.__ permit laws is an important responsibility of building inspectors. The permit process ensures that all necessary safety standards __142.__, which in turn protects the community from property damages and dangerous hazards.

To view a list of permits that might apply to your project, please visit renviewtown.com/permits.

139. (A) Namely
(B) Similarly
(C) Therefore
(D) However

140. (A) Contractors may charge extra for overtime.
(B) This commonly held belief is actually false.
(C) Most building inspectors also work as contractors.
(D) The cost of the project may increase seasonally.

141. (A) Questioning
(B) Eliminating
(C) Enforcing
(D) Reviewing

142. (A) are met
(B) to meet
(C) meeting
(D) have met

Questions 143-146 refer to the following webpage.

**Star Credit Purchase Points**

Star Credit would like to offer its credit card holders the ___143.___ points program in the world. ___144.___ . Members can even double their points by shopping at any of the two hundred specially ___145.___ stores. Points can be redeemed in exchange for gift cards at any of those two hundred stores. ___146.___ , points can be used on www.travelone.com to book flights and hotel rooms, and rent cars. To apply for Star Credit's points program, simply fill out the following form and click submit.

143. (A) comprehension
     (B) most comprehensive
     (C) comprehensive
     (D) most comprehensively

144. (A) With every purchase you make with your Star Credit Card, you can earn up to 100 points.
     (B) Points can only be used to lower your monthly interest rates on all credit card purchases.
     (C) Program members must not have applied for a Star Credit Card in the past.
     (D) Furthermore, program members can receive in-store discounts on all their purchases.

145. (A) select
     (B) selects
     (C) selected
     (D) selection

146. (A) Therefore
     (B) Regardless
     (C) In addition
     (D) For instance

## PART 7

**Directions:** In this part you will read a selection of texts, such as magazine and newspaper articles, e-mails, and instant messages. Each text or set of texts is followed by several questions. Select the best answer for each question and mark the letter (A), (B), (C), or (D) on your answer sheet.

**Questions 147-148** refer to the following website.

http://www.premiuminsurance.com

| Home | Policies | My Account | Sign Out |

Welcome back, Tom Schwarz! Now, you can easily access all your policy information with Premium Insurance's new website. Please take a moment to familiarize yourself with our website's features.

- Additional payment methods and online receipts of all payments
- Easy access to all your policy information in one place
- Upgraded security and timed log-outs to protect your sensitive information
- New customer service tools, such as an updated FAQ and a live chat function
- Simple online forms to update address and telephone information

**147.** Who most likely is Mr. Schwarz?

(A) An insurance salesman
(B) An insurance customer
(C) A web designer
(D) An insurance claims representative

**148.** What is NOT mentioned as a feature of the new website?

(A) Group insurance applications
(B) New customer service tools
(C) Consolidated information
(D) Improved Internet security

**Questions 149-151** refer to the following information.

---

### Affluence Pharmaceuticals

Manuel Rodriguez
Lead Researcher

A highly sought-after leader in today's pharmaceutical industry, Mr. Rodriquez had overseen all major research projects at Affluence Pharmaceuticals for the last five years. Mr. Rodriguez joined Affluence seven years ago and was quickly recognized for his great talent and vision. He was promoted to lead researcher and has since drastically improved employee productivity by more than 20%.

Mr. Rodriguez has been invited to speak at numerous conferences and was even honored at last year's Pharma Vision Conference as the keynote speaker. He also works as a consultant for Techtron University's medical department where he has contributed to numerous academic projects. Prior to joining Affluence, Mr. Rodriguez immigrated from Mexico and attended Stratford University where he graduated with honors.

---

**149.** What is the purpose of the information?
- (A) To outline a university program
- (B) To announce an employee promotion
- (C) To introduce a company employee
- (D) To celebrate an employee's retirement

**150.** What is NOT indicated about Mr. Rodriguez?
- (A) He is employed as a university professor.
- (B) He previously lived in Mexico.
- (C) He has improved employee performance.
- (D) He is an experienced public speaker.

**151.** What is suggested about Mr. Rodriguez's career?
- (A) He often receives awards for his great work ethic.
- (B) He completed two degrees before he applied for a job.
- (C) He worked as an intern prior to being hired as lead researcher.
- (D) He was not hired as lead researcher at first.

*GO ON TO THE NEXT PAGE*

March 7 — the local mayor's office has just released the details of the Budding Futures Internship Program for Park County students. Led by the program director, Milly Andrews, the program is designed to give senior high school students a taste of what it's like working in a public office. --[1]--.

Mayor Steven Greenhorn announced the internship program last year. "I think it's important to include teenagers in public affairs," he said in an interview. "It may help them decide what course of study they want to pursue in college." --[2]--.

According to the newly released details, Milly Andrews will select fifteen students from fifteen schools across the county. Based on their areas of interest, the chosen students will be assigned various jobs in the mayor's downtown office. --[3]--. The program will last eight weeks during the summer.

Applications for the program will be available on the mayor's website at the beginning of next week. --[4]--. The selected interns will be announced in early May.

**152.** What is suggested about the Budding Futures Internship Program?

(A) It is available nationwide.
(B) It is a brand new program.
(C) It is for university students.
(D) It is led by Steven Greenhorn.

**153.** According to Mr. Greenhorn, what is the main goal of the internship program?

(A) Teaching students about elections
(B) Establishing a community of volunteers
(C) Providing students with well-paying jobs
(D) Guiding students in their future education

**154.** In which of the positions marked [1], [2], [3], and [4] does the following sentence best belong?

"Students are encouraged to collect at least one reference in advance."

(A) [1]
(B) [2]
(C) [3]
(D) [4]

## ASPIRE UNLIMITED

As a client of our firm, you
- have access to around-the-clock surveillance
- pay a reasonable monthly fee with no additional costs
- can improve your office's security needs

We provide
- custom installations of CCTV equipment
- regular maintenance of all cameras and alarm systems
- 24-hour remote monitoring of your office
- fingerprint scanning technology for all entrances (additional charges will apply)
- access to Aspire's website for all your billing needs

**155.** What is one of the services offered by Aspire Unlimited?

(A) Office cleaning
(B) CCTV monitoring
(C) Website development
(D) Heating system maintenance

**156.** What is mentioned about fingerprint scanning technology?

(A) It is purchased on a weekly basis.
(B) It is one of Aspire's unique services.
(C) It can be purchased for an extra fee.
(D) It can be added to an account by phone.

ROUGE TOWNSHIP. March 3 — Rouge Township officials have recently announced a new development proposal for an amusement park that will be located on Rouge Lake's 4000-acre waterfront.

The new amusement park is expected to include numerous rollercoasters, an extensive aquarium, a waterpark, and a pavilion for live music. Several local businesses, such as Rotary Automobiles, Pancake House Restaurants, and Maverick Beverages have agreed to sponsor the park's development.

Following the release of the development proposal, several local activists have expressed concerns about effect the park will have on the waterfront's delicate ecosystem. "We can assure you that all precautions will be taken," Lead Developer, Jan Freedman, said in an interview yesterday. "The park will be located far enough away from the beach and the bike trails that it will have little effect on the surrounding wildlife."

Other Rouge Township residents have expressed excitement about the potential increase in business the new park will bring to the Rouge Lake area.

**157.** What is suggested about Rouge Township?

(A) It currently has a large tourism industry.

(B) It is home to a famous water park.

(C) Some of its residents disagree with the proposal.

(D) Much of the local wildlife is endangered.

**158.** What feature of the amusement park is NOT mentioned?

(A) Its large on-site aquarium

(B) Its location at the waterfront

(C) A place for live performances

(D) The gift shops and kiosks

## Maintenance Services

The maintenance department of Fairsview Condos is available to make routine repairs to your condo and all shared spaces, most of which are available at no charge to residents. The following services are free of charge and must be booked two weeks in advance.

- Bathroom fixtures, such as showerheads, faucets, and toilet parts may be replaced once every two years. Free repairs of any broken components can be arranged once per year.
- Doors and windows, including window screens, will be repaired as needed at any time of the year.
- Fan filters above stoves and smoke detectors can be replaced every six months. Air conditioners are allotted one free cleaning service per year.
- For a full list of services, please visit our website. Reservations can be made by filling out a request form at www.fairsviewcondos.com/maintenance.

**159.** For whom is the information most likely intended?

(A) Real estate agents
(B) Employees at a building management company
(C) Landlords of a retirement home
(D) Residents at a complex

**160.** How often can bathroom fixtures be repaired at no cost?

(A) Once a month
(B) Every six months
(C) Once a year
(D) At any time

**161.** According to the information, how can readers arrange to have something repaired?

(A) By filling out an online form
(B) By calling a department
(C) By speaking to a landlord
(D) By signing up on a sheet

**Questions 162-163** refer to the following text message chain.

**Ron Parks [8:03]:**
Jim, can I get your input on the changes Jennifer asked me to make to tomorrow's presentation?

**Jim Webber [8:05]:**
Sure. What do you need?

**Ron Parks [8:07]:**
Can I e-mail you the new proposal? I've highlighted the changes in red, but I'm not sure if these reflect our full range of advertising services.

**Jim Webber [8:08]:**
I'm afraid not. I'm just about to meet a client for dinner. How about I stop by your hotel room after?

**Ron Parks [8:09]:**
That would be OK. Then I can show you the PowerPoint presentation I've made as well.

**Jim Webber [8:10]:**
OK, great. What room are you in?

**Ron Parks [8:10]:**
Room 506. See you then!

**162.** Who most likely is Mr. Parks?

(A) An advertiser
(B) A hotel receptionist
(C) An art collector
(D) An IT specialist

**163.** At 8:08, what does Mr. Webber most likely mean when he writes, "I'm afraid not"?

(A) He is worried about a presentation.
(B) He doesn't have time to review a document.
(C) He does not agree with some changes.
(D) He did not request the changes to be made.

**Questions 164-167** refer to the following e-mail.

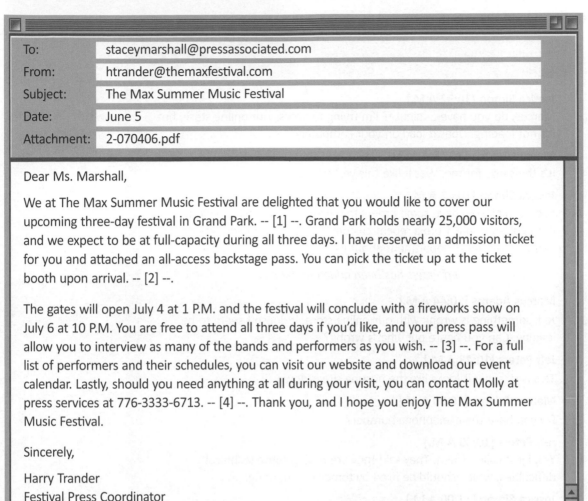

To: staceymarshall@pressassociated.com

From: htrander@themaxfestival.com

Subject: The Max Summer Music Festival

Date: June 5

Attachment: 2-070406.pdf

Dear Ms. Marshall,

We at The Max Summer Music Festival are delighted that you would like to cover our upcoming three-day festival in Grand Park. -- [1] --. Grand Park holds nearly 25,000 visitors, and we expect to be at full-capacity during all three days. I have reserved an admission ticket for you and attached an all-access backstage pass. You can pick the ticket up at the ticket booth upon arrival. -- [2] --.

The gates will open July 4 at 1 P.M. and the festival will conclude with a fireworks show on July 6 at 10 P.M. You are free to attend all three days if you'd like, and your press pass will allow you to interview as many of the bands and performers as you wish. -- [3] --. For a full list of performers and their schedules, you can visit our website and download our event calendar. Lastly, should you need anything at all during your visit, you can contact Molly at press services at 776-3333-6713. -- [4] --. Thank you, and I hope you enjoy The Max Summer Music Festival.

Sincerely,

Harry Trander
Festival Press Coordinator

164. Who most likely is Ms. Marshall?

(A) A customer
(B) A journalist
(C) A band manager
(D) A performer

165. What was sent with the e-mail?

(A) An admission ticket
(B) A parking voucher
(C) A schedule of performances
(D) A backstage press pass

166. According to the e-mail, what is a notable feature of the festival?

(A) It may accommodate more than 25,000 people.
(B) It will include jazz dance performances.
(C) It will end with a special fireworks display.
(D) It may include free camping services.

167. In which of the positions marked [1], [2], [3], and [4] does the following sentence best belong?

"It is our first festival and we have many bands lined up."

(A) [1]
(B) [2]
(C) [3]
(D) [4]

GO ON TO THE NEXT PAGE

Questions 168-171 refer to the following online chat discussion.

**Jessica Simon [10:32 A.M.]**
Marcus, do you have a minute? I'm trying to access our online store, but it's not loading. Does it load on your computer?

**Marcus Adams [10:40 A.M.]**
It's the same for me. Was it like this yesterday?

**Jessica Simon [10:42 A.M.]**
I don't think so. I have some orders that were placed online yesterday. But I got an e-mail from a repeat customer who said our site was down. Can you ask the IT department about it?

*Jeff Peters has been added to the chat.*

**Marcus Adams [10:44 A.M.]**
Jeff, something is wrong with our online store. It doesn't seem to be loading. Can you figure out what's wrong?

**Jeff Peters [10:48 A.M.]**
This is strange. It looks like the hosting site is down.

**Marcus Adams [10:50 A.M.]**
Do you have their telephone number?

**Jeff Peters [10:55 A.M.]**
Yes, I just called them. They said they are having some technical difficulties, which should be fixed by tomorrow morning.

**Jessica Simon [11:00 A.M.]**
OK, I have a meeting with the sales manager shortly. I'll let him know about this problem.

**168.** What problem does Ms. Simon report?

(A) Sales cannot be made online currently.
(B) The online store includes wrong information.
(C) A customer wants to return some items.
(D) A product is no longer listed on the website.

**169.** From whom did Ms. Simon learn about the problem?

(A) A department head
(B) A customer
(C) An IT manager
(D) An assistant

**170.** At 10:50, what does Mr. Adams most likely mean when he writes, "Do you have their telephone number"?

(A) He is requesting some information.
(B) He wants Mr. Peters to call a company.
(C) He would like a directory updated.
(D) He is worried he will get lost.

**171.** What will Ms. Simon most likely do next?

(A) Call some customers
(B) Purchase items online
(C) Attend a meeting
(D) Contact a hosting site

Questions 172-175 refer to the following article.

## Employment Weekly Column
## Job Fairs

Job fairs are a quick and easy way to hire new employees. However, holding a job fair may be a costly event, especially if you're only hiring a few employees. Consider the following advice to determine if holding a job fair is right for your company.

### How many employees are you hiring?

If your company is planning to hire a large group of employees, a job fair might be right for you. Job fairs can bring in a large number of applicants. However, if you're only interested in finding a few new workers, the number of applicants at a job fair may overwhelm human resources departments, making the hiring process even harder.

### Is there a good location to hold the job fair?

High schools and universities are popular places to hold job fairs, but if your company is seeking more experienced candidates, schools are probably not the right place. It is critical to hold the job fair in a place where you can attract suitable employees, such as business conventions. Unfortunately, business conventions are only held at certain times of the year.

### Can you hire employees another way?

Online job advertisement websites have changed the way people search for jobs. Prior to your company's hiring season, human resources staff members may be able to post job openings on numerous websites. This would garner a lot of attention and allow your company to list the experience requirements applicants must meet.

### Is the cost worth it?

Before holding a job fair, consider the cost of the event. You may need to pay to rent a suitable space and would need to provide refreshments and application packages. If your hiring needs could be met by free online websites, a job fair may not be worth it.

---

**172.** What is the article about?

(A) Tips for increasing a worker's productivity
(B) Websites used to hire employees
(C) Methods of increasing the chances of being hired
(D) Strategies for efficient and economical recruitment

**173.** According to the article, what is a good reason to hold a job fair?

(A) To hire specialized workers
(B) To fill a large number of positions
(C) To provide employees with experience
(D) To promote the brand of a company

**174.** The word "critical" in paragraph 3, line 2, is closest in meaning to

(A) urgent
(B) essential
(C) creative
(D) negative

**175.** What is mentioned as an alternative way of finding job candidates?

(A) Advertising in local newspapers
(B) Using employment websites
(C) Holding job fairs at the office
(D) Sending out mass e-mails

GO ON TO THE NEXT PAGE

---

## Publisher Instructs the Next Generation

January 10 — Since his retirement last year, publisher and editor Jim Frank has run the Department of Publishing Studies at Western University. Frank is best known for his role at Maxwell Publishing House where he worked as a senior editor on numerous projects, including the publication of several successful series.

Jim Frank joined Western University as both a department head and a professor. He developed new courses such as E-publishing, Writing for the Web, and International Rights Management. Students who wish to work in the publishing industry as editors, book designers, or literary agents have benefited greatly from his wisdom.

As a result of Frank's hard work, Western University has also founded its first ever publishing internship. Students have been matched with editors, designers, and agents during three-week programs. Additionally, Frank has organized numerous events in which industry professionals have given presentations at the university on various topics. Because of Frank's innovation and connections, the publishing program at Western University has become one of the best in the country.

---

| From: | beth@ricorspublishing.com |
|-------|---------------------------|
| To: | jimfrank@westernuniversity.com |
| Date: | February 25 |
| Subject: | E-Publishing Panel |

Dear Mr. Frank,

Margaret Stevenson is currently doing her internship here at Ricors Publishing House. She mentioned that you're putting together another panel of guest speakers for your students next month. I'd love to join the panel if you still have any openings. As the director of e-publishing here at Ricors, I'm sure I'd be able to give some great information on working in this field.

I will be busy next week attending a conference overseas, but you can leave a message with my assistant and I'll get back to you the following week. My number is 443-223-0911 Ext. 3367.

I look forward to hearing from you.

Sincerely,

Beth Smith,
Director of E-Publishing,
Ricors Publishing House.

**176.** What does the article mainly discuss?

(A) A company's business practices
(B) An editor's career change
(C) A publisher's new series
(D) A student internship program

**177.** What is one contribution Jim Frank has made to the university?

(A) More courses have become available to students.
(B) A student employment website has been developed.
(C) A scholarship foundation has been established.
(D) A computer lab has recently opened.

**178.** Why did Ms. Smith send the e-mail?

(A) She is replying to a phone message.
(B) She would like to join a speaking event.
(C) She is looking for more interns.
(D) She wants to register in a course.

**179.** Who most likely is Ms. Stevenson?

(A) A director at Ricors Publishing House
(B) A student at Western University
(C) A guest speaker in a publishing course
(D) A former editor at Maxwell Publishing House

**180.** What does Ms. Smith say about her schedule?

(A) She can reschedule her meetings.
(B) She is not available for the panel in March.
(C) She can be reached only during the day.
(D) She will be away on business next week.

**MEMO**
**Free Cloud Services**

As you know, Roth Computer Sales has recently partnered with L&B Tech to improve our company's efficiency and file storage. In order to make saving and sharing files easier, we plan to install L&B's Cloud Software program on all our systems.

L&B's Cloud Software allows employees to store files of any size without taking up too much computer memory. Employees can easily send large files in seconds without worrying about slow upload speeds. Additionally, employees who bring their company laptops on business trips will be able to access their files remotely. Furthermore, L&B Cloud Software is extremely secure, so employees can rest assured that any sensitive files will be safe.

To use this new software, simply complete the setup, register with your company e-mail, and start storing and sending files. The service will be available on April 10 at 9 A.M. If you have any questions or concerns about setting up or using the new software, please contact Michael Brown in the IT Department at extension 3342 or by e-mail at michaelbrown@rothcomputers.com.

| To: | michaelbrown@rothcomputers.com |
| --- | --- |
| From: | sandrabell@rothcomputers.com |
| Date: | April 12 |
| Subject: | Cloud Software |

Dear Mr. Brown,

I tried calling you at your extension, but you did not answer. I'm writing to request assistance with the new L&B Cloud Software. I set up my account on the first day the service was available, but today I was unable to find any of the files in my account. It seems that all of the files I uploaded have been deleted, as my account is empty. Since these files include very important sales figures from last quarter, I really need to access them immediately. Can you give me an idea about how to recover these files? It would be great if you could stop by my office sometime today.

Sandra Bell

**181.** What is the purpose of the memo?

(A) To announce a change in a policy
(B) To remind employees to back up computers
(C) To give information about a new program
(D) To explain a new set of rules

**182.** In the memo, the word "sensitive" in paragraph 2, line 5, is closest in meaning to

(A) cautious
(B) responsive
(C) surprising
(D) confidential

**183.** What is stated as a benefit of L&B Cloud Software?

(A) It reduces cost.
(B) It saves a company time.
(C) It is free to install.
(D) It scans documents for mistakes.

**184.** What problem is Ms. Bell having?

(A) She has forgotten her password.
(B) Her computer has crashed.
(C) All files have gone missing.
(D) She cannot access a server.

**185.** When did Ms. Bell set up her account?

(A) On April 10
(B) On April 11
(C) On April 12
(D) On April 13

| From: | oemerson@sommerfield.com |
| To: | mfernandez@rkdistribution.br |
| Subject: | demonstration |
| Date: | August 5 |

Dear Ms. Fernandez,

My plane landed in Sao Paulo and I am e-mailing you from a waiting room in the airport. Unfortunately, the large suitcase that I had checked has been misplaced. Even though I have printed summaries of all the items right here in my carry-on bag, the sample products for the demonstration are in the missing luggage. Airport staff informed me that they need at least three days to locate the bags and deliver them to where I am staying. That means, of course, that I will not have them in time for the demonstration scheduled for the day after tomorrow.

Once I reach my hotel, I will fax the summaries to your company. If it is not too much trouble, could we possibly postpone the demonstration for another two days? Please contact me about this as soon as possible.

Sincerely,

Oscar Emerson

---

### Missing Baggage Claim Form

We would like to extend our deepest apologies for our mishandling of your belongings and any inconveniences it caused. The information you provide below will assist us greatly. Please provide a clear description of every piece of luggage as well as a list of the items inside each piece. This will definitely help expedite the entire process.

| Claim No.: | 341567S/3 |
| Name of Passenger: | Oscar Emerson |
| E-mail: | oemerson@sommerfield.com |

**Permanent address:**

409 Jackson Lane
Cleveland, OH, 44103
United States of America

**Temporary address (Until August 12):**

Piquiri Hotel
Av. Paulista 1209
Sao Paulo, Brazil
01310-060

| Flight No. | Date | From | To |
|---|---|---|---|
| MTC971 | August 3 | Toledo | Buenos Aires |
| BTA302 | August 5 | Buenos Aires | Sao Paulo |

| Suitcase Type: Large leather bag, zipper, shoulder strap | Manufacturer: Riggs | Color: Brown |

**Contents (Please be as specific as possible):**

| Description | Number |
|---|---|
| Running shoes, tennis shoes, golf shoes, baseball shoes, high-top basketball sneakers | 12 pairs |
| Top Guy brand Man's suits | 2 |
| Greyvalley brand digital camera with battery charger | 1 |
| Trousers, shorts, socks, etc. | 6 |
| South American pocket-sized travel guides | 2 |

From: airportlostfoundoffice@spinternat.com
To: oemerson@sommerfield.com
Subject: claim 341567S/3
Date: August 6

Dear Mr. Emerson,

We are delighted to inform you that your missing suitcase has been located with all the items you listed. It will arrive at the temporary address you provided between 1:00 P.M. and 3:00 P.M. on August 7.

We truly appreciate your patience and understanding.

Regards,

Sao Paulo International Airport Lost and Found

**186.** What does Mr. Emerson indicate about the product summaries?

(A) They will be sent by fax.
(B) They are not ready yet.
(C) They are longer than expected.
(D) They need to be printed out.

**187.** What does Mr. Emerson ask Ms. Fernandez to do?

(A) Deliver product samples
(B) Submit an order form
(C) Reschedule a meeting
(D) Drive him to the hotel

**188.** What does Mr. Emerson want to demonstrate?

(A) Bicycle tires
(B) Athletic shoes
(C) Image software
(D) Coffee makers

**189.** In the form, the word "expedite" in paragraph 1, line 4, is closest in meaning to

(A) discover
(B) modify
(C) elaborate
(D) accelerate

**190.** Where will the delivery be sent?

(A) To Cleveland
(B) To Toledo
(C) To Sao Paulo
(D) To Buenos Aires

GO ON TO THE NEXT PAGE

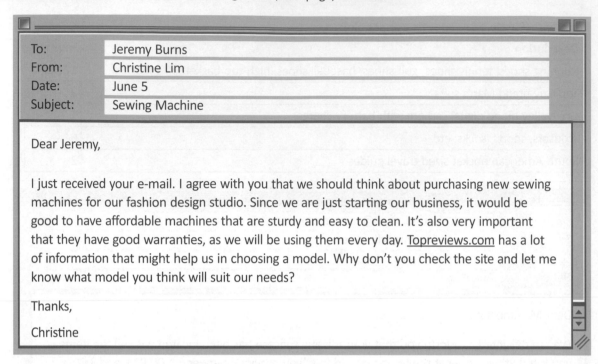

To: Jeremy Burns
From: Christine Lim
Date: June 5
Subject: Sewing Machine

Dear Jeremy,

I just received your e-mail. I agree with you that we should think about purchasing new sewing machines for our fashion design studio. Since we are just starting our business, it would be good to have affordable machines that are sturdy and easy to clean. It's also very important that they have good warranties, as we will be using them every day. Topreviews.com has a lot of information that might help us in choosing a model. Why don't you check the site and let me know what model you think will suit our needs?

Thanks,

Christine

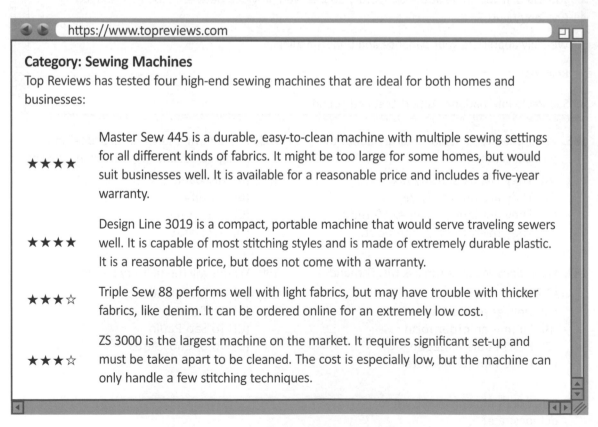

https://www.topreviews.com

**Category: Sewing Machines**

Top Reviews has tested four high-end sewing machines that are ideal for both homes and businesses:

★★★★ Master Sew 445 is a durable, easy-to-clean machine with multiple sewing settings for all different kinds of fabrics. It might be too large for some homes, but would suit businesses well. It is available for a reasonable price and includes a five-year warranty.

★★★★ Design Line 3019 is a compact, portable machine that would serve traveling sewers well. It is capable of most stitching styles and is made of extremely durable plastic. It is a reasonable price, but does not come with a warranty.

★★★☆ Triple Sew 88 performs well with light fabrics, but may have trouble with thicker fabrics, like denim. It can be ordered online for an extremely low cost.

★★★☆ ZS 3000 is the largest machine on the market. It requires significant set-up and must be taken apart to be cleaned. The cost is especially low, but the machine can only handle a few stitching techniques.

**Fashion in Park Falls**
By Zander Cornelli

December 20—Residents of Park Falls who monitor the latest trends in fashion were excited about attending the upscale fashion event held in the Park Falls Convention Center last week. Numerous companies that have made Park Falls the home of their growing businesses participated in the 10th Park Falls Fashion Festival. Over twenty fashion studios were showcased in the event, several of which are owned by local residents.

Rose Designs, which has been in the area for over twenty years, kicked off the festival with some incredible winter apparel. The show was followed by a presentation by Kim Miller, the owner of Accessories Forever. In-Style Fashions and Turnbull Jeans, which have been in business for six months and three years respectively, were newcomers to the festival. All items featured during the fashion shows are available for sale on company websites.

191. What is indicated about the ZS 3000?

(A) It is commonly used in homes.
(B) It has an extended warranty.
(C) It can be transported easily.
(D) It has limited functions.

192. What do all the machines mentioned on the webpage have in common?

(A) They are compact and portable.
(B) They are affordable prices.
(C) They come in various colors.
(D) They can be repaired easily.

193. What sewing machine did Mr. Burns most likely recommend to Ms. Lim?

(A) Master Sew 445
(B) Design Line 3019
(C) Triple Sew 88
(D) ZS 3000

194. In the article, in paragraph 1, line 1, the word "monitor" is closest in meaning to

(A) believe in
(B) observe
(C) supervise
(D depend on

195. What company mentioned in the article do Ms. Lim and Mr. Burns most likely work for?

(A) Rose Designs
(B) Accessories Forever
(C) In-Style Fashions
(D) Turnbull Jeans

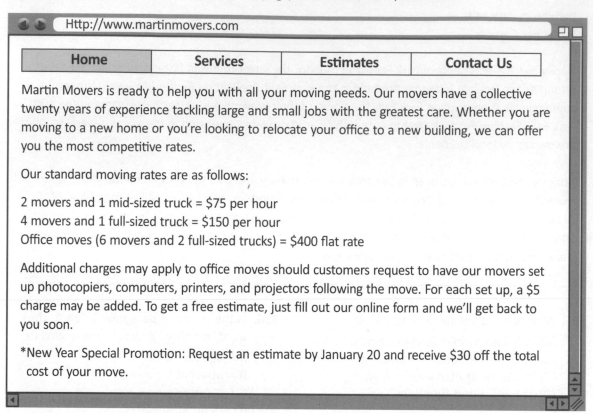

Http://www.martinmovers.com

| Home | Services | Estimates | Contact Us |
|---|---|---|---|

Martin Movers is ready to help you with all your moving needs. Our movers have a collective twenty years of experience tackling large and small jobs with the greatest care. Whether you are moving to a new home or you're looking to relocate your office to a new building, we can offer you the most competitive rates.

Our standard moving rates are as follows:

2 movers and 1 mid-sized truck = $75 per hour
4 movers and 1 full-sized truck = $150 per hour
Office moves (6 movers and 2 full-sized trucks) = $400 flat rate

Additional charges may apply to office moves should customers request to have our movers set up photocopiers, computers, printers, and projectors following the move. For each set up, a $5 charge may be added. To get a free estimate, just fill out our online form and we'll get back to you soon.

*New Year Special Promotion: Request an estimate by January 20 and receive $30 off the total cost of your move.

---

**Martin Movers**
**Estimate Request Form**

| Date | January 10 |
|---|---|
| Name | Connor Goldsmith |
| E-mail address | connor@goldsmithlegal.com |
| Telephone | 409-333-2314 |
| Moving from:<br>Moving to: | 54 First Avenue, New York City<br>889 Fallsview Lane, New York City |
| Moving date | February 23 |
| Items to be moved | 8 desks, 8 computers, 3 printers, 1 photocopier, 1 refrigerator, 1 conference table, 25 office chairs |
| Additional comments | My law office is moving to a new location. As we have our own IT employee, we will not require anyone to set up our equipment. Thus, I believe your standard flat rate will apply. Please contact me by e-mail to confirm the price and finalize the reservation. |

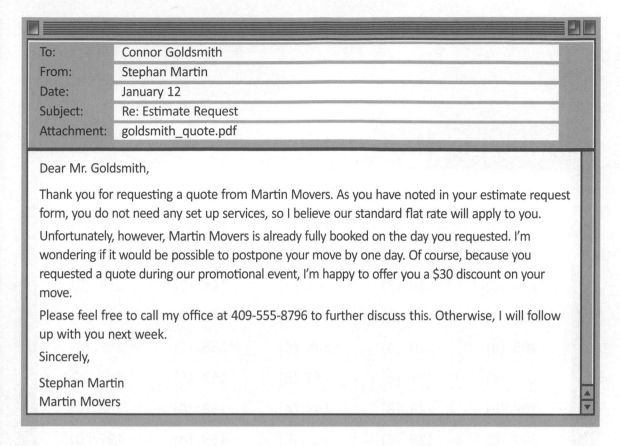

To: Connor Goldsmith
From: Stephan Martin
Date: January 12
Subject: Re: Estimate Request
Attachment: goldsmith_quote.pdf

Dear Mr. Goldsmith,

Thank you for requesting a quote from Martin Movers. As you have noted in your estimate request form, you do not need any set up services, so I believe our standard flat rate will apply to you.

Unfortunately, however, Martin Movers is already fully booked on the day you requested. I'm wondering if it would be possible to postpone your move by one day. Of course, because you requested a quote during our promotional event, I'm happy to offer you a $30 discount on your move.

Please feel free to call my office at 409-555-8796 to further discuss this. Otherwise, I will follow up with you next week.

Sincerely,

Stephan Martin
Martin Movers

**196.** In the webpage, the word "tackling" in paragraph 1, line 2, is closest in meaning to

(A) repairing
(B) handling
(C) considering
(D) entertaining

**197.** What is NOT mentioned about office moves?

(A) Six movers will be involved.
(B) More than one truck will be used.
(C) Estimates will be provided at no cost.
(D) It must be booked at least two weeks in advance.

**198.** What does Mr. Goldsmith mention about his company?

(A) It will discard several items.
(B) It will downsize its office space.
(C) It requires an additional mover.
(D) It employs an IT specialist.

**199.** If Mr. Goldsmith uses Martin Movers, how much will he be charged for his move?

(A) $75
(B) $150
(C) $370
(D) $400

**200.** What is suggested about Martin Movers?

(A) It is booked solid on February 23.
(B) It is located in New York City.
(C) It has five trucks in its fleet.
(D) It charges extra for work done on weekends.

**Stop! This is the end of the test. If you finish before time is called, you may go back to Parts 5, 6, and 7 and check your work.**

# ANSWERS ACTUAL TEST 1

| | | | | |
|---|---|---|---|---|
| **101.** (B) | **121.** (C) | **141.** (C) | **161.** (A) | **181.** (C) |
| **102.** (C) | **122.** (B) | **142.** (A) | **162.** (A) | **182.** (D) |
| **103.** (A) | **123.** (A) | **143.** (B) | **163.** (B) | **183.** (B) |
| **104.** (D) | **124.** (B) | **144.** (A) | **164.** (B) | **184.** (C) |
| **105.** (A) | **125.** (D) | **145.** (C) | **165.** (D) | **185.** (A) |
| **106.** (B) | **126.** (A) | **146.** (C) | **166.** (C) | **186.** (A) |
| **107.** (A) | **127.** (B) | **147.** (B) | **167.** (A) | **187.** (C) |
| **108.** (B) | **128.** (B) | **148.** (A) | **168.** (A) | **188.** (B) |
| **109.** (C) | **129.** (C) | **149.** (C) | **169.** (B) | **189.** (D) |
| **110.** (C) | **130.** (D) | **150.** (A) | **170.** (B) | **190.** (C) |
| **111.** (B) | **131.** (D) | **151.** (D) | **171.** (C) | **191.** (D) |
| **112.** (C) | **132.** (A) | **152.** (B) | **172.** (D) | **192.** (B) |
| **113.** (C) | **133.** (A) | **153.** (D) | **173.** (B) | **193.** (A) |
| **114.** (B) | **134.** (C) | **154.** (D) | **174.** (B) | **194.** (B) |
| **115.** (B) | **135.** (C) | **155.** (B) | **175.** (B) | **195.** (C) |
| **116.** (D) | **136.** (D) | **156.** (C) | **176.** (B) | **196.** (B) |
| **117.** (D) | **137.** (B) | **157.** (C) | **177.** (A) | **197.** (D) |
| **118.** (A) | **138.** (A) | **158.** (D) | **178.** (B) | **198.** (D) |
| **119.** (C) | **139.** (D) | **159.** (D) | **179.** (B) | **199.** (C) |
| **120.** (A) | **140.** (B) | **160.** (C) | **180.** (D) | **200.** (A) |

# ACTUAL TEST 2

## READING TEST

In the Reading Test, you will read a variety of texts and answer several different types of reading comprehension questions. The entire Reading test will last 75 minutes. There are three parts, and directions are given for each part. You are encouraged to answer as many questions as possible within the time allowed.

You must mark your answers on the separate answer sheet. Do not write your answers in your test book.

## PART 5

**Directions:** A word or phrase is missing in each of the sentences below. Four answer choices are given below each sentence. Select the best answer to complete the sentence. Then mark the letter (A), (B), (C), or (D) on your answer sheet.

**101.** Ms. Parker plans to interview the applicants ------- because she understands the position better than anybody.

(A) hers
(B) herself
(C) she
(D) her

**102.** Tax rebates will be given to public servants ------- the State of California.

(A) within
(B) until
(C) during
(D) since

**103.** Interested parties can -------- register online for this weekend's seminar on real estate investing.

(A) very
(B) least
(C) easily
(D) more

**104.** The promotion will ------- employees with upgraded benefits, company cars, and more vacation days.

(A) provide
(B) earn
(C) contrast
(D) loan

**105.** Office staff at Morin Legal Services ------- work four days a week, from Monday to Thursday.

(A) norm
(B) norms
(C) normal
(D) normally

**106.** Items can be exchanged ------- they are returned within one week following the date of purchase.

(A) or
(B) if
(C) nor
(D) but

**107.** According to this newspaper article, earnings at BTR Electronics last quarter were ------- than expected.

(A) lowest
(B) lowering
(C) lower
(D) low

**108.** Everyone ------- the store owner took a week-long vacation in the summertime last year.

(A) out of
(B) other
(C) except
(D) between

**109.** Even though all her landscape paintings are of actual places, Doris Clements puts a great deal of ------- into her work.

(A) imagine
(B) imaginative
(C) imagination
(D) imaginary

**110.** The receptionist will provide the ------ client list to all sales personnel this afternoon.

(A) frequent
(B) updated
(C) certain
(D) monitored

**111.** The spring training course was developed to help sales employees think more -------.

(A) create
(B) creative
(C) creativity
(D) creatively

**112.** Before attempting to assemble this table, you should ------- the instructions.

(A) direct
(B) review
(C) gather
(D) program

**113.** Ms. Jannel, the director of customer relations, ------- the poor reviews the company has received online at the staff meeting tomorrow.

(A) had been addressing
(B) is addressing
(C) will be addressed
(D) should be addressed

**114.** Larson Motors aims to improve its public image ------- the guidance of publicist Cynthia Morison of M&T Public Relations.

(A) under
(B) either
(C) among
(D) beyond

**115.** When --------- to any new clients, don't forget to mention Beckingham's promotional event next week.

(A) spoken
(B) speaking
(C) spoke
(D) to speak

**116.** Tickets for Friday night's play at the Alexander Theater sold out quickly because the production --------- two famous actors from this area.

(A) feature
(B) features
(C) to feature
(D) featuring

**117.** The Thompson Art Gallery will extend its hours of operation ------- on August 1.

(A) will begin
(B) has begun
(C) beginner
(D) beginning

**118.** Donald Mahoney is in charge of the supplies ------- to all plumbers working for Grady Pipe Repairs.

(A) distribute
(B) distribution
(C) distributes
(D) is distributed

**119.** The CEO is known for being ambitious as he expressed his ------- in an interview with *Today Business Magazine* last fall.

(A) interferences
(B) prevention
(C) views
(D) exchange

**120.** Anna Sanchez, founding editor of *Financial Monthly*, has quickly earned the respect of practically ------- in the financial industry.

(A) everyone
(B) anything
(C) whatever
(D) each other

**121.** As stated in the reviews, the theater's new performance was ------- a big hit.

(A) clear
(B) clearly
(C) clearer
(D) clearing

**122.** ------- our hiring committee reads all the resumes, we will compile a list of 20 candidates to invite in for interviews.

(A) Compared to
(B) As soon as
(C) So that
(D) Not only

**123.** The concert was a huge success and drew a crowd of over 5,000 to Moose Park and Recreation Center, -------- the cold weather.

(A) while
(B) whereas
(C) notwithstanding
(D) moreover

**124.** The research staff at Pullford Pharmaceuticals will be using the conference room as its office ------- the renovation period.

(A) opposite
(B) beside
(C) during
(D) with

125. As stated on the company's website, clients who wish to cancel their membership ------- it expires must pay a fee.

(A) before
(B) how
(C) why
(D) either

126. Although the job description is ------- to those at other firms, this job has a much higher salary.

(A) similar
(B) likable
(C) reflected
(D) considerate

127. Access to the research laboratory will be limited to senior employees to ensure ------- with all safety regulations.

(A) activation
(B) fulfillment
(C) compliance
(D) indication

128. If the window had been broken during installation, Riley's Building Supplies ------- to replace it at no charge.

(A) would have offered
(B) has offered
(C) is being offered
(D) would have been offered

129. Prior to reviewing -------, the town council agreed to three proposals in principle.

(A) specifics
(B) specify
(C) specific
(D) specifically

130. Administrators at the Ben Phillips Hospital maintain that ------- to the facility will make many medical procedures more efficient.

(A) continuations
(B) increments
(C) deviations
(D) enhancements

## PART 6

**Directions:** Read the texts that follow. A word, phrase, or sentence is missing in parts of each text. Four answer choices for each question are given below the text. Select the best answer to complete the text. Then mark the letter (A), (B), (C), or (D) on your answer sheet.

**Questions 131-134** refer to the following article.

March 3 — After nearly three years of planning, the largest stadium in Harpville will begin construction. The Expo Stadium will be located on Harpville's majestic waterfront and will have a capacity of up to ten thousand seats. ___131.___. The project is expected to take three years to complete. It will be located amongst several other new developments currently ___132.___ on the waterfront. According to Marshal Thomas, president of the Harpville Sports Association, the new stadium is a ___133.___. "We're going to need a large stadium to accommodate our growing sports clubs," Mr. Thomas said. "___134.___, we'll also be able to use the stadium for concerts and circus performances."

131. (A) Developers are unsure how long it will take to complete the project.
(B) The stadium will be moved from the waterfront to the outskirts of the city.
(C) It will also include over 100 press viewing rooms that hold up to ten people each.
(D) Delays occurred when the mayor refused to fund the city's development plans.

132. (A) to construct
(B) are constructing
(C) were constructed
(D) being constructed

133. (A) necessity
(B) nuisance
(C) risk
(D) bargain

134. (A) On the other hand
(B) In other words
(C) In the first place
(D) As a result

**Questions 135-138** refer to the following press release.

Meredith Hobson, CEO and founder of Hobson Dining, Trenton's oldest family dining franchise, announced that she ___135.___ $6,500 towards renovations to the Jasper Community Center in the city's downtown region. The funds were generated from ticket sales for a banquet held last Friday evening at her ___136.___. Ms. Hobson will present the management staff of the center with a check at a special ceremony scheduled to take place tomorrow afternoon at 2:00. ___137.___ the past 25 years, Ms. Hobson has organized a number of successful fund-raising events for community services and charities. ___138.___.

135. (A) will donate
 (B) donated
 (C) might donate
 (D) donating

136. (A) gallery
 (B) hotel
 (C) academy
 (D) restaurant

137. (A) Despite
 (B) Over
 (C) Between
 (D) Beneath

138. (A) The Jasper Community Center has programs for both children and adults.
 (B) The opening ceremony at the center will be done by 2:30 P.M.
 (C) However, last Friday's event was, without a doubt, her most successful one.
 (D) Ms. Hobson plans to open a branch in uptown Trenton sometime next year.

**Questions 139-142** refer to the following meeting summary.

Our monthly meeting commenced at 4:30 P.M. The meeting's purpose was to discuss the advantages and disadvantages of ___139.___ LGQ International Shipping. Max Powel led the debate on the possible move by stressing the importance of furthering LGQ's current growth patterns. He explained that LGQ has grown to be one of the most successful ___140.___ and that it ships the largest number of electronics in the country.

___141.___ . According to recent reports, the traveling distance from the closest harbor is becoming costly ___142.___ LGQ begins to grow. Staff members discussed some possible solutions, but a final decision was not reached. Mr. Powel will do some more research and present his findings at the next meeting.

139. (A) acquiring
(B) joining
(C) promoting
(D) relocating

140. (A) distribute
(B) distributing
(C) distributors
(D) distributes

141. (A) Mr. Powel also outlined the challenges LGQ is experiencing as a result of its growth.
(B) The CEO then proceeded to discuss the advantages of the new facilities.
(C) Next, shareholders were invited to conduct a vote to decide the date.
(D) Mr. Powel directed employees to consider how operations would be conducted.

142. (A) now
(B) why
(C) just as
(D) ever since

**Questions 143-146** refer to the following e-mail.

---

**From:** tina@lindcosmetics.com
**To:** mia@mymailnow.com
**Date:** September 8
**Subject:** Order 445009

Dear Ms. Kramar,

Thank you for writing to inquire about your order. According to our records, you ordered one tube of Lind SPF 50 Sunscreen, one bottle of Lind 500 Hand Cream, and two bottles of Lind Ultrashine Shampoo from our website on September 1. Your products were scheduled to arrive on September 5. I was surprised to hear that you have not received ‾‾‾‾. **143.**

‾‾‾‾. **144.** According to their schedule, your products will arrive on September 10. If your order is not delivered by that day, feel free ‾‾‾‾ **145.** us again.

I sincerely apologize for this inconvenience. Our shipping methods are usually fast and affordable. This situation is quite ‾‾‾‾. **146.** I hope it will not discourage you from shopping at Lind Cosmetics.

Thank you,

Tina Speller
Lind Cosmetics

---

**143.** (A) it
(B) one
(C) them
(D) some

**144.** (A) We would like to invite you to visit our store.
(B) Please leave a review on our website.
(C) We are currently sold out of that particular product.
(D) I have contacted the shipping company on your behalf.

**145.** (A) contacted
(B) to contact
(C) contacting
(D) contact

**146.** (A) similar
(B) exciting
(C) unusual
(D) welcome

## PART 7

**Directions:** In this part you will read a selection of texts, such as magazine and newspaper articles, e-mails, and instant messages. Each text or set of texts is followed by several questions. Select the best answer for each question and mark the letter (A), (B), (C), or (D) on your answer sheet.

**Questions 147-148** refer to the following advertisement.

| Item for Sale | Price | Location |
|---|---|---|
| Model A7000 Flamesburg Barbecue | $450 | Los Angeles, CA |

**Item Description:**
Purchased new three years ago. Original cost was $700 and came with a two-year warranty.
Grill pieces are charred. Buyer can purchase new ones on the Flamesburg website.
Exterior is in great condition. (Pictures available upon request)
Price is negotiable. Willing to deliver anywhere in the Los Angeles area.
E-mail rjohnson@mail.com if you have any questions.

**147.** What is NOT indicated about the barbecue?

(A) It comes in the original box.
(B) It needs new parts.
(C) Its price is not set.
(D) Its warranty has expired.

**148.** What is the seller willing to do?

(A) Reserve the item for up to a month
(B) Provide instructions on how to use the item
(C) Deliver anywhere in the country
(D) Send photographs to potential buyers

**Questions 149-150** refer to the following notice.

We are delighted to announce that Cordelia Winters has joined IPM Talent as an associate agent. Ms. Winters is a graduate of Roden University's public relations program. While studying at Roden, she founded the university's first student-run magazine. Following graduation, she completed an internship at UV Media and Talent, a prestigious agency that represents a wide variety of musicians, authors, professional athletes, and actors. Ms. Winters has undergone exceptional training and will be a great asset to our growing team of agents. Please join us in conference room B tomorrow morning at 10:00 A.M. to welcome her to the team.

**149.** Where is the notice most likely posted?
(A) In an advertising firm
(B) In a university
(C) In a music studio
(D) In a talent agency

**150.** What are employees invited to do tomorrow?
(A) Participate in a conference
(B) Greet a new employee
(C) Visit a competitor
(D) Meet some new clients

Questions 151-152 refer to the following text message chain.

**Tim Peterson [11:03 A.M.]**
Hey, Amanda. Can you update me on the Sampson Lane job?

**Amanda Ray [11:10 A.M.]**
We've cleared out the main floor and the garage. We're just starting on the second floor of the house now.

**Tim Peterson [11:12 A.M.]**
Is that all? What time do you think you'll be done? We have a move scheduled for 3:00 P.M.

**Amanda Ray [11:15 A.M.]**
We're behind schedule. When the estimate was done, it didn't take into account the old furniture in the garage.

**Tim Peterson [11:20 A.M.]**
Really? Who did the estimate?

**Amanda Ray [11:21 A.M.]**
Matthew did before he went on vacation.

**Tim Peterson [11:23 A.M.]**
OK. Contact me at 1:00 P.M. with a progress report. I'll decide then if I need to call in another crew for the afternoon job.

SEND

*Type your message . . .*

**151.** What type of business does Ms. Ray work for?

(A) A real estate agency
(B) A furniture store
(C) A moving company
(D) A truck rental service

**152.** At 11:12, what does Mr. Peterson mean when he says, "Is that all"?

(A) He wants to know the address of a house.
(B) He thinks the employees are working slowly.
(C) He is surprised because the price is very cheap.
(D) He wants to confirm that everything is loaded on the truck.

**Questions 153-154** refer to the following letter.

Rutherford Eye Clinic
54 Rutherford Avenue
Los Angeles, California

14 March

Katrina Serova
123 Colonel Lane
Los Angeles, California

Dear Ms. Serova,

It is important to us here at Rutherford Eye Clinic that all our customers receive advanced notice of changes to our policies. As of August 1, all routine yearly eye exams will no longer be covered by most major insurance providers. To help offset the cost, we are reducing our fees by $15 per exam. Please see the enclosed list of affected insurance providers.

In some select cases, we are willing to provide eye exams to children free of charge should your family have a history of prior exams with us. Please contact our billing manager Maggie Wilson at 445-987-0023 to inquire about this service or if you have any questions.

Sincerely,

Dr. Nadia Fortuni
Rutherford Eye Clinic

**153.** Why was the letter sent to Ms. Serova?

(A) To announce a billing change
(B) To advertise a new service
(C) To confirm an appointment
(D) To inform of a missed exam

**154.** What is indicated about Rutherford Eye Clinic?

(A) It wants to hire new staff members.
(B) It has extended its hours of operation.
(C) It caters to clients from all around the world.
(D) It will offer free exams to certain customers.

Questions 155-157 refer to the following article.

## Westpoint Shopping Mall to Begin Construction

By Melanie Rosenberg, Staff Writer

March 23 — Yesterday, in a press conference at Mayor Zanga's office downtown, the mayor announced the city's approval of development plans for a new shopping mall. According to the mayor, Westpoint Shopping Mall will be located at Park Road and Wilson Street. --[1]--.

The shopping mall is a joint project between the City of Forks and Windsor Partners, a private development corporation. The mall will include over 200 hundred new stores, 55 restaurants, and a department store. --[2]--. Windsor Partners will be in charge of executing construction and overseeing initial operations.

"The City of Forks has never had a major shopping center," Mr. Johnson of Windsor Partners said in an interview. "By building this state-of-the-art facility, the people of Forks will see an increase in jobs and tourism." --[3]--.

Many retailers have already signed contracts with Windsor Partners to reserve store space in the mall. However, some small business owners have expressed worry that they will lose business once the shopping mall opens. --[4]--. "My store has been in business for two generations," Michelle Stevens of Shoe Blitz said. "My customers are loyal, but I won't be able to compete with shopping mall prices."

**155.** What does Windsor Partners hope to attract to Forks?

(A) Foreign students
(B) A supermarket
(C) More tourists
(D) New small businesses

**156.** Who most likely is Michelle Stevens?

(A  A newspaper reporter
(B) A retail store owner
(C) A city official
(D) A property developer

**157.** In which of the positions marked [1], [2], [3], and [4] does the following sentence best belong?

"Last year, a fire consumed the auto factory located there, leaving the site open to new development."

(A) [1]
(B) [2]
(C) [3]
(D) [4]

**Questions 158-160** refer to the following information.

Simone Decourte
*Kites at Sunset*
Mobile Installation, painted sheet metal and rods
1984

*Kites at Sunset* is one of the most popular mobile installations by Simone Decourte. Decourte revolutionized mobile art in the 1970s by including portable motors to create movement. *Kites at Sunset* is part of a larger series constructed by Decourte between 1970 to 1988. It has been featured in The Museum of Abstract Art in Milan, The Contemporary Art Gallery in New York City, and The New Art Movement Museum in London. Decourte originally donated the piece to the University of Montenegro. It remained there for 10 years before being acquired by Maxwell George of the Wilson Fine Art Museum where it has remained as part of our permanent collection. Before her death, Decourte said *Kites at Sunset* was her "most vibrant piece ever created."

**158.** How does the information describe Simone Decourte?

(A) She was attentive to details.
(B) She created a lot of art work.
(C) She was an innovative artist.
(D) She worked for the poor.

**159.** Where is the information posted?

(A) At the Museum of Abstract Art
(B) At the Wilson Fine Art Museum
(C) At the Contemporary Art Gallery
(D) At the New Art Movement Museum

**160.** What is NOT stated about *Kites at Sunset*?

(A) The artist regarded it as one of her best works.
(B) It has traveled to several places.
(C) It was owned by a university.
(D) It took almost two decades to complete the piece.

Questions 161-163 refer to the following e-mail.

| To: | Jan Andrews |
| From: | Michael Pitelli |
| Date: | March 7 |
| Subject: | Updates for March 8 |

Ms. Andrews,

I've had to make a few minor changes to your schedule for tomorrow. Your meeting with potential client Jeff Woods has been canceled. His assistant suggested March 10 as a possible date to meet. Since you're flying back that morning, you're free in the afternoon. Would you like me to set up the appointment? Please have a look at your updated schedule below. I've replaced Mr. Woods's appointment with your budget review. Please let me know if this doesn't work for you.

| Time | Appointment | Attendees |
| --- | --- | --- |
| 8:30 A.M. | Staff Meeting | Departments A and B |
| 9:45 A.M. | Conference Call with Washington Partners | Jessica Bowers, Tom Park |
| 10:30 A.M. | Budget Review | Ally Strenski |
| 1:30 P.M. | Meeting about Conference Itinerary | Joshua Wilson |
| 4:00 P.M. | Leave for your 7:00 flight to Chicago | |

I have printed out your e-ticket and put it in your company mailbox. Good luck on your trip.

Best,

Michael

161. Why was the e-mail sent?
(A) To cancel an appointment next month
(B) To provide a travel itinerary
(C) To update a daily schedule
(D) To provide documents for a meeting

162. What will happen on March 10?
(A) Mr. Pitelli will fly to Washington.
(B) Ms. Andrews will attend a conference.
(C) Mr. Woods will hold a budget review.
(D) Ms. Andrews will return from Chicago.

163. At what time was Mr. Woods expected?
(A) 8:35 A.M.
(B) 9:45 A.M.
(C) 10:30 A.M.
(D) 1:30 P.M.

**Questions 164-167** refer to the following e-mail.

---

| To: | Employees of Winfred Financial |
| --- | --- |
| From: | Sandra Burns |
| Date: | October 24 |
| Subject: | New regulations |

Dear employees,

As you know, the Ministry of Health and Environment has introduced a new set of laws for work places in order to help reduce the amount of energy consumed during the winter months. In accordance with these new regulations, Winfred Financial will program its heating system during the winter. As such, you will not be able to regulate the temperature of your office at any time. The system will heat the building to 19°C on weekdays, which will be maintained throughout the day. It will then lower to 13°C at the end of each day. By following this new regulation, we should see a 10% reduction in the cost of our utility bills.

As some of you work on weekends, management has decided that offices on the 5th floor will be able to control the temperature manually. Weekend workers may request a change of office with their department managers. We simply ask that the rooms not be heated any warmer than 19°C.

Sincerely,

Sandra Burns,
General Manager

---

**164.** What is the purpose of the e-mail?

(A) To announce an upcoming change in the workplace
(B) To inform employees of a scheduled inspection
(C) To encourage employees to choose new office furniture
(D) To offer managers the opportunity to get a promotion

**165.** The word "maintained" in paragraph 1, line 5, is closest in meaning to

(A) confirmed
(B) repaired
(C) taken
(D) kept

**166.** What is mentioned as a benefit of the new regulation?

(A) It will improve employee work efficiency.
(B) It can allow the company to hire more workers.
(C) It will help the company save money.
(D) It can be applied to public and private companies.

**167.** What are employees who work on weekends advised to do?

(A) E-mail Ms. Burns directly
(B) Request office changes
(C) Alter their work schedules
(D) Work at home on weekends

Questions 168-171 refer to the following online chat discussion.

**Mary Renold [2:02 P.M.]**
Hello, Ben. Can you spare a moment? I want to double-check an inventory report with you.

**Ben Jeffries [2:03 P.M.]**
No problem.

**Mary Renold [2:04 P.M.]**
According to the report, we only have two A75 Canpro notebooks left. We've been selling a lot of that model lately. Should I order more?

**Ben Jeffries [2:06 P.M.]**
That's not necessary. The new A76 model has just come out, so we're going to carry that model instead. I ordered 50 of the new ones, but they haven't come in yet.

**Mary Renold [2:10 P.M.]**
Oh, OK, Thanks for explaining that.

**Ben Jeffries [2:11 P.M.]**
Next week, we'll start displaying them on the shelves, so make sure to print the product information for the displays.

**Mary Renold [2:12 P.M.]**
Sure. I'll get right on that.

**168.** At 2:03 P.M., what does Mr. Jeffries most likely mean when he writes, "No Problem"?

(A) He agrees with Ms. Renold's idea.
(B) He is available to answer Ms. Renold's question.
(C) He wants to set up a meeting with Ms. Renold.
(D) He did exactly as Ms. Renold requested.

**169.** What is mentioned about Mr. Jeffries?

(A) He already ordered some items.
(B) He downloaded some information.
(C) He set up some products today.
(D) He visited a supplier last week.

**170.** What type of business do Mr. Jeffries and Ms. Renold work for?

(A) A computer repair business
(B) A delivery company
(C) An electronics store
(D) A software developer

**171.** What will Mr. Jeffries and Ms. Renold do next week?

(A) Renovate a storefront
(B) Hold a sale for new products
(C) Return some obsolete items
(D) Set up some product displays

**Questions 172-175** refer to the following article.

June 15 — The Walter Horman Estate, the home of deceased millionaire Walter Horman, was recently purchased by the City of Rogerton. According to Malika Trenton, director of the Rogerton Historical Society, the estate will undergo light renovations and restorations before being turned into a local museum. --[1]--. According to Trenton, "The Horman family has included all of the original decorations and furnishings for visitors to enjoy."

Over the last several decades, the Walter Horman Estate has been unoccupied. Instead, the property was available for private party rentals and weddings. Some major film companies have even shot scenes at the estate. However, the cost of keeping the grounds in good condition proved to be too much for the family. --[2]--. Stephen Horman, grandson of the late Walter Horman, said, "It was a tough choice to make. The estate has been in our family for generations, but selling it was the best way to ensure its upkeep." The rest of the Horman family has expressed satisfaction that the estate will be turned into a museum. --[3]--.

The Rogerton Historical Society intends to develop guided tours of the estate rooms, while still providing access to the gardens for private parties. Visitors to the estate can learn the history of the Horman family from its early immigrant beginning to its rise in society as the owner of one of the first food processing companies in the country. --[4]--. Tours are expected to begin next spring. Anyone interested in purchasing passes or learning about the estate's history can visit www. walterhormanestate.com/info.

**172.** What is suggested about the Walter Horman Estate?

(A) It was built by Walter Horman's father.
(B) It is expensive to reserve for parties.
(C) It will have its appliances upgraded.
(D) It includes the original furniture.

**173.** According to the article, what was difficult for the Horman family?

(A) Turning the property into a park
(B) Maintaining the estate
(C) Finding furniture for the rooms
(D) Locating a suitable buyer

**174.** According to the article, what will remain the same about the estate?

(A) It will be owned by the Horman family.
(B) Its exterior walls will be used for security.
(C) Its buildings will serve as guest houses.
(D) Its outdoor property will be available for rent.

**175.** In which of the positions marked [1],[2],[3], and [4] does the following sentence best belong?

"They are pleased the memory of Walter Horman will be preserved."

(A) [1]
(B) [2]
(C) [3]
(D) [4]

| To: | samadams@adamsroofing.com |
| From: | ginachoi@homeimprovementmonthly.com |
| Date: | January 3 |
| Subject: | Home Improvement Monthly |

Dear Mr. Adams,

As a special New Year promotion, *Home Improvement Monthly* will be offering discounted prices for new advertisers in our magazine. *Home Improvement Monthly* has a readership of over 20,000 print subscriptions. Your advertisement will reach each subscriber in print as well as our many online subscribers. With our services, you can increase your business!

This offer is valid until March 1. Our price packages are outlined below, and our designers are ready to create color advertisements according to your specifications. To purchase any of our packages, please reply by e-mail or visit us at www.homeimprovementmonthly.com/advertisements/orders.

| Package | Advertisement Format | Monthly Price |
|---------|---------------------|---------------|
| 1 | One full-page print ad plus banner website ad | $300 |
| 2 | One half-page print ad plus half-banner website ad | $275 |
| 3 | One half-page print ad plus corner website ad | $250 |
| 4 | One quarter-page print ad plus corner website ad | $225 |

Sincerely,

Gina Choi
Advertising Coordinator
*Home Improvement Monthly*

| To: | ginachoi@homeimprovementmonthly.com |
| From: | samadams@adamsroofing.com |
| Date: | January 5 |
| Subject: Re: | Home Improvement Monthly |

Dear Ms. Choi,

Thank you for e-mailing me about your promotion. My business partner and I are interested in placing an ad in your magazine. However, I have some questions about your quarter-page print ad. I've purchased a copy of your magazine and looked at the advertisements. I noticed that some are in the front of the magazine and some are in the back. I'm wondering what determines the location of the ad? Do we need to pay additional fees to have our ad located in the front?

Thank you in advance for answering these questions.

Sincerely,

Sam Adams
Co-owner
Adams Roofing

**176.** Why did Ms. Choi e-mail Mr. Adams?

(A) To announce a new advertising opportunity
(B) To offer a promotional discount on subscriptions
(C) To encourage him to hire a marketing agency
(D) To inform him of a change in a contract

**177.** What is suggested about *Home Improvement Monthly*?

(A) Some of its issues were delivered late.
(B) Its advertisers do not pay for subscriptions.
(C) It will put out two issues every month starting next year.
(D) Some of its subscribers only pay for the website version.

**178.** What is mentioned about *Home Improvement Monthly's* designers?

(A) They can provide custom work.
(B) They require additional fees.
(C) They also design the company website.
(D) They are unavailable until March.

**179.** In the second e-mail, the word "placing" in paragraph 1, line 2, is closest in meaning to

(A) hiring
(B) putting
(C) assigning
(D) calculating

**180.** What package does Mr. Adams most likely want?

(A) Package 1
(B) Package 2
(C) Package 3
(D) Package 4

**Questions 181-185** refer to the following e-mails.

| | |
|---|---|
| To: | mpordeski@mailme.com |
| From: | imranandal@pearsonmedicalresearch.com |
| Date: | April 12 |
| Subject: | Pearson Medical Research Position |
| Attachment: | contract |

Dear Ms. Pordeski,

I enjoyed speaking with you during your telephone interview, and I'm delighted to offer you a position on our team as a research assistant. As I'm sure you're aware, you will be working with the top medical researchers in the country using the most advanced equipment. Your education in both biology and engineering will be a great asset during your six-month contract.

As I mentioned to you, our company works jointly with Austin University. Thus, you will need to know your way around both our company headquarters and the laboratories at the university. As such, I would like to arrange an orientation for you and our other new researchers. You mentioned that you're finishing up your final year of your degree, so I'd like to arrange a time that does not interfere with your schedule. Please let me know which days in May you are available.

Please note, this position is an internship. Your wages will be $200 a week and the occasional work expenses will be reimbursed. However, following the six-month period, there will be permanent employment for our top interns. To finalize your acceptance of these terms, please sign and return the attached contract. Andrew Baxter, our human resources manager, will contact you if there are any problems.

Thank you, and I look forward to working with you!

Imran Andal
Lead Researcher
Pearson Medical Research

| To: | Intern Group |
| From: | imranandal@pearsonmedicalresearch.com |
| Date: | April 24 |
| Subject: | Orientation |

Dear Research Interns,

Since most of you are not available at the same time, I'd like to hold two orientations, one on May 11 and the second on May 16. The May 16 orientation is scheduled on a weekend to accommodate the students in the group. However, if you're not a student, you will be expected to attend the May 11 orientation. Both orientations will start at 9 A.M. at our company headquarters. After a tour, we will have lunch at Buffy's Bistro and then make our way over to the university. Please bring a photo ID in order to gain admittance to the university labs.

Thank you, and I'm looking forward to meeting you all!

Imran Andal,
Lead Researcher,
Pearson Medical Research

**181.** Why did Mr. Andal write to Ms. Pordeski?

(A) To negotiate a contract
(B) To invite her to apply for a job
(C) To provide medical assistance
(D) To offer her an internship

**182.** What document is Ms. Pordeski asked to return?

(A) An employer reference
(B) A signed contract
(C) A program application
(D) A university transcript

**183.** What is indicated about new staff at Pearson Medical Research?

(A) They may work from home.
(B) Their tax forms must be submitted online.
(C) They will not be paid for their work.
(D) Their performance will be evaluated.

**184.** Why might Andrew Baxter contact Ms. Pordeski?

(A) To review company regulations
(B) To resolve a contract issue
(C) To ask for additional references
(D) To explain payment procedures

**185.** When will Ms. Pordeski most likely attend the orientation?

(A) May 11
(B) May 15
(C) May 16
(D) May 19

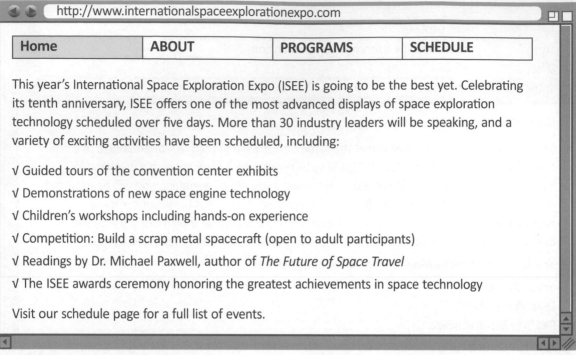

http://www.internationalspaceexplorationexpo.com

| Home | ABOUT | PROGRAMS | SCHEDULE |

This year's International Space Exploration Expo (ISEE) is going to be the best yet. Celebrating its tenth anniversary, ISEE offers one of the most advanced displays of space exploration technology scheduled over five days. More than 30 industry leaders will be speaking, and a variety of exciting activities have been scheduled, including:

√ Guided tours of the convention center exhibits

√ Demonstrations of new space engine technology

√ Children's workshops including hands-on experience

√ Competition: Build a scrap metal spacecraft (open to adult participants)

√ Readings by Dr. Michael Paxwell, author of *The Future of Space Travel*

√ The ISEE awards ceremony honoring the greatest achievements in space technology

Visit our schedule page for a full list of events.

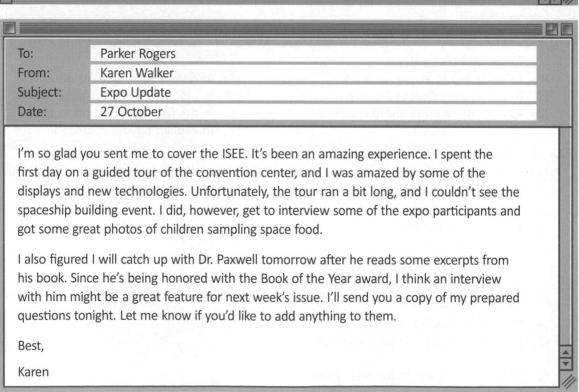

| To: | Parker Rogers |
| From: | Karen Walker |
| Subject: | Expo Update |
| Date: | 27 October |

I'm so glad you sent me to cover the ISEE. It's been an amazing experience. I spent the first day on a guided tour of the convention center, and I was amazed by some of the displays and new technologies. Unfortunately, the tour ran a bit long, and I couldn't see the spaceship building event. I did, however, get to interview some of the expo participants and got some great photos of children sampling space food.

I also figured I will catch up with Dr. Paxwell tomorrow after he reads some excerpts from his book. Since he's being honored with the Book of the Year award, I think an interview with him might be a great feature for next week's issue. I'll send you a copy of my prepared questions tonight. Let me know if you'd like to add anything to them.

Best,

Karen

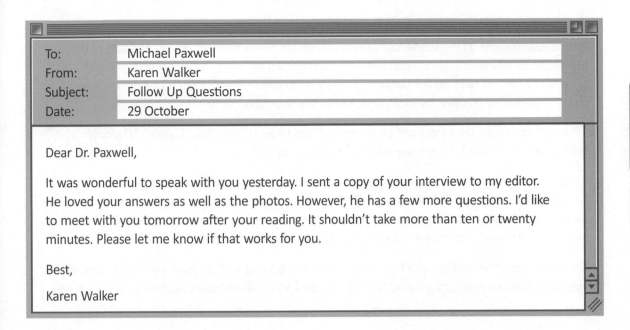

To:        Michael Paxwell
From:      Karen Walker
Subject:   Follow Up Questions
Date:      29 October

Dear Dr. Paxwell,

It was wonderful to speak with you yesterday. I sent a copy of your interview to my editor. He loved your answers as well as the photos. However, he has a few more questions. I'd like to meet with you tomorrow after your reading. It shouldn't take more than ten or twenty minutes. Please let me know if that works for you.

Best,

Karen Walker

**186.** What is indicated about ISEE?

(A) It was originally designed for students.
(B) It is held multiple times per year.
(C) It has existed for several years.
(D) It has moved to a new venue.

**187.** Who most likely is Ms. Walker?

(A) A publisher
(B) An astronaut
(C) A scientist
(D) A journalist

**188.** According to Ms. Walker, what conference activity was she unable to attend?

(A) A demonstration
(B) A craft competition
(C) A guided tour
(D) A workshop

**189.** In the first e-mail, the word "figured" in paragraph 2, line 1, is closest in meaning to

(A) decided
(B) involved
(C) represented
(D) performed

**190.** What is suggested about Dr. Paxwell?

(A) He has won several awards this year.
(B) He will give multiple presentations at the expo.
(C) He is a well-known newspaper editor.
(D) He gives demonstrations every year.

BREDENBURY (June 11) — Bredenbury town officials sat down today to discuss the fate of the Mossomin Bridge which has been in need of major repairs for years. Today's meeting was the first of several expected talks on the subject. Although an extensive restoration is one option, several complications may compel the town to demolish the structure.

"The cost to restore the bridge will be too great," said town planner Ilkay Tidsale. "The only financially feasible option I can see is replacing the structure."

According to Malcolm Vonda, a well-known structural engineer, traffic flow must also be taken into consideration. "Highway 209 will soon have two additional lanes, making it a four-lane highway. The Mossomin Bridge cannot accommodate such a huge increase in the number of vehicles," Vonda says. "I see no other alternative but to build a bigger, modern structure."

The town council would like input from residents on this issue as well. Anyone wishing to share their views can attend a public forum next Monday at 4:30 P.M. at Akber Square, in front of the town hall.

## Letters to the Editor

June 12 — Yesterday's article concerning the future of the Mossomin Bridge prompted me to write this response. The bridge is more than just a bridge; it is an integral part of Bredenbury's culture. For this reason, the town must keep the structure intact. Plus, considering the high revenues generated annually by tourism industry, the short-term costs needed to restore this landmark will prove to be beneficial in the end.

Pierre Atherton, founding member of the Bredenbury Preservation Society (BPS)

| To: | members@bredenburypressoc.org |
| From: | isabellecharlebois@bredenburypressoc.org |
| Date: | June 23 |
| Subject: | update on Mossomin Bridge |

Dear BPS Members,

Congratulations! Thanks to our organization's undeniably strong presence at the town council event, combined with the countless e-mails, letters, and calls to the members of town council, it appears that the bridge is safe from demolition. According to an article in today's *Bredenbury Herald*, the town has decided to relocate Mossomin Bridge to the south end of the town where only pedestrians will be allowed to use it. The bridge will not be open to motorized vehicles.

All of you should feel proud for speaking out and expressing your concerns last Monday. Your actions definitely influenced the town's decision. Great work!

Thank you once again,

Isabelle Charlebois, President
Bredenbury Preservation Society

**191.** In the article, what is indicated about the town of Bredenbury?

(A) It will increase its yearly budget.
(B) It is going to upgrade a road.
(C) It is enforcing local parking laws.
(D) It will offer special tours to attract tourists.

**192.** What is NOT implied about Mr. Atherton?

(A) He works with Mr. Vonda.
(B) He disagrees with Ms. Tisdale.
(C) He read the June 11 newspaper article.
(D) He values a town landmark.

**193.** In the e-mail, the word "countless" in paragraph 1, line 2, is closest in meaning to

(A) unreported
(B) registered
(C) numerous
(D) ambiguous

**194.** Why does Ms. Charlebois congratulate BPS members?

(A) They helped influence a town's decision.
(B) They elected a new vice president.
(C) They were the subjects of a front-page news story.
(D) They raised additional funds for town projects.

**195.** What is suggested about BPS members?

(A) They helped repair a structure.
(B) Many of them spoke out at Akber Square.
(C) Many of them reside in the south end.
(D) They meet on the first Monday of every month.

**Questions 196-200** refer to the following webpage, receipt, and review.

http://www.grandcanyonexploreadventure.com

| Home | Tours | Reservations | Customer Service |

For over 20 years, our experienced pilots have been conducting spectacular, one of a kind sightseeing tours of the incredible Grand Canyon. Our trips are available for groups of up to six passengers and can be conducted in English, French, Spanish, and Chinese. Take a look at our trip itineraries below and then visit our reservations page for more information about pricing.

• Grand Canyon Helicopter Tour — Available every day from 14:30 P.M. – 15:30 P.M. Spend your afternoon flying over the magnificent Grand Canyon in a helicopter. You will see amazing views of the Hoover Dam, Lake Mead, and the surrounding desert.

• Grand Canyon Helicopter Tour & Lunch — Available every day from 11:30 A.M. – 15:00 P.M. See all the incredible aerial sights listed in the Grand Canyon Helicopter Tour. Following your flight, you will descend 4,000 feet to the canyon floor and enjoy a picnic lunch served on the shore of the Colorado River.

• Ultimate Grand Canyon Tour Package — Available every day from 11:30 A.M. – 18:00 P.M. Enjoy all the benefits of our other packages, including an aerial tour and a picnic lunch. Following lunch, you can explore the historical Native American lands before returning to your helicopter for a second flight to watch the beautiful sunset. Join us for a complimentary steak dinner at the Explore and Adventure Lodge.

---

http://www.grandcanyonexploreadventure.com/reservations/customerreceipt

**Customer Reservation Receipt**

| | |
|---|---|
| Date of purchase: | August 3 |
| Customer name: | June Thompson |
| Reference number: | 877573999 |

| Reservation Details | No. of Passengers | Payment Total |
|---|---|---|
| Ultimate Grand Canyon Tour Package (August 27 departure) | 6 x $80 | $480 |

| | |
|---|---|
| Payment Method: | Credit Card |
| Card Number: | 111222-359229 |
| Cardholder's Name: | June Thompson |
| Card Expiry Date: | 07/20 |

Please retain a copy of this receipt for your records. We recommend that you print a copy and bring it with you on the day of your tour. Furthermore, we recommend that you arrive one hour in advance of your departure time in order to be briefed on all safety precautions.

**196.** What is true about the Grand Canyon Helicopter Tour & Lunch Package?

(A) It is designed for large groups.
(B) It includes lunch in a restaurant.
(C) It is the most frequently purchased tour.
(D) It brings the guests over the Hoover Dam and Lake Mead.

**197.** What time and day must Ms. Thompson's group arrive for their tour?

(A) At 10:30 A.M. on August 3
(B) At 11:30 A.M. on August 3
(C) At 10:30 A.M. on August 27
(D) At 14:30 P.M. on August 27

**198.** What does Grand Canyon Explore and Adventure recommend Ms. Thompson to do?

(A) Write a review on their website
(B) Pay via bank transfer
(C) Bring some food with them
(D) Save a copy of her receipt

**199.** What is suggested about Ms. Thompson's tour?

(A) Ms. Thompson paid for it in cash.
(B) It featured a kayak tour along a river.
(C) The guide was rude and unprofessional.
(D) It concluded with a free meal.

**200.** According to Ms. Thompson, how much should her group have been charged?

(A) $80
(B) $350
(C) $400
(D) $450

**Stop! This is the end of the test. If you finish before time is called, you may go back to Parts 5, 6, and 7 and check your work.**

| | | | | |
|---|---|---|---|---|
| **101.** (B) | **121.** (B) | **141.** (A) | **161.** (C) | **181.** (D) |
| **102.** (A) | **122.** (B) | **142.** (C) | **162.** (D) | **182.** (B) |
| **103.** (C) | **123.** (C) | **143.** (C) | **163.** (C) | **183.** (D) |
| **104.** (A) | **124.** (C) | **144.** (D) | **164.** (A) | **184.** (B) |
| **105.** (D) | **125.** (A) | **145.** (B) | **165.** (D) | **185.** (C) |
| **106.** (B) | **126.** (A) | **146.** (C) | **166.** (C) | **186.** (C) |
| **107.** (C) | **127.** (C) | **147.** (A) | **167.** (B) | **187.** (D) |
| **108.** (C) | **128.** (A) | **148.** (D) | **168.** (B) | **188.** (B) |
| **109.** (C) | **129.** (A) | **149.** (D) | **169.** (A) | **189.** (A) |
| **110.** (B) | **130.** (D) | **150.** (B) | **170.** (C) | **190.** (B) |
| **111.** (D) | **131.** (C) | **151.** (C) | **171.** (D) | **191.** (B) |
| **112.** (B) | **132.** (D) | **152.** (B) | **172.** (D) | **192.** (A) |
| **113.** (B) | **133.** (A) | **153.** (A) | **173.** (B) | **193.** (C) |
| **114.** (A) | **134.** (A) | **154.** (D) | **174.** (D) | **194.** (A) |
| **115.** (B) | **135.** (A) | **155.** (C) | **175.** (C) | **195.** (B) |
| **116.** (B) | **136.** (D) | **156.** (B) | **176.** (A) | **196.** (D) |
| **117.** (D) | **137.** (B) | **157.** (A) | **177.** (D) | **197.** (C) |
| **118.** (B) | **138.** (C) | **158.** (C) | **178.** (A) | **198.** (D) |
| **119.** (C) | **139.** (D) | **159.** (B) | **179.** (B) | **199.** (D) |
| **120.** (A) | **140.** (C) | **160.** (D) | **180.** (D) | **200.** (C) |

# ACTUAL TEST

**3**

## READING TEST

In the Reading Test, you will read a variety of texts and answer several different types of reading comprehension questions. The entire Reading test will last 75 minutes. There are three parts, and directions are given for each part. You are encouraged to answer as many questions as possible within the time allowed.

You must mark your answers on the separate answer sheet. Do not write your answers in your test book.

## PART 5

**Directions:** A word or phrase is missing in each of the sentences below. Four answer choices are given below each sentence. Select the best answer to complete the sentence. Then mark the letter (A), (B), (C), or (D) on your answer sheet.

**101.** The ------- of additional city councilors will take place at the beginning of next year.

(A) appoint
(B) appoints
(C) appointed
(D) appointment

**102.** The president of Northern Star Footwear stated that ------ is drafting a proposal for a business merger.

(A) him
(B) he
(C) his
(D) himself

**103.** Ms. Wilson should update her itinerary before she ------- for her trip overseas.

(A) will leave
(B) leaves
(C) leaving
(D) left

**104.** According to the report, the recent ------- with the city mayor's office did not progress favorably.

(A) negotiator
(B) negotiations
(C) negotiated
(D) negotiates

**105.** Several of the candidates were given interviews, but only a few of ------- were chosen for the positions.

(A) we
(B) us
(C) our
(D) ourselves

**106.** The merger was successful because all the partners played a role in ------- planning the deal.

(A) strategy
(B) strategic
(C) strategized
(D) strategically

**107.** After completing his degree at an American university, Paul Bouchard ------- to Paris to teach at a local school.

(A) visited
(B) returned
(C) occurred
(D) related

**108.** Please ensure all deliveries are brought to the side ------- of the supermarket.

(A) entrant
(B) entered
(C) entering
(D) entrance

**109.** The urban planners met several times a week to discuss plans for the upcoming downtown development -------.

(A) statement
(B) permission
(C) project
(D) ability

**110.** The sales position will be open to new graduates, ------- means applicants must have completed a degree program.

(A) whoever
(B) who
(C) which
(D) whatever

**111.** Courses at the company ------- to both seasonal hires and long-term employees.

(A) are offered
(B) have offered
(C) an offer
(D) offering

**112.** The Benson Music School is situated just ------- the Roland Dental Clinic on Boyd Avenue.

(A) into
(B) over
(C) among
(D) past

**113.** Following a mandatory probationary period, full-time employees are ------- to receive benefits.

(A) beneficial
(B) eligible
(C) convenient
(D) relevant

**114.** The Weston Grant ------- outstanding research conducted in the science and technology field.

(A) recognizes
(B) assumes
(C) reassures
(D) moderates

**115.** Every staff member is given an employee handbook so they can ------- remind themselves of procedures.

(A) consecutively
(B) standardly
(C) namely
(D) easily

**116.** Sanford Shoes is the most popular outlet in the city because its products are always durable, ------- priced, and fashionable.

(A) reason
(B) reasoning
(C) reasonable
(D) reasonably

**117.** All staff at Brennan's are ------- to discuss your home decorating needs either in person or over the phone.

(A) delighting
(B) delighted
(C) delights
(D) delight

**118.** Rose Textile Manufacturers uses the ------- latest manufacturing equipment and materials.

(A) so
(B) more
(C) very
(D) much

**119.** All Libby brand refrigerators come with a two-year guarantee -------- stated otherwise.

(A) whereas
(B) below
(C) neither
(D) unless

**120.** The community thanks you for your ------- in keeping Acorn Valley Apartments clean and safe.

(A) participant
(B) participation
(C) participate
(D) participated

**121.** The interest rates were a key ------- in the CEO's decision to switch to the Emerald Bank.

(A) factor
(B) position
(C) instructor
(D) composition

**122.** The health inspector will arrive at an unforeseen date ------- ensure the conditions of the inspection are fair.

(A) even if
(B) in order to
(C) after all
(D) given that

**123.** Peter Nugent's novel was made into an adventure movie two years ago after Winston Studios obtained -------- from Nugent's grandson.

(A) permission
(B) suggestion
(C) comparison
(D) registration

**124.** The mayor's office has issued a statement ------- the use of tax revenue to repair roads in the coming year.

(A) excluding
(B) during
(C) following
(D) regarding

**125.** The Delbert Condominium Tower is
------- located within walking distance of
two subway stations.

(A) conveniently
(B) consistently
(C) continually
(D) commonly

**126.** Interns should ------- new applications if
they wish to apply for any of the new
full-time positions.

(A) reply
(B) submit
(C) vacate
(D) oppose

**127.** Ms. Houlahan's revised draft of
Reynold Manufacturing's mission
statement expresses the goals of the
company --------.

(A) precise
(B) more precise
(C) preciseness
(D) precisely

**128.** ------- the park is open during the
summer months, the public is
restricted from accessing certain areas.

(A) While
(B) When
(C) For
(D) But

**129.** ------- the education level of Paul
Rogers, it is no wonder that he is the
highest-paid speaker at the convention.

(A) About
(B) Given
(C) Upon
(D) Since

**130.** Considering all the hot weather we're
having, the number of people using
public swimming pools is ------- to
increase.

(A) covered
(B) sought
(C) limited
(D) bound

## PART 6

**Directions:** Read the texts that follow. A word, phrase, or sentence is missing in parts of each text. Four answer choices for each question are given below the text. Select the best answer to complete the text. Then mark the letter (A), (B), (C), or (D) on your answer sheet.

**Questions 131-134** refer to the following information.

At Echo Stationery Supplies, we try to ship your orders as quickly as we can. If you have concerns that your shipment has been delayed, please ___131.___ our shipping policies. Our expected delivery time may range from 4 days up to 4 weeks, which depends on the method of shipping customers choose during checkout. ___132.___ . We try to ensure our shipping estimates are accurate; however, some orders may take ___133.___ to arrive at your door. If you have found that your order is excessively ___134.___ , do not hesitate to contact us immediately. We promise to look into the problem and let you know the status of your shipment.

131. (A) note
(B) send
(C) prepare
(D) require

132. (A) Returned items will be eligible for exchanges only, not refunds.
(B) Contact our specialists to get an updated list of all of our new products.
(C) An approximate delivery date is indicated on your receipt.
(D) Visit our online feedback section and let us know how well we served you.

133. (A) length
(B) lengthy
(C) longer
(D) longest

134. (A) different
(B) delayed
(C) overpriced
(D) greater

April 24

After months of discussions, Nackawic Town Council has finally approved an agreement with DRTL Enterprises. Under the terms of the agreement, DRTL **135.** the 30-acre lot on the east end of Barrett Street. The detailed proposal calls for the building of both retail shops and offices in the area. Nackawic's mayor, Leona Hovey, is optimistic that the project will bring **136.** benefits to the town and surrounding areas. "It is expected to create 300 full-time jobs," says Hovey. "For a while, I felt the ongoing postponements would force us to cancel the project all together." **137.** . DRTL spokesperson, Jeff Perkins believes the development will take three years to finish. At the same time, he cautions people that there may be more setbacks. "Of course, we provided the town council with our very best **138.** , but even so, we have no way of predicting everything that will happen," Perkins said.

**135.** (A) to develop
(B) will develop
(C) has developed
(D) could have developed

**136.** (A) economic
(B) unforeseen
(C) environmental
(D) frequent

**137.** (A) While the town is eager to get moving on this, delays are inevitable for major developments like this.
(B) Local residents, however, have approached us with legitimate concerns about the high noise levels construction will create.
(C) Members of town council are set to vote on four different proposals from well-known architects.
(D) Despite the town's promise to grant the developers a contract, they may now have to look at other options.

**138.** (A) argument
(B) background
(C) estimate
(D) combination

Roderick Opera House has announced that it will lengthen its run of Melanie Beck's new musical, *The Birth of Jazz*. Due to an increase in ___139.___ for tickets, the show will be playing nightly until the end of August. The announcement was unexpected, as the musical received ___140.___ criticism from renowned musical theater critic Jeffrey O'pry.

___141.___. However, last week the show was sold out three nights in a row. According to representatives of the opera house, the show has been attracting an older crowd who may not normally attend musicals. The new attendees are ___142.___ excited about hearing the great jazz numbers reinvented by Beck.

**139.** (A) demand
(B) demanded
(C) demanding
(D) to demand

**140.** (A) brilliant
(B) deep
(C) harsh
(D) prompt

**141.** (A) Guests at the musical were mostly from out of town.
(B) The final show will be held on August 24.
(C) Following the review, ticket sales dropped dramatically.
(D) Similarly, the theater has been suffering for years.

**142.** (A) apparent
(B) more apparent
(C) apparentness
(D) apparently

**Questions 143-146** refer to the following e-mail.

---

**From:** Customer Care

**To:** Paul Kanagawa

**Date:** October 16

**Subject:** Welcome to Atlantic Music Trends

**Attachment:** Form

Dear Mr. Kanagawa,

Thank you very much for subscribing to *Atlantic Music Trends*! ___143.___ you will have detailed information about upcoming music classes, festivals, and concerts happening all over Canada's Atlantic coast. You can expect your first issue at your door by the 20th. ___144.___. After that, every issue will be sent out during the first week of the month. With this subscription, you will also have unlimited ___145.___ to online videos, song recordings, articles, schedules, and even ticketing information for concerts. All you have to do is log on to our website using the user ID and eight-digit passwords listed ___146.___ the bottom line of the attached enrollment form.

Sincerely,

Veronica Van Zeyl

Customer Representative

---

143. (A) Now
    (B) Afterward
    (C) Then
    (D) Meanwhile

144. (A) Please notify us if it does not arrive by that date.
    (B) To subscribe, please phone during regular business hours.
    (C) The next festival will take place in Moncton in mid-November.
    (D) We invite readers to submit reviews of concerts for publication.

145. (A) accessing
    (B) accesses
    (C) accessed
    (D) access

146. (A) for
    (B) about
    (C) on
    (D) at

## PART 7

**Directions:** In this part you will read a selection of texts, such as magazine and newspaper articles, e-mails, and instant messages. Each text or set of texts is followed by several questions. Select the best answer for each question and mark the letter (A), (B), (C), or (D) on your answer sheet.

**Questions 147-148** refer to the following notice.

*Jen's Salon and Spa*

**Holiday Information**

- Spa hours will be extended from November 20 to January 20.
  (Monday — Saturday 10 A.M. to 10 P.M.)
- Please note, the spa will be closed from December 24 – 29.
- As always, cancellations must be made 24 hours in advance to avoid cancelation fees.

**147.** What is the purpose of the notice?

(A) To advertise a new service
(B) To explain a schedule
(C) To announce a sale
(D) To offer a refund

**148.** What is stated about cancellations?

(A) The spa requires advance notice of cancellations.
(B) Customers can cancel appointments online.
(C) A service fee is always applied to cancellations.
(D) Holiday appointments cannot be cancelled.

**Questions 149-150** refer to the following notice.

---

**Notice for Eastpoint Community Residents**

As of next month, our weekly community newsletter will be going paperless. In an effort to protect the environment and reduce the amount of paper we use, the newsletter will now be available online only.

Anyone who currently has a small business advertisement in the newsletter is encouraged to contact the newsletter editor for an updated contract at 900-555-3434. The first online newsletter is scheduled to be on www.eastpointcommunity.com/newsletter on November 1. We hope you enjoy this new convenient way to receive your weekly newsletter.

Sincerely,

Eastpoint Community Newsletter Team

---

**149.** What change will be made to the newsletter?

(A) It will merge with another publication.
(B) It will be delivered faster.
(C) It will run less frequently.
(D) It will no longer be printed on paper.

**150.** According to the notice, why might advertisers contact the editor?

(A) To sign a new contract
(B) To receive a discount
(C) To upgrade a membership
(D) To change a listing

---

### Unpaid Spring Training Session
### 9:30 A.M. to 4:30 P.M.

**9:30 A.M.: Meet and Greet**

Meet your managers as well as your fellow new employees. Enjoy coffee and donuts as you watch a short introduction video to the company.

**10:30 A.M.: Rules and Procedures**

Pick up your employee handbook and review the rules and procedures with the office manager. A short question and answer session will be included.

**12:00 P.M.: Lunch Break**

A light buffet lunch of sandwiches, salads, and desserts will be catered in the conference room. Vegetarian options will be provided for employees.

**1:00 P.M.: Department Shadowing**

Employees will visit their respective departments and receive hands-on training from an assigned veteran employee.

**3:30 P.M.: Desk Assignments**

Employees will be shown to their desks and given an opportunity to set up their company accounts and e-mails. IT will be available for any problems that may arise.

---

**151.** For whom is the session most likely intended?

(A) Company CEOs
(B) Computer technicians
(C) New office employees
(D) Department transfers

**152.** What portion of the session involves IT specialists?

(A) Meet and Greet
(B) Rules and Procedures
(C) Department Shadowing
(D) Desk Assignments

**153.** What is NOT indicated about the session?

(A) It is an unpaid event.
(B) It lasts for one work day.
(C) It is run by the HR director.
(D) It includes refreshments.

**Questions 154-157** refer to the following report.

---

**Rengrew Bedding**

Weekly Status Report: September 5-9
Prepared by: Alexander Corbin, Project Coordinator

**Accomplished this Week:**

- Got in touch with four manufacturers in Mexico who currently produce bedding products. --[1]--. E-mailed them design specifications for our new bedding sets along with questions about production pricing, turnaround time, fabric availability, and shipping costs.

- According to the replies, P&M Textiles appears to be the best candidate. --[2]--. Additionally, Sammy Ruiz, a client services manager, e-mailed me promptly. Her responses to my questions were very detailed and professional. I believe she would ensure this transition is both smooth and efficient.

- The other three companies either did not have access to our preferred fabrics or they could not meet our supply demand. --[3]--. As a result, we will no longer be able to consider them.

**Plans for Next Week:**

- Contact P&M Textiles to set up a conference call about payment and shipping terms. --[4]--.

- Review final designs for all products and request revisions if need be. Meet with the design team to discuss any changes.

---

**154.** What is suggested about Rengrew Bedding?

(A) It has just hired a new manager.
(B) It is a brand new company in Mexico.
(C) It has its own factories on-site.
(D) It is getting ready to launch new products.

**155.** According to the report, what did Mr. Corbin do during the week of September 5?

(A) Finalized some design information
(B) Assessed potential business partners
(C) Visited a manufacturer in person
(D) Requested a payment be delayed

**156.** What is mentioned about Ms. Ruiz?

(A) She is new to P&M Textiles.
(B) She suggested some changes.
(C) She contacted some businesses.
(D) She is easy to work with.

**157.** In which of the positions marked [1], [2], [3], and [4] does the following sentence best belong?

"It is located further south than most companies, but it has the capacity to meet our supply needs."

(A) [1]
(B) [2]
(C) [3]
(D) [4]

## Grand Avenue Hotel: Banquet Services

Thank you for choosing Grand Avenue Hotel for your banquet. Please fill out the information below. One of our guest services representatives will contact you to confirm your reservation and request payment information.

Reservation Name: _____  Event Date: _____
E-mail: _____  Business Phone: _____
Personal Phone: _____

**Room Preference:**
[    ] Diamond Room (up to 100 guests) [    ] Rose Room (up to 150 guests)
[    ] Starlight Room (up to 200 guests)

**Requested Layout:**
[    ] Dinner (round tables and chairs)  [    ] Dinner and Dance (tables and a dance floor)
[    ] Dinner and Speech (tables and a stage) [    ] Other : _____

**Food and Beverages:**
[    ] Full-Service Buffet and Dessert Bar  [    ] Three-Course Catered Dinner

AV Equipment Required: [    ] Yes [    ] No  Explain: _____
Hotel Accommodation for Guests: [    ] Yes [    ] No  Number of Rooms: _____

---

**158.** According to the form, what will Grand Avenue Hotel staff do?

(A) E-mail brochures with room photos
(B) Assist customers with setup and cleanup
(C) Offer free accommodation vouchers to guests
(D) Contact customers about payment information

**159.** What is implied about Grand Avenue Hotel's banquet services?

(A) It requires payment for the use of audio-visual equipment.
(B) It will arrange the room to suit the event.
(C) It provides discounted hotel rooms to banquet guests.
(D) It offers free live music for dinner and dance events.

Questions 160-162 refer to the following job advertisement.

---

https://www.employmentfind.com

**Find Employment Online**

*Build Your Career Today!*

The real estate business can be hard when you're working alone. At Team Real Estate, you are not alone! Our large network of real estate agents makes showing and selling properties easy. By sharing information on potential buyers in our database, we sell more properties than any other agency in the country. Our shared commission rates encourage our team members to work together to get the job done.

Complete our new real estate training seminar and apply for your real estate license. If you're successful, you may be offered a full-time contract position with full benefits.

Education and experience will be considered before you are offered a contract. University degrees are a plus, but high school graduates may also apply. Applicants must have access to their own vehicle, as driving to and from local properties is a must.

To apply for this position, please click the button below. You'll need to input your e-mail address, phone number, and upload your resume. Only those selected for interviews will be contacted. Prior to interviews, we recommend that all candidates familiarize themselves with our company policies. Please visit www.teamrealestate.com/careers to learn more about this.

[ Apply Now ]

---

**160.** What duty is suggested as part of the job?

(A) Listing clients on a shared database
(B) Offering advice on upgrading properties
(C) Attracting clients through phone calls
(D) Coordinating a mentorship program

**161.** According to the advertisement, what is requested for a contract position?

(A) A college diploma
(B) A real estate license
(C) Marketing experience
(D) Employment references

**162.** According to the advertisement, why should applicants visit the Team Real Estate website?

(A) To learn about Team Real Estate's procedures
(B) To apply for a contract position with benefits
(C) To upload a resume and references
(D) To inquire about the time of a training session

## 50 Years of Community Service

March 27 — Professor Abraham Drew is known in the local community not for his years as a teacher of psychology or for his numerous papers published in academic journals, but for his dedication to community outreach. Fifty years ago, Mr. Drew founded the first after-school program for local children, which has helped numerous children in the city. The program, which started as a baseball camp for troubled boys, has since grown into Homework Helpers for elementary school-aged children, Art on the Street for teenagers, and Give Back, a charity in which individuals and businesses organize food drives for the homeless. "I never thought my after-school program would develop into all these unique programs," Mr. Drew said, "but there was so much community interest. Everywhere, people were looking for a way to help out."

After 50 years of service, Mr. Drew will retire from both his job as a professor and as program coordinator. His grandson, Michael Drew, will retain control of the programs. "I'm very happy to continue what my grandfather started," Michael Drew said. "He's a great man, and the community needs the work he has done."

Mr. Drew's volunteers will host a retirement party to honor him next month at Wilfred Park. The party will include performances by local bands, food prepared by local restaurants, and a small fireworks show. The mayor will present Mr. Drew with a Lifetime Service Achievement Award as thanks for his years of giving back to the community. For details about this event, please visit www. wilfredpark.com/events/April.

**163.** Why most likely was the article written?

(A) To celebrate the founding of a city
(B) To encourage readers to donate to charity
(C) To announce the closing of a community business
(D) To highlight the achievements of a local figure

**164.** The word "retain" in paragraph 2, line 2, is closest in meaning to

(A) contribute to
(B) agree with
(C) remember
(D) keep

**165.** What is NOT suggested about Abraham Drew?

(A) He started a baseball camp for boys.
(B) He instructs students at a university.
(C) He will open another school next year.
(D) He inspired others to do charity work.

**166.** What is stated about the party at Wilfred Park?

(A) Local comedy acts will perform.
(B) The city will host the celebration.
(C) Participants can attend for a small fee.
(D) Mr. Drew will be honored with an award.

Questions 167-168 refer to the following text message chain.

**Pedro Alando [11:00 A.M.]:**
Ms. Wilson, please check your e-mail. I sent you an updated contract.

**Tina Wilson [11:02 A.M.]:**
OK, thank you. Has the payment scale been updated as well?

**Pedro Alando [11:03 A.M.]:**
Certainly. Because you've been with us for longer than a year, you will now be paid $100 dollars for every color photo you take for our magazine instead of $80.

**Tina Wilson [11:05 A.M.]:**
Excellent. Thank you for clarifying that. I'll have a look at the contract, sign it, and send it back shortly.

**Pedro Alando [11:08 A.M.]:**
Fantastic. We are very pleased you have decided to work with us for another year.

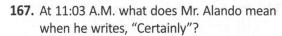

SEND

**167.** At 11:03 A.M. what does Mr. Alando mean when he writes, "Certainly"?

(A) He will send an e-mail one more time.
(B) He is sure of the success of a plan.
(C) He is willing to share some information.
(D) He made a previously agreed-upon change.

**168.** Who most likely is Ms. Wilson?

(A) A contract lawyer
(B) A magazine editor
(C) A photographer
(D) A journalist

**Questions 169-171** refer to the following e-mail.

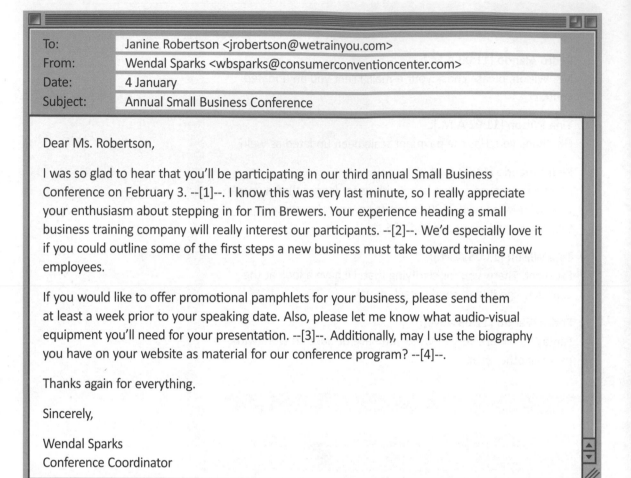

To: Janine Robertson <jrobertson@wetrainyou.com>
From: Wendal Sparks <wbsparks@consumerconventioncenter.com>
Date: 4 January
Subject: Annual Small Business Conference

Dear Ms. Robertson,

I was so glad to hear that you'll be participating in our third annual Small Business Conference on February 3. --[1]--. I know this was very last minute, so I really appreciate your enthusiasm about stepping in for Tim Brewers. Your experience heading a small business training company will really interest our participants. --[2]--. We'd especially love it if you could outline some of the first steps a new business must take toward training new employees.

If you would like to offer promotional pamphlets for your business, please send them at least a week prior to your speaking date. Also, please let me know what audio-visual equipment you'll need for your presentation. --[3]--. Additionally, may I use the biography you have on your website as material for our conference program? --[4]--.

Thanks again for everything.

Sincerely,

Wendal Sparks
Conference Coordinator

**169.** Why did Mr. Sparks most likely send the e-mail?

(A) To propose an itinerary change
(B) To ask for an updated schedule
(C) To send a belated invitation
(D) To recognize an offer of acceptance

**170.** What is suggested about Mr. Brewers?

(A) He attends conferences every year.
(B) He is unable to speak at a conference.
(C) He works as an event coordinator.
(D) He started his own small business.

**171.** In which of the positions marked [1], [2], [3], and [4] does the following sentence best belong?

"If you'd prefer to use a different text, please e-mail it to me."

(A) [1]
(B) [2]
(C) [3]
(D) [4]

**Questions 172-175** refer to the following text message chain.

---

**Jan Swanson**        4 September, 2:35
Jonathan, have you sent order #2256 out for delivery?
If not, we need to add another identical set of personalized pens and paper to it.

**Jonathan Gruer**        4 September, 2:37
The order is still in the storeroom, but it'll take at least two more days to produce the custom pens and paper.

**Jan Swanson**        4 September, 2:38
Is it possible to get it done sooner? The customer said it's urgent.

**Jonathan Gruer**        4 September, 2:40
Let's check with someone from manufacturing.

*Rowena MacArthur has been added to the chat.*

**Jonathan Gruer**        4 September, 2:41
Rowena, do you have time for a rush order? It's a duplicate of order #2256.

**Rowena MacArthur**    4 September, 2:43
I think I can get it done by tomorrow morning. Is that OK?

**Jan Swanson**        4 September, 2:44
Yes, that works. Thanks a lot!

---

**172.** What type of products does the company sell?

(A) Watches
(B) Stationery
(C) Furniture
(D) Electronics

**173.** Why does Mr. Gruer contact Ms. MacArthur?

(A) To pass on a customer complaint
(B) To find out where a staff meeting will be held
(C) To determine where an order has been shipped to
(D) To inquire about the timeframe for some work

**174.** What does the customer want to do?

(A) Double an order
(B) Cancel a delivery
(C) Return a damaged item
(D) Update payment information

**175.** At 2:44, what does Ms. Swanson most likely mean when she writes, "that works"?

(A) She can reschedule some appointments.
(B) She is impressed with a new product.
(C) A deadline will be acceptable for a customer.
(D) Some new items will be advertised online.

| To: | msimpson@tristarinternational.com |
| From: | bookings@stonewallhotel.com |
| Date: | May 17 |
| Subject: | Booking CV1124 |

Dear Ms. Simpson,

Thank you for selecting Stonewall Hotel for your company's annual workshop. As you indicated on your online reservation, 12 king-sized ocean view suites have been booked for your group. Since the purpose of your visit is to conduct a business workshop, I have also reserved our executive lounge and conference room at no extra charge.

According to your online reservation, your check-in date will be August 5 and your check-out will be August 8. A charge of $109 dollars for each room per night will be added to your final bill. Your reservation number is CV1124. Please ensure you record this number as you will need it should you request any changes to your reservation.

As you know, Stonewall Hotel includes many additional features and activities. If your group wish to take a complimentary surfing lesson, I suggest reserving a spot in advance. Furthermore, we offer complimentary breakfasts, room service packages, and have just opened up Stonewall Grill, a brand new steak restaurant located next to the lobby.

Thank you for choosing Stonewall Hotel. We look forward to serving you.

Booking Services, Stonewall Hotel

| To: | bookings@stonewallhotel.com |
| From: | msimpson@tristarinternational.com |
| Date: | May 19 |
| Subject: Re: | Booking CV1124 |

Dear booking services staff,

I am writing to let you know that there were a few errors with my reservation. My reservation number is CV1124. I indicated 10 junior-sized suites when I reserved online, but your e-mail says something different. Additionally, I also paid for a catered lunch during my group's hiking trip on August 6, but that was not mentioned in your e-mail. Please make sure this service has been booked in addition to updating the correct room size. I would appreciate it if you notified me about this issue as soon as possible.

Thank you for your assistance.

Sincerely,

Margo Simpson
Office of the CEO
Tristar International

**176.** What is the purpose of the first e-mail?

(A) To confirm a group reservation
(B) To inform of a new policy
(C) To assist in making a reservation
(D) To provide a free upgrade

**177.** What is suggested about Stonewall's surfing lessons?

(A) They are available only in the mornings.
(B) They are a new service.
(C) They are being offered temporarily.
(D) They are a popular feature.

**178.** What information in the hotel's records is missing?

(A) The lounge has been reserved.
(B) The group will arrive on August 5.
(C) A catering service is booked.
(D) The room bill has been prepaid.

**179.** What can be inferred about the group from Tristar International?

(A) It consists of 12 members.
(B) It will go hiking on the second day of the workshop.
(C) It will have dinner at the Stonewall Grill.
(D) It will arrive a day later than the reservation states.

**180.** In the second e-mail, the word "issue" in paragraph 1, line 6, is closest in meaning to

(A) alteration
(B) selection
(C) price
(D) problem

## Heber Birdwatching Club

April 2 — The Northville Recreation Board recently announced the creation of the Heber Park Birdwatching Club at Heber Wildlife Park. The birdwatching club will meet from Friday through Sunday, from 1 P.M. until 3 P.M. The club meetings will run all summer long and will feature a number of lookout sites located on the Heber Trails. Each participant should dress appropriately for hiking on the trails and bring a supply of drinking water. Cameras are allowed for participants who want to photograph the numerous bird species located in Heber Wildlife Park. Up to 10 members may join the club, and those interested can sign up with the club coordinator, Mindy Beckett (334-998-0034).

## June Weekend Activities at Heber Wildlife Park

- **Friday**   – 12:00 P.M. Children's Picnic (Camp and Recreation Park)
    – 2:00 P.M. Heber Birdwatching Club (Squirrel Trail)
    – 4:00 P.M. T&V Industries Weekly Baseball Game (Diamond)

- **Saturday**   – 2:00 P.M. Heber Birdwatching Club (Squirrel Trail)
    – 4:00 P.M. Barbecue Madness (East Pavilion on June 10 and 24 only)

- **Sunday**   – 10:00 A.M. Nature Watercolor Painting (Gallery Building, $15 per person)
    – 2:00 P.M. Heber Birdwatching Club (Squirrel Trail)
    – 4:00 P.M. Level A Soccer (Soccer field)
    – 6:00 P.M. Music at the Park (West Pavilion)

For more information on any of the above events, please visit www.heberwildlifepark.com or call 556-332-0989.

**181.** What is the purpose of the notice?

(A) To inform of a new activity at Heber Wildlife Park

(B) To announce a new coordinator for the Heber Birdwatching Club

(C) To apologize for the cancelation of an event at Heber Wildlife Park

(D) To advertise a new position at the Northville Recreation Board

**182.** In the notice, the word "run" in paragraph 1, line 3, is closest in meaning to

(A) jog

(B) continue

(C) roam

(D) grow

**183.** What is suggested about the birdwatching club in June?

(A) It has 12 members.

(B) It requires participants to bring cameras.

(C) Its meeting time has been changed.

(D) Its coordinator will be absent.

**184.** What activity will only occur twice in June?

(A) T&V Industries Baseball Game

(B) Barbecue Madness

(C) Nature Watercolor Painting

(D) Music at the Park

**185.** What is indicated about Heber Wildlife Park?

(A) Its pavilions have all been upgraded.

(B) Its campground is open all year round.

(C) It includes a lake and a water fountain.

(D) It has special programs for children.

**Questions 186-190** refer to the following advertisement, e-mail, and website feedback.

Toronto Tours

**Toronto, Ontario**

To celebrate its first year of business, Toronto Tours is offering a special 20% discount on Culture of Toronto tours booked between April 5 and May 5. This is our most popular tour and is offered every Friday. The following is breakdown of our standard itinerary.

▶ The Royal Ontario Museum: Start at the famous Royal Ontario Museum. Enjoy some of the most beautiful art in the world in the ROM's many modern galleries. See the latest archeological discoveries on display and a number of large dinosaur species. April's special exhibit: 18th Century Maps.

▶ The Hockey Hall of Fame: Head over to the Hockey Hall of Fame and see Canada's greatest hockey legends remembered in numerous video exhibits. Learn the history of Canada's favorite sport, and view memorabilia that belonged to players of the past.

▶ The Danforth Festival: Conclude your tour at the Danforth Festival. Enjoy a taste of Greek culture at this energetic street party. Sample food from Toronto's many Greek restaurants while you enjoy live music and dancing. (Until April 20)

Note: The final portion of the tour will be subject to changes depending on which festivals are taking place downtown. Additionally, all entrance fees are covered in your package price, but food and beverage costs are extra.

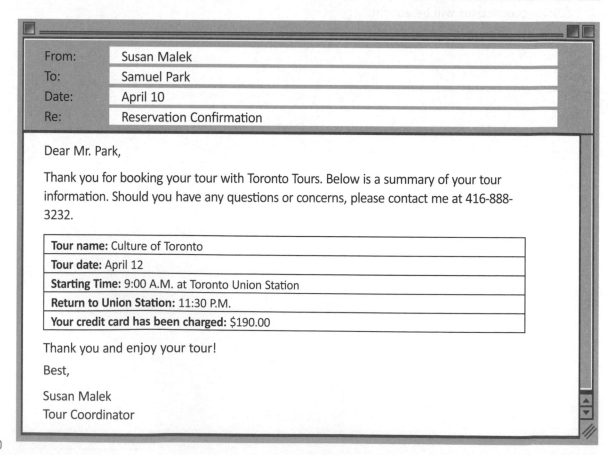

| From: | Susan Malek |
| To: | Samuel Park |
| Date: | April 10 |
| Re: | Reservation Confirmation |

Dear Mr. Park,

Thank you for booking your tour with Toronto Tours. Below is a summary of your tour information. Should you have any questions or concerns, please contact me at 416-888-3232.

| **Tour name:** Culture of Toronto |
| **Tour date:** April 12 |
| **Starting Time:** 9:00 A.M. at Toronto Union Station |
| **Return to Union Station:** 11:30 P.M. |
| **Your credit card has been charged:** $190.00 |

Thank you and enjoy your tour!

Best,

Susan Malek
Tour Coordinator

**Customer Feedback:**

This was my first time using Toronto Tours, and I found the tour to be much more impressive than the sightseeing bus tour I took the last time I visited Toronto. This company sure understands how to treat tourists' interest in the city's unique history and culture. Francis Weltz, our tour guide, was extremely helpful in getting us to and from locations as well as ensuring speedy entry to the listed stops. The only downside of the tour was the rainy weather, which made it hard to enjoy the final stop. As a result, I wish an alternate destination would've been available in the event of poor weather.

Posted by: Samuel Park

**186.** What is suggested about Toronto Tours?

(A) It operates several tour programs.
(B) It has been open for several years.
(C) It will stop offering summer tours.
(D) It has added a new sightseeing tour.

**187.** According to the advertisement, what does Toronto Tours offer clients?

(A) Vouchers for food and beverages
(B) Upgraded travel options
(C) Discounts on group packages
(D) Admission fees to museums

**188.** What is suggested about Mr. Park's tour?

(A) It included return airfare from Greece.
(B) It visited four main stops.
(C) It was purchased at a discount.
(D) It was originally developed for local artists.

**189.** In the website feedback, the word "treat" in paragraph 1, line 3, is closest in meaning to

(A) serve
(B) increase
(C) decide
(D) ignore

**190.** What portion of the tour was Mr. Park dissatisfied with?

(A) Seeing off at Union Station
(B) The Royal Ontario Museum
(C) The Hockey Hall of Fame
(D) The Danforth Festival

# European Manufacturing Commission

4th Annual Convention
Rowensburg Conference Center
Berlin, Germany
Saturday, October 10

| Tentative Schedule | | |
| --- | --- | --- |
| **Time** | **Location** | |
| 9:00 A.M. – 9:30 A.M. | Greetings and Opening Speech by EMC Chairman Alek Sorvenski in the Cranz Banquet Room | |
| 10:00 A.M. – 11:30 A.M. | Strauss Room | Whitman Room |
| | Textile Factory Management Techniques<br>— Hans Tiskawet | Advanced Coloration and Bleaching Technologies<br>— Michelle Perdeu |
| 1:00 P.M. – 2:30 P.M. | Outsourcing and Overseas Management<br>— Rowena Wentworth | Upgrading and Maintaining Equipment<br>— Spencer Defiore |
| 3:00 P.M. – 4:30 P.M. | Establishing Contacts with International Clothing Distributors<br>— Anita Pitelli | International Shipping Strategies<br>— Thao Lee |

• Speakers must confirm their availability with Johanna Swartz (jswartz@emc.com) no later than August 28. Failure to report availability will result in an automatic change of speaker.

• Speakers will be given complimentary accommodation at the Deluxe Grand Hotel for one night. Please fill out the attached form and return it to Berta Joven by September 5. If you are traveling with a colleague or an assistant, you will need to book another room at an additional charge. Please indicate that on the form.

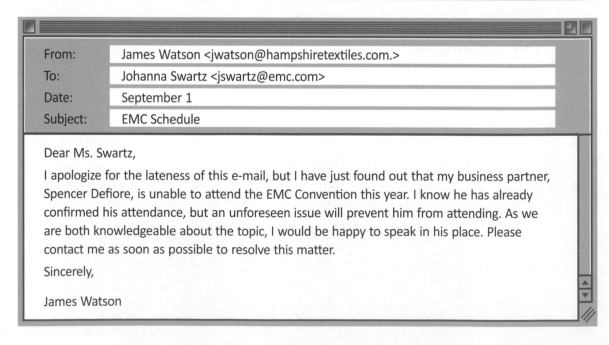

| From: | James Watson <jwatson@hampshiretextiles.com.> |
| --- | --- |
| To: | Johanna Swartz <jswartz@emc.com> |
| Date: | September 1 |
| Subject: | EMC Schedule |

Dear Ms. Swartz,

I apologize for the lateness of this e-mail, but I have just found out that my business partner, Spencer Defiore, is unable to attend the EMC Convention this year. I know he has already confirmed his attendance, but an unforeseen issue will prevent him from attending. As we are both knowledgeable about the topic, I would be happy to speak in his place. Please contact me as soon as possible to resolve this matter.

Sincerely,

James Watson

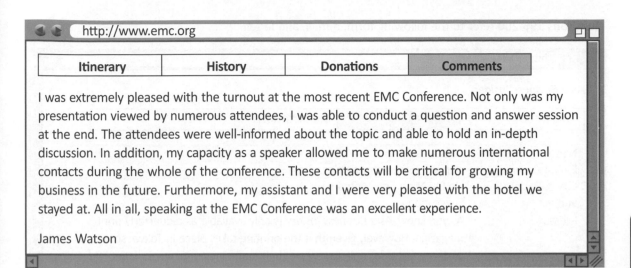

**191.** What industry is the focus of the conference?

(A) Shipping
(B) Dairy
(C) Electronics
(D) Fabrics

**192.** According to the schedule, what are presenters expected to do?

(A) Pay for hotel accommodation
(B) Arrive in Berlin by October 8
(C) Ship some presentation materials
(D) Confirm their participation in an event

**193.** What topic will Mr. Watson most likely speak about?

(A) Textile Factory Management Techniques
(B) Outsourcing and Overseas Management
(C) Upgrading and Maintaining Equipment
(D) International Shipping Strategies

**194.** In the review, the word "capacity" in paragraph 1, line 4, is closest in meaning to

(A) role
(B) time
(C) perspective
(D) experience

**195.** What is probably true about Mr. Watson?

(A) He operates several manufacturing plants in Germany.
(B) He booked a second room at the Deluxe Grand Hotel.
(C) He attends the EMC conference every year.
(D) He changed his topic to a more difficult one.

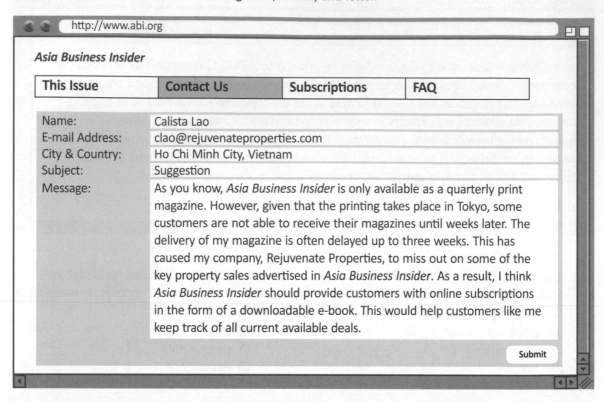

http://www.abi.org

*Asia Business Insider*

| This Issue | Contact Us | Subscriptions | FAQ |

| | |
|---|---|
| Name: | Calista Lao |
| E-mail Address: | clao@rejuvenateproperties.com |
| City & Country: | Ho Chi Minh City, Vietnam |
| Subject: | Suggestion |
| Message: | As you know, *Asia Business Insider* is only available as a quarterly print magazine. However, given that the printing takes place in Tokyo, some customers are not able to receive their magazines until weeks later. The delivery of my magazine is often delayed up to three weeks. This has caused my company, Rejuvenate Properties, to miss out on some of the key property sales advertised in *Asia Business Insider*. As a result, I think *Asia Business Insider* should provide customers with online subscriptions in the form of a downloadable e-book. This would help customers like me keep track of all current available deals. |

Submit

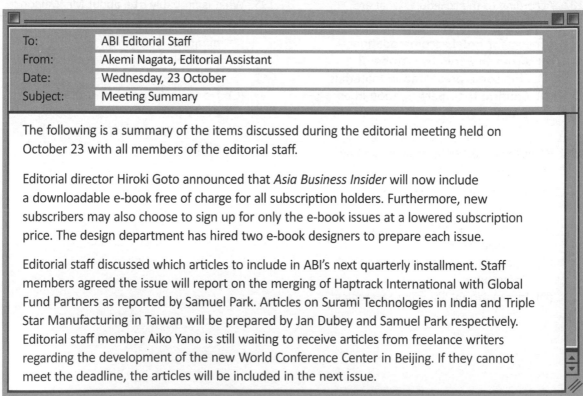

| To: | ABI Editorial Staff |
|---|---|
| From: | Akemi Nagata, Editorial Assistant |
| Date: | Wednesday, 23 October |
| Subject: | Meeting Summary |

The following is a summary of the items discussed during the editorial meeting held on October 23 with all members of the editorial staff.

Editorial director Hiroki Goto announced that *Asia Business Insider* will now include a downloadable e-book free of charge for all subscription holders. Furthermore, new subscribers may also choose to sign up for only the e-book issues at a lowered subscription price. The design department has hired two e-book designers to prepare each issue.

Editorial staff discussed which articles to include in ABI's next quarterly installment. Staff members agreed the issue will report on the merging of Haptrack International with Global Fund Partners as reported by Samuel Park. Articles on Surami Technologies in India and Triple Star Manufacturing in Taiwan will be prepared by Jan Dubey and Samuel Park respectively. Editorial staff member Aiko Yano is still waiting to receive articles from freelance writers regarding the development of the new World Conference Center in Beijing. If they cannot meet the deadline, the articles will be included in the next issue.

## Asia Business Insider
## January • Vol. 7 • Number 1

Letter from the Editor,

This issue celebrates the launch of *Asia Business Insider*'s e-book series. Subscribers can now download fully designed e-books that include all aspects of our print versions. The January issue will cover numerous business deals taking place in Asia. It will also include the launch of our new Editor's Commentary section in which the editorial staff will respond to questions and comments placed online.

Make sure to keep an eye out for our next issue in which we cover all the pertinent details surrounding the plans for the World Conference Center in Beijing. Make sure to sign up on our website for a chance to win free tickets to the center's grand opening business conference next year.

Hiroki Goto

**196.** What is true about Ms. Lao?

(A) She only buys property in Vietnam.
(B) Her ideas were implemented by ABI.
(C) She subscribes to several Japanese magazines.
(D) Her articles often appear in ABI.

**197.** Who will be discussing Surami Technologies?

(A) Hiroki Goto
(B) Samuel Park
(C) Jan Dubey
(D) Akemi Nagata

**198.** What is suggested about Aiko Yano?

(A) She joined ABI as an e-book designer.
(B) She did not receive some articles on time.
(C) She co-writes articles with Samuel Park.
(D) She was absent from the June 1 meeting.

**199.** What is indicated about *Asia Business Insider*?

(A) It has developed a new column.
(B) Its subscribers are mostly located in Vietnam.
(C) It will relocate to Beijing, China.
(D) It prints six issues per year.

**200.** What is mentioned about ABI's website?

(A) It is only for ABI subscribers.
(B) It will be upgraded next year.
(C) It is available in seven different languages.
(D) It will host a give-away for subscribers.

**Stop! This is the end of the test. If you finish before time is called, you may go back to Parts 5, 6, and 7 and check your work.**

# ANSWERS ACTUAL TEST 3

| | | | | |
|---|---|---|---|---|
| 101. (D) | 121. (A) | 141. (C) | 161. (B) | 181. (A) |
| 102. (B) | 122. (B) | 142. (D) | 162. (A) | 182. (B) |
| 103. (B) | 123. (A) | 143. (A) | 163. (D) | 183. (C) |
| 104. (B) | 124. (D) | 144. (A) | 164. (D) | 184. (B) |
| 105. (B) | 125. (A) | 145. (D) | 165. (C) | 185. (D) |
| 106. (D) | 126. (B) | 146. (C) | 166. (D) | 186. (A) |
| 107. (B) | 127. (D) | 147. (B) | 167. (D) | 187. (D) |
| 108. (D) | 128. (A) | 148. (A) | 168. (C) | 188. (C) |
| 109. (C) | 129. (B) | 149. (D) | 169. (D) | 189. (A) |
| 110. (C) | 130. (D) | 150. (A) | 170. (B) | 190. (D) |
| 111. (A) | 131. (A) | 151. (C) | 171. (D) | 191. (D) |
| 112. (D) | 132. (C) | 152. (D) | 172. (B) | 192. (D) |
| 113. (B) | 133. (C) | 153. (C) | 173. (D) | 193. (C) |
| 114. (A) | 134. (B) | 154. (D) | 174. (A) | 194. (A) |
| 115. (D) | 135. (B) | 155. (B) | 175. (C) | 195. (B) |
| 116. (D) | 136. (A) | 156. (D) | 176. (A) | 196. (B) |
| 117. (B) | 137. (A) | 157. (B) | 177. (D) | 197. (C) |
| 118. (C) | 138. (C) | 158. (D) | 178. (C) | 198. (B) |
| 119. (D) | 139. (A) | 159. (B) | 179. (B) | 199. (A) |
| 120. (B) | 140. (C) | 160. (A) | 180. (D) | 200. (D) |

# ACTUAL TEST

# 4

## READING TEST

In the Reading Test, you will read a variety of texts and answer several different types of reading comprehension questions. The entire Reading test will last 75 minutes. There are three parts, and directions are given for each part. You are encouraged to answer as many questions as possible within the time allowed.

You must mark your answers on the separate answer sheet. Do not write your answers in your test book.

## PART 5

**Directions:** A word or phrase is missing in each of the sentences below. Four answer choices are given below each sentence. Select the best answer to complete the sentence. Then mark the letter (A), (B), (C), or (D) on your answer sheet.

**101.** Thanks to the ------- recommendation from his previous employer, Derrick was immediately offered the managerial position.

(A) impress
(B) impression
(C) impressive
(D) impresses

**102.** Nemis Air is no longer ------- to transport freight to the northern regions.

(A) license
(B) licensed
(C) licenses
(D) licensing

**103.** Jerome tried to get tickets to tomorrow's game, but they are ------- sold out.

(A) complete
(B) completed
(C) completing
(D) completely

**104.** Nobody can enter this office ------- proper authorization.

(A) without
(B) unless
(C) only
(D) although

**105.** The annual charity banquet hosted by the Fredericton Children Aid Society is ------- to take place at the Grand Marian Hotel on December 7.

(A) given
(B) scheduled
(C) found
(D) considered

**106.** The owner's manual includes detailed ------- on cleaning this microwave.

(A) instructions
(B) computers
(C) posters
(D) fixings

**107.** The city purchased the ------- building on Balena Street to convert it into an elementary school.

(A) approaching
(B) adjustable
(C) vacant
(D) united

**108.** Customers must provide ------- at the counter or prescriptions will not be filled.

(A) paid
(B) payers
(C) payment
(D) pays

**109.** The company will not reimburse staff for travel expenses unless original receipts are presented ------- upon returning.

(A) mainly
(B) formerly
(C) nearly
(D) immediately

**110.** The *Stickney Entertainment Guide* is, without a doubt, the most reliable source ------- finding the best places to eat in this region.

(A) around
(B) for
(C) as
(D) through

**111.** Mr. Tolliver, the head mechanic, started the repairs by ------- this morning, but two more staff were available to help him after lunch.

(A) he
(B) his
(C) him
(D) himself

**112.** For optimal results, the manufacturer ------- applying this exterior paint when the weather is sunny.

(A) reminds
(B) recognizes
(C) recommends
(D) registers

**113.** Instructors at Darthmouth College have to submit their final student evaluations ------- the last day of this month.

(A) in anticipation of
(B) already
(C) before
(D) so as to

**114.** The Fitzgerald Theater is being renovated so concert organizers for Roland Gagnon's band are ------- seeking another venue.

(A) actively
(B) activity
(C) active
(D) activate

**115.** Once the conveyor belt was fixed, the factory was ------- to continue production.

(A) valuable
(B) responsible
(C) able
(D) possible

**116.** Someone should tell Mr. Sinopoli that ------- car is parked in the section reserved for shopping center customers.

(A) he
(B) him
(C) his
(D) himself

**117.** Ratzenberg Motorcycles will benefit greatly ------- the proposed acquisition by Shefferville Auto.

(A) from
(B) to
(C) on
(D) about

**118.** The application forms we received yesterday ------- have to be reviewed by one of the division heads.

(A) lately
(B) evenly
(C) ever
(D) still

**119.** If bad weather forces a cancellation of the baseball game, full refunds will be issued to ------- who have purchased tickets.

(A) those
(B) which
(C) them
(D) whichever

**120.** Even though tourism revenue in this region usually ------- during the cold winter months, it always recovers in the warm spring.

(A) declines
(B) delays
(C) impacts
(D) impedes

**121.** One important ------- the new personnel manager is responsible for is meeting regularly with factory workers to discuss safety matters.

(A) initiative
(B) initiating
(C) initiation
(D) initiator

**122.** Ms. Gaitor is ------- with implementing policies that led to a significant increase in the number of clients.

(A) credited
(B) scored
(C) agreed
(D) relied

**123.** Tickets to the gallery can be purchased online at a ------- reduced price.

(A) slightest
(B) slighted
(C) slighting
(D) slightly

**124.** Our division ------- last week's policy meeting, but there was a conflict with the schedule.

(A) can attend
(B) must have attended
(C) should attend
(D) would have attended

**125.** Mr. Gleason opted to lease office space on Queen Street instead of Morley Lane, ------- a view of the lake.

(A) prefer
(B) preferring
(C) preferred
(D) preference

**126.** ------- for next year's Grondin Literature Award must be received by the selection committee by the end of March.

(A) Subscriptions
(B) Nominations
(C) Supporters
(D) Venues

**127.** In an effort to make the team less ------- the manager sent all the sales charts to everyone as e-mail attachments rather than printing out hardcopies.

(A) waste
(B) wasteful
(C) wastefully
(D) wasting

**128.** Ms. Wilson must contact the bank manager ------- she needs a little more time for the payment.

(A) if
(B) soon
(C) only
(D) then

**129.** Besides speedy delivery, friendly service is something ------- the management of Caron Courier will never sacrifice.

(A) where
(B) that
(C) when
(D) then

**130.** The editor of the sports section is more ------- about the articles she approves than the other editors.

(A) prominent
(B) punctual
(C) rigorous
(D) selective

**Directions:** Read the texts that follow. A word, phrase, or sentence is missing in parts of each text. Four answer choices for each question are given below the text. Select the best answer to complete the text. Then mark the letter (A), (B), (C), or (D) on your answer sheet.

**Questions 131-134** refer to the following article.

**Bold Move by Popular Shop**

CASTLEBAR — Flavor Fun, Castlebar's oldest and most popular yoghurt restaurant, has introduced a truly unanticipated change as the result of a growing number of ‾‾‾‾‾. The restaurant's owner
131.
decided to introduce a policy that many find to be unusual. For the past two weeks, customers have not been permitted to work on laptops while eating in the restaurant. Flavor Fun is the first and only restaurant in the city to implement such a policy aimed at encouraging customers to leave the restaurant after eating. By making customers spend ‾‾‾‾‾ time at a table, the restaurant has
132.
increased its daily sales by over 20 percent, and customers did not have to wait for a place to sit.
‾‾‾‾‾. Now, some other popular eating spots throughout Castlebar ‾‾‾‾‾ similar changes.
133.                                                                                      134.

131. (A) staff
(B) prices
(C) complaints
(D) deliveries

132. (A) some
(B) less
(C) any
(D) much

133. (A) Customers will receive free coffee during the trial period.
(B) The new policy has already proven popular with customers.
(C) Flavor Fun also has an outdoor patio for dining.
(D) Owners believe new staff need more training before starting work.

134. (A) considers
(B) to consider
(C) being considered
(D) are considering

Questions 135-138 refer to the following letter.

**Do You Use a Hearing Aid? Contact Knapton Technologies Today!**

In August, Knapton Technologies will begin a detailed consumer study on behalf of Hearing 1000. For this huge undertaking, our team is __135.__ more than 300 individuals who wear hearing aids. All participants must have a doctor prescribed device that they began wearing no more than three years ago __136.__ the beginning of the study. __137.__. If you are interested, we ask that you visit us online at www.knaptontechnologies.com/hearingaidstudy and complete our short survey. One of our staff members will be contacting qualified applicants. Every participant __138.__ a gift voucher valued at $200 upon completing of this study.

135. (A) seeking
     (B) insuring
     (C) promoting
     (D) showing

136. (A) except for
     (B) as
     (C) because of
     (D) at

137. (A) A hard copy of the prescription must be presented for confirmation.
     (B) New batteries will be available for all participants.
     (C) We request that payment for your prescription is provided on the spot.
     (D) The prescription will be filled immediately after submission.

138. (A) will receive
     (B) had received
     (C) to receive
     (D) to be received

Questions 139-142 refer to the following press release.

Next month, the national headquarters of Zaki Ltd., Japan's top manufacturer of ___139.___, will relocate to 117 Aoyagi Street, where a modern office building was recently renovated. Zaki will ___140.___ the top seven floors of the Aoyagi Building. In this new location, the staff will enjoy over 90,000 square meters of beautiful office space and convenient amenities.

___141.___ "That is the perfect place to display our latest high-tech refrigerators and ovens." said Kaori Akiba, spokesperson for Zaki. Ms. Akiba noted that the design and engineer divisions will remain in ___142.___ original spot in the Ogawa Building.

139. (A) furniture
    (B) apparel
    (C) wallpaper
    (D) appliances

140. (A) sell
    (B) paint
    (C) occupy
    (D) photograph

141. (A) Zaki's products are known for their cutting-edge designs and energy efficiency.
    (B) Zaki also plans to lease additional retail space on the first floor of the building.
    (C) Zaki was listed in the *Tokyo Times* as one of the top 20 places to work in Asia.
    (D) Zaki stock doubled in value immediately following the announcement.

142. (A) it
    (B) their
    (C) what
    (D) any

---

**To:** Kaori Sazaki <ssawaki601@e-mail.co.jp>

**From:** Customer Service <customerserv@elsworth.co.uk>

**Date:** Thursday, 16 October 8:56 P.M.

**Subject:** inquiry about website

Dear Ms. Sazaki:

We would like to thank you for leaving a comment in the feedback section of our website regarding the instruction booklet for the EW2500 digital camera. You indicated that the instructions on how to upload an image to a phone or mobile device is confusing and we completely agree with you ____143. that point. ____144.. Our publications division has ____145. made some revisions to the section that details the specific software and cable needed to transfer an image from your particular camera. We have made the ____146. version of the instruction booklet available on our website. You can find it under the New Digital Camera section. If you prefer a print version, we will gladly send it by regular mail but delivery will take at least one week.

Sincerely,

Lirim Kilgore

Customer Service Agent

Elsworth Camera Company

---

**143.** (A) all
(B) on
(C) what
(D) of

**144.** (A) The EW2500 digital camera is currently our most popular item.
(B) We can send you the complete instructions via e-mail if you wish.
(C) Other customers have submitted feedback about the same issue.
(D) Most of our customers are based in the southern regions of Asia.

**145.** (A) instead
(B) likewise
(C) therefore
(D) nevertheless

**146.** (A) original
(B) updated
(C) absolute
(D) focused

**Directions:** In this part you will read a selection of texts, such as magazine and newspaper articles, e-mails, and instant messages. Each text or set of texts is followed by several questions. Select the best answer for each question and mark the letter (A), (B), (C), or (D) on your answer sheet.

**Questions 147-148** refer to the following text message.

From: Ron Kapoor, 553-0304
To: Zelda Vincenti

Zelda, I left my schedule book in the office. I have to meet a client at 2:00, but I can't remember the exact location. I'm just about to leave Denny's Grill and had planned to go straight to the meeting. Can you check my book and send me the address?

**147.** Why did Mr. Kapoor send a text message to Ms. Vincenti?

(A) To ask if she found his briefcase
(B) To inquire about a canceled meeting
(C) To request that she send him an address
(D) To make a restaurant reservation

**148.** What will Mr. Kapoor probably do next?

(A) Leave a restaurant
(B) Go to his office
(C) Check a website
(D) Call a client

**Questions 149-150** refer to the following advertisement.

The American chapter of Ancient Worlds Archaeological Foundation seeks two full-time interns to assist with our archaeological dig near Siem Reap, Cambodia.

Candidates must have completed a four-year degree in archaeological studies or must be currently enrolled in their 4th year of an archaeology program.

Research experience is a must, and candidates with hands-on field training will be given preference.

Applicants must be willing to travel to the dig site during the months of August through October. Accommodation and flights will be paid for by the foundation.

Interns will be paid a lump sum at the end of the trip. At the discretion of the project coordinator, interns may be hired as full-time employees following the dig's conclusion.

**149.** What is indicated about the American chapter of Ancient Worlds Archaeological Foundation?
(A) It wants to hire one part-time intern.
(B) It conducts digs in foreign countries.
(C) It does not pay its interns except for travel expenses.
(D) It was founded three years ago.

**150.** What is NOT a qualification for the position?
(A) University education
(B) Willingness to travel
(C) Field training
(D) Computer knowledge

**Questions 151-153** refer to the following memo.

**To:** Timmons Medical Research Staff
**From:** Anderson Baxtor, Director of Employee Relations
**Re:** Presentation
**Date:** 5 April

Attention all staff members,

Next Thursday, 13 April, we will have a special presentation in auditorium 203. Maria Sergios is a senior researcher at the University of Westwood, where she has conducted research for the last five years. She headed the development of a new series of vaccines in addition to partnering with researchers in London, England to work on the development of several new treatments for cancer. Before joining the University of Westwood, Sergios made a name for herself at the Institute of Medical Research in Sydney, Australia. There, I had the chance to learn from her during several ground-breaking projects. Ms. Sergios will be here in Vancouver next week and has agreed to share her latest publication on laboratory techniques with us. All staff members are required to attend the presentation.

**151.** What does the memo discuss?
  (A) Plans to found a new lab
  (B) A new job opening
  (C) A scientist's career
  (D) Deadlines for a project

**152.** Where is Timmons Medical Research located?
  (A) In London
  (B) In Sydney
  (C) In Westwood
  (D) In Vancouver

**153.** What does Mr. Baxtor indicate about Ms. Sergios?
  (A) She is his former mentor.
  (B) She is moving to Vancouver.
  (C) She will join his research team.
  (D) She will open her own laboratory.

**Questions 154-155** refer to the following text message chain.

**Jamal Myers 10:30 A.M.**

Hi, Ferguson. I'm still at Davis Printers waiting for our two banners. Could you go ahead and begin setting up? I put the key to the room in the top right drawer of my desk.

**Ferguson Boyd 10:33 A.M.**

Found it. I'm leaving now.

**Jamal Myers 10:35 A.M.**

Thanks a lot. I know the award ceremony doesn't start until 1:30, but we need to double-check all the equipment.

**Ferguson Boyd 10:40 A.M.**

Just to make sure, we will be having the ceremony in the former city hall building on Elliot Street, right? Not the new one on Queen Street?

**Jamal Myers 10:42 A.M.**

Correct. Right after the ceremony, a photographer will take photos of the winners on the front lawn. That is why I ordered an additional banner to be used outside. I will catch up with you at the former city hall building as soon as I get the banners.

**Ferguson Boyd 10:45 A.M.**

OK. See you in a little while!

**154.** At 10:33 A.M., what does Mr. Boyd most likely mean when he writes, "Found it"?

(A) He will pass on the information a client needs.

(B) He noticed Davis Printers while driving.

(C) He has the key to the venue in his hand.

(D) He is looking at a phone number in a directory.

**155.** Where most likely is Mr. Boyd going next?

(A) To the train station

(B) To company headquarters

(C) To a print shop

(D) To the old city hall

Holt Golf and Country Club
34 Russet Drive
Edmonton, Alberta
www.holtgolf.ca

24 April

Mr. Henry MacArthur
220 Washington Avenue
Edmonton, Alberta

Dear Mr. MacArthur,

Thank you for purchasing a membership to Holt Golf and Country Club. --[1]--. From May 1 until September 30, in addition to having your choice of tee-off time, you will have full access to our lounge, restaurant, and spa. Furthermore, carbonated beverages are complimentary in all our cafés. Simply show your membership card when you order. --[2]--.

In addition to all these incredible services, Holt Golf and Country Club is announcing yet another service for its members. From now until the end of August, all members may invite guests for a round of golf on our extensive course. This feature is available from 8 A.M. until 4 P.M. only. Guest reservations must be made 24 hours in advance. --[3]--.

If you have any questions or concerns, please contact our customer service hotline at 900-555-3344. --[4]--.

Sincerely,

Mitchel Walker

**156.** What is true about Holt golf and Country Club?

(A) It offers its members free drinks.
(B) It only opens during the spring.
(C) It offers discount memberships.
(D) It hosts seasonal parties.

**157.** According to the letter, what will be different after August?

(A) Members cannot access the spa.
(B) Members may not bring guests.
(C) Golf tee-off times will be earlier.
(D) Golf lessons will be available.

**158.** In which of the positions marked [1], [2], [3], and [4] does the following sentence best belong?

"This year, you will be able to enjoy all our premium services."

(A) [1]
(B) [2]
(C) [3]
(D) [4]

**Questions 159-162** refer to the following article.

Milan (July 14) — Roberto Pelini, lead designer at Marshenco Fashions, one of Europe's top design companies, has announced he will retire from his role at the company. --[1]--.

Since first accepting the position 10 years ago, Roberto Pelini has worked hard to make Marshenco Fashions one of the most-recognized names in the industry. Because of Pelini's passion and eye for design, Marshenco has become a favorite among celebrities and his designs can often be seen both on the runway and the red carpet. --[2]--. The company's success has even allowed for the founding of a sister company, Marshenco Accessories.

Irina Morova, former designer at Ruvera Design, will assume the position of lead designer at Marshenco. Morova has more than 10 years of experience heading a major fashion company. Her work has been featured in numerous fashion festivals, magazines, and has clothed some of Europe's top singers and actors. --[3]--.

Following his departure from Marshenco, Roberto Pelini will partner with Sophia Bertuski to found a new independent fashion house. Pelini is quoted as saying, "I look forward to working with Sophia. Her creative vision is similar to my own." --[4]--.

**159.** What is the purpose of the article?

(A) To report on a company's closure
(B) To announce a change in a company's leadership
(C) To advertise a new job opening at a company
(D) To publicize a new line of products

**160.** What is indicated about Marshenco?

(A) It is based in North America.
(B) It was purchased by Pelini.
(C) It owns Ruvera Design.
(D) It founded a second company.

**161.** What is mentioned about Irina Morova?

(A) She will become Pelini's business partner.
(B) Her career at Ruvera Design was successful.
(C) She originally worked as a runway model.
(D) Her designs are for average consumers.

**162.** In which of the positions marked [1], [2], [3], and [4] does the following sentence best belong?

"There is no news as to when Pelini's new lines will be available to the public."

(A) [1]
(B) [2]
(C) [3]
(D) [4]

## The First Annual Waterfront Food Truck Festival!

Ajax Food and Beverage Association is pleased to announce the first ever Waterfront Food Truck Festival. From Monday August 8 through Sunday August 14, the Ajax waterfront will host a number of local food trucks. Guests can enjoy live music, prizes, and children's entertainment between the hours of 11 A.M. and 6 P.M. Food truck items can be sampled for discount prices.

Famous Participating Food Trucks:

♦ Rio Tacos — Enjoy fresh appetizers and a variety of tacos and nachos
♦ Barbecue Madness — Marinated pork ribs, chicken wings, and pulled pork
♦ Benny's Fries — French fries topped with your choice of ingredients

Admission is free for all participants. Parking will be available on a limited basis, so make sure to get there early.

For a complete list of participating food trucks, visit www.ajaxwaterfront.com/foodtruckfestival.

**163.** What is being advertised?

(A) A restaurant's grand opening
(B) A concert in the park
(C) An auto show
(D) A new community event

**164.** What is mentioned about the participating food trucks?

(A) They will travel to various cities.
(B) They will distribute free gifts.
(C) They will be open all day.
(D) They will sell food at reduced prices.

**165.** What are participants encouraged to do?

(A) Arrive at the site early
(B) Leave their cars at home
(C) Pay an admission fee
(D) Camp at the waterfront

**Questions 166-169** refer to the following e-mail.

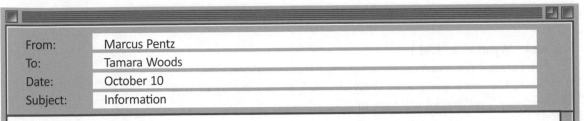

From: Marcus Pentz
To: Tamara Woods
Date: October 10
Subject: Information

Hi Tamara,

Thank you so much for covering for Samira while she's away visiting family. Prior to leaving for her trip abroad, she was working on advertisements for two local properties. According to her files, she has put together the following descriptions:

776 Marshall Avenue is a three-story home situated on Lake Scougog. It features four bedrooms, upgraded kitchen appliances, a fully furnished basement, and a wooden fireplace. It is situated in a quiet area, but is within walking distance of local schools.

9902 Fenton Street is a three-bedroom home with a large yard and an in-ground swimming pool. A garage was recently built on the property and can hold up to two cars. The home is located near all major shopping malls and the university.

I'm going to send over Samira's files, so you can update her descriptions and add any relevant information. These properties, along with photographs, must be submitted to *Scougog Weekly*'s real estate editor by Friday. Please let me know if you have any questions or concerns.

Regards,

Marcus Pentz
Pentz Real Estate

**166.** Why was the e-mail sent?

(A) To request some files
(B) To give some job instructions
(C) To provide payment information
(D) To ask for some local contacts

**167.** What is suggested about Samira?

(A) She often travels abroad.
(B) She purchased a new home.
(C) She works for a newspaper.
(D) She has gone on vacation.

**168.** What is NOT mentioned about the property on Fenton Street?

(A) It has a big yard and a swimming pool.
(B) It was previously listed on a website.
(C) It includes a newly built garage.
(D) It is close to many important amenities.

**169.** According to the e-mail, what is indicated about *Scougog Weekly*?

(A) It will feature the selections Ms. Woods must update.
(B) It comes out every Friday.
(C) It charges fees based on property prices.
(D) It is distributed to local residents free of charge.

**Blake Wyatt [3:23 P.M.]**

Ms. Parker, I just found out there's going to be a parade on First Street. The area is going to be really crowded, so the repaving of your restaurant's parking lot will have to wait.

**Janice Parker [3:26 P.M.]**

So does that mean you won't be coming in at all?

**Blake Wyatt [3:28 P.M.]**

No, we'll still be there. We can help get the basement storage rooms finished.

**Janice Parker [3:31 P.M.]**

OK, great. How long do you think it will take to get everything done down there?

**Blake Wyatt [3:32 P.M.]**

I'll check now.

*Tim Robins has been added to the conversation.*

**Blake Wyatt [3:35 P.M.]**

Tim, how far have you gotten on the basement project?

**Tim Robins [3:40 P.M.]**

Well, things were running smoothly until we found some water damage in the southeast corner. It looks like a big cleanup job.

**Blake Wyatt [3:42 P.M.]**

What if my crew gave you a hand tomorrow?

**Tim Robins [3:44 P.M.]**

That might get us back on schedule. We might even be able to install the new refrigerators.

**Janice Parker [3:45 P.M.]**

If you're moving the fridges, you'll need access to the service entrance behind the building. I think you still have the key, right?

**Blake Wyatt [3:47 P.M.]**

Yes, I've got it. Are there any spots behind the building where the guys can park for the day?

**Janice Parker [3:50 P.M.]**

There might not be any free if there's a parade. You should probably park in the empty lot on Fifth Avenue.

**170.** What does Mr. Wyatt suggest will interrupt tomorrow's work?

(A) A public holiday
(B) A street event
(C) A lost delivery
(D) A lack of equipment

**171.** At 3:40 P.M. what does Mr. Robins most likely mean when he writes, "It looks like a big cleanup job."?

(A) His crew usually does the cleaning.
(B) Some damage was significant.
(C) He does not like his current job.
(D) His crew's project is too complicated.

**172.** Who most likely is Ms. Parker?

(A) A restaurant owner
(B) A construction worker
(C) A parking attendant
(D) An appliance manufacturer

**173.** What is one topic Mr. Wyatt asks about?

(A) Directions to another entrance
(B) The location of a building key
(C) The time of a local event
(D) The location of parking spaces

GO ON TO THE NEXT PAGE

Questions 174-175 refer to the following webpage.

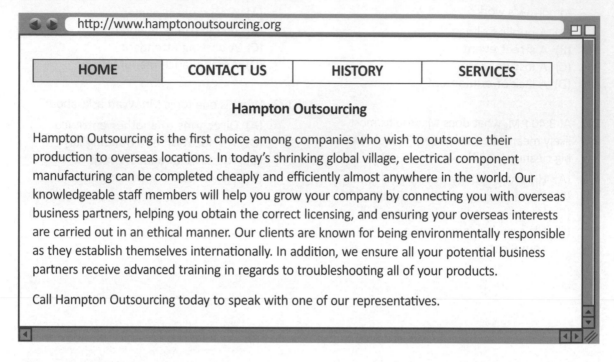

**174.** Who most likely will be a customer of Hampton Outsourcing?

(A) Call center workers
(B) Insurance brokers
(C) Environmental agencies
(D) Home appliance companies

**175.** What is NOT mentioned as a strength of Hampton Outsourcing?

(A) Superior employee training
(B) Knowledge of licensing
(C) Environmentally conscious procedures
(D) Familiarity with export taxes

**Questions 176-180** refer to the following letter and voucher.

| To: | Raphael Rosario <rosario@ebookmail.com> |
|---|---|
| From: | Janelle Parik <jparik@alliancepremiumairways.com> |
| Subject: | Your Flight |
| Date: | 6 January |
| Attachment: | voucher |

Dear Mr. Rosario,

Thank you for sharing your experience with Alliance Premium Airways Customer Service. I am sorry to learn about your negative experience on January 2. According to the online form you completed, you had reserved a business class seat on a third-party website, but you were forced to fly economy class because your reservation had been lost.

I have contacted the website you used to book your flight. Apparently, there was a computer malfunction, which caused some prior bookings to be deleted. Unfortunately, this resulted in some seats being resold. I understand that you have already received a partial refund, but I'd like to offer you an additional coupon for your troubles. Please see the attachment for more information.

Sincerely,

Janelle Parik,
Customer Service Manager
Alliance Premium Airways

---

### Alliance Premium Airways Voucher
#### $200 off your next flight

Details: Alliance Premium Airways would like to offer you $200 off your next flight. Please note, this coupon may only be used for international return flights. This coupon is good until December 31 of this year. You may use this coupon at any Alliance Premium Airways kiosk or online at www.alliancepremiumairways.com.

Voucher Number: YY7732999938          Date Issued: January 6
Issuing office: ___ Vancouver ___Edmonton ___Montreal _X_ Toronto

---

**176.** Why did Ms. Parik send the e-mail?

(A) To reply to an online complaint
(B) To provide a job contract
(C) To cancel an airline ticket
(D) To inquire about a trip

**177.** What does Ms. Parik indicate happened on January 2?

(A) She solved a seating problem.
(B) A flight was unnecessarily delayed.
(C) Many business class seats were empty.
(D) Mr. Rosario got a seat in a lower class.

**178.** What is suggested about Mr. Rosario?

(A) He requested a last-minute flight change.
(B) He flew from Vancouver to Toronto.
(C) He paid for his flight in advance.
(D) He usually flies economy class.

**179.** In the voucher, the word "good" in paragraph 1, line 2, is closest in meaning to

(A) high quality
(B) lucky
(C) well behaved
(D) valid

**180.** Where most likely is Ms. Parik's office located?

(A) Vancouver
(B) Edmonton
(C) Montreal
(D) Toronto

GO ON TO THE NEXT PAGE

Questions 181-185 refer to the following webpage and customer review.

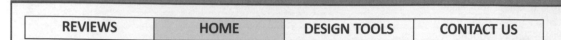

| REVIEWS | HOME | DESIGN TOOLS | CONTACT US |

Flyer Frenzy, the best online flyer generator for businesses large and small!

With Flyer Frenzy, you can create custom flyers for your business. Whether you are advertising the opening of your business or simply trying to generate awareness about your services, Flyer Frenzy has everything you need to design the perfect flyer.

**Step 1: Design Your Flyer**
Our online generator has numerous customizable templates. Browse through our categories and select the right template for you. All our fonts are easy to change with just the click of a mouse. If you want to accent your design with images, we have over 10,000 stock photos you can use at no extra cost. Furthermore, you can upload your own designs and logos to use along with any of our fonts.

**Step 2: Select A Quantity**
At Flyer Frenzy, we can print as few as 25 flyers for each order. However, the more flyers you order, the less you pay for each one.

| Quantity | Price Per Item |
|----------|----------------|
| 25-300 | 20 cents |
| 300-1,000 | 15 cents |
| 1,001-1,500 | 10 cents |
| 1,501 or more | 5 cents |

**Step 3: Purchase A Digital Copy**
For an extra flat fee of $50, you can download a digital copy of your design. This design is perfect for featuring on your business's website, as part of an e-mail newsletter, or as a printed advertisement.

**Step 4: Finalize Your Order**
Orders take five days to process; however, large orders may take longer to prepare. In the event that there are delays, you will be notified by e-mail.

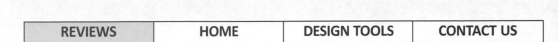

| REVIEWS | HOME | DESIGN TOOLS | CONTACT US |

★ ★ ★ ★ ★ Flyer Frenzy has great services!

I own a local shoe store downtown and had been finding it hard to spread the word about our upcoming sales event. I decided to design my own flyer using Flyer Frenzy's online generator. I found it very easy to use, and the designs were very elegant. I ended up ordering 1,000 flyers. I also purchased a digital copy of my design and used it on my website. Our sales event was a big success. Many customers said they'd heard about it from the flyers they'd seen posted around town. I am extremely pleased with Flyer Frenzy's services. They are much better than some of the other online generators I browsed, and their templates were much more sophisticated. I will definitely be using Flyer Frenzy again in the future!

Jen Tristan

**181.** According to the webpage, what does the online generator allow users to do?

(A) Add images
(B) Include web links
(C) Select paper type
(D) Design a logo

**182.** What is mentioned on the webpage about Flyer Frenzy?

(A) It delivers products free of charge.
(B) It offers digital files for an extra fee.
(C) It allows users to see each other's designs.
(D) It only takes orders in person at a store.

**183.** What is indicated about Ms. Tristan?

(A) She received more flyers than she ordered.
(B) Her order was delayed by a few days.
(C) She received a fifty dollar discount.
(D) She paid fifteen cents per flyer.

**184.** What is suggested about Ms. Tristan's store?

(A) It advertises solely online.
(B) It put flyers up around town.
(C) It holds sales every month.
(D) It gives discounts for online orders.

**185.** According to the review, why does Ms. Tristan prefer Flyer Frenzy's services over other companies?

(A) They have faster delivery times.
(B) They have better design features.
(C) They use better quality paper.
(D) They are cheaper to use.

GO ON TO THE NEXT PAGE

| From: | linda@mailmail.com |
| --- | --- |
| To: | billing@startelecom.com |
| Date: | April 23 |
| Subject: | Bill Number 3788292 |

Dear Customer Service,

I am writing in regards to an unusually high cell phone bill I received in March. The amount listed on my phone bill was $155.33. Previously, my bill ranged between $80 and $90 per month.

I have already paid the bill to avoid any late fees, but I am interested in knowing why I was charged so much. My bill did not show any details to explain these charges. I know I recently upgraded my data usage, which would cost extra, but I also canceled the insurance policy I had for all my devices. These two costs should have balanced each other out if my request for cancellation was handled properly.

Please call me about this matter at 333-0967-5563. I am available to speak only in the afternoons after 3:30 P.M.

Sincerely,

Linda Albert

Customer Service Contact Log Sheet
Date: April 24

| Representative Name | Account Number | Call Time | Resolved? Y/N |
| --- | --- | --- | --- |
| Michael Park | BG44532 | 9:33 A.M. | Yes |
| June Bartholdi | GH30993 | 10:42 A.M. | Yes |
| Nadia Kapoor | TZ33221 | 3:23 P.M. | No |
| Brooklyn Smith | GS17649 | 3:45 P.M. | No |

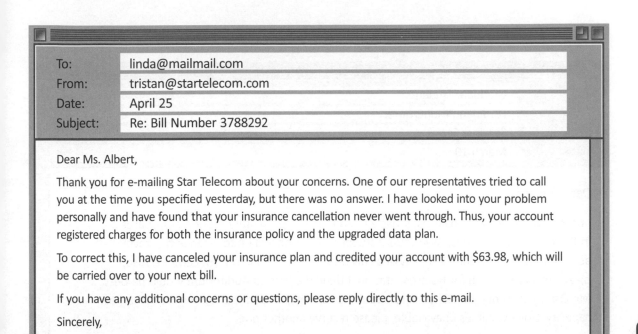

To: linda@mailmail.com
From: tristan@startelecom.com
Date: April 25
Subject: Re: Bill Number 3788292

Dear Ms. Albert,

Thank you for e-mailing Star Telecom about your concerns. One of our representatives tried to call you at the time you specified yesterday, but there was no answer. I have looked into your problem personally and have found that your insurance cancellation never went through. Thus, your account registered charges for both the insurance policy and the upgraded data plan.

To correct this, I have canceled your insurance plan and credited your account with $63.98, which will be carried over to your next bill.

If you have any additional concerns or questions, please reply directly to this e-mail.

Sincerely,

Tristan Mathews

Star Telecom Customer Support

**186.** Why was the first e-mail sent?

(A) To cancel a service
(B) To request another bill
(C) To ask about an invoice
(D) To register for an account

**187.** What is suggested about Ms. Albert?

(A) She previously worked for Star Telecom.
(B) She called a Star Telecom customer service representative.
(C) She correctly identified Star Telecom's mistake.
(D) She wants to close her account with Star Telecom.

**188.** Who called Ms. Albert on April 24?

(A) Michael Park
(B) June Bartholdi
(C) Nadia Kapoor
(D) Brooklyn Smith

**189.** In the second e-mail, in paragraph 1, line 4, the word "registered" is closest in meaning to

(A) enrolled
(B) recorded
(C) matched
(D) allowed

**190.** What does Mr. Mathews indicate in his e-mail?

(A) Some services will be offered for free.
(B) Ms. Kapoor will call Ms. Albert tomorrow.
(C) Ms. Albert's bill will decrease next month.
(D) Customers will be charged for cancellations.

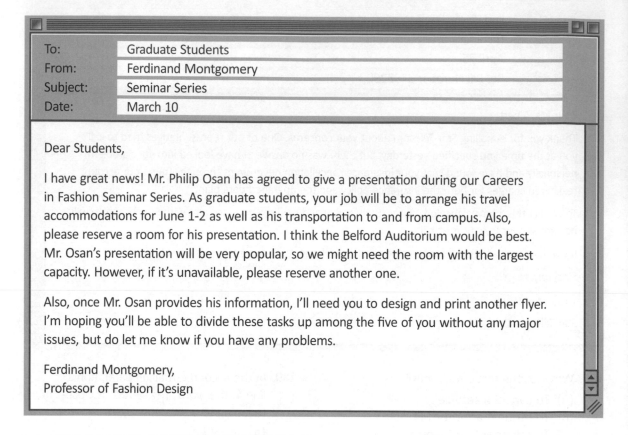

To: Graduate Students
From: Ferdinand Montgomery
Subject: Seminar Series
Date: March 10

Dear Students,

I have great news! Mr. Philip Osan has agreed to give a presentation during our Careers in Fashion Seminar Series. As graduate students, your job will be to arrange his travel accommodations for June 1-2 as well as his transportation to and from campus. Also, please reserve a room for his presentation. I think the Belford Auditorium would be best. Mr. Osan's presentation will be very popular, so we might need the room with the largest capacity. However, if it's unavailable, please reserve another one.

Also, once Mr. Osan provides his information, I'll need you to design and print another flyer. I'm hoping you'll be able to divide these tasks up among the five of you without any major issues, but do let me know if you have any problems.

Ferdinand Montgomery,
Professor of Fashion Design

---

The College of Fashion and Design's
Careers in Fashion Seminar Series Presents:

## Mr. Philip Osan
## CEO and Lead Designer of Bath Fashion House

Fashion Design and Technology
June 1, 3:30 P.M.
Westmont Auditorium

Over the years, many fashion houses have switched from hand-drawn designs to fashion design software programs. As up-and-coming designers, you must be aware of all the newest innovations in fashion design software. How can you keep up to date on the newest software trends? One possible solution is to become fluent in each new program. However, that may be costly and time-consuming. There are several ways to predict which programs will be major players in the future of fashion design. I will share my insights regarding the technological trends in the fashion industry.

From: Robert Parker
To: Rosa Hernandez
Date: May 28

Rosa, I'm at the copy center in the Hurtz Building to print the flyers, but I noticed something is missing. It seems that Mr. Osan's photograph was deleted. Can you fix the flyer and e-mail me the new version as soon as possible? The copy center closes in less than an hour and Dr. Montgomery asked me to drop the flyers off at his office tonight.

191. What is suggested about the Westmont Auditorium?

    (A) It is not available on June 1.
    (B) It is the location for all seminar presentations.
    (C) It has fewer seats than the Belford Auditorium.
    (D) It has a new projector system.

192. In the e-mail, the word "issues" in paragraph 2, line 3, is closest in meaning to

    (A) conflicts
    (B) periodicals
    (C) distributions
    (D) announcements

193. What is Mr. Osan's presentation about?

    (A) New trends in design software
    (B) Advancements in sewing machines
    (C) Learning drawing techniques
    (D) Characteristics of fashion houses

194. What problem does Mr. Parker mention?

    (A) A location has been changed.
    (B) The flyer is missing an image.
    (C) A work history is incorrect.
    (D) The time of an event is wrong.

195. Who most likely is Ms. Hernandez?

    (A) Lead designer at Bath Fashion House
    (B) A fashion design software developer
    (C) A professor at The College of Fashion and Design
    (D) A graduate student at The College of Fashion and Design

## Trenton Air Conditioning

## Air Conditioning Units

Trenton Air Conditioning has been providing businesses with affordable air conditioning units for over 15 years. We have provided numerous local cafés, restaurants, and supermarkets with reliable cooling solutions. All our units include cleaning services and repairs at your request, and should your unit be unsatisfactory in any way, we will replace it at no extra cost. Delivery to any location in the Sydney area and setup are both absolutely free of charge. A two-year contract must be signed by the business owner, and monthly payment plans are available.

Air Conditioning Unit Options:

| Contract Option | Model | Type | Room size in square meters (m²) | Cost Per Month |
|---|---|---|---|---|
| Bronze | GP-A3000 | Ceiling | 9-25 | $55.00 |
| Silver | GP-A4000 | Standing | 26-55 | $75.00 |
| Gold | GP-A9999 | Ceiling | 55-100 | $95.00 |
| Platinum | GP-AR300 | Ceiling | 100-200 | $115.00 |

Contact us for a free service quote today by visiting www.trentonaircon.com or calling one of our knowledgeable customer service agents at 1-800-444-2323.

## Trenton Air Conditioning — Customer Service Quote Form

| | |
|---|---|
| Name: | Medina Prias |
| Business: | Medina's Café |
| E-mail: | medina@mailme.com |
| Date: | 23 April |
| Remarks: | I'm writing to inquire about your air conditioning units. The restaurant next to my café is currently using one of your units, and the owner, Mr. Smithe, highly recommends your services. |
| | Right now, the air conditioner in my café is nearly 10 years old. Just keeping up with the repairs and cleaning is costing a fortune. I think it would be much cheaper to just rent from your company. Since my café is quite small with only 22 square meters, I think one of your cheaper packages would be suitable. However, I will rely on your recommendation about this. Also, can you make sure any unit you recommend comes with a remote control. Our current air conditioner does not have one. Thank you, and I look forward to hearing from you. |

## Customer Review

I have been a customer of Trenton Air Conditioning for a year, and I have to say that I am very pleased with their services. I was very surprised to receive a 10 percent discount on my first year of service thanks to Trenton's referral program. Apparently, if you give the name of the person who connected you with Trenton, both parties will automatically receive a discount. Furthermore, I am very pleased with the contract conditions, which have allowed me to change my unit based on my business's needs. After my business went through an expansion, I called Trenton and the customer service representative agreed to upgrade my unit to a larger package. The new unit turned up only two days later and was installed free of charge even though the type changed from ceiling to standing. I highly recommend Trenton for their great business practices and customer service.

Medina Prias, Owner of Medina's Café

---

**196.** What information about Trenton Air Conditioning is NOT included in the advertisement?

(A) The energy efficiency
(B) The monthly costs
(C) The room sizes
(D) The model numbers

**197.** What is probably true about Mr. Smithe?

(A) He can save on air conditioning for his restaurant.
(B) He purchased a café next to his restaurant.
(C) He received one year free service from Trenton Air Conditioning.
(D) He will upgrade his air conditioning unit next year.

**198.** What is suggested about Medina's Café?

(A) It is owned by Mr. Smithe.
(B) It moved to a new location.
(C) It features nightly entertainment.
(D) It increased its size recently.

**199.** Which contract option is Ms. Prias currently using?

(A) Bronze
(B) Silver
(C) Gold
(D) Platinum

**200.** In the review, the phrase "turned up" in paragraph 1, line 7, is closest in meaning to

(A) removed
(B) considered
(C) designed
(D) arrived

**Stop! This is the end of the test. If you finish before time is called, you may go back to Parts 5, 6, and 7 and check your work.**

# ANSWERS  ACTUAL TEST 4

| | | | | |
|---|---|---|---|---|
| **101.** (C) | **121.** (A) | **141.** (B) | **161.** (B) | **181.** (A) |
| **102.** (B) | **122.** (A) | **142.** (B) | **162.** (D) | **182.** (B) |
| **103.** (D) | **123.** (D) | **143.** (B) | **163.** (D) | **183.** (D) |
| **104.** (A) | **124.** (D) | **144.** (C) | **164.** (D) | **184.** (B) |
| **105.** (B) | **125.** (B) | **145.** (C) | **165.** (A) | **185.** (B) |
| **106.** (A) | **126.** (B) | **146.** (B) | **166.** (B) | **186.** (C) |
| **107.** (C) | **127.** (B) | **147.** (C) | **167.** (D) | **187.** (C) |
| **108.** (C) | **128.** (A) | **148.** (A) | **168.** (B) | **188.** (D) |
| **109.** (D) | **129.** (B) | **149.** (B) | **169.** (A) | **189.** (B) |
| **110.** (B) | **130.** (D) | **150.** (D) | **170.** (B) | **190.** (C) |
| **111.** (D) | **131.** (C) | **151.** (C) | **171.** (B) | **191.** (C) |
| **112.** (C) | **132.** (B) | **152.** (D) | **172.** (A) | **192.** (A) |
| **113.** (C) | **133.** (B) | **153.** (A) | **173.** (D) | **193.** (A) |
| **114.** (A) | **134.** (D) | **154.** (C) | **174.** (D) | **194.** (B) |
| **115.** (C) | **135.** (A) | **155.** (D) | **175.** (D) | **195.** (D) |
| **116.** (C) | **136.** (D) | **156.** (A) | **176.** (A) | **196.** (A) |
| **117.** (A) | **137.** (A) | **157.** (B) | **177.** (D) | **197.** (A) |
| **118.** (D) | **138.** (A) | **158.** (A) | **178.** (C) | **198.** (D) |
| **119.** (A) | **139.** (D) | **159.** (B) | **179.** (D) | **199.** (B) |
| **120.** (A) | **140.** (C) | **160.** (D) | **180.** (D) | **200.** (D) |

ACTUAL TEST

5

## READING TEST

In the Reading Test, you will read a variety of texts and answer several different types of reading comprehension questions. The entire Reading test will last 75 minutes. There are three parts, and directions are given for each part. You are encouraged to answer as many questions as possible within the time allowed.

You must mark your answers on the separate answer sheet. Do not write your answers in your test book.

## PART 5

**Directions:** A word or phrase is missing in each of the sentences below. Four answer choices are given below each sentence. Select the best answer to complete the sentence. Then mark the letter (A), (B), (C), or (D) on your answer sheet.

---

**101.** The colorful team uniforms were provided by Danchester Tires, ------- sister company.

(A) we
(B) our
(C) us
(D) ours

**102.** The family's visa will be processed as soon as all necessary travel ------- are received.

(A) document
(B) documents
(C) documented
(D) documenting

**103.** In his speech, the CEO of Grandstead Pharmaceuticals ------- mentioned the director of the research division as a contributor to the company's success.

(A) thoroughly
(B) utterly
(C) specifically
(D) densely

**104.** Joanne's managerial techniques are quite ------- from her predecessor's.

(A) different
(B) differently
(C) difference
(D) differences

**105.** Wearing a safety harness is not an option for roofers at Delbert Contractors but rather a -------.

(A) training
(B) fulfillment
(C) speculation
(D) requirement

**106.** One of our plumbers will ------- how to replace a Malton DR sink drain quickly and easily.

(A) demonstrate
(B) respond
(C) inquire
(D) visit

**107.** Bramwell Carpets does not issue refunds of any kind so be sure to measure the floor space ------- before purchasing.

(A) careful
(B) caring
(C) carefully
(D) cares

**108.** ------- annual profits are high or low, they still provide important economic information for business analysts.

(A) Whether
(B) Either
(C) Despite
(D) Even

**109.** The report provides a detailed ------- between the old Argo motorcycle design and the new Grandford one.

(A) comparable
(B) comparison
(C) compared
(D) comparative

**110.** ------- speak to a customer service agent, please stay on the line.

(A) For
(B) Across
(C) With
(D) To

**111.** The storage space in the new warehouse is more than ------- for three hundred bicycles.

(A) able
(B) great
(C) sure
(D) enough

**112.** Applying for a family visa in this country is a long and ------- process.

(A) complicate
(B) complicated
(C) complication
(D) complicatedness

**113.** Leading automotive experts maintain that Woykin Oil filters deliver ------- results.

(A) exceptionally
(B) exceptional
(C) exception
(D) exceptions

**114.** A credit card statement or phone bill can be ------- of residency.

(A) process
(B) analysis
(C) proof
(D) basis

115. Mr. Bolduc ------- asked Gabriella to organize the workshop, but then assigned the task to Louise.
    (A) initial
    (B) initially
    (C) initialize
    (D) initialized

116. Job candidates need to submit three letters of recommendation ------- the completed application.
    (A) too
    (B) in addition
    (C) moreover
    (D) along with

117. Even though Mr. Buono has never worked in refrigerator repair, his knowledge of refrigeration systems is -------.
    (A) extensive
    (B) clever
    (C) considered
    (D) eager

118. The flowchart on page six describes the ------- of duties among the different project managers.
    (A) support
    (B) attention
    (C) division
    (D) statement

119. These seeds will produce the biggest tomatoes but not ------- the healthiest ones.
    (A) expectedly
    (B) necessarily
    (C) preventively
    (D) permanently

120. While the store does not issue refunds, customers can exchange any item for something ------- in amount to the original sales price.
    (A) equivalent
    (B) profitable
    (C) deliberate
    (D) controlled

121. This newspaper photograph shows the mayor of Otterbury sitting ------- the prime minister.
    (A) from
    (B) reverse
    (C) opposite
    (D) distant

122. The decision to launch a new line of footwear was ------- the results of some market research.
    (A) such as
    (B) adjacent to
    (C) except for
    (D) based on

123. The Alderburn Employment Center is the only building on this block that is ------- to people in wheelchairs.
    (A) access
    (B) accessibly
    (C) accessible
    (D) accessibility

124. Dr. Darius is striving ------- the look of his office and is going to put a painting in the waiting room.
    (A) to enhance
    (B) enhances
    (C) is enhancing
    (D) enhanced

**125.** Players ------- teams did not make it to the finals can watch the game for free.

(A) its
(B) which
(C) whose
(D) more

**126.** Local officials ------- farmers that the pesticide sprayed on the potato crops was harmless to humans.

(A) assured
(B) arranged
(C) described
(D) committed

**127.** Factory laborers at Langford Manufacturing ------- to work 30 minutes more each day to offset rising production costs.

(A) agreeing
(B) to agree
(C) agreement
(D) have agreed

**128.** ------- Samuel's work experience in three continents, it was no surprise that the CEO put him in charge of the overseas project.

(A) Since
(B) Given
(C) Among
(D) Upon

**129.** A person who was not raised in this community may not understand the historical ------- on the Steinhauer Street Bridge.

(A) signify
(B) significant
(C) significance
(D) significantly

**130.** Jennifer has more seniority than Bill at the company, ------- she is much younger than him.

(A) as if
(B) so that
(C) in case
(D) even though

## PART 6

**Directions:** Read the texts that follow. A word, phrase, or sentence is missing in parts of each text. Four answer choices for each question are given below the text. Select the best answer to complete the text. Then mark the letter (A), (B), (C), or (D) on your answer sheet.

**Questions 131-134** refer to the following e-mail.

**To:** <nina_haidara@kmail.net>
**From:** <duron_charette@wrnpharmaceuticals.com>
**Date:** September 7
**Subject:** Head of Research position

Dear Ms. Haidara,

WRN Pharmaceuticals is delighted to invite you to come in for a second interview next week. Since this is the second stage, our hiring committee will be speaking to only the top five applicants whom we feel are most ___131.___ for this challenging position. Our entire committee agrees that you possess almost all the ___132.___ we need. We trust that you are still interested in the position. ___133.___, would you be available for an appointment next Wednesday at 2:30? Also, as part of the interview, we would like you to prepare a written research proposal related to one of the topics discussed at the first interview as well as a 10-minute presentation. ___134.___.

Best regards,

Duron Charette
WRN Pharmaceuticals
304-677-2426 ext. 18

131. (A) suiting
     (B) suitable
     (C) suit
     (D) suits

132. (A) agreements
     (B) performances
     (C) qualities
     (D) promotions

133. (A) Despite that
     (B) If so
     (C) However
     (D) For example

134. (A) Our current research head will train you in your new duties.
     (B) The CEO will be delighted to provide you with a letter of reference.
     (C) You need to complete your current research project before Wednesday.
     (D) We are looking forward to hearing your vision for a future project.

**Questions 135-138** refer to the following the letter.

---

Chantal Youldon

302 Moline Street

Delavan, IL

61735

Dear Ms. Youldon,

We would like to remind you that the time for another eye examination is soon approaching.
_135._. Eye specialists _136._ having your vision checked at least once a year. _137._, eye problems
can be detected early and the prescription for your eyeglasses can also be updated. Our number
one _138._ is providing our patients with the best vision possible. We will follow up this letter
with a phone call in a few days. Please phone us at (309) 754-3231 if you would like to make an
appointment. Thank you very much.

The Eye Care Team

Herrin Street Eye Clinic

---

**135.** (A) We recently expanded our waiting room to include a larger play area for children.
(B) Our records indicate that it has been eleven months since your last saw Dr. Hoban.
(C) Exercise and a healthy diet also have an impact on the condition of your eyes.
(D) Our office updated its website to include a convenient online appointment system.

**136.** (A) recommending
(B) had recommended
(C) recommend
(D) will recommend

**137.** (A) Nevertheless
(B) In this way
(C) For example
(D) Likewise

**138.** (A) manner
(B) opinion
(C) condition
(D) priority

*Parrsboro Herald*

Local News

(12 June) — On Tuesday afternoon, Parrsboro City Mayor Deborah Middleton announced city council's decision to implement one-on-one training programs for aspiring city bus drivers. ____ 139. , she stated that 20 new drivers will be needed before the end of the year. Speaking at a press conference, she stressed that there is an urgent ____ 140. for new drivers to replace those who are set to retire soon. The announcement ____ 141. with approval by most city officials. Councilor Stephen Digby of Truro Region, however, continues to speak out against the city funding costly training programs when graduates of the Wolfville College of Vehicle Operations, just 50 km west of Parrsboro, are already qualified to fill the positions. ____ 142. .

139. (A) Specifically
(B) Undoubtedly
(C) Regardless
(D) Besides

140. (A) settlement
(B) reduction
(C) demand
(D) difficulty

141. (A) will be meeting
(B) to meet
(C) had been meeting
(D) was met

142. (A) He believes the current buses can be improved to allow more seats.
(B) He wants the city to hire staff already skilled in the field.
(C) He feels the test to become a certified driver is too easy to pass.
(D) He expects the high fuel costs will lead to higher bus rates.

**Questions 143-146** refer to the following letter.

---

**To:** Frans Vanek

**From:** Michelle Sekera

**Date:** 14 July

**Subject:** Good morning.

I learned of your upcoming _____ from a colleague. Even though the position of chief recruiter at
143.

our newly-opened office in Oslo officially _____ on August 2, I would like to take a moment now to
144.

wish you the very best in your new career. If you require any assistance, please do not hesitate to

contact me. I am well aware that this type of transition, while exciting, is also extremely _____.
145.

Your work performance here in Paris at Chara Fashion as assistant hiring director has always been

outstanding. _____. Congratulations and good luck!
146.

Sincerely,

Michelle Sekera

---

143. (A) trip
    (B) event
    (C) award
    (D) promotion

144. (A) begins
    (B) began
    (C) has begun
    (D) could begin

145. (A) challenging
    (B) challenge
    (C) challenger
    (D) challenges

146. (A) The Oslo office is a little smaller with a
        big parking lot.
    (B) I'm still conducting interviews for all
        the new positions.
    (C) You could ask about staff discounts at
        clothing shops.
    (D) I am certain that you will be successful
        in your new position.

## PART 7

**Directions:** In this part you will read a selection of texts, such as magazine and newspaper articles, e-mails, and instant messages. Each text or set of texts is followed by several questions. Select the best answer for each question and mark the letter (A), (B), (C), or (D) on your answer sheet.

**Questions 147-148** refer to the following receipt.

Park Home Outfitters
229 Park Road South
Edmonton, Alberta
(777) 223-4455

Date: May 12                    Time: 10:37
Items
3345    La Roux 4-Seat Sofa      $499.00
3348    La Roux Armchair         $199.00
3355    La Roux Footstool        $99.00
4489    D&F 6-drawer Dresser
        4 $79.00/ea              $316.00
1223    Star Designs pillow
        2 $19.00/ea              $38.00
Subtotal                         $1151.00
Tax (5%)                         $57.55
Total                            $1208.55
Paid by credit card             $1208.55
Total number of items purchased: 9

Returns may be made for all non-sale items within 60 days of purchase.
To view our return policy, please visit
www.parkhomeoutfitters.ca/returns.
*******************

Sign up for a membership on our website and receive up to 50% off on
select online purchases. Offer ends June 28.
*******************

Thank you for shopping at Park Home Outfitters.

**147.** What kind of store most likely is Park Home Outfitters?

(A) A furniture store
(B) A fabric outlet
(C) A construction company
(D) A clothing store

**148.** According to the receipt, how can customers get a discount?

(A) By applying for a membership
(B) By showing a coupon
(C) By completing a survey
(D) By purchasing two or more items

GO ON TO THE NEXT PAGE

**Questions 149-150** refer to the following e-mail.

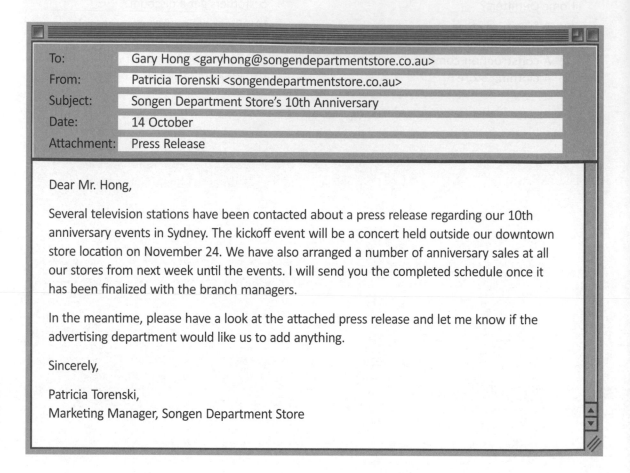

To: Gary Hong <garyhong@songendepartmentstore.co.au>
From: Patricia Torenski <songendepartmentstore.co.au>
Subject: Songen Department Store's 10th Anniversary
Date: 14 October
Attachment: Press Release

Dear Mr. Hong,

Several television stations have been contacted about a press release regarding our 10th anniversary events in Sydney. The kickoff event will be a concert held outside our downtown store location on November 24. We have also arranged a number of anniversary sales at all our stores from next week until the events. I will send you the completed schedule once it has been finalized with the branch managers.

In the meantime, please have a look at the attached press release and let me know if the advertising department would like us to add anything.

Sincerely,

Patricia Torenski,
Marketing Manager, Songen Department Store

149. What is the purpose of the e-mail?
(A) To make a list of items for sale
(B) To reschedule a live music event
(C) To invite a coworker to attend an event
(D) To give an update on a promotional plan

150. What does Ms. Torenski promise to send later?
(A) A recent news article
(B) A schedule of store discounts
(C) A list of television stations
(D) A revised press release

**Questions 151-152** refer to the following article.

---

**Around Town**

---

Town Books owner Cynthia Purdel has announced her plans to open a second bookstore at 667 Brookside Avenue. The building, located across from Brookside Elementary School, was once the home of Smithton Bakery. Ms. Purdel's new bookstore, which has yet to be named, is scheduled to open in the spring of next year. The bookstore will include an extensive children's section, which Ms. Purdel hopes it will attract numerous customers from Brookside Elementary School. Ms. Purdel's original bookstore, Town Books, is located on 5th Avenue and houses genres that are targeted to adult readers.

---

**151.** What is the purpose of the article?

(A) To discuss the closing of a business
(B) To profile a successful bakery owner
(C) To report on a store's relocation
(D) To announce the opening of a new business

**152.** What is indicated about the new store on Brookside Avenue?

(A) It is located across from a popular bakery.
(B) It is scheduled to open this year.
(C) It is Ms. Purdel's first business venture.
(D) It is expected to receive business from students.

# St. Michael's Hospital Research Gala

St. Michael's Hospital will host a gala to benefit continued medical research. The gala will be held at the Grand Renaissance Hotel; however, the day has been changed due to a hotel booking error. Instead of September 20, the event will be held on October 5, from 5:00 P.M. until 8:00 P.M. Please note the following information before attending.

**Directions to Grand Renaissance Hotel from Central Station:**

Drive north on Parcelle Boulevard and turn right onto Meadow Drive. Turn left onto Bath Avenue and continue for five blocks before turning right onto Smithview Road. The Grand Renaissance Hotel is located across from the Mary Rose Theater. The gala will be held in Banquet Room 1A.

**Parking Information:**

Parking is available free of charge in the underground parking lot. Please ensure you have the parking pass that was issued along with your gala ticket. Otherwise, you will be responsible for paying for parking.

**153.** What has changed about the event?

(A) The cost
(B) The location
(C) The sponsor
(D) The date

**154.** Where is Central Station located?

(A) Meadow Drive
(B) Bath Avenue
(C) Parcelle Boulevard
(D) Smithview Road

**155.** What is indicated about the Grand Renaissance Hotel's parking?

(A) Gala guests will have to pay for parking.
(B) The parking lot is located across the street.
(C) Parking is free with a guest pass.
(D) The hotel has a shared parking garage.

**Questions 156-157** refer to the following text message chain.

---

**Steven Yoon  4:45 P.M.**
Jennifer tried to call you about the meeting with the CEO tomorrow. She's wondering if you can call her back.

**Roger Martinez  4:50 P.M.**
I'm in the warehouse right now. Do you think she's worried the reports won't be finished in time?

**Steven Yoon  4:52 P.M.**
It's possible.

**Roger Martinez  4:54 P.M.**
Well, I'm checking the warehouse alarm system now. I got called away, because it seems to be acting up again.

**Steven Yoon  4:57  P.M.**
Do you want me to call the security company?

**Roger Martinez  5:00 P.M.**
I think I can fix it myself. Can you tell Jennifer to stop by my office at 5:30? I think we should discuss her concerns tonight before we go home.

**Steven Yoon  5:01 P.M.**
OK. No problem.

---

ACTUAL TEST 5

PART 7

**156.** At 4:50 P.M. what does Mr. Martinez most likely mean when he writes, "I'm in the warehouse right now"?

(A) He will not be in tomorrow.
(B) He has a delivery to make.
(C) He needs to speak with Mr. Yoon.
(D) He cannot call Jennifer.

**157.** What task is Mr. Yoon asked to do?

(A) Contact the CEO
(B) Set up a meeting
(C) Call a technician
(D) Leave the office

October 10

Peter Stephenson
45 Ramsay Avenue
Cleveland, Ohio

Dear Mr. Stephenson:

Thank you very much for deciding to attend the very first International Magazine Festival that will take place in Paris, France. We received your registration. --[1]--. As requested, we billed your credit card to include both admission to the event as well as the extra fee needed to reserve a table for your display. Immediately upon arrival, we will show you to your table and also present you with a name badge that will allow you to receive discounts at any beverage and food vendors at the festival. --[2]--.

We would like to remind you that accommodation is not included in the festival admission price. To reserve a room in the neighborhood, please visit www.parishotels.com. You may be able to book a room at 25% off the regular rate by providing proof that you are participating in our festival. --[3]--.

Enclosed, please find a map of this particular area of Paris. This will allow you to acquaint yourself with the neighborhood. The map also includes the area's most popular restaurants and hotels. --[4]--.

Again, thank you and we hope the International Magazine Festival turns out to be a rewarding experience for you.

Sincerely,

Nicole Desjardins,
Festival Coordinator

**158.** Why was the letter sent?

(A) To offer a partial refund
(B) To inform of an address change
(C) To explain a procedure
(D) To acknowledge registration

**159.** What is Mr. Stephenson advised to review ahead of time?

(A) A local map
(B) A meeting agenda
(C) Contract terms
(D) Flight times

**160.** In which of the positions marked [1], [2], [3], and [4] does the following sentence best belong?

"This letter is suitable verification so simply present it to the clerk when you check in."

(A) [1]
(B) [2]
(C) [3]
(D) [4]

**Unforeseeable Delays for the Hammer Electronics 8000 Series**

By Sophia Miachi

Last week, Hammer Electronics, the world's leading producer of smart phones, announced a delay in the launch of its new 8000 Series smart phone line. Industry professionals and customers alike were shocked by the news. Hammer Electronics enthusiasts took to social media to express their frustration with the cancellation of the much-anticipated 8000 Series.

According to Hammer representatives, the 8000 Series, which will consist of three individual models and various companion technologies, has been delayed due to unforeseeable problems with the company's new screen design. --[1]--. While the prototypes were initially approved, the first batch of devices were unable to pass safety tests. --[2]--. This may be due to a flaw in the glass used to construct the screens, which makes the internal components vulnerable to overheating.

In addition to not passing the inspections, Hammer's new line has proven to be less durable than the company intended. Because of the flawed materials, the 8000 Series has proven to be quite delicate. --[3]--.

Hammer Electronics is now looking at alternative materials and plans to release the 8000 Series next year. --[4]--. However, the company may have already lost many of its eager customers.

**161.** What is indicated about Hammer Electronics?

(A) It is a top producer of smart phone technology.
(B) It will sell the 8000 Series at a discount.
(C) It is moving its headquarters to another country.
(D) It will continue producing a flawed design.

**162.** What is NOT mentioned as a problem with the 8000 Series design?

(A) The screens have flawed glass.
(B) The devices may overheat.
(C) The materials are too expensive.
(D) The devices are fragile.

**163.** Why will Hammer Electronics release the 8000 Series next year?

(A) They need to address a patent issue.
(B) Their inspections have been rescheduled.
(C) Some factories need to be upgraded.
(D) They need enough time to find new materials.

**164.** In which of the positions marked [1], [2], [3], and [4] does the following sentence best belong?

"For a company that prides itself on durable products, releasing this line of devices would be an embarrassment."

(A) [1]
(B) [2]
(C) [3]
(D) [4]

**Questions 165-168** refer to the following text message chain.

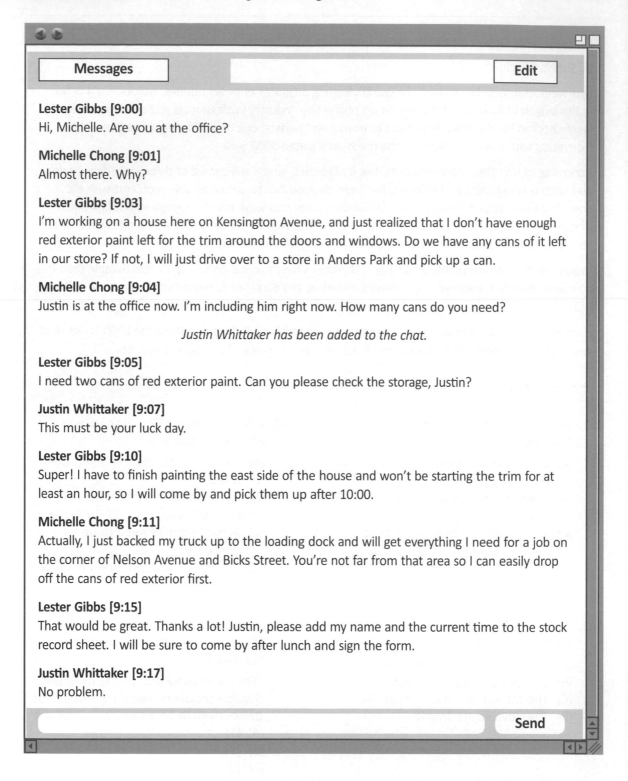

**Messages**                                             **Edit**

**Lester Gibbs [9:00]**
Hi, Michelle. Are you at the office?

**Michelle Chong [9:01]**
Almost there. Why?

**Lester Gibbs [9:03]**
I'm working on a house here on Kensington Avenue, and just realized that I don't have enough red exterior paint left for the trim around the doors and windows. Do we have any cans of it left in our store? If not, I will just drive over to a store in Anders Park and pick up a can.

**Michelle Chong [9:04]**
Justin is at the office now. I'm including him right now. How many cans do you need?

*Justin Whittaker has been added to the chat.*

**Lester Gibbs [9:05]**
I need two cans of red exterior paint. Can you please check the storage, Justin?

**Justin Whittaker [9:07]**
This must be your luck day.

**Lester Gibbs [9:10]**
Super! I have to finish painting the east side of the house and won't be starting the trim for at least an hour, so I will come by and pick them up after 10:00.

**Michelle Chong [9:11]**
Actually, I just backed my truck up to the loading dock and will get everything I need for a job on the corner of Nelson Avenue and Bicks Street. You're not far from that area so I can easily drop off the cans of red exterior first.

**Lester Gibbs [9:15]**
That would be great. Thanks a lot! Justin, please add my name and the current time to the stock record sheet. I will be sure to come by after lunch and sign the form.

**Justin Whittaker [9:17]**
No problem.

Send

**165.** What type of business does Mr. Gibbs probably work for?

(A) A home improvement contractor
(B) An Internet provider
(C) A plastics manufacturer
(D) A fast food restaurant

**166.** Where does Ms. Chong say she will go next?

(A) To Anders Park
(B) To Kensington Avenue
(C) To Bicks Street
(D) To Nelson Avenue

**167.** At 9:07 A.M. what does Mr. Whittaker most likely mean when he writes, "This must be your lucky day"?

(A) There is enough money for a new project.
(B) The directions to the house are easy to follow.
(C) The exact number of cans needed is in stock.
(D) He will be able to help Mr. Gibbs in the evening.

**168.** What does Mr. Gibbs ask Mr. Whittaker to do?

(A) Fill in the main details on a form
(B) Place some items on a shelf
(C) Set up a consultation with a client
(D) Send an invoice to a local business

## BizNet
### *Networking at the click of a mouse!*

BizNet is the latest development in online networking services. Quick, affordable, and easy-to-use, BizNet can connect you with industry professionals and help you land the job of your dreams. Our online services allow you to track trends in the job market as well as get up-to-date information on business conferences in your area.

In cooperation with our sister network, StudyNet, you get numerous advanced features, such as:
- A simple résumé builder that allows you to create a perfect résumé in minutes
- An extensive list of businesses and search tools for finding the right job opening
- A library of videos on everything from applying to interviewing for your dream job
- Weekly matching services that pair you up with new jobs based on your skills

For more information, visit www.biznet.com.

**169.** How would a customer most likely use BizNet?

(A) To shop for online services
(B) To find employment at a company
(C) To complete tax documents
(D) To advertise the services of a company

**170.** What is suggested about the company that developed BizNet?

(A) Its representatives can be contacted by telephone.
(B) It has a reputation for helping home businesses.
(C) It was founded by a large sales corporation.
(D) It has more than one networking website.

**171.** What is NOT mentioned as a feature of BizNet?

(A) A library of videos
(B) A résumé generator
(C) Tickets to conferences
(D) Employment search tools

Questions 172-175 refer to the following notice.

**Lake Porticole Beach and Campground (LPBC)**

Lake Porticole Beach and Campground will be open this spring & summer season beginning April 10 through September 1. Please note, however, LPBC reserves the right to impose additional restrictions on campers. Due to the repeated occurrence of dry weather, campers may be prohibited from having open campfires at certain times. This does not apply to the use of camping stoves and barbecues for cooking, however. When fires are permitted, campers must purchase pre-cut wood from the park. Cutting down trees will not be permitted at any time.

Lake Porticole Beach may be accessed by non-campers for day visits for a small fee. Beach goers may arrive as early as 8 A.M. and stay until 5 P.M. Group tickets may be booked in advance for a discount. Additionally, the park offers guided tours of the Lake Porticole Museum, a historical estate originally owned by Sir William Marks. Tickets for the museum can be purchased at the front gate on the day of the tour.

**Payment and Reservations**
• For campsite reservations, call 888-341-0867. Campsites are $65.00 per night. A non-refundable deposit of $30.00 must be made at the time of reservation. This deposit goes toward the cost of your stay.
• Beach day passes for non-campers can be purchased upon arrival for $8.00 per person. Groups of more than 15 can receive a 20% discount if reservations are made in advance.
• Lake Porticole Museum tickets are available for $7.00 per person. Tours are offered three times per day at 11 A.M., 1 P.M., and 3 P.M.

**172.** What is announced in the notice?
(A) A new policy
(B) A business's closing
(C) An increase in fees
(D) An operation schedule

**173.** What is indicated about visiting Lake Porticole's campground?
(A) Campers can be fined for littering in the forest.
(B) Campers might not be able to have campfires.
(C) To see the museum, campers must be part of a group.
(D) To access the beach, campers need to pay another fee.

**174.** What is mentioned about the Lake Porticole's non-camping services?
(A) Museum tickets can be reserved.
(B) Beach visitors can stay overnight on weekends.
(C) Parasols are offered to beach visitors free of charge.
(D) Groups can get a discount when visiting the beach.

**175.** What happens when a campsite reservation is canceled?
(A) A reservation fee is lost.
(B) A payment is refunded.
(C) A bill will be sent.
(D) A membership will be downgraded.

GO ON TO THE NEXT PAGE

10 March

Ms. Kelly Norstram
Simpson Publishing
Human Resources Department
55 Center St.
Sydney, Australia

Dear Ms. Norstram,

I would like to take this opportunity to submit my application for the editorial director position at Simpson Publishing in its new Sydney office. As you can see from my enclosed résumé, I have extensive experience in the editorial field, including five years as head editor at *Lush Magazine* and three years as an editorial assistant at the *Sydney Times* newspaper.

Aside from this experience, I also have a Bachelor's degree in Journalism and a Master's degree in Publishing Studies. Furthermore, I believe I would add a new dimension to the editorial director position given that I am also a published author of seven children's books. I believe that my unique combination of experience will contribute greatly to the company.

Thank you very much for your time. I look forward to speaking with you.

Sincerely,

Adrian Perdu

| To: | Simpson Publishing Editorial Staff |
|-----|-----------------------------------|
| From: | Adrian Perdu |
| Date: | April 30 |
| Subject: | Some Reminders |

Editorial Staff Members,

It has been nearly a year since we first proposed our new line of educational children's books. I'd like to commend you all on your hard work on this series. With our publication date fast approaching, I'd just like to remind everyone of a few things.

First, please ensure you communicate with designers weekly regarding the overall design of our books. It is important that you give them your input and guidance in bringing our collective vision to fruition.

Second, some freelance proofreaders have fallen behind on their deadlines. Please make sure you contact them regularly and if need be, hire additional freelancers to complete the work.

Finally, as the release of our series will include a website launch, I'd like everyone to submit a biography for the "about us" section. A simple biography of about 100 words will suffice.

Thank you all for your continued hard work, and I look forward to launch day!

Adrian

**176.** What is one purpose of the letter?

(A) To inquire about a starting salary
(B) To list some professional qualifications
(C) To provide an employment reference
(D) To ask about the location of a job

**177.** In the letter, the word "dimension" in paragraph 2, line 2, is closest in meaning to

(A) demand
(B) precedent
(C) matter
(D) characteristic

**178.** Why did Mr. Perdu write the e-mail?

(A) To praise workers for getting tasks done
(B) To stress the importance of some duties
(C) To motivate employees to take on extra work
(D) To inform new hires of special procedures

**179.** What is stated about Simpson Publishing?

(A) It publishes primarily e-books.
(B) It employs editors in seven countries.
(C) It will discontinue some publications.
(D) It will introduce its staff on its website.

**180.** What is suggested about Mr. Perdu?

(A) He previously worked as a book designer.
(B) He was hired by Simpson Publishing one year ago.
(C) He moved to the US for a job opportunity.
(D) He no longer writes books for children.

**Questions 181-185** refer to the following e-mail and business plan.

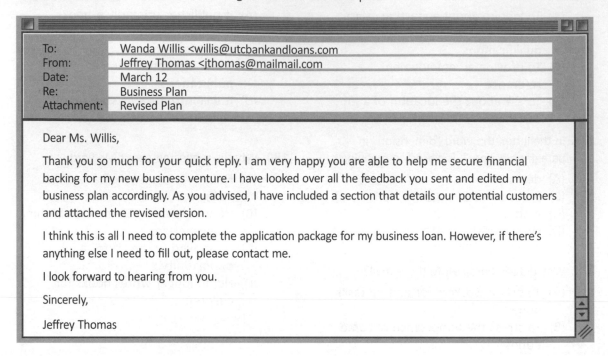

| To: | Wanda Willis <willis@utcbankandloans.com |
| From: | Jeffrey Thomas <jthomas@mailmail.com |
| Date: | March 12 |
| Re: | Business Plan |
| Attachment: | Revised Plan |

Dear Ms. Willis,

Thank you so much for your quick reply. I am very happy you are able to help me secure financial backing for my new business venture. I have looked over all the feedback you sent and edited my business plan accordingly. As you advised, I have included a section that details our potential customers and attached the revised version.

I think this is all I need to complete the application package for my business loan. However, if there's anything else I need to fill out, please contact me.

I look forward to hearing from you.

Sincerely,

Jeffrey Thomas

---

**Revised Business Plan: The Brim**

**Section 1. Purpose**

Downtown Portside has become a bustling business district, filled with numerous office buildings, banks, and department stores. My business, The Brim, will be located near the prestigious courthouse, a busy area of the downtown core. We hope to offer a wide variety of international gourmet coffees at affordable prices, while also providing a relaxing atmosphere to enjoy our gourmet lunch items.

**Section 2. Target Market**

The Brim will serve business professionals working downtown. Because there are so many law offices and banks within walking distance, our customers are likely to visit our coffee house in the mornings, during break times, and at lunch. Furthermore, weekend customers will consist of shoppers who are visiting the nearby Portside Department Store.

**Section 3. Timeline**

The Brim is scheduled to open on June 1. We expect the following preparations to be completed by:

| March 28 | Sign the lease and apply for a business permit |
| April 10 | Renovate the dining area and upgrade the kitchen |
| April 20 | Hire staff and complete employee training |
| May 15 | Finalize the menu, order inventory, and plan the grand opening |

**Section 4. Marketing Plan**

Please see the attached spread sheet for our detailed marketing plans prior to opening and after.

**181.** What is the purpose of the e-mail?

(A) To review the guidelines of a permit
(B) To send feedback about some financial data
(C) To request advice on writing a business plan
(D) To respond to a requested revision

**182.** In the e-mail, the word "secure" in paragraph 1, line 1, is closest in meaning to

(A) guard
(B) obtain
(C) save
(D) fasten

**183.** What section of the business plan was added?

(A) Section 1
(B) Section 2
(C) Section 3
(D) Section 4

**184.** What type of business does Mr. Thomas plan to start?

(A) A loan company
(B) A department store
(C) A law office
(D) A gourmet café

**185.** According to the business plan, what information was submitted separately?

(A) A detailed estimate of expected profits
(B) Contact information for employment references
(C) A list of ways the business will advertise
(D) Recommendations for renovation companies

**Questions 186-190** refer to the following webpage, e-mail, and form.

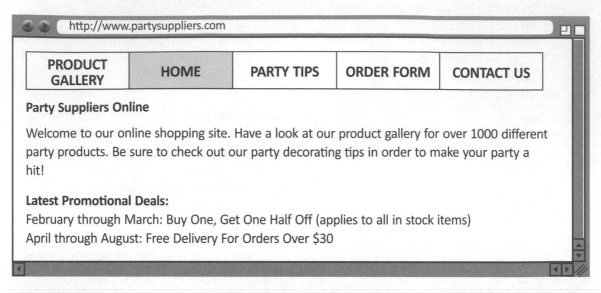

http://www.partysuppliers.com

| PRODUCT GALLERY | HOME | PARTY TIPS | ORDER FORM | CONTACT US |

**Party Suppliers Online**

Welcome to our online shopping site. Have a look at our product gallery for over 1000 different party products. Be sure to check out our party decorating tips in order to make your party a hit!

**Latest Promotional Deals:**
February through March: Buy One, Get One Half Off (applies to all in stock items)
April through August: Free Delivery For Orders Over $30

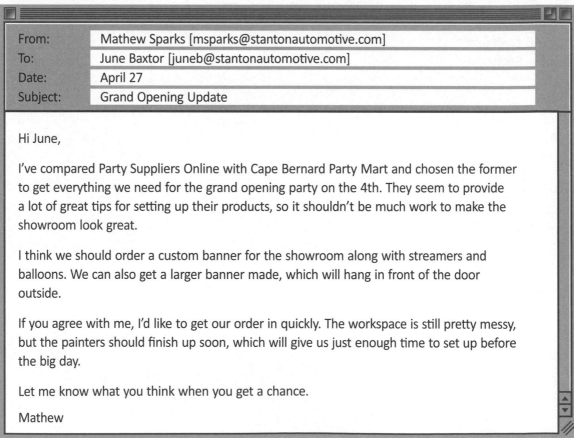

| From: | Mathew Sparks [msparks@stantonautomotive.com] |
| To: | June Baxtor [juneb@stantonautomotive.com] |
| Date: | April 27 |
| Subject: | Grand Opening Update |

Hi June,

I've compared Party Suppliers Online with Cape Bernard Party Mart and chosen the former to get everything we need for the grand opening party on the 4th. They seem to provide a lot of great tips for setting up their products, so it shouldn't be much work to make the showroom look great.

I think we should order a custom banner for the showroom along with streamers and balloons. We can also get a larger banner made, which will hang in front of the door outside.

If you agree with me, I'd like to get our order in quickly. The workspace is still pretty messy, but the painters should finish up soon, which will give us just enough time to set up before the big day.

Let me know what you think when you get a chance.

Mathew

**Order Number:** 112233265
**Contact Info:** Mathew Sparks (444) 232-0916
**Delivery To:** Stanton Automotive Dealership, 14 Brooks Lane, Atlantic City
**Delivery Window:** 01-02 May, 09:00-13:00

| Quantity | Product Code | Description |
|---|---|---|
| 1 | YZ0933 | Custom Banner (3 feet long) |
| 1 | YZ0955 | Custom Banner (6 feet long) |
| 12 | GH3345 | Rainbow Balloons 12 per pack |
| 2 | BB3200 | Streamers (white) |
| | | Total: $104.50 |

**Note:** All our custom banners are printed at our manufacturing headquarters in Baltimore. Those items will be shipped into Atlantic City from Baltimore instead of our Port Edward store, which means you will have two separate shipments. Should you have any questions, do not hesitate to call us immediately.

186. What is indicated about Party Suppliers Online?

(A) It provides complimentary product samples.
(B) It offers decorating advice to customers.
(C) It recently opened up another store.
(D) It will expand its product line next year.

187. What is probably true about Stanton Automotive Dealership's order?

(A) It will be delivered for free.
(B) It includes foreign products.
(C) It includes half-price items.
(D) It will be refunded in May.

188. Why does Mr. Sparks probably prefer to schedule a delivery quickly?

(A) He needs time to purchase more items.
(B) He wants to take advantage of a promotion.
(C) He needs some workers to help clean up.
(D) He wants to have enough time to set up.

189. What product will most likely be placed outside Stanton Automotive Dealership?

(A) Custom Banner 3ft
(B) Custom Banner 6ft
(C) Rainbow Balloons
(D) Streamers

190. According to the form, where most likely will the balloons be shipped from?

(A) Baltimore
(B) Atlantic City
(C) Cape Bernard
(D) Port Edward

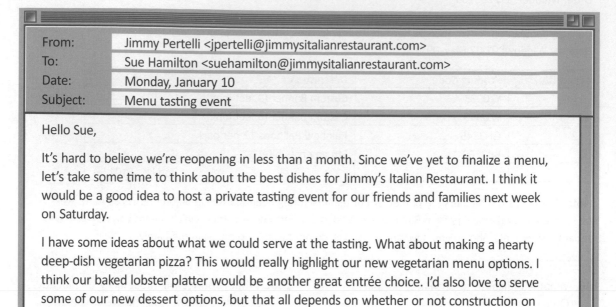

From: Jimmy Pertelli <jpertelli@jimmysitalianrestaurant.com>
To: Sue Hamilton <suehamilton@jimmysitalianrestaurant.com>
Date: Monday, January 10
Subject: Menu tasting event

Hello Sue,

It's hard to believe we're reopening in less than a month. Since we've yet to finalize a menu, let's take some time to think about the best dishes for Jimmy's Italian Restaurant. I think it would be a good idea to host a private tasting event for our friends and families next week on Saturday.

I have some ideas about what we could serve at the tasting. What about making a hearty deep-dish vegetarian pizza? This would really highlight our new vegetarian menu options. I think our baked lobster platter would be another great entrée choice. I'd also love to serve some of our new dessert options, but that all depends on whether or not construction on the pastry station is completed. In the event that it's not, how about serving some of our new organic ice cream flavors topped with your amazing chocolate sauce? I will leave it all up to you, though. As head chef, you have complete freedom.

Finally, I'd love to offer our guests an ice-cream making demonstration after the tasting. Let me know if you think that would be possible.

Thanks,

Jimmy

---

### Jimmy's Italian Restaurant Tasting Menu
### Saturday, January 15

Caprese Salad with mozzarella cheese and fresh basil
Coconut Shrimp
Baked Garlic Bread
Vegetarian Pasta with tomato sauce
Baked Lobster Platter smothered in melted butter
Rib eye Fire-Grilled Steak served with roasted potatoes
Jimmy's Famous Puff Pastries

## Tasting Comment Card

**Name:** Fran Humphrey

**Please comment on your tasting experience at Jimmy's Italian Restaurant.**

I enjoyed the appetizers very much. The salad, however, had too much balsamic dressing for my taste. The vegetarian pasta dish was quite good, but I found the noodles to be a bit overcooked. The baked lobster, on the other hand, was the best I've ever tasted. I found the steak to be a bit rare, but the potatoes were seasoned very nicely. The dessert was perhaps too sweet for me, but I thought the pastry was cooked to perfection. I also enjoyed the ice cream making demonstration, though I wish we could've tasted some of the flavors.

**191.** What is the purpose of the menu tasting?

(A) To select dishes for a new menu
(B) To prepare for a restaurant inspection
(C) To audition new cooking staff
(D) To decide who will be head chef

**192.** In the e-mail, the word "hearty" in paragraph 2, line 1, is closest in meaning to

(A) sincere
(B) aromatic
(C) satisfying
(D) original

**193.** What is true about the tasting menu?

(A) It showcases only old menu items.
(B) It lists several new ice cream flavors.
(C) It is only available to customers on weekends.
(D) It includes an entrée suggested by Mr. Pertelli.

**194.** Which menu item was most likely Ms. Humphrey's favorite?

(A) The salad
(B) The pasta
(C) The lobster
(D) The steak

**195.** What is suggested about the pastry station?

(A) It was too large for the kitchen.
(B) It was moved to another location.
(C) It was damaged in a renovation.
(D) It was completed on time.

**Questions 196-200** refer to the following advertisement, e-mail, and text message.

**Hartford Opera House**
**45 Bellview Street**
**New York City**
www.hartfordoperahouse.com

The Hartford Opera House is pleased to announce an exciting schedule of events that will take place this summer. We will be featuring everything from concerts to stage plays, so we are sure to have something for you. Tickets will be available on our website for each event, and seasonal passes may be purchased for a lump sum. Seasonal pass holders will be able to attend as many events as they wish and bring up to three guests at a time free of charge.

Schedule of Events:

June 23 — The Miller Brothers Classical Ensemble
July 3 — Stand-Up Comedy by Alan Brewer
July 4 — *Into the Jungle*, an award-winning musical featuring songs by Catrina Belford
July 10 — *Women of Egypt*, a stage play directed by Tommy Wilson

For a complete summer schedule, please visit www.hartfordoperahouse.com.

---

| To: | Lila Sampson |
| --- | --- |
| From: | Roderick Kelly |
| Cc: | June Varek |
| Subject: | Your Trip to Meadworth Paper and Packaging |
| Date: | June 2 |

Dear Ms. Sampson,

We at Meadworth Paper and Packaging are looking forward to your visit to our company headquarters from July 2 to July 4. We are very pleased that your company has agreed to discuss the terms of a possible merger between our two businesses.

In addition to providing you with a tour of our factory and offices, we have an exciting schedule planned for you, which will include a lunch with our CEO, a trip to Westflower Golf Club, and an excursion at the Harbor Yacht Club. We have also scheduled an evening at our local opera house for some live entertainment on your last night. We hope you will enjoy your trip, and if you need anything else, please let me know.

Sincerely

Roderick Kelly
Meadworth Paper and Packaging

From: Varek

To: Kelly

The weather forecast predicts rain during our trip to the golf club with Ms. Sampson next week. I think it would be best if you switched the golf club visit with the opera house event. This will change the opera house event we'll attend, but there's no need to buy new tickets. I'm allowed to bring a few guests free of charge.

**196.** What is suggested about the Hartford Opera House?

(A) It is merging with another company.
(B) It gives away free seasonal passes.
(C) It is located next to a golf club.
(D) It schedules a variety of events.

**197.** What is Ms. Sampson scheduled to do during her visit?

(A) Discuss a new deal
(B) Review a contract
(C) Consult a lawyer
(D) Present a product

**198.** What opera house event was Ms. Sampson originally scheduled to attend?

(A) A classical music performance
(B) A live comedy performance
(C) A popular musical
(D) A stage play about Egypt

**199.** What does Mr. Kelly need to reschedule?

(A) A boat trip
(B) A game of golf
(C) A lunch meeting
(D) A factory tour

**200.** Why most likely does Ms. Varek not need to purchase tickets?

(A) The event they will attend is free for everyone.
(B) Ms. Sampson has not approved the schedule yet.
(C) Ms. Varek already has a seasonal pass for the opera house.
(D) Mr. Kelly must wait for some tickets to be refunded.

Stop! This is the end of the test. If you finish before time is called, you may go back to Parts 5, 6, and 7 and check your work.

167

# ANSWERS ACTUAL TEST 5

| | | | | |
|---|---|---|---|---|
| 101. (B) | 121. (C) | 141. (D) | 161. (A) | 181. (D) |
| 102. (B) | 122. (D) | 142. (B) | 162. (C) | 182. (B) |
| 103. (C) | 123. (C) | 143. (D) | 163. (D) | 183. (B) |
| 104. (A) | 124. (A) | 144. (A) | 164. (C) | 184. (D) |
| 105. (D) | 125. (C) | 145. (A) | 165. (A) | 185. (C) |
| 106. (A) | 126. (A) | 146. (D) | 166. (B) | 186. (B) |
| 107. (C) | 127. (D) | 147. (A) | 167. (C) | 187. (A) |
| 108. (A) | 128. (B) | 148. (A) | 168. (A) | 188. (D) |
| 109. (B) | 129. (C) | 149. (D) | 169. (B) | 189. (B) |
| 110. (D) | 130. (D) | 150. (B) | 170. (D) | 190. (D) |
| 111. (D) | 131. (B) | 151. (D) | 171. (C) | 191. (A) |
| 112. (B) | 132. (C) | 152. (D) | 172. (D) | 192. (C) |
| 113. (B) | 133. (B) | 153. (D) | 173. (B) | 193. (D) |
| 114. (C) | 134. (D) | 154. (C) | 174. (D) | 194. (C) |
| 115. (B) | 135. (B) | 155. (C) | 175. (A) | 195. (D) |
| 116. (D) | 136. (C) | 156. (D) | 176. (B) | 196. (D) |
| 117. (A) | 137. (B) | 157. (B) | 177. (D) | 197. (A) |
| 118. (C) | 138. (D) | 158. (D) | 178. (B) | 198. (C) |
| 119. (B) | 139. (A) | 159. (A) | 179. (D) | 199. (B) |
| 120. (A) | 140. (C) | 160. (C) | 180. (B) | 200. (C) |

ACTUAL
TEST

**6**

## READING TEST

In the Reading Test, you will read a variety of texts and answer several different types of reading comprehension questions. The entire Reading test will last 75 minutes. There are three parts, and directions are given for each part. You are encouraged to answer as many questions as possible within the time allowed.

You must mark your answers on the separate answer sheet. Do not write your answers in your test book.

## PART 5

**Directions:** A word or phrase is missing in each of the sentences below. Four answer choices are given below each sentence. Select the best answer to complete the sentence. Then mark the letter (A), (B), (C), or (D) on your answer sheet.

**101.** The shelves in the east warehouse must be ------- stocked for the holiday season.

(A) full
(B) fully
(C) fuller
(D) fullest

**102.** ------- to the swimming pool is reserved for guests staying in one of our deluxe suites.

(A) Access
(B) Accessed
(C) Accessing
(D) Accessible

**103.** Mr. Takashi admits that ------- is expected to take on more managerial duties.

(A) he
(B) his
(C) him
(D) himself

**104.** At the end of the month, Davisville Incorporated is ------- its Internet provider.

(A) changing
(B) attending
(C) holding
(D) turning

**105.** Better City Travel offers bicycle tours ------- Skiff Lake at very reasonable rates.

(A) between
(B) along
(C) below
(D) apart

**106.** Of all snow tires, Marten's new MR-200 is, without a doubt, the most durable -------.

(A) that
(B) any
(C) one
(D) either

**107.** As the amount of orders increased significantly, Lawford's Coffee Shop was able to ------- new deals with its suppliers.

(A) negotiating
(B) negotiates
(C) negotiated
(D) negotiate

**108.** Pandora Hair Design offers employees ------- opportunities to advance their careers.

(A) plenty
(B) each
(C) very
(D) many

**109.** Highway 56 between Greenville and Trenton has been blocked off ------- fallen power poles.

(A) so that
(B) as a result
(C) in order to
(D) because of

**110.** It is impossible to rent an apartment in the Dorchester Building without a ------- from a current tenant.

(A) referring
(B) referred
(C) referral
(D) refer

**111.** A green sticker will be placed on the windshield ------- after the inspection of the vehicle is complete.

(A) when
(B) only
(C) still
(D) most

**112.** Since two managers have opted for early retirement, it is ------- to find replacements by July 30.

(A) necessitating
(B) necessary
(C) necessarily
(D) necessities

**113.** The cargo elevator in the south end of the building will not be in operation ------- further notice.

(A) until
(B) onto
(C) since
(D) all

**114.** The weight indicated on the outside of this package is ------- accurate.

(A) fairness
(B) fairest
(C) fairly
(D) fair

GO ON TO THE NEXT PAGE

115. David sent a link to a website that has a ------- of information on engine repair.

(A) wealth
(B) height
(C) labor
(D) fame

116. To find the easiest route to Simmons, Darthmouth, and nearby towns, be sure to look at an ------- map.

(A) update
(B) updated
(C) updates
(D) updating

117. The hiring committee will start reviewing résumés ------- the application deadline has passed.

(A) how
(B) nor
(C) now that
(D) whether

118. On her television show, Gloria Van Cingel, the well-known art critic, ------- paintings from a variety of periods.

(A) analysis
(B) analyzer
(C) analyzes
(D) analyzing

119. The installation of several self-checkout kiosks in the Redford Supermarket is expected to create changes ------- the number of employees.

(A) in
(B) again
(C) positions
(D) ultimately

120. Compared to everyone else, Donald prepared himself for the real estate license exam in a ------- short period of time.

(A) surprised
(B) surprise
(C) surprisingly
(D) surprising

121. The production supervisor of Gleason Shoes is ------- of all the factory's operations.

(A) aware
(B) current
(C) serious
(D) alert

122. The tourism ------- of Cape Breton Island has dramatically improved ever since the harbor was reopened last year.

(A) economical
(B) economic
(C) economize
(D) economy

123. Someone from Renforth Building Supplies asked us to ------- the type of lumber needed for the project.

(A) personify
(B) magnify
(C) specify
(D) testify

124. Fitzgerald Air offers flights to over 200 destinations ------- northern Canada.

(A) toward
(B) throughout
(C) regarding
(D) aboard

**125.** The beginners' guitar class at the Lesterville Academy fills up quickly so we recommend filling out an online ------- form.

(A) enrollment
(B) inventory
(C) complaint
(D) solicitation

**126.** On Friday, Lancaster Incorporated's newly ------- vice president will address his staff for the first time.

(A) appoint
(B) appoints
(C) appointed
(D) appointing

**127.** The head of public relations must be continually in contact with the media, so Randolph Industries ------- someone with exceptional communication skills.

(A) seeking
(B) is seeking
(C) are sought
(D) have been sought

**128.** Ms. Laporte's approach to organizing a fundraising event is ------- different from Ms. Halloway's.

(A) haltingly
(B) intimately
(C) permissibly
(D) markedly

**129.** Recently, Kingston has experienced a huge increase in the number of residents, ------- are international students.

(A) inasmuch as
(B) the reason being
(C) because of them
(D) most of whom

**130.** To help the staff of the Carrington Inn make your stay more -------, please fill out a guest feedback form and leave it at the front desk.

(A) knowledgeable
(B) considerable
(C) enjoyable
(D) available

## PART 6

**Directions:** Read the texts that follow. A word, phrase, or sentence is missing in parts of each text. Four answer choices for each question are given below the text. Select the best answer to complete the text. Then mark the letter (A), (B), (C), or (D) on your answer sheet.

**Questions 131-134** refer to the following e-mail.

**To:** sandrabae@gladstoneresearch.com.au

**From:** markjohnson@sydneyunienergy.au

**Date:** 15 May

**Subject:** Thank you!

Dear Dr. Bae,

Thank you very much for _____ our main research center last Friday. Your expert advice, as always,
**131.**
_____. Our entire engineering team benefited greatly from your presentation on the exciting new
**132.**
advances in energy generation and consumption systems for industrial facilities. This fall, our
department plans to hire five more engineering researchers. Would _____ mind leading a training
**133.**
session on the topic you spoke of last week? _____. We will look forward to your prompt response
**134.**
so that details can be discussed.

Sincerely,

Mark Johnson

131. (A) calling
   (B) opening
   (C) visiting
   (D) staffing

132. (A) appreciates
   (B) will be appreciated
   (C) is appreciating
   (D) was appreciated

133. (A) his
   (B) yours
   (C) you
   (D) he

134. (A) All engineers must adhere to our center's strict regulations.
   (B) A large number of candidates have impressive résumés.
   (C) If you can, it would undoubtedly prove beneficial to the new staff.
   (D) With your feedback, we will be able to build it quickly.

**Questions 135-138** refer to the following article.

GEARY (April 5) — This morning, the National Transportation Authority announced that a $41 million grant has been awarded to Weston Valley Air Travel Network. Thanks to this ___135.___, the dream of having two airports in Weston Valley will soon be realized. Many residents in the region welcome news of this expansion to the current air service. ___136.___. Business owners throughout the Weston Valley are truly delighted. Jennifer Rossignol, a local business owner, expressed her delight with the grant earlier today. "This is fantastic news for someone like myself ___137.___ has to travel to Toronto frequently on business," says Rossignol. "We have had no choice ___138.___ years but to endure a four-hour bus ride into the city, but soon, I will be able to board a plane and be there in under an hour."

135. (A) funding
(B) policy
(C) design
(D) strategy

136. (A) Weston Valley Air Travel Network confirmed that the project must be delayed.
(B) Passengers will have access to more parking spaces at one of the airports.
(C) This development is expected to create over 500 jobs at both airports.
(D) Air fares for most regional flights, however, will most likely be raised.

137. (A) likewise
(B) another
(C) then
(D) who

138. (A) for
(B) with
(C) about
(D) on

**Questions 139-142** refer to the following e-mail.

To: Arnold Mallory [amallory@channel6news.net]

From: Melinda Calhoun [mcalhoun@channel6news.net]

Re: Fantastic reviews

Date: March 21

Dear Arnold,

The managerial division here at Channel 6 News was positively excited to read sensational reviews of our program in both the *Moncton Gazette* and *Uptown Entertainment*. All of us agree that your work here has been nothing but ------- . **139.** For this reason, Channel 6 News is truly delighted ------- **140.** you a yearly bonus that will be added to your next monthly paycheck on March 30. ------- , **141.** your current salary will be raised by 12% effective April 1. Since you took over as head news anchor last November, our number of regular viewers has tripled. ------- . **142.** We could not have achieved any of this without your outstanding performance. On behalf of everyone at Channel 6 News, thank you for your hard work and dedication.

Melinda

**139.** (A) withdrawn
(B) matched
(C) affordable
(D) exceptional

**140.** (A) to award
(B) an award
(C) it awarded
(D) that awards

**141.** (A) For example
(B) In addition
(C) Nevertheless
(D) On the other hand

**142.** (A) Channel 6 News has also received fabulous reviews in national newspapers.
(B) An assistant news anchor will be hired sometime next month.
(C) Our team will meet next week to discuss changes to your show.
(D) You are one of two employees who are entitled to an annual bonus.

**Questions 143-146** refer to the following article.

---

**Electronics Trade Show**

(25 August) The annual Global Electronics Trade Show came to Tokyo on Saturday, 23 August for the fifth consecutive year. ____143.___. As was the case last year, China was the most ___144.___ represented nation. ___145.___, organizers reported that the number of South American companies was significantly higher than previous years. Another noticeable change at this year's ___146.___ was the fact that the majority of companies showcased kitchen appliances rather than the usual entertainment electronics.

---

143. (A) Volunteers at the event were not required to pay the registration fee.
    (B) Product demonstrations will be held in three different auditoriums.
    (C) The event featured over 500 companies from every corner of the world.
    (D) Recruiters collected résumés from university students in attendance.

144. (A) heavy
    (B) heavily
    (C) heavier
    (D) heaviness

145. (A) Moreover
    (B) Rather
    (C) Instead
    (D) Thus

146. (A) class
    (B) demonstration
    (C) event
    (D) ceremony

## PART 7

**Directions:** In this part you will read a selection of texts, such as magazine and newspaper articles, e-mails, and instant messages. Each text or set of texts is followed by several questions. Select the best answer for each question and mark the letter (A), (B), (C), or (D) on your answer sheet.

**Questions 147-148** refer to the following notice.

To our dear customers,

We are happy to announce that we will be hosting a weekly talent night starting in October. The event will be held every Wednesday from 6:00 P.M. until 8:00 P.M. and the stage will be set up on the first floor of our café.

Participants may sing, play instruments, or read poetry. Make sure to arrive early to sign up for a twenty-minute slot. All participants will be allowed free coffee or tea for the duration of the event.

For more information, please visit our website at www.cafémaria.com or call us at 777-4367.

**147.** Where would the notice most likely appear?

(A) In a subway station
(B) In a music book
(C) At a coffee house
(D) At a doctor's office

**148.** According to the notice, what will participants receive?

(A) Discount coupons
(B) A small payment
(C) A participation certificate
(D) Free beverages

Questions 149-150 refer to the following invoice.

**Eastview Convention Center**
**55 Lakeview Road**
**Seattle, Washington**

| | |
|---|---|
| **Date:** April 12<br>**Invoice number:** 9800032 | **Bill To:**<br>Trisha Baxter<br>Pure Motorcycles<br>90 Yamer Street<br>Orlando, Florida |

Invoice for the Eastview Convention Center's Annual Automotive Show from June 25 – June 27.

| Item: | Rate: | Total: |
|---|---|---|
| Convention Booth (30 square feet) | $100.00/day | $300.00 |
| **Additional Services:** | | |
| 3 display tables | $10.00/unit | $30.00 |
| Storage | $30.00/unit | $120.00 |
| Computer rental | $20.00/unit | $20.00 |
| 55-inch television rental | $30.00/unit | $30.00 |
| Show passes | $20.00/person | $200.00 |
| | **Subtotal:** | $700.00 |
| | **Tax:** | $45.50 |
| | **Total:** | $745.50* |

*Please visit your online account to arrange payment by April 20.

**149.** What is NOT included in the cost of the event?

(A) Passes to the show
(B) Display tables
(C) Television rental
(D) Setup and cleanup

**150.** What is Ms. Baxter asked to do?

(A) Sign up for a membership
(B) Mail a check to the venue
(C) Settle an invoice
(D) Confirm the number of participants

**Jennifer Porter [11:23 A.M.]**
Hi, Raphael. Were you able to stop by the Rickter Avenue property this weekend?

**Raphael Morez [11:25 A.M.]**
Yes, I went on Saturday. Since most of our photographers will be working at events every day, are you sure we need such a big place?

**Jennifer Porter [11:27 A.M.]**
The rooms are large, but as we expand, we'll need the space.

**Raphael Morez [11:28 A.M.]**
That might not happen for a few years, though.

**Jennifer Porter [11:30 A.M.]**
Yes, but we should be thinking about our long-term goals for the company. The Rickter Avenue property will give us a chance to finally develop an on-site studio.

**Raphael Morez [11:32 A.M.]**
You're right. We'll definitely need the extra space once we start offering portrait services.

**151.** At what kind of business do the people most likely work?

(A) A photography company
(B) A fashion design house
(C) An event planning business
(D) An art gallery

**152.** At 11:32 A.M., what does Mr. Morez most likely mean when he writes, "You're right"?

(A) A location is too far from the city.
(B) The building will help the company meet its goals.
(C) Much interior design work is needed in the building.
(D) The property has some significant flaws.

**To:** Tristan Starr
**From:** Emilia Simpson
**Date:** June 2
**Re:** Walton Shopping Center contract

Hi Tristan,

I just got an e-mail from Marcus Pine about the budget proposal you sent him yesterday. Apparently, several of the figures are incorrect. It seems you included the initial figures we presented to him during our first advertising pitch on May 6 and not the figures we later agreed on during negotiations on May 20.

Mr. Pine was hoping to present the advertising plan to his superiors on June 5. He mentioned that there are several other agencies that have sent him proposals, and he will select one of them instead if we cannot get this paperwork done by June 3. Since I'm just about to fly to our Chicago office, I'm hoping you can handle this right away. Please send Mr. Pine the revised proposal and e-mail me when you get his response.

Sincerely,

Emilia

**153.** Why was the e-mail written?

(A) To request a vacation
(B) To introduce an applicant
(C) To announce a policy change
(D) To point out some mistakes

**154.** When was the proposal modified?

(A) On May 6
(B) On May 20
(C) On June 3
(D) On June 5

**155.** What would Ms. Simpson like Mr. Starr to do?

(A) Make a phone call
(B) Issue a refund
(C) Send a document
(D) Speak with a manager

Restaurant sales are down in Plymouth County. According to a report in the *Plymouth Journal*, sales have dropped by more than 15 percent this winter. The drop has shocked many restaurant owners, especially since the winter holidays usually increase restaurant business. Bob Fulton, owner of Little Italy Eatery, attributed the drop to an increase in wholesale prices as one factor of the drop. "With the prices of everything going up, we've had to increase our prices as well," Mr. Fulton said in an interview. "Most customers just don't want to pay that much for a meal." To encourage more business, many local restaurants have joined forces to develop membership programs. These programs provide customers with discounts at numerous restaurants in the county.

**156.** According to the article, why have restaurant sales dropped?

(A) The weather has become unpleasant.

(B) The costs have risen too high.

(C) Newer restaurants have been built.

(D) Many local jobs have been lost.

**157.** How are restaurant owners responding to the trend?

(A) By improving the quality of the food

(B) By decreasing the number of workers

(C) By working with other restaurants

(D) By launching television advertisements.

Questions 158-161 refer to the following online chat discussion.

**Rita Frasier [2:23 P.M.]**
Ms. Norton, do you have a minute? Thomas and I are unclear about our assignments. Last year, I was in charge of developing the seasonal training program, but Thomas was assigned the exact same job this year.

**Patrina Norton [2:25 P.M.]**
Yes, everyone needs a chance to work on developing their own programs for human resources.

**Rita Frasier [2:26 P.M.]**
So, we will no longer use the materials I developed last year?

**Patrina Norton [2:28 P.M.]**
That's right. Thomas is expected to develop new materials that will be used this year.

**Thomas Woods [2:30 P.M.]**
But what if I would like to use some of Rita's ideas?

**Patrina Norton [2:33 P.M.]**
Program development is part of the job.

**Thomas Woods [2:35 P.M.]**
Yes, but Rita's program was excellent last year. I would hate all her hard work to go to waste.

**Patrina Norton [2:39 P.M.]**
If Rita is OK with it, I think you could use some of her materials so long as you update them where appropriate. Let me review last year's materials first and get back to you.

**Rita Frasier [2:41 P.M.]**
What if Thomas and I worked together on the project?

**Patrina Norton [2:44 P.M.]**
I don't think that will be necessary.

**Rita Frasier [2:45 P.M.]**
OK, I understand.

**Thomas Woods  [2:46 P.M.]**
Let us know when you've decided. Thanks.

158. Who most likely is Ms. Norton?
   (A) A financial planner
   (B) A human resources manager
   (C) A company intern
   (D) An advertising consultant

159. What is suggested about Ms. Frasier?
   (A) She developed a successful training program last year.
   (B) She usually works with Mr. Woods on projects.
   (C) She is pleased with this year's assignment.
   (D) She will take over Ms. Norton's job next year.

160. At 2:33 P.M., what does Ms. Norton most likely mean when she writes, "Program development is part of the job"?
   (A) Her job duties include program development.
   (B) She believes Ms. Frasier is better suited for the job.
   (C) She disagrees with Mr. Woods's suggestion.
   (D) Her contract with the company needs revising.

161. What will most likely happen next?
   (A) Ms. Frasier will contact a supervisor.
   (B) Mr. Woods will begin working on a project.
   (C) Mr. Woods and Ms. Frasier will have a meeting.
   (D) Ms. Norton will look at some old materials.

**To:** Tamika Keynes
**From:** Marcel Ventrue
**Re:** Information
**Date:** April 22

I'm writing in regard to the service quote you requested on our website. I'm delighted you're interested in Lawn and Garden Care's extensive range of services. --[1]--. I can assure you that we are the top landscaping company in the city. We service many local businesses, such as hotels and country clubs. --[2]--. We also maintain the extensive lawns at Memorial Stadium downtown.

I have attached the service quote you requested. --[3]--. The quote is based on weekly lawn maintenance services for The Renolds Gallery. In the event that you require additional services, such as garden planting or tree removal, you would be charged extra. --[4]--. Have a look at the quote and I will be in touch early next week to answer any questions you might have.

Sincerely,

Marcel Ventrue

162. What is the purpose of the e-mail?
    (A) To change a schedule
    (B) To respond to a request
    (C) To send a blueprint
    (D) To submit an application

163. For what kind of business does Ms. Keynes most likely work?
    (A) An art gallery
    (B) A stadium
    (C) A country club
    (D) A hotel

164. What is mentioned in the e-mail?
    (A) Ms. Keynes is a new employee at Lawn and Garden Care.
    (B) Lawn and Garden Care is a new business.
    (C) Ms. Keynes will hear from Mr. Ventrue next week.
    (D) Mr. Ventrue visited Ms. Keynes' business.

165. In which of the positions marked [1], [2], [3], and [4] does the following sentence best belong?

    "However, all additional services will be discounted should you sign a two-year contract with us."
    (A) [1]
    (B) [2]
    (C) [3]
    (D) [4]

Questions 166-168 refer to the following article.

**Parker Wallace to Join Adventure Software**
By Amy Swanson, *The Daily Chat*

NEW YORK (24 February) — Parker Wallace has announced he will join the new start-up Adventure Software. Wallace, who has been developing software applications for five years now, is best known as the creator of Marble FM, a music sharing application. Marble FM accumulated over three million downloads in just two years, leading Wallace to become one of the most sought-after developers in the industry.

Despite turning down jobs at Liquid Apps and T&B Developers, Wallace has made the surprising move and accepted an offer to join a company that is less than two years old. "When I met Alan Pike of Adventure Software, I knew he and I shared the same goals," Wallace recently said at the launch of his latest app. "He and I are both passionate about music, and he had some great ideas for future projects. I am extremely confident that we'll be putting out hot new products in the next year."

Wallace's newest app, Marble Video, has already generated over 500,000 downloads in less than a month. The tech world will be expecting big things from the partnership between Wallace and Pike, starting with the rerelease of an upgraded version of Pike's Smart Symphony on March 30.

**166.** Who most likely is Mr. Pike?

(A) A film director
(B) A symphony composer
(C) A music video producer
(D) A software company owner

**167.** What most likely is true about Ms. Swanson?

(A) She was formerly employed at Liquid Apps.
(B) She attended the launch of Marble Video.
(C) She purchased a copy of Marble FM.
(D) She met with Mr. Pike at an event.

**168.** What is indicated about Smart Symphony?

(A) It is an already existing app.
(B) It was originally developed by T&B Developers.
(C) It will be limited to 500,000 copies.
(D) It will feature elements of Marble FM.

Questions 169-171 refer to the following brochure.

**Energy Savers**

Are you paying high utility bills during the summer or winter months? With Energy Savers, you can find the energy solutions that will save you money. Contact us for your free four-step consultation.

**1. Determine your energy needs**

Our qualified energy consultants will visit your home to determine what your energy needs are. You will be asked to complete a detailed survey regarding the number of hours you spend at home, your desired temperatures during each season, and your cooking and cleaning habits.

**2. Home inspection**

Once our consultants determine your needs, they will inspect the windows, walls, and doors of your home to ensure proper insulation. They will also test your heating, cooling, and lighting systems for weaknesses. Unlike other companies, Energy Savers will prepare a detailed report of flaws and make suggestions for improvements.

**3. Choose your upgrades**

Our consultants will discuss the recommended upgrades for your home while keeping your budget in mind. We can help you choose and install everything from double-paned glass for your windows to solar panels on your roof.

**4. Installations**

Our team will work around your schedule to install your upgrades. However, most installations take several days to complete. You will see instant savings on your utility bills and the best part is those savings never end. You will continue to save money for years to come. Should you have problems with your upgrades within the first year, Energy Savers will fix them free of charge.

**169.** What is the purpose of the brochure?

(A) To announce a new type of energy
(B) To compare two energy companies
(C) To advertise a company's services
(D) To discuss the benefits of insulation

**170.** What is NOT examined during the home consultation?

(A) The number of hours the home is occupied
(B) The home owner's preferred temperatures
(C) The efficiency of heating systems
(D) The current cost of monthly utilities

**171.** What does the brochure suggest is one disadvantage of the upgrades?

(A) The upgrades are costly to purchase.
(B) It takes time to install all the features.
(C) Home owners must be present during the installations.
(D) Monthly bills will not decrease for a year.

**Questions 172-175** refer to the following article.

---

**Newmont Technology Convention to Launch World Tour**

March 5 — The Newmont Technology Convention (NTC) is scheduled to make the first stop on its world tour next month. The convention is one of the world's largest technology exhibitions and features everything from medical technology to aerospace engineering demonstrations. The NTC was founded in Sydney, Australia by Newmont Industries and its CEO, Barret Michaels. --[1]--. Every year, over 30,000 people visit the Sydney convention to see some of the most innovative technologies that have not yet reached the market.

The NTC commonly hosts scientists from all over the world, but this is the first year it will become an international traveling exhibition. --[2]--. Mr. Michaels stated in an interview, "We're very excited about this expansion. When we started the convention 10 years ago, we had no idea it would grow to be the biggest technology event in the world. -- [3]--. We're extremely happy to kick off our six-country tour in London, England next month. We're already expecting a huge crowd."

The U.S., Brazil, Japan, Germany, and South Africa will also host the NTC during its tour. Tickets to most of the tour dates are already sold out. --[4]--. "Industry professionals in both Canada and France have already reached out to us with proposals," Mr. Michaels said. "We're optimistic that other countries will make similar proposals."

---

**172.** What is true about Newmont Industries?

(A) It helped establish the Newmont Technology Convention.
(B) It has offices in England, Brazil, and Japan.
(C) It is the leading developer of medical technology.
(D) It buys and sells aerospace engineering equipment.

**173.** What is stated about the convention in Sydney?

(A) It took five years to become popular.
(B) It employs over 30,000 workers.
(C) It features technologies that cannot be purchased.
(D) It was the second location for the exhibition.

**174.** Where will the next Newmont Technology Convention be held?

(A) In France
(B) In England
(C) In Brazil
(D) In Japan

**175.** In which of the positions marked [1], [2], [3], and [4] does the following sentence best belong?

"If the NTC tour is successful, Mr. Michaels plans to add additional locations to next year's tour."

(A) [1]
(B) [2]
(C) [3]
(D) [4]

**Questions 176-180** refer to the following letter and survey.

Grand Palace Hotel
Koh Samui, Thailand

Bethanie Sparks
44 Brock Road,
Toronto, ON L1T 4W2

Dear Ms. Sparks,

Thank you for choosing the Grand Palace Hotel as your accommodation from October 12 to October 25. According to our records, you purchased your stay as part of our Vacation in Thailand package, which celebrated our hotel's 50th anniversary. We are conducting a short survey regarding this package. We would appreciate your completion of the enclosed survey and its return in the self-addressed envelope. If you respond by January 2, you will receive a 10% discount on your next trip as our thanks. However, should you send it back after that deadline, we would still like to enter you into a draw for a free night's stay in any of our hotels.

Sincerely,

Rita Lao
Grand Palace Hotel

---

### Grand Palace Hotel, Thailand
**By participating in this survey, you can assist us in providing the best possible services to all our guests.**

**Name:** Bethanie Sparks | **Date:** 28 November

1. May we call you to discuss your answers further?
• Yes, phone number_____ • NO

2. How would you rate the quality of our facilities and services?
• Poor • Fair • Average • Good • Excellent

**Please explain your response:** I found my room to be luxurious and clean. The food in the restaurant was also excellent. However, when I ordered room service, the food was always delivered quite late.

3. How would you rate our amenities?

• Poor • Fair • Average • Good • Excellent

**Please explain your response:** I enjoyed the variety of the activities you had to offer. During my stay, I was able to go scuba diving, cave exploring, attend a dance lesson, and even take a tour of the local markets. There were so many exciting things to do!

**176.** Why did Ms. Lao write to Ms. Sparks?

   (A) To notify of a late payment

   (B) To reschedule a hotel stay

   (C) To request some customer feedback

   (D) To respond to a complaint

**177.** What is indicated about the Grand Palace Hotel?

   (A) Its head office is located in Thailand.

   (B) It plans to build a hotel in Toronto.

   (C) It wants to expand its recreational activities.

   (D) It launched a promotion to celebrate an anniversary.

**178.** In the letter, the word "conducting" in paragraph 1, line 3, is closest in meaning to

   (A) administering

   (B) authorizing

   (C) behaving

   (D) transferring

**179.** What will Ms. Sparks most likely receive from the Grand Palace Hotel?

   (A) A discount coupon

   (B) Entry into a contest

   (C) Free scuba diving lessons

   (D) A free night's stay

**180.** What does Ms. Sparks mention about the Grand Palace Hotel?

   (A) Its staff did not help her solve a problem.

   (B) It has a wide range of activities for guests.

   (C) Its food was of poor quality.

   (D) It has a great location in a large city.

**Questions 181-185** refer to the following notice and form.

| To: | Employees of Tombes Financial Monthly |
| From: | Tombes Publications Acquisition Board |
| Re: | Tombes-Parker Business and Finance |
| Date: | 6 March |

As you have been made aware, *Tombes Financial Monthly* plans to officially merge with *Parker Business Magazine* on April 27. This merger will be an exciting opportunity for both companies. *Parker Business Magazine* is one of the top three business publications and specializes in reporting on international business issues and trends. This merger will allow us to create the first-ever business and finance magazine, which we're sure will boost our publication to the number 1 spot. In addition, with our larger staff, we'll now be able to put out biweekly editions and generate more sales.

Department managers will meet during the week of April 2 to work out some of the details of the merger as well as the renovation of our brand-new office space downtown. If you have any concerns you'd like to raise during the meetings, please send an e-mail to the relevant department manager in advance.

Tombes Publications Acquisitions Board

| Department | Date / Time | Department Managers |
|---|---|---|
| **Editorial** | Monday, April 2 9:00 A.M. – 1:00 P.M. | Joanne Steele, Editorial Director *(Tombes Financial Monthly)* / Tommy Renaldo, Editor-in-Chief *(Parker Business Magazine)* |
| **Design** | Tuesday, April 3 10:00 A.M. – 2:00 P.M. | Samuel Westford, Lead Designer *(Tombes Financial Monthly)* / Wendy Skeller, Head of Design *(Parker Business Magazine)* |
| **Administrative** | Wednesday, April 4 11:00 A.M. – 4:00 P.M. | Annabelle Cordel, Office Manager *(Tombes Financial Monthly)* / Steven Parinon, Office Manager *(Parker Business Magazine)* |
| **Public Relations** | Thursday, April 5 09:30 A.M. – 12:00 P.M. | Laini Peterson, Lead Advertiser *(Tombes Financial Monthly)* / Sandy Baxter, Head of Advertising *(Parker Business Magazine)* |

*All meetings will take place at *Tombes Financial Monthly* in the relevant department.
*Steven Parinon will retire prior to the merger. Annabelle Cordel has been selected run the new office following the merger. All department managers are expected to attend the meeting on April 4, which will be in conference room A to accommodate the number of attendees.

**181.** What is one purpose of the memo?

(A) To remind of changes to a financial plan

(B) To explain why some employees were let go

(C) To announce the retirement of an office manager

(D) To note the benefits of an upcoming merger

**182.** According to the memo, what is *Parker Business Magazine*'s area of expertise?

(A) Local finance

(B) Company mergers

(C) Government policies

(D) International business

**183.** What is suggested about the employees of Tombes-Parker Business and Finance?

(A) They have been asked to retire early.

(B) They will be able to apply for management positions.

(C) They will relocate to a new office building.

(D) They all need to attend the meeting on April 6.

**184.** What is indicated about Mr. Westford?

(A) He plans to take over the position of office manager.

(B) He will discuss some e-mailed questions at his meeting.

(C) He organized the merger between the two magazines.

(D) He chose the location for the new company headquarters.

**185.** What will happen at a meeting on April 4?

(A) A greater number of participants will be present.

(B) Mr. Parinon will be absent from the discussion.

(C) The CEO of *Parker Business Magazine* will give a presentation.

(D) Employees will be informed of their new job assignments.

**Individuals Needed for Mini Focus Groups**

Dressler Marketing, the biggest market research company in Edmonton, is recruiting people between the ages of 21 and 70 for a study focused on travel. The event will take place in the conference center of the Sanderson Hotel, 48 Emery Avenue, during the second week of June. The study begins by viewing a series of short travel-related videos followed by small group discussions that are facilitated by our moderators. The entire session will last three hours and compensation will be provided for all who participate. Anyone interested can phone Dressler at 409-5321-8082. Be sure to mention study 73. To determine if a caller is eligible to take part in this study, he or she will be asked to remain on the line and respond to a few screening questions.

---

Roland,

Dressler Marketing really appreciates you taking time out from your busy work schedule to assist with our market research project for Pacific Adventures at the Sanderson Hotel. You will be facilitating four mini focus groups composed of five people each. Since the focus is travelling along Canada's west coast, our client insists that we locate individuals with extensive travel experience, either for business or leisure, in that region.

Schedule of Sessions from 3:00 to 6:00 P.M.

**Age Range/Date**
21-35 Tuesday, June 9
36-45 Wednesday, June 10
46-60 Thursday, June 11
61-70 Friday, June 12

Upon arrival, participants will be given yellow name tags. Make sure their name tags are clearly visible at all times during the study, especially when making the video recordings of the members' discussions. This will allow Dressler to refer to individuals by their names when submitting our findings and recommendations to Pacific Adventures.

Each of the four video clips centers on a different aspect of Pacific Adventures:

**Video Clip 1:** Group Discussion of Whale-watching tours
**Video Clip 2:** One-Day Kayaking Adventures
**Video Clip 3:** Popular Mountain Resorts
**Video Clip 4:** Hiking Adventures in Whistler Mountain

Nina Hernandez

| To: | rothschild@pacificadventures.ca |
| --- | --- |
| From: | nhernandez@dressler.ca |
| Date: | 28 June |
| Subject: | Study 73 |
| Attachment: | Study 73 findings |

Dear Mr. Rothschild

I am contacting to notify you that the research you requested last month for a specific target market has been completed. As the attached report indicates, one theme was the favorite of all focus groups. This theme represents an overview of the most popular places for travelers to stay. To ensure that we have covered all the key aspects in our findings, we would like to view the video with you and your representatives and have a lengthy discussion on it. Please inform us of a convenient time and date to meet.

Best regards,

Nina Hernandez
Head of Client Services, Dressler Marketing

**186.** What is NOT suggested about the participants of the mini focus groups?

(A) They will receive a payment.
(B) They need to answer questions when they call.
(C) They must be experienced travelers.
(D) They are hotel employees.

**187.** In the Instructions, paragraph 1, line 4, the word "locate" is the closest in meaning to

(A) remark
(B) believe
(C) find
(D) check

**188.** What is indicated about study 73?

(A) It will be held at Dressler's headquarters.
(B) It includes four groups of the same size.
(C) It centers solely on water leisure.
(D) It will be completed in two days.

**189.** According to the instructions, why were the participants provided with name tags?

(A) So that the marketing company can identify them easily.
(B) So that each registration number matches with the correct name.
(C) So that they would be able to find their seats quickly.
(D) So that they would be permitted to enter the conference center.

**190.** Based on the results of the study, what video clip was the most popular?

(A) Video Clip 1
(B) Video Clip 2
(C) Video Clip 3
(D) Video Clip 4

| St. John Art Gallery Upcoming Exhibitions | | |
|---|---|---|
| Dates | Title of Exhibition | Brief Description |
| 11 April – 20 August | Recycled Materials as Sculptures | People usually see recycled materials as mere scrap piles. However, as this exhibition featuring the works of 10 artists throughout South America shows, any material can be transformed into breathtaking sculptures. |
| 28 April – 3 October | The Portraits of Athletes | This watercolor collection features beautiful paintings of professional athletes by artists from every corner of the globe. |
| 5 June – 29 November | More than Just Trees | This remarkable collection of photographs and paintings by artists throughout Africa and several Mediterranean nations captures the mesmerizing power of forests. |
| 11 June – 14 July | The History of Food in Art | Through video recordings, sculptures, photographs, and paintings, this unique exhibition traces the history of food in Europe from the 15th to the 19th century. |

Tickets can be purchased through our website or by sending an e-mail to banderson@ stjohnartgallery.org. To learn about our wonderful membership plans, simply go to our website and click on "Become a St. John Art Gallery Member!" Members receive two free tickets to the exhibition of their choice.

| From: | Chevon Jabar <CJabar@rogerstalent.ca> |
|---|---|
| To: | Belinda Anderson <banderson@stjohnartgallery.org> |
| Subject: | thank you |
| Date: | March 10 |

I am e-mailing to say thank you for the two free tickets to "The History of Food in Art." I also need another ticket for this event for my division head, Helena Lafleur. I assume the gallery has a record of my credit card details, so please bill the same card and send the tickets to the same address.

I would like to thank your staff for providing such fantastic exhibitions.

Chevon Jabar

| From: | Belinda Anderson <banderson@stjohnartgallery.org> |
|---|---|
| To: | Chevon Jabar <CJabar@rogerstalent.ca> |
| Subject: | a cancelled exhibition |
| Date: | March 14 |

Dear Mr. Jabar,

St. John Art Gallery would like to thank you for your patronage during the past seven years. We are truly sorry that the exhibition you and your colleague planned to see was cancelled due to circumstances beyond our control. However, we have already scheduled a replacement exhibition of black and white photographs. It is scheduled to run during the exact same dates (11 June – 14 July) and is called "The Working Classes of Latin America." I have already sent a new program guide in the mail to your office. Please let me know which exhibition you would like to see instead.

Thank you for your understanding in this matter.

Sincerely yours,

Belinda Anderson
St. John Art Gallery

**191.** According to the website, what do all of the exhibitions have in common?

(A) They showcase works from various nations.
(B) They showcase paintings from Mediterranean countries.
(C) They include video presentations.
(D) They include sculptures.

**192.** What is indicated about Mr. Jabar?

(A) He donated a collection for an exhibition.
(B) He is currently employed as an art instructor.
(C) He has already seen three of the exhibits.
(D) He is a paid member of the art gallery.

**193.** Which exhibition has been canceled?

(A) Recycled Materials as Sculptures
(B) The Portraits of Athletes
(C) More Than Just Trees
(D) The History of Food in Art

**194.** In the second e-mail, the word "run" in paragraph 1, line 4, is closest in meaning to

(A) direct
(B) remove
(C) be shown
(D) be announced

**195.** What did Ms. Anderson do for Mr. Jabar?

(A) Bill his credit card
(B) Mail an updated program guide
(C) Upgrade his membership
(D) Reschedule a social event

| | |
|---|---|
| To: | Marcus Lount; Gabriella Sanchez; Daniel Wilkes |
| From: | Shelly Dorcas |
| Date: | July 16, 9:09 A.M. |
| Subject: | business space |
| Attachment: | available properties |

Hi everyone,

I really enjoyed last Friday's lunch with you at the Davisville Grill. I am truly excited about opening our first Miami branch of Ebbet Construction Equipment Rentals. As Miami's housing market grows more and more each day, I am sure that we are all eager to attract our very first customers and start advising companies on the equipment that is most suitable for their projects and objectives.

I appreciate all the input you offered on the most appropriate business space. Using the budget and criteria you suggested, I searched for spaces at www.vanzylerealty.com. I found several possible spaces and compiled them into a list. That document is attached. Please have a look at it and get back to me with any comments you may have.

Shelly Dorcas, Ebbet Construction Equipment Rentals

### 13990 Gifford Way
Suburban two-story rental facility. Second floor office suites. Parking lot can accommodate up to 100 automobiles. Located across from Devon City's main bus terminal and near a large number of hotels used by business travelers. Half an hour from downtown Miami.
Monthly lease: $975

### 1389 Singleton Highway
Large retail space located in the heart of downtown Miami. Large sign on building makes it high visible to highway motorists. Building includes large storage facilities for parts and equipment. The newly installed air conditioning unit is guaranteed to keep you comfortable during the hot summers.
Monthly lease: $1,150

### 7643 Beckford Avenue
Third-floor retails and office space. Located uptown within Miami's main business district. Located on the same street as two major shopping centers. Facility includes state-of-the-art security alarm system. Printer/scanner/fax/color copier on-site for company use.
Monthly lease: $1,050

### 6094 Wilmot Drive
Single-story building. Comes with small office space. Land contract is also offered for property immediately behind facility. Located on the city's east side in lovely Ryerson Park, a prime Miami development site for condominium towers.
Monthly lease: $825

| To: | Shelly Dorcas; Marcus Lount; Gabriella Sanchez |
|---|---|
| From: | Daniel Wilkes |
| Date: | July 20, 11:23 A.M. |
| Re: | business space |

Hi everyone,

Thank you very much, Shelly, for all your work in narrowing our search to the options in the list you provided. I'm certain the strategy meeting held last Friday was quite productive. My apologies for not being there, but I was called to Boston all of a sudden on an urgent business matter. Also, I have to say thank all of you for being patient in waiting for my response to this important e-mail discussion.

Marcus, while I truly appreciate the need to save money on an inexpensive suburban facility, our company should not ignore the significance of having a facility conveniently located downtown as more and more homes are being built in that area.

I am also in agreement with Gabriella's idea that our company needs a booth at Miami's upcoming housing fair. Next week, I will be flying to Miami to visit relatives so I will look into the matter then. Also, while in Miami, I am scheduled to have lunch with a local realtor who worked for our company up until two years ago. Thank you, Shelly, for reminding me that Helen Richardson now resides in Miami. I'm sure she will have useful insights for us.

Daniel Wilkes, Ebbet Construction Equipment Rentals

**196.** Who most likely is Ms. Dorcas?

(A) A real estate expert
(B) An official in Miami Housing Bureau
(C) A construction equipment specialist
(D) A cook at Davisville Grill

**197.** What is one property feature mentioned in the attachment?

(A) An energy-efficient heating system
(B) A newly-installed carpet in the office
(C) A large cafeteria for employees
(D) A location close to housing development

**198.** What is suggested about Mr. Wilkes?

(A) He will fly to Miami tomorrow morning.
(B) He is renting some property in Boston.
(C) He did not make it to the Davisville Grill meeting.
(D) He plans to apply for a managerial position.

**199.** What is indicated about Ms. Sanchez?

(A) She suggested an idea to her colleagues by e-mail.
(B) She used to live in downtown Miami.
(C) She will meet a former colleague.
(D) She started her own equipment rental business.

**200.** Which property does Mr. Wilkes most likely favor?

(A) 13990 Gifford Way
(B) 1389 Singleton Highway
(C) 7643 Beckford Avenue
(D) 6094 Wilmot Drive

**Stop! This is the end of the test. If you finish before time is called, you may go back to Parts 5, 6, and 7 and check your work.**

| | | | | |
|---|---|---|---|---|
| 101. (B) | 121. (A) | 141. (B) | 161. (D) | 181. (D) |
| 102. (A) | 122. (D) | 142. (A) | 162. (B) | 182. (D) |
| 103. (A) | 123. (C) | 143. (C) | 163. (A) | 183. (C) |
| 104. (A) | 124. (B) | 144. (B) | 164. (C) | 184. (B) |
| 105. (B) | 125. (A) | 145. (A) | 165. (D) | 185. (A) |
| 106. (C) | 126. (C) | 146. (C) | 166. (D) | 186. (D) |
| 107. (D) | 127. (B) | 147. (C) | 167. (B) | 187. (C) |
| 108. (D) | 128. (D) | 148. (D) | 168. (A) | 188. (B) |
| 109. (D) | 129. (D) | 149. (D) | 169. (C) | 189. (A) |
| 110. (C) | 130. (C) | 150. (C) | 170. (D) | 190. (C) |
| 111. (B) | 131. (C) | 151. (A) | 171. (B) | 191. (A) |
| 112. (B) | 132. (D) | 152. (B) | 172. (A) | 192. (D) |
| 113. (A) | 133. (C) | 153. (D) | 173. (C) | 193. (D) |
| 114. (C) | 134. (C) | 154. (B) | 174. (B) | 194. (C) |
| 115. (A) | 135. (A) | 155. (C) | 175. (D) | 195. (B) |
| 116. (B) | 136. (C) | 156. (B) | 176. (C) | 196. (C) |
| 117. (C) | 137. (D) | 157. (C) | 177. (D) | 197. (D) |
| 118. (C) | 138. (A) | 158. (B) | 178. (A) | 198. (C) |
| 119. (A) | 139. (D) | 159. (A) | 179. (A) | 199. (A) |
| 120. (C) | 140. (A) | 160. (C) | 180. (B) | 200. (B) |

# ACTUAL TEST

## 中譯+解析

# PART 5

聘僱關係一終止，所有的員工都會拿到推薦函及遣散費。

字彙
receive 收到
severance pay 資遣費
termination 終止
employment 僱用

**101** All employees will receive _____ letters and severance pay upon termination of employment.

(A) recommends
(B) recommendation*
(C) recommended
(D) recommending

空格為及物動詞 receive 的受詞，選項 (B) 的名詞 recommendation 可與 letters 結合，成為複合名詞「推薦信」作為 receive 的受詞，故為正確答案。因為空格在名詞 letters 前方，可能會考慮選擇 (C) 和 (D)，作為形容詞修飾名詞。但無論是「被推薦的信」或是「正在推薦的信」，語意上皆不通順，因此都不是答案。

• recommend (v.) 推薦　　recommendation (n.) 推薦

* 高頻率複合名詞：
travel document 旅行文件
account number 帳號　　construction delay 工程延誤
return policy 退貨規定　　expiration date 有效期限，到期日
product information 產品資訊
information distribution 資訊流通；資訊發布　　retail sales 零售銷售額
client satisfaction 客戶滿意（度）

---

史蒂文斯先生在「文具與紙的世界」為公司挑了一些新用品。

字彙
supplies 用品
stationery 文具

**102** Mr. Stevens picked up some new supplies for the office _____ Stationery and Paper World.

(A) but
(B) as
(C) at*
(D) after

本題要找出適當的介系詞。空格後方為購買用品的地點：文具與紙的世界（Stationery and Paper World），因此答案選 (C) at，意思為「在……」，才符合句意。在多益測驗中，常常出現以「We ＋ at ＋公司名稱」作為主詞的句子。

---

需要有人盡快來修影印機。

字彙
repair 修理

**103** _____ needs to come and repair the photocopier as soon as possible.

(A) Someone*
(B) Us
(C) They
(D) Any

空格為主詞的位置，因此作為受詞的 (B) 和作為形容詞的 (D) 都不能選。空格後方為單數動詞 needs，所以 (C) They 為複數主詞，也是不正確的選項，答案應為 (A)。在新制多益中，主詞與動詞單複數須一致，為常見的基本題型。

---

公司的新軟體設計成可自動更新至最新的版本。

**104** The company's new software is designed to update to the most recent version _____.

(A) automate
(B) automatic
(C) automated
(D) automatically*

空格中應填入副詞來修飾動詞 update，故 (D) 為正確選項。

• automate 使自動化　　automatic 自動的　　automatically 自動地

**105** The new policies are designed to curb lateness and _____ employee accountability.

(A) promote*　　　　　(B) declare
(C) obtain　　　　　　(D) benefit

根據句意，訂定政策的目的在於「遏止遲到」和「提升員工責任感」，因此答案應為 (A)。

- **promote** 提升，促進　**declare** 聲明　**obtain** 獲得　**benefit** 有益於

新政策訂定的目的是要遏止遲到及提升員工責任感。

字彙
**policy** 政策
**curb** 遏止，控制
**lateness** 遲到
**accountability** 負有責任

---

**106** Most employees have cited the positive work _____ as the reason they have remained with the company.

(A) reconstruction　　　(B) environment*
(C) employment　　　　(D) position

員工續留公司的理由為「正向的工作環境」。work 經常和 (B) environment 結合成複合名詞「工作環境」，故為正確答案。

- **reconstruction** 重建　**environment** 環境　**employment** 就業　**position** 職位

\* as 的相關用法：
**work as** 擔任　**regard A as B**（將 A 看作 B）
**treat A as B**（將 A 當作 B 對待）　**use A as B**（將 A 當成 B 使用）
**come as a shock**（令人震驚的事件）

大多數的員工以「正向的工作環境」作為他們續留公司的理由。

字彙
**cite A as B**（引用 A 作為 B）
**positive** 正面的；積極的
**reason** 理由
**remain** 留在

---

**107** Martin's Coffee _____ over 300 shops across Canada by next summer.

(A) will have*　　　　(B) has
(C) is having　　　　(D) has had

副詞片語 next summer 表示時間。由此線索，可知本句應用未來式，因此答案為 (A)。在此補充，當 have 表示「擁有」時，不能用進行式。

\* 不能使用進行式的動詞：
表擁有的動詞：**have, own, possess**
表喜惡的動詞：**love, like, hate**
表認知的動詞：**know, recognize**

到了明年夏天，馬汀咖啡在加拿大各地將擁有超過300家店面。

---

**108** This law was passed to protect citizens _____ own and operate small businesses.

(A) for　　　　　　　(B) who*
(C) those　　　　　　(D) as

空格前方為 citizens，表示先行詞為「人」，因此空格中應填入關係代名詞 who 作為主詞，引導關係子句。在此補充，過往考題中，who 作為關係代名詞是答案的機率很高。

這個法律的通過是為了保護擁有並經營小型企業的人。

字彙
**law** 法律
**pass** 通過
**protect** 保護
**own** 擁有
**operate** 經營，管理

與新供應商的會議已經重新安排，提早在週三舉行。

字彙
supplier 供應商
reschedule 重新安排時間

**109** The meeting with our new supplier has been rescheduled for an _____ time on Wednesday.

(A) hardly
(B) comfortably
(C) early*
(D) eagerly

本句應為「提早在週三開會」語意上較為完整。與時間相關的副詞中，(C) 最合適，故為正確答案。

• hardly 幾乎不　comfortably 舒適地　eagerly 渴望地，熱切地

---

哈沃史塔克公司作為電信電纜供應商，已建立了快速客戶服務的聲譽。

字彙
provider 供應者
prompt 及時的，迅速的

**110** Haverstock Telephone & Cable has built a _____ as a provider of prompt customer service.

(A) privilege
(B) character
(C) reputation*
(D) consequence

空格為 build 的受詞，四個選項皆為名詞，都可以填入空格作為受詞。但根據句意，應為「建立供應商的聲譽」語意上較為完整，因此答案為 (C)。

• privilege 特權　character 個性　reputation 名聲　consequence 結果

\* 與 reputation 搭配的動詞：
have/earn/establish/build a reputation 擁有／贏得／創立／建立聲譽

---

員工手冊簡要說明了處理客訴的正確流程。

字彙
handbook 手冊
proper 正確的；適當的
procedure 程序，手續
handle 處理
complaint 抱怨，投訴

**111** The employee handbook _____ the proper procedure for handling customer complaints.

(A) outlining
(B) outlines*
(C) to outline
(D) is outlined

本句的句構為：主詞（The ... handbook）＋空格＋受詞（the ... procedure），也就是 S ＋ V ＋ O 的句型。因此答案應為現在式動詞 outlines，故 (B) 為正確答案。

• outline 概述

---

藍道先生決定在休息室安裝新的自動販賣機，供大家使用。

字彙
install 安裝
vending machine 自動販賣機

**112** Mr. Randal has decided to install new vending machines in the lounge _____ everyone to use.

(A) if
(B) to
(C) for*
(D) until

根據句意，應為「為了」每個人使用最為適當。因此答案為 (C) 介系詞 for，表「為了……」。to ＋ V 則形成不定詞，如本題的 to use。和上述相關的還有虛主詞的句型：「It ... for ＋人 ... to ＋ V」，表「做某件事對某人而言是……」，可知 to ＋ V 形成不定詞，而 for ＋人則作為意義上的主詞。

**113** Smith International Trading's department managers _____ conduct employee satisfaction surveys.

(A) lively
(B) harshly
(C) routinely*
(D) vastly

本句應為「定期進行員工滿意度調查」語意上較為完整，四個副詞中，(C) 為最適當的答案。

- lively 活潑的，生動的　harshly 嚴厲地　routinely 定期地，例行地　vastly 非常

\* 現在簡單式表示習慣或常態，常和下方頻率副詞搭配使用：
routinely, regularly, normally, always, usually, generally, often

史密斯國際貿易公司的部門主管定期進行員工滿意度調查。

**字彙**
department 部門
satisfaction 滿意
survey 問卷調查

---

**114** The consulting firm _____ several procedural changes that would improve the shipping company's efficiency.

(A) proposing
(B) proposed*
(C) proposal
(D) proposals

本句空格的位置應填入主要動詞，才符合英文句子「主詞＋動詞」的基本結構，因此選項 (B) 正確。

- propose 提議　proposal 企劃案

顧問公司提出幾個異動程序的建議，以改善貨運公司的效率。

**字彙**
consulting 專職顧問的
firm 公司
procedural 程序的
change 變動
improve 改善
shipping 貨運，運送
efficiency 效率

---

**115** The main responsibility of the volunteers is to help visitors _____ their way around the exhibition hall.

(A) do
(B) find*
(C) put
(D) ask

根據句意，志工職責是在展覽廳內協助「帶路」，語意上較為完整，因此答案為 (B)。

志工的主要職責，就是協助遊客在展覽廳裡找到路。

**字彙**
responsibility 責任
find one's way around . . .
找到……的途徑

---

**116** Please retain this e-mail as _____ that your payment information has been entered into our system.

(A) confirm
(B) confirmed
(C) confirmable
(D) confirmation*

介系詞 as 後方要接名詞，且 that 子句作為同位語，補充說明前方空格的資訊，再次確認空格應填名詞，故 (D) 正確。confirmation 是抽象名詞，idea 和 suggestion 也同屬於抽象名詞。

- confirm 確認　confirmable 可確定的　confirmation 確定

請保留本電子郵件，作為您的款項資料已輸入本公司系統的確認依據。

**字彙**
retain 保留，留住
payment 款項
enter 輸入

德拉果女士大約十年前就開始在這家銀行服務，自此一直擔任副經理的職位。

字彙
decade 十年
assume 擔任

**117** Ms. Derlago started working at this bank almost a decade ago and has _____ assumed the role of assistant manager.

(A) ever  (B) yet
(C) so  (D) since*

本題使用現在完成式，用來說明「過去特定的時間點（a decade ago）到現在持續發生的事情」。因此空格中填入副詞 since，故選項 (D) 最為適當。

* since 的相關用法：
**連接詞**：連接 S＋V 子句，表示「自……以來」或「因為……」
**介系詞**：後接名詞，表「自從……」或「自……以後」的意思
**副詞**：表示「此後」

---

巴恩斯先生正在嘗試取得一些推薦函，以取得醫院的職務。

字彙
attempt 試圖
collect 取；收集
several 數個
reference 推薦函
gain 獲得

**118** Mr. Barns is attempting to collect several references _____ for gaining employment at the hospital.

(A) required*  (B) requiring
(C) requires  (D) will require

因為空格前方省略了 which (= references) are，可知關係子句的句構為被動語態，表達 references（推薦函）是被需要的，所以答案應為過去分詞 required，故 (A) 正確。在主動語態中，require 為及物動詞，因此主動語態進行式 requiring 的後方必須接受詞，故 (B) 不能選。

---

在市區內進行營建工程的法規全都條列在市府的許可網頁上。

字彙
limit 範圍
list 列出
permit 許可

**119** The _____ for building within the city limits are all listed on the city's permit website.

(A) probabilities  (B) allowances
(C) regulations*  (D) varieties

句子後段的 permit，意思為「許可（證）」，最適合搭配的單字為 regulation，故 (C) 正確。在此補充，在多益測驗中，經常出現選項 (B) 的 allowance，常見的意思有「零用錢；限額」，例如：a baggage allowance of 20 kg（行李重量 20 公斤的限額）。

● **probability** 可能性  **allowance** 允許  **regulation** 規定
**variety** 多樣化

---

在奧斯丁科技大學所進行的研究被認為是全國最先進的。

字彙
advanced 先進的

**120** _____ at Austin Tech University is considered the most advanced in the country.

(A) Research*  (B) Researchers
(C) Researched  (D) Researches

空格為主詞的位置，可以考慮皆為名詞的 (A) 或 (B) 為答案。但是由於動詞為 is considered，所以答案應為單數名詞 research，故 (A) 正確。在此補充，research 為不可數名詞，不能寫成複數形。

● **research** 研究  **researcher** 研究者
* 常見不可數名詞如下：
**information, advice, progress, access, funding, correspondence, news, luggage/baggage, furniture, equipment, gear, clothing, merchandise, machinery, scenery, poetry, change（零錢）, software, hardware, kitchenware, glassware, eyewear, footwear, sportswear**

**121** Covington Ice Cream attributes its recent surge in sales to the addition of its newest flavor _____ its advertising campaigns.

(A) as for
(B) even so
(C) rather than*
(D) after all

to 後方為銷售量激增的原因——推出新口味，根據句意，空格後應為「比較」另一個銷量激增的可能原因——廣告活動，因此 (C) rather than（是 A 而不是 B）為最適當的答案。

- **as for . . .** 至於……　**even so** 儘管如此
  **rather than . . .** 而不是……　**after all** 畢竟

柯文頓冰淇淋將最近銷售量的激增歸因於推出新口味，而不是廣告活動之故。

字彙
**attribute A to B**
把 A 歸因於 B
**surge** 激增
**addition** 增加的人或物
**flavor** 口味

**122** The service at Wallace Limos improved _____ after the customer surveys were conducted.

(A) tightly
(B) markedly*
(C) manageably
(D) separately

「問卷調查後」，服務有 (A) 緊緊地 (B) 顯著地 (C) 易處理地 (D) 各自地改善，根據句意，選擇 (B) 語意上較為完整。請同時熟記 (B) 的同義詞 conspicuously（醒目地，顯眼地）。

在進行客戶滿意度調查後，華倫斯豪華禮車公司的服務顯著地改善了。

字彙
**improve** 改善

**123** These computers are reserved for people searching _____ employment opportunities in downtown London.

(A) for*
(B) up
(C) as
(D) to

只要知道 search 經常搭配的介系詞為 for，表「尋找……」，就能迅速找出答案為 (A)。

* 後接 search 與 look 相關片語補充：
**search for = look for** 尋找　**look up a word in a dictionary** 查字典
**look up to** 敬重

這些電腦保留給那些在倫敦市中心尋找就業機會的人使用。

字彙
**reserve** 保留，預約
**opportunity** 機會

**124** Please ensure that you have written all your information _____, as an error could result in a long delay in the process.

(A) affordably
(B) precisely*
(C) unitedly
(D) decisively

逗點後方為「出錯的後果」，根據句意，本句應該是叮嚀對方「請正確地填寫（避免出錯）」語意上較為完整，因此答案為 (B)。

- **affordably** 負擔得起地　**precisely** 精確地　**unitedly** 聯合地
  **decisively** 決然地，果斷地

請確認您已經正確地填寫所有資料，因為一個錯誤就可能導致手續的長期延誤。

字彙
**result in** 導致，造成
**delay** 延誤，延遲
**process** 手續，程序

朱恩・奧斯丁以前僱員的角度來書寫，因此她那篇有關 THP 電廠擴建計畫的文章相當獨特。

**字彙**
**expansion** 擴展，擴建
**unique** 獨特的
**former** 前任的

---

**125** June Austin's article on THP Power's expansion plans was very unique due to her _____ as a former employee.

(A) detail         (B) prospect
(C) investment      (D) perspective*

由於曾為 THP 電廠的前僱員，她的 (A) 細節 (B) 前途 (C) 投資 (D) 觀點，得以「寫成獨特的文章」，選項 (D) 最為適當。

---

人力資源部的職員能夠在不需部門主管的介入下，解決他們之間的問題。

**字彙**
**human resources**
人力資源（部）
**solve** 解決
**intervention** 介入，調停
**department** 部門

---

**126** Human resources employees were able to solve the problem among _____ without intervention from the department manager.

(A) themselves*      (B) theirs
(C) their           (D) they

本題要從人稱代名詞中找出適當的格。空格前方為介系詞 among，為重要的解題線索，表示空格應填受格，因此答案為 (A)。句意上，由於重複提及了主詞 human resources employees，所以改用反身代名詞 themselves 表示。

---

布朗先生熟知跨國企業政策，所以我們最好向他詢問。

**字彙**
**when it comes to . . .**
當談到……時
**policy** 政策

---

**127** Mr. Brown is _____ when it comes to international company policies, so we had better ask him.

(A) appropriate      (B) knowledgeable*
(C) undeveloped     (D) triumphant

連接詞 so 表示「所以」，連接前後兩句話，所以逗點前方的內容，應為後方的原因。根據句意，當結論為「最好向他詢問」，前方應為「因為他的學識豐富」較符合文意，因此 (B) 為最適當的答案。

- **appropriate** 適當的    **knowledgeable** 博學的
  **undeveloped** 未開發的    **triumphant** 勝利的

---

保單持有人一收到損壞修復帳單，即可提出車險的索賠。

**字彙**
**insurance** 保險
**claim**（對保險公司）索賠
**policy owner** 保單持有人
**bill** 帳單
**damage** 損害

---

**128** Car insurance claims must be made _____ policy owners receive bills for damages.

(A) as well as       (B) as soon as*
(C) in regard to      (D) in addition to

「一收到損壞修復帳單，即可提出車險的索賠」最符合句意，因此答案為 (B)。在此補充，介系詞 to 的後方必須連接名詞，但空格後方為「主詞＋動詞」的句構，因此 (C) 和 (D) 皆無法填入空格中。

- **as well as** 和    **as soon as** 一……就……
  **in regard to . . .** 關於……    **in addition to . . .** 除了……外

**129** With such a beautiful beach and huge assortment of art galleries, Adelaine Town is quite a _____ tourist spot.

(A) offering　　　　　(B) proposing

(C) promising*　　　　(D) identifying

逗點前方為「觀光景點」的特徵，形容詞 promising 意思為「棒的；有潛力的」，最適合用來修飾 tourist spot，所以 (C) 正確。

- **promising** 前景看好的　**identify** 認出

艾德蘭鎮擁有漂亮的海灘和豐富的各類藝廊，是相當棒的景點。

字彙
**huge** 數量多的；巨大的
**assortment** 各種各樣的
**spot** 地點

---

**130** The marketing department arranged to have weekly meetings to ensure a _____ effort is made on the new project.

(A) mundane　　　　(B) transitional

(C) reduced　　　　(D) concentrated*

「每週都要開會的原因」應為「確保在新專案上全力以赴」語意上較為完整，因此答案為 (D)。(A) 中的 mundane 為高難度單字，幾乎未曾出現在以往的多益測驗中，但在最近的考題中，卻出現了這樣的單字。

- **mundane** 世俗的，平凡的　**transitional** 轉變的，過渡的
  **reduced** 減少的　**concentrated** 全力以赴的

\* 名詞 effort 的相關用法：
**make an effort** 努力
**in an effort to** 為……而努力去
**a joint/group effort** 共同合作
**a concerted effort** 齊心協力

行銷部門安排了週會的舉行，以確保大家在新專案上全力以赴。

字彙
**arrange** 安排
**weekly** 每週的
**ensure** 確保，保證
**effort** 努力

# PART 6

**字彙**
extended 延伸的
at least 至少
receive 收到
additional 額外的
be responsible for
為……負責
application 申請（書）
qualify 具有資格
lottery 抽獎
draw 抽（籤）

Questions 131-134 refer to the following information.

**Extended Vacations**

Employees who have been with Star Packaging for at least two years may be ‾‾131.‾‾ to receive an additional five days of summer vacation. ‾‾132.‾‾ . Department managers will be responsible for reviewing the applications and those ‾‾133.‾‾ who qualify will have their names entered into a lottery system. Those who have been at the company for five years or longer will be given ‾‾134.‾‾ , and up to fifteen names will be drawn from the lottery.

-------------------------------------------------

長假

所有在星辰包裝公司服務至少兩年以上的員工，都符合多休五天暑假的資格。同仁可填寫申請表，並繳回給主管。部門主管將負責審查這些申請表。符合資格的人選名單將投入抽獎系統中。在公司服務滿五年或五年以上者將給予優先考量。系統將抽出最多 15 個名額。

**131** (A) prominent
(B) cooperative
(C) exclusive
(D) eligible*

空格需搭配後方的 to，根據前後文意，本句應為「擁有休長假的資格」語意上較為完整，因此答案為 (D)。be eligible to + V 表「有資格做某事」，請熟記這常用片語。

- **prominent** 顯著的　**cooperative** 合作的　**exclusive** 獨家的
  **eligible (to + V)** 有資格做……的

**132**
(A) 同仁可填寫申請表，並繳回給主管。
(B) 舉例來說，所有長期員工將獲得額外的福利待遇。
(C) 但是，少數有功同仁才會獲得績優加薪。
(D) 管理部門很高興地宣布已經聘僱了新同仁。

(A) Employees can fill out an application and return it to their manager.*
(B) For example, all long-term employees will receive additional benefits packages.
(C) However, competitive salary raises will be given to a few deserving employees.
(D) Management is pleased to announce that new employees have been hired.

空格後方的句子為「部門主管將負責審查這些申請表」，因此空格中應填入與「申請表」、「部門主管」相關的內容，故選 (A) 語意上較為完整。

- **benefit** 福利，津貼　**competitive** 具競爭力的
  **raise** 加薪　**deserving** 有功的　**management** 管理（部門）
  **announce** 宣布　**hire** 聘用

**133**　(A) candidates*
(B) awardees
(C) suppliers
(D) occupants

本句應為「繳交申請表的同仁中，符合資格的人選」，語意上較為完整，因此選項 (A) 最為適當。

- **candidate** 人選；候選者　　**awardee** 受獎者　　**supplier** 供應商
**occupant** 居住者

---

**134**　(A) prefer
(B) preferred
(C) preference*
(D) preferential

根據本句的結構，空格應為名詞作為 given 的受詞。對公司服務滿五年或以上者「提供優先權」，語意上較為完整，選項 (C) 的名詞 preference 在文法上和語意上都是最適合的答案。

- **prefer** 更喜歡　　**preferred** 更合意的　　**preference** 優先權
**preferential** 優惠的

字彙

celebrate 慶祝
anniversary 週年紀念
coverage 新聞報導
insightful 有深刻見解的
commentary 評論
human-interest 人情味
celebration 慶祝活動
hold 舉辦
take part in . . . 參加……
first-hand 第一手的，直接的
demonstration 示範
state-of-the-art 最先進的
equipment 設備
attend 參加，出席
register 登記
occasion 時機，場合

Questions 135-138 refer to the following notice.

**Channel 8 News Turns 60!**

On March 15, Channel 8 News, the city's number one news source, celebrates its sixtieth anniversary. That's six decades of studio and live ------. For well over half a century, we at Channel
<sub>135.</sub>
8 News ------ our viewers breaking news coverage, insightful
<sub>136.</sub>
commentaries, and wonderful human-interest stories from across the city and region. We would like to invite you, our loyal viewers, to our celebration. On March 15, we will hold an open house from 4:30 P.M. to 6:00 P.M. at our studio on Kingsley Street. Take part in a studio tour and see first-hand what goes on behind the scenes and watch a demonstration of our state-of-the-art broadcasting equipment. ------. There is no charge to attend this event, but you
<sub>137.</sub>
do have to register. We hope to see you all at this ------ occasion.
<sub>138.</sub>

------

第八新聞頻道60歲了！

全市首要的新聞來源，第八新聞頻道將於3月15慶祝成立60週年紀念。這是電視公司與現場轉播節目的第 60 年。超過半世紀以來，第八新聞頻道為觀眾們提供了即時新聞報導、見解深刻的評論以及來自全市及各地的精采人文故事。我們想邀請身為忠實觀眾的您參加我們的慶祝活動。3 月 15 日當天下午 4:30 至 6:30，我們將開放金斯利街的攝影棚供民眾參觀。來參加攝影棚導覽，第一線目睹幕後狀況，參觀我們最先進播放設備的操作示範。您甚至還有機會見到我們的新聞主播，並與他們對談。活動完全免費，但需登記報名。我們希望能在這個特別的時刻見到大家。

**135** (A) concerts
(B) discussions
(C) programming*
(D) teaching

第一句中出現電視台（Channel 8 News），因此空格中應填入與「電視節目」有關的單字，(C) 為最適當的答案。

• **discussion** 討論　**programming** （電視，廣播）轉播

**136**

(A) offers
(B) offering
(C) will offer
(D) have offered*

空格所在的句子中已有主詞 we，但少了主要動詞，所以空格應填入主要動詞，因此可以直接刪除選項 (B)。從過去某個時間點（60 年前）直到現在為止「都在提供」新聞，因此要從其他選項中找出現在完成式，答案為 (D)。

- **offer** 提供

---

**137**

(A) The station will remain a vital part of this city for years to come.
(B) You will even have the chance to meet and talk with our news anchors.*
(C) This celebration will be the third one to take place in March.
(D) Channel 8 News will be acquired by a national news network in a few months.

空格前面提到了「參觀攝影棚的內容」，例如參觀最先進播放設備的操作示範，因此補充說明參觀內容的 (B) 最為適當。

- **station** 廣播電台；電視台　　**remain** 保持，仍是　　**vital** 重要的　　**chance** 機會　　**acquire** 購得；獲得

(A) 這個電視台在未來幾年，仍然會是全市重要的一份子。
(B) 您甚至還有機會見到我們的新聞主播，並與他們對談。
(C) 這個慶祝活動會是三月所舉辦的第三場。
(D) 第八新聞頻道在將來幾個月內將被一間全國新聞網收購。

---

**138**

(A) special*
(B) specialize
(C) especially
(D) specialization

限定詞（this）＋空格＋名詞（occasion），空格中只能填入形容詞，故 (A) 正確。

- **special** 特別的　　**specialize** 專攻　　**especially** 尤其是　　**specialization** 專門化

字彙

reminder 提醒
resident 住戶，居民
obtain 取得
permit 許可
exterior 外部的
improvement 改善
currently 目前地
external 外面的
authorize 批准，許可
in advance 預先
assume 以為，假定為
contractor 承包商
arrange 安排
property 房地產
owner 所有人
inspector 檢查員
site 地點，場所
fine 罰款
issue 核發
responsibility 責任
ensure 確保，保證
in turn 進而
hazard 危險
apply to . . . 適用於……

Questions 139-142 refer to the following information.

This is just a reminder that residents of Archer Court are required to obtain a permit for any exterior home-improvement projects. Interior changes do not currently need a permit. ___139___, all external jobs, large and small, must be authorized in advance.

In the past, some residents have assumed that their contractors are responsible for arranging permits. ___140___. In truth, property owners must obtain the necessary permits themselves. Building inspectors may visit a site at any time, and if the property owner does not have a permit, fines may be issued.

___141___ permit laws is an important responsibility of building inspectors. The permit process ensures that all necessary safety standards ___142___, which in turn protects the community from property damages and dangerous hazards.

To view a list of permits that might apply to your project, please visit renviewtown.com/permits.

---------------------------------------------------------------

這通知是要提醒雅契府的住戶們，若要進行任何住家外圍整修必須先取得許可。屋內整修目前不需許可，但是所有外圍工程，不論大小，必須事先獲得批准。

過去，部分住戶認為承包商必須負責申請許可。這個普遍認定的想法其實是錯的。事實上，資產所有人必須自行取得必要的許可。建物檢查員將隨時走訪施工處，如果資產所有人未持許可，將處以罰款。

建物檢查員重要的職責就是執行許可法規。這個許可申請程序可確保施工整修符合所有必要的安全標準，進而保護整個社區免於房舍毀損及危險的隱憂。

欲察看各工程適用之許可清單，請上 renviewtown.com/permits 查詢。

**139**
(A) Namely
(B) Similarly
(C) Therefore
(D) However*

本題要找出適當的連接副詞。「住家外圍整修需要許可證」、「屋內整修目前不需許可」，前後文為轉折語氣，因此答案為 (D)。

* **namely** 即是，那就是　　**similarly** 同樣地　　**therefore** 因此

---

**140**
(A) Contractors may charge extra for overtime.
(B) This commonly held belief is actually false.*
(C) Most building inspectors also work as contractors.
(D) The cost of the project may increase seasonally.

請掌握空格前後方的文意。「過去，部分住戶認為承包商必須負責申請許可」，但是「事實上，資產所有人必須自行取得必要的許可」。根據文意，可以得知空格前句為錯誤的認知，因此 (B) 為最適當的答案。

* **charge** 索費　　**overtime** 超時　　**false** 不正確的，謬誤的
  **seasonally** 季節性地

(A) 承包商可因超時而加價。
(B) 這個普遍認定的想法其實是錯的。
(C) 大多數的建物檢查員也是承包商。
(D) 工程的費用可能隨季節調漲。

---

**141**
(A) Questioning
(B) Eliminating
(C) Enforcing*
(D) Reviewing

本句應為「建物檢查員的職責就是依法執行許可法規」，語意上較為完整，因此 (C) 為最適當的答案。

* **question** 質疑　　**eliminate** 排除　　**enforce** 執行　　**review** 審閱

---

**142**
(A) are met*
(B) to meet
(C) meeting
(D) have met

空格為 that 子句中的動詞部分，(B) 和 (C) 皆不是動詞，可以直接刪除這兩個選項。由於 that 子句為被動語態，需符合 S ＋ be 動詞＋ p.p.（過去分詞）的句構，所以要選 (A)，表示「合乎標準」。在主動語態的句子中，由於 meet 為及物動詞，後方需連接受詞，因此無法填入 (D)。

字彙

**purchase** 消費，購買
**offer** 提供
**holder** 持有者
**redeem** 兌換成（現金）
**in exchange for**
作為……的交換
**book** 預訂
**flight** 航班
**rent** 租用
**apply for** 申請
**fill out** 填寫
**submit** 提交

Questions 143-146 refer to the following webpage.

## Star Credit Purchase Points

Star Credit would like to offer its credit card holders the ‾‾‾‾‾ 143. points program in the world. ‾‾‾‾‾ 144. . Members can even double their points by shopping at any of the two hundred specially ‾‾‾‾‾ 145. stores. Points can be redeemed in exchange for gift cards at any of those two hundred stores. ‾‾‾‾‾ 146. , points can be used on www.travelone.com to book flights and hotel rooms, and rent cars. To apply for Star Credit's points program, simply fill out the following form and click submit.

------------------------------------------------------------

星辰信用卡消費點數

星辰信用卡欲提供信用卡持卡人全球範圍最廣的集點專案。您使用星辰信用卡所進行的每一筆消費，最高可賺進 100 點。會員在 200 家特選商店中的任何一家購物，甚至可以得到雙倍點數。點數可於這 200 家商店中兌換成禮品卡。此外，點數還可用於 www.travelone.com 預訂班機、飯店房間及租車。欲申請星辰集點專案，只要填寫以下表格，並點擊「送出」即可。

**143** (A) comprehension
(B) most comprehensive*
(C) comprehensive
(D) most comprehensively

定冠詞（the）＋空格＋名詞（points program），空格中應填入形容詞。由於句子的最後方為 in the world，應為「世界上最……」，語意上較為完整，因此可以得知空格應填入形容詞最高級，故 (B) 正確。

- **comprehension** 理解　　**comprehensive** 全面的
  **comprehensively** 全面地

**144**
(A) With every purchase you make with your Star Credit Card, you can earn up to 100 points.*
(B) Points can only be used to lower your monthly interest rates on all credit card purchases.
(C) Program members must not have applied for a Star Credit Card in the past.
(D) Furthermore, program members can receive in-store discounts on all their purchases.

(A) 您使用星辰信用卡所進行的每一筆消費，最高可賺進100點。
(B) 點數僅可用於降低信用卡消費的月利率。
(C) 專案會員必須在以前從未申請過星辰信用卡。
(D) 此外，專案會員的所有消費均可享店內優惠折扣。

針對集點專案進行簡單的介紹後，後句提到「會員甚至可以得到雙倍點數」，因此空格應填入專案「基本回饋」才符合文意，故選項 (A) 正確。雖然空格後方似乎可以連接 (D) 選項中的內容，但是 (D) 選項前方並未提及任何和它相關的內容，在此不適合以 furthermore 連接。

- **earn** 賺得；贏得　**lower** 降低，減少　**interest rate** 利率
  **furthermore** 再者　**in-store** 商店內的

**145**
(A) select
(B) selects
(C) selected*
(D) selection

本題空格用來修飾後方的名詞 stores，因此要從 (C) 和 (D) 當中選出答案，用來作為形容詞。空格前方為副詞 specially，強調行為本身是「特別地」，因此應使用含被動意義的過去分詞 selected（被挑選的）較為適當，答案為 (C)。一般而言，若前方已是副詞，就不會使用名詞再修飾後方名詞，故 (D) 錯。

- **select** 挑選　**selection** 選集

**146**
(A) Therefore
(B) Regardless
(C) In addition*
(D) For instance

空格前方提到點數取得與使用方法，空格後接著說出「其他點數可適用的網站」，因此表示「額外資訊」的 (C) 為最適當的答案。

- **therefore** 因此　**regardless** 無論如何　**in addition** 此外
  **for instance** 舉例來說

# PART 7

## 字彙

policy 保險單
account 帳戶
access 取得；進入
insurance 保險
familiarize 使熟悉
feature 特點
additional 更多的，額外的
payment 付款；款項
method 方式
receipt 收據
security 安全
timed 定時的
sensitive 機密的

Questions 147-148 refer to the following website.

http://www.premiuminsurance.com

| Home | Policies | My Account | Sign Out |
|------|----------|------------|----------|

Welcome back, Tom Schwarz! Now, [147] you can easily access all your policy information with Premium Insurance's new website. Please take a moment to familiarize yourself with our website's features.

• Additional payment methods and online receipts of all payments
• [148 (C)] Easy access to all your policy information in one place
• [148 (D)] Upgraded security and timed log-outs to protect your sensitive information
• [148 (B)] New customer service tools, such as an updated FAQ and a live chat function
• Simple online forms to update address and telephone information

--------------------------------------------------

http://www.premiuminsurance.com

| 首頁 | 保險單 | 我的帳戶 | 登出 |
|------|--------|----------|------|

湯姆·施瓦茲，歡迎回來！現在，您可以使用優質保險公司的新網頁輕鬆地取得所有保單資料。請用一點時間熟悉本網頁的特點。

• 更多付款方式及所有款項的線上收據
• 在同一個地方就可輕鬆取得您所有的保單資料
• 升級的安全措施及定時登出以保護您的機密資料
• 全新客服工具，像是最新的常見問答與即時客服通訊功能
• 簡單的線上表格，可更新地址與聯絡電話資料

施瓦茲先生最有可能是誰？

(A) 保險業務員
(B) 保險客戶
(C) 網頁設計師
(D) 理賠專員

## 字彙
representative 代表人員

**147** Who most likely is Mr. Schwarz?

(A) An insurance salesman
(B) An insurance customer*
(C) A web designer
(D) An insurance claims representative

本題提及關鍵人名湯姆·施瓦茲，網頁的第二句表示，施瓦茲先生可使用該保險公司的新網頁，輕鬆地取得所有保單資料（You can easily access all your policy information with Premium Insurance's new website.），由此可以得知答案為 (B)。

在與 insurance 有關的文章中，經常出現 policy，表示「保險單」，也可以解釋為保險契約書或保險商品

**148** What is NOT mentioned as a feature of the new website?

(A) Group insurance applications*
(B) New customer service tools
(C) Consolidated information
(D) Improved Internet security

解題時，請先找出提及特色的段落，並對照各個選項的內容，再刪除文章中提及的選項。第二項 Easy access to all your policy information in one place 符合選項 (C) 的敘述；第三項 Upgraded security 符合選項 (D) 的敘述；第四項 New customer service tools 符合選項 (B) 的內容，因此本題的答案應為 (A)。

下列何者不是文中所提到的新網頁特點？

(A) 團體保險的申請
(B) 新客服工具
(C) 整合的資料
(D) 加強的網路安全性

字彙
application 申請（書）
consolidated 整合的
improved 改進的

---

Questions 149-151 refer to the following information.

## Affluence Pharmaceuticals

Manuel Rodriguez
Lead Researcher

A highly sought-after leader in today's pharmaceutical industry, Mr. Rodriquez had overseen all major research projects at Affluence Pharmaceuticals for the last five years. Mr. Rodriguez joined Affluence seven years ago and was quickly recognized for his great talent and vision. [151] He was promoted to lead researcher and [150 (C)] has since drastically improved employee productivity by more than 20%.

[150 (D)] Mr. Rodriguez has been invited to speak at numerous conferences and was even honored at last year's Pharma Vision Conference as the keynote speaker. [150 (A)] He also works as a consultant for Techtron University's medical department where he has contributed to numerous academic projects. Prior to joining Affluence, [150 (B)] Mr. Rodriguez immigrated from Mexico and attended Stratford University where he graduated with honors.

---

富裕製藥

曼努爾・羅德里格斯
首席研究員

羅德里格斯先生是現今製藥產業廣受歡迎的領導者，在過去的五年來一直督導富裕製藥所有主要的研究計畫。羅德里格斯先生在七年前加入富裕製藥，很快就以其優秀的才能與遠見獲得讚賞。他被拔擢為首席研究員，從此還大大地提高了 20% 以上的員工產能。

羅德里格斯先生已經受邀在多場的會議中演說，並於去年的藥理願景會議上榮任主講人。他也擔任泰創大學醫學系的顧問，為許多學術計畫提供意見。在加入富裕製藥前，羅德里格斯先生移居自墨西哥，於斯特拉福特大學求學，並在那以優等成績畢業。

字彙
affluence 富裕
pharmaceutical
藥品；製藥的
sought-after
（因品質高）受歡迎的
industry 產業；工業
oversee 監督，管理
be recognized for . . .
因……受到讚賞
promote 晉升
drastically 大大地
productivity 生產力
numerous 許多的
honor 受……表揚
department 系所；部門
contribute 貢獻
academic 學術的
prior to . . . 在……之前
immigrate 移居
attend 上（大學）

這份資料的目的是什麼？

(A) 概述一個大學課程
(B) 宣布員工升遷
(C) 介紹公司員工
(D) 慶祝員工退休

字彙
outline 概述
announce 宣布
promotion 升遷，晉升
introduce 介紹
celebrate 慶祝
retirement 退休

**149** What is the purpose of the information?

(A) To outline a university program
(B) To announce an employee promotion
(C) To introduce a company employee*
(D) To celebrate an employee's retirement

第一段主要說明羅德里格斯先生的工作成果；第二段則簡述了他的經歷，根據前後文意，(C) 為最適當的答案。文章的目的大多會出現在文章的前半部，但有時也會出現本題這樣的題型，需要先理解整篇文意後，才能進行解題。

下列何者與羅德里格斯先生無關？

(A) 他受僱為大學教授。
(B) 他之前住在墨西哥。
(C) 他增進了員工績效。
(D) 他是位經驗豐富的演說者。

字彙
employ 僱用
previously 先前地
performance 成果，績效
experienced 經驗豐富的

**150** What is NOT indicated about Mr. Rodriguez?

(A) He is employed as a university professor.*
(B) He previously lived in Mexico.
(C) He has improved employee performance.
(D) He is an experienced public speaker.

解題時，請刪除文章中提及的選項。(B) 出現在最後一句的「Mr. Rodriguez immigrated from Mexico . . .」(C) 出現在第一段最後「. . . has since drastically improved employee productivity by more than 20%」；由第二段的「Mr. Rodriguez has been invited to speak at numerous conferences . . .」可以推測出 (D)，因此本題的答案應為 (A)。

文章第二段提到：「He also works as a consultant for Techtron University's medical department . . .」，可得知他在大學擔任顧問而非教授，故 (A) 錯。

關於羅德里格斯先生的職涯，文中提及了什麼？

(A) 他常因優異的職業道德而獲獎。
(B) 他在應徵工作前完成了兩個學位。
(C) 他在受聘為首席研究員之前擔任實習生。
(D) 他一開始並非以首席研究員身分受僱。

字彙
award 獎
ethic 道德
degree 學位
apply for . . . 申請……
hire 聘用

**151** What is suggested about Mr. Rodriguez's career?

(A) He often receives awards for his great work ethic.
(B) He completed two degrees before he applied for a job.
(C) He worked as an intern prior to being hired as lead researcher.
(D) He was not hired as lead researcher at first.*

閱讀文章時，請將焦點放在題目的 career。第一段中提到他在七年前進入公司，提拔為首席研究員後（He was promoted to lead researcher . . .），大大提升了員工的產能，可得知他並非一開始就是首席研究員，因此 (D) 為最適當的答案。

**Questions 152-154 refer to the following article.**

March 7—the local mayor's office has just released the details of the Budding Futures Internship Program for Park County students. 152 (C), (D) Led by the program director, Milly Andrews, the program is designed to give senior high school students a taste of what it's like working in a public office. --[1]--.

152 (B) Mayor Steven Greenhorn announced the internship program last year. "I think it's important to include teenagers in public affairs," he said in an interview. 153 "It may help them decide what course of study they want to pursue in college." --[2]--.

152 (B) According to the newly released details, Milly Andrews will select 15 students from 15 schools across the county. Based on their areas of interest, the chosen students will be assigned various jobs in the mayor's downtown office. --[3]--. The program will last eight weeks during the summer.

Applications for the program will be available on the mayor's website at the beginning of next week. --[4]--. The selected interns will be announced in early May.

---

3 月 7 日——本地市長辦公室剛公布了給帕克縣學生的「嶄露未來實習計畫」的細節。由專案主任米莉・安德魯斯所主導，這個計畫設計的目的就是為了提供高中學生從事公職的體驗。

史蒂芬・格林霍恩市長去年就發表了這個實習計畫。「我認為將青少年納入公共事務是很重要的。」他在一場訪談中說，「這有助於他們決定想在大學進行的研究課程。」

根據新公布的細節，米莉・安德魯斯將自全縣 15 所學校中挑選出 15 位學生。根據他們的興趣，獲選的學生將分配至市中心市長辦公室中擔任各種職務。這個計畫將於暑假期間持續進行八週。

本計畫的申請表於下週一開始即放在市長網站上。我們鼓勵學生事先準備至少一封的推薦函，將於五月初宣布獲選的實習生。

**字彙**
mayor 市長
release 發表
detail 細節
lead 領導
senior 高年級的
taste 感受，體驗
announce 宣布，公告
affair 事務
course 課程
pursue 進行；追求
according to . . . 根據……
select 挑選
based on 根據
assign 分派
last 持續

下列何者與「嶄露未來實習計畫」有關？

(A) 全國適用。
(B) 是全新的計畫。
(C) 提供給大學生。
(D) 由史蒂芬·格林霍恩主導。

字彙
nationwide 全國的

**152** What is suggested about the Budding Futures Internship Program?

(A) It is available nationwide.
(B) It is a brand new program. *
(C) It is for university students.
(D) It is led by Steven Greenhorn.

(C) 和 (D) 可以由第一段印證為錯誤選項：「Led by the program director, Milly Andrews, the program is designed to give senior high school students a taste of what it's like working in a public office.」(A) 可以由第三段的「Milly Andrews will select 15 students from 15 schools across the county」得知為錯誤的選項；由第二段的 Mayor Steven Greenhorn announced the internship program last year 和第三段的 According to the newly released details，可以得知答案應為 (B)。

根據格林霍恩先生所言，這個實習計畫的主要目標是什麼？

(A) 教導學生有關選舉事宜
(B) 建立志工社群
(C) 提供學生待遇優渥的工作
(D) 在學生未來的教育中引導他們

字彙
election 選舉
establish 建立，創建

**153** According to Mr. Greenhorn, what is the main goal of the internship program?

(A) Teaching students about elections
(B) Establishing a community of volunteers
(C) Providing students with well-paying jobs
(D) Guiding students in their future education *

第二段中引用了格林霍恩市長的訪問「It may help them decide what course of study they want to pursue in college.」，表示該實習計畫有助於學生決定想在大學進行的研究課程，因此 (D) 為最適當的答案。

下列句子最適合出現在[1]、[2]、[3]、[4]的哪個位置中？
「我們鼓勵學生事先準備至少一封的推薦函。」

(A) [1]
(B) [2]
(C) [3]
(D) [4]

字彙
encourage 鼓勵
collect 取；收集
reference 推薦函
in advance 預先

**154** In which of the positions marked [1], [2], [3], and [4] does the following sentence best belong?

"Students are encouraged to collect at least one reference in advance."

(A) [1]
(B) [2]
(C) [3]
(D) [4] *

題目句的內容屬於「申請相關資料」的一部分，最適合放入最後一段申請程序說明 [4] 當中，答案為 (D)。

Questions 155-156 refer to the following webpage.

# ASPIRE UNLIMITED

As a client of our firm, you
- have access to around-the-clock surveillance
- pay a reasonable monthly fee with no additional costs
- can improve your office's security needs

We provide
- [155] custom installations of CCTV equipment
- regular maintenance of all cameras and alarm systems
- [155] 24-hour remote monitoring of your office
- [156] fingerprint scanning technology for all entrances (additional charges will apply)
- access to Aspire's website for all your billing needs

---

無盡嚮往保全公司

做為本公司客戶，您
- 可獲得日夜不斷的監控
- 支付合理月費，不需額外費用
- 能改善貴公司的保全需求

本公司提供
- 監視攝影器材的客製化安裝
- 所有攝影機與警報系統的定期保養
- 24 小時遠端監控貴公司
- 所有入口的指紋掃描技術（需支付額外費用）
- 可使用嚮往公司網站，處理所有帳單

**字彙**
aspire 嚮往；渴望
unlimited 無限的
access （使用某物的）權利
around-the-clock 日夜不斷的
surveillance 監視，看守
pay 支付
reasonable 合理的
fee 費用
additional 額外的
cost 費用
installation 安裝
equipment 設備
maintenance 維修，保養
remote 遙遠的
monitoring 監視
fingerprint 指紋
entrance 出入口
billing 帳單

---

**155** What is one of the services offered by Aspire Unlimited?

(A) Office cleaning
(B) CCTV monitoring*
(C) Website development
(D) Heating system maintenance

第二段中提到保全公司提供的服務。第一項為 custom installations of CCTV equipment，第三項為 24-hour remote monitoring of your office，由這兩項可以確認答案為 (B)。

下列何者是「無盡嚮往」所提供的服務之一？

(A) 清理辦公室
(B) 監視攝影機的監視
(C) 網頁開發
(D) 暖氣系統維修

---

**156** What is mentioned about fingerprint scanning technology?
(A) It is purchased on a weekly basis.
(B) It is one of Aspire's unique services.
(C) It can be purchased for an extra fee.*
(D) It can be added to an account by phone.

閱讀題目時，請特別留意關鍵字 fingerprint scanning technology。第二段第四項中寫道：「fingerprint scanning technology for all entrances (additional charges will apply)」，表示要另外付費購買，因此答案為 (C)。在 Part 7 中，線索常出現在括號（ ）、星號＊或是 Note 當中。

* 答案改寫：additional → extra
　　　　　　charge → fee

文中提到何者與指紋掃描技術有關？

(A) 以每週支付方式購買。
(B) 嚮往公司獨特的服務之一。
(C) 可以額外費用購買。
(D) 可以電話告知方式加入帳戶中。

**字彙**
unique 獨特的
extra 額外的
account 帳戶

Questions 157-158 refer to the following article.

ROUGE TOWNSHIP. March 3 – Rouge Township officials have recently announced a new development proposal for [158 (B)] an amusement park that will be located on Rouge Lake's 4000-acre waterfront.

[158 (A), (C)] The new amusement park is expected to include numerous rollercoasters, an extensive aquarium, a water park, and a pavilion for live music. Several local businesses, such as Rotary Automobiles, Pancake House Restaurants, and Maverick Beverages have agreed to sponsor the park's development.

[157] Following the release of the development proposal, several local activists have expressed concerns about effect the park will have on the waterfront's delicate ecosystem. "We can assure you that all precautions will be taken," Lead Developer, Jan Freedman, said in an interview yesterday. "The park will be located far enough away from the beach and the bike trails that it will have little effect on the surrounding wildlife."

Other Rouge Township residents have expressed excitement about the potential increase in business the new park will bring to the Rouge Lake area.

--------------------------------------------------------

胭脂鎮 3 月 3 日——胭脂鎮官員最近宣布了一個 4,000 公頃胭脂湖濱水區的遊樂園開發企劃案。

這個新遊樂園預計有多座雲霄飛車、一座大型水族館、親水公園以及供現場音樂演奏的涼亭。數間當地商家，像是扶輪汽車、鬆餅屋餐館和小牛飲料都同意贊助遊樂園的開發。

在開發案宣布後，幾位當地激進分子對遊樂園的興建表達了關切，他們認為遊樂園會對濱水區脆弱的生態系統造成影響。「我們向大家保證將採取所有的預防措施。」開發負責人珍·佛德曼昨天在一場訪談中說，「這座遊樂園會與海灘及自行車道保持足夠的距離，所以對周遭野生動植物造成的影響極微。」

胭脂鎮其他居民，則對新遊樂園即將為胭脂湖區所帶來的潛在商機利益，表達了興奮之意。

**157** What is suggested about Rouge Township?

(A) It currently has a large tourism industry.

(B) It is home to a famous water park.

(C) Some of its residents disagree with the proposal.*

(D) Much of the local wildlife is endangered.

第三段中寫道：「Following the release of the development proposal, several local activists have expressed concerns . . .」，顯示有一部分當地的居民對開發案表示憂慮，因此 (C) 為最適當的答案。

\* 答案改寫：local activists → residents

下列何者與胭脂鎮有關？

(A) 目前有大規模的觀光產業。

(B) 是知名親水公園所在地。

(C) 部分居民反對該開發計畫。

(D) 大多數的當地野生動植物正瀕臨絕種。

字彙
**tourism** 觀光（業）
**disagree** 不認同
**endanger** 使處於險境，危及

---

**158** What feature of the amusement park is NOT mentioned?

(A) Its large on-site aquarium

(B) Its location at the waterfront

(C) A place for live performances

(D) The gift shops and kiosks*

解題時，請先找出文章中與「遊樂園特點」有關的敘述（第一段和第二段），對照各選項的內容，並刪除文章中提及的選項。(A) 和 (C) 出現在第二段「The new amusement park is expected to include numerous rollercoasters, an extensive aquarium, a water park, and a pavilion for live music.」；可以由第一段的「an amusement park that will be located on Rouge Lake's 4000-acre waterfront」確認 (B)，因此本題的答案應為 (D)。

下列何者不是文中所提到的新遊樂園特點？

(A) 大規模水族館

(B) 位於濱水區

(C) 有現場表演的場地

(D) 禮品店與售貨亭

字彙
**on-site** 現場的
**performance** 表演
**kiosk**
（販售商品的）小亭或機器

**maintenance** 維修，保養
**department** 公寓
**condo (condominium)**
公寓大樓
**routine** 定期的，例行的
**repair** 修理
**at no charge** 免費
**free of charge** 免費
**fixture** 設備
**showerhead** 蓮蓬頭
**faucet** 水龍頭
**part** 零件
**replace** 更換，替換
**component** 零件
**arrange** 安排
**including** 包含
**smoke detector**
煙霧偵測器
**allot** 分配
**reservation** 預約

**Questions 159-161 refer to the following information.**

# Maintenance Services

159 The maintenance department of Fairsview Condos is available to make routine repairs to your condo and all shared spaces, most of which are available at no charge to residents. The following services are free of charge and must be booked two weeks in advance.

- Bathroom fixtures, such as showerheads, faucets, and toilet parts may be replaced once every two years. 160 Free repairs of any broken components can be arranged once per year.
- Doors and windows, including window screens, will be repaired as needed at any time of the year.
- Fan filters above stoves and smoke detectors can be replaced every six months. Air conditioners are allotted one free cleaning service per year.
- For a full list of services, please visit our website. 161 Reservations can be made by filling out a request form at www.fairsviewcondos.com/maintenance.

---

## 維修服務

費爾斯維公寓大樓的維修部，專為您的公寓及所有公共空間提供定期修繕服務，大部分的服務可免費提供給住戶。以下的服務將不收取任何費用，但必須提早兩週預約。

- 浴室設備，像是蓮蓬頭、水龍頭與馬桶零件每兩年可更換一次。任何毀損零件每年可免費修理一次。
- 門窗，包括紗窗，需要時，隨時可修理。
- 爐子上方的風扇濾網及煙霧偵測器每六個月可更換一次。冷氣機每年可享免費清理一次。
- 欲知完整服務清單，請參考網頁。預約可於網站 www.fairsviewcondos.com/maintenance 填寫申請表即可。

**159** For whom is the information most likely intended?

(A) Real estate agents
(B) Employees at a building management company
(C) Landlords of a retirement home
(D) Residents at a complex*

由文章的第一句「The maintenance department of Fairsview Condos is available to make routine repairs to your condo and all shared spaces, most of which are available at no charge to residents.」，可以確認答案為 (D)。單字 condo 為 condominium 的縮寫，表示「公寓大廈」。

\* 答案改寫：condo → complex

這則資訊最有可能是給誰看的？

(A) 房地產仲介
(B) 大樓管理公司的員工
(C) 養老院的房東
(D) 公寓大樓的住戶

字彙
**real estate** 不動產
**management** 管理
**landlord** 房東
**complex** 綜合大樓

---

**160** How often can bathroom fixtures be repaired at no cost?

(A) Once a month
(B) Every six months
(C) Once a year*
(D) At any time

閱讀文章時，請特別留意題目關鍵字 bathroom fixtures。第一項中便提到浴室設備免費維修週期（Free repairs of any broken components can be arranged once per year.），由此可以得知答案為 (C)。

浴室的設備可多久免費修理一次？

(A) 一個月一次
(B) 每六個月一次
(C) 一年一次
(D) 隨時

---

**161** According to the information, how can readers arrange to have something repaired?

(A) By filling out an online form*
(B) By calling a department
(C) By speaking to a landlord
(D) By signing up on a sheet

請掌握本題的重點為「安排修繕事宜」。最後一項中提到，網站上載明所有的服務項目，請於網站填寫申請表（Reservations can be made by filling out a request form at www.fairsviewcondos.com/maintenance.），因此答案為 (A)。

根據這則資訊，讀者要如何安排修繕事宜？

(A) 填寫線上表格
(B) 打電話給部門
(C) 告訴房東
(D) 在表單上簽名

字彙
input 投入；輸入
change 變動
highlight 強調
reflect 表現，反映
stop by 順路拜訪

Questions 162-163 refer to the following text message chain.

**Ron Parks [8:03]:** Jim, can I get your input on the changes Jennifer asked me to make to tomorrow's presentation?

**Jim Webber [8:05]:** Sure. What do you need?

**Ron Parks [8:07]:** [163] Can I e-mail you the new proposal? I've highlighted the changes in red, but [162] I'm not sure if these reflect our full range of advertising services.

**Jim Webber [8:08]:** I'm afraid not. [163] I'm just about to meet a client for dinner. How about I stop by your hotel room after?

**Ron Parks [8:09]:** That would be OK. Then I can show you the PowerPoint presentation I've made as well.

**Jim Webber [8:10]:** OK, great. What room are you in?

**Ron Parks [8:10]:** Room 506. See you then!

--------------------------------------------------

| | |
|---|---|
| 榮恩・帕克斯 [8:03] | 吉姆，珍妮佛要我修改明天的簡報，可以請你幫我一下嗎？ |
| 吉姆・韋伯 [8:05] | 當然。你需要什麼？ |
| 榮恩・帕克斯 [8:07] | 我可以用電子郵件把新企劃案寄給你嗎？我已經把修改處用紅色標示出來了，但是我不確定這些是否能呈現我們所有的廣告服務。 |
| 吉姆・韋伯 [8:08] | 恐怕不行。我正要出門和客戶吃晚餐。那結束後，我到飯店找你好嗎？ |
| 榮恩・帕克斯 [8:09] | 可以喔。那我剛好可以把已經做好的投影片簡報一起給你看。 |
| 吉姆・韋伯 [8:10] | 好，那太好了。你的房號是？ |
| 榮恩・帕克斯 [8:10] | 506 號房。到時候見！ |

帕克斯先生有可能是誰？

(A) 廣告商
(B) 飯店接待員
(C) 藝術收藏家
(D) 資訊科技專家

字彙
receptionist 接待員

**162** Who most likely is Mr. Parks?

(A) An advertiser*
(B) A hotel receptionist
(C) An art collector
(D) An IT specialist

本題詢問的重點為「職業」，並在文章中找尋相關資訊。帕克斯先生於 8 點 07 分傳送的訊息中寫道：「I'm not sure if these reflect our full range of advertising services.」，由此可以得知答案為 (A)。

在8:08時，韋伯先生說的「恐怕不行」是什麼意思？

(A) 他擔心簡報。
(B) 他沒有時間審視文件。
(C) 他不認同一些修改。
(D) 他沒有要求做修改。

字彙
review 審閱
request 要求

**163** At 8:08, what does Mr. Webber most likely mean when he writes, "I'm afraid not"?

(A) He is worried about a presentation.
(B) He doesn't have time to review a document.*
(C) He does not agree with some changes.
(D) He did not request the changes to be made.

在某些狀況中，若對方回答「I'm afraid not.」就表示 No，是鄭重回絕的意思。前一封訊息中，帕克斯先生問：「Can I e-mail you the new proposal?」，詢問可否寄給對方企劃書，對方回答「正要出門和客戶吃晚餐」，根據文意，(B) 為最適當的答案。

**Questions 164-167 refer to the following e-mail.**

**To:** staceymarshall@pressassociated.com
**From:** htrander@themaxfestival.com
**Subject:** The Max Summer Music Festival
**Date:** June 5
**Attachment:** 2-070406.pdf

Dear Ms. Marshall,

[164, 167] We at The Max Summer Music Festival are delighted that you would like to cover our upcoming three-day festival in Grand Park. -- [1] --. Grand Park holds nearly 25,000 visitors, and we expect to be at full-capacity during all three days. I have reserved an admission ticket for you and [165] attached an all-access backstage pass. You can pick the ticket up at the ticket booth upon arrival. -- [2] --.

The gates will open July 4 at 1 P.M. and [166] the festival will conclude with a fireworks show on July 6 at 10 P.M. You are free to attend all three days if you'd like, and your press pass will allow you to interview as many of the bands and performers as you wish. -- [3] --. For a full list of performers and their schedules, you can visit our website and download our event calendar. Lastly, should you need anything at all during your visit, you can contact Molly at press services at 776-3333-6713. -- [4] --. Thank you, and I hope you enjoy The Max Summer Music Festival.

Sincerely,

Harry Trander
Festival Press Coordinator

--------------------------------------------------------------------------------

收件者：staceymarshall@pressassociated.com
寄件者：htrander@themaxfestival.com
主旨：麥克斯夏日音樂祭
日期：6 月 5 日
附件：2-070406.pdf

親愛的馬歇爾女士，

麥克斯夏日音樂季很高興您願意報導即將於大公園舉辦的三天音樂祭活動。這是我們的第一場音樂祭，我們安排了許多樂團。大公園可容納近 25,000 名遊客。我們希望在這三天中能達到全滿狀況。我已為您保留一張入場券，並附上後臺全場通行證。您可以在抵達時於售票亭領取。

出入口將於 7 月 4 日下午一點開放，而音樂祭將以 7 月 6 日晚間十點的煙火秀畫下句點。您可以隨意自由參加這三天的活動。您的媒體通行證可以讓您採訪任何樂團以及表演者。至於完整的表演者與演出時間表，可至我們的網站查詢並下載。最後，如果您在採訪期間有任何需要，都可以聯絡媒體服務處的莫莉，電話是 776-3333-6713。感謝您，希望您會喜歡麥克斯夏日音樂祭。

活動媒體統籌
哈利·崔德 敬上

馬歇爾女士有可能是誰？

(A) 顧客
(B) 記者
(C) 樂團經理
(D) 表演者

字彙
journalist 記者

**164** Who most likely is Ms. Marshall?

(A) A customer
(B) A journalist*
(C) A band manager
(D) A performer

此郵件中的收件人馬歇爾女士，也就是文中的第二人稱 you。從郵件的第一句「We at The Max Summer Music Festival are delighted that you would like to cover . . .」，感謝對方願意採訪，因此答案為 (B)。

---

這封電子郵件中還附上了什麼？

(A) 入場券
(B) 停車券
(C) 表演時間表
(D) 後臺全場通行證

字彙
voucher 票券

**165** What was sent with the e-mail?

(A) An admission ticket
(B) A parking voucher
(C) A schedule of performances
(D) A backstage press pass*

閱讀文章時，請特別留意題目的關鍵字「隨電子郵件附上的東西」。第一段中提到：「. . . attached an all-access backstage pass」，由此可以確認答案為 (D)。

---

根據這封電子郵件，這個音樂祭顯著的特色是什麼？

(A) 可容納超過25,000人。
(B) 將包括爵士舞表演。
(C) 將以特殊煙火表演作為結束。
(D) 包含免費露營服務。

字彙
notable 顯著的
accommodate 容納

**166** According to the e-mail, what is a notable feature of the festival?

(A) It may accommodate more than 25,000 people.
(B) It will include jazz dance performances.
(C) It will end with a special fireworks display.*
(D) It may include free camping services.

閱讀文章時，請掌握本題重點為「活動的特色」。由第二段中 the festival will conclude with a fireworks show，表示將以煙火秀作為結束，因此答案為 (C)。

* 答案改寫：conclude → end
　　　　　　 show → display

---

下列句子最適合出現在[1]、[2]、[3]、[4]的哪個位置中？
「這是我們的第一場音樂祭，我們安排了許多樂團。」

(A) [1]
(B) [2]
(C) [3]
(D) [4]

**167** In which of the positions marked [1], [2], [3], and [4] does the following sentence best belong?

"It is our first festival and we have many bands lined up."

(A) [1]*
(B) [2]
(C) [3]
(D) [4]

請在前一句話中，找尋插入句中代名詞 It 所代表的單字。若將句子填入〔1〕當中，It 即用來表示 our upcoming three-day festival，最符合句意，故 (A) 正確。

**Questions 168-171 refer to the following online chat discussion.**

**Jessica Simon [10:32 A.M.]** Marcus, do you have a minute? [168] I'm trying to access our online store, but it's not loading. Does it load on your computer?

**Marcus Adams [10:40 A.M.]** It's the same for me. Was it like this yesterday?

**Jessica Simon [10:42 A.M.]** I don't think so. I have some orders that were placed online yesterday. But [168,169] I got an e-mail from a repeat customer who said our site was down. Can you ask the IT department about it?

*Jeff Peters has been added to the chat.*

**Marcus Adams [10:44 A.M.]** Jeff, something is wrong with our online store. It doesn't seem to be loading. Can you figure out what's wrong?

**Jeff Peters [10:48 A.M.]** This is strange. It looks like the hosting site is down.

**Marcus Adams [10:50 A.M.]** Do you have their telephone number?

**Jeff Peters [10:55 A.M.]** [170] Yes, I just called them. They said they are having some technical difficulties, which should be fixed by tomorrow morning.

**Jessica Simon [11:00 A.M.]** OK, [171] I have a meeting with the sales manager shortly. I'll let him know about this problem.

-------------------------------------------------------------

潔西卡‧賽門 [ 上午 10:32 ]　馬可仕，你有空嗎？我試著要進入我們的網路商店，但它無法載入。你的電腦可以載入嗎？

馬可仕‧亞當斯 [ 上午 10:40 ]　我也一樣。昨天就這樣了嗎？

潔西卡‧賽門 [ 上午 10:42 ]　我不這麼認為。我這裡有幾張昨天在網路下的訂單。不過我收到一位老顧客的電子郵件，說我們的網頁當機了。你可以向資訊科技部詢問一下嗎？

傑夫‧彼得斯加入聊天。

馬可仕‧亞當斯 [ 上午 10:44 ]　傑夫，我們的網路商店有問題，好像無法載入。你可以弄清楚是怎麼回事嗎？

傑夫‧彼得斯 [ 上午 10:48 ]　這就怪了。看起來好像是網路寄存網站當機了。

馬可仕‧亞當斯 [ 上午 10:50 ]　你有他們的電話嗎？

傑夫‧彼得斯 [ 上午 10:55 ]　有，我剛打電話給他們了。他們說他們碰到了一些技術上的問題，應該明天早上前就可以修好。

潔西卡‧賽門 [ 上午 11:00 ]　好，我一會兒要和業務主管開會，我會告訴他這個問題的。

---

**字彙**
**access** 進入
**load** 載入
**order** 訂單
**repeat customer** 老顧客
**add** 加入，增加
**figure out** 弄清楚
**fix** 修復

賽門女士呈報了什麼問題？

(A) 目前無法在網路上販賣商品。

(B) 網路商店有錯誤訊息。

(C) 一個顧客想要退還一些商品。

(D) 有一項產品不會再列在網站上了。

字彙

**item** 物品

**no longer** 不再

---

**168** What problem does Ms. Simon report?

(A) Sales cannot be made online currently.*

(B) The online store includes wrong information.

(C) A customer wants to return some items.

(D) A product is no longer listed on the website.

賽門女士在第一封訊息中寫道：「I'm trying to access our online store, but it's not loading.」，且由「I got an e-mail from a repeat customer who said our site was down.」，可以推知客戶不能在網站下單，故答案為 (A)。

---

賽門女士從誰得知這個問題？

(A) 部門主管

(B) 顧客

(C) 資訊科技部主管

(D) 助理

字彙

**head** 主管

**assistant** 助理

---

**169** From whom did Ms. Simon learn about the problem?

(A) A department head

(B) A customer*

(C) An IT manager

(D) An assistant

閱讀文章時，請把焦點放在賽門女士的訊息內容。10 點 42 分傳送的訊息中寫道：「I got an e-mail from a repeat customer who said our site was down.」，表示由顧客電郵得知網路商店出了問題，因此答案為 (B)。

---

在10:50時，當亞當斯先生寫道：「你有他們的電話嗎？」，他的意思是？

(A) 他要求一些資料。

(B) 他要彼得斯先生打電話給一家公司。

(C) 他想要更新名錄。

(D) 他擔心他會迷路。

字彙

**directory** 名錄

---

**170** At 10:50, what does Mr. Adams most likely mean when he writes, "Do you have their telephone number"?

(A) He is requesting some information.

(B) He wants Mr. Peters to call a company.*

(C) He would like a directory updated.

(D) He is worried he will get lost.

題目句後方，彼得斯先生回答剛才已經打過電話（Yes, I just called them.），因此 (B) 為最適當的答案。

---

賽門女士接下來最有可能做什麼？

(A) 打電話給一些顧客

(B) 在網路上買東西

(C) 參加會議

(D) 聯絡網路寄存網站

字彙

**purchase** 購買

**contact** 聯絡

---

**171** What will Ms. Simon most likely do next?

(A) Call some customers

(B) Purchase items online

(C) Attend a meeting*

(D) Contact a hosting site

閱讀時，請把焦點放在賽門女士的訊息內容。最後一封訊息中寫道：「I have a meeting with the sales manager shortly.」，表示她待會要去開會，因此答案應為 (C)。

Questions 172-175 refer to the following article.

# Employment Weekly Column
# Job Fairs

Job fairs are a quick and easy way to hire new employees. However, holding a job fair may be a costly event, especially if you're only hiring a few employees. [172] Consider the following advice to determine if holding a job fair is right for your company.

## How many employees are you hiring?

[173] If your company is planning to hire a large group of employees, a job fair might be right for you. Job fairs can bring in a large number of applicants. However, if you're only interested in finding a few new workers, the number of applicants at a job fair may overwhelm human resources departments, making the hiring process even harder.

----

字彙

employment 就業
hire 聘用
hold 舉辦
costly 昂貴的
event 活動
consider 考量
determine 決定
applicant 應徵者；申請者
be interested in . . .
對……感興趣的
overwhelm 使……受不了
human resources
人力資源（部）

----

每週就業專欄
就業博覽會

就業博覽會是一種快速又簡單招聘新員工的方法。但是，舉辦就業博覽會可能是非常花錢的活動，尤其是如果您只打算招聘幾位員工而已。將以下的建議列入考量，再決定舉辦就業博覽會是不是適合貴公司。

您打算招聘多少員工？
如果貴公司打算招聘一大群員工，那就業博覽會就很適合您了。就業博覽會可以吸引許多應徵者，但如果您只有意找幾位新員工，那就業博覽會的應徵者數量可能會讓貴公司的人力資源部應接不暇，反而使整個招聘過程變得更麻煩。

**Is there a good location to hold the job fair?**

High schools and universities are popular places to hold job fairs, but if your company is seeking more experienced candidates, schools are probably not the right place. It is critical to hold the job fair in a place where you can attract suitable employees, such as business conventions. Unfortunately, business conventions are only held at certain times of the year.

**175 Can you hire employees another way?**

175 Online job advertisement websites have changed the way people search for jobs. Prior to your company's hiring season, human resources staff members may be able to post job openings on numerous websites. This would garner a lot of attention and allow your company to list the experience requirements applicants must meet.

**Is the cost worth it?**

Before holding a job fair, consider the cost of the event. You may need to pay to rent a suitable space and would need to provide refreshments and application packages. If your hiring needs could be met by free online websites, a job fair may not be worth it.

----------------------------------------------------------------------------

有沒有適合舉辦就業博覽會的場地？

高中和大學都是舉辦就業博覽會很受歡迎的場地，但如果貴公司找的是經驗豐富的應徵者，那學校可能就不是適合之處了。在一個能吸引到合適應徵者的場所而舉辦的就業博覽會是很重要的，像是商務會議。但遺憾的是，商務會議只在每年的特定時間舉行。

您可以透過其他方式招聘員工嗎？

線上就業廣告網站已經改變了人們找工作的方式。在貴公司的招募季之前，人力資源部的人員可以在數個網站上貼出職缺公告。這可引起許多關注，也讓貴公司列出應徵者所必須符合的資歷條件。

這筆花費值得嗎？

在舉辦就業博覽會前，考慮一下活動的花費。您可能需要租借一個合適的場地，還得提供茶點和申請資料。如果免費網站就可以符合您的招聘需求，那舉辦就業博覽會就不值得了。

**172** What is the article about?

(A) Tips for increasing a worker's productivity
(B) Websites used to hire employees
(C) Methods of increasing the chances of being hired
(D) Strategies for efficient and economical recruitment*

從標題即可得知文章內容與「就業」有關，但是由於四個選項都提到了相關的內容，請務必一一檢視確認。第一段中：「Consider the following advice to determine if holding a job fair is right for your company.」，且整篇討論舉辦就業博覽會是否合乎效益與成本，因此 (D) 為最適當的答案。

＊答案改寫：advice → strategy

這篇文章是有關什麼？
(A) 增進員工生產力的要訣
(B) 用來聘僱員工的網站
(C) 增進錄取機會的方法
(D) 有效率又省錢的招募策略

字彙
productivity 生產力
method 方法
strategy 策略
efficient 有效率的
economical 省錢的，經濟實惠的
recruitment 招募

---

**173** According to the article, what is a good reason to hold a job fair?

(A) To hire specialized workers
(B) To fill a large number of positions*
(C) To provide employees with experience
(D) To promote the brand of a company

閱讀文章時，請務必先掌握本題的重點為「要舉辦就業博覽會的原因」。第二段「If your company is planning to hire a large group of employees, a job fair might be right for you.」，可以得知公司如欲進行大規模招募，便適合舉辦就業博覽會。因此 (B) 為最適當的答案。

根據這篇文章，要舉辦就業博覽會的原因是什麼？
(A) 招聘專業員工
(B) 填補大量職缺
(C) 提供員工經驗
(D) 宣傳公司品牌

字彙
position 職位
promote 宣傳，促銷

---

**174** The word "critical" in paragraph 3, line 2, is closest in meaning to

(A) urgent
(B) essential*
(C) creative
(D) negative

本句的意思應為「重要的是在適當地點舉辦就業博覽會」。因此若要替換成選項中的單字，最相似的意思為 (B) essential。

第三段、第二行的「critical」與下列哪一個意思最接近？
(A) 緊急的
(B) 重要的
(C) 有創造力的
(D) 負面的

字彙
urgent 緊急的
essential 重要的；必要的
negative 負面的

---

**175** What is mentioned as an alternative way of finding job candidates?

(A) Advertising in local newspapers
(B) Using employment websites*
(C) Holding job fairs at the office
(D) Sending out mass e-mails

關於其他招聘員工的方法（Can you hire employees another way?），在第四段中提到還可以透過網路（Online job advertisement websites），因此答案應為 (B)。

何者是找到求職者的另一種方式？
(A) 在當地報紙上刊廣告
(B) 利用就業網站
(C) 在公司舉辦就業博覽會
(D) 寄出大量電子郵件

字彙
alternative 可選擇的
mass 大量

233

Questions 176-180 refer to the following article and e-mail.

### [176] Publisher Instructs the Next Generation

January 10—Since his retirement last year, publisher and editor Jim Frank has run the Department of Publishing Studies at Western University. Frank is best known for his role at Maxwell Publishing House where he worked as a senior editor on numerous projects, including the publication of several successful series.

Jim Frank joined Western University as both a department head and a professor. [177] He developed new courses such as E-publishing, Writing for the Web, and International Rights Management. Students who wish to work in the publishing industry as editors, book designers, or literary agents have benefited greatly from his wisdom.

As a result of Frank's hard work, Western University has also founded its first ever publishing internship. [179] Students have been matched with editors, designers, and agents during three-week programs. Additionally, Frank has organized numerous events in which industry professionals have given presentations at the university on various topics. Because of Frank's innovation and connections, the publishing program at Western University has become one of the best in the country.

--------------------------------------------------------------

### 出版人指導下一代

1月10日——出版商兼編輯吉姆‧法蘭克從去年退休以來，就接掌了西部大學的出版研究學系。法蘭克以他在麥克斯威爾出版社所擔任的角色聞名，他在那裡擔任許多專案的資深編輯，其中包括了幾部暢銷套書的出版。

吉姆‧法蘭克以系主任及教授之姿加入西部大學。他開發了一些新課程，像是數位出版，網頁寫作和國際版權管理。有意在出版界擔任編輯、圖書設計師或作家經紀人的學生都從他的學識中獲益良多。

由於法蘭克的努力，西部大學也創立了有史以來第一個出版實習職。學生們在三週的實習計畫中和編輯、設計師及經紀人相互搭配。除此之外，法蘭克還安排了許多活動，讓業界專家在大學中發表各種不同主題的演說。因為法蘭克的創新與人脈，西部大學的出版課程已成了全國最棒的一門相關課程。

**From:** beth@ricorspublishing.com
**To:** jimfrank@westernuniversity.com
**Date:** February 25
**Subject:** E-Publishing Panel

Dear Mr. Frank,

[179] Margaret Stevenson is currently doing her internship here at Ricors Publishing House. She mentioned that you're putting together another panel of guest speakers for your students next month. [178] I'd love to join the panel if you still have any openings. As the director of e-publishing here at Ricors, I'm sure I'd be able to give some great information on working in this field.

[180] I will be busy next week attending a conference overseas, but you can leave a message with my assistant and I'll get back to you the following week. My number is 443-223-0911 Ext. 3367.

I look forward to hearing from you.

Sincerely,

Beth Smith,
Director of E-Publishing,
Ricors Publishing House

------------------------------------------------------------------------

寄件者：beth@ricorspublishing.com
收件者：jimfrank@westernuniversity.com
日期：2 月 25 日
主旨：數位出版專題小組

親愛的法蘭克先生，

瑪格莉特‧史蒂文森目前正在瑞克斯出版社實習。她提到您正在為學生安排下個月的客座講者。如果您還有缺額的話，我很樂意加入這個專題小組。身為瑞克斯出版的數位出版主管，我確信我能夠提供一些該領域工作的重要資訊。

下週我將忙於參加海外會議，但您可以跟我的助理留言，我將於隔週回覆。我的電話是 443-223-0911 轉分機 3367。

期待收到您的回信。

瑞克斯出版社數位出版主管
貝斯‧史密斯敬上

字彙
**panel** 專題小組
**put together** 安排；組合
**opening** 空缺
**field** 領域
**Ext.** 分機
（extension 的縮寫）
**look forward to V-ing**
期待做……

這篇文章主要是在討論什麼？

(A) 一家公司的業務活動
(B) 一位編輯的職涯變化
(C) 一家出版商的新套書
(D) 一個學生實習計畫

**字彙**
**practice** 業務（活動）

**176** What does the article mainly discuss?

(A) A company's business practices
(B) An editor's career change*
(C) A publisher's new series
(D) A student internship program

文章主旨的關鍵線索，通常就在報導（第一篇）的標題。由標題：「Publisher Instructs the Next Generation（出版人指導下一代）」，可以推測應為某出版人士在職業生涯上的轉變，因此 (B) 為最適當的答案。

---

下列何者是吉姆·法蘭克對大學的貢獻之一？

(A) 學生可修到更多課程。
(B) 開發學生就業網站。
(C) 建立獎學金基金會。
(D) 最近開設一間電腦室。

**字彙**
**contribution** 貢獻
**available** 可得到的
**employment** 就業
**scholarship** 獎學金
**establish** 建立
**lab**（電腦）室；實驗室

**177** What is one contribution Jim Frank has made to the university?

(A) More courses have become available to students.*
(B) A student employment website has been developed.
(C) A scholarship foundation has been established.
(D) A computer lab has recently opened.

報導（第一篇）第二段中介紹了吉姆·法蘭克的經歷和貢獻，由「He developed new courses . . .」可以確認答案為 (A)。

---

史密斯女士為何要寄這封電子郵件？

(A) 她要回覆一通電話留言。
(B) 她想參加演講活動。
(C) 她在找更多實習生。
(D) 她想報名課程。

**字彙**
**reply to** 回覆
**register** 登記報名

**178** Why did Ms. Smith send the e-mail?

(A) She is replying to a phone message.
(B) She would like to join a speaking event.*
(C) She is looking for more interns.
(D) She wants to register in a course.

本題詢問的是史密斯女士撰寫郵件（第二篇）的目的。文章或電郵前半部的內容常表示作者的目的，因此閱讀時要特別注意。第二篇文章的第一段提到，史密斯女士聽說法蘭克先生下個月將安排客座講師團隊，如尚有空缺，希望自己也能加入（I'd love to join the panel if you still have any openings.），因此答案應為 (B)。

**179** Who most likely is Ms. Stevenson?

(A) A director at Ricors Publishing House

(B) A student at Western University*

(C) A guest speaker in a publishing course

(D) A former editor at Maxwell Publishing House

閱讀文章時，請特別留意史蒂文森小姐。由郵件（第二篇）開頭「Margaret Stevenson is currently doing her internship here at Ricors Publishing House.」可以得知她在「實習」。報導（第一篇）第三段中提到了西部大學推行了出版實習計畫，後方接著說參與此項計畫，可以與編輯、設計師及經紀人相互搭配（Students have been matched with editors, designers, and agents during three-week programs.），因此答案應為 (B)。

---

**180** What does Ms. Smith say about her schedule?

(A) She can reschedule her meetings.

(B) She is not available for the panel in March.

(C) She can be reached only during the day.

(D) She will be away on business next week.*

從史密斯女士所撰寫的郵件（第二篇）第二段，她提到行程表，由「I will be busy next week attending a conference overseas . . .」可以確認答案為 (D)。

---

史蒂文森小姐可能是誰？

(A) 瑞克斯出版社的主管

(B) 西部大學的學生

(C) 出版課程的客座講者

(D) 麥克斯威爾出版社的前編輯

字彙
former 前任的

---

史密斯女士提到有關她行程表的什麼？

(A) 她可以重新安排會議。

(B) 她三月沒有時間出席客座講師小組。

(C) 只能在白天聯絡到她。

(D) 她下週將出差，不在公司。

字彙
reschedule 重新安排時間
reach 聯絡

**字彙**
efficiency 效率
storage 儲存
in order to . . . 為了……
install 安裝
store (v.) 存放
remotely 遠距離地
extremely 非常，極度地
rest assured 放心
sensitive 敏感的
register 登記，註冊
extension 分機

Questions 181-185 refer to the following memo and e-mail.

## MEMO
## Free Cloud Services

As you know, Roth Computer Sales has recently partnered with L&B Tech to improve our company's efficiency and file storage. [181] In order to make saving and sharing files easier, we plan to install L&B's Cloud Software program on all our systems.

L&B's Cloud Software allows employees to store files of any size without taking up too much computer memory. [183] Employees can easily send large files in seconds without worrying about slow upload speeds. Additionally, employees who bring their company laptops on business trips will be able to access their files remotely. Furthermore, L&B Cloud Software is extremely secure, so employees can rest assured that any sensitive files will be safe.

To use this new software, simply complete the setup, register with your company e-mail, and start storing and sending files. [185] The service will be available on April 10 at 9 A.M. If you have any questions or concerns about setting up or using the new software, please contact Michael Brown in the IT Department at extension 3342 or by e-mail at michaelbrown@rothcomputers.com.

---

備忘錄
免費雲端服務

正如各位所知，羅斯電腦最近與 L&B 科技合作，以改善本公司的電腦效率及檔案儲存。為了讓儲存檔案與分享檔案更便利，我們計畫在公司所有系統上安裝 L&B 雲端軟體。

L&B 雲端軟體可讓員工儲存各種容量的檔案，而不會佔據太多電腦記憶體的空間。員工可以輕鬆地在短時間內傳送大型檔案，而不用擔心緩慢的上載速度。除此之外，帶著筆記型電腦出差的員工也能夠自遠端讀取資料。再者，L&B 雲端軟體相當安全，所以員工可以放心任何敏感性檔案都會安全無虞。

欲使用新軟體，只要完成設定，以您在公司的電子信箱註冊，即可開始儲存與傳送檔案。這個服務將於 4 月 30 日上午九點起生效。如果您對於設定或使用這個新軟體有任何問題或疑慮，請撥打分機 3342 或寄電子郵件到 michaelbrown@rothcomputers.com 與資訊科技部的麥可・布朗聯絡。

**To:** michaelbrown@rothcomputers.com
**From:** sandrabell@rothcomputers.com
**Date:** April 12
**Subject:** Cloud Software

Dear Mr. Brown,

I tried calling you at your extension, but you did not answer. I'm writing to request assistance with the new L&B Cloud Software. [185] I set up my account on the first day the service was available, but today I was unable to find any of the files in my account. [184] It seems that all of the files I uploaded have been deleted, as my account is empty. Since these files include very important sales figures from last quarter, I really need to access them immediately. Can you give me an idea about how to recover these files? It would be great if you could stop by my office sometime today.

Sandra Bell

-------------------------------------------------------------------------

收件者：michaelbrown@rothcomputers.com
寄件者：sandrabell@rothcomputers.com
日期：4 月 12 日
主旨：雲端軟體

親愛的布朗先生，

我試著打分機電話給您，但您沒有接電話。我寫信是想請求關於新 L&B 雲端軟體的協助。我在服務生效的第一天就設定了帳戶，但今天我的帳號內卻找不到任何檔案。我所上傳的檔案好像全都被刪除了，因為我的帳戶裡是空的。由於這些檔案內含上一季很重要的銷售數據，我真的需要馬上取得。您可以告訴我該如何回復這些檔案嗎？如果您今天有空到我辦公室的話就太好了。

珊卓·貝爾

字彙
**assistance** 協助
**account** 帳戶
**delete** 刪除
**empty** 空的
**quarter** 季
**immediately** 立即地
**recover** 恢復

這個備忘錄的目的是什麼？

(A) 宣布政策的異動
(B) 提醒員工備份電腦檔案
(C) 提供新軟體的資訊
(D) 說明一套新規定

字彙
announce 宣布
remind 提醒

**181** What is the purpose of the memo?

(A) To announce a change in a policy
(B) To remind employees to back up computers
(C) To give information about a new program*
(D) To explain a new set of rules

文章（第一篇）的第一段提到為了讓儲存檔案與分享檔案更便利，羅斯電腦將與 L&B 科技公司合作，安裝新的軟體（In order to make saving and sharing files easier, we plan to install L&B's Cloud Software program on all our systems.），因此 (C) 為最適當的答案。在文章的前半部，大多可以找到文章的目的。

---

備忘錄中，第二段、第五行的「sensitive」與下列哪一個意思最接近？

(A) 小心的
(B) 反應的
(C) 令人驚訝的
(D) 機密的

字彙
cautious 小心的
responsive 反應的
confidential 機密的

**182** In the memo, the word "sensitive" in paragraph 2, line 5, is closest in meaning to

(A) cautious
(B) responsive
(C) surprising
(D) confidential*

單字所在的句子內容為維護「敏感性」檔案的安全。根據文意，填入表示「祕密的，機密的」的單字 confidential 最為適當，故 (D) 正確。classified 亦為時常使用的同義字。

---

下列何者是 **L&B** 雲端軟體的優點之一？

(A) 減少成本。
(B) 節省公司時間。
(C) 免費安裝。
(D) 可審視出文件中的錯誤。

字彙
benefit 利益，好處
reduce 減少
mistake 錯誤

**183** What is stated as a benefit of L&B Cloud Software?

(A) It reduces cost.
(B) It saves a company time.*
(C) It is free to install.
(D) It scans documents for mistakes.

閱讀備忘錄（第一篇）時，請找出有關題目關鍵字 L&B 雲端軟體的優點。在第二段提到了多項優點，由「Employees can easily send large files in seconds without worrying about slow upload speeds.」可以確認答案為 (B)。

**184** What problem is Ms. Bell having?

(A) She has forgotten her password.

(B) Her computer has crashed.

(C) All files have gone missing.*

(D) She cannot access a server.

貝爾女士正遭遇什麼問題？

(A) 她忘記自己的密碼。

(B) 她的電腦當機了。

(C) 所有檔案不見了。

(D) 她無法進入伺服器。

閱讀貝爾女士所撰寫的郵件（第二篇）時，請特別留意「問題點」。電郵中間表示檔案好像被刪除了（It seems that all of the files I uploaded have been deleted, as my account is empty.），因此 (C) 為最適當的答案。

**185** When did Ms. Bell set up her account?

(A) On April 10*

(B) On April 11

(C) On April 12

(D) On April 13

貝爾女士何時設定她的帳戶？

(A) 4月10日

(B) 4月11日

(C) 4月12日

(D) 4月13日

由貝爾女士所撰寫的郵件（第二篇）前半部「I set up my account on the first day the service was available . . . 」，表示在服務上線的首日便建立了帳戶。回頭至備忘錄（第一篇）中尋找「服務上線日」，可以由第三段「The service will be available on April 10 at 9 A.M.」得知答案應為 (A)。

**demonstration** 展示
**unfortunately**
不幸地，遺憾地
**misplace** 誤置，丟失
**even though** 雖然，儘管
**summary** 一覽（表），摘要
**item** 物品
**carry-on** 隨身攜帶的
**missing** 遺失的
**luggage** 行李
**inform** 告知
**locate** 找出
**deliver** 寄送，運送
**postpone** 延後

**Questions 186-190 refer to the following e-mails and form.**

**From:** oemerson@sommerfield.com
**To:** mfernandez@rkdistribution.br
**Subject:** demonstration
**Date:** August 5

Dear Ms. Fernandez,

My plane landed in Sao Paulo and I am e-mailing you from a waiting room in the airport. Unfortunately, the large suitcase that I had checked has been misplaced. Even though I have printed summaries of all the items right here in my carry-on bag, [188] the sample products for the demonstration are in the missing luggage. Airport staff informed me that they need at least three days to locate the bags and deliver them to where I am staying. That means, of course, that I will not have them in time for the demonstration scheduled for the day after tomorrow.

Once I reach my hotel, [186] I will fax the summaries to your company. If it is not too much trouble, [187] could we possibly postpone the demonstration for another two days? Please contact me about this as soon as possible.

Sincerely,

Oscar Emerson

-------------------------------------------------------------------------

寄件者：oemerson@sommerfield.com
收件者：mfernandez@rkdistribution.br
主旨：展示
日期：8 月 5 日

親愛的費南德茲女士，

我的班機已降落於聖保羅，我正從機場的候機室寫這封電子郵件給您。很不幸地，我所託運的大行李被弄丟了。雖然我已經將隨身行李中的所有樣品一覽表列印出來，但是展示的商品樣本都在遺失的行李中。機場員工告訴我，他們至少需要三天的時間才能找到行李，並送到我住的地方。那也表示，我來不及在安排於後天的展示會前拿到它們了。

一旦我到了飯店，就把樣品一覽表傳真到貴公司。如果不是太麻煩的話，是不是可以將展示會延後兩天？請盡快與我聯絡。

奧斯卡·艾默生 敬上

# Missing Baggage Claim Form

We would like to extend our deepest apologies for our mishandling of your belongings and any inconveniences it caused. The information you provide below will assist us greatly. Please provide a clear description of every piece of luggage as well as a list of the items inside each piece. This will definitely help expedite the entire process.

Claim No: 341567S/3
Name of Passenger: Oscar Emerson
E-mail: oemerson@sommerfield.com

## Permanent address:

409 Jackson Lane
Cleveland, OH, 44103
United States of America

## Temporary address (Until August 12):

Piquiri Hotel
Av. Paulista 1209
[190] Sao Paulo, Brazil
01310-060

| Flight No. | Date | From | To |
|---|---|---|---|
| MTC971 | August 3 | Toledo | Buenos Aires |
| BTA302 | August 5 | Buenos Aires | Sao Paulo |

Suitcase Type: Large leather bag, zipper, shoulder strap

Manufacturer: Riggs  Color: Brown

## Contents (Please be as specific as possible):

| Description | Number |
|---|---|
| [188] Running shoes, tennis shoes, golf shoes, baseball shoes, high-top basketball sneakers | 12 pairs |
| Top Guy brand Man's suits | 2 |
| Greyvalley brand digital camera with battery charger | 1 |
| Trousers, shorts, socks, etc. | 6 |
| South American pocket-sized travel guides | 2 |

--------------------------------------------------------

## 行李遺失單

我們要為本公司不當處理您的物品，因而造成的不便表達最深的歉意。以下您所提供的資料將提供我們莫大的協助。請詳細描述每一件行李的外觀，以及行李內所有物品的清單，這將有助於加速整個處理流程。

申請編號 3415673S/3
旅客姓名 奧斯卡‧艾默生
電子信箱 oemerson@sommerfield.com

永久地址：
美國俄亥俄州克里夫蘭市44103傑克森巷409號

暫時地址（至8月12日止）：
01310-060
巴西聖保羅保利斯塔大道1209號
皮基里飯店

| 航班號碼 | 日期 | 起點 | 終點 |
|---|---|---|---|
| MTC971 | 8月3日 | 托雷多 | 布宜諾斯艾利斯 |
| BTA302 | 8月5日 | 布宜諾斯艾利斯 | 聖保羅 |

| 行李箱類型 | 大型皮革包，附拉鍊、肩帶 | | |
|---|---|---|---|
| 製造商 | 里格斯 | 顏色 | 棕色 |

內容物（請盡可能詳述）：

| 說明 | 數量 |
|---|---|
| 慢跑鞋、網球鞋、高爾夫球鞋、棒球鞋、高筒籃球鞋 | 12雙 |
| 頂槍牌男士西裝 | 2 |
| 灰谷牌數位相機及充電器 | 1 |
| 長褲、短褲、襪子等 | 6 |
| 南美旅遊口袋指南手冊 | 2 |

字彙
**be delighted to . . .**
樂意……
**arrive** 抵達
**appreciate** 感激
**patience** 耐心
**lost and found** 失物招領

**From:** airportlostfoundoffice@spinternat.com
**To:** oemerson@sommerfield.com
**Subject:** claim 341567S/3
**Date:** August 6

Dear Mr. Emerson,

We are delighted to inform you that your missing suitcase has been located with all the items you listed. [190] It will arrive at the temporary address you provided between 1:00 P.M. and 3:00 P.M. on August 7. We truly appreciate your patience and understanding.

Regards,

Sao Paulo International Airport Lost and Found

------------------------------------------------------------------------------

寄件者：airportlostfoundoffice@spinternat.com
收件者：oemerson@sommerfield.com
主旨：341567S/3 申請
日期：8月6日

親愛的艾默生先生，

我們很高興通知您，您所遺失的行李以及列舉的所有物品都已經找到了。
將於8月7日下午一點至三點之間送抵您所提供的暫時地址。

我們誠摯地感謝您的耐心等候與體諒。

聖保羅國際機場失物招領處 敬上

**186** What does Mr. Emerson indicate about the product summaries?

(A) They will be sent by fax.*
(B) They are not ready yet.
(C) They are longer than expected.
(D) They need to be printed out.

請閱讀艾默生先生所撰寫的電子郵件（第一篇），並特留意題目關鍵字 the product summaries。由第二段「I will fax the summaries to your company.」，可以確認答案為 (A)。

關於樣品一覽表，艾默生先生提及了什麼？

(A) 將以傳真寄送。
(B) 還沒寫好。
(C) 比預期的要長。
(D) 需要列印出來。

字彙
**indicate** 表明，指出
**expect** 預期

**187** What does Mr. Emerson ask Ms. Fernandez to do?

(A) Deliver product samples
(B) Submit an order form
(C) Reschedule a meeting*
(D) Drive him to the hotel

電子郵件（第一篇）的寄件人為艾默生先生，收件人為費南德茲女士，第二段艾默生先生詢問是否可以將展示延後兩天（could we possibly postpone the demonstration for another two days?），並請對方回覆，因此 (C) 為最適當的答案。

* 答案改寫：**postpone → reschedule**

艾默生先生要求費南德茲女士做什麼？

(A) 遞送商品樣本
(B) 送交訂單
(C) 重新安排會議
(D) 送他去飯店

字彙
**submit** 提交

**188** What does Mr. Emerson want to demonstrate?

(A) Bicycle tires
(B) Athletic shoes*
(C) Image software
(D) Coffee makers

閱讀文章時，請掌握解題關鍵為「展示品」。艾默生先生所撰寫的郵件（第一篇）中的第一段「the sample products for the demonstration are in the missing luggage」，表示展示品為「遺失物」。在行李遺失單（第二篇）的詳細內容中，值得注意的有 running shoes, tennis shoes, golf shoes, baseball shoes, high-top basketball sneakers，表示展示品應為各種運動鞋，故 (B) 為正確答案。

艾默生先生要展示的是什麼？

(A) 腳踏車輪胎
(B) 運動鞋
(C) 影像軟體
(D) 咖啡機

字彙
**athletic** 運動的

表格中，第一段、第四行的「expedite」與下列哪一個意思最接近？

(A) 發現
(B) 修改
(C) 詳述
(D) 加快

字彙

**modify** 修改
**elaborate** 詳細說明
**accelerate** 加快

貨運要送到哪裡？

(A) 克里夫蘭
(B) 托雷多
(C) 聖保羅
(D) 布宜諾斯艾利斯

字彙

**delivery** 運送（的物品）

**189** In the form, the word "expedite" in paragraph 1, line 4, is closest in meaning to

(A) discover
(B) modify
(C) elaborate
(D) accelerate*

expedite 的意思為「使迅速；加快」，選項中可以替換的單字為 accelerate，故 (D) 正確。

**190** Where will the delivery be sent?

(A) To Cleveland
(B) To Toledo
(C) To Sao Paulo*
(D) To Buenos Aires

機場寄送的電郵（第三篇）中寫道：「It will arrive at the temporary address you provided . . . 」，由此可以得知會將行李送往「暫時住址」。由於選項的內容為特定的地名，要從申請表格（第二篇）中找尋答案。第二篇中 Temporary address 所寫的地名為 (C)。

**Questions 191-195 refer to the following e-mail, webpage, and article.**

**To:** Jeremy Burns
**From:** Christine Lim
**Date:** [195] June 5
**Subject:** Sewing Machine

Dear Jeremy,

I just received your e-mail. I agree with you that we should think about purchasing new sewing machines for our fashion design studio. [195] Since we are just starting our business, [193] it would be good to have affordable machines that are sturdy and easy to clean. It's also very important that they have good warranties, as we will be using them every day. Topreviews.com has a lot of information that might help us in choosing a model. Why don't you check the site and let me know what model you think will suit our needs?

Thanks,

Christine

------------------------------------------------------------

收件者：傑若米・伯恩斯
寄件者：克莉絲汀・琳姆
日期：6月5日
主旨：縫紉機

親愛的傑若米，

我剛收到您的電子郵件。我同意您的看法，我們應該考慮為服裝設計工作室添購新縫紉機。既然我們的事業剛起步，能買到堅固耐用，好清理又價格合理的機器應該是很棒的。因為我們每天都會使用縫紉機，具良好保固也是很重要的。頂尖評論 Topreviews.com 上有很多資訊，有助於我們挑選型號。您何不看一下網頁，再告訴我您認為哪一個型號符合我們的需求？

感恩

克莉絲汀

https://www.topreviews.com

**Category: Sewing Machines**

Top Reviews has tested four high-end sewing machines that are ideal for both homes and businesses:

★★★★ Master Sew 445 is [193] a durable, easy-to-clean machine with multiple sewing settings for all different kinds of fabrics. It might be too large for some homes, but would suit businesses well. [192,193] It is available for a reasonable price and [193] includes a five-year warranty.

★★★★ Design Line 3019 is a compact, portable machine that would serve traveling sewers well. It is capable of most stitching styles and is made of extremely durable plastic. [192] It is a reasonable price, but does not come with a warranty.

★★★☆ Triple Sew 88 performs well with light fabrics, but may have trouble with thicker fabrics, like denim. It can be ordered online for [192] an extremely low cost.

★★★☆ ZS 3000 is the largest machine on the market. It requires significant set-up and must be taken apart to be cleaned. [192] The cost is especially low, but [191] the machine can only handle a few stitching techniques.

-------------------------------------------------------------------

https://www.topreviews.com

**類別：縫紉機**

頂尖評論測試了四款適合家庭與商用的高檔縫紉機：

★★★★ 縫製大師 445 是一款耐用，易清理的機器，具多種縫紉設定，適合縫紉各種不同布料。對部分家庭來說，機身可能太大，卻相當適合商業使用。價格合理，還附有五年保固。

★★★★ 設計系列 3019 是一款小巧，可攜式機器。適合作為行動式縫紉機。能縫製大多數車線款式，本機器以非常耐用的塑料製成。價格合理，但無保固。

★★★☆ 三倍縫製 88 善於縫製輕薄布料，處理較厚重布料，如丹寧布可能略為不便。線上訂購可獲超低價格優惠。

★★★☆ ZS 3000 是市面上最大型機器。需要精確的裝設，必須拆解才能清理。價格特別低廉，但該機器只能處理一些縫製技巧。

## Fashion in Park Falls

By Zander Cornelli

[195] December 20—Residents of Park Falls who monitor the latest trends in fashion were excited about attending the upscale fashion event held in the Park Falls Convention Center last week. Numerous companies that have made Park Falls the home of their growing businesses participated in the 10th Park Falls Fashion Festival. Over twenty fashion studios were showcased in the event, several of which are owned by local residents.

Rose Designs, which has been in the area for over twenty years, kicked off the festival with some incredible winter apparel. The show was followed by a presentation by Kim Miller, the owner of Accessories Forever. [195] In-Style Fashions and Turnbull Jeans, which have been in business for six months and three years respectively, were newcomers to the festival. All items featured during the fashion shows are available for sale on company websites.

字彙
resident 居民
monitor 關注；監測
trend 潮流
upscale 高級的，高檔的
participate in 參與
showcase 使展現
kick off 開始
incredible
極好的；令人難以置信的
apparel 服裝
be followed by . . .
接連……
respectively 分別地，各自地
newcomer 新來的人

------------------------------------------------------------

帕克弗爾斯時裝秀

詹德·科奈里 撰稿

12 月 20 日——向來關注最新時尚潮流的帕克佛爾斯居民，對於參加上週在帕克佛爾斯會議中心所舉辦的高級時尚活動，都感到興奮不已。多家自帕克佛爾斯發跡成長的公司都參與了第十屆帕克佛爾斯時尚季。超過 20 家服裝工作室在活動中亮相，其中數家工作室還是當地居民所開設的。

在當地超過 20 年的玫瑰設計，以絕美的冬季服飾揭開時尚秀序幕。緊接著登場的是永恆配件的老闆金·米勒的展示。開業六個月的 In 潮流服飾與開業三年的湯布爾牛仔褲，則是這場時尚秀的新人。時尚秀中展示的所有商品均在各公司網站上販售。

---

**191** What is indicated about the ZS 3000?

(A) It is commonly used in homes.

(B) It has an extended warranty.

(C) It can be transported easily.

(D) It has limited functions.*

閱讀文章時，請特別留意關鍵字 ZS 3000。網頁（第二篇）最後一段「the machine can only handle a few stitching techniques」，由此可知該型號機器功能有限，答案為 (D)。

\* 答案改寫：a few → limited, technique → function

下列何者與 **ZS 3000** 有關？

(A) 普遍在家庭中使用。

(B) 有延長保固。

(C) 容易搬運。

(D) 功能有限。

字彙
commonly 普遍地
extended 延長的；延伸的
transport 運送；運輸
limited 有限的
function 功能

網站上所提到的機器有什麼共同點？

(A) 都小巧可攜。
(B) 價格合理。
(C) 有各種顏色。
(D) 容易修理。

字彙
in common 共同（特點）
come in 有（不同種類）

**192** What do all the machines mentioned on the webpage have in common?

(A) They are compact and portable.
(B) They are affordable prices.*
(C) They come in various colors.
(D) They can be repaired easily.

網頁（第二篇）中，可以看到各類機器的相關說明，每項說明的後方都表示為「合理或低價」（a reasonable price, an extremely low cost, The cost is especially low），由此可以確認答案為 (B)。

伯恩斯先生最有可推薦琳姆女士哪一款縫紉機？

(A) 縫製大師445
(B) 設計系列3019
(C) 三倍縫製88
(D) ZS 3000

**193** What sewing machine did Mr. Burns most likely recommend to Ms. Lim?

(A) Master Sew 445*
(B) Design Line 3019
(C) Triple Sew 88
(D) ZS 3000

關鍵人名即為電子郵件（第一篇）的寄件人和收件人，閱讀郵件時，請特別留意琳姆小姐開出的條件。郵件中間寫道：「. . . it would be good to have affordable machines that are sturdy and easy to clean. It's also very important that they have good warranties, as we will be using them every day.」，開出了四項條件。請再對照網頁（第二篇）中縫製大師 445 的評論：「durable, easy-to-clean machine, a reasonable price, includes a five-year warranty」，可以確認答案為 (A)。

文章中，第一段、第一行的「monitor」與下列哪一個意思最接近？

(A) 相信
(B) 觀察
(C) 監督
(D) 依賴

字彙
observe 觀察
supervise 監督
depend on . . . 依賴……

**194** In the article, in paragraph 1, line 1, the word "monitor" is closest in meaning to

(A) believe in
(B) observe*
(C) supervise
(D) depend on

單字所在的句子內容為居民「關注最新時尚潮流」。根據文意，選項中最適合填入的單字為 (B) observe。

琳姆女士與伯恩斯先生最有可能在文章中的哪一家公司服務？

(A) 玫瑰設計
(B) 永恆配件
(C) In潮流服飾
(D) 湯布爾牛仔褲

**195** What company mentioned in the article do Ms. Lim and Mr. Burns most likely work for?

(A) Rose Designs
(B) Accessories Forever
(C) In-Style Fashions*
(D) Turnbull Jeans

本題必須綜合分析報導（第三篇）和電子郵件（第一篇）才能解題。第一篇電郵的前半部提及「Since we are just starting our business」，且發信日期為六月。而第三篇報導於十二月發布，報導的第二段「In-Style Fashions and Turnbull Jeans, which have been in business for six months and three years respectively」，將兩篇文章進行對照後，可以得知兩人工作的 In 潮流服飾創業時間為六個月，故答案為 (C)。

Questions 196-200 refer to the following webpage, online order form, and e-mail.

Http://www.martinmovers.com

| **Home** | **Services** | **Estimates** | **Contact Us** |
|---|---|---|---|

Martin Movers is ready to help you with all your moving needs. Our movers have a collective twenty years of experience tackling large and small jobs with the greatest care. Whether you are moving to a new home or you're looking to relocate your office to a new building, we can offer you the most competitive rates.

Our standard moving rates are as follows:

2 movers and 1 mid-sized truck = $75 per hour

4 movers and 1 full-sized truck = $150 per hour

197 (A),(B),199 Office moves (6 movers and 2 full-sized trucks) = $400 flat rate

Additional charges may apply to office moves should customers request to have our movers set up photocopiers, computers, printers, and projectors following the move. For each set up, a $5 charge may be added. 197 (C) To get a free estimate, just fill out our online form and we'll get back to you soon.

*New Year Special Promotion: Request an estimate by January 20 and receive $30 off the total cost of your move.

------------------------------------------------

Http://www.martinmovers.com

| 首頁 | 服務 | 估價 | 聯絡我們 |
|---|---|---|---|

馬丁搬家公司準備好提供您所有搬遷需求的協助。本搬家公司謹慎處理大小搬遷工作上已有 20 年的經驗。不論您是搬新家，還是打算將公司遷至新大樓，我們都能提供您最具競爭力的價格。

我們的標準搬遷費用如下：

兩位搬運工人和一部中型卡車＝每小時 75 元

四位搬運工人和一部大型卡車＝每小時 150 元

辦公營業處所搬遷（六位工人和兩部大型卡車）＝均一價 400 元

關於辦公營業處所搬遷，顧客若於搬遷後要求搬運工人裝設影印機、電腦、印表機、投影機，將酌收額外費用。每裝設一台機器，將多收五元。欲申請免費估價，只要填寫線上表格，我們將盡快回覆給您。

＊新年特別促銷活動：在 1 月 20 日前申請估價，將抵扣 30 元搬遷費。

**Martin Movers**
**Estimate Request Form**

| Date | January 10 |
|---|---|
| Name | Connor Goldsmith |
| E-mail address | connor@goldsmithlegal.com |
| Telephone | 409-333-2314 |
| Moving from:<br>Moving to: | 54 First Avenue, New York City<br>889 Fallsview Lane, New York City |
| [200] Moving date | February 23 |
| Items to be moved | 8 desks, 8 computers, 3 printers, 1 photocopier, 1 refrigerator, 1 conference table, 25 office chairs |
| Additional comments | My law office is moving to a new location. As [198] we have our own IT employee, we will not require anyone to set up our equipment. Thus, [199] I believe your standard flat rate will apply. Please contact me by e-mail to confirm the price and finalize the reservation. |

馬丁搬家公司
估價申請表

| 日期 | 1 月 10 日 |
|---|---|
| 姓名 | 康納·金史密斯 |
| 電子信箱 | connor@goldsmithlegal.com |
| 電話 | 409-333-3214 |
| 搬遷起始地：<br>搬遷目的地： | 紐約市第一大道 54 號<br>紐約市秋景巷 889 號 |
| 搬遷日期 | 2 月 23 日 |
| 搬遷物品 | 八張書桌，八台電腦，三台印表機，一台影印機，一台冰箱，一張會議桌，25 張辦公椅。 |
| 其他意見 | 本律師事務所將搬至新址。因為本公司有自己的資訊科技員工，所以我們不需要任何人員裝設設備。因此我相信應適用貴公司的標準均一價。請以電子郵件與我聯繫以確認價格，並確認預約登記。 |

**To:** Connor Goldsmith
**From:** Stephan Martin
**Date:** January 12
**Subject:** Re: Estimate Request
**Attachment:** goldsmith_quote.pdf

Dear Mr. Goldsmith,

Thank you for requesting a quote from Martin Movers. As you have noted in your estimate request form, you do not need any set up services, so [199] I believe our standard flat rate will apply to you.

Unfortunately, however, [200] Martin Movers is already fully booked on the day you requested. I'm wondering if it would be possible to postpone your move by one day. Of course, because you requested a quote during our promotional event, [199] I'm happy to offer you a $30 discount on your move.

Please feel free to call my office at 409-555-8796 to further discuss this. Otherwise, I will follow up with you next week.

Sincerely,

Stephan Martin
Martin Movers

------------------------------------------------------------

收件者：康納・金史密斯
寄件者：史帝芬・馬丁
日期：1 月 12 日
主旨：回覆：申請估價
附件：goldsmith_quote.pdf

親愛的金史密斯先生，

感謝您申請馬丁搬家公司估價。正如您於估價申請表所提到的，貴公司不需要任何的裝設服務，所以我相信我們的標準均一價應適用於貴公司。

然而，遺憾的是，您申請的當天，馬丁搬家公司已經登記額滿了。我不知道貴公司的搬遷是否可延後一天。當然，您是在我們促銷活動期間提出的估價申請，我很樂意提供您 30 元的搬遷服務折扣。

歡迎來電 409-555-8796 至本公司以進一步討論相關事宜。或者，我將於下週與您做後續連繫。

馬丁搬家公司
史帝芬・馬丁 敬上

字彙
**attachment** 附件
**quote** 報價
**postpone** 延後
**promotional** 促銷的
**event** 活動
**feel free to . . .**
無須拘束做……
**otherwise** 不然，否則
**follow (sth) up**
追查後續狀況

253

網頁中，第一段、第二行的
「tackling」與下列哪一個意
思最接近？

(A) 修理
(B) 處理
(C) 考慮
(D) 款待

字彙
handle 處理
entertain 款待

**196** In the webpage, the word "tackling" in paragraph 1, line 2, is closest in meaning to

(A) repairing
(B) handling*
(C) considering
(D) entertaining

請先從文中，找出單字所在的句子。句子的內容為擁有「處理大小搬遷工作」的經驗，因此 (B) 為最適當的答案。

下列何者與辦公營業處所搬
遷無關？

(A) 將有六位搬運工人參與。
(B) 將使用一部以上的卡車。
(C) 免費提供估價。
(D) 必須提早兩週前預約。

字彙
involve 牽涉，包含
at no cost 免費
at least 至少
in advance 提早，預先

**197** What is NOT mentioned about office moves?

(A) Six movers will be involved.
(B) More than one truck will be used.
(C) Estimates will be provided at no cost.
(D) It must be booked at least two weeks in advance.*

請由搬家公司的網頁（第一篇）中找尋與 office moves（辦公營業處所搬遷）有關的段落，對照各選項的內容，並刪除文章中提及的選項。(A) 和 (B) 出現在 Office moves (6 movers and 2 full-sized trucks)；可以由下一段末行中的「To get a free estimate, just fill out our online form and we'll get back to you soon.」確認與 (C) 內容相符，因此本題的答案應為 (D)。

金史密斯先生提及有關他公
司的什麼？

(A) 將丟棄幾樣物品。
(B) 將縮減辦公空間。
(C) 需要多一名搬運工人。
(D) 聘用資訊科技專業人員。

字彙
discard 丟棄
downsize 縮減
employ 僱用

**198** What does Mr. Goldsmith mention about his company?

(A) It will discard several items.
(B) It will downsize its office space.
(C) It requires an additional mover.
(D) It employs an IT specialist.*

金史密斯先生所填寫的詢價表格（第二篇）中，由最後一欄內容「we have our own IT employee」，可以得知答案為 (D)。

**199** If Mr. Goldsmith uses Martin Movers, how much will he be charged for his move?

(A) $75
(B) $150
(C) $370*
(D) $400

金史密斯先生估價申請表（第二篇）中表示不需要協助安裝設備，之後寫道：「I believe your standard flat rate will apply.」，表示應該可以適用均一價格。第三篇的郵件第二段提到，在促銷活動期間的估價申請，可以提供 30 元的折扣（I'm happy to offer you a $30 discount on your move.）。從公司網頁（第一篇）「辦公營業處所搬遷」中，可以確認費用為 400 元均一價，再扣除 30 元後，答案應為 (C)。

**200** What is suggested about Martin Movers?

(A) It is booked solid on February 23.*
(B) It is located in New York City.
(C) It has five trucks in its fleet.
(D) It charges extra for work done on weekends.

由第三篇的郵件第二段「Martin Movers is already fully booked on the day you requested.」，可以得知本郵件收件人所指定的搬遷日期，預約已全數額滿。再從估價申請表（第二篇）中，確認搬遷的日期為 2 月 23 日，因此答案為 (A)。

如果金史密斯先生聘用馬丁搬家公司，那他的搬遷費用是多少錢？

(A) 75元
(B) 150元
(C) 370元
(D) 400元

下列何者與馬丁搬家公司有關？

(A) 2月23日的預約已額滿。
(B) 位於紐約市。
(C) 搬運車隊共有五部卡車。
(D) 週末加班需額外收費。

字彙
solid 持續不間斷的
be located in . . . 位於……
fleet 車隊

# ACTUAL TEST 2

## 中譯+解析

# PART 5

帕克女士打算自己面試那些應徵者，因為她比任何人都了解這個職務。

字彙
**position** 職務；職位

**101** Ms. Parker plans to interview the applicants _____ because she understands the position better than anybody.

(A) hers       (B) herself*

(C) she       (D) her

請先看空格前的部份：主詞（Ms. Parker）＋動詞（plans）＋受詞（to interview the applicants）為結構完整的句子，因此空格不需要填入表示主格的 she 或是受格的 her；所有格代名詞 hers，表「她的物品」語意也不合。空格中應填入表「親自」的反身代名詞 (B)，用來修飾前方句子。

---

退稅將發還給在加州的公務員。

字彙
**tax** 稅
**rebate**（政府的）部分退款
**public servant** 公務員，公僕

**102** Tax rebates will be given to public servants _____ the State of California.

(A) within*       (B) until

(C) during       (D) since

空格後方為特定的地點，因此空格應為表地理位置概念的介系詞，(A) 為最適當的答案。

• **within** 在……之內    **during** 在……期間    **since** 自從

---

有興趣的團體可以方便地在線上報名本週末不動產投資的研討會。

字彙
**party** 團體
**register** 報名，註冊
**real estate** 不動產
**investing** 投資

**103** Interested parties can _____ register online for this weekend's seminar on real estate investing.

(A) very       (B) least

(C) easily*       (D) more

空格位在助動詞（can）＋動詞（register）之間，因此要填入副詞，用來修飾動詞 register。本句應為「可以方便地登記」語意上較為完整，因此 (C) 為最適當的答案。

• **least** 最小；最少

---

本晉升將提供員工更優的福利、公司配車及更多的休假日。

字彙
**promotion** 晉升
**benefit** 福利

**104** The promotion will _____ employees with upgraded benefits, company cars, and more vacation days.

(A) provide*       (B) earn

(C) contrast       (D) loan

本句意思應為升遷能為員工「提供」許多好處，語意上較為完整，因此 (A) 為最適當的答案。在使用上，請熟記 provide 句型為：「provide ＋東西／好處＋ with ＋人」。

• **provide** 提供    **earn** 賺取    **contrast** 對比，對照    **loan** 借出；貸與

* 動詞＋ A ＋ with ＋ B 的句型：
**provide/supply/furnish/present A with B** 將 B 提供／贈與給 A

**105** Office staff at Morin Legal Services _____ work four days a week, from Monday to Thursday.

(A) norm (B) norms
(C) normal (D) normally*

主詞（Office . . . Services）＋不及物動詞（work）為結構完整的句子，因此空格中應填入副詞，用來修飾動詞 work，答案為 (D)。

- norm 規範　　normal 正常的　　normally 通常

\* 當主詞為類似的個體所結合而成的集合體（集合名詞）時，動詞後方不能加上表第三人稱單數的 s，常見集合名詞如下：
staff, family, audience, committee, team, class, the police, the public, the press, the crowd

\* 現在簡單式一般表示常態，常和下方頻率副詞搭配使用：
routinely, regularly, normally, always, usually, generally, often

莫林法律事務所的員工通常一週工作四天，從週一到週四。

字彙
legal 法律的

**106** Items can be exchanged _____ they are returned within one week following the date of purchase.

(A) or (B) if*
(C) nor (D) but

空格後方為商品可以交換的「條件」，因此答案應為 (B)。

\* 表時間或條件的副詞子句：
假設未來發生的事情，條件句仍須用現在簡單式。
表示時間的連接詞：when, while, before, after, as soon as, until, once
表示條件的連接詞：if, unless, as long as

如果商品在購買後一週內退還，均可換貨。

字彙
item 物品
exchange 交換

**107** According to this newspaper article, earnings at BTR Electronics last quarter were _____ than expected.

(A) lowest (B) lowering
(C) lower* (D) low

介系詞 than 用來表示比較，由於空格後方為 than，因此空格中應填入比較級 lower，故 (C) 正確。

- lowering 天空陰沉的　　low 低的

根據這篇文章報導，BTR電子上一季的利潤比預期低。

字彙
earnings（公司）利潤
electronics 電子（裝置）
quarter 季度

**108** Everyone _____ the store owner took a week-long vacation in the summertime last year.

(A) out of (B) other
(C) except* (D) between

本句文意應為「除了店主外，每個人在去年夏季都休了一個禮拜的假。」，因此空格最適合填入介系詞 except，答案為 (C)。

- except 除……以外

除了店主外，每個人在去年夏季都休了一個禮拜的假。

儘管桃樂絲・克來門特的風景畫都出自真實的地點，她仍在作品中投入了大量的想像力。

字彙
**actual** 真實的
**a great deal of** 大量的

---

**109** Even though all her landscape paintings are of actual places, Doris Clements puts a great deal of _____ into her work.

(A) imagine      (B) imaginative

(C) imagination*      (D) imaginary

本題要找出適當的詞性。空格位置為介系詞 of 的受詞，因此只能填入名詞 imagination，答案為 (C)。

- **imagine** 想像    **imaginative** 富有想像力的    **imagination** 想像力
  **imaginary** 虛構的，想像中的

\* 表示「大量」的相關用法：
**a large amount of / a great deal of** ＋不可數名詞＋單數動詞（＝ much）
**a number of** ＋可數名詞＋複數動詞（＝ many）

---

接待員今天下午將會把更新的顧客名單交給所有的業務人員。

字彙
**personnel**
（公司的）全體人員

---

**110** The receptionist will provide the _____ client list to all sales personnel this afternoon.

(A) frequent      (B) updated*

(C) certain      (D) monitored

根據句意，提供給業務人員的名單應為「最新的，更新後的」較為適當，因此答案為 (B)。certain 可以放在名詞的前方，意思為「某個，某些」，但並不會和定冠詞 the 搭配使用（the 用於表示特定的名詞），因此 (C) 不是答案。

- **frequent** 頻繁的    **certain** 某個；某些    **monitored** 被監視的

---

春季培訓課程設立的目的是為了幫助業務同仁能更創意地思考。

字彙
**training** 訓練
**course** 課程

---

**111** The spring training course was developed to help sales employees think more _____.

(A) create      (B) creative

(C) creativity      (D) creatively*

「使役動詞（help）＋受詞（sales employees）＋受詞補語（think）」為結構完整的句型，因此 (A) 與 (C) 可以刪除。答案應為 (D) creatively，因為它可用來修飾作為受詞補語的動詞 think。

- **creativity** 創造力    **creatively** 有創意地

\* 適用於「動詞＋受詞（人）＋ to ＋ V」句型的動詞：
**enable** 使能夠    **allow** 允許    **permit** 准許    **advise** 建議
**instruct** 指導    **encourage** 鼓勵    **remind** 提醒    **convince** 說服
**invite** 邀請    **require** 要求    **request** 請求    **urge** 敦促
**order** 命令    **persuade** 勸服

請注意，help 亦屬上述句型，但後方的 to 在美式英語用法中被省略。

---

在試著組裝這張桌子前，你應該查看一下安裝說明。

字彙
**attempt** 試圖
**assemble** 組裝
**instruction** 操作指南

---

**112** Before attempting to assemble this table, you should _____ the instructions.

(A) direct      (B) review*

(C) gather      (D) program

本句應為「組裝桌子前，應該查看一下安裝說明」，語意上較為完整。因此 (B) 為最適當的答案。

- **direct** 指揮    **review** 查看，查閱    **gather** 收集    **program** 課程；節目

**113** Ms. Jannel, the director of customer relations, _____ the poor reviews the company has received online at the staff meeting tomorrow.

(A) had been addressing    (B) is addressing*

(C) will be addressed    (D) should be addressed

客服部主管雅內爾女士將在明天的員工會議上，提出公司於網路上收到的不良評價。

由選項的內容，可以得知本題要考的是時態。address 可以用來表示「對……説話；處理（問題）」。由於空格後方為受詞，因此要從 (A) 和 (B) 當中找出答案。句子最後方的 tomorrow 為表未來的時間副詞，因此答案應為 (B)。請特別熟記，可以用現在式 be + V-ing 和 be going to 來表示未來時態。

• **address** 對……講話；處理

---

**114** Larson Motors aims to improve its public image _____ the guidance of publicist Cynthia Morison of M&T Public Relations.

(A) under*    (B) either

(C) among    (D) beyond

拉森汽車在公關人員辛希亞‧莫里森和M&T公關公司的指導下努力改善公共形象。

字彙
**aim to** 力求
**guidance** 指導；引導
**publicist** 公關人員
**public relations** 公共關係

本題只要知道片語 under the guidance of 的意思為「在……的指導之下」，就能輕鬆解題，故答案為 (A)。

* 「under +名詞」的用法：
**under + the direction/name/pressure/warranty/new management of**
在……的指導／名義／施壓／保證／新的管理之下

---

**115** When _____ to any new clients, don't forget to mention Beckingham's promotional event next week.

(A) spoken    (B) speaking*

(C) spoke    (D) to speak

在和新客戶談話時，別忘了提到貝金漢下週的促銷活動。

字彙
**promotional** 促銷的

本句屬於分詞構句，也就是原本「When +主詞+動詞」的句型中省略了主詞，並將動詞改成分詞的形式，因此答案應為 (B)。句型結構（before/after/when/while/since/though + V-ing）經常出現在考題中。

---

**116** Tickets for Friday night's play at the Alexander Theater sold out quickly because the production _____ two famous actors from this area.

(A) feature    (B) features*

(C) to feature    (D) featuring

亞歷山大劇院週五晚上的演出票券很快就銷售一空了，因為這場演出的主角是本地兩位知名演員。

字彙
**play** 戲劇
**production** 演出

空格位在連接詞 because 後方的子句當中，子句的主詞為第三人稱單數形（the production），空格應填主要動詞，因此可以直接刪除 (C) 和 (D)。因主詞與動詞的數應一致，所以答案為 (B)。

• **feature** 由……主演

湯普森藝廊將自8月1日起延長營業時間。

**字彙**
extend 延長
operation 營業；運轉

**117** The Thompson Art Gallery will extend its hours of operation _____ on August 1.

(A) will begin　　　　　(B) has begun
(C) beginner　　　　　(D) beginning*

(D) beginning 用來表示從特定時間點開始的狀況。用分詞 beginning 是因為空格前方省略了 which are。starting 和 effective 也有相同的用法，亦可填入空格。

- beginner 初學者

---

唐諾·馬哈尼負責將用品分發給所有格雷迪水管維修公司的水管工。

**字彙**
supplies 用品
plumber 水管工

**118** Donald Mahoney is in charge of the supplies _____ to all plumbers working for Grady Pipe Repairs.

(A) distribute　　　　　(B) distribution*
(C) distributes　　　　　(D) is distributed

根據句意，the supplies _____ 為片語「be in charge of」的受詞，因此答案應為名詞 (B)，supplies 和 distribution 可以組合為複合名詞。

- distribute (v.) 分發，分配　　distribution (n.) 分發，分配

* 高難度 & 高頻率的複合名詞：
attendance record 出勤紀錄　　budget constraints 預算限制
building modification 大樓裝修　　contingency plan 緊急應變計畫
business correspondence 商業書信　　earnings growth 利益成長
consumer awareness 消費者意識　　installment payment 分期付款
maternity leave 產假　　media coverage 媒體報導　　utility bill 水電費
power failure 停電　　savings plan 儲蓄計畫

---

由於這位執行長去年秋天在《今日商業雜誌》的訪談中表達了個人觀點，而以頗具雄心而聞名。

**字彙**
be known for 以……聞名
ambitious
雄心勃勃的，具抱負的

**119** The CEO is known for being ambitious as he expressed his _____ in an interview with *Today Business Magazine* last fall.

(A) interferences　　　　　(B) prevention
(C) views*　　　　　(D) exchange

根據句意，應為「表達看法」，故選項 (C) 正確。

- interference 干涉　　prevention 預防　　view 觀點　　exchange 交換

* 常與 express 一起使用的動詞：
express concern about 表達關心／擔憂
express fears/doubts/reservations 表達恐懼／懷疑／存疑
express interest/surprise/regret 表示興趣／驚訝／後悔

---

《財務月刊》的創刊編輯，安娜·桑切斯很快就贏得了金融界中幾乎所有人的敬重。

**字彙**
found 創立
financial 金融的
practically 幾乎，差不多

**120** Anna Sanchez, founding editor of *Financial Monthly*, has quickly earned the respect of practically _____ in the financial industry.

(A) everyone*　　　　　(B) anything
(C) whatever　　　　　(D) each other

代名詞 (A) 和 (B) 都可以作為介系詞 of 的受詞，但根據句意，本句應為「受到大家的尊敬」較為適當，因此答案為 (A)。

- whatever 任何事物　　each other 彼此

**121** As stated in the reviews, the theater's new performance was
_____ a big hit.

(A) clear　　　　　　　(B) clearly*
(C) clearer　　　　　　(D) clearing

本句主詞（the . . . performance）＋ be 動詞（was）＋主詞補語（a big hit）為結構完整的 S ＋ V ＋ SC 句型，因此空格中應填入副詞 (B)，用來修飾 be 動詞 was。

以前考題中曾出現過 It is predominantly through . . . 表「主要是藉由……」，同樣是以副詞修飾 be 動詞。

• **clear** 明顯的　　**clearly** 明顯地

如評論中所述，劇院的新表演顯然大受歡迎。

**字彙**
**performance** 表演

---

**122** _____ our hiring committee reads all the resumes, we will compile a list of 20 candidates to invite in for interviews.

(A) Compared to　　　(B) As soon as*
(C) So that　　　　　　(D) Not only

根據句意，順序應為委員會看完履歷表後，才編製應徵者名單，因此 (B) 為最適當的連接詞。在此補充，(D) 的意思為「不僅……而且……」，通常會寫成 not only . . . (but) also 的結構。

• **compared to** 相較於……　　**as soon as** 一……就……　　**so that** 為了

我們的招聘委員會一看完所有履歷表，就會編製出一份 20 位應徵者的名單，邀請參加面試。

**字彙**
**hiring** 召募
**committee** 委員會
**compile** 編製，彙編
**candidate** 應徵者；候選人

---

**123** The concert was a huge success and drew a crowd of over 5,000 to Moose Park and Recreation Center, _____ the cold weather.

(A) while　　　　　　(B) whereas
(C) notwithstanding*　(D) moreover

本句應為「儘管天氣寒冷，這場音樂會仍然非常成功」語意上較為適當。(A)、(B)、(C) 皆可以考慮，但是 (A) 和 (B) 為連接詞，後方必須連接「主詞＋動詞」，而空格後方為名詞片語 the cold weather，因此應選擇介系詞 (C) 作為答案。

\* 高難度介系詞：
**excluding** 不包括　　**regarding (= about, concerning)** 關於
**following** 在……之後　　**barring** 除……之外　　**considering** 考慮
**prior to (= before)** 先前的　　**according to** 根據　　**based on** 根據
**in terms of** 就……而言　　**in/with regard to** 關於　　**regardless of** 不管

儘管天氣寒冷，這場音樂會仍然非常成功，吸引了超過 5,000 名的群眾到麋鹿公園暨休閒活動中心觀賞。

**字彙**
**huge** 巨大的
**draw** 吸引

---

**124** The research staff at Pullford Pharmaceuticals will be using the conference room as its office _____ the renovation period.

(A) opposite　　　　　(B) beside
(C) during*　　　　　(D) with

period 用來表示「期間」，為本題的重要解題線索。本句應為在整修「期間」，把會議室當作辦公室使用，語意上較為適當，因此答案為 (C)。請務必熟記 during 的後方要接表「期間」的名詞，for 的用法則為 for ＋數詞＋表單位的名詞，表示「達多久時間」。

• **opposite** 相反的；對面的　　**beside** 在……旁邊
\* 以介系詞表示時間的用法：
**for** ＋數字＋名詞（**for three years**）
**during** ＋名詞（**during the vacation**）
**since** ＋時間點（**since 1998**）

寶福德製藥廠的研究同仁將於整修期間，把會議室當作辦公室使用。

**字彙**
**research** 研究
**pharmaceutical** 製藥公司
**renovation** 整修

如公司網頁所述，客戶如欲在到期日前取消會員資格，必須付一筆費用。

**字彙**
state 說明，陳述
expire 到期

**125** As stated on the company's website, clients who wish to cancel their membership _____ it expires must pay a fee.

(A) before*　　　　　　(B) how
(C) why　　　　　　　(D) either

從 who 到 expires 為關係代名詞所引導的子句，用來修飾 clients。空格後方為另一個子句：主詞（it）＋動詞（expires），因此空格應填入連接詞 (A)，來引導子句。

- either 兩者之一

---

雖然該職務說明與其他家公司類似，但這份工作的薪資卻高出許多。

**字彙**
description 說明，描述
salary 薪水

**126** Although the job description is _____ to those at other firms, this job has a much higher salary.

(A) similar*　　　　　　(B) likable
(C) reflected　　　　　　(D) considerate

本題只要知道「similar ＋ to ＋名詞」的意思為「和……類似」，就可以輕鬆解題。

- similar 類似的　likable 可愛的　reflected 反射的
  considerate 體貼的
* be 動詞＋形容詞＋ to ＋名詞：
be accessible to ＋人 可用的；可取得的　be adjacent to 臨近的
be attractive to ＋人 對人有吸引力的　be available to ＋人 可取得的
be close to 接近的　be equivalent to 等同的
be committed to = be dedicated to = be devoted to 致力於
be identical to 相同的　be native to ＋區域 原產於
be subject to (laws/rules) 視法律／法規而定
be subject to approval 取決於（某人）同意／批准

---

為確保遵守安全規定，僅限資深員工才能進入研究室。

**字彙**
access 取得；進入
laboratory 實驗室
limit 限制
senior 資深的
ensure 確保，保證
safety 安全性
regulation 規定

**127** Access to the research laboratory will be limited to senior employees to ensure _____ with all safety regulations.

(A) activation　　　　　　(B) fulfillment
(C) compliance*　　　　　(D) indication

本題的解題線索為 regulations，意思是「規定，規章」，因此答案應為表示「遵守」規則的名詞 compliance，故答案為 (C)。在此補充，意思同為「遵守；順從」的片語還有 be in compliance with、be compliant with 與 comply with，也請務必熟記。

- activation 活化　fulfillment 實現　compliance 遵守；順從
  indication 暗示

**128** If the window had been broken during installation, Riley's Building Supplies _____ to replace it at no charge.

(A) would have offered*     (B) has offered

(C) is being offered        (D) would have been offered

本句屬於與過去事實相反的假設語氣，句型為：「If ＋主詞＋ had ＋ p.p. ，主詞＋ would/should/could ＋ have ＋ p.p.」，空格中可以選擇填入 (A) 或 (D)。但是由於萊立建材 (Riley's Building Supplies) 即為負責更換的「執行者」，所以答案應為主動語態的 (A)。

* 與現在事實相反的假設語氣
If ＋主詞＋動詞過去式，主詞＋ would/should/could/might ＋原形動詞
* 與過去事實相反的假設語氣
If ＋主詞＋ had ＋ p.p. ，主詞＋ would/should/could/might ＋ have ＋ p.p.

如果窗戶在安裝期間損壞，萊立建材會提供免費更換。

字彙
**installation** 安裝
**replace** 更換
**at no charge** 免費

---

**129** Prior to reviewing _____, the town council agreed to three proposals in principle.

(A) specifics*           (B) specify

(C) specific            (D) specifically

空格為及物動詞 review 的受詞，因此可以填入名詞 (A)。

• **specifics** 細節    **specify** 詳細說明    **specific** 具體的，明確的
**specifically** 具體地

在具體審查細節前，市議會原則上同意這三個提案。

字彙
**prior to . . .** 在……之前
**council** 地方議會
**principle** 原則

---

**130** Administrators at the Ben Phillips Hospital maintain that _____ to the facility will make many medical procedures more efficient.

(A) continuations       (B) increments

(C) deviations         (D) enhancements*

根據句意，「增加效率」的原因應為「提升設施」較為適當，因此空格中應填入 (D)，語意上較為完整。

• **continuation** 連續    **increment** （金錢的）增加    **deviation** 誤差
**enhancement** 提升
* 常與介系詞 to 搭配使用的名詞：
**solution/exposure/response/trip/answer/visit/approach/access ＋ to ＋名詞**

班・菲利浦醫院管理人堅持設備的提升，將使許多醫療程序更有效率。

字彙
**administrator** 管理人
**maintain** 堅持；維持
**facility** 設備
**medical** 醫療的
**procedure** 程序，步驟
**efficient** 有效率的

**nearly** 幾乎
**construction** 建設
**be located on** 位於……
**majestic** 壯麗的；雄偉的
**waterfront** 濱水區，水邊地
**capacity** 容量
**up to** 高達……
**currently** 目前地；現今
**association** 協會
**accommodate** 容納
**performance** 表演；成果

Questions 131-134 refer to the following article.

March 3—After nearly three years of planning, the largest stadium in Harpville will begin construction. The Expo Stadium will be located on Harpville's majestic waterfront and will have a capacity of up to ten thousand seats. ___131___. The project is expected to take three years to complete. It will be located amongst several other new developments currently ___132___ on the waterfront. According to Marshal Thomas, president of the Harpville Sports Association, the new stadium is a ___133___. "We're going to need a large stadium to accommodate our growing sports clubs," Mr. Thomas said. "___134___, we'll also be able to use the stadium for concerts and circus performances."

---

3月3日──經過將近三年的籌劃，哈普維爾最大的體育場即將動工。世博體育場將設於哈普維爾壯麗的海濱，可容量10,000個座位。同時，還有超過100個媒體採訪室，每間可容納10人之多。這項工程預計花三年的時間完工，即將座落於其他目前正在濱海區興建的新建築區中。根據哈普維爾運動協會理事長馬歇爾‧湯瑪士表示，新體育場絕對是必要之建設。「我們需要一座大型體育場來容納逐漸增加的運動社團。」湯瑪士先生說，「另一方面，我們也能把體育場用在音樂會和馬戲團表演上。」

---

**131**

(A) 開發業者不確定要花多久時間才能完成這項工程。

(B) 體育場將從濱海區搬到市郊。

(C) 同時，還有超過100個媒體採訪室，每間可容納10人之多。

(D) 市長拒絕為市區開發計畫提供資金，就產生了延誤。

(A) Developers are unsure how long it will take to complete the project.

(B) The stadium will be moved from the waterfront to the outskirts of the city.

(C) It will also include over 100 press viewing rooms that hold up to ten people each.*

(D) Delays occurred when the mayor refused to fund the city's development plans.

空格在施工規模（ten thousand seats）和施工時間（three years to complete）之間，最適合填入的句子為「針對體育場建設進一步的說明」，故 (C) 正確。

- **unsure** 不確定　**outskirts** 市郊，郊區　**include** 包括
  **press** 媒體，新聞界　**hold** 容納　**delay** 延遲　**occur** 發生
  **mayor** 市長　**refuse** 拒絕　**fund** 提供資金

**132** (A) to construct
(B) are constructing
(C) were constructed
(D) being constructed*

本句的動詞部分已有 **will be located**，因此可以優先刪除含動詞部分的 (B) 和 (C)。空格應用來作為 **developments** 的後位修飾，因此答案為 (D)，指「正被建設的」新建築區。原本的句子應為 **developments that are being constructed**，當中省略了 **that are**。

- **construct** 興建

---

**133** (A) necessity*
(B) nuisance
(C) risk
(D) bargain

空格後方為「為我們需要」（**We're going to need**），由此可以推測出答案為 (A)。

- **necessity** 必需品　**nuisance** 麻煩事　**risk** 風險　**bargain** 便宜貨

---

**134** (A) On the other hand*
(B) In other words
(C) In the first place
(D) As a result

根據文意，空格前方為需要體育場的主因，空格後方則補充「其他的」原因，因此表示「另一方面」的 (A) 為最適當的答案。

- **on the other hand** 另一方面　**in other words** 換句話說
  **in the first place** 起初　**as a result** 因此

**Questions 135-138 refer to the following press release.**

Meredith Hobson, CEO and founder of Hobson Dining, Trenton's oldest family dining franchise, announced that she ____ 135. $6,500 towards renovations to the Jasper Community Center in the city's downtown region. The funds were generated from ticket sales for a banquet held last Friday evening at her ____ 136. Ms. Hobson will present the management staff of the center with a check at a special ceremony scheduled to take place tomorrow afternoon at 2:00. ____ 137. the past 25 years, Ms. Hobson has organized a number of successful fund-raising events for community services and charities. ____ 138.

---

翠登最早的家庭式餐飲加盟連鎖店——霍布森餐飲，其創辦人兼執行長梅雷迪斯·霍布森宣布，她將為市中心賈斯伯社區活動中心的整修工程捐贈 6,500 元。這筆款項來自上週五晚上在其餐館所舉辦的晚宴售票所得。霍布森女士將在預定於明天下午 2:00 所舉辦的特別典禮上將支票贈送給中心的管理人員。在過去的 25 年間來，霍布森女士已經為社區服務與慈善團體籌辦了多場成功的募款活動。但無疑地，上週五的活動是最成功的一場。

---

**135** (A) will donate*
(B) donated
(C) might donate
(D) donating

空格位在動詞的部分，因此無法填入 (D)。由文章中段「Ms. Hobson will present the management staff of the center with a check . . .」，說明了霍布森女士「未來」的動作，因此答案應為表未來式的 (A)。

• **donate** 捐贈

**136** (A) gallery
(B) hotel
(C) academy
(D) restaurant*

第一句提到了公司名稱（Meredith Hobson, CEO and founder of Hobson Dining）和公司性質（Trenton's oldest family dining franchise），由此可以得知應和餐飲有關，答案為 (D)。

• **gallery** 藝廊　**hotel** 飯店　**academy** 學院

---

**137** (A) Despite
(B) Over*
(C) Between
(D) Beneath

本句文意應為過去 25 年「間」的事蹟，因此空格中最適合填入表示「在……期間」的介系詞 (B)。

• **despite** 儘管……　**beneath** 在……下方

---

**138** (A) The Jasper Community Center has programs for both children and adults.
(B) The opening ceremony at the center will be done by 2:30 P.M.
(C) However, last Friday's event was, without a doubt, her most successful one.*
(D) Ms. Hobson plans to open a branch in uptown Trenton sometime next year.

前面的句子提到「成功募資的活動」，因此根據文意，後方應填入 (C)，以 one 代替「其中一場的募資活動」，補充說明上週五那場是「過去最成功的活動」，最為適當。

• **without a doubt** 毫無疑問地　**branch** 分店

**(A)** 賈斯伯社區活動中心有針對小孩和大人的課程。
**(B)** 中心的開幕典禮將於下午 **2:30** 結束。
**(C)** 但無疑地，上週五的活動是最成功的一場。
**(D)** 霍布森女士計畫於明年某個時間在翠登上城開設分店。

## 字彙

**monthly** 每月的
**commence** 開始
**purpose** 目的
**advantage** 優點
**disadvantage** 缺點
**shipping** 運輸，運輸業
**debate** 討論；辯論
**possible** 可能的
**stress** 強調
**further** 提升，促進
**growth** 成長
**ship** 運送
**electronics** 電子產品
**distance** 距離
**harbor** 碼頭
**costly** 昂貴的
**solution** 解決方案
**reach** 達到
**present** 報告；呈現

Questions 139-142 refer to the following meeting summary.

Our monthly meeting commenced at 4:30 P.M. The meeting's purpose was to discuss the advantages and disadvantages of ‾‾‾‾‾. 139. LGQ International Shipping. Max Powel led the debate on the possible move by stressing the importance of furthering LGQ's current growth patterns. He explained that LGQ has grown to be one of the most successful ‾‾‾‾‾ and that it ships the largest 140. number of electronics in the country.

‾‾‾‾‾. According to recent reports, the traveling distance from the 141. closest harbor is becoming costly ‾‾‾‾‾ LGQ begins to grow. Staff 142. members discussed some possible solutions, but a final decision was not reached. Mr. Powel will do some more research and present his findings at the next meeting.

---

我們的月會在下午 4:30 開始。這個會議的目的是為了討論 LGQ 國際貨運公司遷址的優缺點。麥克斯·鮑威爾以著眼於提升 LGQ 目前成長模式的重要性，帶領大家討論遷址的可能性。他解釋 LGQ 已經成長為最成功的分銷商之一，同時也配送全國最大量的電子產品。

鮑威爾先生也大致說明了 LGQ 因成長而正在經歷的挑戰。根據最近的報告顯示，就在 LGQ 開始成長時，往來最近港口的成本也變高了。員工們討論了一些可能的解決方案，但仍未達成最後決議。鮑威爾先生將進行更多研究，並於下次會議中報告他的研究結果。

---

**139**　(A) acquiring
(B) joining
(C) promoting
(D) relocating*

後方句子接著提到「討論遷址的可能性（possible move）」，根據文意，本句的重點應為「搬遷」的優缺點，語意上較為連貫，因此答案為 (D)。

• **acquire** 取得　**promote** 宣傳　**relocate** 搬遷

**140**

(A) distribute
(B) distributing
(C) distributors*
(D) distributes

空格是形容詞 successful 修飾的對象，因此要填入名詞，故 (C) 正確。

• **distribute** 分發　　**distributor** 分銷商

---

**141**

(A) Mr. Powel also outlined the challenges LGQ is experiencing as a result of its growth.*
(B) The CEO then proceeded to discuss the advantages of the new facilities.
(C) Next, shareholders were invited to conduct a vote to decide the date.
(D) Mr. Powel directed employees to consider how operations would be conducted.

**(A)** 鮑威爾先生也大致說明了 **LGQ** 因成長而正在經歷的挑戰。
**(B)** 執行長接著討論了新設施的優點。
**(C)** 接下來，股東受邀進行投票決定日期。
**(D)** 鮑威爾先生指示員工思考要如何進行運作。

空格前段的句子提到「LGQ 已經成長為最成功的分銷商之一」；後方則表示「LGQ 成長伴隨而來的運輸成本問題」，(A) 句中的 challenges 與 growth 分別呼應到前後文的成長與成本，因此 (A) 最為適當答案。

• **outline** 概述　　**challenge** 挑戰　　**experience** 經歷
**as a result of** 由於……　　**proceed** 進行　　**facilities** 設備
**shareholder** 股東　　**invite** 邀請　　**conduct** 進行　　**vote** 投票
**direct** 指示　　**consider** 思考　　**operation** 運轉，操作

---

**142**

(A) now
(B) why
(C) just as*
(D) ever since

本句應為「就在 LGQ 開始成長時，往來最近港口的成本也變高了」，最符合文意，因此 (C) just as（就當，就在）為最合適的答案。在此補充，若空格中填入 ever since（自從），後方必須要連接過去式。

字彙
inquire 詢問
be scheduled to 預定
feel free to
無須拘束做（某事）
sincerely 由衷地
apologize for
為……道歉，認錯
inconvenience 不便
method 方法
affordable 負擔得起的
situation 狀況
discourage 使卻步；使沮喪
cosmetics 化妝品

**Questions 143-146 refer to the following e-mail.**

From: tina@lindcosmetics.com
To: mia@mymailnow.com
Date: September 8
Subject: Order 445009

Dear Ms. Kramar,

Thank you for writing to inquire about your order. According to our records, you ordered one tube of Lind SPF 50 Sunscreen, one bottle of Lind 500 Hand Cream, and two bottles of Lind Ultrashine Shampoo from our website on September 1. Your products were scheduled to arrive on September 5. I was surprised to hear that you have not received ___143___.

___144___. According to their schedule, your products will arrive on September 10. If your order is not delivered by that day, feel free ___145___ us again.

I sincerely apologize for this inconvenience. Our shipping methods are usually fast and affordable. This situation is quite ___146___. I hope it will not discourage you from shopping at Lind Cosmetics.

Thank you,

Tina Speller
Lind Cosmetics

----------------------------------------

寄件者：tina@lindcosmetics.com
收件者：mia@mymailnow.com
日期：9月8日
主旨：訂單445009

親愛的克拉瑪女士，

感謝您來信詢問訂單狀況。根據我們的紀錄顯示，您在9月1日於本公司網站訂購了一條林德SPF50防曬乳，一瓶林德500護手霜，兩瓶超亮澤洗髮精。您的商品預定在9月5日送達。知道您還未收到商品，讓我深感驚訝。

我已經代您聯絡了運送公司。根據他們的行程表，您的商品將於9月10日送達。如果您所訂購的東西到那天仍未送抵，可以再次與我們聯繫。

本人衷心地為這次的不便致歉。本公司的配送方式通常快速又便宜。這次的狀況相當特殊，希望不會因此讓您對林德化妝品卻步。

感謝您

林德化妝品
蒂娜·史伯樂

**143**

(A) it
(B) one
(C) them*
(D) some

當選項皆為代名詞時，請從前方句子中找出所代指的東西為何。由前句可以得知代名詞所指為為複數形名詞 products，因此答案為 (C)。

---

**144**

(A) We would like to invite you to visit our store.
(B) Please leave a review on our website.
(C) We are currently sold out of that particular product.
(D) I have contacted the shipping company on your behalf.*

空格後方的內容為「查詢後的到貨行程表」(their schedule)，根據文意 their 應指的是插入句中的 the shipping company，因此填入 (D) 最為適當。

- **leave** 留下　**contact** 聯絡　**on (one's) behalf** 代表某人

(A) 我們想邀請您光臨本店。
(B) 請在本公司網站上留下評論。
(C) 這個特定商品目前已售完。
(D) 我已經代您聯絡了運送公司。

---

**145**

(A) contacted
(B) to contact*
(C) contacting
(D) contact

只要知道慣用片語 feel free to ＋原形動詞，意思為「無須拘束做（某事）」，就能輕鬆找出答案為 (B)。在此補充，本句也可以替換成 don't hesitate to ＋原形動詞，請務必熟記。

---

**146**

(A) similar
(B) exciting
(C) unusual*
(D) welcome

此電郵針對延遲配送商品道歉，前方句子提到「配送方式通常 (usually) 快速又便宜」，最能與此內容形成對比的為選項 (C)。

- **similar** 相似的　**unusual** 特殊的，不尋常的

Questions 147-148 refer to the following advertisement.

| Item for Sale | Price | Location |
|---|---|---|
| Model A7000 | $450 | Los Angeles, CA |
| Flamesburg Barbecue | | |

**Item Description:**

147 (D) Purchased new three years ago. Original cost was $700 and came with a two-year warranty.

Grill pieces are charred. 147 (B) Buyer can purchase new ones on the Flamesburg website.

Exterior is in great condition. (148 Pictures available upon request)

147 (C) Price is negotiable. Willing to deliver anywhere in the Los Angeles area.

E-mail rjohnson@mail.com if you have any questions.

--------------------------------------------------------------------

| 商品待售 | 價格 | 地點 |
|---|---|---|
| 火焰鎮烤肉架型號 A7000 | 450 元 | 加州洛杉磯 |

商品說明：

三年前全新購入。原價 700 元，附兩年保固。

烤架組件已燒焦。買方可於火焰鎮網站上購買新品。

外觀狀況良好（可應要求提供照片）。

價錢可議。可配送洛杉磯地區各處。

若有疑問，可寄電子郵件至 rjohnson@mail.com。

---

下列何者與烤肉架無關？

(A) 以原始的箱子包裝。
(B) 需要新零件。
(C) 價格未定。
(D) 已逾保固期。

**147** What is NOT indicated about the barbecue?

(A) It comes in the original box.*
(B) It needs new parts.
(C) Its price is not set.
(D) Its warranty has expired.

解題時，請將烤肉架的具體說明（Item Description），對照各選項的內容，再刪除文章中提及的選項。(D) 出現在前半部說明當中「Purchased new three years ago. Original cost was $700 and came with a two-year warranty.」。(B) 出現在「Buyer can purchase new ones (= grill pieces) on the Flamesburg website.」；可由「Price is negotiable.」確認 (C)，因此本題的答案為 (D)。

\* 答案改寫：negotiable → not set

---

賣方願意做什麼事？

(A) 保留商品一個月
(B) 提供商品使用說明
(C) 配送至全國各地
(D) 提供照片給可能的買方

**148** What is the seller willing to do?

(A) Reserve the item for up to a month
(B) Provide instructions on how to use the item
(C) Deliver anywhere in the country
(D) Send photographs to potential buyers*

閱讀文章時，請特別留意「賣家的想法」。文章中提到：「Pictures available upon request」，表示如有需要，賣家可以提供照片作為參考，因此 (D) 為最適當的答案。

**Questions 149-150 refer to the following notice.**

[149] We are delighted to announce that Cordelia Winters has joined IPM Talent as an associate agent. Ms. Winters is a graduate of Roden University's public relations program. While studying at Roden, she founded the university's first student-run magazine. Following graduation, she completed an internship at UV Media and Talent, a prestigious agency that represents a wide variety of musicians, authors, professional athletes, and actors. Ms. Winters has undergone exceptional training and will be a great asset to our growing team of agents. [150] Please join us in conference room B tomorrow morning at 10:00 A.M. to welcome her to the team.

----

我們很高興宣布寇蒂莉亞‧溫特斯加入 IPM 演藝經紀公司，成為合夥經紀人。溫特斯女士畢業自羅丹大學公共關係學程。在羅丹就學時，她就創辦了該大學第一本由學生主辦的雜誌。畢業後，她在 UV 媒體暨演藝經紀公司實習，那是一家代理各方人才——音樂家、作家、職業運動員和演員的知名經紀公司。溫特斯女士受過優秀的訓練，將成為我們茁壯中的經紀團隊的一大資產。請於明天上午 10 點到 B 會議室一同歡迎她的加入。

---

**149** Where is the notice most likely posted?

(A) In an advertising firm
(B) In a university
(C) In a music studio
(D) In a talent agency*

由第一句「We are delighted to announce that Cordelia Winters has joined IPM Talent as an associate agent.」，可以得知答案為 (D)。

這個公告最可能出現在哪裡？
(A) 廣告公司
(B) 大學
(C) 錄音室
(D) 演藝經紀公司

---

**150** What are employees invited to do tomorrow?

(A) Participate in a conference
(B) Greet a new employee*
(C) Visit a competitor
(D) Meet some new clients

請特別留意題目關鍵時間點 tomorrow。通知最後一句要求明天到 B 會議室一同歡迎新進員工（Please join us in conference room B tomorrow morning at 10:00 A.M. to welcome her to the team.），因此答案應為 (B)。

＊答案改寫：welcome → greet

員工受邀明天要做何事？
(A) 參加會議
(B) 歡迎新同事
(C) 拜訪競爭對手
(D) 與新客戶見面

字彙
garage 車庫
behind schedule 進度落後
estimate 估計
take into account
將……列入考量
crew 工作人員

Questions 151-152 refer to the following text message chain.

**Tim Peterson [11:03 A.M.]**
Hey, Amanda. Can you update me on the Sampson Lane job?

**Amanda Ray [11:10 A.M.]**
We've cleared out the main floor and the garage. We're just starting on the second floor of the house now.

**Tim Peterson [11:12 A.M.]**
Is that all? [152] What time do you think you'll be done? [151] We have a move scheduled for 3:00 P.M.

**Amanda Ray [11:15 A.M.]**
We're behind schedule. When the estimate was done, it didn't take into account the old furniture in the garage.

**Tim Peterson [11:20 A.M.]**
Really? Who did the estimate?

**Amanda Ray [11:21 A.M.]**
Matthew did before he went on vacation.

**Tim Peterson [11:23 A.M.]**
OK. Contact me at 1:00 P.M. with a progress report. I'll decide then if I need to call in another crew for the afternoon job.

SEND

*Type your message . . .*

-------------------------------------------------------------------

**提姆・彼得森　　[上午 11:03]**
嗨，阿曼達。妳可以跟我報告桑普森・蘭恩那裡的最新工作進度嗎？

**阿曼達・瑞　　[上午 11:10]**
我們已經清空主層樓和車庫。現在才剛開始屋子的二樓部分。

**提姆・彼得森　　[上午 11:12]**
就這樣？你們認為什麼時候可以做完？我們在下午三點還有安排另一家要搬的。

**阿曼達・瑞　　[上午 11:15]**
我們進度落後。當初估算時，沒有考慮到車庫裡的舊家具。

**提姆・彼得森　　[上午 11:20]**
真的嗎？是誰做的估算。

**阿曼達・瑞　　[上午 11:21]**
馬修在休假前做的。

**提姆・彼得森　　[上午 11:23]**
好。下午一點時再跟我報告進度。到時候，我會決定要不要再找一組人幫忙下午的工作。

送出

輸入您的訊息……

**151** What type of business does Ms. Ray work for?

(A) A real estate agency
(B) A furniture store
(C) A moving company*
(D) A truck rental service

提姆·彼得森於上午 11 點 12 分傳送的訊息中寫道:「We have a move scheduled for 3:00 P.M.」。由訊息內容可以推測出收發這封訊息的人,可能都在與「搬家」有關的公司內工作,因此答案為 (C)。

瑞女士在哪個行業服務?

(A) 不動產仲介
(B) 家具店
(C) 搬家公司
(D) 卡車租賃服務

字彙
**real estate** 不動產
**rental** 租賃

**152** At 11:12, what does Mr. Peterson mean when he says "Is that all"?

(A) He wants to know the address of a house.
(B) He thinks the employees are working slowly.*
(C) He is surprised because the price is very cheap.
(D) He wants to confirm that everything is loaded on the truck.

題目句後方詢問大概幾點可以完成(What time do you think you'll be done?),屬於催促的口氣,因此 (B) 為最適當的答案。

11:12時,彼得森先生說的「就這樣?」是什麼意思?

(A) 他想知道房子的地址。
(B) 他認為員工工作進度緩慢。
(C) 他很驚訝,因為價格很便宜。
(D) 他想確認所有東西都裝上卡車了。

字彙
**load** 裝載

字彙
advanced 提前的
routine 例行的
cover 承保
provider 提供者
offset 補償
reduce 減少，降低
enclosed 附上的
affected 受影響的
select 特定的
prior 先前的
inquire 詢問

Questions 153-154 refer to the following letter.

Rutherford Eye Clinic
54 Rutherford Avenue
Los Angeles, California
14 March
Katrina Serova
123 Colonel Lane
Los Angeles, California

Dear Ms. Serova,

[153] It is important to us here at Rutherford Eye Clinic that all our customers receive advanced notice of changes to our policies. As of August 1, all routine yearly eye exams will no longer be covered by most major insurance providers. To help offset the cost, we are reducing our fees by $15 per exam. Please see the enclosed list of affected insurance providers.

[154] In some select cases, we are willing to provide eye exams to children free of charge should your family have a history of prior exams with us. Please contact our billing manager Maggie Wilson at 445-987-0023 to inquire about this service or if you have any questions.

Sincerely,

Dr. Nadia Fortuni
Rutherford Eye Clinic

------------------------------------------------------------

拉賽福眼科診所
加州洛杉磯拉賽福大道 54 號

3 月 14 日

卡崔娜·薩若娃
加州洛杉磯上校巷 123 號

親愛的薩諾娃女士，

對拉賽福眼科診所來說，讓所有客戶提前收到本診所規定異動的通知，是非常重要的。自 8 月 1 日起，大多數主要的保險公司將不再給付所有年度例行視力檢查。為了補償這筆費用，本診所的每項檢查將減少 15 元的費用。請查看隨信附上受影響的保險公司名單。

在部分特定狀況下，如果您的家人曾在本診所檢查過，我們很樂意免費提供兒童視力檢查。若有任何問題，請來電 445-987-0023 與帳務管理員梅姬·威爾森洽詢該服務。

拉賽福眼科診所
娜迪亞·佛特尼醫師敬上

**153** Why was the letter sent to Ms. Serova?

(A) To announce a billing change*
(B) To advertise a new service
(C) To confirm an appointment
(D) To inform of a missed exam

通知第一段寫道:「It is important to us here at Rutherford Eye Clinic that all our customers receive advanced notice of changes to our policies.」,由此可以推測出應為政策變更相關的內容。第一段對此補充說明,因為大多數保險公司將不再給付所有年度例行視力檢查,該診所為受到影響的客戶,提供費用折扣作為補償,因此答案為 (A)。

這封信為什麼會寄給薩諾娃女士?

(A) 為了通知收費異動
(B) 為了宣傳新服務項目
(C) 為了確認預約
(D) 為了通知未做的檢查

字彙
appointment 預約

---

**154** What is indicated about Rutherford Eye Clinic?

(A) It wants to hire new staff members.
(B) It has extended its hours of operation.
(C) It caters to clients from all around the world.
(D) It will offer free exams to certain customers.*

第二段提到特定狀況下,只要孩童的家人先前曾在診所內做過檢查,孩童就能享有免費視力檢查。(In some select cases, we are willing to provide eye exams to children free of charge should your family have a history of prior exams with us.),因此 (D) 為最適當的答案。

* 答案改寫:provide → offer
　　　　　 free of charge → free

下列何者與拉賽福眼科診所有關?

(A) 它想聘僱新員工。
(B) 它延長了營業時間。
(C) 它服務了來自全世界各地的客戶。
(D) 它為特定客戶提供免費服務。

字彙
extend 延長
cater to 提供……服務

Questions 155-157 refer to the following article.

# Westpoint Shopping Mall to Begin Construction

By Melanie Rosenberg, Staff Writer

March 23—Yesterday, in a press conference at Mayor Zanga's office downtown, the mayor announced the city's approval of development plans for a new shopping mall. According to the mayor, [157] Westpoint Shopping Mall will be located at Park Road and Wilson Street. --[1]--.

The shopping mall is a joint project between the City of Forks and Windsor Partners, a private development corporation. The mall will include over 200 hundred new stores, 55 restaurants, and a department store. --[2]--. Windsor Partners will be in charge of executing construction and overseeing initial operations.

"The City of Forks has never had a major shopping center," Mr. Johnson of Windsor Partners said in an interview. "By building this state-of-the-art facility, [155] the people of Forks will see an increase in jobs and tourism." --[3]--.

Many retailers have already signed contracts with Windsor Partners to reserve store space in the mall. [156] However, some small business owners have expressed worry that they will lose business once the shopping mall opens. --[4]--. "My store has been in business for two generations," Michelle Stevens of Shoe Blitz said. "My customers are loyal, but I won't be able to compete with shopping mall prices."

-------------------------------------------------------------------

### 西點購物商場動工

撰稿人梅蘭妮·羅森伯格

3月23日——昨天，在贊加市市長市中心辦公室的記者會中，市長宣布市府通過了一個新購物商場的開發計畫。根據市長表示，西點購物商場將座落在公園路與威爾森街上。去年一場大火燒毀了該地的汽車製造廠，空下了那塊地供新開發案使用。

這個購物商場是福克斯市與私人開發企業——溫莎公司的一項合作計畫。這個商場將容納200多間新商店、55家餐廳和一間百貨公司。溫莎公司將負責工程的執行，並監督初期的營運。

「福克斯市一直沒有大型的購物商場，」溫莎公司的強生先生在一場訪談中提到。「藉著建造這座最先進的商場，福克斯的人們也會看到工作機會與觀光業的提升。」

許多零售業者已經和溫莎公司簽約，以保留商場中的店面。但是部分小型企業主也表達了商場一旦開幕，他們就會沒生意可做的憂慮。「我的店面已經經營了兩代，」巴利茲鞋店的蜜雪兒·史蒂文斯說，「我的顧客都很忠實，但還是敵不過購物商場的價格。」

**155** What does Windsor Partners hope to attract to Forks?

(A) Foreign students
(B) A supermarket
(C) More tourists*
(D) New small businesses

在第三段採訪中，提到了關鍵字溫莎公司的期望（the people of Forks will see an increase in jobs and tourism），(C) 選項的 tourists 呼應 tourism，故 (C) 為正確答案。

溫莎公司希望為福克斯市帶來什麼？

(A) 外國學生
(B) 超市
(C) 更多觀光客
(D) 新小型企業

字彙
attract 吸引

**156** Who most likely is Michelle Stevens?

(A) A newspaper reporter
(B) A retail store owner*
(C) A city official
(D) A property developer

閱讀文章時，請特別留意關鍵人名蜜雪兒・史蒂文斯。第四段中提到了小型企業主的擔憂（However, some small business owners have expressed worry that they will lose business once the shopping mall opens.），緊接著就是鞋店店主史蒂文斯小姐的採訪內容，因此答案為 (B)。

蜜雪兒・史蒂文斯最有可能是誰？

(A) 報紙記者
(B) 零售店老闆
(C) 市府官員
(D) 土地開發業者

字彙
property 地產

**157** In which of the positions marked [1], [2], [3], and [4] does the following sentence best belong?

"Last year, a fire consumed the auto factory located there, leaving the site open to new development."

(A) [1]*
(B) [2]
(C) [3]
(D) [4]

本插入句表示「選擇在此空地施工的理由」。文章第一段中先說明了施工所在位置（Westpoint Shopping Mall will be located at Park Road and Wilson Street.），根據文意，本句適合放在商場位置說明的正後方，故 (A) 正確。

下列句子最適合出現在[1]、[2]、[3]、[4]的哪個位置中？
「去年一場大火燒毀了該地的汽車製造廠，空下了那塊地供新開發案使用。」

(A) [1]
(B) [2]
(C) [3]
(D) [4]

字彙
consume 燒毀
auto 汽車

字彙

**installation** 裝置；安裝
**sheet metal** 金屬薄片
**rod** 棒，杆
**revolutionize**
顛覆，徹底改革
**portable** 可攜式
**movement** 行動
**construct** 建造
**abstract** 抽象
**contemporary** 當代的
**originally** 起初地
**donate** 捐贈
**acquire** 購得，取得
**permanent** 永久的
**vibrant** 充滿熱力的

Questions 158-160 refer to the following information.

Simone Decourte
*Kites at Sunset*
Mobile Installation, painted sheet metal and rods
1984

*Kites at Sunset* is one of the most popular mobile installations by Simone Decourte. [158] Decourte revolutionized mobile art in the 1970s by including portable motors to create movement. *Kites at Sunset* is part of a larger series constructed by Decourte between 1970 to 1988. [160 (B)] It has been featured in The Museum of Abstract Art in Milan, The Contemporary Art Gallery in New York City, and The New Art Movement Museum in London. [160 (C)] Decourte originally donated the piece to the University of Montenegro. [159] It remained there for 10 years before being acquired by Maxwell George of the Wilson Fine Art Museum where it has remained as part of our permanent collection. Before her death, [160 (A)] Decourte said *Kites at Sunset* was her "most vibrant piece ever created."

-----------------------------------------------------------------

西蒙・黛珂
《日落風箏》
行動裝置藝術，彩繪金屬片與金屬棒
1984

《日落風箏》是西蒙・黛珂最受歡迎的行動裝置藝術之一。黛珂在 1970 年代時，運用可攜式馬達創造出行動感的方式，徹底顛覆了行動藝術。《日落風箏》是黛珂在 1970 至 1988 年間，所創造的較大型系列中的其中一部分。曾於米蘭的抽象藝術美術館、紐約當代藝術美術館、倫敦新趨勢藝術美術館展出。黛珂原本將《日落風箏》捐給蒙特內哥羅大學，它在那裡展示了十年，最後由威爾森美術館的麥斯威爾・喬治購得，成為本館永久收藏品之一。在她離世前，黛珂曾說《日落風箏》是「她畢生所創作出最充滿熱力的作品」。

**158** How does the information describe Simone Decourte?

(A) She was attentive to details.
(B) She created a lot of art work.
(C) She was an innovative artist.*
(D) She worked for the poor.

文章前半部「Decourte revolutionized mobile art in the 1970s」，表示黛珂於 1970 年代的創作徹底顛覆了行動藝術，因此 (C) 為最適當的答案。

這份資料是如何描述西蒙・黛珂的？

(A) 她很留意細節。
(B) 她創作出很多作品。
(C) 她是個具創新風格的藝術家。
(D) 她為窮人服務。

字彙
attentive 留意的
detail 細節
innovative 創新的

---

**159** Where is the information posted?

(A) At the Museum of Abstract Art
(B) At the Wilson Fine Art Museum*
(C) At the Contemporary Art Gallery
(D) At the New Art Movement Museum

本題必須閱讀數個句子後，才能順利解題。文章的後半部提到《日落風箏》先贈送給蒙特內哥羅大學，十年之後又被威爾森美術館買走（It remained there for 10 years before being acquired by Maxwell George of the Wilson Fine Art Museum），成為我們的（our = Wilson Fine Art Museum）永久收藏（where it has remained as part of our permanent collection），因此答案應為 (B)。

這份資料張貼在那裡？

(A) 抽象藝術美術館
(B) 威爾森美術館
(C) 當代藝術美術館
(D) 新趨勢藝術美術館

---

**160** What is NOT stated about *Kites at Sunset*?

(A) The artist regarded it as one of her best works.
(B) It has traveled to several places.
(C) It was owned by a university.
(D) It took almost two decades to complete the piece.*

解題時，將各選項的內容對照相關段落，並刪除文章中提及的選項。(A) 出現在最後一句「Decourte said *Kites at Sunset* was her "most vibrant piece ever created."」；(B) 可以從文章中段得知「It has been featured in The Museum of Abstract Art in Milan, The Contemporary Art Gallery in New York City, and The New Art Movement Museum in London.」(C) 可由「Decourte originally donated the piece to the University of Montenegro.」確認，因此本題的答案應為 (D)。

下列何者與《日落風箏》無關？

(A) 藝術家視其為她最佳作品之一。
(B) 已經流傳至數處。
(C) 曾被大學取得。
(D) 用了將近20年的時間完成這件作品。

字彙
regard 將……認為

字彙

minor 些微的；次要的
potential 潛在的
assistant 助理
set up 安排
appointment 約會
replace 更改
budget 預算
attendee 出席者
conference call 電話會議
itinerary 行程表
leave for 前往
flight 航班

Questions 161-163 refer to the following e-mail.

**To:** Jan Andrews
**From:** Michael Pitelli
**Date:** March 7
[161] **Subject:** Updates for March 8

Ms. Andrews,

I've had to make a few minor changes to your schedule for tomorrow. Your meeting with potential client Jeff Woods has been canceled. [162] His assistant suggested March 10 as a possible date to meet. [162] Since you're flying back that morning, you're free in the afternoon. Would you like me to set up the appointment? Please have a look at your updated schedule below. [163] I've replaced Mr. Woods's appointment with your budget review. Please let me know if this doesn't work for you.

| Time | Appointment | Attendees |
|------|-------------|-----------|
| 8:30 A.M. | Staff Meeting | Departments A and B |
| 9:45 A.M. | Conference Call with Washington Partners | Jessica Bowers, Tom Park |
| [163] 10:30 A.M. | Budget Review | Ally Strenski |
| 1:30 P.M. | Meeting about Conference Itinerary | Joshua Wilson |
| 4:00 P.M. | Leave for your 7:00 [162] flight to Chicago | |

I have printed out your e-ticket and put it in your company mailbox. Good luck on your trip.

Best,
Michael

------------------------------------------------------------------

收件者：珍‧安德魯斯
寄件者：麥可‧貝特利
日期：3月7日
主旨：3月8日最新情況

安德魯斯女士，

我為您明天的行程表做了些微的異動。您與潛在客戶傑夫‧伍茲的會議已經取消了。他的助理建議3月10日或許可以碰面。由於您當天早上即搭機返回，當天下午有空。您要我敲定那個會面嗎？請看一下以下更新後的行程表。我已經將伍茲先生的會議改成預算審查。請告訴我這樣是否可行。

| 時間 | 會議 | 與會者 |
|------|------|--------|
| 上午 8:30 | 員工會議 | A 與 B 部門 |
| 上午 9:45 | 與華盛頓公司電話會議 | 潔西卡‧鮑爾、湯姆‧帕克 |
| 上午 10:30 | 預算審查 | 艾利‧斯特倫斯基 |
| 下午 1:30 | 討論會議行程 | 約書亞‧威爾森 |
| 下午 4:00 | 前往搭七點的班機至芝加哥 | |

我已經將您的電子機票列印出來，放在公司的信箱了。旅途順利。

麥可敬上

**161** Why was the e-mail sent?

(A) To cancel an appointment next month
(B) To provide a travel itinerary
(C) To update a daily schedule*
(D) To provide documents for a meeting

在電子郵件的主旨，通常就有與目的相關的關鍵線索。由 Subject: Updates for March 8，可以得知答案應為 (C)。

為什麼會寄這封電子郵件？

(A) 要取消下個月的會議
(B) 提供旅遊行程表
(C) 更新日常行程表
(D) 提供會議資料

**162** What will happen on March 10?

(A) Mr. Pitelli will fly to Washington.
(B) Ms. Andrews will attend a conference.
(C) Mr. Woods will hold a budget review.
(D) Ms. Andrews will return from Chicago.*

閱讀文章時，請特別留意題目的關鍵時間點 March 10。在第一段中寫道：「His assistant suggested March 10 as a possible date to meet.」，表示 3 月 10 日可以進行會議，並補充說因為您（郵件收件人：安德魯斯女士）預計於當天早上即搭機返回（Since you're flying back that morning）。且行程表中有前往芝加哥的班機（flight to Chicago），因此答案為 (D)。

3月10日會發生什麼事？

(A) 貝特利先生將飛到華盛頓。
(B) 安德魯斯女士要參加會議。
(C) 伍茲先生將舉行預算審查。
(D) 安德魯斯女士將自芝加哥返回。

字彙
**attend** 參加，出席

**163** At what time was Mr. Woods expected?

(A) 8:35 A.M.
(B) 9:45 A.M.
(C) 10:30 A.M.*
(D) 1:30 P.M.

請務必掌握題目解題關鍵為「伍茲先生原本幾點要參加會議」。第一段中寫道：「I've replaced Mr. Woods's appointment with your budget review.」，表示將會議換成了預算審核。由行程表中的 10:30 A.M. Budget Review，可以得知伍茲先生原本預定的開會時間為 10:30 A.M.，因此答案為 (C)。

伍茲先生原本幾點要到？

(A) 上午8:35
(B) 上午9:45
(C) 上午10:30
(D) 下午1:30

**financial** 金融的；財務的
**regulation** 規定
**ministry** (政府的) 部
**environment** 環境
**introduce** 推行
**reduce** 減少
**consume** 消耗
**in accordance with . . .**
與……一致
**program** 設定
**regulate** 控制，調整
**temperature** 溫度
**maintain** 維持
**lower** 比……低
**reduction** 刪減，降低
**utility bill** 水電費帳單
**management** 管理部
**manually** 手動地
**change (n.)** 異動，改變

Questions 164-167 refer to the following e-mail.

**To:** Employees of Winfred Financial
**From:** Sandra Burns
**Date:** October 24
[164] **Subject:** New regulations

Dear employees,

As you know, the Ministry of Health and Environment has introduced a new set of laws for work places in order to help reduce the amount of energy consumed during the winter months. [164] In accordance with these new regulations, Winfred Financial will program its heating system during the winter. As such, you will not be able to regulate the temperature of your office at any time. The system will heat the building to 19°C on weekdays, which will be maintained throughout the day. It will then lower to 13°C at the end of each day. [166] By following this new regulation, we should see a 10% reduction in the cost of our utility bills.

As some of you work on weekends, management has decided that offices on the 5th floor will be able to control the temperature manually. [167] Weekend workers may request a change of office with their department managers. We simply ask that the rooms not be heated any warmer than 19°C.

Sincerely,

Sandra Burns,
General Manager

--------------------------------------------------------------------

收件者：溫弗雷德金融全體員工
寄件者：珊卓·伯恩斯
日期：10 月 24 日
主旨：新規定

親愛的全體同仁，

正如各位所知道的，為了減少冬季能源的消耗量，衛生暨環境部已經推行了一套適用於辦公場所的新法規。為配合新規定，溫弗雷德金融將於冬季期間設定暖氣系統。確切地來說，就是各位無法隨時調整辦公室的溫度。平日時，這個系統會讓整棟大樓的溫度上升到攝氏 19 度，然後一整天都維持在 19 度的狀況下。到了每天下班時，就會降到攝氏 13 度。依循這個新規定，我們應該會看到電費減少了 10%。

由於部分同仁會在週末時上班，管理部已經決定五樓的辦公室將可手動控溫。週末上班的同仁可向部門主管提出辦公室異動的申請。我們只要求辦公室的溫度不要超過攝氏 19 度即可。

總經理
珊卓·伯恩斯 敬上

**164** What is the purpose of the e-mail?

(A) To announce an upcoming change in the workplace*
(B) To inform employees of a scheduled inspection
(C) To encourage employees to choose new office furniture
(D) To offer managers the opportunity to get a promotion

由電子郵件的主旨，可以推測出郵件應為規定相關的變動內容（Subject: New regulations）。第一段中的「In accordance with these new regulations, Winfred Financial will program its heating system during the winter.」，為針對新規定的具體說明，因此 (A) 為最適當的答案。

這封電子郵件的目的是什麼？

(A) 宣布辦公場所即將出現的變動
(B) 通知員工排定的檢測
(C) 鼓勵員工挑選新辦公家具
(D) 提供主管升遷機會

字彙
workplace 辦公場所
inspection 檢測
opportunity 機會
promotion 晉升

---

**165** The word "maintained" in paragraph 1, line 5, is closest in meaning to

(A) confirmed
(B) repaired
(C) taken
(D) kept*

單字所在句的重點為「維持」整日的溫度，因此答案應為表示「保持」的 kept，故 (D) 正確。

第一段、第五行的「maintained」與下列哪一個意思最接近？

(A) 確認
(B) 修理
(C) 拿取
(D) 保持

字彙
confirm 確認

---

**166** What is mentioned as a benefit of the new regulation?

(A) It will improve employee work efficiency.
(B) It can allow the company to hire more workers.
(C) It will help the company save money.*
(D) It can be applied to public and private companies.

第一段末句寫道：「By following this new regulation, we should see a 10% reduction in the cost of our utility bills.」，表示新規定將能減少電費，因此答案為 (C)。

\* 答案改寫：cost → money

文中提到下列何者是新規定的好處？

(A) 將改善員工工作效率。
(B) 可讓公司聘用更多員工。
(C) 幫公司省錢。
(D) 可適用於公家與私人企業。

字彙
benefit 好處，利益
efficiency 效率
hire 聘用
save 節省
apply to . . . 適用於……

週末上班的員工被建議做什麼事？

**(A)** 直接寄電子郵件給伯恩斯女士
**(B)** 提出更換辦公司的申請
**(C)** 更動工作時間表
**(D)** 週末在家工作

字彙
**alter** 改變

字彙
**spare** 撥出時間
**inventory** 庫存，存貨
**come out** 推出
**carry** 有……出售
**shelf** 架子
**get right on . . .**
馬上開始……

**167** What are employees who work on weekends advised to do?

(A) E-mail Ms. Burns directly
(B) Request office changes*
(C) Alter their work schedules
(D) Work at home on weekends

閱讀文章時，請特別留意題目關鍵字 weekends。第二段中提到了週末加班者適用的特殊條款──可向部門主管提出辦公室異動的申請（Weekend workers may request a change of office with their department managers.），因此答案應為 (B)。

---

Questions 168-171 refer to the following online chat discussion.

**Mary Renold [2:02 P.M.]**
Hello, Ben. 168 Can you spare a moment?
I want to double-check an inventory report with you.

**Ben Jeffries [2:03 P.M.]**
No problem.

**Mary Renold [2:04 P.M.]**
According to the report, 170 we only have two A75 Canpro notebooks left. We've been selling a lot of that model lately. Should I order more?

**Ben Jeffries [2:06 P.M.]**
That's not necessary. The new A76 model has just come out, so we're going to carry that model instead. 169 I ordered 50 of the new ones, but they haven't come in yet.

**Mary Renold [2:10 P.M.]**
Oh, OK. Thanks for explaining that.

**Ben Jeffries (2:11 P.M.]**
171 Next week, we'll start displaying them on the shelves, so make sure to print the product information for the displays.

**Mary Renold [2:12 P.M.]**
Sure. I'll get right on that.

| 瑪莉・瑞諾德 [ 下午 2:02 ] | 嗨，班。可以撥出點時間來嗎？我想要再跟你仔細核對一下庫存報告。 |
|---|---|
| 班・傑傅瑞 [ 下午 2:03 ] | 沒問題。 |
| 瑪莉・瑞諾德 [ 下午 2:04 ] | 根據這份報告，我們只剩兩台康普 A75 筆記型電腦了。我們最近賣出很多台這型號的電腦。我要再多訂嗎？ |
| 班・傑傅瑞 [ 下午 2:06 ] | 沒必要。新的型號 A76 剛推出。我們要改賣那個型號。我已經訂了 50 台新的。不過還沒到貨。 |
| 瑪莉・瑞諾德 [ 下午 2:10 ] | 喔，好的。感謝你的說明。 |
| 班・傑傅瑞 [ 下午 2:11 ] | 我們下禮拜開始就要在架上展示，所以一定要把產品資料印出來供展示用。 |
| 瑪莉・瑞諾德 [ 下午 2:12 ] | 好的。我馬上就著手進行。 |

**168** At 2:03 P.M., what does Mr. Jeffries most likely mean when he writes, "No Problem"?

(A) He agrees with Ms. Renold's idea.

(B) He is available to answer Ms. Renold's question.*

(C) He wants to set up a meeting with Ms. Renold.

(D) He did exactly as Ms. Renold requested.

請務必確認題目句「No problem」前方所提及的內容為何。瑞諾德女士表示，想要再次確認對方現在是否有空回答庫存問題（Can you spare a moment? I want to double-check an inventory report with you.），因此 (B) 為最適當的答案。

下午2:03時，傑傅瑞先生說的「沒問題」是什麼意思？

(A) 他贊同瑞諾德女士的想法。

(B) 他方便回答瑞諾德女士的問題。

(C) 他想要安排與瑞諾德女士的會議。

(D) 他完全照著瑞諾德女士的要求做。

字彙
exactly 確切地

下列何者與傑傳瑞先生有關？

(A) 他已經訂購了一些商品。
(B) 他下載了一些資料。
(C) 他今天安置了一些產品。
(D) 他上週拜訪了一位供應商。

**字彙**
**supplier** 供應商

**169** What is mentioned about Mr. Jeffries?

(A) He already ordered some items.*
(B) He downloaded some information.
(C) He set up some products today.
(D) He visited a supplier last week.

閱讀文章時，請特別留意「傑傳瑞先生的行動」。在 2 點 06 分的訊息中「I ordered 50 of the new ones . . .」，由此可以得知答案為 (A)。

---

傑傳瑞先生與瑞諾德女士從事哪一種行業？

(A) 電腦修理公司
(B) 貨運公司
(C) 電子用品店
(D) 軟體開發業者

**字彙**
**electronics** 電子用品

**170** What type of business do Mr. Jeffries and Ms. Renold work for?

(A) A computer repair business
(B) A delivery company
(C) An electronics store*
(D) A software developer

在前半段訊息中，瑞諾德女士提到了庫存報告，表示某一款的筆電僅剩下兩台（. . . we only have two A75 Canpro notebooks left），表示販售中的電子商品庫存已不夠，因此 (C) 為最適當的答案。

---

傑傳瑞先生與瑞諾德女士下週要做什麼？

(A) 整修店面
(B) 為新產品舉辦銷售會
(C) 退還過時的商品
(D) 擺設商品陳列

**字彙**
**storefront** 店面
**obsolete** 過時的

**171** What will Mr. Jeffries and Ms. Renold do next week?

(A) Renovate a storefront
(B) Hold a sale for new products
(C) Return some obsolete items
(D) Set up some product displays*

閱讀文章時，請特別留意題目關鍵時間點 next week。2 點 11 分的訊息中「Next week, we'll start displaying them on the shelves . . .」，由此可以得知答案應為 (D)。

Questions 172-175 refer to the following article.

June 15—The Walter Horman Estate, the home of deceased millionaire Walter Horman, was recently purchased by the City of Rogerton. According to Malika Trenton, director of the Rogerton Historical Society, the estate will undergo light renovations and restorations before being turned into a local museum. --[1]--. According to Trenton, 172 "The Horman family has included all of the original decorations and furnishings for visitors to enjoy."

Over the last several decades, the Walter Horman Estate has been unoccupied. Instead, the property was available for private party rentals and weddings. Some major film companies have even shot scenes at the estate. 173 However, the cost of keeping the grounds in good condition proved to be too much for the family. --[2]--. Stephen Horman, grandson of the late Walter Horman, said, "It was a tough choice to make. The estate has been in our family for generations, but selling it was the best way to ensure its upkeep." 175 The rest of the Horman family has expressed satisfaction that the estate will be turned into a museum. --[3]--.

174 The Rogerton Historical Society intends to develop guided tours of the estate rooms, while still providing access to the gardens for private parties. Visitors to the estate can learn the history of the Horman family from its early immigrant beginning to its rise in society as the owner of one of the first food processing companies in the country. --[4]--. Tours are expected to begin next spring. Anyone interested in purchasing passes or learning about the estate's history can visit www.walterhormanestate.com/info.

字彙

**estate** 莊園；地產
**deceased** 已故的
**millionaire** 百萬富翁
**renovation** 整修
**restoration** 修復
**unoccupied** 閒置的
**property** 房產
**rental** 出租
**shoot** 拍攝
**condition** 狀況
**prove to . . .** 證明是……
**late** 已故的
**make a choice** 做決定
**generation** 世代
**ensure** 確保
**upkeep** 保養（費）
**rest** 其餘的人
**express** 表達
**satisfaction** 滿意
**intend** 打算，想要
**access** 使用某物的權利
**immigrant** 移民
**rise** 發跡；上升
**processing** 加工；處理

---

6 月 15 日──已故百萬富翁華特‧霍爾曼的家「華特‧霍爾曼莊園」最近被羅傑頓市府收購。根據羅傑頓歷史協會主任瑪莉卡‧崔頓表示，在轉型為在地博物館前，將對莊園進行小幅整修與修復。崔頓表示：「霍爾曼家擁有所有的原始裝潢與家具，可供遊客欣賞。」

數幾十年來，「華特‧霍爾曼莊園」一直無人入住。倒是提供給私人宴會租用與婚禮使用。一些大型電影公司甚至將莊園當作拍攝場景。然而，讓莊園保持良好狀態的維護費用對該家族來說太高了。華特‧霍爾曼的孫子，史蒂芬‧霍爾曼說：「這是個很困難的決定。我們家族已經擁有這個莊園好幾個世代了，但賣掉莊園才是確保它永續保存的最佳方式。」霍爾曼家族的其他人也對莊園將轉型為博物館表達滿意。他們很高興華特‧霍爾曼的回憶能被保存下來。

羅傑頓歷史協會打算開發莊園房舍的導覽之旅，同時也繼續提供花園舉辦私人宴會。來到莊園的遊客可以了解霍爾曼家族的歷史，從早期移民到成為全國第一波食品加工公司企業主之一 的發跡史。預計自明年春天起開放參觀。有興趣購買門票或了解莊園歷史的人，可至 www.walterhormanestate.com/info 查詢。

下列何者與華特·霍爾曼莊園有關？

(A) 由華特霍爾曼的父親所建。
(B) 預約莊園作派對使用很昂貴。
(C) 其中設備將升級。
(D) 包含原有的家具。

字彙
reserve 預約
appliance 裝置，設備

**172** What is suggested about the Walter Horman Estate?

(A) It was built by Walter Horman's father.
(B) It is expensive to reserve for parties.
(C) It will have its appliances upgraded.
(D) It includes the original furniture.*

第一段中提到霍爾曼家擁有原始裝潢與家具（The Horman family has included all of the original decorations and furnishings for visitors to enjoy.），因此 (D) 為最適當的答案。

---

根據文章內容，霍爾曼家族覺得什麼很困難？

(A) 將房產改成公園
(B) 維護莊園
(C) 為房舍找家具
(D) 找到適當買主

字彙
maintain 維護
locate 找出

**173** According to the article, what was difficult for the Horman family?

(A) Turning the property into a park
(B) Maintaining the estate*
(C) Finding furniture for the rooms
(D) Locating a suitable buyer

請特別留意題目關鍵字 difficult。第二段中「However, the cost of keeping the grounds in good condition proved to be too much for the family.」，由此可以確認答案為 (B)。

* 答案改寫：keep . . . in good condition → maintain

---

根據文章內容，莊園的哪個部分將維持不變？

(A) 仍為霍爾曼家族擁有。
(B) 外牆將做為防禦使用。
(C) 建築將做為客房使用。
(D) 外面的地產可供租用。

字彙
own 擁有
security 防禦，保安

**174** According to the article, what will remain the same about the estate?

(A) It will be owned by the Horman family.
(B) Its exterior walls will be used for security.
(C) Its buildings will serve as guest houses.
(D) Its outdoor property will be available for rent.*

請務必掌握本題的關鍵為「維持現狀的部分」。最後一段提到莊園仍可作為派對場地租用（The Rogerton Historical Society intends to develop guided tours of the estate rooms, while still providing access to the gardens for private parties.），因此 (D) 為最適當的答案。

* 答案改寫：garden → outdoor property

**175** In which of the positions marked [1], [2], [3], and [4] does the following sentence best belong?

"They are pleased the memory of Walter Horman will be preserved."

(A) [1]
(B) [2]
(C) [3]*
(D) [4]

前方句子中必須要有插入句人稱代名詞 they 所代表的對象。第二段中寫道:「The rest of the Horman family has expressed satisfaction that the estate will be turned into a museum.」,當中的 The rest of the Horman family 可以用 they 代替。另外,句中的 has expressed satisfaction 與題目插入句的 be pleased 情緒互相呼應,因此 (C) 為最適當的答案。

下列句子最適合出現在[1]、[2]、[3]、[4]的哪個位置中?
「他們很高興華特·霍爾曼的回憶能被保存下來。」

(A) [1]
(B) [2]
(C) [3]
(D) [4]

字彙
**preserve** 保存,維護

**improvement** 改善，加強
**readership** 讀者們
**reach** 到達
**subscriber** 訂閱者
**valid** 有效的
**outline** 簡述，概述
**specification** 規格
**quarter** 四分之一
**coordinator** 統籌者

**Questions 176-180 refer to the following e-mails.**

**To:** samadams@adamsroofing.com
**From:** ginachoi@homeimprovementmonthly.com
**Date:** January 3
**Subject:** Home Improvement Monthly

Dear Mr. Adams,

176 As a special New Year promotion, *Home Improvement Monthly* will be offering discounted prices for new advertisers in our magazine. *Home Improvement Monthly* has a readership of over 20,000 print subscriptions. 177 Your advertisement will reach each subscriber in print as well as our many online subscribers. With our services, you can increase your business!

This offer is valid until March 1. Our price packages are outlined below, and 178 our designers are ready to create color advertisements according to your specifications. To purchase any of our packages, please reply by e-mail or visit us at www.homeimprovementmonthly. com/advertisements/orders.

| Package | Advertisement Format | Monthly Price |
|---------|---------------------|---------------|
| 1 | One full-page print ad plus banner website ad | $300 |
| 2 | One half-page print ad plus half-banner website ad | $275 |
| 3 | One half-page print ad plus corner website ad | $250 |
| 4 | 180 One quarter-page print ad plus corner website ad | $225 |

Sincerely,

Gina Choi
Advertising Coordinator
*Home Improvement Monthly*

-------------------------------------------------------------------------------

收件者：samadams@adamsroofing.com
寄件者：ginachoi@homeimprovementmonthly.com
日期：1 月 3 日
主旨：《家居裝飾月刊》

親愛的亞當斯先生，

《家居裝飾月刊》將提供本雜誌新廣告商優惠價，做為新年促銷活動。《家居裝飾月刊》擁有超過 20,000 的紙本訂閱量。您的廣告將以平面形式傳達給所有訂閱戶，以及廣大電子訂閱戶。有了我們的服務，貴公司的業績絕對可以增加。

這個優惠只到 3 月 1 日有效。我們的優惠方案簡述如下。本雜誌的美術設計已經準備好要根據您所需的規格設計出彩色廣告。欲購買任何優惠套組，請以電子郵件回覆，或上網 www.homeimprovementmonthly.com/advertisements/orders。

| 套組 | 廣告格式 | 月費 |
|------|----------|------|
| 1 | 一則全頁平面廣告加橫幅網頁廣告 | 300 元 |
| 2 | 一則半頁平面廣告加半橫幅網頁廣告 | 275 元 |
| 3 | 一則半頁平面廣告加網頁截角廣告 | 250 元 |
| 4 | 一則 1/4 頁平面廣告加網頁截角廣告 | 225 元 |

《家居裝飾月刊》
廣告統籌
吉娜・崔敬上

---

**To:** ginachoi@homeimprovementmonthly.com
**From:** samadams@adamsroofing.com
**Date:** January 5
**Subject:** Re: Home Improvement Monthly

Dear Ms. Choi,

Thank you for e-mailing me about your promotion. My business partner and I are interested in placing an ad in your magazine. However, I have some questions about [180] your quarter-page print ad. I've purchased a copy of your magazine and looked at the advertisements. I noticed that some are in the front of the magazine and some are in the back. I'm wondering what determines the location of the ad. Do we need to pay additional fees to have our ad located in the front?

Thank you in advance for answering these questions.

Sincerely,

Sam Adams
Co-owner
Adams Roofing

--------------------------------------------------------------

收件者：ginachoi@homeimprovementmonthly.com
寄件者：samadams@adamsroofing.com
日期：1 月 5 日
主旨：回覆：《家居裝飾月刊》

親愛的崔女士，

感謝您寄電子郵件告知貴雜誌的促銷活動。我的商業合夥人和我頗有興趣在貴雜誌刊登廣告。不過，我對您的 1/4 頁平面廣告有些疑問。我買了一份雜誌，也看了廣告。我發現有些廣告在雜誌的前頁，而有些卻刊在後頁。我想了解決定廣告刊登位置的因素是什麼。如果我們想把自己的廣告刊在前頁，是不是需要額外付費？

在此先感謝您的回答。

亞當斯屋頂工程 共同經營人
山姆・亞當斯 敬上

字彙
**location** 位置
**in advance** 預先
**roofing** 蓋或維修屋頂

崔女士為什麼要寄這封電子
郵件給亞當斯先生？

**(A)** 告知一個新的廣告機會
**(B)** 提供訂閱促銷優惠
**(C)** 鼓勵他僱用行銷公司
**(D)** 通知合約上的異動

字彙
**opportunity** 機會
**promotional** 促銷的
**hire** 僱用

**176** Why did Ms. Choi e-mail Mr. Adams?

(A) To announce a new advertising opportunity*
(B) To offer a promotional discount on subscriptions
(C) To encourage him to hire a marketing agency
(D) To inform him of a change in a contract

本題詢問的是第一封電子郵件（第一篇）的撰寫目的。由電郵第一句「As a special New Year promotion, *Home Improvement Monthly* will be offering discounted prices for new advertisers in our magazine.」，可以得知後方的內容應與「新年的廣告促銷活動」有關，因此答案應為 (A)。

---

下列何者與《家居裝飾月刊》
有關？

**(A)** 有幾期晚送達。
**(B)** 廣告商可免費訂閱。
**(C)** 自明年起將每月發行兩期。
**(D)** 部分訂閱戶只訂電子版。

**177** What is suggested about *Home Improvement Monthly*?

(A) Some of its issues were delivered late.
(B) Its advertisers do not pay for subscriptions.
(C) It will put out two issues every month starting next year.
(D) Some of its subscribers only pay for the website version.*

將崔女士所撰寫的第一封電郵（第一篇），與各選項的內容進行對照。在第一段中寫道廣告會透過平面形式與網路形式傳達給訂閱者（Your advertisement will reach each subscriber in print as well as our many online subscribers.），由此可以推測出答案應為 (D)。

---

下列何者與《家居裝飾月刊》
的美術設計有關？

**(A)** 他們可提供客製化服務。
**(B)** 他們要求額外費用。
**(C)** 他們也設計公司網頁。
**(D)** 他們要到三月才有空。

字彙
**custom** 訂做的
**unavailable**
（因忙於他事而）沒空的

**178** What is mentioned about *Home Improvement Monthly*'s designers?

(A) They can provide custom work.*
(B) They require additional fees.
(C) They also design the company website.
(D) They are unavailable until March.

閱讀第一篇文章時，請特留意題目關鍵字 designer。第二段中寫道：「our designers are ready to create color advertisements according to your specifications」，表示可以依照客戶的要求製作彩色廣告，因此答案應為 (A)。

**179** In the second e-mail, the word "placing" in paragraph 1, line 2, is closest in meaning to

(A) hiring
(B) putting*
(C) assigning
(D) calculating

先掃描文章確認單字所在的位置（第二篇電郵），本句的文意應為「放置」廣告。因此意思最接近的單字應為 put，表示「放在某個地點或位置」，故答案為 (B)。

**180** What package does Mr. Adams most likely want?

(A) Package 1
(B) Package 2
(C) Package 3
(D) Package 4*

由亞當斯先生所撰寫的電郵（第二篇）中的 your quarter-page print ad，再將此部分對照第一封郵件（第一篇）中所提及的各類方案。綜合兩邊內容後發現應為第四個方案 One quarter-page print ad plus corner website ad，因此可以確認答案為 (D)。

在第二封電子郵件中，第一段、第二行的「**placing**」與下列哪一個意思最接近？

(A) 僱用
(B) 放置
(C) 分配
(D) 計算

字彙
**assign** 分配
**calculate** 計算

亞當斯先生最有可能採用哪一個方案？

(A) 第一套組
(B) 第二套組
(C) 第三套組
(D) 第四套組

字彙

medical 醫學的
assistant 助理
advanced 先進的
biology 生物
asset 優勢
jointly 共同地
thus 因此
headquarters 總部
laboratory 實驗室
degree 學位
interfere 妨礙
note 注意
wage 薪資,工資
occasional 偶爾的
expense 支出,費用
reimburse 核銷
permanent 長期的
employment 受僱
finalize 最後確定
acceptance 接受
human resources
人力資源(部)
look forward to V-ing
期待做……

Questions 181-185 refer to the following e-mails.

**To:** mpordeski@mailme.com
**From:** imranandal@pearsonmedicalresearch.com
**Date:** April 12
[181] **Subject:** Pearson Medical Research Position
**Attachment:** contract

Dear Ms. Pordeski,

I enjoyed speaking with you during your telephone interview, and I'm delighted to offer you a position on our team as a research assistant. As I'm sure you're aware, you will be working with the top medical researchers in the country using the most advanced equipment. Your education in both biology and engineering will be a great asset during your six-month contract.

As I mentioned to you, our company works jointly with Austin University. Thus, you will need to know your way around both our company headquarters and the laboratories at the university. As such, I would like to arrange an orientation for you and our other new researchers. [185] You mentioned that you're finishing up your final year of your degree, so I'd like to arrange a time that does not interfere with your schedule. Please let me know which days in May you are available.

[181] Please note, this position is an internship. Your wages will be $200 a week and the occasional work expenses will be reimbursed. However, [183] following the six-month period, there will be permanent employment for our top interns. [182] To finalize your acceptance of these terms, please sign and return the attached contract. [184] Andrew Baxter, our human resources manager, will contact you if there are any problems.

Thank you, and I look forward to working with you!

Imran Andal
Lead Researcher
Pearson Medical Research

收件者：mpordeski@mailme.com
寄件者：imranandal@pearsonmedicalresearch.com
日期：4 月 12 日
主旨：培生醫學研究職位
附件：合約

親愛的波多斯基女士，

與您在電話面試中相談甚歡。我很高興能提供您本團隊研究助理一職。我想您知道，您將與全國最頂尖的醫學研究員合作，有機會使用最先進的設備。在六個月的合約期間中，您在生物與工程學中的教育背景將會是一大優勢。

正如我向您提過的，本公司與奧斯丁大學合作。因此您需要了解本公司總部與大學實驗室周邊的路徑。更確切地說，我將為您與其他新進研究員安排一場新進員工訓練。您提過您即將結束大四課程，所以我會安排一個不會妨礙到您行程的時間。麻煩您告訴我五月的哪一天是方便的。

請注意這個職位是實習職。您的薪資是每週 200 元，偶爾職務上的支出也可核銷。不過在六個月實習期間後，我們將提供長期職位給表現優異的實習生。請在附件中的合約上簽名並寄回，以確定您已接受這些條款。若有任何問題，本公司人力資源部經理安德魯‧百克斯特將與您聯絡。

感謝您，並期待與您共事。

培生醫學研究所 首席研究員
伊姆蘭‧安鐸

**To:** Intern Group
**From:** imranandal@pearsonmedicalresearch.com
**Date:** April 24
**Subject:** Orientation

Dear Research Interns,

Since most of you are not available at the same time, I'd like to hold two orientations, one on May 11 and the second on May 16. [185] The May 16 orientation is scheduled on a weekend to accommodate the students in the group. However, if you're not a student, you will be expected to attend the May 11 orientation. Both orientations will start at 9 A.M. at our company headquarters. After a tour, we will have lunch at Buffy's Bistro and then make our way over to the university. Please bring a photo ID in order to gain admittance to the university labs.

Thank you, and I'm looking forward to meeting you all!

Imran Andal,
Lead Researcher,
Pearson Medical Research

- - - - - - - - - - - - - - - - - - - - - - - - - - - - - - - - - - - - - - - - - - - - - - - - - - - - -

收件者：實習生群組
寄件者：imranandal@pearsonmedicalresearch.com
日期：4 月 24 日
主旨：新進員工訓練

親愛的實習研究員，

由於您們當中有大多數人無法挪出同一時間來，我打算舉辦兩場新進員工訓練，一場在 5 月 11 日，第二場在 5 月 16 日。5 月 16 日那場新進員工訓練之所以安排在週末，是為了給群組中的學生參加的。若您不是學生身分，我們希望您參加 5 月 11 日的新進員工訓練。兩場訓練講習都將於當天上午九點在本公司總部舉行。在導覽後，我們將於巴夫小館用餐。之後，我們再走路到大學區。請攜帶附照片的證件，以方便進入大學實驗室。

感謝各位，期待見到大家。

培生醫學研究所 首席研究員
伊姆蘭·安鐸

**181** Why did Mr. Andal write to Ms. Pordeski?

(A) To negotiate a contract
(B) To invite her to apply for a job
(C) To provide medical assistance
(D) To offer her an internship*

本題詢問的是第一封電郵（第一篇）的撰寫目的。由電郵主旨 Pearson Medical Research Position 及第三段第一行，「Please note, this position is an internship.」，可得知答案為 (D)。

安鐸先生為什麼要寫信給波多斯基女士？

(A) 協商合約內容
(B) 邀她應徵工作
(C) 提供醫療協助
(D) 提供她實習職

字彙
**negotiate** 協商
**assistance** 協助

**182** What document is Ms. Pordeski asked to return?

(A) An employer reference
(B) A signed contract*
(C) A program application
(D) A university transcript

請由收件人為波多斯基女士的第一封電郵中，找尋寄件人要求的事項。在第三段中「To finalize your acceptance of these terms, please sign and return the attached contract.」請對方也就是波多斯基女士，在附件的合約書上簽名後寄回，因此答案應為 (B)。

波多斯基女士被要求寄回什麼文件？

(A) 僱主推薦信
(B) 已簽名的合約
(C) 課程申請表
(D) 大學成績單

字彙
**reference** 推薦信
**transcript** 成績單

下列何者與培生醫學研究所
新職員有關？

(A) 他們可以在家工作。
(B) 他們的稅單必須上網提交。
(C) 他們無法獲得薪資。
(D) 他們的表現會受到評估。

字彙
tax 稅
performance 表現
evaluate 評估

**183** What is indicated about new staff at Pearson Medical Research?

(A) They may work from home.
(B) Their tax forms must be submitted online.
(C) They will not be paid for their work.
(D) Their performance will be evaluated.*

培生醫學研究一方撰寫了第一封電郵（第一篇），通知波多斯基女士
獲得了實習的機會。在第三段中提到在實習結束後，表現最優秀的實
習生將能轉為正職（following the six-month period, there will be
permanent employment for our top interns），因此可以推測出實習
生的表現會被評估，故答案為 (D)。

---

安德魯・百克斯特為什麼可能
會聯絡波多斯基女士？

(A) 檢閱公司規定
(B) 解決合約問題
(C) 要求更多推薦信
(D) 說明付款流程

字彙
regulation 規定
resolve 解決
issue 問題；議題
procedure 流程

**184** Why might Andrew Baxter contact Ms. Pordeski?

(A) To review company regulations
(B) To resolve a contract issue*
(C) To ask for additional references
(D) To explain payment procedures

閱讀文章時，請特別留意題目關鍵人名 Andrew Baxter。由第一封
電郵（第一篇）第三段中「Andrew Baxter, our human resources
manager, will contact you if there are any problems (about your
contract).」，表示如有任何相關合約問題，可以聯繫他，因此答案應為
(B)。

\* 答案改寫：problem → issue

---

波多斯基女士最有可能參加
哪一天的新進員工訓練？

(A) 5月11日
(B) 5月15日
(C) 5月16日
(D) 5月19日

**185** When will Ms. Pordeski most likely attend the orientation?

(A) May 11
(B) May 15
(C) May 16*
(D) May 19

閱讀文章時，請特別留意題目「職前訓練的時間」。第二封電郵為
發給所有實習生的郵件（第二篇），當中的第一段提到了 (A) 和 (C)
的時間，但後方補充說明學生可以參加的時間為 (C)（The May 16
orientation is scheduled on a weekend to accommodate the
students in the group.）。回頭看到第一封郵件（第一篇），第二段中
寫道：「You mentioned that you're finishing up your final year of
your degree」，表示波多斯基女士還是名學生，所以要參加 5 月 16 那
場的訓練，因此答案為 (C)。

**Question 186-190 refer to the following webpage and e-mails.**

http://www.internationalspaceexplorationexpo.com

| HOME | ABOUT | PROGRAMS | SCHEDULE |

This year's International Space Exploration Expo (ISEE) is going to be the best yet. [186] Celebrating its tenth anniversary, ISEE offers one of the most advanced displays of space exploration technology scheduled over five days. More than 30 industry leaders will be speaking, and a variety of exciting activities have been scheduled, including:

√ Guided tours of the convention center exhibits
√ Demonstrations of new space engine technology
√ Children's workshops including hands-on experience
√ [188] Competition: Build a scrap metal spacecraft (open to adult participants)
√ [190] Readings by Dr. Michael Paxwell, author of *The Future of Space Travel*
√ The ISEE awards ceremony honoring the greatest achievements in space technology

Visit our schedule page for a full list of events.

------------------------------------------------------------

http://www.internationalspaceexplorationexpo.com

| 首頁 | 關於我們 | 活動 | 活動時間表 |

今年的國際太空探索博覽會 (ISEE) 將會是有史以來最棒的一場。為了慶祝十週年紀念，ISEE 預計以五天的時間，推出最先進的太空探索科技展覽。將有 30 多位的業界領袖演講，並安排各種精彩的活動，包括：

V 會議中心展示導覽
V 新太空引擎科技展示
V 兒童工作坊，包括手作體驗
V 建造廢金屬太空船比賽（成人可參加）
V《太空旅行的未來》作者，麥可・帕克斯維爾博士朗讀會
V ISEE 頒獎典禮，表揚太空科技中最傑出的成就

完整活動清單，請參考網頁活動時間表。

**To:** Parker Rogers
**From:** Karen Walker
**Subject:** Expo Update
**Date:** 27 October

[187] I'm so glad you sent me to cover the ISEE. It's been an amazing experience. I spent the first day on a guided tour of the convention center, and I was amazed by some of the displays and new technologies. [188] Unfortunately, the tour ran a bit long, and I couldn't see the spaceship building event. I did, however, get to interview some of the expo participants and got some great photos of children sampling space food.

I also figured [190] I will catch up with Dr. Paxwell tomorrow after he reads some excerpts from his book. Since he's being honored with the Book of the Year award, I think an interview with him might be a great feature for next week's issue. I'll send you a copy of my prepared questions tonight. Let me know if you'd like to add anything to them.

Best,

Karen

--------------------------------------------------------------------------

收件者：帕克·羅傑斯
寄件者：凱倫·沃克
主旨：博覽會事項更新
日期：10 月 27 日

我很高興您派我去採訪 ISEE。這是個很棒的經驗。我在會議中心的導覽中度過了第一天。一些展示與新科技都讓我感到驚奇。遺憾的是，導覽的時間有點長，我沒看到建造太空船的活動。不過我訪問了幾位博覽會的參與者，也拍到了孩子們品嚐太空食物的精彩照片。

我想，明天在帕克斯維爾博士讀完他書中一些摘錄後，我應該可以採訪到他。由於他剛榮獲年度最佳書籍獎，我想他的訪談或許可以成為下週刊號中，一則很棒的特別報導。我今晚會寄一份準備好的採訪問題給您過目。麻煩告訴我，您是否要增加任何訪談問題。

凱倫 敬上

**To:** Michael Paxwell
**From:** Karen Walker
**Subject:** Follow Up Questions
**Date:** 29 October

Dear Dr. Paxwell,

It was wonderful to speak with you yesterday. I sent a copy of your interview to my editor. He loved your answers as well as the photos. However, he has a few more questions. [190] I'd like to meet with you tomorrow after your reading. It shouldn't take more than ten or twenty minutes. Please let me know if that works for you.

Best,

Karen Walker

----------------------------------------------------------------

收件者：麥可·帕克斯維爾
寄件者：凱倫·沃克
主旨：後續採訪問題
日期：10 月 29 日

親愛的帕克斯維爾博士，

昨天能與您對談，真是太棒了。我寄了一份訪談稿給我的編輯。他非常喜歡您的對答及照片。不過他還有一些問題想請教您。我希望明天能在您的導讀後與您會面。應該不會超過 10 或 20 分鐘，請告訴我您是否可行。

凱倫·沃克 敬上

---

**186** What is indicated about ISEE?

(A) It was originally designed for students.
(B) It is held multiple times per year.
(C) It has existed for several years.*
(D) It has moved to a new venue.

網頁（第一篇）針對關鍵字 ISEE 進行說明。第一段寫道：「Celebrating its tenth anniversary, ISEE offers one of the most advanced displays of space exploration technology scheduled over five days.」，由此可以推測出 ISEE 已舉辦多年，答案為 (C)。

下列何者與ISEE有關？

(A) 最初是為學生設計的。
(B) 一年舉辦多次。
(C) 已經存在多年。
(D) 遷至新會場。

字彙
originally 起初地
multiple 多個的
exist 存在
venue 會場

沃克女士有可能是誰？

(A) 出版商
(B) 太空人
(C) 科學家
(D) 記者

字彙
**astronaut** 太空人

**187** Who most likely is Ms. Walker?

(A) A publisher
(B) An astronaut
(C) A scientist
(D) A journalist*

沃克女士所撰寫的第一封郵件（第二篇）中，第一句「I'm so glad you sent me to cover the ISEE.」，表示沃克女士「前往採訪」ISEE，推知她應為記者，因此答案應為 (D)。

---

根據沃克女士表示，她沒有參加到哪一個會議活動？

(A) 展示
(B) 手工製作比賽
(C) 導覽
(D) 工作坊

字彙
**craft** 手工製作，工藝

**188** According to Ms. Walker, what conference activity was she unable to attend?

(A) A demonstration
(B) A craft competition*
(C) A guided tour
(D) A workshop

由沃克女士所撰寫的第一封郵件（第二篇）、第一段中「Unfortunately, the tour ran a bit long, and I couldn't see the spaceship building event.」，由此可以得知她錯過了「建造太空船比賽」。再看到活動網頁（第一篇）中的 Competition: Build a scrap metal spacecraft，更可以確認答案為 (B)。

* 答案改寫：building → craft

---

在第一封電子郵件中，第二段、第一行的「**figured**」與下列哪一個意思最接近？

(A) 決定
(B) 參與
(C) 代表
(D) 執行

字彙
**represent** 代表
**perform** 執行

**189** In the first e-mail, the word "figured" in paragraph 2, line 1, is closest in meaning to

(A) decided*
(B) involved
(C) represented
(D) performed

單字所在句的文意應為沃克女士「決定要」訪問對方。根據句意，選項中最適合替換的字為 (A) decided。

---

文中提到何者與帕克斯維爾博士有關？

(A) 他今年獲得了好幾個獎項。
(B) 他將在博覽會發表好幾場演講。
(C) 他是著名的報紙編輯。
(D) 他每年都做示範。

字彙
**well-known** 知名的

**190** What is suggested about Dr. Paxwell?

(A) He has won several awards this year.
(B) He will give multiple presentations at the expo.*
(C) He is a well-known newspaper editor.
(D) He gives demonstrations every year.

由網頁（第一篇）活動介紹的第五點：「Readings by Dr. Michael Paxwell」，以及第二篇的電郵「I will catch up with Dr. Paxwell tomorrow after he reads some excerpts from his book.」，可以得知隔天（10 月 28 日）將有一場「朗讀活動」。且第三篇電郵的「I'd like to meet with you (= Dr. Paxwell) tomorrow after your reading.」，可以得知隔天（10 月 30 日）又有一場朗讀活動，因此綜合前述內容，帕克斯維爾博士有多場演講，故答案應為 (B)。

Questions 191-195 refer to the following article, newspaper editorial, and e-mail.

**BREDENBURY** (June 11)—Bredenbury town officials sat down today to discuss the fate of the Mossomin Bridge which has been in need of major repairs for years. Today's meeting was the first of several expected talks on the subject. Although an extensive restoration is one option, several complications may compel the town to demolish the structure.

192 (B) "The cost to restore the bridge will be too great," said town planner Ilkay Tidsale. "The only financially feasible option I can see is replacing the structure."

According to Malcolm Vonda, a well-known structural engineer, traffic flow must also be taken into consideration. "191 Highway 209 will soon have two additional lanes, making it a four-lane highway. The Mossomin Bridge cannot accommodate such a huge increase in the number of vehicles," Vonda says. "I see no other alternative but to build a bigger, modern structure."

The town council would like input from residents on this issue as well. 195 Anyone wishing to share their views can attend a public forum next Monday at 4:30 P.M. at Akber Square, in front of the town hall.

--------------------------------------------------------

布雷登伯里（6月11日）──布雷登伯里市鎮官員今天坐下來討論，數年來一直需要大規模維修的莫撒敏大橋的命運。今天的會議是該議題預訂議程中的第一場。雖然大規模的修復是其中一個選項，但幾個難題可能會迫使市鎮府拆除整座橋的結構。

「修復整座橋的成本太高了，」城市規劃師伊爾凱·緹黛絲爾說，「我看到的是，汰換橋的結構是唯一財政上可行的方案。」

根據知名結構工程師麥爾坎·汪達表示，交通流量也必須納入考量。「209號高速公路即將增加兩線道，成為四線道公路，但莫撒敏大橋無法容納如此多的車輛增加。」汪達說，「除了建造一座更大更現代化的橋樑外，我看不出還有其他選擇。」

市鎮議會也希望廣納居民們對這個議題的看法。所有想要表達自己意見者，可以參加下週一下午4:30在市鎮府前阿克巴廣場所舉辦的公共論壇。

字彙
fate 命運
in need of . . . 需要……
extensive 大規模的；廣泛的
restoration 修復，重建
complication 困難
compel 迫使，強迫
demolish 拆除
structure 結構
restore 修復
financially 財政上
feasible 可行的
traffic flow 交通流量
take into consideration . . .
將……列入考量
lane 車道，線道
alternative 選擇
input （意見上的）貢獻
resident 居民

# Letters to the Editor

[192 (C)] June 12—Yesterday's article concerning the future of the Mossomin Bridge prompted me to write this response. **The bridge is more than just a bridge;** [192 (D)] it is an integral part of Bredenbury's culture. For this reason, the town must keep the structure intact. Plus, considering the high revenues generated annually by tourism industry, [192 (B)] the short-term costs needed to restore this landmark will prove to be beneficial in the end.

Pierre Atherton, founding member of the Bredenbury Preservation Society (BPS)

----------------------------------------------------------------

## 給編輯的信

6 月 12 日——昨天有關莫撒敏大橋的未來一文，促使我寫下這篇回應。這座橋不只是一座橋；它是布雷登伯里文化不可或缺的一部分。為此，本鎮必須保留這座橋的結構是完整的。除此之外，考量觀光業每年所帶來的高收益，修復這座地標的短期成本最終將證明是有利的。

布雷登伯里保護協會（BPS）創始會員 皮爾·阿瑟頓

**To:** members@bredenburypressoc.org
**From:** isabellecharlebois@bredenburypressoc.org
**Date:** June 23
**Subject:** update on Mossomin Bridge

Dear BPS Members,

Congratulations! Thanks to our organization's undeniably strong presence at the town council event, combined with the countless e-mails, letters, and calls to the members of town council, it appears that the bridge is safe from demolition. According to an article in today's *Bredenbury Herald*, the town has decided to relocate Mossomin Bridge to the south end of the town where only pedestrians will be allowed to use it. The bridge will not be open to motorized vehicles.

[195] All of you should feel proud for speaking out and expressing your concerns last Monday. [194] Your actions definitely influenced the town's decision. **Great work!**

Thank you once again,

Isabelle Charlebois, President
Bredenbury Preservation Society

----------------------------------------

收件者：members@bredenburypressoc.org

寄件者：isabellecharlebois@bredenburypressoc.org

日期：6 月 23 日

主旨：莫撒敏大橋的最新狀況

親愛的 BPS 會員，

恭喜大家！由於本會在市鎮議會上的強勢表現，加上無數的電子郵件、信件、與致電給市議會議員，看起來大橋免於被拆除的命運。根據今天《布雷登伯里先驅報》的一篇文章指出，市鎮府已經決定要將莫撒敏橋大重新安置到本鎮的最南端，僅供行人使用，而不開放給汽機車使用。

全體會員都該為上週一的勇於發聲、表達意見而自豪。各位的行動確實影響了市鎮府的決定。表現得太好了！

再次感謝各位

布雷登伯里保護協會會長

伊莎貝爾·查爾鮑伊斯

---

**191** In the article, what is indicated about the town of Bredenbury?

(A) It will increase its yearly budget.

(B) It is going to upgrade a road.*

(C) It is enforcing local parking laws.

(D) It will offer special tours to attract tourists.

報導（第一篇）的第三段訪問中「Highway 209 will soon have two additional lanes, making it a four-lane highway.」，由此可以確認答案為 (B)。

\* 答案改寫：highway → road

文章中，下列何者指的是布雷登伯里市鎮？

(A) 它將增加年度預算。

(B) 它將提升一條道路品質。

(C) 它將實行本地停車規定。

(D) 它將提供特別導覽以吸引觀光客。

字彙
enforce（強制）實行，執行

下列何者不是在說阿瑟頓先生?

**(A)** 他和汪達先生共事。

**(B)** 他不認同緹黛絲爾女士的看法。

**(C)** 他看了6月11日報紙的報導。

**(D)** 他很重視市府地標。

字彙

**value** 尊重，重視

**192** What is NOT implied about Mr. Atherton?

(A) He works with Mr. Vonda.*

(B) He disagrees with Ms. Tidsale.

(C) He read the June 11 newspaper article.

(D) He values a town landmark.

請閱讀阿瑟頓先生所撰寫的文章（第二篇）。由「June 12—Yesterday's article concerning the future of the Mossomin Bridge prompted me to write this response.」可以推測出阿瑟頓先生已看過 6 月 11 的報導，故 (C) 不能選；由 it is an integral part of Bredenbury's culture 可以推測出 (D)。同時，綜合報導（第一篇）第二段的「The cost to restore the bridge will be too great," said town planner Ilkay Tidsale.」和第二篇後半段中的「the short-term costs needed to restore this landmark will prove to be beneficial in the end」，可以推測出阿瑟頓先生和緹黛絲爾女士意見不同，故 (B) 也不能選，因此本題的答案應為 (A)。

在電子郵件中，第一段、第二行的「**countless**」與下列哪一個意思最接近?

**(A)** 未經報導的

**(B)** 已登記的

**(C)** 許多的

**(D)** 含糊不清的

字彙

**unreported** 未經報導的

**registered** 已登記的，登記過的

**ambiguous** 含糊不清的

**193** In the e-mail, the word "countless" in paragraph 1, line 2, is closest in meaning to

(A) unreported      (B) registered

(C) numerous*      (D) ambiguous

countless 的意思為「無數的，數不盡的」，選項中最適合替換的單字為 numerous，故答案為 (C)。

查爾鮑伊斯女士為什麼要恭喜**BPS**會員?

**(A)** 他們影響了一個鎮的決定。

**(B)** 他們選出了一位新副會長。

**(C)** 他們是頭版新聞的主角。

**(D)** 他們為市鎮工程另外募款。

字彙

**elect** 選舉

**raise** 募（款）

**fund** 資金

**194** Why does Ms. Charlebois congratulate BPS members?

(A) They helped influence a town's decision.*

(B) They elected a new vice president.

(C) They were the subjects of a front-page news story.

(D) They raised additional funds for town projects.

本題詢問的是查爾鮑伊斯女士寫郵件給 BPS 會員（第三篇）的目的。第一段中提到莫撒敏大橋最新的狀況，接著在第二段表示「各位（會員）的行動確實影響了一個鎮的決定」，因此 (A) 為最適當的答案。

**195** What is suggested about BPS members?

(A) They helped repair a structure.

(B) Many of them spoke out at Akber Square.*

(C) Many of them reside in the south end.

(D) They meet on the first Monday of every month.

請先閱讀收信人為 BPS 會員的郵件（第三篇）。在最後一段寫道：「All of you should feel proud for speaking out and expressing your concerns last Monday.」，而與 Monday 有關的內容，可以從報導（第一篇）的最後一句得到確認「Anyone wishing to share their views can attend a public forum next Monday at 4:30 at Akber Square, in front of the town hall.」，因此可以得知答案應為 (B)。

下列何者與BPS會員有關？

(A) 他們協助修復了一座建築結構。

(B) 其中很多人在阿克巴廣場發聲。

(C) 其中很多人住在南端。

(D) 他們在每個月的第一個星期一聚會。

字彙
reside in . . . 居住於……

---

**Questions 196-200 refer to the following webpage, receipt, and review.**

http://www.grandcanyonexploreadventure.com

| **Home** | **Tours** | **Reservations** | **Customer Service** |
|---|---|---|---|

For over 20 years, our experienced pilots have been conducting spectacular, one of a kind sightseeing tours of the incredible Grand Canyon. Our trips are available for groups of up to six passengers and can be conducted in English, French, Spanish, and Chinese. Take a look at our trip itineraries below and then visit our reservations page for more information about pricing.

● Grand Canyon Helicopter Tour — Available every day from 14:30 P.M. – 15:30 P.M. Spend your afternoon flying over the magnificent Grand Canyon in a helicopter. [196] You will see amazing views of the Hoover Dam, Lake Mead, and the surrounding desert.

● Grand Canyon Helicopter Tour & Lunch — Available every day from 11:30 A.M. – 15:00 P.M. [196] See all the incredible aerial sights listed in the Grand Canyon Helicopter Tour. Following your flight, you will descend 4,000 feet to the canyon floor and enjoy a picnic lunch served on the shore of the Colorado River.

● [197] Ultimate Grand Canyon Tour Package — Available every day from 11:30 A.M. – 18:00 P.M. Enjoy all the benefits of our other packages, including an aerial tour and a picnic lunch. Following lunch, you can explore the historical Native American lands before returning to your helicopter for a second flight to watch the beautiful sunset. [199] Join us for a complimentary steak dinner at the Explore and Adventure Lodge.

字彙
experienced 經驗豐富的
pilot 飛行員
conduct 帶領；導覽；進行
spectacular 令人驚嘆的；壯麗的
one of a kind 獨特的
sightseeing 觀光
incredible 極好的
magnificent 雄偉的
aerial （從飛機上的）空中的
flight 飛行
descend 下降
shore 岸，濱
ultimate 終極的
lodge 山林小屋

http://www.grandcanyonexploreadventure.com

| 首頁 | 行程 | 預約 | 客戶服務 |

● 20 多年以來，我們經驗豐富的飛行員一直導覽著令人驚嘆、獨特的大峽谷觀光行程，讓遊客一覽無遺大峽谷絕佳的景緻。我們的行程可提供給高達六位乘客的團體，還可用英文、法文、西班牙文與中文進行導覽。請參考以下的行程表，再到我們的預約網頁了解更多價格相關的資訊。

● 大峽谷直升機之旅——每天下午 2:30 至 3:30。搭直升機飛越壯麗的大峽谷來度過您的午後時光。您將可看到胡佛水壩，米德湖和周遭沙漠的絕妙景致。

● 大峽谷直升機含午餐之旅——每天上午 11:30 至下午 3:00。參觀「大峽谷直升機之旅」中所有驚人的空中景色。在這趟空中導覽之後，您將下降 4,000 英呎至峽谷底床，於科羅拉多河岸邊享用野餐式的午餐。

● 終極大峽谷套裝行程——每天上午 11:30 至晚上 6:00。享受我們其他行程的所有特點，包括空中之旅與野餐式午餐。午餐後，您可盡情探索歷史上美國原住民的家園，再次回到直升機進行第二趟飛行，觀賞美麗的夕陽。參加本行程，還可獲贈探索與冒險小屋的牛排晚餐。

---

**字彙**
receipt 收據
purchase 購買
reference 參考
payment 付款，款項
departure 出發
expiry 終止
retain 保留，留住
recommend 建議
in advance 預先
in order to . . . 為了……
brief (v.) 為……提供簡報
safety 安全
precaution 預防措施

---

http://www.grandcanyonexploreadventure.com/reservations/customerreceipt

**Customer Reservation Receipt**

| Date of purchase: | August 3 |
|---|---|
| Customer name: | June Thompson |
| Reference number: | 877573999 |

| Reservation Details | No. of Passengers | Payment Total |
|---|---|---|
| 197, 200 Ultimate Grand Canyon Tour Package (August 27 departure) | 6 x $80 | $480 |

| 199 Payment Method: | Credit Card |
|---|---|
| Card Number: | 111222-359229 |
| Cardholder's Name: | June Thompson |
| Card Expiry Date: | 07/20 |

198 Please retain a copy of this receipt for your records.
We recommend that you print a copy and bring it with you on the day of your tour. Furthermore, 197 we recommend that you arrive one hour in advance of your departure time in order to be briefed on all safety precautions.

## 客戶預約收據

購買日期：8 月 3 日

客戶姓名：瓊恩‧湯普森

編號：877573999

| 預約細項 | 乘客數量 | 付款總額 |
|---|---|---|
| 終極大峽谷套裝行程<br>（8 月 27 日出發） | 6 X 80 元 | 480 元 |

付款方式：信用卡

卡號：111222-359229

持卡人姓名：瓊恩‧湯普森

卡片到期日：7 月 20 日

請保留一份收據作為記錄。我們建議您影印一份，於行程當天隨身攜帶。此外，我們也建議您在出發前一個小時抵達，以了解所有安全注意事項。

---

http://www.grandcanyonexploreadventure.com/customerservice/customerreviews

| **Home** | **Tours** | **Reservation** | **Customer Service** |
|---|---|---|---|

**Grand Canyon Explore and Adventure Customer Review:**

Overall, I was not very pleased with Grand Canyon Explore and Adventure. I originally reserved the Ultimate Grand Canyon Tour Package for six passengers. However, one of the passengers came down with the flu unexpectedly. [200] Grand Canyon Explore and Adventure refused to refund his ticket, meaning we were forced to pay the full price with only five passengers. Furthermore, despite arriving at the requested time, our departure was delayed by an extra thirty minutes, which cut into our exploration time. The only redeeming factor of the trip was our tour guide, Beth Richards, who was well-spoken and friendly. All in all, I would not recommend Grand Canyon Explore and Adventure to anyone.
June Thompson, August 29

---

http://www.grandcanyonexploreadventure.com/customerservice/customerreviews

| 首頁 | 行程 | 預約 | 客戶服務 |
|---|---|---|---|

**大峽谷探索與冒險公司客戶評論：**

整體來說，我對大峽谷探索與冒險公司的服務不是很滿意。我一開始訂了六個人的「終極大峽谷套裝行程」。但其中一位乘客意外地染上流行性感冒病倒了。大峽谷探索與冒險公司卻拒絕退票，意思是，我們五個人被迫付了全額。除此之外，即使我們在要求的時間抵達，我們出發的時間還是延誤了半個小時，而且這還佔用到我們的探險時間。這趟旅程唯一的補償就是我們的導遊，貝絲‧李察斯，她談吐得體又親切。總而言之，我不推薦大峽谷探索與冒險公司給各位。

瓊恩‧湯普森 8 月 29 日

字彙
overall 整體的，總的
come down with
染上……而病倒
flu 流行性感冒
unexpectedly
無預期地，意外地
refund 退款
despite 儘管
cut into 占用
exploration 探險
redeeming 補償的
factor 因素
all in all 總而言之

有關大峽谷直升機含午餐的
套裝行程，下列何者為真？

**(A)** 為大型團體而設計。
**(B)** 包含在餐廳用餐。
**(C)** 最暢銷的行程。
**(D)** 帶客人飛越胡佛水壩與米
德湖。

字彙
**frequently** 頻繁地

---

**196** What is true about the Grand Canyon Helicopter Tour & Lunch Package?

(A) It is designed for large groups.
(B) It includes lunch in a restaurant.
(C) It is the most frequently purchased tour.
(D) It brings the guests over the Hoover Dam and Lake Mead. *

本題要先找出題目關鍵字 Grand Canyon Helicopter Tour & Lunch（大峽谷直升機含午餐之旅）的說明，網頁中（第一篇），針對該行程介紹為 See all the incredible aerial sights listed in the Grand Canyon Helicopter Tour。再對照 Grand Canyon Helicopter Tour（大峽谷直升機之旅）的介紹「You will see amazing views of the Hoover Dam, Lake Mead, and the surrounding desert.」，可以得知題目所問的行程也會看到胡佛水壩與米德湖，故答案應為 (D)。

---

湯普森女士一行人必須在哪
一天幾點到達出發地點？

**(A)** 8月3日上午**10:30**
**(B)** 8月3日上午**11:30**
**(C)** 8月27日上午**10:30**
**(D)** 8月27日下午**2:30**

---

**197** What time and day must Ms. Thompson's group arrive for their tour?

(A) At 10:30 A.M. on August 3
(B) At 11:30 A.M. on August 3
(C) At 10:30 A.M. on August 27 *
(D) At 14:30 P.M. on August 27

湯普森女士的收據（第二篇）中寫道：「Ultimate Grand Canyon Tour Package, August 27 departure」，由此可以推測出答案可能為 (C) 或 (D)。

另外，在收據後方的注意事項中有「we recommend that you arrive one hour in advance of your departure time in order to be briefed on all safety precautions」（建議在出發時間前一個小時抵達），再從網頁（第一篇）中找出 Ultimate Grand Canyon Tour Package（終極大峽谷套裝行程）的時間：「Ultimate Grand Canyon Tour Package — Available every day from 11:30 A.M. – 18:00 P.M.」，因此湯普森女士應該要比 11:30 提早一小時到達，答案應為 (C)。

---

大峽谷探索與冒險公司建議
湯普森女士做什麼？

**(A)** 在網站上寫評論
**(B)** 透過銀行轉帳付款
**(C)** 自行攜帶食物
**(D)** 保留一份收據

字彙
**bank transfer** 銀行轉帳

---

**198** What does Grand Canyon Explore and Adventure recommend Ms. Thompson to do?

(A) Write a review on their website
(B) Pay via bank transfer
(C) Bring some food with them
(D) Save a copy of her receipt*

第二篇的收據有「Please retain a copy of this receipt for your records.」，請保管好此收據作為紀錄，因此 (D) 為最適當的答案。

**199** What is suggested about Ms. Thompson's tour?

(A) Ms. Thompson paid for it in cash.
(B) It featured a kayak tour along a river.
(C) The guide was rude and unprofessional.
(D) It concluded with a free meal.*

請從收據（第二篇）中，確認湯普森女士的行程細項。看到 Payment Method: Credit Card，即可將 (A) 刪除。從網頁中找出旅遊商品的名稱 Ultimate Grand Canyon Tour Package，在最後一段中提到「Join us for a complimentary steak dinner at the Explore and Adventure Lodge.」，因此答案應為 (D)。

\* 答案改寫：complimentary → free
　　　　　　 steak dinner → meal

下列何者與湯普森女士的行程有關？

**(A)** 湯普森女士以現金付款。
**(B)** 主打河上獨木舟之旅。
**(C)** 導遊非常無禮又不專業。
**(D)** 以一份免費餐點畫下句點。

字彙
**rude** 無禮的
**conclude** 結束

**200** According to Ms. Thompson, how much should her group have been charged?

(A) $80
(B) $350
(C) $400*
(D) $450

湯普森女士的收據（第二篇）上寫道結帳總額為美金 480 元。在選項中無法找到這個金額，因此要從其他文章中找出導致差額的根據。評論（第三篇）中提到有一名同伴因流感無法參加，但由於旅遊公司拒絕退費，因此最後仍支付了全額（Grand Canyon Explore and Adventure refused to refund his ticket, meaning we were forced to pay the full price with only five passengers.），而實際上她那團應該支付五名的費用即可（5 x $80），答案為 (C)。

根據湯普森女士表示，他們那團應該要收多少錢才對？

**(A)** 80元
**(B)** 350元
**(C)** 400元
**(D)** 480元

字彙
**charge** 索費

# ACTUAL TEST
# 中譯+解析

## PART 5

明年初將舉行增額市議員的任命。

**字彙**
additional 額外的
councilor 市議員

**101** The _____ of additional city councilors will take place at the beginning of next year.

(A) appoint      (B) appoints
(C) appointed      (D) appointment*

「定冠詞（The）＋空格＋介系詞（of）」的結構中，空格應填入名詞，因此答案只能選 (D)。

- appoint (v.) 任命，指派    appointment (n.) 任命，指派

---

北星鞋業董事長表示他正在草擬一份企業合併的企劃案。

**字彙**
footwear 鞋類
state 表示，陳述
draft 草擬
proposal 企劃案

**102** The president of Northern Star Footwear stated that _____ is drafting a proposal for a business merger.

(A) him      (B) he*
(C) his      (D) himself

本題要從人稱代名詞中找出適當的格，空格的位置為 that 子句的主詞，因此答案應為 (B)。

---

威爾森女士在出國旅遊前應更新她的旅遊行程。

**字彙**
overseas 海外

**103** Ms. Wilson should update her itinerary before she _____ for her trip overseas.

(A) will leave      (B) leaves*
(C) leaving      (D) left

表時間或條件的從屬子句，即便主要子句表示未來發生的事情，仍要使用現在簡單式。因此答案為 (B)。

- leave 離開

* 表時間或條件的副詞子句：假設未來發生的事情，條件句仍須使用現在簡單式
* 表示時間的連接詞：when, while, before, after, as soon as, until, once
* 表示條件的連接詞：if, unless, as long as

---

根據報導，最近與市長辦公室的協商進行得並不順利。

**字彙**
mayor 市長
progress 進展
favorably 順利地

**104** According to the report, the recent _____ with the city mayor's office did not progress favorably.

(A) negotiator      (B) negotiations*
(C) negotiated      (D) negotiates

定冠詞（the）＋形容詞（recent）＋空格，空格中應填入名詞 (A) 或 (B)，但根據句意，本句應為「近期的協商」較為適當，因此答案為 (B)。

- negotiator 談判者    negotiation (n.) 協商，談判
  negotiate (v.) 協商，談判

**105** Several of the candidates were given interviews, but only a few of _____ were chosen for the positions.

(A) we            (B) us*
(C) our          (D) ourselves

介系詞 of 後方必須連接受詞，因此空格中可以填入表受格的 us，故 (B) 正確。

因為所有夥伴都在策略性地規劃交易中扮演要角，合併才能成功。

好幾位應徵者接受面試，但只有我們幾位獲得了那個職位。

字彙
**candidate** 應徵者；候選人

---

**106** The merger was successful because all the partners played a role in _____ planning the deal.

(A) strategy          (B) strategic
(C) strategized       (D) strategically*

當題目的考點為詞性時，請務必先掌握好題目句子的結構。空格為介系詞 in 的受詞，後方已連接了動名詞 planning 作為受詞，因此空格要用副詞修飾動名詞，答案應為 (D)。

• **strategy** 策略    **strategic** 策略的；戰略的    **strategize** 制訂策略
  **strategically** 策略性地

因為所有夥伴都在策略性地規劃交易中扮演要角，合併才能成功。

字彙
**merger** 合併
**play a role** 在……中扮演要角
**deal** 交易

---

**107** After completing his degree at an American university, Paul Bouchard _____ to Paris to teach at a local school.

(A) visited          (B) returned*
(C) occurred        (D) related

空格後方使用介系詞 to，又接地點巴黎，以表示目的地。(A) 的後方必須直接連接地點作為受詞，因此可以直接刪除此選項；(C) 和 (D) 並不符合句意，(occur to ＋人) 的意思為「使人……想起」，relate A to B 表示「A 和 B 有關」，因此 (B) 才是答案。

• **visit** 拜訪    **return** 返回    **occur to** 想到    **be related to . . .** 與……有關

在美國大學取得學位之後，保羅‧布查德回到巴黎，在當地學校任教。

字彙
**degree** 學位

---

**108** Please ensure all deliveries are brought to the side _____ of the supermarket.

(A) entrant         (B) entered
(C) entering       (D) entrance*

定冠詞（the）＋形容詞（side）＋空格，空格中應填入名詞 (A) 或 (D)，但根據句意，本句應為「側邊的入口，側門」較為適當，因此答案為 (D)。

• **entrant** 新職員；參賽者    **enter** 進入    **entrance** 入口

請確保所有運送的貨物都送到超市的側門。

字彙
**ensure** 確保，保證
**delivery** 運送（的貨物）

城市規劃師每週碰面數次，討論即將進行的市中心開發計畫。

**字彙**

**upcoming** 即將到來的
**development** 開發，發展

---

**109** The urban planners met several times a week to discuss plans for the upcoming downtown development _____.

(A) statement　　　　　(B) permission
(C) project*　　　　　　(D) ability

根據句意，本句的重點為「城市規劃師討論市中心開發……」，因此後方應為「開發計畫」，語意上較為完整，答案為 (C)。

* **statement** 聲明，陳述　**permission** 許可　**ability** 能力

---

銷售職位將開放給應屆畢業生應徵，這表示求職者必須已經完成學位。

**字彙**

**mean** 意指

---

**110** The sales position will be open to new graduates, _____ means applicants must have completed a degree program.

(A) whoever　　　　　　(B) who
(C) which*　　　　　　　(D) whatever

逗點前後各連接一個句子（前方為主要子句），先確認兩個子句的關係。空格後方為動詞 means（表示），因此空格應為它的主詞，且用來代表前方整個句子，也就是說，原本要以連接詞（and）加主詞（it）的形式連接前後兩句子（此時的 it 即代表前方整個句子），但沒有 and 和 it 這個選項，因此可以使用關係代名詞，選項能代表先行詞為事物的僅能選擇 which，故答案 (C) 正確。whoever 和 whatever 前方不需要先行詞，故不能選。

* **whoever** 任何……的人　**whatever** 任何……的事物

---

公司課程均提供給季節性聘用人員與長期聘僱員工。

**字彙**

**seasonal** 季節性的
**hire** 新僱員

---

**111** Courses at the company _____ to both seasonal hires and long-term employees.

(A) are offered*　　　　(B) have offered
(C) an offer　　　　　　(D) offering

空格位在動詞的位置，因此可以優先考慮選擇 (A) 或 (B)。課程「被提供給」兩種員工，因此答案要使用被動語態的 are offered，選項 (A) 正確。

* 授與動詞的句型中，所需的介系詞有 to 或 for：
**give, teach, show, lend, pass, offer** ＋直接受詞＋ **to** ＋間接受詞
**buy, make, find, get** ＋直接受詞＋ **for** ＋間接受詞

---

班森音樂學校就位於鮑伊德大道上，會經過羅蘭牙醫診所。

**字彙**

**situate** 使位於
**dental** 牙醫的
**clinic** 診所

---

**112** The Benson Music School is situated just _____ the Roland Dental Clinic on Boyd Avenue.

(A) into　　　　　　　　(B) over
(C) among　　　　　　　(D) past*

本句應為「一過診所後便是音樂學校」，語意上較為完整，因此答案為 (D)。

* **past** 經過

**113** Following a mandatory probationary period, full-time employees are _____ to receive benefits.

(A) beneficial    (B) eligible*

(C) convenient   (D) relevant

本題只要知道 be eligible to 此片語的意思為「具有⋯⋯資格」，就能輕鬆解題。在此補充片語 be eligible for ＋名詞，亦為相同的意思，請特別熟記。

- **beneficial** 有利的 **eligible** 有⋯⋯資格的 **convenient** 方便的
  **relevant** 相關的

\* be 動詞＋形容詞＋ to ＋ V 的用法：

**be able to** . . . 能夠做⋯⋯ **be anxious to** . . . 渴望做⋯⋯
**be due to** . . . 預計⋯⋯ **be willing to** . . . 樂意做⋯⋯
**be afraid to** . . . 害怕做⋯⋯ **be liable to** . . . 很可能做⋯⋯
**be reluctant to** . . . 勉強做⋯⋯

全職員工通過規定的試用期後，就有資格享有福利。

字彙
**mandatory** 必須履行的
**probationary** 試用的

---

**114** The Weston Grant _____ outstanding research conducted in the science and technology field.

(A) recognizes*   (B) assumes

(C) reassures    (D) moderates

本句應為「給予優秀研究之獎學金」，語意上較為完整。因此正確答案為 (A)，表示認可（所以才給予獎勵）。

- **recognize** 表揚，賞識 **assume** 認為，假定 **reassure** 使⋯⋯安心
  **moderate** 減輕，變緩和

威斯頓獎學金表揚在科學和科技領域的傑出研究。

字彙
**grant** 獎學金
**outstanding** 傑出的
**field** 領域

---

**115** Every staff member is given an employee handbook so they can _____ remind themselves of procedures.

(A) consecutively  (B) standardly

(C) namely     (D) easily*

空格位在助動詞 can 和動詞 remind 之間，因此本題要找出適合填入空格中的副詞，以修飾動詞。根據句意，本句應為「輕鬆地提醒自己作業程序」，因此答案為 (D)。在此補充，(A) 經常使用的型態為 for three consecutive days（連續三天）；(C) 表「也就是」時可以與 or 替換使用。

- **consecutively** 連續地 **standardly** 標準地 **namely** 即，也就是

每位員工都發給一本員工手冊，這樣就可以輕鬆地提醒自己作業程序。

字彙
**handbook** 手冊

---

**116** Sanford Shoes is the most popular outlet in the city because its products are always durable, _____ priced, and fashionable.

(A) reason    (B) reasoning

(C) reasonable  (D) reasonably*

空格後方為形容詞 priced（定價的），因此空格中應填入副詞，用來修飾形容詞，因此答案為 (D)。

- **reasoning** 推論 **reasonable** 合理的 **reasonably** 合理地

山福鞋店是本市最受歡迎的商店，因為它的產品耐穿、價錢合理而且款式流行。

字彙
**outlet** 專賣店，經銷點
**durable** 耐用的
**priced** 定價的

布倫南全體員工都很樂意當面，或在電話中與您討論居家裝潢需求。

**字彙**
in person 親自

**117** All staff at Brennan's are _____ to discuss your home decorating needs either in person or over the phone.

(A) delighting　　(B) delighted*　　(C) delights　　(D) delight

be 動詞常連接形容詞，描述主詞的狀態，因此可以直接刪除動詞詞性的 (C) 和 (D)。因為表達人（= All staff）的感覺應該用過去分詞 delighted，故答案為 (B)。
「人＋ be delighted/pleased/happy to ＋原形動詞」為慣用句型，意思為「人因……而感到快樂、樂意去做……」，請特別熟記。

• delighting （事物）令人開心的　　delighted 感到開心的

---

玫瑰紡織廠使用的正是最新的生產設備和材料。

**字彙**
textile 紡織品
manufacturer 製造商
manufacturing 生產；製造業

**118** Rose Textile Manufacturers uses the _____ latest manufacturing equipment and materials.

(A) so　　　　(B) more　　　　(C) very*　　　　(D) much

空格位在形容詞最高級 latest 的前方，因此答案應為 (C)，用於比較級的 more 不會跟形容詞最高級連用，故 (B) 錯。
very 放在形容詞最高級的前方＋名詞表強調，例如 the very man，意思為「正是這名男子」。在此補充，very 不能用來修飾動詞，所以不能寫出「I very thank you.」這種句子。

* 常和形容詞最高級一起使用的字詞：
quite / by far the _____ est, the _____ est ever
the single / very _____ est

---

除非另有說明，否則所有立比品牌冰箱都享有兩年保固。

**字彙**
come with . . . 附有……
otherwise 除此之外

**119** All Libby brand refrigerators come with a two-year guarantee _____ stated otherwise.

(A) whereas　　(B) below　　　(C) neither　　(D) unless*

本句應為「除非另有說明‧立比冰箱都享有兩年保固」語意上較為完整。因此答案為 (D)。

• whereas 然而　　unless 除非
* unless 的用法
unless otherwise indicated 除非另有說明
unless otherwise agreed 除非另有協議
unless otherwise noted 除非另有提及
unless I'm mistaken 除非我弄錯了
unless you have further questions 除非您還有其他問題

---

社區感謝您參與維持橡實谷公寓的清潔與安全。

**120** The community thanks you for your _____ in keeping Acorn Valley Apartments clean and safe.

(A) participant　　　　　(B) participation*
(C) participate　　　　　(D) participated

所有格人稱代名詞（your）＋空格＋介系詞（in），空格中可以填入名詞 (A) 或 (B)，但根據句意，感謝您的「參與」較為適當，因此答案為 (B)。

• participant 參與者　　participation 參與　　participate 參加
* 可以與 in 搭配使用的名詞：
change in . . . 在……有所改變　　experience in . . . 在……的經驗
rise/increase in . . . 在……方面提升/增加
decrease/fall/reduction in . . . 在……方面減少/下降/降低
delay in . . . 在……方面延誤
difficulty/interest/pleasure in . . . 在……方面有困難/興趣/感到愉悅

**121** The interest rates were a key _____ in the CEO's decision to switch to the Emerald Bank.

(A) factor*　　　　　　(B) position
(C) instructor　　　　 (D) composition

本句應為「總裁決定轉換銀行的關鍵因素在於利率」，較符合文意，因此 (A) 為最適當的答案。

• **factor** 因素　**position** 職位　**instructor** 教練　**composition** 構成

利率是總裁決定要轉換到綠寶石銀行的關鍵因素。

字彙
**interest rate** 利率
**switch** 轉換

---

**122** The health inspector will arrive at an unforeseen date _____ ensure the conditions of the inspection are fair.

(A) even if　　　　　　(B) in order to*
(C) after all　　　　　(D) given that

根據句意，空格後方應表示「衛生檢測員不定期來訪的目的」，因此表目的的片語 in order to 最為適當，因此答案為 (B)。

• **even if . . .** 即使……　**in order to . . .** 為了……　**after all** 畢竟
　**given that . . .** 考慮到……

衛生檢測員將不定期來訪，以確保檢測狀況是公平的。

字彙
**inspector** 檢測員
**unforeseen**
不定期的，無法預期的
**inspection** 檢測

---

**123** Peter Nugent's novel was made into an adventure movie two years ago after Winston Studios obtained _____ from Nugent's grandson.

(A) permission*　　　　(B) suggestion
(C) comparison　　　　 (D) registration

根據文意，若要將小說翻拍成電影，必須先取得著作權者的「許可」，因此答案應為 (A)。

• **permission** 許可　**suggestion** 建議　**comparison** 比較
　**registration** 登記，註冊

* 經常與 obtain 搭配使用的名詞：
**obtain advice/information** 取得建議／資訊
**obtain approval** 獲得核准
**obtain admission to . . .** 獲得入場許可至……
**obtain a patent** 取得專利
**obtain (secure) employment** 得到工作
**obtain a copy of the report** 拿到一份報告

溫斯頓電影製片公司在取得彼得・努甘特孫子的同意後，於兩年前將他的小說拍成冒險片。

字彙
**obtain** 取得，獲得

---

**124** The mayor's office has issued a statement _____ the use of tax revenue to repair roads in the coming year.

(A) excluding　　　　　(B) during
(C) following　　　　　(D) regarding*

空格後方為聲明（statement）的相關訊息，因此答案應為表示「關於……」的 (D)。類似的用法還有 concerning/about/as to/pertaining to，請務必一併熟記。

• **excluding . . .** 除……之外　**following . . .** 接著的
　**regarding . . .** 關於……

市長辦公室發表了明年將以稅收來修補道路的相關聲明。

字彙
**issue** 發表
**statement** 聲明
**tax revenue** 稅收

戴伯特公寓塔樓位於兩個
地鐵站步行距離內的便利
之處。

**字彙**
**condominium** 公寓
**locate** 使位於
**walking distance** 步行距離

**125** The Delbert Condominium Tower is _____ located within walking distance of two subway stations.

(A) conveniently*　　(B) consistently
(C) continually　　　(D) commonly

根據句意，本句要表達的是「位置的條件」。空格中最適合填入的單字為 conveniently，故 (A) 正確。be conveniently located 意思為「位於便利之處」，經常出現在考題中。

- **conveniently** 方便地　**consistently** 持續地　**continually** 不斷地　**commonly** 一般地

---

實習生若想應徵任何新的全
職工作，都需要繳交新的申
請表。

**126** Interns should _____ new applications if they wish to apply for any of the new full-time positions.

(A) reply　　　　(B) submit*
(C) vacate　　　(D) oppose

根據句意，本句應為「繳交應徵函」，語意上較為完整，因此答案為 (B)。在此補充，若 apply 的後方直接連接受詞，意思為「塗抹，敷」；若後方並未連接介系詞 for，而是連接 to 時（apply to），則表示「適用於……」的意思。

- **reply** 回覆　**submit** 繳交，提交　**vacate** 空出　**oppose** 反對

---

胡拉漢女士修改的雷諾製造
使命聲明的草稿中，精確地
表達了公司的目標。

**字彙**
**revise** 修訂
**draft** 草稿
**manufacturing** 製造業
**mission** 使命，任務
**express** 表達

**127** Ms. Houlahan's revised draft of Reynold Manufacturing's mission statement expresses the goals of the company _____.

(A) precise　　　　(B) more precise
(C) preciseness　　(D) precisely*

本句的結構為：主詞（Ms. Houlahan's . . . statement）＋及物動詞（expresses）＋受詞（the . . . company），屬於完整的句型，因此本句可以省略掉空格的位置。空格中只能填入副詞 precisely 修飾動詞 expresses，故答案為 (D)。

- **precise** 精確的　**preciseness** 精確性　**precisely** 精確地

---

雖然公園在夏季月分開放，
但民眾仍然不得進入某些特
定區域。

**字彙**
**restrict** 限制
**access** 進入

**128** _____ the park is open during the summer months, the public is restricted from accessing certain areas.

(A) While*　　　(B) When
(C) For　　　　(D) But

逗點前後句的內容為相反的概念（open ↔ restricted），因此表示「轉折」的連接詞 while 為最適當的答案，故選 (A)。雖然 (D) 也是代表「轉折」的意思，但在表示兩句為對比的狀況時，不能放在句首。

**129** _____ the education level of Paul Rogers, it is no wonder that he is the highest-paid speaker at the convention.

(A) About            (B) Given*

(C) Upon             (D) Since

空格到逗點前的內容應為「羅傑斯先生可以收取最多演講費的原因」，語意上較為適當。因此答案應為 (B) Given，意思為「有鑑於……」。這裡使用的 given 為介系詞，同義詞為 considering。

有鑑於保羅・羅傑斯的學歷，難怪他是會議中演講費最高的講者。

字彙
**education** 教育
**it is no wonder that . . .**
難怪……

---

**130** Considering all the hot weather we're having, the number of people using public swimming pools is _____ to increase.

(A) covered         (B) sought

(C) limited          (D) bound*

本題只要知道慣用片語 be bound to 的意思為「必定會……」，就能輕鬆找出答案為 (D)。請一併熟記同義片語 be sure to。

• **cover** 涵蓋    **seek** 試圖；尋找    **limit** 限制

\* **be bound to = be sure to；be certain to** 必定會……

\* **a bus/train bound for . . .** 公車/火車正要前往……

考量到我們面臨的炎熱天氣，使用公共泳池的人數勢必會增加。

字彙
**considering . . .** 考量到……

## PART 6

## 字彙

**stationery** 文具
**shipment** （運送的）貨品
**delay** 延誤，延遲
**policy** 規定；政策
**range from A up to B**
從 A 到 B 的範圍內變化
**depend on . . .**
依……狀況而定
**method** 方式
**ensure** 保證
**estimate** 預估
**accurate** 準確的
**excessively** 過度地
**hesitate** 猶豫，遲疑
**status** 狀態，情況

Questions 131-134 refer to the following information.

At Echo Stationery Supplies, we try to ship your orders as quickly as we can. If you have concerns that your shipment has been delayed, please ‾‾131.‾‾ our shipping policies. Our expected delivery time may range from 4 days up to 4 weeks, which depends on the method of shipping customers choose during checkout. ‾‾132.‾‾ . We try to ensure our shipping estimates are accurate; however, some orders may take ‾‾133.‾‾ to arrive at your door. If you have found that your order is excessively ‾‾134.‾‾ , do not hesitate to contact us immediately. We promise to look into the problem and let you know the status of your shipment.

--------------------------------------------------------

在回音文具用品公司，我們努力盡快配送您所訂購的商品。如果您擔心貨物已延遲寄送，請注意本公司的運送規定。依據顧客於結帳時所選擇的運送方式，本公司預計的運送時間會自四天至四週不等。預估的運送日期會明列於收據上。我們盡力確保預估的運送時間是準確的。但是，有些訂單運送時間會較久。若您發現您的訂單延遲過久，請立即與我們聯絡。我們承諾會找出問題所在，並告知配送進度。

**131** (A) note*
(B) send
(C) prepare
(D) require

根據文意，本句應為「如果您擔心貨物已延遲寄送，請注意本公司的運送規定」，語意上較為適當，因此適合填入空格中的單字為 note，表「留意，注意」，答案為 (A)。

● **note** 注意　　**require** 要求

**132**
(A) Returned items will be eligible for exchanges only, not refunds.
(B) Contact our specialists to get an updated list of all of our new products.
(C) An approximate delivery date is indicated on your receipt.*
(D) Visit our online feedback section and let us know how well we served you.

空格前方提到配送進度，會隨著結帳時選擇的付款方式有所不同，空格後方則提到了預估的運送時間(shipping estimates)，因此這兩句中間，只有 (C) 提及運送日期，所以最適合填入空格。

- **item** 物品　**eligible . . .** 具……資格的　**exchange** 更換
　**refund** 退款　**product** 產品　**approximate** 大概的，近似的
　**indicate** 標示，表明　**receipt** 收據

(A) 退換物品只能更換，無法退款。
(B) 聯絡專員，以取得更新後的新產品清單。
(C) 預估的運送日期會明列於您的收據上。
(D) 查看線上回饋專區，告訴我們您有多滿意本公司的服務。

**133**
(A) length
(B) lengthy
(C) longer*
(D) longest

英文通常會以「It takes long.」或是「It takes a long time.」表示「花費較多的時間」。因為選項中並沒有 long，所以選擇 long 的比較級 longer，答案為 (C)。

- **length** 長度　**lengthy** 冗長的

**134**
(A) different
(B) delayed*
(C) overpriced
(D) greater

全文為針對「配送」的說明。根據文意，當配送「延遲」過久時，可以聯絡撰寫本文的一方，語意上較為適當，故答案選 (B)。

- **overpriced** 訂價過高的

Questions 135-138 refer to the following article.

April 24

After months of discussions, Nackawic Town Council has finally approved an agreement with DRTL Enterprises. Under the terms of the agreement, DRTL ------ the 30-acre lot on the east end
135.
of Barrett Street. The detailed proposal calls for the building of both retail shops and offices in the area. Nackawic's mayor, Leona Hovey, is optimistic that the project will bring ------ benefits to the
136.
town and surrounding areas. "It is expected to create 300 full-time jobs," says Hovey. "For a while, I felt the ongoing postponements would force us to cancel the project all together." ------ . DRTL
137.
spokesperson, Jeff Perkins believes the development will take three years to finish. At the same time, he cautions people that there may be more setbacks. "Of course, we provided the town council with our very best ------ , but even so, we have no way of
138.
predicting everything that will happen," Perkins said.

--------------------------------------------------------------

4 月 24 日

經過數月的討論，納卡維克市市鎮議會終於通過與 DRTL 企業的協議。依據協議條款，DRTL 將會開發巴雷特街東邊街尾的那塊 30 英畝的空地。詳細的企劃案需要取得該區零售商店與辦公室的屋舍才能訂定。納卡維克市市長里奧納·哈維對於這個計畫能對全市與周遭區域所帶來的經濟利益感到樂觀。「本開發案預期將創造 300 個全職職缺。」哈維說，「有一度我以為持續的延宕會迫使我們取消這整個計畫。」雖然全鎮都渴望能進行這個案子，但像這類的大型開發案，延遲是不可避免的。DRTL 發言人，傑夫·柏金斯認為這個開發案將花上三年才能完工。同時，他警告大家可能會有更多的挫折發生。柏金斯說：「當然，我們把最好的預測結果提供給鎮議會參考，但即便如此，我們還是無法預期任何可能會發生的事。」

**135**
(A) to develop
(B) will develop*
(C) has developed
(D) could have developed

由於空格位在句子的動詞部分，因此可以直接刪除 (A)。由第一句的 approved an agreement，可以得知市鎮議會已經通過並預計要進行開發，因此答案為未來式的 (B)。

---

**136**
(A) economic*
(B) unforeseen
(C) environmental
(D) frequent

本句文意為「開發計畫能對全市與周遭區域帶來經濟利益」，最適合填入的形容詞為 economic，故答案為 (A)。

- **economic** 經濟的　　**unforeseen** 無法預料的　　**environmental** 環境的

---

**137**
(A) While the town is eager to get moving on this, delays are inevitable for major developments like this.*
(B) Local residents, however, have approached us with legitimate concerns about the high noise levels construction will create.
(C) Members of town council are set to vote on four different proposals from well-known architects.
(D) Despite the town's promise to grant the developers a contract, they may now have to look at other options.

本句接在「因為計畫延宕而感到擔憂」的後方，因此空格中最適合填入和計劃延誤相關的句子，(A) 句中的「delays」呼應到前句的 postponements，故為正確答案。

- **eager** 渴望的　　**delay** 延誤，延遲　　**inevitable** 不可避免的
  **resident** 居民　　**approach** 找……商量　　**legitimate** 合理的，正當的
  **construction** 營造，建設　　**be set to . . .** 準備要……
  **architect** 建築師　　**grant** 給予，授予　　**contract** 合約
  **option** 選擇（項）

(A) 雖然全市都渴望能進行這個案子，但像這類的大型開發案，延遲是不可避免的。
(B) 然而，當地居民以合理的懷疑與我們討論工程將帶來的強烈噪音。
(C) 鎮議會成員將針對知名建築師所提出的四個企劃案來投票。
(D) 雖然市鎮府承諾授予開發者一紙合約，但他們現在仍須看看其他的選擇。

---

**138**
(A) argument
(B) background
(C) estimate*
(D) combination

根據文意，「雖然將最好的預測結果提供給鎮議會參考，仍無法預期任何可能會發生的事。」，語意上較為完整，因此答案應為 (C)。

- **argument** 爭論　　**background** 背景　　**estimate** 預測
  **combination** 結合

字彙

lengthen 延長
nightly 每夜的
unexpected
突如其來的，出乎意料的
criticism 批評
renowned 知名的
critic 評論家
sold out 售完
in a row 連續地
representative 代表人員
attract 吸引
normally 通常
attendee 出席者
number 短曲，短歌
reinvent 重新改造

Questions 139-142 refer to the following article.

Roderick Opera House has announced that it will lengthen its run of Melanie Beck's new musical, *The Birth of Jazz*. Due to an increase in ----- for tickets, the show will be playing nightly until the end of August. The announcement was unexpected, as the musical received ----- criticism from renowned musical theater critic Jeffrey O'pry.

----- However, last week the show was sold out three nights in a row. According to representatives of the opera house, the show has been attracting an older crowd who may not normally attend musicals. The new attendees are ----- excited about hearing the great jazz numbers reinvented by Beck.

---

羅德里克歌劇院宣布將延長梅蘭妮·貝克的新音樂劇《爵士之生》的演出時間。由於門票需求增加，直至八月底前，每天晚上都將演出。這突如其來的宣布，讓音樂劇受到知名音樂劇評論家傑佛瑞·歐普瑞的嚴厲批評。在評論後，門票的銷售量急遽地下滑。然而，上週連續三晚的票都銷售一空。根據歌劇院代表的說法，這個演出吸引了一群原本不看音樂劇的長者。而新觀眾也顯然對於能聽到貝克重新創作的絕美爵士樂曲感到興奮不已。

**139** (A) demand*
(B) demanded
(C) demanding
(D) to demand

介系詞 in 後方需要連接受詞，因此答案為名詞的 (A)。依照文法規則，也可以把動名詞 (C) 納入考量範圍，但是如果選項中已有適當的名詞，則不會選擇動名詞的形態。

• demand 要求　demanding 苛求的

**140** (A) brilliant
(B) deep
(C) harsh*
(D) prompt

如果對於歌劇延長演出「感到突如其來的」，可推論公演的評價應該不太好。因此用來表示「嚴厲的」的 harsh 為最適當的答案，故選 (C)。

• brilliant 傑出的　deep 深的　harsh 嚴厲的　prompt 迅速的

**141** (A) Guests at the musical were mostly from out of town.

(B) The final show will be held on August 24.

(C) Following the review, ticket sales dropped dramatically.*

(D) Similarly, the theater has been suffering for years.

空格前方提到知名評論家的嚴厲的評價（harsh criticism from renowned musical theater critic），因此空格內應填入伴隨的結果：售票量下降。且從空格後方表轉折語氣的 However，提到「全數銷售一空（the show was sold out）」，更可以確定空格的內容應為「售票量大幅下降」，答案為 (C)。

- **hold** 舉行　**following . . .** 在……之後　**drop** 下滑，下降　**dramatically** 大幅地；劇烈地　**similarly** 同樣地 **suffer** 受損失，受害

(A) 音樂劇的來賓大多數都是從外地來的。

(B) 最後一場演出將於8月24日舉行。

(C) 在評論後，門票的銷售量急遽地下滑。

(D) 同樣地，劇院也受害多年。

**142** (A) apparent

(B) more apparent

(C) apparentness

(D) apparently*

本題要找出最適合填入句中的詞性。空格所在句是一個結構完整的句子，因此答案為副詞 apparently，用來修飾形容詞 excited。若空格位在 be 和過去分詞之間，答案則為副詞，請特別熟記這個規則。

- **apparent** 明顯的　**apparentness** 明顯　**apparently** 顯然地

Questions 143-146 refer to the following e-mail.

**From:** Customer Care
**To:** Paul Kanagawa
**Date:** October 16
**Subject:** Welcome to Atlantic Music Trends

**Attachment:** Form

Dear Mr. Kanagawa,

Thank you very much for subscribing to *Atlantic Music Trends*! ------ 143. you will have detailed information about upcoming music classes, festivals, and concerts happening all over Canada's Atlantic coast. You can expect your first issue at your door by the 20th. ------ 144. . After that, every issue will be sent out during the first week of the month. With this subscription, you will also have unlimited ------ 145. to online videos, song recordings, articles, schedules, and even ticketing information for concerts. All you have to do is log on to our website using the user ID and eight-digit passwords listed ------ 146. the bottom line of the attached enrollment form.

Sincerely,

Veronica Van Zeyl
Customer Representative

--------------------------------------------------------------------------------

寄件者：顧客服務部
收件者：保羅·神奈川
日期：10 月 16 日
主旨：歡迎加入大西洋音樂趨勢
附件：表格

親愛的神奈川先生，

感謝您訂閱《大西洋音樂趨勢》！您現在將獲得所有關於音樂活動的詳細資訊，像是即將到來的音樂課程、音樂節以及在加拿大大西洋沿岸各地所舉辦的演唱會。您將於20號收到您的第一期刊物。若未於該天送達，請通知我們。之後，每期刊物將於當月的第一週寄出。藉著訂閱本刊，您也可以無限地觀看線上影片、唱片、文章、時程表，甚至是演唱會的售票資訊。您只需要用帳號及附件註冊申請表末的八位數密碼登入網站即可。

顧客服務部代表
維若妮卡·范澤 敬上

**143**
(A) Now*
(B) Afterward
(C) Then
(D) Meanwhile

根據文意，本句應為訂閱後，「從此刻起，現在」神奈川先生可以享有的權限，因此 (A) 為最適當的答案。

- **afterward** 之後　**meanwhile** 同時

---

**144**
(A) Please notify us if it does not arrive by that date.*
(B) To subscribe, please phone during regular business hours.
(C) The next festival will take place in Moncton in mid-November.
(D) We invite readers to submit reviews of concerts for publication.

空格前方提到了「首期刊物的寄送日期為 20 號」。根據文意，推測後方插入句應為如未在「此日期」收到的相關叮嚀，因此填入 (A) 的內容最為適當。

- **notify** 通知　**submit** 提交　**publication** 刊登，出版

(A) 若未於該天送達，請通知我們。
(B) 如欲訂購，請於上班時間來電。
(C) 下個慶典將於11月中在蒙克頓舉行
(D) 我們邀請讀者投稿演唱會的評論以供刊登。

---

**145**
(A) accessing
(B) accesses
(C) accessed
(D) access*

及物動詞（have）＋形容詞（unlimited）＋空格，當中的空格僅能填入名詞 (D)，用來作為動詞的受詞。當 access 作為動詞來使用時，後方不用加上介系詞 to，直接連接受詞即可。

---

**146**
(A) for
(B) about
(C) on*
(D) at

本題要找出適當的介系詞。答案應為 (C)，用來表示「在線（line）的上方」。在此補充，介系詞 across/along/over 也經常與 line 搭配使用。

# PART 7

**字彙**
extend 延長
cancellation 取消
avoid 避免

Questions 147-148 refer to the following notice.

*Jen's Salon and Spa*

**Holiday Information**

- Spa hours will be extended from November 20 to January 20. (Monday — Saturday 10 A.M. to 10 P.M.).
- Please note, the spa will be closed from December 24 – 29.
- As always, [148] cancellations must be made 24 hours in advance to avoid cancellation fees.

- - - - - - - - - - - - - - - - - - - - - - - - - - - - - - - - - - - - - - - - - - - - - - - -

珍的水療沙龍                                                                          假日公告

- 自 11 月 20 日至 1 月 20 日將延長水療時間。
  （星期一至星期六上午 10 點至晚上 10 點）
- 請注意，水療將於 12 月 24 日至 29 日期間暫停營業。
- 如同以往，取消需於 24 小時前提出，以免產生取消費用。

---

這則公告的目的是什麼？

(A) 為新的服務打廣告
(B) 說明時間表
(C) 宣布促銷
(D) 提供退款

**字彙**
advertise 為……打廣告
refund 退款

**147** What is the purpose of the notice?

(A) To advertise a new service
(B) To explain a schedule*
(C) To announce a sale
(D) To offer a refund

公告的第一項寫道「延長水療營業時間」，第二項寫道「水療未營業時間」，綜合兩項的內容，(B) 為最適當的答案。

---

下列何者與取消有關？

(A) 取消水療要事先告知。
(B) 顧客可以線上取消預約。
(C) 取消皆需支付服務費。
(D) 假日預約無法取消。

**字彙**
advance 事先的
apply to . . . 適用於……

**148** What is stated about cancellations?

(A) The spa requires advance notice of cancellations.*
(B) Customers can cancel appointments online.
(C) A service fee is always applied to cancellations.
(D) Holiday appointments cannot be canceled.

公告中的第三項提及 cancellations，表示若於二十四小時前取消水療預約，就不會收取手續費（cancellations must be made 24 hours in advance to avoid cancellation fees），因此答案應為 (A)。

Questions 149-150 refer to the following notice.

**Notice for Eastpoint Community Residents**

[149] As of next month, our weekly community newsletter will be going paperless. In an effort to protect the environment and reduce the amount of paper we use, the newsletter will now be available online only.

[150] Anyone who currently has a small business advertisement in the newsletter is encouraged to contact the newsletter editor for an updated contract at 900-555-3434. The first online newsletter is scheduled to be on www.eastpointcommunity.com/newsletter on November 1. We hope you enjoy this new convenient way to receive your weekly newsletter. Sincerely,

Eastpoint Community Newsletter Team

--------------------------------------------------------------------

東點社區居民公告

自下個月起，本社區週訊將改為無紙化。為致力保護環境及減少用紙量，週訊僅提供數位版。

任何目前在週訊上刊登小型商業廣告的人，請來電 900-555-3434 與週訊編輯聯絡以更新合約。第一份線上週訊預定於 11 月 1 日上傳至 www.eastpointcommunity.com/newsletter。希望您會喜歡以這新穎便利的方式收到您的週訊。

東點社區週訊團隊　敬上

**字彙**
resident 居民
in an effort to . . . 致力……，試圖……
environment 環境
editor 編輯
contract 合約

---

**149** What change will be made to the newsletter?

(A) It will merge with another publication.
(B) It will be delivered faster.
(C) It will run less frequently.
(D) It will no longer be printed on paper.*

閱讀文章時，請特別留意題目關鍵字 change。公告的第一句「As of next month, our weekly community newsletter will be going paperless.」，由此可以得知週訊將不再印出紙本，因此答案為 (D)。

週訊將有何種改變？
(A) 將與另一份刊物合併。
(B) 寄送速度會更快。
(C) 較不頻繁出刊。
(D) 不再印出紙本。

**字彙**
merge 合併
publication 出版物，刊物

---

**150** According to the notice, why might advertisers contact the editor?

(A) To sign a new contract*
(B) To receive a discount
(C) To upgrade a membership
(D) To change a listing

公告第二段提到目前有刊登廣告者，請與編輯聯絡更新合約（Anyone who currently has a small business advertisement in the newsletter is encouraged to contact the newsletter editor for an updated contract at 900-555-3434.），因此答案為 (A)。

根據公告，廣告客戶為什麼要和編輯聯絡？
(A) 簽署新合約
(B) 獲得優惠折扣
(C) 會員升級
(D) 修改清單

**字彙**
listing 清單

Questions 151-153 refer to the following agenda.

### 153 (A), (B) Unpaid Spring Training Session
#### 9:30 A.M. to 4:30 P.M.

### 9:30 A.M.: Meet and Greet
151 Meet your managers as well as your fellow new employees. Enjoy coffee and donuts as you watch a short introduction video to the company.

### 10:30 A.M.: Rules and Procedures
Pick up your employee handbook and review the rules and procedures with the office manager. A short question and answer session will be included.

### 12:00 P.M.: 153 (D) Lunch Break
A light buffet lunch of sandwiches, salads, and desserts will be catered in the conference room. Vegetarian options will be provided for employees.

### 1:00 P.M.: Department Shadowing
Employees will visit their respective departments and receive hands-on training from an assigned veteran employee.

### 3:30 P.M.: Desk Assignments
Employees will be shown to their desks and given an opportunity to set up their company accounts and e-mails. 152 IT will be available for any problems that may arise.

-----------------------------------------------------------------------

#### 春季免費教育訓練講習
#### 上午9:30至下午4:30

**上午 9:30：相見歡**
與主管以及新同事見面。在觀看公司介紹短片的同時，可享用咖啡和甜甜圈。

**上午 10:30：規章與程序**
領取員工手冊，和部門主管一起檢閱規章與程序。包含簡短問答時間。

**中午 12:00：午休**
將於會議室提供三明治、沙拉和甜點的輕食自助式午餐，並提供素食餐。

**下午 1:00：部門觀摩**
員工將參觀各自部門，由指派的資深員工進行實務訓練。

**下午 3:30：辦公桌分配**
員工將被帶往個人辦公桌，設定公司帳號與電子郵件。任何疑問可隨時詢問資訊工程人員。

**151** For whom is the session most likely intended?

(A) Company CEOs
(B) Computer technicians
(C) New office employees*
(D) Department transfers

由日程表的第一項「Meet your managers as well as your fellow new employees.」，可以確答案為 (C)。這句話中的 fellow，意思為「同事的，同輩的」。

---

**152** What portion of the session involves IT specialists?

(A) Meet and Greet
(B) Rules and Procedures
(C) Department Shadowing
(D) Desk Assignments*

閱讀文章時，請特別留意題目關鍵字 IT specialist。由日程表的最後一項「IT will be available for any problems that may arise.」，可以確認當為新員工設定電郵時，有疑問可隨時詢問資訊工程人員，故 (D) 正確。

---

**153** What is NOT indicated about the session?

(A) It is an unpaid event.
(B) It lasts for one work day.
(C) It is run by the HR director.*
(D) It includes refreshments.

解題時，先將各選項的內容對照內文，並刪除文章中提及的選項。(A) 出現在標題 Unpaid Spring Training Session 當中；(B) 出現在 9:30 A.M. to 4:30 P.M. 當中；(D) 可以由 Lunch Break 的說明來確認，因此本題的答案應為 (C)。

這個講習針對的對象是誰？

(A) 公司執行長
(B) 電腦技術員
(C) 新任辦公室員工
(D) 調動部門的員工

字彙
**technician** 技術員
**transfer** 轉調人員

---

講習中的哪一部分與資訊工程人員有關？

(A) 相見歡
(B) 規章與程序
(C) 部門觀摩
(D) 辦公桌分配

字彙
**portion** 部分
**involve** 涉及

---

以下何者與講習無關？

(A) 是免費的活動。
(B) 時間為一個工作天。
(C) 由人力資源部主管負責。
(D) 包含茶點。

字彙
**last** 持續
**refreshment** 茶點

字彙
bedding 寢具
status 狀況
coordinator 統籌者
accomplish 完成
manufacturer 製造商
currently 目前地
specification 規格
production 生產
pricing 價格
turnaround 交貨時間
fabric 織品，布料
availability 可得性
shipping 運送
textile 紡織品
appear 看起來
promptly 迅速地，立即地
ensure 保證
transition 過渡（時期）
efficient 有效率的
preferred 偏好的
meet 符合
supply 供應
demand 需求
as a result 因此
consider 考慮
term 期限
revision 修訂

Questions 154-157 refer to the following report.

**Rengrew Bedding**

Weekly Status Report: September 5–9
Prepared by: Alexander Corbin, Project Coordinator

155, 157 **Accomplished this Week:**

- Got in touch with four manufacturers in Mexico who currently produce bedding products. --[1]--. 154 E-mailed them design specifications for our new bedding sets along with questions about production pricing, turnaround time, fabric availability, and shipping costs.

- According to the replies, 157 P&M Textiles appears to be the best candidate. --[2]--. Additionally, Sammy Ruiz, a client services manager, e-mailed me promptly. 156 Her responses to my questions were very detailed and professional. I believe she would ensure this transition is both smooth and efficient.

- The other three companies either did not have access to our preferred fabrics or they could not meet our supply demand. --[3]--. As a result, we will no longer be able to consider them.

**Plans for Next Week:**

- Contact P&M Textiles to set up a conference call about payment and shipping terms. --[4]--.

- Review final designs for all products and request revisions if need be. Meet with the design team to discuss any changes.

--------------------------------------------------------------------

倫格魯寢具

每週狀況報告：9月5日至9日
撰寫人：專案統籌 亞歷山卓·科賓

本週成果：

- 與墨西哥目前生產寢具產品的四間製造商聯繫。以電子郵件將我們新寢具的設計規格與生產價格、交貨時間、布料取得以及運費等相關問題寄給對方。

- 根據回覆，看起來 P&M 紡織廠應是最佳選擇。它的地理位置比大多數公司偏南許多，但生產力可滿足我們的供應需求。此外，客戶服務部主管珊米·露意茲回覆電子郵件的速度迅速。對於問題的回覆既詳盡又專業。我相信她能確保過渡時期進行得平順又有效率。

- 其他三間公司不是無法取得我們想要的布料，就是無法達到供應的要求。所以，就不再將其列入考慮。

下週規劃：

- 與 P&M 紡織廠聯繫，以電話會議的方式討論付款與運送期限。

- 檢視所有產品的最後設計，且於必要時要求修改。與設計團隊開會討論修改。

**154** What is suggested about Rengrew Bedding?

(A) It has just hired a new manager.
(B) It is a brand new company in Mexico.
(C) It has its own factories on-site.
(D) It is getting ready to launch new products. *

本週的第一項成果為「E-mailed them design specifications for our new bedding sets along with questions about production pricing, turnaround time, fabric availability, and shipping costs.」，提及新的寢具，包含其設計規格到運費等項目，因此 (D) 為最適當的答案。

下列何者與倫格魯寢具有關？

(A) 剛聘僱一位新主管。
(B) 在墨西哥是間全新的公司。
(C) 有自己的工廠。
(D) 準備好要推出新產品。

字彙
own 自己的
factory 工廠
launch 推出

---

**155** According to the report, what did Mr. Corbin do during the week of September 5?

(A) Finalized some design information
(B) Assessed potential business partners *
(C) Visited a manufacturer in person
(D) Requested a payment be delayed

請務必掌握本題要問的是「本週成果（Accomplished this Week）」。綜合文中的三項內容，推知科賓先生接洽四間可能合作的廠商並一一評估，可以得知答案應為 (B)。

根據報告，科賓先生在9月5日那週做了什麼？

(A) 定案一些設計資料
(B) 評估可能的生意伙伴
(C) 親自參觀工廠
(D) 申請延後付款

字彙
finalize 定案，最終確定
assess 評估
in person 親自
delay 延遲，延誤

---

**156** What is mentioned about Ms. Ruiz?

(A) She is new to P&M Textiles.
(B) She suggested some changes.
(C) She contacted some businesses.
(D) She is easy to work with. *

閱讀文章時，請特別留意題目關鍵人名露意茲女士（Ms. Ruiz）。第二項提到了 P&M 紡織廠的回覆，當中寫道這位女士的回覆十分迅速，內容也很詳盡與專業（Her responses to my questions were very detailed and professional.），表示她很好共事，因此 (D) 為最適當的答案。

文中提到何者與露意茲女士有關？

(A) 她剛到P&M紡織廠上班。
(B) 她提出了變更的建議。
(C) 她聯絡了一些公司。
(D) 好共事。

字彙
be easy to . . . 容易做……

---

**157** In which of the positions marked [1], [2], [3], and [4] does the following sentence best belong?

"It is located further south than most companies, but it has the capacity to meet our supply needs."

(A) [1]
(B) [2] *
(C) [3]
(D) [4]

題目句為針對「特定公司的（位置、產能）評價」。根據文意，插入句放入「本週成果（Accomplished this Week）」下且與可能合作的廠商相關，為較適當的位置。同時在插入句前方的句子中，必須要有代名詞 It 所代表的對象，而 [2] 的前方便提到了公司名稱 P&M Textiles，因此答案應為 (B)。

下列句子最適合出現在[1]、[2]、[3]、[4]的哪個位置中？
「它的地理位置比大多數公司偏南許多，但生產力可滿足我們的供應需求。」

(A) [1]
(B) [2]
(C) [3]
(D) [4]

字彙
capacity 生產力

字彙
banquet 宴席
representative 代表人員
confirm 確認
reservation 預約
preference 偏愛
layout 布置
equipment 設備
accommodation 住宿

Questions 158-159 refer to the following form.

# Grand Avenue Hotel: Banquet Services

Thank you for choosing Grand Avenue Hotel for your banquet. Please fill out the information below. [158] One of our guest services representatives will contact you to confirm your reservation and request payment information.

Reservation Name: _____

Event Date: _____

E-mail: _____

Business Phone: _____ Personal Phone: _____

**Room Preference:**

[  ] Diamond Room (up to 100 guests)

[  ] Rose Room (up to 150 guests)

[  ] Starlight Room (up to 200 guests)

[159] **Requested Layout:**

[  ] Dinner (round tables and chairs)

[  ] Dinner and Dance (tables and a dance floor)

[  ] Dinner and Speech (tables and a stage)

[  ] Other : _____

**Food and Beverages:**

[  ] Full-Service Buffet and Dessert Bar

[  ] Three-Course Catered Dinner

AV Equipment Required: [  ] Yes [  ] No

Explain: _____

Hotel Accommodation for Guests: [  ] Yes [  ] No

Number of Rooms: _____

------------------------------------------------------------

## 格蘭大道飯店：宴會服務

感謝您選擇格蘭大道飯店為宴會地點。請填寫以下資料。本公司客戶服務代表人員將與您連絡，以確認預約及請求付款資訊。

預約姓名：_____　　活動日期：_____

電子郵件：_____　　公司電話：_____

個人電話：_____

**宴會廳偏好：**

[  ] 鑽石廳（人數上限 100 人）　　　[  ] 玫瑰廳（人數上限 150 人）

[  ] 星光廳（人數上限 200 人）

**需要的布置：**

[  ] 晚宴（圓桌與椅子）　[  ] 晚宴與舞會（餐桌與舞池）

[  ] 晚宴與致詞（餐桌與舞台）　[  ] 其他：_____

**餐點與飲料：**

[  ] 全套服務自助餐與甜點吧　[  ] 三道菜式晚餐

視聽設備需求：[  ] 是 [  ] 否　說明：_____

賓客飯店住宿：[  ] 是 [  ] 否　房間數：_____

**158** According to the form, what will Grand Avenue Hotel staff do?

(A) E-mail brochures with room photos

(B) Assist customers with setup and cleanup

(C) Offer free accommodation vouchers to guests

(D) Contact customers about payment information*

閱讀文章時，請特別留意「飯店員工的工作內容」。表格第一段中的：「One of our guest services representatives will contact you to confirm your reservation and request payment information.」，表示代表人員會與填表人聯絡，確認預約內容與請求付款資訊，因此答案應為 (D)。

\* 答案改寫：representative → staff

---

根據表單，格蘭大道飯店的員工將做什麼事？

**(A)** 以電子郵件寄出含房間照片的手冊

**(B)** 協助客戶布置與清理

**(C)** 提供賓客免費住宿券

**(D)** 聯絡客戶有關付款資訊

字彙
**assist** 協助
**setup** 布置
**voucher** 票券

---

**159** What is implied about Grand Avenue Hotel's banquet services?

(A) It requires payment for the use of audio-visual equipment.

(B) It will arrange the room to suit the event.*

(C) It provides discounted hotel rooms to banquet guests.

(D) It offers free live music for dinner and dance events.

Requested Layout（需要的布置）的該段說明中，有晚宴、晚宴與舞會、晚宴與致詞三種，因此可以得知會場中的桌椅會依據活動的特性，有不同的安排，因此答案應為 (B)。

下列何者與格蘭大道飯店的服務有關？

**(A)** 要求支付視聽器材使用費。

**(B)** 將安排適合活動的場地。

**(C)** 提供宴會賓客飯店住宿折扣。

**(D)** 於晚宴和舞會提供免費現場音樂演奏。

ACTUAL TEST 3

PART 7 中譯＋解析

Questions 160-162 refer to the following job advertisement.

https://www.employmentfind.com
**Find Employment Online**
***Build Your Career Today!***

The real estate business can be hard when you're working alone. At Team Real Estate, you are not alone! Our large network of real estate agents makes showing and selling properties easy. [160] By sharing information on potential buyers in our database, we sell more properties than any other agency in the country. Our shared commission rates encourage our team members to work together to get the job done.

[161] Complete our new real estate training seminar and apply for your real estate license. If you're successful, you may be offered a full-time contract position with full benefits.

Education and experience will be considered before you are offered a contract. University degrees are a plus, but high school graduates may also apply. Applicants must have access to their own vehicle, as driving to and from local properties is a must.

To apply for this position, please click the button below. You'll need to input your e-mail address, phone number, and upload your resume. Only those selected for interviews will be contacted. Prior to interviews, we recommend that all candidates familiarize themselves with our company policies. [162] Please visit www.teamrealestate.com/careers to learn more about this.

**Apply Now**

--------------------------------------------------------------------

http://www.employmentfind.com

線上求職
今天就打造您的事業！

當您單打獨鬥時，房地產這一行會是艱辛的。在團隊房地產，您不孤單！本公司大型房地產仲介網絡，讓房地產的展示與銷售變簡單了。藉由分享資料庫中潛在買家的資訊，我們比國內其他仲介賣出更多的房地產。我們共享的佣金鼓勵團隊成員一同努力完成工作。

完成我們新的房地產教育訓練研習，並申請房地產執照。如果成功地申請到執照，那您就可以獲得一份附有完整福利的全職合約職位。

在您獲得合約之前，學歷與經歷將列入考量。大學學歷尤佳，但是高中畢業生亦可應徵。應徵者必須自備交通工具，因為開車來回當地房產為工作所需。

請點選以下按鍵來應徵職位。您需要輸入電子郵件信箱、電話號碼並上傳履歷表。只有通過書面篩選者會獲得通知。面試前，建議所有應徵者先自行了解本公司法規。更多資訊，請至公司網址 www.teamrealestate.com 查詢。

立即申請

**160** What duty is suggested as part of the job?

(A) Listing clients on a shared database*
(B) Offering advice on upgrading properties
(C) Attracting clients through phone calls
(D) Coordinating a mentorship program

閱讀文章時，請特別留意題目關鍵「仲介工作的內容」。第一段中的「By sharing information on potential buyers in our database, we sell more properties than any other agency in the country.」，提到該公司仲介會分享潛在買家的資訊到資料庫內，因此 (A) 為最適當的答案。

下列何者為這份工作的職責之一？

(A) 將客戶名單分享至共用資料庫中
(B) 提供改進宅第的建議
(C) 以電話方式吸引客戶
(D) 協調督導計畫

---

**161** According to the advertisement, what is requested for a contract position?

(A) A college diploma
(B) A real estate license*
(C) Marketing experience
(D) Employment references

第二段中提到完成教育訓練並申請房地產證照（Complete our new real estate training seminar and apply for your real estate license.），並表示如果成功完成上述要求，就可能得到全職工作的職缺，因此答案為 (B)。

根據廣告，下列何者為合約職位所要求的條件？

(A) 大學文憑
(B) 房地產執照*
(C) 行銷經驗
(D) 推薦函

字彙
diploma 文憑
reference 推薦函，參考資料

---

**162** According to the advertisement, why should applicants visit the Team Real Estate website?

(A) To learn about Team Real Estate's procedures*
(B) To apply for a contract position with benefits
(C) To upload a resume and references
(D) To inquire about the time of a training session

閱讀文章時，請特別留意解題關鍵在 website。最後一段的「Please visit www.teamrealestate.com/careers to learn more about this.」，當中的 this 即為前方句子中提到的 company policies，因此 (A) 為最適當的答案。

根據廣告，求職者為什麼要上團隊房地產公司的網站？

(A) 了解團隊房地產公司的常規
(B) 應徵具福利的合約職位
(C) 上傳履歷表與推薦函
(D) 詢問教育訓練講習的時間

字彙
procedure 常規；程序
inquire 詢問

字彙
community 社區
psychology 心理學
publish 發表，出版
academic 學術的
journal 期刊
dedication 致力，奉獻
outreach 拓展
found 創辦
troubled
麻煩的，問題叢生的
charity 慈善（機構）
individual 個人
organize 籌辦，組織
the homeless 無家可歸的人
unique 獨特的
retire 退休
retain 保持
retirement 退休
honor 表揚，給與榮耀
fireworks show 煙火秀
present 頒發
achievement 成就
award 獎

**Questions 163-166 refer to the following article.**

### [163] 50 Years of Community Service

March 27 — [163, 165 (B)] Professor Abraham Drew is known in the local community not for his years as a teacher of psychology or for his numerous papers published in academic journals, but for his dedication to community outreach. Fifty years ago, Mr. Drew founded the first after-school program for local children, which has helped numerous children in the city. [165 (A)] The program, which started as a baseball camp for troubled boys, has since grown into Homework Helpers for elementary school-aged children, Art on the Street for teenagers, and Give Back, a charity in which individuals and businesses organize food drives for the homeless. "I never thought my after-school program would develop into all these unique programs," Mr. Drew said, "but [165 (D)] there was so much community interest. Everywhere, people were looking for a way to help out."

After 50 years of service, Mr. Drew will retire from both his job as a professor and as program coordinator. His grandson, Michael Drew, will retain control of the programs. "I'm very happy to continue what my grandfather started," Michael Drew said. "He's a great man, and the community needs the work he has done."

[165 (D)] Mr. Drew's volunteers will host a retirement party to honor him next month at Wilfred Park. The party will include performances by local bands, food prepared by local restaurants, and a small fireworks show. [166] The mayor will present Mr. Drew with a Lifetime Service Achievement Award as thanks for his years of giving back to the community. For details about this event, please visit www.wilfredpark.com/events/April.

------------------------------------------------

### 社區服務50年

3月27日——亞伯拉罕·德魯教授在當地頗負盛名，不是因為他擔任心理學教授多年，或於學術期刊發表許多論文，而是因為他致力於社區擴展的原故。50年前，德魯先生為當地孩童創辦了第一個課後計畫，幫助了全市許多孩童。該計畫以為問題男童創立的棒球營起，現在已經發展成「國小學童的作業幫手」、「給青少年的街頭藝術」以及「回饋」，一個個人與企業為遊民籌辦食物募捐行動的慈善機構。「我從沒想過自己的課後計畫可以發展成這些獨特的計畫。」德魯先生說，「而是有太多來自社區的關注。到處都有人在尋求幫助他人擺脫困難的方法。」

在服務50年後，德魯先生即將自教職與計畫統籌的職位上退休。他的孫子麥可·德魯繼續管理這些計畫。「我很開心能延續祖父所創立的一切。」麥可·德魯說，「他是個很棒的人，而社區需要他所做的這一切。」

下個月，德魯先生的志工群，將於威爾弗瑞德公園舉辦一個退休派對來表揚他。派對將包括當地樂團的表演、當地餐廳所提供的美食以及一場小型煙火秀。市長將頒發終身服務成就獎給德魯先生，以感謝他多年來對社區的貢獻。更多活動相關資訊，請上網站 www.wilfredpark.com/events/april 查詢。

**163** Why most likely was the article written?

(A) To celebrate the founding of a city
(B) To encourage readers to donate to charity
(C) To announce the closing of a community business
(D) To highlight the achievements of a local figure*

在文章的前半部，大多會出現文章的目的；若文章為報導，標題本身就是解題的線索。由標題可以推測報導應該和社區服務五十年（50 Years of Community Service）的人相關的故事。且報導的第一句：「Professor Abraham Drew is known in the local community not for his years as a teacher of psychology or for his numerous papers published in academic journals, but for his dedication to community outreach.」，更可確定報導的目的是為了彰顯德魯教授於當地的貢獻，因此答案應為 (D)。

為什麼會有這篇文章？

(A) 慶祝城市的創立
(B) 鼓勵讀者捐款給慈善機構
(C) 宣布當地社區企業的結束營業
(D) 彰顯當地人物的成就

字彙
**founding** 創立
**donate** 捐款
**highlight** 彰顯；強調
**figure** 人物

---

**164** The word "retain" in paragraph 2, line 2, is closest in meaning to

(A) contribute to
(B) agree with
(C) remember
(D) keep*

單字所在句的重點，應為往後將由孫子「繼續」管理計畫，因此最適合替換的單字應為 keep，答案為 (D)。

第二段、第二行的「**retain**」與下列哪一個意思最接近？

(A) 貢獻
(B) 同意
(C) 記住
(D) 保持

字彙
**contribute** 貢獻

---

**165** What is NOT suggested about Abraham Drew?

(A) He started a baseball camp for boys.
(B) He instructs students at a university.
(C) He will open another school next year.*
(D) He inspired others to do charity work.

報導第一段詳細說明了關鍵人名 Abraham Drew（亞伯拉罕·德魯）的經歷，請對照各選項的內容，並刪除文章中提及的選項。(A) 出現在「The program, which started as a baseball camp for troubled boys」當中；(B) 可以由下確認：「Professor Abraham Drew is known in the local community not for his years as a teacher of psychology.」；由「there was so much community interest. Everywhere, people were looking for a way to help out」和最後一段的 Mr. Drew's volunteers 可以推測出 (D)，因此本題的答案應為 (C)。

下列何者不是指亞伯拉罕·德魯？

(A) 他創立了男童棒球營。
(B) 他在大學教學。
(C) 明年將開設另一間學校。
(D) 他啟發他人進行慈善工作。

字彙
**instruct** 指導
**inspire** 給……啟發；激勵

---

**166** What is stated about the party at Wilfred Park?

(A) Local comedy acts will perform.
(B) The city will host the celebration.
(C) Participants can attend for a small fee.
(D) Mr. Drew will be honored with an award.*

閱讀文章時，請特別留意解題關鍵為 Wilfred Park。最後一段中提到在公園舉辦派對有關的內容，由「The mayor will present Mr. Drew with a Lifetime Service Achievement Award as thanks for his years of giving back to the community.」，可以確認答案為 (D)。

下列何者說的是在威爾弗瑞德公園所舉辦的派對？

(A) 當地喜劇節目將演出。
(B) 市府將主辦慶祝活動。
(C) 參加者需支付小額費用。
(D) 將頒獎給德魯先生。

字彙
clarify 釐清，弄清楚
shortly 不久

Questions 167-168 refer to the following text message chain.

**Pedro Alando [11:00 A.M.]:**

Ms. Wilson, please check your e-mail. I sent you an updated contract.

**Tina Wilson [11:02 A.M.]:**

OK, thank you. [167] Has the payment scale been updated as well?

**Pedro Alando [11:03 A.M.]:**

[167] Certainly. Because you've been with us for longer than a year, [168] you will now be paid $100 dollars for every color photo you take for our magazine instead of $80.

**Tina Wilson [11:05 A.M.]:**

Excellent. Thank you for clarifying that. I'll have a look at the contract, sign it, and send it back shortly.

**Pedro Alando [11:08 A.M.]:**

Fantastic. We are very pleased you have decided to work with us for another year.

| SEND |
| --- |

---------------------------------------------------------------------

**佩德羅・艾倫多 [ 上午 11:00 ]：**

威爾森女士，請查看您的電子信箱。我已經將更新後的合約寄給您了。

**蒂娜・威爾森 [ 上午 11:02 ]：**

好的，謝謝您。酬勞等級也更新了嗎？

**佩德羅・艾倫多 [ 上午 11:03 ]：**

當然。因為您已經和我們合作超過一年，所以您現在為本雜誌所拍攝的彩色照片，每張費用將從 80 元調為 100 元。

**蒂娜・威爾森 [ 上午 11:05 ]：**

太棒了。感謝您弄清楚這部分。我會看看合約，簽名後盡快寄回。

**佩德羅・艾倫多 [ 上午 11:08 ]：**

太好了。很高興您明年能繼續和我們一起合作。

| 送出 |
| --- |

**167** At 11:03 A.M. what does Mr. Alando mean when he writes, "Certainly"?

(A) He will send an e-mail one more time.
(B) He is sure of the success of a plan.
(C) He is willing to share some information.
(D) He made a previously agreed-upon change.*

題目句是針對問句「Has the payment scale been updated as well?（酬勞等級也更新了嗎？）」的回覆，可以推測雙方先前已達成酬勞調整的協議，因此 (D) 為最適當的答案。

在上午**11:03**時，艾倫多先生所寫的「當然」是什麼意思？

(A) 他會再寄一次電子郵件。
(B) 他確定計畫成功。
(C) 他願意分享一些資訊。
(D) 他做了先前商議的修訂。

字彙
**previously** 之前地

**168** Who most likely is Ms. Wilson?

(A) A contract lawyer
(B) A magazine editor
(C) A photographer*
(D) A journalist

本題要找出與「職業」有關的解題線索。上午 11 點 03 分傳給威爾森女士的訊息中寫道：「you will now be paid $100 dollars for every color photo you take for our magazine instead of $80」，當中提到「拍攝彩色照片」，因此威爾森女士最有可能的職業為攝影師，答案為 (C)。

威爾森女士最有可能是誰？

(A) 合約律師
(B) 雜誌編輯
(C) 攝影師
(D) 記者

字彙
**editor** 編輯

Questions 169-171 refer to the following e-mail.

**To:** Janine Robertson <jrobertson@wetrainyou.com>
**From:** Wendal Sparks <wbsparks@consumerconventioncenter.com>
**Date:** 4 January
**Subject:** Annual Small Business Conference

Dear Ms. Robertson,

169 I was so glad to hear that you'll be participating in our third annual Small Business Conference on February 3. --[1]--. 170 I know this was very last minute, so I really appreciate your enthusiasm about stepping in for Tim Brewers. Your experience heading a small business training company will really interest our participants. --[2]--. We'd especially love it if you could outline some of the first steps a new business must take toward training new employees.

If you would like to offer promotional pamphlets for your business, please send them at least a week prior to your speaking date. Also, please let me know what audio-visual equipment you'll need for your presentation. --[3]--. Additionally, 171 may I use the biography you have on your website as material for our conference program? --[4]--.

Thanks again for everything.

Sincerely,

Wendal Sparks
Conference Coordinator

--------------------------------------------------------------------------------

收件者：珍妮‧羅賓森 (jrobertson@wetrainyou.com)
寄件者：溫戴爾‧史帕克斯 (wbsparks@consumerconventioncenter.com)
日期：1 月 4 日
主旨：年度小型企業會議

親愛的羅賓森女士，

很開心聽到您將出席即將於 2 月 3 日舉辦的第三屆年度小型企業會議。我知道時間已經逼近了，所以非常感謝您那麼熱心地頂替提姆‧布維爾斯。您在管理小型教育訓練公司上的經驗，絕對會引起與會者的興趣。若您能夠概述新公司在訓練新員工時，必須採取的基本步驟，一定會深受歡迎。

若您有意提供貴公司的宣傳手冊，請至少於演講前一週送來。同時，也請告知我們您演講時所需的視聽器材。此外，我可以將您網站上的個人簡介用為會議活動的資料嗎？若您偏好使用不同的簡介，請以電子郵件寄給我。

再次感謝您所做的一切。

會議統籌
溫戴爾‧史帕克斯敬上

**169** Why did Mr. Sparks most likely send the e-mail?

(A) To propose an itinerary change
(B) To ask for an updated schedule
(C) To send a belated invitation
(D) To recognize an offer of acceptance*

電郵第一句「I was so glad to hear that you'll be participating in our third annual Small Business Conference on February 3.」，由此可以得知撰寫郵件的主要目的為「向對方的參與表達欣喜與感謝之意」，因此 (D) 為最適當的答案。

史帕克斯先生為什麼要寄這封電子郵件？

(A) 提出行程異動
(B) 要求更新後的時程表
(C) 寄一封過時的邀請函
(D) 接受對方同意參與

字彙
**belated** 過時的
**invitation** 邀請（函）
**recognize** 認可；辨別
**acceptance** 接受

---

**170** What is suggested about Mr. Brewers?

(A) He attends conferences every year.
(B) He is unable to speak at a conference.*
(C) He works as an event coordinator.
(D) He started his own small business.

閱讀文章時，請特別留意關鍵人名布維爾斯先生（Mr. Brewers）。第一段中表示即使時間上過於倉促，對方（羅賓森女士）仍願意代替提姆·布維爾斯演講，真的非常感謝對方（I know this was very last minute, so I really appreciate your enthusiasm about stepping in for Tim Brewers.），可知布維爾斯先生無法在會議演講，因此 (B) 為最適當的答案。

下列何者與布維爾斯先生有關？

(A) 他每年都出席會議。
(B) 他無法在會議中演講。
(C) 他擔任活動統籌。
(D) 他創立了自己的小型公司。

---

**171** In which of the positions marked [1], [2], [3], and [4] does the following sentence best belong?

"If you'd prefer to use a different text, please e-mail it to me."

(A) [1]
(B) [2]
(C) [3]
(D) [4]*

根據文意，插入句前方的句子必須提到有關「文字使用」的內容，因此插入句應放在詢問「是否可以使用對方網站中的個人簡歷」之後。插入句的 texts 對應到前句的 biography，故答案為 (D)。

下列句子最適合出現在[1]、[2]、[3]、[4]的哪個位置中？
「若您偏好使用不同的簡介，請以電子郵件寄給我。」

(A) [1]
(B) [2]
(C) [3]
(D) [4]

字彙
identical 完全相同的
personalized 客製化的
storeroom 儲藏室
urgent 緊急的
manufacturing 生產，製造
rush 緊急的，匆忙的
rush order 緊急訂單
duplicate 複製品
work 行得通

Questions 172-175 refer to the following text message chain.

**Jan Swanson**　　　　　4 September, 2:35
Jonathan, have you sent order #2256 out for delivery?
If not, [172, 174] we need to add another identical set of personalized pens and paper to it.

**Jonathan Gruer**　　　　4 September, 2:37
The order is still in the storeroom, but it'll take at least two more days to produce the custom pens and paper.

**Jan Swanson**　　　　　4 September, 2:38
Is it possible to get it done sooner? The customer said it's urgent.

**Jonathan Gruer**　　　　4 September, 2:40
Let's check with someone from manufacturing.

*Rowena MacArthur has been added to the chat.*

**Jonathan Gruer**　　　　4 September, 2:41
[173] Rowena, do you have time for a rush order? [174] It's a duplicate of order #2256.

**Rowena MacArthur**　　4 September, 2:43
[175] I think I can get it done by tomorrow morning. Is that OK?

**Jan Swanson**　　　　　4 September, 2:44
Yes, [175] that works. Thanks a lot!

--------------------------------------------------------------------------------

珍·史雲森　　　　　　9 月 4 日 2:35
強納森，你把訂單編號 2256 的東西送去寄了嗎？
如果還沒，我們需要再加一套一樣的客製化原子筆和紙。

強納森·格魯爾　　　　9 月 4 日 2:37
這張訂單還在儲藏室，但是生產客製化的原子筆和紙，需要再花至少兩天的時間。

珍·史雲森　　　　　　9 月 4 日 2:38
有可能盡快完成嗎？客戶說急著要。

強納森·格魯爾　　　　9 月 4 日 2:40
要跟生產部的人確認一下。

羅溫娜·麥克阿瑟加入談話。

強納森·格魯爾　　　　9 月 4 日 2:41
羅溫娜，妳有空處理一張緊急訂單嗎？和訂單編號 2256 是一樣的東西。

羅溫娜·麥克阿瑟　　　9 月 4 日 2:43
我想我明天早上可以做好。這樣可以嗎？

珍·史雲森　　　　　　9 月 4 日 2:44
好，可以的。太感謝了！

## 172 What type of products does the company sell?

(A) Watches
(B) Stationery*
(C) Furniture
(D) Electronics

第一則訊息中寫道：「we need to add another identical set of personalized pens and paper to it」，當中提到解題線索——筆和紙，可以推知該公司販售文具，因此答案為 (B)。

## 173 Why does Mr. Gruer contact Ms. MacArthur?

(A) To pass on a customer complaint
(B) To find out where a staff meeting will be held
(C) To determine where an order has been shipped to
(D) To inquire about the timeframe for some work*

格魯爾先生在 2 點 41 分所傳的訊息中寫道：「Rowena, do you have time for a rush order?」，詢問對方是否有時間處理緊急訂單，因此 (D) 為最適當的答案。

## 174 What does the customer want to do?

(A) Double an order*
(B) Cancel a delivery
(C) Return a damaged item
(D) Update payment information

2 點 35 分訊息中的 another identical set，意思是指再加一套一樣的客製化的原子筆和紙，2 點 41 分的訊息中的 a duplicate of order，意思是和前述訂單一樣的東西，由此可知答案應為 (A)。

\* 答案改寫：duplicate → double

## 175 At 2:44, what does Ms. Swanson most likely mean when she writes, "that works"?

(A) She can reschedule some appointments.
(B) She is impressed with a new product.
(C) A deadline will be acceptable for a customer.*
(D) Some new items will be advertised online.

根據文意，題目中的「that works」是回答上一則訊息：「明天早上可以做好急單。這樣可以嗎？」的回覆，因此 (C) 為最適當的答案。

---

這間公司販售哪一類商品？

(A) 手錶
(B) 文具
(C) 家具
(D) 電器

字彙
stationery 文具
electronics 電器用品

格魯爾先生為什麼和麥克阿瑟女士聯絡？

(A) 轉告顧客投訴
(B) 查詢員工會議的開會地點
(C) 確定訂單物品運送地點
(D) 詢問一些工作的期限

字彙
complaint 抱怨
determine 確定，決定
timeframe 期限；時間範圍

客戶想要做什麼？

(A) 訂單加倍
(B) 取消運送
(C) 退還受損商品
(D) 更新付款資料

字彙
damaged 受損的

在2:44時，史雲森女士說「可以的」是什麼意思？

(A) 她可以重新安排預約時間。
(B) 她對於新產品印象深刻。
(C) 完工時間對顧客來說是可接受的。
(D) 有些新產品將在網路上打廣告。

字彙
be impressed with . . .
對……印象深刻
acceptable 可接受的

字彙

annual 年度的
reservation 預約
suite 套房
purpose 目的
executive
給重要人物使用的
at no extra charge
不另收費
ensure 保證，確保
complimentary 附贈的
spot 地點
in advance 預先
furthermore 再者

Questions 176-180 refer to the following e-mails.

**To:** msimpson@tristarinternational.com
**From:** bookings@stonewallhotel.com
**Date:** May 17
[176] **Subject:** Booking CV1124

Dear Ms. Simpson,

Thank you for selecting Stonewall Hotel for your company's annual workshop. [176] As you indicated on your online reservation, 12 king-sized ocean view suites have been booked for your group. Since the purpose of your visit is to conduct a business workshop, I have also reserved our executive lounge and conference room at no extra charge.

According to your online reservation, [179] your check-in date will be August 5 and your check-out will be August 8. A charge of $109 dollars for each room per night will be added to your final bill. Your reservation number is CV1124. Please ensure you record this number as you will need it should you request any changes to your reservation.

As you know, Stonewall Hotel includes many additional features and activities. [177] If your group wish to take a complimentary surfing lesson, I suggest reserving a spot in advance. Furthermore, we offer complimentary breakfasts, room service packages, and have just opened up Stonewall Grill, a brand new steak restaurant located next to the lobby.

Thank you for choosing Stonewall Hotel. We look forward to serving you.

Booking Services, Stonewall Hotel

----------------------------------------------------------------

收件者：msimpson@tristarinternational.com
寄件者：bookings@stonewallhotel.com
日期：5 月 17 日
主旨：訂房號 CV1124

親愛的辛普森女士，

感謝您選擇石牆飯店舉辦貴公司的年度研習。如同您在線上預約時所指示，已經為貴公司預訂了 12 間特大床海景套房。由於您來訪的目的是辦理企業研習，我也已經預約了免費貴賓休息室與會議廳。

根據線上預約顯示，您的入住日期為 8 月 5 日，退房則是 8 月 8 日。每晚單房的費用是 109 元，將於最終帳單一併結算。您的訂房號碼是 CV1124。請記下這個號碼，若您要求任何異動，需要提供這個號碼。

如您所知，石牆飯店涵蓋許多其他的特點與活動。若貴公司有意參加免費衝浪課程，建議您事先預約。再者，我們提供免費早餐、客房服務套餐，還有大廳旁全新開幕的牛排餐廳——石牆燒烤餐廳。

感謝您選擇石牆飯店。期待為您服務。
石牆飯店 訂房服務部

---

**To:** bookings@stonewallhotel.com
**From:** msimpson@tristarinternational.com
**Date:** May 19
**Subject:** Re: Booking CV1124
Dear booking services staff,

I am writing to let you know that there were a few errors with my reservation. My reservation number is CV1124. [179] I indicated 10 junior-sized suites when I reserved online, **but your e-mail says something different. Additionally,** [178] I also paid for a catered lunch during [179] my group's hiking trip on August 6, but that was not mentioned in your e-mail. Please make sure this service has been booked in addition to updating the correct room size. I would appreciate it if you notified me about this issue as soon as possible.

Thank you for your assistance.

Sincerely,

Margo Simpson
Office of the CEO
Tristar International

收件者：bookings@stonewallhotel.com
寄件者：msimpson@tristarinternational.com
日期：5 月 19 日
主旨：回覆：訂房號 CV1124

訂房服務部，您好：

寫這封信是為了告知我的訂單出現了一些錯誤。我的訂房編號是 CV1124。在線上預約時，我所指定的是 10 間小套房，但您信中所說的卻不是這樣。除此之外，我已經支付了本公司 8 月 6 日健行行程的午餐，您卻未在信中提到此事。除了更新正確的房型外，也請確認這項服務已經預約完成。若您能盡快地告知這問題的後續處理狀況，本人將非常感激。

感謝您的協助。

三星國際公司
執行長辦公室 馬柯·辛普森敬上

字彙
**error** 錯誤
**cater** 為……提供飲食
**appreciate** 感謝
**notify** 告知
**issue** 問題
**assistance** 協助

ACTUAL TEST **3** PART **7** 中譯＋解析

第一封電子郵件的目的是什麼？

**(A)** 確認團體預約
**(B)** 告知新規定
**(C)** 協助預約
**(D)** 提供免費升等

字彙
**policy** 政策；規定
**assist** 協助
**make a reservation** 預約

**176** What is the purpose of the first e-mail?

(A) To confirm a group reservation*
(B) To inform of a new policy
(C) To assist in making a reservation
(D) To provide a free upgrade

由標題 Subject: Booking CV1124 可以得知郵件內容應與「預約」有關。且由第一段中的「As you indicated on your online reservation, 12 king-sized ocean view suites have been booked for your group.」，可以得知來信目的為確認團體預約，答案應為 (A)。

---

下列何者與石牆的衝浪課程有關？

**(A)** 只提供上午時段。
**(B)** 是新服務項目。
**(C)** 只是暫時提供。
**(D)** 是受歡迎的主打項目。

字彙
**temporarily** 暫時地

**177** What is suggested about Stonewall's surfing lessons?

(A) They are available only in the mornings.
(B) They are a new service.
(C) They are being offered temporarily.
(D) They are a popular feature.*

閱讀文章時，請特別留意題目關鍵字 surfing lessons。第一封郵件（第一篇）的第三段中提到石牆飯店提供各式各樣的活動，如果想要參加衝浪課程（If your group wish to take a complimentary surfing lesson），建議提前預約（I suggest reserving a spot in advance）。由此可以推測出因為衝浪課程很受歡迎，如果不先預約的話，可能會沒有位置，因此 (D) 為最適當的答案。

---

飯店的記錄遺漏了什麼資料？

**(A)** 已經預約了休息室。
**(B)** 將於8月5號抵達。
**(C)** 已經預訂了餐食服務。
**(D)** 已經預付了房費。

字彙
**prepay** 預付

**178** What information in the hotel's records is missing?

(A) The lounge has been reserved.
(B) The group will arrive on August 5.
(C) A catering service is booked.*
(D) The room bill has been prepaid.

閱讀文章時，請特別留意「記錄中遺漏的內容」。第二封郵件（第二篇）的中間「I also paid for a catered lunch during my group's hiking trip on August 6, but that was not mentioned in your e-mail.」，表示訂房人員並未在郵件中提到與預訂午餐有關的內容，因此答案應為 (C)。

**179** What can be inferred about the group from Tristar International?

(A) It consists of 12 members.
(B) It will go hiking on the second day of the workshop.*
(C) It will have dinner at the Stonewall Grill.
(D) It will arrive a day later than the reservation states.

本題的關鍵字為 Tristar International，請閱讀由他們所撰寫的第二封郵件（第二篇）。在前半部中的「I indicated 10 junior-sized suites when I reserved online，因此可知將有 10 人入住，所以先刪除 (A)。綜合第二篇中間的 my group's hiking trip on August 6 和第一篇中第二段的 your check-in date will be August 5，可以得知健行日在入住飯店的第二天，答案應為 (B)。

**180** In the second e-mail, the word "issue" in paragraph 1, line 6, is closest in meaning to

(A) alteration
(B) selection
(C) price
(D) problem*

請找出單字所在的句子，並掌握句意。根據文意，本句應為針對房型與餐食服務的「問題」，希望對方能盡快通知，選項中最適合替換的單字為 problem，故 (D) 正確。

在右側邊欄

文中可推論出三星國際公司什麼？

(A) 由12位成員組成。
(B) 研習第二天要去健行。
(C) 將於石牆燒烤餐廳吃晚餐。
(D) 會比預約時間晚一天抵達。

字彙
consist of . . . 由……組成
state 陳述

在第二封電子郵件中，第一段、第六行的「issue」與下列哪一個意思最接近？

(A) 變更
(B) 選擇
(C) 價格
(D) 問題

字彙
alteration 變更
selection 選擇

Questions 181-185 refer to the following notice and calendar.

**Heber Birdwatching Club**

April 2 — [181] The Northville Recreation Board recently announced the creation of the Heber Park Birdwatching Club at Heber Wildlife Park. [183] The birdwatching club will meet from Friday through Sunday, from 1 P.M. until 3 P.M. The club meetings will run all summer long and will feature a number of lookout sites located on the Heber Trails. Each participant should dress appropriately for hiking on the trails and bring a supply of drinking water. Cameras are allowed for participants who want to photograph the numerous bird species located in Heber Wildlife Park. Up to 10 members may join the club, and those interested can sign up with the club coordinator, Mindy Beckett (334-998-0034).

-----------------------------------------------------------------

賀伯賞鳥社

4 月 2 日 —— 諾斯維爾休閒處最近宣布，在賀伯野生動物園創立了賀伯公園賞鳥社。賞鳥社聚會時間為週五至週日下午 1:00 至 3:00。社團聚會將持續整個夏季，並以賀伯步道上多處賞鳥點為主要特色。每位參加者需穿著適合步道健行的服裝，並自行攜帶飲用水。參加者欲拍攝賀伯野生動物園中的各種鳥類，可攜帶相機。參加上限人數為 10 人，有意參加者，可向社團統籌明蒂‧貝克特報名（334-998-0034）。

## June Weekend Activities at Heber Wildlife Park

- **Friday** — [185]12:00 P.M. Children's Picnic (Camp and Recreation Park)
  - [183]2:00 P.M. Heber Birdwatching Club (Squirrel Trail)
  - 4:00 P.M. T&V Industries Weekly Baseball Game (Diamond)

- **Saturday** — [183]2:00 P.M. Heber Birdwatching Club (Squirrel Trail)
  - [184]4:00 P.M. Barbecue Madness (East Pavilion on June 10 and 24 only)

- **Sunday** - 10:00 A.M. Nature Watercolor Painting (Gallery Building, $15 per person)
  - [183]2:00 P.M. Heber Birdwatching Club (Squirrel Trail)
  - 4:00 P.M. Level A Soccer (Soccer field)
  - 6:00 P.M. Music at the Park (West Pavilion)

For more information on any of the above events, please visit www.heberwildlifepark.com or call 556-332-0989.

----------------------------------------------------------------

賀伯野生動物園六月週末活動表

- 星期五 ── 中午 12:00 兒童野餐（營地與休閒公園）
  ── 下午 2:00 賀伯賞鳥社（松鼠步道）
  ── 下午 4:00 T&V 企業每週棒球賽（鑽石球場）

- 星期六 ── 下午 2:00 賀伯賞鳥社（松鼠步道）
  ── 下午 4:00 瘋燒烤（東亭，僅限 6 月 10 日與 6 月 24 日）

- 星期日 ── 上午 10:00 自然水彩畫（美術館大樓，每人 15 元）
  ── 下午 2:00 賀伯賞鳥社（松鼠步道）
  ── 下午 4:00 A 級足球（足球場）
  ── 下午 6:00 公園音樂會（西亭）

更多與上述活動相關資訊，請上網站 www.heberwildlifepark.com 或來電 556-332-0989。

----

**181** What is the purpose of the notice?

(A) To inform of a new activity at Heber Wildlife Park*

(B) To announce a new coordinator for the Heber Birdwatching Club

(C) To apologize for the cancellation of an event at Heber Wildlife Park

(D) To advertise a new position at the Northville Recreation Board

公告（第一篇）的第一段中「The Northville Recreation Board recently announced the creation of the Heber Park Birdwatching Club at Heber Wildlife Park.」，由此可以得知答案應為 (A)。在文章的前半部，大多會出現與文章主旨有關的解題線索。

這則公告的目的是什麼？

(A) 告知賀伯野生動物園的新活動

(B) 宣布賀伯賞鳥社的新統籌人員

(C) 為賀伯野生動物園取消的活動致歉

(D) 宣傳諾斯維爾休閒處的新職缺

----

**182** In the notice, the word "run" in paragraph 1, line 3, is closest in meaning to

(A) jog

(B) continue*

(C) roam

(D) grow

單字所在句的意思應為夏天賞鳥社仍會「持續進行」。根據句意，選項中最適合替換的單字為 continue，故選 (B)。

在公告中，第一段、第三行的「run」與下列哪一個意思最接近？

(A) 慢跑

(B) 持續

(C) 漫步

(D) 成長

字彙
continue 持續
roam 漫步

下列何者與六月的賞鳥社有關？

(A) 有12位成員。
(B) 要求參加者攜帶相機。
(C) 見面時間有異動。
(D) 社團統籌將不會出席。

**183** What is suggested about the birdwatching club in June?

(A) It has 12 members.
(B) It requires participants to bring cameras.
(C) Its meeting time has been changed.*
(D) Its coordinator will be absent.

本題必須綜合野生動物園六月的時間表（第二篇）和有關賞鳥社的公告（第一篇）後，才能順利解題。第一篇的第一段「The birdwatching club will meet from Friday through Sunday, from 1 P.M. until 3 P.M.」；而第二篇中賞鳥的時間為 2:00 P.M.，綜合兩者內容後，可以得知賞鳥時間已改，答案為 (C)。

---

下列哪一項活動只在六月舉辦兩次？

(A) T&V企業棒球賽
(B) 瘋燒烤
(C) 自然水彩畫
(D) 公園音樂會

**184** What activity will only occur twice in June?

(A) T&V Industries Baseball Game
(B) Barbecue Madness*
(C) Nature Watercolor Painting
(D) Music at the Park

請從野生動物園六月的時間表（第二篇）中找出「只進行兩次的活動」。在時間表星期六的說明 Barbecue Madness (East Pavilion on June 10 and 24 only)，可知答案應為 (B)。

---

下列何者與賀伯野生動物園有關？

(A) 它的涼亭全都改善了。
(B) 營區全年開放。
(C) 有湖和噴水池。
(D) 有給小朋友的特別活動。

**185** What is indicated about Heber Wildlife Park?

(A) Its pavilions have all been upgraded.
(B) Its campground is open all year round.
(C) It includes a lake and a water fountain.
(D) It has special programs for children.*

本題的關鍵字為 Heber Wildlife Park，在該野生公園六月的時間表（第二篇）中，星期五的活動有 Children's Picnic，由此可以推測出答案應為 (D)。

Toronto Tours

## ★★★★★
## Toronto, Ontario

[186] To celebrate its first year of business, [188] Toronto Tours is offering a special 20% discount on Culture of Toronto tours booked between April 5 and May 5. [186] This is our most popular tour and is offered every Friday. The following is breakdown of our standard itinerary.

▶ The Royal Ontario Museum: Start at the famous Royal Ontario Museum. Enjoy some of the most beautiful art in the world in the ROM's many modern galleries. See the latest archeological discoveries on display and a number of large dinosaur species. April's special exhibit: 18th Century Maps.

▶ The Hockey Hall of Fame: Head over to the Hockey Hall of Fame and see Canada's greatest hockey legends remembered in numerous video exhibits. Learn the history of Canada's favorite sport, and view memorabilia that belonged to players of the past.

▶ [190] The Danforth Festival: Conclude your tour at the Danforth Festival. Enjoy a taste of Greek culture at this energetic street party. Sample food from Toronto's many Greek restaurants while you enjoy live music and dancing. (Until April 20)

Note: The final portion of the tour will be subject to changes depending on which festivals are taking place downtown. Additionally, [187] all entrance fees are covered in your package price, but food and beverages costs are extra.

--------------------------------------------------------

多倫多旅行社

## ★★★★★
### 安大略省多倫多

為慶祝創業第一年,只要在4月5日至5月5日間訂購多倫多文化團之旅,多倫多旅行社就提供八折的特別優惠。這是本旅行社最受歡迎的行程,每週五開團。以下是標準行程的細目說明。

安大略皇家博物館:以著名的安大略皇家博物館為起點。在安大略皇家博物館多個現代美術館內,享受世界絕美的藝術品。參觀展出中的最新考古發現與許多大型恐龍物種。四月特別展:18世紀地圖。

曲棍球名人堂:前進曲棍球名人堂,觀賞影片中深受世人懷念的加拿大最佳曲棍球傳奇人物。了解加拿大最受歡迎運動的歷史,看看過往球員的重要收藏品。

丹福斯節:在丹福斯節為旅程畫下句點。在活力四射的街道派對感受希臘文化。當你享受現場演奏音樂與舞蹈的同時,品嚐由多倫多多家希臘餐館所提供的餐點。(至4月20日止)

備註:旅遊的最後一項行程,將視市中心舉辦的慶典活動有所異動。另外,套裝行程費用僅含全部門票,餐點及飲料需自付。

字彙
**breakdown** 明細
**itinerary** 旅行行程
**archeological** 考古學的
**dinosaur** 恐龍
**species** 物種
**exhibit** 展覽
**head (v.)** 出發
**memorabilia** 收藏品
**conclude** 結束
**energetic** 充滿活力的
**portion** 部分
**be subject to . . .**
視……而定,依照
**depending on . . .**
以……情況而定

**From:** Susan Malek

**To:** Samuel Park

[188] **Date:** April 10

**Re:** Reservation Confirmation

Dear Mr. Park,

Thank you for booking your tour with Toronto Tours. Below is a summary of your tour information. Should you have any questions or concerns, please contact me at 416-888-3232.

| | |
|---|---|
| **Tour name:** Culture of Toronto | |
| **Tour date:** April 12 | |
| **Starting Time:** 9:00 A.M. at Toronto Union Station | |
| **Return to Union Station:** 11:30 P.M. | |
| **Your credit card has been charged:** $190.00 | |

Thank you and enjoy your tour!

Best,

Susan Malek

Tour Coordinator

----------------------------------------------------------------------------

寄件者：蘇珊・梅勒克

收件者：山謬・帕克

日期：4 月 10 日

回覆：確認預約

親愛的帕克先生，

感謝您訂購多倫多旅行社的行程。以下是您的行程摘要。若有任何問題或疑慮，請來電 416-888-3232 與我聯絡。

行程名稱：多倫多文化之旅

行程日期：4 月 12 日

出發時間：上午 9:00，多倫多聯合車站

返回聯合車站時間：晚上 11:30

信用卡支付金額：190 元

感謝您，祝您旅途愉快！

旅遊統籌

蘇珊・梅勒克 敬上

**Customer Feedback:**

This was my first time using Toronto Tours, and I found the tour to be much more impressive than the sightseeing bus tour I took the last time I visited Toronto. This company sure understands how to treat tourists' interest in the city's unique history and culture. Francis Weltz, our tour guide, was extremely helpful in getting us to and from locations as well as ensuring speedy entry to the listed stops. [190] The only downside of the tour was the rainy weather, which made it hard to enjoy the final stop. As a result, I wish an alternate destination would've been available in the event of poor weather.

Posted by: Samuel Park

--------------------------------------------------------------

顧客意見回饋：

這是我第一次參加多倫多旅行社的行程，我發現本次旅遊比我上回到多倫多參加的觀光巴士行程，更令我印象深刻。這家旅行社的確了解如何滿足遊客在這座城市中，對其獨特的歷史與文化的興趣。我們的導遊法蘭西斯·威爾茲在往返地點的接送上幫了很大的忙，也讓大家能快速進入行程上列出的景點。行程中唯一掃興的是雨天，讓大家無法好好的享受最後一個行程。因此，我希望貴公司能規劃一個天氣不佳時的備案景點。

張貼者：山謬·帕克

字彙
**impressive** 令人印象深刻的
**sightseeing** 觀光
**treat** 對待，款待
**downside** 缺點
**alternate** 替代的
**destination** 目的地

關於多倫多旅行社，文中暗示什麼？

**(A)** 它有好幾個旅遊行程。
**(B)** 已經營業數年了。
**(C)** 不再提供夏季旅遊行程。
**(D)** 新增了一個觀光旅遊行程。

字彙
**operate** 營業，運作

**186** What is suggested about Toronto Tours?

(A) It operates several tour programs.*
(B) It has been open for several years.
(C) It will stop offering summer tours.
(D) It has added a new sightseeing tour.

本題的關鍵字為 Toronto Tours，閱讀文章時，請注意由他們撰寫的廣告（第一篇）。第一段中 This is our most popular tour，為「最受歡迎的行程」，代表除此之外還有其他的行程，因此答案為 (A)。在此補充，由第一句話 To celebrate its first year of business，可以得知 (B) 不是答案。

根據廣告，多倫多旅行社提供給顧客什麼？

**(A)** 餐點與飲料券
**(B)** 升級的旅遊項目
**(C)** 團體旅遊行程的優惠折扣
**(D)** 博物館的門票

字彙
**voucher** 票券

**187** According to the advertisement, what does Toronto Tours offer clients?

(A) Vouchers for food and beverages
(B) Upgraded travel options
(C) Discounts on group packages
(D) Admission fees to museums*

本題必須要掌握旅行社所提供的「服務」。廣告（第一篇）的最後一段中「all entrance fees are covered in your package price, but food and beverage costs are extra」，表示行程包含門票的費用，但是顧客必須自行負擔餐食與飲料的費用，因此 (D) 為最適當的答案。

* 答案改寫：entrance → admission

下列何者與帕克先生參加的旅行團有關？

**(A)** 包含從希臘回來的機票。
**(B)** 參觀了四個主要的景點。
**(C)** 以折扣價購買。
**(D)** 原本是為了當地藝術家而開發的。

字彙
**airfare** 飛機票價
**originally** 原本，起初

**188** What is suggested about Mr. Park's tour?

(A) It included return airfare from Greece.
(B) It visited four main stops.
(C) It was purchased at a discount.*
(D) It was originally developed for local artists.

本題必須綜合兩篇文章的內容，才能順利解題。由第一篇第一段的「Toronto Tours is offering a special 20% discount on Culture of Toronto tours booked between April 5 and May 5」，和第二篇郵件的撰寫日期（Date: April 10），推測出該行程是在優惠期間訂購的，可以找出答案為 (C)。

**189** In the website feedback, the word "treat" in paragraph 1, line 3, is closest in meaning to

(A) serve*
(B) increase
(C) decide
(D) ignore

單字所在句的文意為「旅行社非常了解如何滿足遊客的興趣」，接著又提及導遊高品質的服務。根據句意，選項中最適合替換的單字為 serve，故選 (A)。

在網站的回饋意見中，第一段、第三行的「treat」與下列哪一個意思最接近？

(A) 款待
(B) 增加
(C) 決定
(D) 忽略

字彙
serve 款待
ignore 忽略

---

**190** What portion of the tour was Mr. Park dissatisfied with?

(A) Seeing off at Union Station
(B) The Royal Ontario Museum
(C) The Hockey Hall of Fame
(D) The Danforth Festival*

本題必須綜合帕克先生回覆的評論（第三篇），以及廣告（第一篇）簡介旅遊行程的內容，才能解題。第三篇的後半部「The only downside of the tour was the rainy weather, which made it hard to enjoy the final stop.」，表示本趟旅程中，唯一的遺憾只有「在最後一個行程」時，氣候狀況不佳。從第一篇內容中找出最後一個行程（destination）為丹福斯節，可以得知答案為 (D)。

帕克先生不滿意哪一部分的行程？

(A) 在聯合車站送別
(B) 安大略皇家博物館
(C) 曲棍球名人堂
(D) 丹福斯節

字彙
dissatisfied 不滿的
see . . . off 為某人送行

Questions 191-195 refer to the following schedule, e-mail, and review.

# European Manufacturing Commission

4th Annual Convention
Rowensburg Conference Center
Berlin, Germany
Saturday, October 10

| Tentative Schedule | | |
| --- | --- | --- |
| Time | Location | |
| 9:00 A.M. – 9:30 A.M. | Greetings and Opening Speech by EMC Chairman Alek Sorvenski in the Cranz Banquet Room | |
| 10:00 A.M. – 11:30 A.M. | Strauss Room | Whitman Room |
| | [191] Textile Factory Management Techniques — Hans Tiskawet | Advanced [191] Coloration and Bleaching Technologies — Michelle Perdeu |
| 1:00 P.M. – 2:30 P.M. | Outsourcing and Overseas Management — Rowena Wentworth | [193] Upgrading and Maintaining Equipment — Spencer Defiore |
| 3:00 P.M. – 4:30 P.M. | Establishing Contacts with International Clothing Distributors — Anita Pitelli | International Shipping Strategies — Thao Lee |

● [192] Speakers must confirm their availability with Johanna Swartz (jswartz@emc.com) no later than August 28. Failure to report availability will result in an automatic change of speaker.

● Speakers will be given complimentary accommodation at the [195] Deluxe Grand Hotel for one night. Please fill out the attached form and return it to Berta Joven by September 5. [195] If you are traveling with a colleague or an assistant, you will need to book another room at an additional charge. Please indicate that on the form.

-----------------------------------------------------

歐洲製造業委員會

第四屆年度大會
德國柏林
羅文斯堡會議中心
10 月 10 日星期六

| 暫定時程表 | | |
| --- | --- | --- |
| 時間 | 地點 | |
| 上午 9:00- 上午 9:30 | 相見歡及開幕演講。主講人：EMC 主席艾立克‧碩文斯基，地點為克蘭茲宴會廳 | |
| 上午 10:00- 上午 11:30 | 史特勞斯廳 | 惠特曼廳 |
| | 紡織工廠管理技巧 —— 漢斯‧提斯卡威特 | 高階染色與漂白科技 —— 蜜雪兒‧普爾德 |

| 下午 1:00-<br>下午 2:30 | 外包與海外管理<br>—— 羅威納‧溫特沃斯 | 機具升級與保養<br>—— 史賓賽‧德斐歐雷 |
|---|---|---|
| 下午 3:00-<br>下午 4:30 | 聯繫國際服飾大盤商<br>—— 安妮塔‧皮特里 | 國際寄送策略<br>—— 李紹 |

● 主講人須於 8 月 28 日前與喬漢娜‧史華茲 (jswartz@emc.com) 確認可出席時間。若未確認可出席時間，將自動更換講者。

● 將提供主講人豪華大飯店免費住宿一晚。請填寫附件表格，並於 9 月 5 日前回傳給柏塔‧喬文。若與同事或助理同行，需自行支付額外的房間費用。請於表格上註明。

---

**From:** James Watson <jwatson@hampshiretextiles.com.>
**To:** Johanna Swartz <jswartz@emc.com>
**Date:** September 1
**Subject:** EMC Schedule

Dear Ms. Swartz,

I apologize for the lateness of this e-mail, but I have just found out that my business partner, Spencer Defiore, is unable to attend the EMC Convention this year. I know he has already confirmed his attendance, but an unforeseen issue will prevent him from attending. [193] As we are both knowledgeable about the topic, I would be happy to speak in his place. Please contact me as soon as possible to resolve this matter.

Sincerely,

James Watson

--------------------------------------------------

寄件者：詹姆斯‧華森 <jwatson@hampshiretextiles.com>
收件者：喬漢娜‧史華茲 <jswartz@emc.com>
日期：9 月 1 日
主旨：EMC 時程表

親愛的史華茲女士，

很抱歉這麼晚才寄這封信，但是我剛剛才發現我的事業夥伴史賓賽‧德斐歐雷今年無法出席 EMC 大會。我知道他已經確認出席，但是一件無法預期的事情讓他無法出席。由於我們兩人對演講主題都很了解，所以我很樂意代替他發表演說。為解決這個事情，請盡速與我聯絡。

詹姆斯‧華森 敬上

字彙
**attendance** 出席
**unforeseen** 無法預期的
**issue** 議題，問題

http://www.emc.org

| Itinerary | History | Donations | Comments |
|---|---|---|---|

I was extremely pleased with the turnout at the most recent EMC Conference. Not only was my presentation viewed by numerous attendees, I was able to conduct a question and answer session at the end. The attendees were well-informed about the topic and able to hold an in-depth discussion. In addition, my capacity as a speaker allowed me to make numerous international contacts during the whole of the conference. These contacts will be critical for growing my business in the future. Furthermore, [195] my assistant and I were very pleased with the hotel we stayed at. All in all, speaking at the EMC Conference was an excellent experience.

James Watson

---

http://www.emc.org

| 日程 | 歷史 | 捐款 | 評論 |
|---|---|---|---|

我對最近舉辦的 EMC 大會出席人數感到非常欣喜。不只有許多與會者聆聽我的演講，在演講的結尾還能進行問答座談。與會者對於講題都非常熟悉，也能進行深入的對談。同時，講者的身分也讓我能在整場研討會中與許多國際人士有所接觸。這些接觸對於我自身未來的事業發展非常重要。另外，我和助理也十分滿意下榻的飯店。整體來說，能在 EMC 大會中演講是個很棒的經驗。

詹姆斯·華森

---

191  What industry is the focus of the conference?

(A) Shipping
(B) Dairy
(C) Electronics
(D) Fabrics*

會議主辦方的行程表（第一篇）中，出現了 Textile, Coloration and Bleaching 等紡織業類別的單字，由此可以得知答案應為 (D)。

## 192

According to the schedule, what are presenters expected to do?

(A) Pay for hotel accommodation
(B) Arrive in Berlin by October 8
(C) Ship some presentation materials
(D) Confirm their participation in an event*

行程表（第一篇）的後半部寫道：「Speakers must confirm their availability with Johanna Swartz (jswartz@emc.com) no later than August 28.」，要求講者確認能否出席，因此答案為 (D)。

* 答案改寫：availability → participation

根據時程表，演說者必須做什麼事？

(A) 支付飯店費用
(B) 於10月8日前抵達柏林
(C) 寄送一些演講資料
(D) 確認能否出席

字彙
ship 寄送

## 193

What topic will Mr. Watson most likely speak about?

(A) Textile Factory Management Techniques
(B) Outsourcing and Overseas Management
(C) Upgrading and Maintaining Equipment*
(D) International Shipping Strategies

各選項的內容皆寫在行程表（第一篇）當中，請將此對照華森先生的郵件（第二篇）的內容，當中表示因為史賓賽・德斐歐先生（Spencer Defiore）有事無法前往進行演說，將由自己代替（As we are both knowledgeable about the topic, I would be happy to speak in his place.）。請再從第一篇行程表中找出「Spencer Defiore」的人名，他演講的主題是機具升級與保養，可以得知答案為 (C)。

華森先生的演講主題可能與何者有關？

(A) 紡織工廠管理技巧
(B) 外包與海外管理
(C) 機具升級與保養
(D) 國際寄送策略

ACTUAL TEST 3
PART 7 中譯＋解析

## 194

In the review, the word "capacity" in paragraph 1, line 4, is closest in meaning to

(A) role*          (B) time
(C) perspective    (D) experience

capacity 除了表示「能力；容量」之外，還有「身分，角色」的意思。本句的句意為講者這個「身分」使他得以接觸各國人士，因此選項中最適合替換的單字為 role，故答案選 (A)。

在評論中，第一段、第四行的「capacity」與下列哪一個意思最接近？

(A) 角色
(B) 時間
(C) 觀點
(D) 經驗

字彙
perspective 觀點

## 195

What is probably true about Mr. Watson?

(A) He operates several manufacturing plants in Germany.
(B) He booked a second room at the Deluxe Grand Hotel.*
(C) He attends the EMC conference every year.
(D) He changed his topic to a more difficult one.

請閱讀華森先生所撰寫的郵件（第二篇）以及評論（第三篇）。第三篇的後半部「my assistant and I were very pleased with the hotel we stayed at」，為與「住宿」有關的內容。從行程表（第一篇）最後一段的「If you are traveling with a colleague or an assistant, you will need to book another room at an additional charge.」，可以確認華森先生為助理訂了另一間房，加上第一篇有提到飯店的名稱為 Deluxe Grand Hotel，因此答案為 (B)。

下列何者與華森先生有關？

(A) 他在德國經營了好幾間製造廠。
(B) 他在豪華大飯店訂了第二個房間。
(C) 他每年都出席EMC大會。
(D) 他將講題更改為較難的題目。

字彙
operate 管理，營運
plant 廠房

Questions 196-200 refer to the following form, e-mail, and letter.

http://www.abi.org

*Asia Business Insider*

| This Issue | Contact Us | Subscriptions | FAQ |
|---|---|---|---|

| | |
|---|---|
| Name: | Calista Lao |
| E-mail Address: | clao@rejuvenateproperties.com |
| City & Country: | Ho Chi Minh City, Vietnam |
| Subject: | Suggestion |
| Message: | As you know, *Asia Business Insider* is only available as a quarterly print magazine. However, given that the printing takes place in Tokyo, some customers are not able to receive their magazines until weeks later. The delivery of my magazine is often delayed up to three weeks. This has caused my company, Rejuvenate Properties, to miss out on some of the key property sales advertised in *Asia Business Insider*. [196] As a result, I think *Asia Business Insider* should provide customers with online subscriptions in the form of a downloadable e-book. This would help customers like me keep track of all current available deals. |

**Submit**

--------------------------------------------------------------------

http://www.abi.org
亞洲企業內幕

| 當期號 | 聯絡我們 | 訂閱 | 常見問題 |
|---|---|---|---|

姓名：克莉絲塔‧廖

電子郵件：clao@rejuvenateproperties.com

城市與國家：越南胡志明市

主旨：建議

訊息：如您所知，《亞洲企業內幕》是平面季刊。但是將印刷流程搬到東京後，有些客戶得在幾週之後才能收到雜誌。我的雜誌寄送通常就延誤三週的時間。這讓我的公司，回春地產，錯失在《亞洲企業內幕》中一些重要地產出售的消息。因此，我認為《亞洲企業內幕》應該提供客戶線上訂閱，提供可下載的電子書。這將有助我們這類的客戶，了解所有目前市場上有的交易。

提交

**To:** ABI Editorial Staff
**From:** Akemi Nagata, Editorial Assistant
**Date:** Wednesday, 23 October
**Subject:** Meeting Summary

The following is a summary of the items discussed during the editorial meeting held on October 23 with all members of the editorial staff.

[196] Editorial director Hiroki Goto announced that *Asia Business Insider* will now include a downloadable e-book free of charge for all subscription holders. Furthermore, new subscribers may also choose to sign up for only the e-book issues at a lowered subscription price. The design department has hired two e-book designers to prepare each issue.

Editorial staff discussed which articles to include in ABI's next quarterly installment. Staff members agreed the issue will report on the merging of Haptrack International with Global Fund Partners as reported by Samuel Park. Articles on [197] Surami Technologies in India and Triple Star Manufacturing in Taiwan will be prepared by Jan Dubey and Samuel Park respectively. Editorial staff member Aiko Yano is still waiting to receive articles from freelance writers regarding the development of the new World Conference Center in Beijing. [198] If they cannot meet the deadline, the articles will be included in the next issue.

--------------------------------------------------------------------

收件者：ABI 編輯部員工
寄件者：編輯助理永田明美
日期：10 月 23 日星期三
主旨：會議摘要

以下是 10 月 23 日編輯部全體同仁出席的編輯會議所討論的事項摘要。

編輯主任後藤寬貴宣布，《亞洲企業內幕》將免費提供所有訂閱者可下載的電子書。另外，新訂閱讀者也能選擇以較低的訂閱價單獨訂購電子版。設計部已經聘請了兩名電子書設計人員來籌備每一期刊物。

編輯部員工討論了哪些文章要放進 ABI 的下一期季刊中。員工同意該期將報導哈普翠克國際公司與全球基金的合併案，該報導由山謬‧帕克所採訪。印度武士科技與台灣三星製造公司的新聞將依序由珍‧杜貝和山謬‧帕克分別報導。編輯部的矢野愛子仍在等自由撰述所報導的北京新世界會議中心的最新情況。如果他們無法在截稿日期前交稿，那報導將納入下一期的內容。

**字彙**
editorial 編輯的
summary 摘要
sign up for . . .
報名加入……
installment
刊物的一部分；安裝
merging 合併
respectively 分別地
development 發展，新情況

ACTUAL TEST 3

PART 7 中譯＋解析

**Asia Business Insider**
**January ▪ Vol. 7 ▪ Number 1**

**字彙**
**launch** 發行
**aspect** 部分
**cover** 報導；涵蓋
**commentary** 評論
**comment** 意見，評論
**keep an eye out for . . .**
留意……
**pertinent** 有關的

Letter from the Editor,

This issue celebrates the launch of *Asia Business Insider*'s e-book series. Subscribers can now download fully designed e-books that include all aspects of our print versions. The January issue will cover numerous business deals taking place in Asia. [199] It will also include the launch of our new Editor's Commentary section in which the editorial staff will respond to questions and comments placed online.

[198] Make sure to keep an eye out for our next issue in which we cover all the pertinent details surrounding the plans for the World Conference Center in Beijing. [200] Make sure to sign up on our website for a chance to win free tickets to the center's grand opening business conference next year.

Hiroki Goto

-------------------------------------------------------------------

《亞洲企業內幕》
1月 ● 第七卷 ● 第一期

編輯的話，

本期將慶賀《亞洲企業內幕》電子版的發行。訂閱者可下載精心設計的電子書，其中包含紙本期刊的所有內容。一月號將報導許多在亞洲發生的企業交易。同時也包含新的編輯評論專區，編輯部員工將於線上回覆提問與評論。

記得留意我們的下一期，在下一期中我們將報導北京世界會議中心計畫的所有相關細節。記得登入網站，就有機會贏得明年會議中心開幕商業研討會議的免費門票。

後藤寬貴

**196** What is true about Ms. Lao?

(A) She only buys property in Vietnam.
(B) Her ideas were implemented by ABI.*
(C) She subscribes to several Japanese magazines.
(D) Her articles often appear in ABI.

請先閱讀廖小姐所撰寫的建議（第一篇）。她於後半部提議 ABI 製作電子書（I think Asia Business Insider should provide customers with online subscriptions in the form of a downloadable e-book）。而 ABI 回覆的郵件（第二篇）中，在第二段提到了製作電子書的相關內容（Editorial director Hiroki Goto announced that *Asia Business Insider* will now include a downloadable e-book free of charge for all subscription holders.）。綜合兩者的內容後，可知廖小姐的意見被付諸實行了，答案應為 (B)。

下列何者與廖女士有關？
(A) 她只在越南購買房地產。
(B) ABI執行了她的構想。
(C) 她訂閱了幾本日本雜誌。
(D) 她的文章常刊登在ABI上。

字彙
**implement** 執行，實施

**197** Who will be discussing Surami Technologies?

(A) Hiroki Goto
(B) Samuel Park
(C) Jan Dubey*
(D) Akemi Nagata

閱讀文章時，請特別留意題目關鍵字 Surami Technologies。在郵件（第二篇）的第三段「Surami Technologies in India and Triple Star Manufacturing in Taiwan will be prepared by Jan Dubey and Samuel Park respectively」，可以確認答案為 (C)。當 respectively 放在兩個或兩個以上的名詞後方，且後方連接說明內容時，意思為「依序地」，若句子加上 respectively，可以使句子的意思更加明確。

誰將報導武士科技公司？
(A) 後藤寬貴
(B) 山謬・帕克
(C) 珍・杜貝
(D) 永田明美

**198** What is suggested about Aiko Yano?

(A) She joined ABI as an e-book designer.
(B) She did not receive some articles on time.*
(C) She co-writes articles with Samuel Park.
(D) She was absent from the June 1 meeting.

閱讀文章時，請特別留意矢野愛子（Aiko Yano）。在第二篇第三段中提到，矢野愛子目前仍在等待自由撰述的報導，如果無法在截稿日前收到，則該報導會改成在下期刊登（If they cannot meet the deadline, the articles will be included in the next issue.），且由第三篇第二段「Make sure to keep an eye out for our next issue in which we cover all the pertinent details surrounding the plans for the World Conference Center in Beijing.」，得知世界會議中心的報導確定改到下期刊登了，可以推測她未能如期收到該報導，故 (B) 正確。

下列何者與矢野愛子有關？
(A) 她以電子書設計人員的身分加入ABI。
(B) 她沒有按時收到一些文章。
(C) 她和山謬・帕克一起撰寫文章。
(D) 她沒有出席6月1日的會議。

關於《亞洲企業內幕》，文中提及了什麼？

(A) 開發了新專欄。
(B) 大部分的訂閱者都在越南。
(C) 將遷至中國北京。
(D) 每年發行六期。

字彙
relocate 搬遷

**199** What is indicated about *Asia Business Insider*?

(A) It has developed a new column. *
(B) Its subscribers are mostly located in Vietnam.
(C) It will relocate to Beijing, China.
(D) It prints six issues per year.

第三篇第一段中寫道：「It will also include the launch of our new Editor's Commentary section in which the editorial staff will respond to questions and comments placed online.」，表示 ABI 開發新的編輯評論專區，因此 (A) 為最適當的答案。

* 答案改寫：* 答案改寫：section → column

---

下列何者與ABI網站有關？
(A) 只提供給ABI訂閱者。
(B) 將於明年升級。
(C) 提供七種不同語言的版本。
(D) 將為訂閱者舉辦贈品活動。

字彙
give-away 贈送，免費分發

**200** What is mentioned about ABI's website?

(A) It is only for ABI subscribers.
(B) It will be upgraded next year.
(C) It is available in seven different languages.
(D) It will host a give-away for subscribers. *

閱讀文章時，請特別留意題目關鍵字 ABI's website。第三篇的後半部「Make sure to sign up on our website at that time for a chance to win free tickets」，強調千萬不要錯過贏得商業研討會議免費門票的機會，因此答案應為 (D)。

* 答案改寫：* 答案改寫：free ticket → give-away

# ACTUAL TEST

## 中譯+解析

## PART 5

由於前僱主的推薦函令人印象深刻，德瑞克立刻得到了那個管理職。

字彙
**thanks to** 由於，幸虧
**recommendation** 推薦（函）
**previous** 之前的
**employer** 僱主
**managerial** 管理的

**101** Thanks to the _____ recommendation from his previous employer, Derrick was immediately offered the managerial position.

(A) impress
(B) impression
(C) impressive*
(D) impresses

定冠詞（the）＋空格＋名詞（recommendation）中，選項中只有形容詞 impressive 可以填入空格中，用來修飾名詞，故 (C) 正確。

- **impress** 給……深刻印象　　**impression** 印象
  **impressive** 令人印象深刻的

\* 表示情緒的現在分詞／過去分詞
— **exciting - excited** 刺激的；感到興奮的
— **confusing - confused** 令人困惑的；感到困惑的
— **surprising - surprised** 令人驚訝的；感到驚訝的
— **frustrating - frustrated** 令人挫敗的；感到挫敗的
— **troubling - troubled** 麻煩的；感到麻煩的
— **boring - bored** 令人厭煩的；感到厭煩的
— **satisfying - satisfied** 令人滿意的；感到滿意的
— **disappointing - disappointed** 令人失望的；感到失望的
— **tiring - tired** 令人疲倦的；感到疲倦的
— **worrying - worried** 令人擔心的；感到擔心的
— **interesting - interested** 有趣的；感興趣的
— **embarrassing - embarrassed** 令人難堪的；感到難堪的
— **pleasing - pleased** 令人愉快的；感到愉快的
— **depressing - depressed** 令人沮喪的；感到沮喪的

---

納米斯航空不再獲准運送貨物到北部地區。

字彙
**transport** 運送
**freight** 貨物
**region** 地區

**102** Nemis Air is no longer _____ to transport freight to the northern regions.

(A) license
(B) licensed*
(C) licenses
(D) licensing

空格與 be 動詞 is 要組合成動詞片語，所以得從 (B) 和 (D) 當中選出答案。而航空公司並非主動「提供」運送貨物的許可，而是「被准許」的對象，因此要使用被動語態，答案為過去分詞 licensed，故 (B) 正確。

- **license** 執照；發給執照

---

傑洛米設法要拿到明天比賽的入場券，但它們已經完全售完了。

**103** Jerome tried to get tickets to tomorrow's game, but they are _____ sold out.

(A) complete
(B) completed
(C) completing
(D) completely*

空格位在 be 動詞與 p.p. 之間，因此空格中只能填入副詞，修飾 sold out，故答案選 (D)。

- **complete** 完全的　　**completely** 完全地

**104** Nobody can enter this office _____ proper authorization.

(A) without*　　　　　　(B) unless
(C) only　　　　　　　　(D) although

本句應為「未經正式許可，無人得以進入這間辦公室。」，語意上較為完整，因此答案為 (A)。考題中，without 經常是正確答案。

未經正式許可，任何人不能進入這間辦公室。

字彙
**proper** 正式的，適當的
**authorization** 許可

---

**105** The annual charity banquet hosted by the Fredericton Children Aid Society is _____ to take place at the Grand Marian Hotel on December 7.

(A) given　　　　　　　(B) scheduled*
(C) found　　　　　　　(D) considered

本句用來表示活動的日程，因此要填入 (B)，變成 be scheduled to，意思為「預計在……」。

• **consider** 考慮

\* 高頻率「be + p.p. + to」句型
**be advised to** ＋原形動詞：被建議去……
**be allowed to** ＋原形動詞：得到許可去……
**be asked to** ＋原形動詞：被要求去……
**be expected to** ＋原形動詞：被期許去……
**be invited to** ＋原形動詞：受邀去……
**be reminded to** ＋原形動詞：被提醒去……
**be required to** ＋原形動詞：被要求去……

弗雷德里克頓兒童扶助協會所舉辦的年度慈善晚宴，預定在**12月7日**於大瑪麗安飯店舉行。

字彙
**annual** 年度的
**charity** 慈善（機構）
**banquet** 宴席
**aid** 救助，支援

---

**106** The owner's manual includes detailed _____ on cleaning this microwave.

(A) instructions*　　　　(B) computers
(C) posters　　　　　　　(D) fixings

本句應為清理微波爐方法的「說明」，語意上較為完整，因此答案為 (A)。如果碰到像本題一樣使用 instructions 時，後方記得要連接介系詞 on。

• **instruction** 說明，指示　　**fixings** 配菜

\* 高頻率「名詞＋ on」用法：
**ban on . . .** 禁止……
**advice on . . .** 勸告……
**reliance on . . .** 信賴……
**focus on . . .** 專注……
**opinion/view on . . .** 對……的見解／看法
**report/news/information on . . .** 有關……的報導／新聞／資訊
**conference/workshop on . . .** 有關……的會議／研討會
**effect/influence on . . .** 對……的效用／影響

擁有者的使用手冊中，包含了如何清潔這台微波爐的詳細說明。

字彙
**manual** 手冊
**detailed** 詳細的

市府買下了巴萊納街上的閒置大樓，將它改成一所國小。

**字彙**

convert 轉變，改成

---

**107** The city purchased the _____ building on Balena Street to convert it into an elementary school.

(A) approaching          (B) adjustable

(C) vacant*              (D) united

空格用來修飾 building，當中必須填入適當的形容詞，因此答案為 (C)，表示「閒置的，空的」。

- **approaching** 接近的   **adjustable** 可調整的   **vacant** 閒置的，空的   **united** 聯合的

---

顧客必須在櫃檯付款，否則無法領取處方箋的藥。

**字彙**

counter 櫃台
prescription 處方箋
fill 按……供應

---

**108** Customers must provide _____ at the counter or prescriptions will not be filled.

(A) paid                (B) payers

(C) payment*         (D) pays

助動詞（must）＋及物動詞（provide）＋空格，空格只能填入名詞作為受詞，所以可選 (B) 或 (C)。然而本句的重點應為顧客們必須「付款」，語意上較為適當，因此答案為 (C)。

- **paid** 已付的   **payer** 付款人   **payment** 款項   **pay** 支付，付款

---

除非員工在一回來就立刻出示原始收據，否則公司將不核銷差旅費用。

**字彙**

reimburse 核銷；補償
expense 費用
unless . . . 除非……
original 原始的，本來的

---

**109** The company will not reimburse staff for travel expenses unless original receipts are presented _____ upon returning.

(A) mainly           (B) formerly

(C) nearly            (D) immediately*

本句的重點應為如要「核銷」差旅費用，也就是領回代墊的差旅費，員工回來後要「馬上」繳交收據，語意上較為適當，因此答案為 (D)。

- **mainly** 主要地   **formerly** 以前地   **nearly** 幾乎   **immediately** 立即地

---

《斯蒂克尼娛樂指南》肯定是找到本地最佳用餐處最可靠的資訊來源。

**字彙**

without a doubt
肯定，毫無疑問地
reliable 可靠的
source 來源

---

**110** The *Stickney Entertainment Guide* is, without a doubt, the most reliable source _____ finding the best places to eat in this region.

(A) around          (B) for*

(C) as               (D) through

空格前方是最可靠的指南，空格後方應說明它可靠的「原因」，因此空格中最適合填入介系詞 for，答案選 (B)。

- **around** 周遭，在……附近   **as** 像……一樣，如同   **through** 穿過

**111** Mr. Tolliver, the head mechanic, started the repairs by _____ this morning, but two more staff were available to help him after lunch.

(A) he
(B) his
(C) him
(D) himself*

空格為介系詞的受詞，因此請直接刪除表主詞的 (A) 和所有格代名詞 (B)。but 表前後文語意上的轉折，後方表示兩名職員可以幫忙，所以空格要填「只靠他自己」因此 (D) 的 himself 為正確答案。(all) by oneself 表示「獨自，沒有其他人」的意思。

今天早上總技師托利弗先生自己開始修理工作，不過午餐後有兩位職員可以來幫他。

字彙
head 帶領的
mechanic 技師

---

**112** For optimal results, the manufacturer _____ applying this exterior paint when the weather is sunny.

(A) reminds
(B) recognizes
(C) recommends*
(D) registers

空格後方有動名詞，因此先看選項中是否有適合搭配動名詞的動詞，接動名詞作為受詞。根據文法規則，(C) 為合適的選項。若根據句意，空格後方為達成最佳效果的「建議」，由此可以確認答案為 (C)。

• **remind** 提醒　　**recognize** 認出　　**recommend** 建議，推薦
**register** 登記，註冊

* 後方連接動名詞（作為受詞）的動詞：
**enjoy, keep, finish, delay, postpone, mind, avoid, deny, give up, admit, consider, suggest**

為了達到最佳效果，製造商建議晴天時再塗上外部漆料。

字彙
optimal 最佳的，最理想的
apply 將……塗、敷在表面
exterior 外部的

---

**113** Instructors at Darthmouth College have to submit their final student evaluations _____ the last day of this month.

(A) in anticipation of
(B) already
(C) before*
(D) so as to

空格後方為「特定的時間點」，因此空格中最適合填入介系詞 before，表示「在……之前」，故答案為 (C)。

• **in anticipation of . . .** 期待……，預計……　　**so as to . . .** 為了……

達特茅斯學院的教師必須於本月最後一天前交出學生期末成績。

字彙
instructor 教師；教練
evaluation 評量，評估

---

**114** The Fitzgerald Theater is being renovated so concert organizers for Roland Gagnon's band are _____ seeking another venue.

(A) actively*
(B) activity
(C) active
(D) activate

空格位在動詞片語 are seeking 之間，因此答案為副詞 actively，用來修飾本句的動詞部分，故答案為 (A)。

• **actively** 積極地，主動地　　**activity** 活動　　**active** 活躍的，積極的
**activate** 活化；啟動

費茲傑羅戲院正在進行整修，因此樂蘭·甘農樂團演唱會的籌辦者正在積極尋找另一個場地。

字彙
renovate 整修
organizer 籌備者，組織者
venue 場地

一旦傳送帶修好，工廠就可以繼續生產了。

字彙
production 生產

**115** Once the conveyor belt was fixed, the factory was _____ to continue production.

(A) valuable　　　　　(B) responsible
(C) able*　　　　　　(D) possible

本題只要知道片語 be able to 的意思為「能夠……」，就能輕鬆解題。possible 不同於 be able to，並非表示「有……的能力」，而是指某件事情「有可能」發生，通常會使用句型 It is possible to . . .。

• **valuable** 有價值的　　**responsible** 負責任的

---

應該有人告訴西諾波利先生，他的車停在給購物中心顧客的預留車位了。

字彙
park (v.) 停車
section 區塊
reserve 保留，預約

**116** Someone should tell Mr. Sinopoli that _____ car is parked in the section reserved for shopping center customers.

(A) he　　　　　　　(B) him
(C) his*　　　　　　(D) himself

本題要從人稱代名詞中找出適當的格。that 子句的主詞為 car，因此空格中最適合填入所有格 his 作為限定詞，限定出車子是誰的，故答案為 (C)。這類的題型，答案經常是所有格代名詞。

---

謝弗維爾汽車公司所提出的收購，將使拉森柏格機車大大獲益。

字彙
benefit from . . .
從……受益
proposed 被提議的
acquisition 收購，取得

**117** Ratzenberg Motorcycles will benefit greatly _____ the proposed acquisition by Shefferville Auto.

(A) from*　　　　　　(B) to
(C) on　　　　　　　(D) about

benefit 為不及物動詞，因此要和介系詞 from 搭配使用，表示「從……獲利」，答案為 (A)。

---

我們昨天收到的申請表，仍需由一位部門主管審查。

字彙
division 部門

**118** The application forms we received yesterday _____ have to be reviewed by one of the division heads.

(A) lately　　　　　　(B) evenly
(C) ever　　　　　　(D) still*

本題要找出適當的副詞。本句的重點應為申請書「仍然」需由一位部門主管審查，較符合文意，因此 (D) 為最適當的答案。在此補充，ever 多用於否定句、疑問句、或是包含 if 在內的句子中。

• **lately** 最近　　**evenly** 平均地　　**ever** 曾經　　**still** 仍然

**119** If bad weather forces a cancellation of the baseball game, full refunds will be issued to _____ who have purchased tickets.

(A) those*　　　　　　　(B) which
(C) them　　　　　　　(D) whichever

選項中，只有 (A) 能作為關係代名詞 who 的先行詞。請直接熟記 those who，意思為「那些……的人們」。

• whichever 無論哪個……

如果惡劣天氣迫使棒球賽取消，已購票的人將獲得全額退款。

字彙
force 強迫，迫使
refund 退款
issue 發給

---

**120** Even though tourism revenue in this region usually _____ during the cold winter months, it always recovers in the warm spring.

(A) declines*　　　　　(B) delays
(C) impacts　　　　　　(D) impedes

本題的解題線索為 even though，代表前後兩個句子的意思相反。逗點後方句子的意思為在春天時「觀光收入回復」，前句就是觀光收入在冬季時「下跌」，才能使兩句話的文意形成對比，因此空格中填入 (A) 最為適當。

• decline 下降，減少　delay 延誤，延遲　impact 影響
impede 妨礙，阻止

雖然這個地區的觀光收入在冬季月分時通常會減少，但在溫暖的春天就會回復。

字彙
tourism 觀光（業）
revenue 收入
recover 回復，恢復

---

**121** One important _____ the new personnel manager is responsible for is meeting regularly with factory workers to discuss safety matters.

(A) initiative*　　　　　(B) initiating
(C) initiation　　　　　(D) initiator

空格為 is responsible 的受詞，因此空格中應填入名詞。根據文意，可以得知空格中要填入與 work 和 project 意思相關的單字，因此答案為 initiative，故 (A) 正確。

• initiative 新措施　initiate (v.) 開始　initiation (n.) 開始；發起
initiator 創始者，發起人

* 以 ive 結尾的名詞：
alternative 選擇　directive 指令　executive 行政主管
initiative 新措施　objective 目標　relative 親戚
representative 代表人員　adhesive 黏著劑　additive 添加物

新人事經理所負責的一個重要措施就是定期和工廠員工開會討論安全事宜。

字彙
personnel 人事部門
regularly 定期地
safety 安全

---

**122** Ms. Gaitor is _____ with implementing policies that led to a significant increase in the number of clients.

(A) credited*　　　　　(B) scored
(C) agreed　　　　　　(D) relied

credit sb with sth（= sb is credited with sth）意思為「將某事的功勞歸功於某人」，通常會使用被動語態。本題只要知道此用法，就能順利解題。

• score 得分　agree 同意　rely 依靠，依賴

蓋特女士的功勞是實施讓顧客數量顯著增加的策略。

字彙
implement 實施
policy 策略
significant 顯著的

美術館的門票可以在網路上以稍微便宜的價格購得。

**字彙**
reduced 降低的

---

**123** Tickets to the gallery can be purchased online at a _____ reduced price.

(A) slightest　　(B) slighted　　(C) slighting　　(D) slightly*

本題結構為：不定冠詞（a）＋空格＋形容詞（reduced）＋名詞（price），空格應用來修飾形容詞，因此答案應為副詞 slightly，故選 (D)，填入後的句意為「稍微便宜的」。

- slightest 最少的　　slight 微小的；少量的　　slighting 輕視的
  slightly 稍微地

---

本部門原本要參加上週的政策會議，但時間上卻撞期而無法參加。

**字彙**
division 部門
conflict 衝突

---

**124** Our division _____ last week's policy meeting, but there was a conflict with the schedule.

(A) can attend　　　　　　(B) must have attended
(C) should attend　　　　 (D) would have attended*

本題的解題線索為 but，用來表示轉折的語氣。根據文意，實際上是因為撞期而無法參加，因此填入 (D) would have p.p. 最為適當，表示「原本會……」。

- attend 參加，出席
* 助動詞 ＋ have ＋ p.p
would have p.p. . . .（當時）原本會……
should have p.p. . . .（當時）原本應該……
must have p.p. . . .（當時）一定是……
might have p.p. . . .（當時）也許是……
could have p.p. . . .（當時）原本可以……

---

格利森先生喜歡湖景，因此選擇租用皇后街的辦公室，而不是在茉雷巷的。

**字彙**
opt 選擇
lease 租用

---

**125** Mr. Gleason opted to lease office space on Queen Street instead of Morley Lane, _____ a view of the lake.

(A) prefer　　(B) preferring*　　(C) preferred　　(D) preference

空格後方表示「理由」，應為格利森先生「喜好」皇后街辦公室的原因。選項中的現在分詞 preferring 表示主動；過去分詞 preferred 則表示被動，原句為 because he preferred a view of the lake，省略了連接詞和主詞後，要將動詞改成現在分詞，因此選擇 (B) 而非 (C)。

- prefer 偏好，較喜歡　　preference 偏好

---

選拔委員會必須在三月底前收到格倫丁文學獎明年的提名。

**字彙**
literature 文學
selection 選拔，選擇
committee 委員會

---

**126** _____ for next year's Grondin Literature Award must be received by the selection committee by the end of March.

(A) Subscriptions　　　　(B) Nominations*
(C) Supporters　　　　　(D) Venues

收件的單位為「選拔委員會」，因此空格中填入 nominations 最符合文意，故答案選 (B)。

- subscription 訂閱　　nomination 提名　　supporter 支持者
  venue 場所
* 高頻率「名詞＋ for」的用法：
hope/desire for . . . 希望/渴望……　　preference for . . . 偏好……
advertisement for . . . ……的廣告
reason/motivation for . . . ……的理由/動機
demand/need for . . . 對……的需求/需要
admiration/respect for . . . 崇拜/尊敬……
reputation for . . . ……的聲譽

**127**

In an effort to make the team less _____, the manager sent all the sales charts to everyone as e-mail attachments rather than printing out hardcopies.

(A) waste        (B) wasteful*

(C) wastefully      (D) wasting

句中使用了使役動詞 make，因此本句的句型應為 make ＋受詞（名詞＝ team）＋受詞補語（形容詞、名詞、原形動詞）。因為空格前方為 little 的比較級 less，所以空格中要填入形容詞，答案應為 (B)。

- **waste** 浪費　**wasteful** 浪費的　**wastefully** 揮霍地

為了讓小組減少浪費，經理沒有將所有的銷售圖表印成紙本，而是以電子郵件的附件寄給大家。

字彙
**in an effort to . . .**
為了……努力
**hardcopy** 紙本

---

**128**

Ms. Wilson must contact the bank manager _____ she needs a little more time for the payment.

(A) if*         (B) soon

(C) only       (D) then

因為空格前後各有一個子句，所以空格中應填入連接詞。選項中只有 (A) 為連接詞。且根據文意：「如果威爾森女士需要多一點時間付款，就必須和銀行經理聯繫。」，空格後方屬於「條件句」，因此可以再次確認答案為 (A)。

如果威爾森女士需要多一點時間付款，就必須和銀行經理聯繫。

---

**129**

Besides speedy delivery, friendly service is something _____ the management of Caron Courier will never sacrifice.

(A) where       (B) that*

(C) when        (D) then

空格前方為先行詞 something，空格後方則為先行詞的相關說明，關係代名詞中有 that 與 which 可以用來代指先行詞為事或物，因此應該填入 (B) 最為適當。

卡隆快遞除了迅速運送外，親切的服務也是他們的管理部所重視的。

字彙
**speedy** 迅速的
**management** 管理（部門）
**courier** 快遞人員；快遞公司
**sacrifice** 犧牲

---

**130**

The editor of the sports section is more _____ about the articles she approves than the other editors.

(A) prominent     (B) punctual

(C) rigorous      (D) selective*

根據文意，本句的重點應為「在核准文章方面更嚴格」，較符合文意，因此答案為 (D)。

- **prominent** 顯著的；重要的　**punctual** 準時的　**rigorous** 嚴格的　**selective** 嚴格篩選的

運動版的編輯對她自己所核准的文章比其他編輯更嚴格。

字彙
**approve** 核准，許可

# PART 6

Questions 131-134 refer to the following article.

## 字彙

**bold move** 大膽之舉
**introduce** 推出；介紹
**unanticipated** 令人意外的
**policy** 規定
**unusual** 不平常的
**permit** 允許，許可
**implement** 實施
**aim** 目標
**throughout** 遍及
**similar** 類似的

## Bold Move by Popular Shop

CASTLEBAR — Flavor Fun, Castlebar's oldest and most popular yoghurt restaurant, has introduced a truly unanticipated change as the result of a growing number of ‾‾‾‾‾. The restaurant's owner 131. decided to introduce a policy that many find to be unusual. For the past two weeks, customers have not been permitted to work on laptops while eating in the restaurant. Flavor Fun is the first and only restaurant in the city to implement such a policy aimed at encouraging customers to leave the restaurant after eating. By making customers spend ‾‾‾‾‾ time at a table, the restaurant has 132. increased its daily sales by over 20 percent, and customers did not have to wait for a place to sit. ‾‾‾‾‾. Now, some other popular 133. eating spots throughout Castlebar ‾‾‾‾‾ similar changes. 134.

---

人氣店家的大膽之舉

卡斯爾巴──因為愈來愈多的客訴，卡斯爾巴最具歷史，也最受歡迎的優格餐廳「趣味餐廳」推出了一個確實令人意外的改變。餐廳老闆決定採用一個許多人都覺得很特別的規定。在過去的兩週以來，顧客在餐廳用餐時，不得使用筆記型電腦做事。趣味餐廳是本市中第一家，也是唯一一家實施這種規定，目的是鼓勵顧客在用餐後隨即離開餐廳。藉由讓顧客在餐桌上耗費較短的時間，這家餐廳每日業績量增加了20%以上。顧客也不用等位子。新規定已經證明受到顧客們的歡迎。現在，卡斯爾巴其他受歡迎的餐飲業者也在考慮進行類似的調整。

---

**131** (A) staff
(B) prices
(C) complaints*
(D) deliveries

根據文意，要找出讓餐廳選擇改變的原因，才能順利解題。空格後方的內容為，「為了讓客人在用餐後隨即離開餐廳，實施了禁止使用筆電的規定」，因此不再需要讓後來的客人等候過久。由此可以推測出，改變的原因應是為了減少客人等候的「不滿」，因此答案為 (C)。

- **complaint** 抱怨 **delivery** 運送，遞送

**132**

(A) some
(B) less*
(C) any
(D) much

根據上下文，本句的重點應是餐廳在禁止顧客用餐時使用筆電後，顧客在餐桌上耗費「較短的」時間，最符合文意，因此答案為 (B)。在此補充，any 多使用於否定句或疑問句當中，或是用於 if 或 whether 子句。

• **less** 較少的

---

**133**

(A) Customers will receive free coffee during the trial period.
(B) The new policy has already proven popular with customers.*
(C) Flavor Fun also has an outdoor patio for dining.
(D) Owners believe new staff need more training before starting work.

(A) 顧客在試賣期間可獲得免費咖啡。
(B) 新規定已經證明受到顧客們的歡迎。
(C) 趣味餐廳也有戶外用餐區。
(D) 老闆們相信新員工在開始工作前，需要更多的訓練。

根據上下文意，由於新規定實施後，顧客也不用等位子，有效減少了等候時間，「新規定已經證明受到顧客們的歡迎」比較符合文意，因此 (B) 為最適當的答案。

• **trial** 試用的　　**dine** 用餐

---

**134**

(A) considers
(B) to consider
(C) being considered
(D) are considering*

空格位在句子動詞的位置，請直接刪除 (B) 和 (C)。主詞 some other popular eating spots 為複數，因此答案應為 (D)。

Questions 135-138 refer to the following letter.

**Do You Use a Hearing Aid? Contact Knapton Technologies Today!**

In August, Knapton Technologies will begin a detailed consumer study on behalf of Hearing 1000. For this huge undertaking, our team is ___135.___ more than 300 individuals who wear hearing aids. All participants must have a doctor prescribed device that they began wearing no more than three years ago ___136.___ the beginning of the study. ___137.___. If you are interested, we ask that you visit us online at www.knaptontechnologies.com/hearingaidstudy and complete our short survey. One of our staff members will be contacting qualified applicants. Every participant ___138.___ a gift voucher valued at $200 upon completing of this study.

--------------------------------------------------------

您使用助聽器嗎？今天就聯絡納普頓科技公司吧！

八月份，納普頓科技公司將代表聽力 1000 開始進行一項詳盡的消費者研究計畫。為了這個大型計劃，本團隊正徵求 300 百多名佩戴助聽器的民眾。所有參與者必須配戴醫生囑咐的器具。配戴時間距本研究計畫起不得超過三年。需出示紙本處方箋，作為確證。如有興趣，請上本公司網站 www.knaptontechnologies.com/hearingaidstudy，並填寫簡短問卷調查。我們的人員將與合格參與者聯絡。每位參與者將於研究完成後獲贈價值 200 元的禮券。

**135** (A) seeking*
(B) insuring
(C) promoting
(D) showing

由文章標題和第一句話，即可得知本文為「找尋使用助聽器的人」，因此空格中填入 (A) 最為適當。

• **seek** 尋找　　**insure** 為……投保　　**promote** 升遷

**136**
(A) except for
(B) as
(C) because of
(D) at*

本句的重點應為「在研究計畫開始時，參與者使用助聽器的時間，不能超過三年」語意較為完整，因此最適當的答案為 (D) at，用來表示「在特定的時間點或狀態」。

- **at the beginning of = at the start of . . .** 在……開始時
  **except for . . .** 除了……外

---

**137**
(A) A hard copy of the prescription must be presented for confirmation.*
(B) New batteries will be available for all participants.
(C) We request that payment for your prescription is provided on the spot.
(D) The prescription will be filled immediately after submission.

(A) 需出示紙本處方箋，作為確證。
(B) 將提供新電池給所有參加者。
(C) 我們要求處方箋的款項必須當場給付。
(D) 送交後將立即根據處方箋配藥。

空格前方句子為「所有參與者必須配戴醫生囑咐的器具」，空格應為對此敘述的説明，因此 (A) 提到紙本處方箋作為醫生開立的確證最為適當，故為正確答案。

- **prescription** 處方箋 　**present** 出示 　**confirmation** 確認
  **payment** 付款 　**fill** 按……供應，依處方箋配藥
  **immediately after** 隨即 　**submission** 提交

---

**138**
(A) will receive*
(B) had received
(C) to receive
(D) to be received

空格位在句子動詞的位置，請直接刪除 (C) 和 (D)。另外，研究完成後，可以獲得商品禮券，此為「未來會發生的事情」，因此答案應為表未來式的 (A)。

字彙
**headquarters** 總部
**relocate** 搬遷
**renovate** 翻新
**square meter** 平方公尺
**amenities** 設施
**spokesperson** 發言人
**note** 提到
**spot** 地點，場所

Questions 139-142 refer to the following press release.

Next month, the national headquarters of Zaki Ltd., Japan's top manufacturer of ⎯⎯⎯, will relocate to 117 Aoyagi Street, where a modern office building was recently renovated. Zaki will ⎯⎯⎯. 140. the top seven floors of the Aoyagi Building. In this new location, the staff will enjoy over 90,000 square meters of beautiful office space and convenient amenities. ⎯⎯⎯ "That is the perfect place to display our latest high-tech refrigerators and ovens." said Kaori Akiba, spokesperson for Zaki. Ms. Akiba noted that the design and engineer divisions will remain in ⎯⎯⎯ original spot in the Ogawa Building.

---

下個月，日本電器製造業龍頭崎企業將搬遷至青柳街 117 號，該處最近剛翻修完成的現代化辦公大樓。崎企業將佔用青柳大樓最上面的七個樓層。在這個新址中，員工們將享用超過 90,000 平方公尺的漂亮辦公空間及便利的設施。崎企業也計劃另外租下大樓一樓的零售空間。「那是展示我們最新高科技冰箱與烤箱的最佳地點。」崎企業的發言人秋葉香織說。秋葉女士提到，設計與工程師部門將留在他們位於小川大樓的原址。

**139**  (A) furniture
(B) apparel
(C) wallpaper
(D) appliances*

本題要選出適合描述公司性質的單字。在文章的後半部提到冰箱和烤箱（high-tech refrigerators and ovens），(D) appliances 可以作為電器通稱，因此為正確答案。

• **apparel** 服裝　**wallpaper** 壁紙　**appliances** 家用電器

**140**  (A) sell
(B) paint
(C) occupy*
(D) photograph

根據上下文，本句應為崎企業「使用」建築物的特定樓層，較符合文意，因此答案為 (C)。

• **occupy** 佔用　**photograph** 攝影；照相

**141**

(A) Zaki's products are known for their cutting-edge designs and energy efficiency.

(B) Zaki also plans to lease additional retail space on the first floor of the building.*

(C) Zaki was listed in the *Tokyo Times* as one of the top 20 places to work in Asia.

(D) Zaki stock doubled in value immediately following the announcement.

(A) 崎企業的產品以尖端設計與省電聞名。

(B) 崎企業也計劃另外租下大樓一樓的零售空間。

(C) 崎企業以亞洲前20名最佳工作場域列於《東京時報》上。

(D) 崎企業的股票在公告後隨即價值倍增。

空格前方介紹了崎企業對「樓層的使用」，因此空格應填入有關「租賃空間」的說明較符合文意，故 (B) 正確。另外，空格後方的句子中提到一樓適合作為產品展示空間，再次確認答案為 (B)。

- **cutting-edge** 尖端的　**energy efficiency** 省電　**lease** 租用　**retail** 零售　**stock** 股票　**immediately following** 隨即

---

**142**

(A) it

(B) their*

(C) what

(D) any

空格後方為形容詞（original）＋名詞（spot），因此空格只能填入所有格代名詞的 (B)、或是不定限定詞的 (D)。根據文意，本句為針對兩個部門（design and engineer divisions）」所在位置的說明，因此答案為 (B)。

字彙

**inquiry** 詢問
**instruction** 操作說明
**indicate** 指出
**device** 裝置
**publication** 出版
**division** 部門
**revision** 修訂
**transfer** 轉換

Questions 143-146 refer to the following e-mail.

**To:** Kaori Sazaki <ssawaki601@e-mail.co.jp>
**From:** Customer Service <customerserv@elsworth.co.uk>
**Date:** Thursday, 16 October 8:56 P.M.

**Subject:** inquiry about website

Dear Ms. Sazaki:

We would like to thank you for leaving a comment in the feedback section of our website regarding the instruction booklet for the EW2500 digital camera. You indicated that the instructions on how to upload an image to a phone or mobile device is confusing and we completely agree with you ‾‾143.‾‾ that point. ‾‾144.‾‾. Our publications division has ‾‾145.‾‾ made some revisions to the section that details the specific software and cable needed to transfer an image from your particular camera. We have made the ‾‾146.‾‾ version of the instruction booklet available on our website. You can find it under the New Digital Camera section. If you prefer a print version, we will gladly send it by regular mail but delivery will take at least one week.

Sincerely,

Lirim Kilgore
Customer Service Agent
Elsworth Camera Company

------------------------------------------------------------------

收件者：佐佐木香織 <ssawaki601@e-mail.com.jp>
寄件者：客戶服務部 <customerserv@elsworth.co.uk>
日期：10 月 16 日星期四晚上 8:56
主旨：查問網站

親愛的佐佐木女士，

我們要感謝您在本公司網站上的回饋欄上，留下有關 EW2500 數位相機使用手冊的意見。您表示，在如何上傳影像到手機或行動裝置的相關說明非常複雜難懂。我們完全認同您對這一點的看法。其他客戶也對同一問題提出了回饋。因此，本公司出版部已經針對相機轉傳影像所需要的特定軟體與傳輸線的說明做出修訂。我們已將更新版的使用手冊放在本公司的網站上。您可以在「新數位相機區」中找到。如果您偏好紙本說明，我們也很樂意以平信寄送給您，但寄送最少需要一週的時間。

埃爾斯沃斯相機公司
客戶服務部專員
立倫‧基爾戈 敬上

**143**

(A) all
(B) on*
(C) what
(D) of

根據上下文，本句應為相機公司「對於」使用説明複雜的回饋表示同意。因此空格中最適合填入介系詞 on，故答案為 (B)。agree with sb on sth 意思為「同意某人關於某事」。

---

**144**

(A) The EW2500 digital camera is currently our most popular item.
(B) We can send you the complete instructions via e-mail if you wish.
(C) Other customers have submitted feedback about the same issue.*
(D) Most of our customers are based in the southern regions of Asia.

(A) EW2500數位相機目前是我們最受歡迎的商品。
(B) 如果您需要，我們可以透過電子郵件將完整的使用説明寄給您。
(C) 其他客戶也對同一問題提出了回饋。
(D) 我們大多數的客戶來自亞洲的南部地區。

空格前方的內容為顧客提出關於相機的問題；空格後方提到修正的説明，因此空格應填入和前後相關的訊息，因此 (C)「其他客戶也對同一問題提出了回饋」，最符合文意，故為正確答案。

- **item** 物品，商品　**complete** 完整的　**submit** 提交
  **issue** 問題，議題　**be based in ...** 立基於……，位於……

---

**145**

(A) instead
(B) likewise
(C) therefore*
(D) nevertheless

空格前後文的脈絡應為：提出問題（使用説明非常複雜難懂）→解決方案（修訂複雜的説明），因此 (C) therefore 為最適當的答案，表示前後文的「因果關係」。

- **instead** 替代　**likewise** 同樣地　**therefore** 因此
  **nevertheless** 儘管如此

---

**146**

(A) original
(B) updated*
(C) absolute
(D) focused

空格前方提到 made some revisions，表示相機公司已經修訂過説明手冊，因此 (B) updated 為最適當的形容詞，表示「更新的」。

- **original** 最初的　**updated** 更新的　**absolute** 絕對的
  **focused** 專心的

# PART 7

**字彙**
exact 確切的

Questions 147-148 refer to the following text message.

**From:** Ron Kapoor, 553-0304
**To:** Zelda Vincenti

Zelda, I left my schedule book in the office. I have to meet a client at 2:00, but I can't remember the exact location. [148] I'm just about to leave Denny's Grill and had planned to go straight to the meeting. [147] Can you check my book and send me the address?

------------------------------------------------

傳訊者：榮恩·卡浦爾，553-0304
收訊者：薩爾達·文森蒂

薩爾達，我把我的日誌本留在辦公室了。我必須在兩點和客戶碰面，但我忘記確切地點了。我正要離開丹尼燒烤店，打算直接去開會。妳可以看一下我的日誌本，把地址傳給我嗎？

---

卡浦爾先生為什麼傳簡訊給文森蒂女士？

(A) 詢問她是否找到了他的公事包
(B) 詢問一個取消的會議
(C) 要她傳一個地址給他
(D) 預約餐廳

**字彙**
briefcase 公事包
inquire 詢問
request 要求
make a reservation 預約

**147** Why did Mr. Kapoor send a text message to Ms. Vincenti?

(A) To ask if she found his briefcase
(B) To inquire about a canceled meeting
(C) To request that she send him an address*
(D) To make a restaurant reservation

訊息中寫道卡浦爾先生忘了帶日誌本，請文森蒂女士把會面地址傳給他（Can you check my book and send me the address?），根據文意，(C) 為最適當的答案。本題必須閱讀全文後，才能掌握文意並順利解題。考題中，時常出現這一類的短篇文章。

---

卡浦爾先生接下來可能會做什麼？

(A) 離開餐廳
(B) 去辦公室
(C) 查網站
(D) 打電話給客戶

**148** What will Mr. Kapoor probably do next?

(A) Leave a restaurant*
(B) Go to his office
(C) Check a website
(D) Call a client

「I'm just about to leave Denny's Grill and had planned to go straight to the meeting.」，表示卡浦爾先生現在正要離開餐廳（Denny's Grill），因此答案為 (A)。

**Questions 149-150 refer to the following advertisement.**

[149] The American chapter of Ancient Worlds Archaeological Foundation seeks two full-time interns to assist with our archaeological dig near Siem Reap, Cambodia.

[150 (A)] Candidates must have completed a four-year degree in archaeological studies or must be currently enrolled in their 4th year of an archaeology program.

Research experience is a must, and [150 (C)] candidates with hands-on field training will be given preference.

[150 (B)] Applicants must be willing to travel to the dig site during the months of August through October. Accommodation and flights will be paid for by the foundation.

Interns will be paid a lump sum at the end of the trip. At the discretion of the project coordinator, interns may be hired as full-time employees following the dig's conclusion.

-------------------------------------------------------------------

古世界考古基金會美國分會徵求兩位全職實習生，協助柬埔寨暹粒附近的考古挖掘工作。

應徵者須取得大學考古學位，或現為考古學系大四學生。

需具研究經驗。具考古現場實際操作經驗者尤佳。

應徵者須願意於八月至十月間這赴至挖掘現場。基金會將提供住宿與機票。

實習生將於行程結束時領取全額薪水。實習生將於挖掘工作結束後，由專案統籌決定是否獲聘為全職員工。

---

**149** What is indicated about the American chapter of Ancient Worlds Archaeological Foundation?
(A) It wants to hire one part-time intern.
(B) It conducts digs in foreign countries.*
(C) It does not pay its interns except for travel expenses.
(D) It was founded three years ago.

由第一段中的「The American chapter of Ancient Worlds Archaeological Foundation seeks two full-time interns to assist with our Archaeological dig near Siem Reap, Cambodia.」，由此可以得知答案為 (B)。在此補充，由此句也可以確認 (A) 為錯誤的選項。

---

**150** What is NOT a qualification for the position?
(A) University education
(B) Willingness to travel
(C) Field training
(D) Computer knowledge*

閱讀文章時，請特別留意「應徵資格」。由第二段的內容可以確認 (A) 是該職位應徵資格之一；由第三段的「candidates with hands-on field training will be given preference」可以確認 (C)；由第四段的「Applicants must be willing to travel to the dig site during the months of August through October.」可以確認 (B)，因此本題的答案為 (D)。

---

字彙
chapter （協會）分部，支會
archaeological 考古學的
foundation 基金會
assist 協助
dig (n.) 挖掘
hands-on 實際操作的
field 實地，野外
training 訓練
preference 偏好，優先
accommodation 住宿
flight 航程，班機
lump sum
一次性支付的金額
discretion 決定權
conclusion 結束

下列何者與古世界考古基金會美國分會有關？
(A) 它想要聘僱一位兼職實習生。
(B) 它在外國進行挖掘工作。
(C) 除了旅費外不另給付實習生薪資。
(D) 在三年前創立。

字彙
except for 除……之外
expense 費用 found 創立

下列何者不是該職務的資格條件？
(A) 大學教育
(B) 旅行意願
(C) 實地訓練
(D) 電腦知識

字彙
qualification 資格

字彙
relation 關係
auditorium 禮堂
senior 資深的
head 負責，率領
development 開發
treatment 治療，療法
make a name for oneself
出名，成名
institute 學院
ground-breaking 開創性的
publication 發表
laboratory 實驗室

Questions 151-153 refer to the following memo.

**To:** Timmons Medical Research Staff
**From:** Anderson Baxtor, Director of Employee Relations
**Re:** Presentation
**Date:** 5 April

Attention all staff members,

Next Thursday, 13 April, we will have a special presentation in auditorium 203. [151] Maria Sergios is a senior researcher at the University of Westwood, where she has conducted research for the last five years. She headed the development of a new series of vaccines in addition to partnering with researchers in London, England to work on the development of several new treatments for cancer. Before joining the University of Westwood, Sergios made a name for herself at the Institute of Medical Research in Sydney, Australia. There, [153] I had the chance to learn from her during several ground-breaking projects. [152] Ms. Sergios will be here in Vancouver next week and has agreed to share her latest publication on laboratory techniques with us. All staff members are required to attend the presentation.

------------------------------------------------------------

收件者：蒂蒙斯醫學研究人員
寄件者：員工關係部主任安德森·巴斯特
回覆：演講
日期：4月5日

所有人員，請注意，

4月13日下週四，我們將在203號禮堂舉辦一場特別的演講。瑪麗亞·賽喬斯是西木大學的資深研究員。過去的五年來，她在那裡進行研究。除了和英國倫敦的研究者合作進行幾項癌症新療法的研發外，她還負責一系列新疫苗的開發。在加入西木大學前，賽喬斯成名於澳洲雪梨的醫學研究院。在那裡，我剛好有機會在幾項開創性的專案中受教於她。賽喬斯女士下週將到溫哥華，並同意與我們分享實驗室技術上的最新成果發表。所有人員都必須參加這場演講。

---

這個備忘錄討論的是什麼？

(A) 創立新實驗室的計畫
(B) 新職缺
(C) 一位科學家的職涯
(D) 專案計畫的截止日期

**151** What does the memo discuss?

(A) Plans to found a new lab
(B) A new job opening
(C) A scientist's career*
(D) Deadlines for a project

第一段提及賽喬斯女士是一位資深研究員（Maria Sergios is a senior researcher）。文章多半為她的相關介紹，因此 (C) 為最適當的答案。

* 答案改寫：researcher → scientist

**152** Where is Timmons Medical Research located?

(A) In London
(B) In Sydney
(C) In Westwood
(D) In Vancouver*

蒂蒙斯醫學研究位於何處？

(A) 倫敦
(B) 雪梨
(C) 西木
(D) 溫哥華

閱讀文章時，請先掌握 Timmons Medical Research 為本備忘錄撰寫人和收件人的研究機構，並留意文章中特定的地名。

由後半部「Ms. Sergios will be here in Vancouver next week」當中的 here = Vancouver，可以找出答案應為 (D)。

---

**153** What does Mr. Baxtor indicate about Ms. Sergios?

(A) She is his former mentor.*
(B) She is moving to Vancouver.
(C) She will join his research team.
(D) She will open her own laboratory.

巴斯特先生提到有關賽喬斯女士的什麼？

(A) 她是他以前的導師。
(B) 她將搬到溫哥華。
(C) 她將加入他的研究團隊。
(D) 她將開設自己的實驗室。

字彙
**former** 前任的

閱讀時，請特別留意撰寫人（第一人稱）的巴斯特先生（Mr. Baxter）。在後半部中，他提到在參與開創性專案時，從賽喬斯女士身上學到很多東西（I had the chance to learn from her during several ground-breaking projects.），由此可以得知答案為 (A)。

ACTUAL TEST **4**

PART **7**

中譯＋解析

字彙

**go ahead** 先去
**set up** 布置，安排
**drawer** 抽屜
**equipment** 設備
**former** 早前的；前任的
**catch up** 趕上

Questions 154-155 refer to the following text message chain.

**Jamal Myers 10:30 A.M.**

Hi, Ferguson. I'm still at Davis Printers waiting for our two banners. Could you go ahead and begin setting up? [154] I put the key to the room in the top right drawer of my desk.

**Ferguson Boyd 10:33 A.M.**

Found it. I'm leaving now.

**Jamal Myers 10:35 A.M.**

Thanks a lot. I know the award ceremony doesn't start until 1:30, but we need to double-check all the equipment.

**Ferguson Boyd 10:40 A.M.**

Just to make sure, [155] we will be having the ceremony in the former city hall building on Elliot Street, right? Not the new one on Queen Street?

**Jamal Myers 10:42 A.M.**

[155] Correct. Right after the ceremony, a photographer will take photos of the winners on the front lawn. That is why I ordered an additional banner to be used outside. I will catch up with you at the former city hall building as soon as I get the banners.

**Ferguson Boyd 10:45 A.M.**

OK. See you in a little while!

---

**賈邁爾‧麥爾斯 上午 [ 10:30 ]**

嗨，弗格森。我還在戴維斯影印店等兩幅橫旗。你可以先去前往布置嗎？我把房間鑰匙放在辦公桌右上的抽屜裡。

**弗格森‧博伊德 上午 [ 10:33 ]**

找到了。我現在就去。

**賈邁爾‧麥爾斯 上午 [ 10:35 ]**

太感謝了。我知道頒獎典禮 1:30 才開始，但我們需要仔細檢查所有設備。

**弗格森‧博伊德 上午 [10:40]**

只是確定一下，我們的頒獎典禮是在埃利奧特街的前市政大樓，對吧？不是皇后街上新的這棟。

**賈邁爾‧麥爾斯 上午 [10:42]**

沒錯。典禮後攝影師會在前面的草地上為獲獎者拍照。這就是我多訂一幅橫旗在外面使用的原因。我一拿到橫旗就趕到前市政大樓跟你會合。

**弗格森‧博伊德 上午 [10:45]**

好。待會兒見！

**154** At 10:33 A.M., what does Mr. Boyd most likely mean when he writes, "Found it"?

(A) He will pass on the information a client needs.
(B) He noticed Davis Printers while driving.
(C) He has the key to the venue in his hand.*
(D) He is looking at a phone number in a directory.

麥爾斯先生在 10 點 30 分的訊息中寫道：「I put the key to the room in the top right drawer of my desk.」，提到鑰匙所在的位置，因此博伊德先生找到的東西就是鑰匙（= it），故 (C) 為最適當的答案。

\* 答案改寫：room → venue

---

上午**10:33**時，博伊德先生說的「找到了」是什麼意思？

(A) 他會把客戶需要的資料傳過去。
(B) 他在開車時有看到戴維斯影印店。
(C) 他拿到了會場的鑰匙。
(D) 他正在找通訊錄上的電話號碼。

字彙
**notice** 注意
**venue** 場地
**directory** 通訊錄

---

**155** Where most likely is Mr. Boyd going next?

(A) To the train station
(B) To company headquarters
(C) To a print shop
(D) To the old city hall*

閱讀文章時，請特別留意博伊德先生前往的「目的地」。博伊德先生在 10 點 40 分傳送的訊息中「we will be having the ceremony in the former city hall building on Elliot Street, right?」，且之後對此的答覆為 Correct（沒錯），由此可以確認答案為 (D)。

\* 答案改寫：former → old

---

博伊德先生接下來有可能去哪裡？

(A) 火車站
(B) 公司總部
(C) 影印店
(D) 舊市政廳

**字彙**
tee-off （高爾夫）開球
access 取得
furthermore 再者
carbonated
碳酸，含二氧化碳的
complimentary 附贈的
incredible 極佳的
extensive 廣闊的
feature 特色，特點

## Holt Golf and Country Club
## 34 Russet Drive
## Edmonton, Alberta
## www.holtgolf.ca

24 April
Mr. Henry MacArthur
220 Washington Avenue
Edmonton, Alberta

Dear Mr. MacArthur,

Thank you for purchasing a membership to Holt Golf and Country Club. --[1]--. From May 1 until September 30, in addition to having your choice of tee-off time, you will have full access to our lounge, restaurant, and spa. Furthermore, [156] carbonated beverages are complimentary in all our cafés. Simply show your membership card when you order. --[2]--.

In addition to all these incredible services, Holt Golf and Country Club is announcing yet another service for its members. [157] From now until the end of August, all members may invite guests for a round of golf on our extensive course. This feature is available from 8 A.M. until 4 P.M. only. Guest reservations must be made 24 hours in advance. --[3]--.

If you have any questions or concerns, please contact our customer service hotline at 900-555-3344. --[4]--.

Sincerely,

Mitchel Walker

---------------------------------------------------------------------------

霍爾特高爾夫暨鄉村俱樂部
亞伯達省埃德蒙頓
羅西特大道 34 號
www.holtgolf.ca

4 月 24 日
亨利·麥克阿瑟先生
亞伯達省埃德蒙頓
華盛頓大道 220 號

親愛的麥克阿瑟先生，

感謝您購買霍爾特高爾夫暨鄉村俱樂部會員。本年度內，您可以享用我們所有的優質服務。自 5 月 1 日起至 9 月 30 日，除了可自選開球時間外，您還可以盡情地使用我們的休息室、餐廳和水療設備。除此之外，我們所有的小餐館都附贈碳酸飲料，您只要在點餐時，出示會員卡即可。

除了這些極佳的服務外，霍爾特高爾夫暨鄉村俱樂部正宣布另一項專屬會員的服務。從現在起至八月底，所有的會員都可以邀請賓客到我們廣闊的球場上打一場高爾夫球。這個特別優惠只限上午八點至下午四點。該服務需提早於 24 小時前預約。

若您有任何問題或疑慮，請來電客服熱線 900-555-3344。
米切爾·沃克 敬上

---

**156** What is true about Holt golf and Country Club?

(A) It offers its members free drinks.*
(B) It only opens during the spring.
(C) It offers discount memberships.
(D) It hosts seasonal parties.

文章第一段末提到了會員的優惠「. . . carbonated beverages are complimentary in all our cafés. Simply show your membership card when you order.」，表示只要出示會員卡，會員即可享有免費的碳酸飲料，因此答案應為 (A)。

\* 答案改寫：beverage → drink
　　　　　　　complimentary → free

有關霍爾特高爾夫暨鄉村俱樂部的敘述，下列何者為真？

(A) 它提供會員免費飲料。
(B) 它只在春季開放。
(C) 它提供優惠的會員資格。
(D) 它舉辦季節性派對。

字彙
**seasonal** 季節性的

---

**157** According to the letter, what will be different after August?

(A) Members cannot access the spa.
(B) Members may not bring guests.*
(C) Golf tee-off times will be earlier.
(D) Golf lessons will be available.

閱讀文章時，請特別留意關鍵時間點 August。第二段中的「From now until the end of August, all members may invite guests for a round of golf on our extensive course.」，表示從現在開始至八月底，可以帶賓客前往打球，因此過了八月之後則無法，答案應為 (B)。

根據信件內容，八月後會有什麼變動？

(A) 會員無法使用水療。
(B) 會員不能帶賓客入場。
(C) 高爾夫球開球時間會提早。
(D) 有高爾夫球課程。

字彙
**access** 使用某物的權利

---

**158** In which of the positions marked [1], [2], [3], and [4] does the following sentence best belong?

"This year, you will be able to enjoy all our premium services."

(A) [1]*
(B) [2]
(C) [3]
(D) [4]

[1] 的後方列出了許多和會員相關的優惠，而插入句中的 all our premium services 即用來預告以下將介紹更為詳細的優惠內容，因此本句最適合填入 [1] 當中，故 (A) 正確。

下列句子最適合出現在[1]、[2]、[3]、[4]的哪個位置中？
「本年度內，您可以享用我們所有的優質服務。」

(A) [1]
(B) [2]
(C) [3]
(D) [4]

字彙

role 角色，職位
recognized 公認的，認可的
industry 產業；工業
passion 熱情
celebrity 名人
founding 創立
assume 就任
numerous 許多的
clothe 為……提供衣服
departure 離開
quote 引述

Questions 159-162 refer to the following article.

Milan (July 14) — [159] Roberto Pelini, lead designer at Marshenco Fashions, one of Europe's top design companies, has announced he will retire from his role at the company. --[1]--.

Since first accepting the position 10 years ago, Roberto Pelini has worked hard to make Marshenco Fashions one of the most-recognized names in the industry. Because of Pelini's passion and eye for design, Marshenco has become a favorite among celebrities and his designs can often be seen both on the runway and the red carpet. --[2]--. [160] The company's success has even allowed for the founding of a sister company, Marshenco Accessories.

Irina Morova, former designer at Ruvera Design, will assume the position of lead designer at Marshenco. Morova has more than 10 years of experience heading a major fashion company. [161] Her work has been featured in numerous fashion festivals, magazines, and has clothed some of Europe's top singers and actors. --[3]--.

Following his departure from Marshenco, [162] Roberto Pelini will partner with Sophia Bertuski to found a new independent fashion house. **Pelini is quoted as saying,** [162] "I look forward to working with Sophia. Her creative vision is similar to my own." --[4]--.

--------------------------------------------------

米蘭（7 月 14 日）——歐洲頂尖設計公司之一的馬軒可時尚，其首席設計師羅伯特·佩利尼已經宣布將自公司的職位退休。

自 10 年前首次接掌該職，羅伯特·佩利尼一直努力讓馬軒可時尚成為業界最知名的品牌之一。由於佩利尼的熱情與設計眼光，馬軒可已經成為名流間最受歡迎的品牌。而佩利尼的設計也常見於伸展台與紅毯上。公司的成功甚至促成了姊妹公司馬軒可飾品的成立。

里維拉設計公司的前任設計師伊莉娜·莫羅娃將接掌馬軒可首席設計師一職。莫羅娃擁有管理大型時尚企業十多年的經驗。她的作品在許多時尚季、雜誌中成為焦點，也曾為一些歐洲頂尖歌手與演員提供服裝。

在離開馬軒可後，羅伯特·佩利尼將與蘇菲亞·伯蘇斯基合夥創立新的獨立時尚坊。引述佩利尼自己說的話，「我很期待與蘇菲亞合作。她頗具創意的眼光與我相近。」至於佩利尼的新時裝作品何時發表，至今尚未有消息傳出。

**159** What is the purpose of the article?

(A) To report on a company's closure
(B) To announce a change in a company's leadership*
(C) To advertise a new job opening at a company
(D) To publicize a new line of products

由第一段第一句中的「Roberto Pelini, lead designer at Marshenco Fashions, one of Europe's top design companies, has announced he will retire from his role at the company.」，可以推測本文主旨應為某間公司的高層人事異動，因此 (B) 為最適當的答案。

**160** What is indicated about Marshenco?

(A) It is based in North America.
(B) It was purchased by Pelini.
(C) It owns Ruvera Design.
(D) It founded a second company.*

由第二段中的「The company's success has even allowed for the founding of a sister company, Marshenco Accessories.」，可知由於公司的成功，讓姊妹公司得以成立，因此答案應為 (D)。

* 答案改寫：sister company → second company

**161** What is mentioned about Irina Morova?

(A) She will become Pelini's business partner.
(B) Her career at Ruvera Design was successful.*
(C) She originally worked as a runway model.
(D) Her designs are for average consumers.

閱讀文章時，請特別留意題目關鍵人名伊莉娜·莫羅娃（Irina Morova）。在第三段中提到了馬軒可時尚首席設計師的繼任者伊莉娜·莫羅娃，並簡短說明了她的經歷與成果（Her work has been featured in numerous fashion festivals, magazines, and has clothed some of Europe's top singers and actors.），由此可以確認答案為 (B)，既然莫羅娃女士為歌手與演員提供服裝，可知她的服飾不是為一般人設計，故 (D) 錯。。

**162** In which of the positions marked [1], [2], [3], and [4] does the following sentence best belong?

"There is no news as to when Pelini's new lines will be available to the public."

(A) [1]
(B) [2]
(C) [3]
(D) [4]*

關於「佩利尼的新時裝作品何時發表」，與最後一段佩利尼往後的計畫（創立新的獨立時尚坊）最為相關，因此 (D) 為最適當的答案。

字彙
waterfront 濱水區
association 協會
a number of 許多的
participating 參加的
appetizer 開胃菜
marinate 浸泡滷汁
pork rib 豬肋排
top with 把⋯⋯放在上
ingredient 食材
admission 入場許可
limited 有限的

Questions 163-165 refer to the following advertisement.

## [163] The First Annual Waterfront Food Truck Festival!

Ajax Food and Beverage Association is pleased to announce the first ever Waterfront Food Truck Festival. From Monday August 8 through Sunday August 14, the Ajax waterfront will host a number of local food trucks. Guests can enjoy live music, prizes, and children's entertainment between the hours of 11 A.M. and 6 P.M. [164] Food truck items can be sampled for discount prices.

Famous Participating Food Trucks:

◆ Rio Tacos —Enjoy fresh appetizers and a variety of tacos and nachos

◆ Barbecue Madness — Marinated pork ribs, chicken wings, and pulled pork

◆ Benny's Fries —French fries topped with your choice of ingredients

Admission is free for all participants. [165] Parking will be available on a limited basis, so make sure to get there early.

For a complete list of participating food trucks, visit www.ajaxwaterfront.com/foodtruckfestival.

-----------------------------------------------------

第一屆年度海濱餐車祭

愛捷克斯餐飲協會很高興宣布有史以來的第一場海濱餐車祭。自 8 月 8 日星期一至 8 月 14 日星期日，愛捷克斯海濱區將邀請許多本地餐車參與。來賓在上午 11:00 至下午 6:00 間可享現場音樂演奏、獎品以及兒童遊樂活動。並可以優惠價試吃餐車上的食物。

與會的知名餐車：
★ 里約墨西哥捲餅——可享新鮮開胃小點，及各式墨西哥捲餅和玉米片
★ 瘋狂燒烤——滷豬肋排、雞翅及手撕豬肉
★ 邦妮薯條——配上您喜愛食材沾醬的薯條

所有入場均免費。停車位有限，請盡早到場。
欲知與會餐車完整名單，請上網站 www.ajaxwaterfront.com/foodtruckfestival。

**163** What is being advertised?

(A) A restaurant's grand opening
(B) A concert in the park
(C) An auto show
(D) A new community event*

由標題 The First Annual Waterfront Food Truck Festival，可以得知為濱海區的活動，(D) 為最適當的答案。

* 答案改寫：first → new
　　　　　　festival → event

這則廣告是在宣傳什麼？

(A) 餐廳的盛大開幕
(B) 公園的音樂會
(C) 汽車展
(D) 新社區活動

---

**164** What is mentioned about the participating food trucks?

(A) They will travel to various cities.
(B) They will distribute free gifts.
(C) They will be open all day.
(D) They will sell food at reduced prices.*

第一段文章中的「Food truck items can be sampled for discount prices.」，表示可以以優惠價格試吃，因此答案應為 (D)。

* 答案改寫：item → food
　　　　　　discount → reduced

文中提到何者與參加的餐車有關？

(A) 將開至各個城市。
(B) 將分發免費禮物。
(C) 全天營業。
(D) 將降價販售食物。

字彙
**distribute** 分發

---

**165** What are participants encouraged to do?

(A) Arrive at the site early*
(B) Leave their cars at home
(C) Pay an admission fee
(D) Camp at the waterfront

文章的後半部，大多會出現建議的事項。當中提到由於停車位有限，建議提早前來（Parking will be available on a limited basis, so make sure to get there early.），由此可以得知答案為 (A)。

* 答案改寫：get → arrive

參加者被鼓勵做什麼事？

(A) 盡早到場
(B) 把自己的車子留在家裡
(C) 付入場費
(D) 在海濱區露營

ACTUAL TEST 4

PART 7 中譯＋解析

## 字彙

cover 頂替
property 房地產
put together 整理；組合
description 說明，敘述
appliance 電器
fully furnished 附家具的
basement 地下室
fireplace 壁爐
in-ground 建在地上的
relevant 相關的
real estate 不動產

Questions 166-169 refer to the following e-mail.

**From:** Marcus Pentz
**To:** Tamara Woods
**Date:** October 10
**Subject:** Information

Hi Tamara,

[167] Thank you so much for covering for Samira while she's away visiting family. Prior to leaving for her trip abroad, she was working on advertisements for two local properties. According to her files, she has put together the following descriptions:

776 Marshall Avenue is a three-story home situated on Lake Scougog. It features four bedrooms, upgraded kitchen appliances, a fully furnished basement, and a wooden fireplace. It is situated in a quiet area, but is within walking distance of local schools.

9902 Fenton Street is a three-bedroom home with [168 (A)] a large yard and an in-ground swimming pool. [168 (C)] A garage was recently built on the property and can hold up to two cars. [168 (D)] The home is located near all major shopping malls and the university.

I'm going to send over Samira's files, so you can update her descriptions and add any relevant information. [169] These properties, along with photographs, must be submitted to *Scougog Weekly*'s real estate editor by Friday. Please let me know if you have any questions or concerns.

Regards,

Marcus Pentz
Pentz Real Estate

----------------------------------------------------------------

寄件者：馬庫斯·潘次
收件者：塔瑪拉·伍茲
日期：10 月 10 日
主旨：資料

嗨，塔瑪拉，

非常感謝妳在莎米拉探視家人時頂替她的職務。在她出國前，她正在做兩家本地房產的廣告。根據她的文件顯示，她已經將下述的說明整理好了：

馬歇爾大道 776 號是一棟位於史古葛湖的三層樓住家。有四間臥房，升級的廚具電器，家具完備的地下室與一座木造壁爐。地處閑靜地區，步行即可抵達本地學校。

芬頓街 9902 號是一棟三房住家，配有大庭院及游泳池。車庫是最近增建的，可容納兩部車。這棟住屋鄰近所有大型購物商場與大學。

我會傳送塔瑪拉的文件過去，這樣妳就可以更新內容，加上相關的資料了。這些房產資料和照片必須在週五前，交給《史古葛週報》的不動產編輯。如果妳有任何問題或疑慮，請告訴我。

潘次不動產
馬庫斯·潘次 敬上

## 166 Why was the e-mail sent?

(A) To request some files
(B) To give some job instructions*
(C) To provide payment information
(D) To ask for some local contacts

郵件第一段中潘次先生提到感謝對方暫代他人的工作，並交代接手的工作內容、截止日期與注意事項。因此 (B) 為最適當的答案。在郵件的主旨或是第一段，通常就會出現郵件寄送目的關鍵線索。但本題必須掌握郵件全文的文意後，才能順利解題，有時也會出現這樣的題型。

為什麼會寄這封電子郵件？

(A) 要求一些文件
(B) 提供工作指令
(C) 提供付款資訊
(D) 要求與本地聯絡人聯繫

字彙
instruction 指令
payment 付款

## 167 What is suggested about Samira?

(A) She often travels abroad.
(B) She purchased a new home.
(C) She works for a newspaper.
(D) She has gone on vacation.*

閱讀文章時，請特別留意題目關鍵 Samira。由第一句的「Thank you so much for covering for Samira while she's away visiting family.」，可以得知 (D) 為最適當的答案。

下列何者與莎米拉有關？

(A) 她常出國。
(B) 她買了一棟新屋。
(C) 她為報社工作。
(D) 她去度假了。

## 168 What is NOT mentioned about the property on Fenton Street?

(A) It has a big yard and a swimming pool.
(B) It was previously listed on a website.*
(C) It includes a newly built garage.
(D) It is close to many important amenities.

第三段中提到了題目關鍵字 Fenton Street，請將各選項的內容對照內文，並刪除當中提及的選項。由第一句 a large yard and an in-ground swimming pool 可以確認 (A)；後方的 A garage was recently built on the property 可以確認 (C)；而下一句的「The home is located near all major shopping malls and the university.」可以確認 (D)，因此本題的答案應為 (B)。

下列何者與芬頓街的住屋無關？

(A) 它有大庭院和一座游泳池。
(B) 它之前刊於網站中。
(C) 它有一間新蓋的車庫。
(D) 它接近許多重要的設施。

字彙
amenities 設施

## 169 According to the e-mail, what is indicated about *Scougog Weekly*?

(A) It will feature the selections Ms. Woods must update.*
(B) It comes out every Friday.
(C) It charges fees based on property prices.
(D) It is distributed to local residents free of charge.

第四段中的「These properties, along with photographs, must be submitted to *Scougog Weekly*'s real estate editor by Friday.」，提到了題目關鍵字《史古葛週報》，由此可知該週報將刊登伍茲女士更新的房產資料與照片，所以答案為 (A)。

根據電子郵件的內容，下列何者指的是《史古葛週報》？

(A) 它會介紹伍茲女士須更新資料的精選房產物件。
(B) 它每週五發行。
(C) 它會依房地產價格收費。
(D) 免費發送給本地居民。

字彙
selection 精選
based on . . . 根據……
resident 居民

Questions 170-173 refer to the text message chain.

**Blake Wyatt [3:23 P.M.]**

Ms. Parker, [170] I just found out there's going to be a parade on First Street. The area is going to be really crowded, so [172] the repaving of your restaurant's parking lot will have to wait.

**Janice Parker [3:26 P.M.]**

So does that mean you won't be coming in at all?

**Blake Wyatt [3:28 P.M.]**

No, we'll still be there. We can help get the basement storage rooms finished.

**Janice Parker [3:31 P.M.]**

OK, great. How long do you think it will take to get everything done down there?

**Blake Wyatt [3:32 P.M.]**

I'll check now.

*Tim Robins has been added to the conversation.*

**Blake Wyatt [3:35 P.M.]**

Tim, how far have you gotten on the basement project?

**Tim Robins [3:40 P.M.]**

Well, [171] things were running smoothly until we found some water damage in the southeast corner. It looks like a big cleanup job.

**Blake Wyatt [3:42 P.M.]**

What if my crew gave you a hand tomorrow?

**Tim Robins [3:44 P.M.]**

That might get us back on schedule. We might even be able to install the new refrigerators.

**Janice Parker [3:45 P.M.]**

If you're moving the fridges, you'll need access to the service entrance behind the building. I think you still have the key, right?

**Blake Wyatt [3:47 P.M.]**

Yes, I've got it. [173] Are there any spots behind the building where the guys can park for the day?

**Janice Parker [3:50 P.M.]**

There might not be any free if there's a parade. You should probably park in the empty lot on Fifth Avenue.

**布萊克・懷特 [ 下午 3:23 ]**
帕克女士,我剛發現第一街將舉辦遊行。該區會非常的擁擠,所以貴餐廳停車場的地面重鋪工程要再等等了。

**珍妮斯・帕克 [ 下午 3:26 ]**
那表示你們不會進來了嗎?

**布萊克・懷特 [ 下午 3:28 ]**
不,我們還是會到。我們會協助完工地下室的儲藏室。

**珍妮斯・帕克 [ 下午 3:31 ]**
好,那太好了。你認為那裡全部弄好要多久時間?

**布萊克・懷特 [ 下午 3:32 ]**
我現在確認一下。

提姆・羅賓斯加入對話。

**布萊克・懷特 [ 下午 3:35 ]**
提姆,地下室的工程,你們做好多少了?

**提姆・羅賓斯 [ 下午 3:40 ]**
嗯,開始一切都很順利,一直到我們發現東南邊角落有幾處進水。那看起來會是個很大的清理工程。

**布萊克・懷特 [ 下午 3:42 ]**
如果我的工作人員明天過去幫你呢?

**提姆・羅賓斯 [ 下午 3:44 ]**
那可以幫我們回歸到預定的進度。我們甚至可能可以安裝新冰箱。

**珍妮斯・帕克 [ 下午 3:45 ]**
如果你要搬動冰箱,就需要使用大樓後面的廠商專用出入口。我想你還留有鑰匙吧?

**布萊克・懷特 [ 下午 3:47 ]**
是的,我有。大樓後面有任何地方可以讓我們的人員在那天停車嗎?

**珍妮斯・帕克 [ 下午 3:50 ]**
如果有遊行的話,恐怕就沒有空位了。你們可能要停到第五大道的空地上。

懷特先生提到什麼會打斷明天的工作？

(A) 國定假日
(B) 街頭活動
(C) 遺失的貨運商品
(D) 設備不足

字彙
interrupt 打斷，阻礙
lack 缺少

**170** What does Mr. Wyatt suggest will interrupt tomorrow's work?

(A) A public holiday　　(B) A street event*
(C) A lost delivery　　(D) A lack of equipment

閱讀時，請特別留意 Mr. Wyatt 的訊息。在 3 點 23 分的訊息中，他提到之後將會有遊行活動（I just found out there's going to be a parade on First Street.），並在後方補充說道對方的地面重鋪工程要再等等，因此答案為 (B)。

* 答案改寫：parade → street event

---

下午3:40時，羅賓斯先生說：「那看起來會是個很大的清理工程。」是什麼意思？

(A) 他的組員通常都在做清理工作。
(B) 有些損害很嚴重。
(C) 他不喜歡自己目前的工作。
(D) 他的組員的工程太複雜了。

字彙
significant 重大的
complicated 複雜的

**171** At 3:40 P.M., what does Mr. Robins most likely mean when he writes, "It looks like a big cleanup job."?

(A) His crew usually does the cleaning.
(B) Some damage was significant.*
(C) He does not like his current job.
(D) His crew's project is too complicated.

題目句前方的句子為「things were running smoothly until we found some water damage in the southeast corner」，提到進水的問題，推測問題相當嚴重，才會接題目句的「很大的清理工程」，因此答案應為 (B)。

---

帕克女士有可能是誰？

(A) 餐廳老闆
(B) 營建工人
(C) 停車場服務員
(D) 電器製造商

字彙
attendant 服務員
appliance 電器
manufacturer 製造商

**172** Who most likely is Ms. Parker?

(A) A restaurant owner*　　(B) A construction worker
(C) A parking attendant　　(D) An appliance manufacturer

第一句懷特先生便向關鍵人名帕克女士（Ms. Parker）說：「. . . the repaving of your restaurant's parking lot will have to wait.」，由此可以推知帕克女士是餐廳老闆，答案為 (A)。

---

懷特先生詢問的其中一個問題是什麼？

(A) 到另一個入口的路線
(B) 大樓鑰匙的下落
(C) 當地活動的時間
(D) 停車位的位置

字彙
directions 路線；方向

**173** What is one topic Mr. Wyatt asks about?

(A) Directions to another entrance
(B) The location of a building key
(C) The time of a local event
(D) The location of parking spaces*

請把重點放在懷特先生（Mr. Wyatt）的訊息上。在他的訊息中出現了數次的問句，當中針對停車場的詢問（Are there any spots behind the building where the guys can park for the day?），即為本題的答案 (D)。

http://www.hamptonoutsourcing.org

| HOME | CONTACT US | HISTORY | SERVICES |
|------|------------|---------|----------|

### Hampton Outsourcing

Hampton Outsourcing is the first choice among companies who wish to outsource their production to overseas locations. In today's shrinking global village, [174] electrical component manufacturing can be completed cheaply and efficiently almost anywhere in the world. Our knowledgeable staff members will help you grow your company by connecting you with overseas business partners, [175 (B)] helping you obtain the correct licensing, and ensuring your overseas interests are carried out in an ethical manner. [175 (C)] Our clients are known for being environmentally responsible as they establish themselves internationally. In addition, [175 (A)] we ensure all your potential business partners receive advanced training in regards to troubleshooting all of your products.

Call Hampton Outsourcing today to speak with one of our representatives.

--------------------------------------------------------------------

http://www.hamptonoutsourcing.org

| 首頁 | 聯絡我們 | 沿革 | 服務項目 |
|------|----------|------|----------|

### 漢普頓外包公司

漢普頓外包公司,對所有希望將生產工作委外至海外各地的公司而言,是所有外包公司的首選。在今日日益縮小的地球村中,幾乎在全世界各地都可以便宜又有效率地完成電子零件的生產。我們知識廣博的同仁藉由幫您連結海外事業夥伴,來協助貴公司成長、輔佐您取得適當的授權、並確保您的海外事業利益以合乎道德的方式進行。我們的客戶在立足於國際的同時,也以維護環保著名。除此之外,我們還向您保證,您所有的潛在事業夥伴都能獲得貴公司所有產品檢修相關的高階訓練。

今天就來電漢普頓外包公司,與我們的代表人員聯絡吧。

字彙
outsource 外包
overseas 海外
location 地點
shrinking 正在縮小的
electrical 電的
component 零件
manufacturing 製造(業)
knowledgeable
博學的,有知識的
connect 連結
obtain 得到,獲得
correct 適當的,合乎規範的
license (v.) 授權
ensure 確保,保證
interest 利益
carry out . . . 執行,進行
ethical 合乎道德的
manner 方式
environmentally
在環境方面地
establish 建立,創辦
potential 潛在的
advanced 進階的
in regards to . . . 關於……
troubleshoot 檢修
representative 代表人員

誰最有可能是漢普頓外包公司的客戶？

**(A)** 客戶服務中心的人員

**(B)** 保險經紀人

**(C)** 環境保護局

**(D)** 家電用品公司

字彙
**broker** 經紀人
**appliance** 電器

**174** Who most likely will be a customer of Hampton Outsourcing?

(A) Call center workers

(B) Insurance brokers

(C) Environmental agencies

(D) Home appliance companies*

由第一段中的「electrical component manufacturing can be completed cheaply and efficiently almost anywhere in the world」，可以得知顧客應為與「生產電器零件」相關的產業，因此答案為 (D)。

---

下列何者不是漢普頓外包公司的強項？

**(A)** 優質的員工訓練

**(B)** 對授權的了解

**(C)** 環保流程

**(D)** 熟悉出口稅制

字彙
**strength** 長處
**superior** 優質的
**conscious**
意識到的，覺察的
**procedure** 程序，手續
**familiarity** 熟悉，了解
**export** 出口
**tax** 稅

**175** What is NOT mentioned as a strength of Hampton Outsourcing?

(A) Superior employee training

(B) Knowledge of licensing

(C) Environmentally conscious procedures

(D) Familiarity with export taxes*

解題時，請將各選項與相關段落進行對照，並刪除文章中提及的選項。(A) 出現在第一段最後一句「we ensure all your potential business partners receive advanced training in regards to troubleshooting all of your products」；(B) 出現在 helping you obtain the correct licensing 當中；由「Our clients are known for being environmentally responsible as they establish themselves internationally.」可以確認 (C)，因此答案應為 (D)。

**Questions 176-180 refer to the following letter and voucher.**

To: Raphael Rosario <rosario@ebookmail.com>
From: Janelle Parik <jparik@alliancepremiumairways.com>
Subject: Your Flight
180 **Date:** 6 January
180 **Attachment:** voucher

Dear Mr. Rosario,

176 Thank you for sharing your experience with Alliance Premium Airways Customer Service. 176, 177 I am sorry to learn about your negative experience on January 2. 177 According to the online form you completed, you had reserved a business class seat on a third-party website, but you were forced to fly economy class because your reservation had been lost.

I have contacted the website you used to book your flight. Apparently, there was a computer malfunction, which caused some prior bookings to be deleted. Unfortunately, this resulted in some seats being resold. 178 I understand that you have already received a partial refund, but I'd like to offer you an additional coupon for your troubles. Please see the attachment for more information.

Sincerely,

Janelle Parik,
Customer Service Manager
Alliance Premium Airways

--------------------------------------------------------------------

收件者：拉斐爾・羅薩里奧 <rosario@ebookmail.com>
寄件者：賈奈兒・帕里克 <jparik@alliancepremiumairways.com>
主旨：您的航班
日期：1月6日
附件：優惠券

親愛的羅薩里奧先生，

感謝您與高優聯盟航空客戶服務部分享您的個人經驗。本人對您在1月2日不愉快的經驗深感抱歉。根據您所填寫的線上表格，您於第三方網站上預訂了商務艙的座位，但由於預約紀錄遺失，只好被迫搭乘經濟艙。

我已聯絡您之前預約班機的網站。顯然地，由於電腦故障，造成早先的預約被刪除。很不幸地，這已經造成了部分座位被轉售。我了解您已獲得部分退款，但我想為您的不便另外提供優惠券。更多資訊，請您參考附件。

高優聯盟航空客戶服務部經理
賈奈兒・帕里克 敬上

字彙
voucher 票券
alliance 聯盟
negative 不愉快的，負面的
third-party 第三方
be forced to . . . 被迫……
apparently 顯然地
malfunction 故障
cause 造成，導致
delete 刪除
result in 造成，導致
partial 部分的
refund 退款
additional 額外的，另外的

## Alliance Premium Airways Voucher
## $200 off your next flight

Details: Alliance Premium Airways would like to offer you $200 off your next flight. Please note, this coupon may only be used for international return flights. This coupon is good until December 31 of this year. You may use this coupon at any Alliance Premium Airways kiosk or online at www.alliancepremiumairways.com.

Voucher Number: YY7732999938          Date Issued: January 6

[180] Issuing office: _____ Vancouver _____ Edmonton
_____ Montreal [180] X Toronto

--------------------------------------------------------

高優聯盟航空優惠券
下一趟航班可折扣200元

詳細說明：高優聯盟航空很樂意為您的下一趟航班提供200元的折扣。請注意，本優惠券僅可用於國際回程航班。有效使用期限於本年度12月31日止。您可於所有高優聯盟航空自動服務機，或線上www.alliancepremiumairways.com使用本優惠券。

票號：YY7732999938          核發日期：1月6日
簽發單位：_____ 溫哥華 _____ 艾德蒙頓 _____ 蒙特婁 _____ 多倫多
                                                    X

---

帕里克女士為什麼會寄這封電子郵件？

**(A)** 回覆線上客訴
**(B)** 提供工作合約
**(C)** 取消機票
**(D)** 詢問旅程

**176** Why did Ms. Parik send the e-mail?

(A) To reply to an online complaint*
(B) To provide a job contract
(C) To cancel an airline ticket
(D) To inquire about a trip

在郵件前半部內容中，通常就可以找到與郵件（第一篇）寄送目的相關的重要線索。第一段帕里克女士表示感謝對方願意分享自身的經驗（Thank you for sharing your experience with Alliance Premium Airways Customer Service.），並提到針對對方不愉快的經驗表示抱歉（I am sorry to learn about your negative experience on January 2.），因此答案應為 (A)。

**177** What does Ms. Parik indicate happened on January 2?

(A) She solved a seating problem.
(B) A flight was unnecessarily delayed.
(C) Many business class seats were empty.
(D) Mr. Rosario got a seat in a lower class.*

請從帕里克女士所撰寫的郵件（第一篇）中，找出有關 1 月 2 日的內容。第一段中帕里克女士便陳述羅薩里奧先生在 1 月 2 日時，發生了有關班機艙等不愉快的經驗（According to the online form you completed, you had reserved a business class seat on a third-party website, but you were forced to fly economy class because your reservation had been lost.），由此可以確認答案為 (D)。

帕里克女士提到1月2日發生什麼事？

(A) 她解決了一個座位問題。
(B) 一架班機沒有理由地延誤了。
(C) 很多商務艙座位是空的。
(D) 羅薩里奧先生拿到了較低艙等的座位。

字彙
unnecessarily
沒有理由地；不必要地

**178** What is suggested about Mr. Rosario?

(A) He requested a last-minute flight change.
(B) He flew from Vancouver to Toronto.
(C) He paid for his flight in advance.*
(D) He usually flies economy class.

郵件（第一篇）的收件人為羅薩里奧先生，第二段中的「I understand that you have already received a partial refund」，提到對方應該已經「收到部分的退款」，表示羅薩里奧先生之前就已經支付了機票的費用，因此 (C) 為最適當的答案。

下列何者與羅薩里奧先生有關？

(A) 他在最後一刻要求更換航班。
(B) 他從溫哥華飛到多倫多。
(C) 他預先支付了航班的錢。
(D) 他通常搭乘經濟艙。

字彙
last-minute 最後一刻的

**179** In the voucher, the word "good" in paragraph 1, line 2, is closest in meaning to

(A) high quality
(B) lucky
(C) well behaved
(D) valid*

請先找出單字所在的句子，並根據文意，選出選項中最適合替換的同義字。「有效使用至 12 月 31 日止」，為符合本句的文意，最適合替換的單字為 valid，故 (D) 正確。

在優惠券中，第一段、第二行的「good」與下列哪一個意思最接近？

(A) 高品質
(B) 幸運的
(C) 表現良好
(D) 有效的

字彙
well behaved 表現良好
valid 有效的

**180** Where most likely is Ms. Parik's office located?

(A) Vancouver
(B) Edmonton
(C) Montreal
(D) Toronto*

解題時，請綜合帕里克女士所撰寫的郵件（第一篇）與附件優惠券（第二篇）的內容。優惠券標示的發行日期為 1 月 6 日，地點在多倫多（見 Issuing office 那行），因此答案應為 (D)。

帕里克女士的辦公室最有可能在哪裡？

(A) 溫哥華
(B) 艾德蒙頓
(C) 蒙特婁
(D) 多倫多

Questions 181-185 refer to the following webpage and customer review.

| REVIEWS | HOME | DESIGN TOOLS | CONTACT US |
|---|---|---|---|

Flyer Frenzy, the best online flyer generator for businesses large and small!

With Flyer Frenzy, you can create custom flyers for your business. Whether you are advertising the opening of your business or simply trying to generate awareness about your services, Flyer Frenzy has everything you need to design the perfect flyer.

**Step 1: Design Your Flyer**

Our online generator has numerous customizable templates. Browse through our categories and select the right template for you. All our fonts are easy to change with just the click of a mouse. [181] If you want to accent your design with images, we have over 10,000 stock photos you can use at no extra cost. Furthermore, you can upload your own designs and logos to use along with any of our fonts.

**Step 2: Select A Quantity**

At Flyer Frenzy, we can print as few as 25 flyers for each order. However, the more flyers you order, the less you pay for each one.

| Quantity | Price Per Item |
|---|---|
| 25-300 | 20 cents |
| [183] 301-1,000 | 15 cents |
| 1,001-1,500 | 10 cents |
| 1,501 or more | 5 cents |

**Step 3: Purchase A Digital Copy**

[182] For an extra flat fee of $50, you can download a digital copy of your design. This design is perfect for featuring on your business's website, as part of an e-mail newsletter, or as a printed advertisement.

**Step 4: Finalize Your Order**

Orders take five days to process; however, large orders may take longer to prepare. In the event that there are delays, you will be notified by e-mail.

| 評論 | 首頁 | 設計工具 | 聯絡我們 |

狂傳單，大小公司行號最佳線上傳單製作器。

有了狂傳單，您可以為自己的公司行號創作客製化傳單。不論您是要宣傳門市的開幕，或只是要吸引大眾對貴公司服務的注意。狂傳單有您設計絕佳傳單所需的一切。

**步驟一：設計您的傳單**
我們的線上製作器有許多可客製的樣板。瀏覽我們的目錄，選出適合您的樣板。只要按一下滑鼠，就可以更改所有字體。如果您想要加上圖像突顯設計，我們有超過 10,000 個庫存圖片可供免費使用。此外，你也可以上傳自己的設計圖像與商標，搭配我們的字體。

**步驟二：選擇數量**
在狂傳單，每筆訂單最少有 25 張傳單。但您訂購的傳單數量愈多，每張的單價就愈便宜。

| 數量 | 每張單價 |
|---|---|
| 25-300 | 20 分錢 |
| 301-1,000 | 15 分錢 |
| 1,001-1,500 | 10 分錢 |
| 1,501 以上 | 5 分錢 |

**步驟三：購買數位版**
只要額外支付單一價 50 元，就可以下載您個人設計的數位版。這個設計非常適合使用於公司的網站上，也可當作電子商訊郵件的一部分，或作為平面廣告。

**步驟四：結單**
訂單需五天時間處理。但大型訂單將耗費更長的準備時間。若有任何延誤，將以電子郵件通知。

| REVIEWS | HOME | DESIGN TOOLS | CONTACT US |

★ ★ ★ ★ ★ Flyer Frenzy has great services!

I own a local shoe store downtown and had been finding it hard to spread the word about our upcoming sales event. I decided to design my own flyer using Flyer Frenzy's online generator. I found it very easy to use, and the designs were very elegant. [183] I ended up ordering 1,000 flyers. I also purchased a digital copy of my design and used it on my website. Our sales event was a big success. [184] Many customers said they'd heard about it from the flyers they'd seen posted around town. I am extremely pleased with Flyer Frenzy's services. [185] They are much better than some of the other online generators I browsed, and their templates were much more sophisticated. I will definitely be using Flyer Frenzy again in the future!

Jen Tristan

字彙
**spread** 傳播；散布
**upcoming** 即將到來的
**elegant** 優美的
**end up V-ing . . .**
最後成為⋯⋯
**extremely** 非常，極度地
**be pleased with . . .**
對⋯⋯感到高興／滿意
**sophisticated** 精緻的
**definitely** 肯定地

| 評論 | 首頁 | 設計工具 | 聯絡我們 |

★ ★ ★ ★ ★ 狂傳單有超棒的服務！

我在市中心開設鞋店，老覺得要把即將舉辦的拍賣活動傳播出去是件很難的事。我決定利用狂傳單的線上製作器來設計傳單。我發現它很容易操作，而且設計也很優美。我最後訂了 1,000 張傳單，還購買了自己設計的數位版，把它用在我的網站上。我們的拍賣活動很成功。很多客人都說，他們是從鎮上到處張貼的傳單上得知我們的活動。我對狂傳單的服務真的很滿意。它比一些我瀏覽過的線上製作器還要好，而且它們的樣板也精緻很多。未來我絕對會再使用狂傳單！

貞・崔斯坦

---

根據網頁內容，線上製作器可以讓使用者做什麼？

(A) 增加圖像
(B) 包含網路連結
(C) 選擇紙張種類
(D) 設計商標

**181** According to the webpage, what does the online generator allow users to do?

(A) Add images*
(B) Include web links
(C) Select paper type
(D) Design a logo

第一篇文章中，步驟一便提到了「線上製作器」的使用方法（If you want to accent your design with images, we have over 10,000 stock photos you can use at no extra cost.），表示客戶可以免費使用圖片放至傳單，因此答案為 (A)。

---

文中提到何者與狂傳單有關？

(A) 它免費寄送產品。
(B) 額外付費就提供電子檔案。
(C) 它讓使用者看到他人的設計。
(D) 它只接受到店現場訂單。

字彙
**in person** 親自，當面

**182** What is mentioned on the webpage about Flyer Frenzy?

(A) It delivers products free of charge.
(B) It offers digital files for an extra fee.*
(C) It allows users to see each other's designs.
(D) It only takes orders in person at a store.

第一篇文章中，在步驟三提到只要額外支付單一價 50 元，就可以下載數位版（For an extra flat fee of $50, you can download a digital copy of your design.），因此答案為 (B)。

\* 答案改寫：copy → file

**183** What is indicated about Ms. Tristan?

(A) She received more flyers than she ordered.
(B) Her order was delayed by a few days.
(C) She received a fifty dollar discount.
(D) She paid fifteen cents per flyer.*

閱讀崔斯坦女士所寫的評價（第二篇）時，請把重點放在「訂購明細」。中間部分寫道：「I ended up ordering 1,000 flyers.」，從網頁（第一篇）中找出對應的價格後，即可得知答案為 (D)。

下列何者與崔斯坦女士有關？
(A) 她收到的傳單比訂購的更多。
(B) 她的訂單延誤了幾天。
(C) 她收到50塊錢的折扣。
(D) 她為每張傳單付了15分錢。

**184** What is suggested about Ms. Tristan's store?

(A) It advertises solely online.
(B) It put flyers up around town.*
(C) It holds sales every month.
(D) It gives discounts for online orders.

崔斯坦女士的評價（第二篇）中寫道：「Many customers said they'd heard about it from the flyers they'd seen posted around town.」，表示有很多顧客是看了從鎮上到處張貼的傳單，才前來活動的，因此 (B) 為最適當的答案。

下列何者與崔斯坦女士的店有關？
(A) 它只在網路上打廣告。
(B) 它在全鎮貼傳單。
(C) 它每個月都舉辦拍賣。
(D) 它提供線上訂購折扣。

字彙
solely 只；唯一的

**185** According to the review, why does Ms. Tristan prefer Flyer Frenzy's services over other companies?

(A) They have faster delivery times.
(B) They have better design features.*
(C) They use better quality paper.
(D) They are cheaper to use.

在評價（第二篇）的後半部中，崔斯坦女士提到她認為狂傳單比其他線上製作器更好用，擁有許多精緻的樣版（They are much better than some of the other online generators I browsed, and their templates were much more sophisticated.），因此答案為 (B)。

根據評論，崔斯坦女士為什麼喜歡狂傳單勝於其他公司？
(A) 它們的運送時間較快。
(B) 它們有較佳的設計。
(C) 它們使用品質較好的紙張。
(D) 它們比較便宜。

Questions 186-190 refer to the following e-mails and log sheet.

**From:** linda@mailmail.com
**To:** billing@startelecom.com
**Date:** April 23
**Subject:** Bill Number 3788292
Dear Customer Service,

I am writing in regards to an unusually high cell phone bill I received in March. The amount listed on my phone bill was $155.33. Previously, my bill ranged between $80 and $90 per month.

I have already paid the bill to avoid any late fees, but [186] I am interested in knowing why I was charged so much. My bill did not show any details to explain these charges. I know I recently upgraded my data usage, which would cost extra, but I also canceled the insurance policy I had for all my devices. [187] These two costs should have balanced each other out if my request for cancellation was handled properly.

Please call me about this matter at 333-0967-5563. [188] I am available to speak only in the afternoons after 3:30 P.M.

Sincerely,

Linda Albert

------------------------------------------------------------------------

寄件者：linda@mailmail.com
收件者：billing@startelecom.com
日期：4月23日
主旨：帳單編號 3788292

親愛的客服人員，

我寫這封信是想告知，我在三月時收到了一封異常高額的手機帳單。列在手機帳單上的金額是 155.33 元。之前，我的帳單金額每個月都在 80 元至 90 元之間。

為了避免延遲繳納費用，我已經繳付帳款了，但我想知道為什麼我會被收取這麼高的金額。我的帳單並未顯示任何明細說明這些費用。我知道我最近提高了使用流量，這會增加費用。但我也取消了所有裝置的保險契約。如果我的取消申請處理得當，那這兩筆費用應該會相互抵消才是。

請來電 333-0967-5563 與我聯繫這件事。我要在下午 3:30 之後才能接電話。

琳達・艾伯特 敬上

**Customer Service Contact Log Sheet**

Date: April 24

| Representative Name | Account Number | Call Time | Resolved? Y/N |
|---|---|---|---|
| Michael Park | BG44532 | 9:33 A.M. | Yes |
| June Bartholdi | GH30993 | 10:42 A.M. | Yes |
| Nadia Kapoor | TZ33221 | 3:23 P.M. | No |
| [188] Brooklyn Smith | GS17649 | 3:45 P.M. | No |

---

客戶服務聯絡記錄表

日期：4月24日

| 代表人員 | 帳號 | 來電時間 | 解決與否 |
|---|---|---|---|
| 麥可·帕克 | BG44532 | 上午9:33 | 是 |
| 朱恩·巴索勒迪 | GH30993 | 上午10:42 | 是 |
| 娜迪亞·卡普爾 | TZ33221 | 下午3:23 | 否 |
| 布魯克林·史密斯 | GS17649 | 下午3:45 | 否 |

**To:** linda@mailmail.com
**From:** tristan@startelecom.com
**Date:** April 25
**Subject:** Re: Bill Number 3788292

Dear Ms. Albert,

Thank you for e-mailing Star Telecom about your concerns. One of our representatives tried to call you at the time you specified yesterday, but there was no answer. I have looked into your problem personally and have found that your insurance cancellation never went through. Thus, [187] your account registered charges for both the insurance policy and the upgraded data plan.

To correct this, [190] I have canceled your insurance plan and credited your account with $63.98, which will be carried over to your next bill.

If you have any additional concerns or questions, please reply directly to this e-mail.

Sincerely,

Tristan Mathews

Star Telecom Customer Support

字彙
log 記錄
representative 代表人員
account 帳戶
resolve 解決

字彙
specify 指明
look into . . . 查看
personally 親自地
go through 被正式通過
register 記錄
credit 把……計入貸方
carry over to . . . 結轉至……
directly 直接地

收件者：linda@mailmail.com
寄件者：tristan@startelecom.com
日期：4月25日
主旨：回覆：帳單編號 3788292

親愛的艾伯特女士，

感謝您來信星辰電信提出您的疑慮。昨天我們一位代表人員在您指定的時間試著打電話給您，但您並沒有接電話。我親自研究了您的問題，發現您的保險取消並未正式通過。因此，您的帳戶同時記錄了保險契約和流量升級方案的費用。

為修正這問題，我已經取消了您的保險計畫，將 63.98 元存入到您的帳戶中，應可轉用到下一次的帳單。

如果您還有其他的疑慮或問題，請直接回覆這封電子郵件。

星辰電信客戶服務部
崔斯坦·馬修斯 敬上

---

為什麼會寄第一封電子郵件？

(A) 取消服務
(B) 申請另一張帳單
(C) 詢問費用清單問題
(D) 註冊帳戶

字彙
**invoice** 費用清單
**register for . . .**
登記報名……

**186** Why was the first e-mail sent?

(A) To cancel a service
(B) To request another bill
(C) To ask about an invoice*
(D) To register for an account

由第一封郵件（第一篇）的第二段中「I am interested in knowing why I was charged so much.」，表示艾伯特女士想要知道為何需要支付這麼多的費用，因此 (C) 為最適當的答案。

---

下列何者與艾伯特女士有關？

(A) 她之前在星辰電信工作。
(B) 她打電話給星辰電信客服代表人員。
(C) 她正確地辨識出星辰電信的失誤。
(D) 她想結束在星辰電信的帳戶。

字彙
**correctly** 正確地
**identify** 辨識

**187** What is suggested about Ms. Albert?

(A) She previously worked for Star Telecom.
(B) She called a Star Telecom customer service representative.
(C) She correctly identified Star Telecom's mistake.*
(D) She wants to close her account with Star Telecom.

本題的關鍵人名為艾伯特女士（Ms. Albert）。在她所撰寫的郵件（第一篇）中，第二段她推測了費用超收的原因（These two costs should have balanced each other out if my request for cancellation was handled properly.）。而在第三篇的第一段中，客服人員證實了她的推測（your account registered charges for both the insurance policy and the upgraded data plan），表示艾伯特女士的推測是正確的，因此 (C) 為最適當的答案。

**188** Who called Ms. Albert on April 24?

(A) Michael Park
(B) June Bartholdi
(C) Nadia Kapoor
(D) Brooklyn Smith*

本題要綜合艾伯特女士撰寫的郵件（第一篇）和客戶服務聯絡紀錄表（第二篇）的內容。第一篇第三段中艾伯特女士說：「I am available to speak only in the afternoons after 3:30 P.M.」，由此確認客服人員可以打電話的時段為 3 點 30 分以後，再確認第二篇的記錄表後，可以發現答案應為 (D)。

誰在4月24當天打電話給艾伯特女士？

(A) 麥可·帕克
(B) 朱恩·巴索勒迪
(C) 娜迪亞·卡普爾
(D) 布魯克林·史密斯

---

**189** In the second e-mail, in paragraph 1, line 4, the word "registered" is closest in meaning to

(A) enrolled
(B) recorded*
(C) matched
(D) allowed

單字所在句的 registered，表示「（帳戶中）記錄」，因此 (B) 為意思最相近的單字。

在第二封電子郵件中，第一段、第四行的「**registered**」與下列哪一個意思最接近？

(A) 註冊入學
(B) 記錄
(C) 相配
(D) 允許

字彙
**enroll** 註冊入學
**match** 相配

---

**190** What does Mr. Mathews indicate in his e-mail?

(A) Some services will be offered for free.
(B) Ms. Kapoor will call Ms. Albert tomorrow.
(C) Ms. Albert's bill will decrease next month.*
(D) Customers will be charged for cancellations.

馬修斯先生撰寫的郵件（第三篇）中，在第二段表示會將多收取的費用退至對方的帳戶，應可轉用到下一次的帳單（I have cancelled your insurance plan and credited your account with $63.98, which will be carried over to your next bill.），因此 (C) 為最適當的答案。

關於馬修斯先生的電子郵件中，文中暗示了什麼？

(A) 有些服務將免費提供。
(B) 卡普爾女士明天會打電話給艾伯特女士。
(C) 艾伯特女士的帳單下個月會減少。
(D) 客戶會因取消而被收費。

字彙
**indicate** 暗示
**decrease** 減少

字彙
graduate student 研究生
arrange 安排，籌備
accommodation 住宿
transportation 運輸
capacity 容量
flyer 傳單
divide 分配
task 任務，工作
issue 問題

Questions 191-195 refer to the following e-mail, flyer, and text message.

**To:** [195] Graduate Students
**From:** Ferdinand Montgomery
**Subject:** Seminar Series
**Date:** March 10

Dear Students,

I have great news! Mr. Philip Osan has agreed to give a presentation during our Careers in Fashion Seminar Series. As graduate students, your job will be to arrange his travel accommodations for June 1-2 as well as his transportation to and from campus. Also, please reserve a room for his presentation. [191] I think the Belford Auditorium would be best. Mr. Osan's presentation will be very popular, so we might need the room with the largest capacity. However, if it's unavailable, please reserve another one.

Also, once Mr. Osan provides his information, I'll need you to design and print another flyer. I'm hoping you'll be able to divide these tasks up among the five of you without any major issues, but do let me know if you have any problems.

Ferdinand Montgomery,
Professor of Fashion Design

------------------------------------------------------------------------

收件者：研究生
寄件者：費迪南‧蒙哥馬利
主旨：系列講座
日期：3 月 10 日

親愛的學生們，

我有個好消息。菲利浦‧奧尚先生已經答應，他會在我們時尚職涯系列講座中發表演說。身為研究生，你們的工作就是安排他在 6 月 1 日至 2 日間的差旅住宿，以及往返校園的交通。另外，請預約供他演講的場地。我想貝爾福德大禮堂會是最佳選擇。奧尚先生的演講應該會大受歡迎，所以我們需要有最大容納空間的場地，但如果無法使用那間，請預約另一間。

此外，一旦奧尚先生提供了他的資料，我需要你們設計，並列印出另一份傳單。我希望你們五個能在沒有什麼太大的爭議下分擔這些工作。但若有任何問題，一定要告訴我。

時尚設計教授
費迪南‧蒙哥馬利

字彙
switch 轉移
hand-drawn 手繪的
up-and-coming 前景好的
innovation 創新，改革
trend 趨勢，潮流
solution 解決方案
fluent 流利的，流暢的
costly 昂貴的
predict 預測
insight 見解

The College of Fashion and Design's
Careers in Fashion Seminar Series Presents:

**Mr. Philip Osan**

**CEO and Lead Designer of Bath Fashion House**

[193] *Fashion Design and Technology*

June 1, 3:30 P.M.

[191] *Westmont Auditorium*

Over the years, many fashion houses have switched from hand-drawn designs to fashion design software programs. As up-and-coming designers, you must be aware of all [193] the newest innovations in fashion design software. How can you keep up to date on [193] the newest software trends? One possible solution is to become fluent in each new program. However, that may be costly and time-consuming. There are several ways to predict which programs will be major players in the future of fashion design. I will share my insights regarding the technological trends in the fashion industry.

-------------------------------------------------------------------

時尚設計學院

時尚職涯系列講座邀請到：

菲利浦・奧尚先生

貝斯時裝公司執行長暨首席設計師

時尚設計與科技

6月1日下午 3:30

維斯蒙特禮堂

這幾年來，許多時裝公司已經將手繪設計的方式，轉換為時裝設計軟體程式。身為前景備受矚目的設計師們，你們必須了解時裝設計軟體中所有最新的創新發展。各位要如何了解最新的軟體趨勢呢？其中一個可能的方法，就是對每個新程式都知之甚詳。但這可能要付出很大的代價，也很耗時。有幾個方式可以預測哪些程式將成為時裝設計中的主流，而我也將分享自己對時尚業中科技趨勢的見解。

**From:** Robert Parker
**To:** Rosa Hernandez
**Date:** May 28

Rosa, I'm at the copy center in the Hurtz Building to print the flyers, but I noticed something is missing. [194] It seems that Mr. Osan's photograph was deleted. [195] Can you fix the flyer and e-mail me the new version as soon as possible? The copy center closes in less than an hour and [195]Dr. Montgomery asked me to drop the flyers off at his office tonight.

----------------------------------------

傳訊者：羅伯特・帕克
收訊者：羅莎・赫南德茲
日期：5 月 28 日

羅莎，我在赫茲大樓的影印中心印傳單。但我發現有個東西遺漏了。奧尚先生的照片好像被刪除了。妳可以盡快修復傳單，把新版本寄給我嗎？影印中心再不到一個小時就要打烊了。蒙哥馬利博士要我今晚把傳單送到他的辦公室。

---

**191** What is suggested about the Westmont Auditorium?

(A) It is not available on June 1.
(B) It is the location for all seminar presentations.
(C) It has fewer seats than the Belford Auditorium.*
(D) It has a new projector system.

閱讀文章時，請特別留意「演說的場地」。第一段中蒙哥馬利教授提到最大最佳的場地為貝爾福德大禮堂（I think the Belford Auditorium would be best.），但如果不行的話，請預約其他的地方（if it's unavailable, please reserve another one），而由演說通知的傳單（第二篇）中，可知場地為維斯蒙特禮堂，故可推測該禮堂的座位比貝爾福德大禮堂少，因此答案應為 (C)。

---

**192** In the e-mail, the word "issues" in paragraph 2, line 3, is closest in meaning to

(A) conflicts*
(B) periodicals
(C) distributions
(D) announcements

單字所在句的意思為，蒙哥馬利教授希望這幾位研究生，在不會有太大的「爭議」下分擔這些工作。為符合文意，最適合替換 issues 的字為 conflicts，答案為 (A)。

**193** What is Mr. Osan's presentation about?

(A) New trends in design software*
(B) Advancements in sewing machines
(C) Learning drawing techniques
(D) Characteristics of fashion houses

傳單（第二篇）中呈現研討會的題目為：時尚設計與科技（Fashion Design and Technology），從傳單正文中的「the newest innovations in fashion design software, the newest software trends」，可以得知奧尚先生的演講和設計軟體趨勢有關，答案應為 (A)。

奧尚先生的演講和什麼有關？

**(A)** 設計軟體的新趨勢
**(B)** 縫紉機的發展
**(C)** 繪畫技巧的學習
**(D)** 時尚公司的特色

字彙
**advancement** 發展
**sewing machine** 縫紉機
**characteristic** 特性

---

**194** What problem does Mr. Parker mention?

(A) A location has been changed.
(B) The flyer is missing an image.*
(C) A work history is incorrect.
(D) The time of an event is wrong.

請參考帕克先生撰寫的訊息（第三篇），當中提到傳單中似乎遺漏了照片（It seems that Mr. Osan's photograph was deleted.），因此答案應為 (B)。

\* 答案改寫：**photograph → image**

帕克先生提到了什麼問題？

**(A)** 地點已經更改了。
**(B)** 傳單上漏了一個圖像。
**(C)** 工作經歷是錯的。
**(D)** 活動時間是錯的。

字彙
**incorrect** 不正確的

---

**195** Who most likely is Ms. Hernandez?

(A) Lead designer at Bath Fashion House
(B) A fashion design software developer
(C) A professor at The College of Fashion and Design
(D) A graduate student at The College of Fashion and Design*

訊息（第三篇）中提到赫南德茲女士（Ms. Hernandez），而帕克先生問：「Can you fix the flyer and e-mail me the new version as soon as possible?」，可以推測兩人應為共同製作傳單的研究生。而最後一句話出現指派此工作的蒙哥馬利教授，而從教授所寫的郵件（第一篇），可以得知收件人為 Graduate Students，更可確定答案為 (D)。

赫南德茲女士有可能是誰？

**(A)** 貝斯時裝公司的首席設計師
**(B)** 時尚設計軟體開發者
**(C)** 時尚設計學院教授
**(D)** 時尚設計學院研究生

## Trenton Air Conditioning
## Air Conditioning Units

Trenton Air Conditioning has been providing businesses with affordable air conditioning units for over 15 years. We have provided numerous local cafés, restaurants, and supermarkets with reliable cooling solutions. All our units include cleaning services and repairs at your request, and should your unit be unsatisfactory in any way, we will replace it at no extra cost. Delivery to any location in the Sydney area and setup are both absolutely free of charge. A two-year contract must be signed by the business owner, and monthly payment plans are available.

### Air Conditioning Unit Options:

| Contract Option | 196(D) Model | Type | 196(C) Room size in square meters (m²) | 196(B) Cost Per Month |
|---|---|---|---|---|
| Bronze | GP-A3000 | Ceiling | 9-25 | $55.00 |
| 199 Silver | GP-A4000 | Standing | 26-55 | $75.00 |
| Gold | GP-A9999 | Ceiling | 55-100 | $95.00 |
| Platinum | GP-AR300 | Ceiling | 100-200 | $115.00 |

Contact us for a free service quote today by visiting www.trentonaircon.com or calling one of our knowledgeable customer service agents at 1-800-444-2323.

---

## 翠登空調
## 空調設備

超過 15 年來，翠登空調一直為公司行號提供合理價格的空調設備。我們提供給許多本地咖啡館、餐廳與超市值得信賴的空調冷卻系統。我們所有的設備可應貴公司要求提供清理服務與修繕。若您對設備有任何的不滿，我們將免費更換。雪梨地區各地的運送與裝設亦免費。企業主須簽訂兩年期合約，我們也提供每月支付方案。

### 空調設備方案：

| 合約方案 | 型號 | 類型 | 房型(以平方公尺計) | 每月費用 |
|---|---|---|---|---|
| 銅 | GP-A3000 | 天花板式 | 9-25 | 55.00 元 |
| 銀 | GP-A4000 | 直立式 | 26-55 | 75.00 元 |
| 金 | GP-A9999 | 天花板式 | 55-100 | 95.00 元 |
| 白金 | GP-AR300 | 天花板式 | 100-200 | 115.00 元 |

洽詢免費報價，可上網 www.trentonaircon.com 或來電 1-800-444-2323 連絡我們內行的客服專員。

**Trenton Air Conditioning —Customer Service Quote Form**

**Name:** Medina Prias
**Business:** Medina's Café
**E-mail:** medina@mailme.com
**Date:** 23 April

**Remarks:** I'm writing to inquire about your air conditioning units. The restaurant next to my café is currently using one of your units, and [197] the owner, Mr. Smithe, highly recommends your services.

Right now, the air conditioner in my café is nearly 10 years old. Just keeping up with the repairs and cleaning is costing a fortune. I think it would be much cheaper to just rent from your company. Since my café is quite small with only 22 square meters, I think one of your cheaper packages would be suitable. However, I will rely on your recommendation about this. Also, can you make sure any unit you recommend comes with a remote control. Our current air conditioner does not have one. Thank you, and I look forward to hearing from you.

-------------------------------------------------------------------------

翠登空調──客服報價單

姓名：麥迪娜·皮拉斯

行號：麥迪娜咖啡

電子郵件：medina@mailme.com

日期：4 月 23 日

註記：我填寫這份表單是想詢問貴公司的空調設備。我咖啡店隔壁的餐廳目前就是使用貴公司的設備。該餐廳老闆，史密斯先生非常推薦貴公司的服務。

目前我餐廳的空調機已經將近 10 年了。光是維修和清理就要花一大筆錢。我想如果向貴公司承租，還比較划算。因為我的咖啡店很小，只有 22 平方公尺，我想應該適用貴公司較便宜的方案，但這部分我還是會依貴公司的建議為主。另外，您可以確認您所推薦的設備是附遙控器的嗎？我目前的空調機並沒有。感謝您，期待您的回覆。

## Customer Review

I have been a customer of Trenton Air Conditioning for a year, and I have to say that I am very pleased with their services. I was very surprised to receive a 10 percent discount on my first year of service thanks to Trenton's referral program. Apparently, [197] if you give the name of the person who connected you with Trenton, both parties will automatically receive a discount. Furthermore, I am very pleased with the contract conditions, which have allowed me to change my unit based on my business's needs. [198] After my business went through an expansion, I called Trenton and the customer service representative agreed to upgrade my unit to a larger package. The new unit turned up only two days later and [199] was installed free of charge even though the type changed from ceiling to standing. I highly recommend Trenton for their great business practices and customer service.

Medina Prias, Owner of Medina's Café

字彙
remark 註記；評論
currently 目前
nearly 幾乎
fortune 一大筆錢
suitable 合適的
rely on . . . 信賴……
recommendation
建議，推薦
come with . . . 附有……
remote 遙控的

字彙
be pleased with . . .
對……感到滿意
referral 轉介
apparently 顯然地
party （契約）一方，當事人
automatically 自動地
furthermore 再者
condition 條款；條件
expansion 擴展
turn up 到來
install 安裝
practice 業務；實施

顧客評論

顧客評論

我成為翠登空調公司的客戶已經一年了。我必須說,我對他們的服務非常滿意。因為翠登的轉介方案,我很驚訝在第一年的保養服務中,就收到了百分之十的優惠折扣。看來,如果您提供了推薦者的姓名,雙方都自動收到折扣。另外,我也對合約條款非常滿意,條約內容讓我可以根據業務需求變更設備。在我的店面擴大後,我打電話給翠登,客服代表答應將我的設備升級成較大型的套組。兩天後新設備就送來了,雖然型式從天花板式換成直立式,但安裝居然免費。因為他們絕佳的經營方式與客服,我極度推薦翠登。

麥迪娜咖啡店主 麥迪娜·皮拉斯

---

下列有關翠登空調的資訊,何者未出現在廣告中?

(A) 節能
(B) 月費
(C) 房間大小
(D) 型號

**196** What information about Trenton Air Conditioning is NOT included in the advertisement?

(A) The energy efficiency*
(B) The monthly costs
(C) The room sizes
(D) The model numbers

解題時,請先將各選項內容與廣告(第一篇)進行對照,再刪除當中提到的選項。由表格第五欄的 Cost Per Month 可以確認 (B);由表格第四欄 Room size in square meters (m²) 可以確認 (C);由表格第二欄 Model 可以確認 (D),因此本題的答案為 (A)。

---

有關史密斯先生,下列何者可能為真?

(A) 他幫他的餐廳在空調上省錢。
(B) 他買下了餐廳旁邊的咖啡店。
(C) 他獲得翠登空調一年免費服務。
(D) 他明年要升級空調設備。

**197** What is probably true about Mr. Smithe?

(A) He can save on air conditioning for his restaurant.*
(B) He purchased a café next to his restaurant.
(C) He received one year free service from Trenton Air Conditioning.
(D) He will upgrade his air conditioning unit next year.

閱讀文章時,請特別留意題目關鍵字史密斯先生(Mr. Smithe)。報價單(第二篇)中,在「the owner, Mr. Smithe, highly recommends your services」,提到了史密斯先生是「推薦人」。而在皮拉斯女士的評論(第三篇)的中間部分「if you give the name of the person who connected you with Trenton, both parties will automatically receive a discount」,表示只要提供推薦人的名字,兩個人都可以獲得翠登空調的折扣,推論史密斯先生因為推薦了翠登給皮拉斯女士,因而也獲得折扣,因此 (A) 為最適當的答案。

**198** What is suggested about Medina's Café?

(A) It is owned by Mr. Smithe.
(B) It moved to a new location.
(C) It features nightly entertainment.
(D) It increased its size recently.*

在咖啡廳老闆皮拉斯女士的評論（第三篇）的中間部分 After my business went through an expansion，由此可以推測出答案應為 (D)。

* 答案改寫：went through an expansion → increased its size

下列何者與麥迪娜咖啡有關？

(A) 為史密斯先生所擁有。
(B) 搬到新址。
(C) 提供夜間娛樂活動。
(D) 最近擴大規模。

---

**199** Which contract option is Ms. Prias currently using?

(A) Bronze
(B) Silver*
(C) Gold
(D) Platinum

選項皆在第一篇廣告中，請綜合皮拉斯女士所寫的評論與廣告（第一篇）的內容，再選出正確答案。在評論（第三篇）的後半部，皮拉斯女士提到翠登空調為她免費更換為直立式冷氣（was installed free of charge even though the type changed from ceiling to standing），而由第一篇空調設備方案中，直立式冷氣屬於銀方案，可以得知答案為 (B)。

皮拉斯女士目前採用的是哪一個合約方案？

(A) 銅
(B) 銀
(C) 金
(D) 白金

---

**200** In the review, the phrase "turned up" in paragraph 1, line 7, is closest in meaning to

(A) removed
(B) considered
(C) designed
(D) arrived*

單字所在句的意思應為新設備兩天後「抵達」，較符合句意，因此最適合填入的單字為 arrived，故 (D) 正確。

在評論中，第一段、第七行的「turned up」與下列哪一個意思最接近？

(A) 移除
(B) 考慮
(C) 設計
(D) 抵達

字彙
**remove** 移除

# ACTUAL TEST

# 5

## TEST
## 中譯+解析

# PART 5

這些彩色團體制服是由我們的子公司，丹徹斯特輪胎所提供的。

字彙
**sister company** 子公司（同一母公司旗下的姐妹公司）

**101** The colorful team uniforms were provided by Danchester Tires, _____ sister company.

(A) we
(B) our*
(C) us
(D) ours

本題要從人稱代名詞中找出適當的格。答案應為所有格 our，用來限定與形容複合名詞 sister company，故 (B) 正確。這類的題型，答案經常是所有格。

---

一旦收到所有旅行必要文件後，將盡快處理這一家的簽證。

字彙
**process** 處理
**receive** 收到

**102** The family's visa will be processed as soon as all necessary travel _____ are received.

(A) document
(B) documents*
(C) documented
(D) documenting

形容詞 necessary 用來修飾空格，因此空格中應填入 (A) 或 (B)，與 travel 結合成複合名詞。因為前方有限定詞 all，且 be 動詞為複數形的 are，因此答案應為 (B)。

- **document** 文件

\* 高頻率複合名詞：

**account number** 帳號　**construction delay** 工程延誤
**return policy** 退貨規定　**expiration date** 有效期限
**product information** 產品資訊
**information distribution** 資訊流通；資訊發布　**retail sales** 零售銷售額
**client satisfaction** 客戶滿意度　**recommendation letter** 推薦信

---

在演講中，格蘭史達製藥廠執行長特別提到研究部主管對於公司成功貢獻良多。

字彙
**pharmaceutical** 製藥業；藥品
**mention** 提到
**research** 研究
**division** 部門
**contributor** 貢獻者

**103** In his speech, the CEO of Grandstead Pharmaceuticals _____ mentioned the director of the research division as a contributor to the company's success.

(A) thoroughly
(B) utterly
(C) specifically*
(D) densely

根據文意，本句的重點應為演講中執行長「特別」提到了某位特定人士的貢獻，語意上較為完整，因此答案為 (C)。

- **thoroughly** 徹底地，完全地　**utterly** 徹底地，完全地
  **specifically** 特別地；具體地　**densely** 密集地；濃密地

---

喬安的管理方法與她的前任大不相同。

字彙
**managerial** 管理的
**predecessor** 前任

**104** Joanne's managerial techniques are quite _____ from her predecessor's.

(A) different*
(B) differently
(C) difference
(D) differences

主詞（Joanne's . . . techniques）＋ be 動詞（are）＋空格，因此空格應填入形容詞作為主詞補語，補充說明喬安管理方法的特質，且副詞 quite 用來修飾形容詞，因此空格中只能填入 (A)。

- **different** 不同的　**differently** 不同地　**difference** 差別，差異

\* 常見的 be 動詞＋形容詞＋介系詞的片語：

**be full of . . .** 充滿……　**be similar to . . .** 和……相似
**be responsible for . . .** 對……負責；是……的起因
**be familiar to . . .** 對……熟悉　**be packed with . . .** 裝滿；擠滿
**be resistant to . . .** 抗、防……的　**be content with . . .** 滿足於……

**105** Wearing a safety harness is not an option for roofers at Delbert Contractors but rather a _____.

(A) training          (B) fulfillment
(C) speculation      (D) requirement*

對等連接詞 but 用來表示轉折語氣，前方出現了 option，意思為「選擇，選項」，因此表「規定」的反義詞 requirement 最為適當，故 (D) 正確。

- **training** 訓練    **fulfillment** 實現    **speculation** 推測
  **requirement** 規定；要求

對戴伯特承建公司的屋頂工人來說，配戴安全背帶不是一個選項而是規定。

字彙
**safety** 安全
**harness** 繫帶
**option** 選擇
**roofer** 屋頂工人
**contractor** 承包商，承建公司

---

**106** One of our plumbers will _____ how to replace a Malton DR sink drain quickly and easily.

(A) demonstrate*      (B) respond
(C) inquire           (D) visit

根據文意，本句應為「水電工人將示範如何更換水槽排水管」，語意上較為完整，因此答案為 (A)。(B) 要連接介系詞 to；(C) 則要和 about 搭配使用。

- **demonstrate** 示範    **respond** 回答    **inquire** 詢問

本公司水電工人將示範如何又快又輕鬆地更換莫爾頓 DR水槽排水管。

字彙
**plumber** 水電工
**replace** 更換
**sink** 水槽
**drain** 排水管

---

**107** Bramwell Carpets does not issue refunds of any kind so be sure to measure the floor space _____ before purchasing.

(A) careful          (B) caring
(C) carefully*       (D) cares

本句即使省略了空格，仍為結構完整的句子，因此空格中最適合填入副詞 carefully 用來修飾動詞 measure，故 (C) 正確。

- **careful** 仔細的    **caring** 有愛心的    **carefully** 仔細地    **care** 在乎

布拉姆威爾地毯公司不核發任何商品退款，因此在購買前務必仔細地丈量地板空間大小。

字彙
**issue** 核發；發給
**refund** 退款
**measure** 測量，丈量

---

**108** _____ annual profits are high or low, they still provide important economic information for business analysts.

(A) Whether*       (B) Either
(C) Despite        (D) Even

本句當中，逗點前後有兩個子句，而兩個子句之間沒有連接詞，因此空格應填入連接詞 whether，表示「不管是……」，故答案為 (A)。在此補充，相關連接詞 either A or B 連接兩個詞性對等的字詞或句子，其意思為「A 或 B 兩者之一」，經常出現在考題當中。(C) 是介系詞而 (D) 是副詞，均不能連接兩個句子。

- **despite ...** 儘管

不論年度獲利高低，他們仍然為商業分析師提供重要的經濟資訊。

字彙
**profit** 利潤，盈利
**economic** 經濟的
**analyst** 分析師

在舊設計的亞果機車與新款
的格蘭福特機車之間，這份
報告提供了詳細的比較。

字彙
detailed 詳細的

**109** The report provides a detailed _____ between the old Argo motorcycle design and the new Grandford one.

(A) comparable          (B) comparison*

(C) compared          (D) comparative

本題句構是「不定冠詞（a）＋形容詞（detailed）＋空格」，空格中只能填入名詞 comparison，故答案選 (B)。

- comparable 可比較的    comparison (n.) 比較，對照
  compare (v.) 比較，對照    comparative 比較的，對比的

\* detailed ＋名詞的高頻率片語
detailed information 詳細資訊     detailed description 詳細說明
detailed assessment 詳細評估     detailed forecast 詳細預測
detailed analysis 詳細分析

---

如欲與客服專員通話，請勿
掛斷。

字彙
stay on the line
別掛斷電話，在線上等候

**110** _____ speak to a customer service agent, please stay on the line.

(A) For          (B) Across

(C) With         (D) To*

根據文意，逗點前方應屬於勿掛斷電話、等候通話的「目的」最為適當，to ＋ V 形成不定詞常表「目的」，因此答案為 (D)。

---

新倉庫的儲存空間存放三百
台腳踏車綽綽有餘。

字彙
storage 儲存
warehouse 倉庫

**111** The storage space in the new warehouse is more than _____ for three hundred bicycles.

(A) able          (B) great

(C) sure         (D) enough*

本題只要知道 enough for / to ＋ V（不定詞）的意思為「足夠……，充分……」，就能輕鬆解題。在此補充，enough 在本句作代名詞，表「足夠的空間」。

- able 能；能幹的    great 極好的    sure 一定的
  enough 足夠的量或程度；足夠的

---

在這國家申請家庭簽證是一
段漫長又複雜的過程。

字彙
apply for . . .
（透過書面或表格形式）申請
process 過程

**112** Applying for a family visa in this country is a long and _____ process.

(A) complicate          (B) complicated*

(C) complication         (D) complicatedness

對等連接詞 and 前後接的字詞的詞性必須一致，and 的前方為形容詞 long，因此 and 的後方也要接形容詞，用來修飾名詞 process，故答案為 (B)。很多考生會誤以為 (A) 為形容詞，因為相同字首的 complete 可以作為動詞（完成）或形容詞（完整的），但請特別熟記 complicate 只能作動詞表「使複雜」。

- complicate 使複雜    complicated 複雜的
  complication 複雜；複雜化    complicatedness 複雜性

**113** Leading automotive experts maintain that Woykin Oil filters deliver _____ results.

(A) exceptionally　　　(B) exceptional*

(C) exception　　　　 (D) exceptions

空格位在 deliver 的受詞位置，且空格又要修飾名詞 results，因此只能填入形容詞 exceptional，故答案為 (B)。

- **exceptionally** 異常地；特別地　**exceptional** 絕佳的，卓越的
  **exception** 例外

那些頂尖的汽車專家堅稱，渥宜津石油公司的過濾器能產生絕佳的成效。

字彙
**leading** 頂尖的，一流的
**automotive** 汽車的
**expert** 專家
**maintain** 堅稱
**deliver** 達到（要求，標準等）

---

**114** A credit card statement or phone bill can be _____ of residency.

(A) process　　　　　(B) analysis

(C) proof*　　　　　 (D) basis

根據文意，本句「空格＋ of residency」應為「居住證明」，語意上較為完整，因此答案為 (C)。

- **process** 過程　**analysis** 分析　**proof** 證明　**basis** 基礎；根據

信用卡帳單明細或電話帳單可做為居住證明。

字彙
**statement** （銀行）對帳單
**bill** 帳單
**residency** 居住

---

**115** Mr. Bolduc _____ asked Gabriella to organize the workshop, but then assigned the task to Louise.

(A) initial　　　　　　(B) initially*

(C) initialize　　　　 (D) initialized

空格位在主詞（Mr. Bolduc）＋動詞（asked）之間，主詞＋動詞為完整的句型結構，故可刪除 (C) 與 (D)，空格中應填入副詞 initially 修飾動詞 asked，所以 (B) 最為適當。

- **initial** 開始的，最初的　**initially** 最初地　**initialize** 初始化
  **initialized** 初始化的

博爾達克先生最初要求加布里埃拉籌辦研討會，但是後來又把這工作分配給露意絲。

字彙
**organize** 組織，安排
**assign** 指派，分配
**task** 任務，工作

---

**116** Job candidates need to submit three letters of recommendation _____ the completed application.

(A) too　　　　　　　(B) in addition

(C) moreover　　　　 (D) along with*

空格中要填入介系詞，用來連接後方的受詞 application，因此答案為 (D)。而根據文意，本句應為「要同時繳交推薦信和申請書」，語意上最為完整，因此可以再次確認答案為 (D)。(B) 應改成 in addition to，才是可以接受詞的介系詞片語。

- **in addition** 此外　**moreover** 此外，並且　**along with ...** 和……一起

求職者需附上三份推薦信，連同完成的申請文件一起繳交。

字彙
**recommendation** 推薦信

雖然博諾先生從來沒做過冰箱維修，但他對冷藏系統的知識卻非常淵博。

字彙
refrigeration 冷藏

**117** Even though Mr. Buono has never worked in refrigerator repair, his knowledge of refrigeration systems is _____.

(A) extensive*　(B) clever　(C) considered　(D) eager

空格中應填入形容詞，用來描述 knowledge。由於 knowledge 屬於抽象名詞，不適合與多用於形容人的 (B) 和 (D) 搭配使用。(C) 的後方必須連接 to be，並加上補充說明，因此答案為 (A)，表示「淵博的」。

• extensive 淵博的；廣泛的　clever 聰明伶俐的
  considered 被考慮的　eager 渴望的

---

第六頁的流程圖說明了各專案主管間的職務分配。

字彙
flowchart 流程圖
describe 描述，說明
duty 職務

**118** The flowchart on page six describes the _____ of duties among the different project managers.

(A) support　(B) attention　(C) division*　(D) statement

根據文意，本句的重點應為「職務分配」，語意上較為適當。空格當中最適合填入的名詞為 division，故答案為 (C)。

• support 支持　attention 注意，留心　division 分配
  statement 聲明

---

這些種子會長出最大、卻不一定是最健康的番茄。

字彙
seed 種子
produce 生產，出產

**119** These seeds will produce the biggest tomatoes but not _____ the healthiest ones.

(A) expectedly　　　　(B) necessarily*
(C) preventively　　　(D) permanently

請特別留意對等連接詞 but，用來表示轉折語氣，biggest 對比後方的 healthiest。本句應為「最大卻不一定是最健康的番茄」，最符合文意，因此 (B) 為最適當的答案。but 搭配 not，表示「不一定是……」。

• expectedly 預期地，意料之中地　necessarily 必然地；必要地
  preventively 預防性地　permanently 永久地

---

雖然店家不提供退款，但顧客可更換與原價等值的任何商品。

字彙
exchange 交換，更換
item 物品，品項

**120** While the store does not issue refunds, customers can exchange any item for something _____ in amount to the original sales price.

(A) equivalent*　(B) profitable　(C) deliberate　(D) controlled

根據文意，本句應為「可更換與原價等值的任何商品」，語意上較為完整，因此答案為 (A)。

• equivalent 相等的　profitable 有盈利的
  deliberate 深思熟慮的；故意的　controlled 克制的；被控制的

* 下列情況要使用後位修飾：
1. 修飾以 thing、body、one、where 結尾的不定代名詞時
   例：something small 小東西；小事情
2. 使用兩個或兩個以上的形容詞修飾名詞時
   例：a friend kind, caring and funny 善良、有愛心且有趣的朋友
3. 修飾語為分詞（現在分詞或過去分詞）作形容詞時
   例：a wall painted in yellow 粉刷成黃色的牆
4. 修飾形容詞最高級後方的名詞時
   例：the best actress alive 現存的最佳女主角

**121** This newspaper photograph shows the mayor of Otterbury sitting _____ the prime minister.

(A) from  (B) reverse

(C) opposite*  (D) distant

根據文意，空格要填入表示位置的介系詞，因此答案為 (C)，用來表示「坐在對面」。

- **reverse** 相反的  **opposite** 在……對面；相對的  **distant** 遙遠的

從新聞照片中看出奧塔貝里市市長坐在首相對面。

字彙
**mayor** 市長
**prime minister** 首相

---

**122** The decision to launch a new line of footwear was _____ the results of some market research.

(A) such as  (B) adjacent to

(C) except for  (D) based on*

由於空格後方的文意為「決定的依據」，因此 (D) 為最適當的答案。

- **such as** 像是，例如  **adjacent to . . .** 鄰近的
  **except for . . .** 除了……以外  **based on . . .** 根據，基於

新鞋款的推出決定，是根據市場研究結果而訂的。

字彙
**launch** 推出，上市
**footwear** 鞋類

---

**123** The Alderburn Employment Center is the only building on this block that is _____ to people in wheelchairs.

(A) access  (B) accessibly

(C) accessible*  (D) accessibility

空格為 that 子句的主詞補語，因此要填入形容詞或是名詞。本句應填入形容詞，表示對輪椅人士而言，是「可以出入的」大樓，較符合文意，故 (C) 正確。

- **access** 進入；接近；使用某物的權利  **accessibly** 可接近地；可得到地
  **accessible** 可接近的；可得到的  **accessibility** 易接近性

* access 的用法：
**access** 當動詞＋地點／資料：進入某處……／使用資料（此時不用加上 to）
**access** 當名詞＋ **to** ＋地點：可以進入……
**accessible** ＋ **to** ＋人物：人可以進入的

埃爾德柏恩就業中心是這一區中，唯一一間方便輪椅人士出入的大樓。

字彙
**employment** 就業

---

**124** Dr. Darius is striving _____ the look of his office and is going to put a painting in the waiting room.

(A) to enhance*  (B) enhances

(C) is enhancing  (D) enhanced

本題只要知道 strive to ＋原形動詞，表示「奮鬥，努力……」，就能輕鬆解題。

- **enhance** 提升；改善

* 受詞為不定詞（to ＋V）的動詞：
**want, hope, plan, decide, expect, wish, promise, afford, agree, pretend, fail, refuse**

戴流士醫生努力提升診所的門面，將於候診室擺放畫作。

字彙
**strive** 努力

未進入決賽的球隊球員可免費觀賞比賽。

**字彙**
make it to . . . 到達（目的）
final 決賽

**125** Players _____ teams did not make it to the finals can watch the game for free.

(A) its          (B) which
(C) whose*      (D) more

根據句型結構，空格到 finals 為關係子句用來修飾 players，因此空格內應填入關係代名詞。players 和 teams 之間的關係可以定義為 their (= players') teams，因此空格中要填入關係代名詞 whose，故答案選 (C)。

---

當地官員向農民保證，噴灑在馬鈴薯作物上的殺蟲劑對人體無害。

**字彙**
pesticide 殺蟲劑
crop 作物
harmless 無害的

**126** Local officials _____ farmers that the pesticide sprayed on the potato crops was harmless to humans.

(A) assured*      (B) arranged
(C) described     (D) committed

根據文意，that 後方的內容應為官員向農夫們「所保證」的話，因此空格中填入 (A) 最符合文意。

• assure 保證    arrange 安排    commit 犯（罪）

* 適用「主詞＋動詞＋人＋ that……」句型的動詞：
tell, inform, notify, convince, instruct, remind

---

藍福製造的工廠員工同意每天多上班30分鐘，以抵銷上升的生產成本。

**字彙**
laborer 勞工，員工
manufacturing 製造（業）
offset 抵銷；補償
rising 上升的

**127** Factory laborers at Langford Manufacturing _____ to work 30 minutes more each day to offset rising production costs.

(A) agreeing      (B) to agree
(C) agreement    (D) have agreed*

本句的句型結構為主詞（Factory laborers at Langford Manufacturing）＋動詞（空格），選項中只有 (D) 為動詞。

• agree 同意    agreement 同意，協議

---

考慮到山繆曾在三大洲的工作經驗，難怪執行長讓他負責海外計畫。

**字彙**
continent 大洲
overseas 海外的，國外的

**128** _____ Samuel's work experience in three continents, it was no surprise that the CEO put him in charge of the overseas project.

(A) Since      (B) Given*
(C) Among    (D) Upon

根據文意，逗點前方的內容即為山繆成為海外計畫負責人的「依據」，因此答案應為介系詞 given，表示「考慮到……」，故答案為 (B)。

**129**  A person who was not raised in this community may not understand the historical _____ on the Steinhauer Street Bridge.

(A) signify  (B) significant
(C) significance*  (D) significantly

「定冠詞（the）＋形容詞（historical）＋空格」的句構中，空格中只能填入名詞 significance，the significance on 的意思為「……的意義，重要性」，故 (C) 正確。

- signify 表示，意味著　significant 有意義的，重要的
  significance 重要性，意義　significantly 顯著地

不是在這個社區長大的人，可能無法理解史坦荷爾街大橋在歷史上的重要性。

字彙
**raise** 養育長大
**historical** 歷史的

---

**130**  Jennifer has more seniority than Bill at the company, _____ she is much younger than him.

(A) as if  (B) so that
(C) in case  (D) even though*

請先理解空格前後句的意思，前句說珍妮佛「年資較長」，後句說她「年輕很多」，由此可知兩句應為對比的概念，因此答案為表轉折的連接詞 even though，故 (D) 正確。

- as if 好像　so that . . . 以便　in case . . . 以防萬一

雖然珍妮佛比比爾年輕很多，但在公司裡珍妮佛比他還資深。

字彙
**seniority** 年資

Questions 131-134 refer to the following e-mail.

**To:** <nina_haidara@kmail.net>
**From:** <duron_charette@wrnpharmaceuticals.com>
**Date:** September 7
**Subject:** Head of Research Position

Dear Ms. Haidara,

WRN Pharmaceuticals is delighted to invite you to come in for a second interview next week. Since this is the second stage, our hiring committee will be speaking to only the top five applicants whom we feel are most _____ for this challenging position. Our
131.
entire committee agrees that you possess almost all the _____ we
132.
need. We trust that you are still interested in the position. _____,
133.
would you be available for an appointment next Wednesday at 2:30? Also, as part of the interview, we would like you to prepare a written research proposal related to one of the topics discussed at the first interview as well as a 10-minute presentation. _____.
134.

Best regards,

Duron Charette
WRN Pharmaceuticals
304-677-2426 ext. 18

--------------------------------------------------

收件者：<nina_haidara@kmail.net>
寄件者：<duron_charette@wrnpharmaceuticals.com>
日期：9 月 7 日
主旨：研究主管職缺

親愛的海德拉女士，

WRN 製藥廠很樂意邀請您下週至本公司進行第二次面試。因為這已經是第二階段，本公司招聘委員會只面談前五名應徵者，這五位是我們認為最適合這個具挑戰性職位的人選。委員會一致同意，您幾乎擁有我們所需的一切特質。我們相信您仍對這個職位感到興趣。若是如此，您下週三下午 2:30 是否有空會面？另外，做為本次面試內容的一部分，希望您可以準備一份書面研究計畫，內容為第一次面試中討論到的其中一個主題，以及一場十分鐘的簡報。很期待能聽到您對未來計畫的願景。

WRN 製藥廠
杜倫・夏爾特 敬上
304-677-2426 轉分機 18

**131**

(A) suiting
(B) suitable*
(C) suit
(D) suits

空格位置為 be 動詞 are 的主詞補語，因此空格中要填入形容詞 suitable，故答案為 (B)。

- suiting 西服料　suitable 適合的　suit 適合；套裝；訴訟

**132**

(A) agreements
(B) performances
(C) qualities*
(D) promotions

本題要選出適當的名詞，用來作為動詞 possess 的受詞。本句大意為「招聘委員會對海德拉女士的評價」，推測海德拉女士具備了一些「特質」，因此答案為 (C)。

- agreement 協議　performance 表現；成果　quality 特質　promotion 晉升

**133**

(A) Despite that
(B) If so*
(C) However
(D) For example

根據文意，本句「我們相信您仍對此職缺感興趣」，後方應為「若是如此」，再麻煩您來面試，語意承接上較為通順，因此答案為 (B)。

- despite . . . 僅管　if so 若是這樣　however 然而　for example 例如，舉例來說

**134**

(A) Our current research head will train you in your new duties.
(B) The CEO will be delighted to provide you with a letter of reference.
(C) You need to complete your current research project before Wednesday.
(D) We are looking forward to hearing your vision for a future project.*

(A) 我們現任研究主管將針對您的新職務進行培訓。
(B) 執行長很樂意幫您寫推薦信。
(C) 您需要在星期三之前完成目前的研究計畫。
(D) 很期待能聽到您對於未來計畫的願景。

文中要求海德拉女士從第一次面試時談論的主題當中，挑選一個主題準備書面研究計畫，(C) 與 (D) 中的 project 呼應到前句的 proposal，均可考慮，但 (C) 句卻要面試中的海德拉女士完成目前的研究計畫，不合應徵時的情境，故 (D) 最為適當。

- train 訓練，培訓　provide 提供　a letter of reference 推薦信　look forward to V-ing . . . 期待做⋯⋯

examination 檢查
approach 接近，臨近
vision 視力
detect 發現，查出
prescription 度數；處方
follow up
對……採取後續行動
make an appointment
約診；預約

Questions 135-138 refer to the following the letter.

Chantal Youldon

302 Moline Street

Delavan, IL

61735

Dear Ms. Youldon,

We would like to remind you that the time for another eye examination is soon approaching. ‗‗‗‗‗ 135. . Eye specialists ‗‗‗‗‗ 136. having your vision checked at least once a year. ‗‗‗‗‗ 137. , eye problems can be detected early and the prescription for your eyeglasses can also be updated. Our number one ‗‗‗‗‗ 138. is providing our patients with the best vision possible.

We will follow up this letter with a phone call in a few days. Please phone us at (309) 754-3231 if you would like to make an appointment. Thank you very much.

The Eye Care Team

Herrin Street Eye Clinic

---

香岱爾・瑤頓
61735 伊利諾州德拉凡市莫林街 302 號

親愛的瑤頓女士，

要提醒您另一次眼睛檢查的時間快到了。本所紀錄顯示，自您上回讓霍班醫生檢查距今已經 11 個月了。眼科專家建議您至少每年檢查視力一次。如此一來，可以盡早檢查出眼睛的問題，也能更新眼鏡度數。本診所的首要考量，就是盡力維持病患最佳視力狀態。過幾天我們將致電以作為本函的後續追蹤。如欲預約，請來電（309）754-3231。感謝您。

赫林街眼科診所 護眼團隊

**135**

(A) We recently expanded our waiting room to include a larger play area for children.

(B) Our records indicate that it has been 11 months since your last saw Dr. Hoban.*

(C) Exercise and a healthy diet also have an impact on the condition of your eyes.

(D) Our office updated its website to include a convenient online appointment system.

(A) 本所最近擴大候診室，增添孩童更大的遊戲區。

(B) 本所記錄顯示，自您上回讓霍班醫生檢查已經11個月了。

(C) 運動及健康飲食也會影響您的眼睛狀況。

(D) 本所更新了官網，包含便利的線上預約系統。

空格前方提醒瑤頓女士要做視力檢查，可以推測插入句應是補充她「檢查週期」相關的內容，因此 (B) 為最適當的答案。

● **expand** 擴大　**indicate** 顯示；指出　**exercise** 運動
**healthy** 健康的　**diet** 飲食，食物
**have an impact on . . .** 對⋯⋯有影響　**condition** 情況，狀況
**convenient** 便利的，方便的

---

**136**

(A) recommending
(B) had recommended
(C) recommend*
(D) will recommend

空格位在句子的動詞部分，(B)、(C)、(D) 可考慮，但本句的內容「專家建議至少每年檢查視力一次」屬於普遍認知的事實，因此答案為表現在簡單式的 (C)。

● **recommend** 建議

---

**137**

(A) Nevertheless
(B) In this way*
(C) For example
(D) Likewise

根據文意，藉由每年至少檢查一次的「這個方式」，可以及早發現眼睛的問題，並更新眼鏡的度數。因此答案為 (B)，意思為「如此一來，以這個方式」。

● **nevertheless** 然而　**in this way** 如此一來　**likewise** 同樣地

---

**138**

(A) manner
(B) opinion
(C) condition
(D) priority*

根據文意，本句想表達的是「盡力維持病患最佳視力狀態」就是「本診所的首要考量」，因此答案應為 (D)。

● **manner** 方式　**opinion** 意見　**priority** 優先（事項）

Questions 139-142 refer to the following article.

*Parrsboro Herald*

Local News

(12 June) — On Tuesday afternoon, Parrsboro City Mayor Deborah Middleton announced city council's decision to implement one-on-one training programs for aspiring city bus drivers. ‾‾‾‾139.‾, she stated that 20 new drivers will be needed before the end of the year. Speaking at a press conference, she stressed that there is an urgent ‾‾‾‾140.‾ for new drivers to replace those who are set to retire soon. The announcement ‾‾‾‾141.‾ with approval by most city officials. Councilor Stephen Digby of Truro Region, however, continues to speak out against the city funding costly training programs when graduates of the Wolfville College of Vehicle Operations, just 50 km west of Parrsboro, are already qualified to fill the positions. ‾‾‾‾142.‾.

-----

《帕斯波羅先趨報》
本地新聞

（6月12日）——星期二下午，帕斯波羅市市長黛博拉·密道頓宣布市議會決定，將為想成為市區公車司機的民眾，進行一對一的培訓計畫。她特別說明年底前需要20名新司機。在記者會談話中，市長強調了聘請新司機來代替即將退休人力的緊急需求。這個宣布獲得多數市府官員的認同。然而，特魯羅區議員史帝芬·迪格比不斷地公開反對市府大筆地提供資金在培訓計畫上，因為離帕斯波羅市西方50公里遠的沃夫維爾汽車營運大學，其畢業生都具備填補該缺額的資格。他要市府聘用熟悉該領域的人才。

**139** (A) Specifically*
(B) Undoubtedly
(C) Regardless
(D) Besides

空格前方的內容為市長在記者會上的宣布——新公車司機培訓，而空格後方則較具體地說明新司機需求的人數與原因，因此空格中適合填入副詞 specifically，答案為 (A)。

• **specifically** 特別地　　**undoubtedly** 毫無疑問地
**regardless** 無論如何　　**besides . . .** 除此之外

**140**

(A) settlement

(B) reduction

(C) demand*

(D) difficulty

單字 demand 可以與空格後方的 for 搭配使用，意思為「……要求，需要，需求」，且根據文意，聘請新司機來代替即將退休人力的「緊急需求」比較通順，故 (C) 正確。

- **settlement of . . .** 在……方面的解決或清算
  **reduction in . . .** 在……方面的減少
  **demand for . . .** 在……方面的需求，要求
  **difficulty in . . .** 在……方面的困難

---

**141**

(A) will be meeting

(B) to meet

(C) had been meeting

(D) was met*

空格為動詞所在的位置，因此無法填入 (B)。其他的選項中，(C) 和 (D) 表過去式，符合文意的時態，但是被動語態的 was met with approval 才是正確的用法，表示「獲得認同」，故 (D) 正確。

---

**142**

(A) He believes the current buses can be improved to allow more seats.

(B) He wants the city to hire staff already skilled in the field.*

(C) He feels the test to become a certified driver is too easy to pass.

(D) He expects the high fuel costs will lead to higher bus rates.

(A) 他相信可以以增加座位來改善目前公車狀況。

(B) 他要市府聘用已熟悉該領域的人才。

(C) 他覺得司機的合格測驗太容易通過。

(D) 他預期高油價將造成較高的公車費用。

請先閱讀空格前方的句子，議員史帝芬·迪格比表示不應該浪費資金去「培訓有意從事公車司機的生手」，因為沃夫維爾汽車營運大學畢業生均有當公車司機的資格，(B) 句的 skilled in the field 呼應到前句的 are already qualified to fill the positions，因此空格應填入 (B) 最符合文意。

- **improve** 改善，提升　**certified** 合格的　**cost** 費用；成本
  **lead to** 導致，造成　**rate** 費用，價格

字彙
colleague 同事
recruiter 招聘人員
officially 正式地
assistance 協助
hesitate 猶豫，躊躇
transition 過渡（時期）
performance 表現
outstanding 傑出的，優異的

Questions 143-146 refer to the following letter.

**To:** Frans Vanek
**From:** Michelle Sekera
**Date:** 14 July
**Subject:** Good morning.

I learned of your upcoming ‾‾‾‾ from a colleague. Even though
                              143.
the position of chief recruiter at our newly-opened office in Oslo
officially ‾‾‾‾ on August 2, I would like to take a moment now
           144.
to wish you the very best in your new career. If you require any
assistance, please do not hesitate to contact me. I am well aware
that this type of transition, while exciting, is also extremely ‾‾‾‾ .
                                                                 145.
Your work performance here in Paris at Chara Fashion as
assistant hiring director has always been outstanding. ‾‾‾‾ .
                                                        146.
Congratulations and good luck!

Sincerely,

Michelle Sekera

------------------------------------------------------------

收件者：法蘭絲·凡奈克
寄件者：蜜雪兒·薩克拉
日期：7 月 14 日
主旨：早安

我從同事那得知你即將升職。雖然奧斯陸新設辦公室的招募主管一職，
將於 8 月 2 日才正式開始，還是先祝福你新工作一切順利。如果需要任
何協助，歡迎與我聯絡，我很清楚這種過渡期，雖然令人興奮，卻也是相
當具挑戰性。你在巴黎查拉時尚擔任副招募總監一職時，工作表現一向
都很傑出。我相信你在新職位上的表現也會很成功的。恭喜你，也祝你
一切順利！

蜜雪兒·薩克拉敬上

**143**
(A) trip
(B) event
(C) award
(D) promotion*

凡奈克先生的職稱從 assistant hiring director 變成 chief recruiter，故表示「升遷」的 (D) 為最適當的答案。

- **award** 獎項　**promotion** 晉升，升職

---

**144**
(A) begins*
(B) began
(C) has begun
(D) could begin

現在的時間根據郵件日期為 7 月 14 日，根據文意，8 月 2 日為「任職新職位」的時間，因此答案應為表「未來」的現在簡單式 (A)。現在簡單式通常不用於談論未來事件，但若談論時刻表、計畫表上確定的計畫或安排時，會用現在簡單式，請特別熟記這項文法規則。

---

**145**
(A) challenging*
(B) challenge
(C) challenger
(D) challenges

空格位置為 is 的補語，補充說明 transition（過渡期）的性質為何，因此空格中只能填入形容詞 challenging 作補語，前方副詞 extremely 則修飾 challenging，故答案選 (A)。

- **challenging** 有挑戰性的　**challenge** 挑戰　**challenger** 挑戰者

---

**146**
(A) The Oslo office is a little smaller with a big parking lot.
(B) I'm still conducting interviews for all the new positions.
(C) You could ask about staff discounts at clothing shops.
(D) I am certain that you will be successful in your new position.*

空格前方提到凡奈克先生「在目前所擔任的職務內表現優異」，「相信凡奈克先生在新職位上的表現也會成功」，較符合句意，因此最適合的答案為 (D)。

- **parking lot** 停車場　**conduct** 進行；實施

(A) 奧斯陸辦公室比較小，但有個大停車場。
(B) 我還在進行所有新職缺的面試事宜。
(C) 你可以問問服飾店的員工折扣。
(D) 我相信你在新職位上的表現也會很成功的。

字彙

**outfitter** 戶外活動用品店
**footstool** 腳凳
**subtotal** 小計
**tax** 稅金
**policy** 規定；政策
**sign up for** 參加
**offer** 折扣，優惠

Questions 147-148 refer to the following receipt.

**Park Home Outfitters**
229 Park Road South
Edmonton, Alberta
(777) 223-4455
Date: May 12                                   Time: 10:37

**Items**

| 3345 | [147] La Roux 4-Seat Sofa | $499.00 |
|------|------|------|
| 3348 | La Roux Armchair | $199.00 |
| 3355 | La Roux Footstool | $99.00 |
| 4489 | D&F 6-drawer Dresser | |
| | 4 $79.00/ea | $316.00 |
| 1223 | Star Designs pillow | |
| | 2 $19.00/ea | $38.00 |
| Subtotal | | $1151.00 |
| Tax (5%) | | $57.55 |
| Total | | $1208.55 |
| Paid by credit card | | $1208.55 |

Total number of items purchased: 9

Returns may be made for all non-sale items within 60 days of purchase.

To view our return policy, please visit www.parkhomeoutfitters.ca/returns.

********************

[148] Sign up for a membership on our website and receive up to 50% off on select online purchases. Offer ends June 28.

********************

Thank you for shopping at Park Home Outfitters.

----------------------------------------------------------------------

公園家戶外活動用品店
亞伯達省艾德蒙頓，公園路南區 229 號
(777) 223-4455
日期：5 月 12 日                                   時間：10:37

品項

| 3345 | 樂路克斯 四人座沙發 | $499.00 |
|------|------|------|
| 3348 | 樂路克斯 扶手椅 | $199.00 |
| 3355 | 樂路克斯 腳凳 | $99.00 |
| 4489 | D&F 六入抽屜櫃 | |
| | 四座（79 元／座） | $316.00 |
| 1223 | 明星設計款枕頭 | |
| | 兩個（19 元／個） | $38.00 |
| 小計 | | $1151.00 |
| 稅（5%） | | $57.55 |
| 總計 | | $1208.55 |
| 信用卡支付金額 | | $1208.55 |

總購買件數：9

非特價商品於購買後 60 天內，皆可接受退貨。退貨規定請至 www.parkhomeoutfitters.ca/returns. 查閱。

*******************************************

上官網加入會員，即可以最高五折優惠購買線上特定商品，優惠至 6 月 28 日。

*******************************************

感謝您購買公園家戶外活動用品店商品。

---

**147** What kind of store most likely is Park Home Outfitters?

(A) A furniture store*
(B) A fabric outlet
(C) A construction company
(D) A clothing store

由商品明細中列出的品項（Sofa, Armchair, Footstool, Dresser, pillow），可以得知該商店販售家具，故答案為 (A)。

公園家戶外用品店可能是哪一種商店？

(A) 家具行
(B) 紡織品商店
(C) 建設公司
(D) 服飾店

字彙
**fabric** 布料，織物
**outlet** 專賣店，經銷點
**construction** 建設

---

**148** According to the receipt, how can customers get a discount?

(A) By applying for a membership*
(B) By showing a coupon
(C) By completing a survey
(D) By purchasing two or more items

閱讀文章時，請特別留意「享有折扣的方式」。收據後方寫道：「Sign up for a membership on our website and receive up to 50% off on select online purchases.」，表示只要加入會員，最高可享有五折的優惠購買線上特定商品，因此答案為 (A)。

* 答案改寫：sign up for → apply for

根據收據，顧客要如何獲得折扣？

(A) 申請會員
(B) 出示折價券
(C) 填寫問卷調查
(D) 購買兩項以上商品

**字彙**
anniversary 週年紀念日
release（發布的）新聞稿
kickoff（活動的）開始
arrange 安排，組織
completed 完整的
finalize 最後確定，定案
branch 分店；分公司
in the meantime 在此期間
attached 附件的
department 部門

Questions 149-150 refer to the following e-mail.

**To:** Gary Hong <garyhong@songendepartmentstore.co.au>
**From:** Patricia Torenski <songendepartmentstore.co.au>
**Subject:** Songen Department Store's 10th Anniversary
**Date:** 14 October
**Attachment:** Press Release

Dear Mr. Hong,

[149] Several television stations have been contacted about a press release regarding our 10th anniversary events in Sydney. **The kickoff event will be a concert held outside our downtown store location on November 24.** [149] We have also arranged a number of anniversary sales at all our stores from next week until the events. [150] I will send you the completed schedule once it has been finalized with the branch managers.

In the meantime, please have a look at the attached press release and let me know if the advertising department would like us to add anything.

Sincerely,

Patricia Torenski,
Marketing Manager, Songen Department Store

--------------------------------------------------------------------

收件者：蓋瑞・洪 <garyhong@songendepartmentstore.co.au>
寄件者：派翠西亞・圖倫斯基 <songendepartmentstore.co.au>
主旨：頌恩百貨公司十週年慶
日期：10 月 14 日
附件：新聞稿

親愛的洪先生，

有關我們在雪梨的十週年慶祝活動新聞稿，已聯絡了數家電視台。週年慶將以音樂會為開幕活動，將於 11 月 24 日在市中心門市外舉辦。自下週起到整個活動期間，我們也在所有分店安排了幾場週年慶特賣會。待分店主管確認後，我會將完整的時程表寄給您。

同時，請參閱附件的新聞稿，若宣傳部需要增添任何資料，再請告知。

頌恩百貨公司行銷經理
派翠西亞・圖倫斯基 敬上

**149** What is the purpose of the e-mail?

(A) To make a list of items for sale
(B) To reschedule a live music event
(C) To invite a coworker to attend an event
(D) To give an update on a promotional plan*

郵件第一段便提到有關週年慶祝活動的消息，寄件人報告最新的籌備狀況──告知已連絡數家電視台（Several television stations have been contacted about a press release regarding our 10th anniversary events in Sydney.），之後他又提及安排週年慶特賣，週年慶活動與特賣都是宣傳計畫之一（anniversary sales = promotional plan），因此 (D) 為最適當的答案。

這封電子郵件的目的是什麼？

(A) 列出出售商品清單
(B) 重新安排現場音樂演奏節目時間
(C) 邀請同事出席活動
(D) 報告宣傳計畫的最新狀況

字彙
**coworker** 同事
**promotional**
廣告宣傳的；促銷的

**150** What does Ms. Torenski promise to send later?

(A) A recent news article
(B) A schedule of store discounts*
(C) A list of television stations
(D) A revised press release

閱讀文章時，請特別留意題目關鍵字 send。郵件第一段圖倫斯基女士提到，待她與分店主管確認後，就會寄出完整的時程表（I will send you the completed schedule once it has been finalized with the branch managers.）。此處的日程表就是前文曾提及的週年慶特賣會（anniversary sales）的日程，因此答案為 (B)。

圖倫斯基女士答應稍後要寄什麼？

(A) 最近的一篇新聞文章
(B) 商店優惠折扣的時程表
(C) 電視台清單
(D) 修改後的新聞稿

**字彙**

**name** 命名；取名
**extensive** 寬闊的
**attract** 吸引
**house** 收藏；安置
**target**
以……為目標（或對象）

Questions 151-152 refer to the following article.

**Around Town**

[151, 152] Town Books owner Cynthia Purdel has announced her plans to open a second bookstore at 667 Brookside Avenue. The building, located across from Brookside Elementary School, was once the home of Smithton Bakery. Ms. Purdel's new bookstore, which has yet to be named, is scheduled to open in the spring of next year. The bookstore will include an extensive children's section, which [152] Ms. Purdel hopes it will attract numerous customers from Brookside Elementary School. Ms. Purdel's original bookstore, Town Books, is located on 5th Avenue and houses genres that are targeted to adult readers.

---

大城小事

城鎮書店老闆辛西亞·普戴爾宣布，她將於布魯克賽德大道 667 號開設第二間書店的計畫。地點就在布魯克賽德小學對面，之前是史密斯頓麵包店的所在地。普戴爾女士的新書店尚未命名，但預計於明年春天開幕。書店將有寬廣的童書區，普戴爾女士希望可以藉此吸引許多布魯克賽德小學的小客人。普戴爾女士原本位於第五大道上的城鎮書店，其藏書類型與營業型態則鎖定成人讀者。

---

這篇文章的目的是什麼？

(A) 討論商店結束營業
(B) 介紹一位成功的烘焙業者
(C) 報告店家搬遷
(D) 宣布新店家開幕

**字彙**

**profile** 簡要介紹
**relocation** 遷移，搬遷

**151** What is the purpose of the article?

(A) To discuss the closing of a business
(B) To profile a successful bakery owner
(C) To report on a store's relocation
(D) To announce the opening of a new business*

由第一句「Town Books owner Cynthia Purdel has announced her plans to open a second bookstore at 667 Brookside Avenue.」，就可以確認答案為 (D)。另外，原本的店並沒有要搬遷，而是再多開一間新的店 (a second bookstore = a new business)，因此 (C) 為錯誤的選項。

---

下列何者與布魯克賽德大道上的商店有關？

(A) 位在一家受歡迎的麵包店的對面。
(B) 預計今年開幕。
(C) 是普戴爾女士的首次創業。
(D) 預期客源為學生。

**字彙**

**venture** 企業；(冒險) 事業

**152** What is indicated about the new store on Brookside Avenue?

(A) It is located across from a popular bakery.
(B) It is scheduled to open this year.
(C) It is Ms. Purdel's first business venture.
(D) It is expected to receive business from students.*

閱讀文章時，請掌握好與 second bookstore 有關的事項。文章中的「Ms. Purdel hopes it will attract numerous customers from Brookside Elementary School.」，表示她希望能吸引很多小學生前來書店，因此 (D) 為最適當的答案。由第一句的 open a second bookstore 可知這不是普戴爾女士的首次創業，故 (C) 不對。

Questions 153-155 refer to the following notice.

## St. Michael's Hospital Research Gala

St. Michael's Hospital will host a gala to benefit continued medical research. The gala will be held at the Grand Renaissance Hotel; however, [153] the day has been changed due to a hotel booking error. Instead of September 20, the event will be held on October 5, from 5:00 P.M. until 8:00 P.M. Please note the following information before attending.

[154] **Directions to Grand Renaissance Hotel from Central Station:**

[154] Drive north on Parcelle Boulevard and turn right onto Meadow Drive. Turn left onto Bath Avenue and continue for five blocks before turning right onto Smithview Road. The Grand Renaissance Hotel is located across from the Mary Rose Theater. The gala will be held in Banquet Room 1A.

**Parking Information:**

[155] Parking is available free of charge in the underground parking lot. Please ensure you have the parking pass that was issued along with your gala ticket. Otherwise, you will be responsible for paying for parking.

------------------------------------------------

### 聖麥克醫院研究盛會

聖麥克醫院將舉辦一場盛會幫助持續性醫療研究。盛會將於大復興飯店舉行，但是由於飯店預約錯誤，必須更動活動日期。活動將由原訂的 9 月 20 日改到 10 月 5 日晚上 5:00 至 8:00。出席前請注意以下資訊。

從中央車站到大復興飯店的交通路線如下：

帕歇爾大道往北行，右轉彌督路。左轉貝絲大街，經過五條街後右轉史密斯維路。大復興飯店就位於瑪莉蘿絲戲院對面。盛會將於 1A 宴會廳舉行。

停車資訊：

地下停車場可免費停車。請確認您攜帶連同盛會入場券一同核發的停車證。否則您須自行支付停車費用。

---

**153** What has changed about the event?

(A) The cost
(B) The location
(C) The sponsor
(D) The date*

由第二句的 the day has been changed due to a hotel booking error，表示由於飯店預約失誤導致日期產生變動，因此答案為 (D)。

\* 答案改寫：day → date

**字彙**
gala 盛會
host 主辦
benefit
使……受益，對……有幫助
continued 持續的
medical 醫學的；醫療的
due to . . . 由於，因為
booking 預約
boulevard 大道
banquet 宴會
ensure 確保
issue 核發，發給
otherwise 否則，不然

這項活動變更了什麼？

(A) 費用
(B) 位置
(C) 贊助商
(D) 日期

**字彙**
sponsor 贊助者

中央車站位於何處？

(A) 彌督路

(B) 貝絲大街

(C) 帕歇爾大道

(D) 史密斯維路

**154** Where is Central Station located?

(A) Meadow Drive

(B) Bath Avenue

(C) Parcelle Boulevard*

(D) Smithview Road

在由中央車站至活動會場的交通路線（Directions to Grand Renaissance Hotel from Central Station）中，提到了從帕歇爾大道往北行，可以推測中央車站就在帕歇爾大道上（Drive north on Parcelle Boulevard），因此答案為 (C)。

---

下列何者與大復興飯店的停車有關？

(A) 盛會貴賓必須支付停車費。

(B) 停車場位於對街。

(C) 有來賓停車證者可免費停車。

(D) 飯店有共用的停車場。

字彙

**shared** 共用的，共享的

**parking garage** 汽車停車場

**155** What is indicated about the Grand Renaissance Hotel's parking?

(A) Gala guests will have to pay for parking.

(B) The parking lot is located across the street.

(C) Parking is free with a guest pass.*

(D) The hotel has a shared parking garage.

請找出有關停車的段落。在最後一段的停車資訊中，提醒賓客記得攜帶停車證，才能免費停車（Please ensure you have the parking pass that was issued along with your gala ticket.），因此 (C) 為最適當的答案。

Questions 156-157 refer to the following text message chain.

**Steven Yoon  4:45 P.M.**
Jennifer tried to call you about the meeting with the CEO tomorrow.
[156] She's wondering if you can call her back.

**Roger Martinez  4:50 P.M.**
I'm in the warehouse right now. Do you think she's worried the reports won't be finished in time?

**Steven Yoon  4:52 P.M.**
It's possible.

**Roger Martinez  4:54 P.M.**
Well, I'm checking the warehouse alarm system now. I got called away, because it seems to be acting up again.

**Steven Yoon  4:57 P.M.**
Do you want me to call the security company?

**Roger Martinez  5:00 P.M.**
I think I can fix it myself. [157] Can you tell Jennifer to stop by my office at 5:30? I think we should discuss her concerns tonight before we go home.

**Steven Yoon  5:01 P.M.**
OK. No problem.

--------------------------------------------------------------------------------

史蒂芬・尹  下午 4:45
珍妮佛來電要跟你說有關明天和執行長開會的事。她想知道你是否可以回電給她。

羅傑・馬丁尼茲  下午 4:50
我現在在倉庫。你覺得她是在擔心報告無法及時完成嗎？

史蒂芬・尹  下午 4:52
有可能。

羅傑・馬丁尼茲  下午 4:54
嗯，我正在檢查倉庫的警報系統。我被叫來，因為系統似乎又出問題了。

史蒂芬・尹  下午 4:57
要我打電話給保全公司嗎？

羅傑・馬丁尼茲  下午 5:00
我想我可以自己修好。你可以告訴珍妮佛，請她 5:30 到我辦公室來一趟嗎？我想，我們應該在今晚下班前討論一下她所擔心的事。

史蒂芬・尹  下午 5:01
好，沒問題。

字彙
warehouse 倉庫
call away 叫走
act up
故障，(機器) 運轉不正常
security 保全
stop by 順路造訪

ACTUAL TEST **5**

PART **7** 中譯＋解析

下午4:50時，馬丁尼茲先生
說，「我現在在倉庫。」他的意
思最有可能是？

**(A)** 他明天不在。

**(B)** 他要送貨。

**(C)** 他需要和尹先生說話。

**(D)** 他無法打電話給珍妮佛。

---

**156** At 4:50 P.M. what does Mr. Martinez most likely mean when he writes, "I'm in the warehouse right now"?

**(A)** He will not be in tomorrow.

**(B)** He has a delivery to make.

**(C)** He needs to speak with Mr. Yoon.

(D) He cannot call Jennifer.*

前一封訊息中提到珍妮佛曾經打電話來過，想確認馬丁尼茲先生現在是否方便回電給她（She's wondering if you can call her back.）。題目中的句子即為對此詢問的回覆，表示他人在倉庫，無法回覆，因此 (D) 為最適當的答案。

---

尹先生被要求做什麼事？

**(A)** 和執行長聯絡

**(B)** 籌備會議

**(C)** 打電話給技術員

**(D)** 離開辦公室

---

**157** What task is Mr. Yoon asked to do?

**(A)** Contact the CEO

(B) Set up a meeting*

**(C)** Call a technician

**(D)** Leave the office

本題的解題關鍵為「馬丁尼茲先生拜託尹先生的內容」。閱讀訊息時，請把焦點放在馬丁尼茲先生的訊息上。他下午 5 點的訊息中寫道：「Can you tell Jennifer to stop by my office at 5:30?」，請求對方告訴珍妮佛，請她順道來一趟辦公室討論公事。(B) 以單字 meeting 來代稱最後一句的 discuss，為最適當的答案。

## Questions 158-160 refer to the following letter.

October 10

Peter Stephenson
45 Ramsay Avenue
Cleveland, Ohio

Dear Mr. Stephenson:

Thank you very much for deciding to attend the very first International Magazine Festival that will take place in Paris, France. 158 We received your registration. --[1]--. As requested, we billed your credit card to include both admission to the event as well as the extra fee needed to reserve a table for your display. Immediately upon arrival, we will show you to your table and also present you with a name badge that will allow you to receive discounts at any beverage and food vendors at the festival. --[2]--.

We would like to remind you that accommodation is not included in the festival admission price. To reserve a room in the neighborhood, please visit www.parishotels.com. 160 You may be able to book a room at 25% off the regular rate by providing proof that you are participating in our festival. --[3]--.

159 Enclosed, please find a map of this particular area of Paris. This will allow you to acquaint yourself with the neighborhood. The map also includes the area's most popular restaurants and hotels. --[4]--.

Again, thank you and we hope the International Magazine Festival turns out to be a rewarding experience for you.

Sincerely,

Nicole Desjardins,
Festival Coordinator

---

10 月 10 日

彼得‧史帝文森
俄亥俄州克里夫蘭拉姆齊大道 45 號

親愛的史帝文森先生，

十分感謝您決定參加在法國巴黎舉辦的第一屆國際雜誌節。我們已經收到您的報名。如您所要求的，我們已將展場入場費及預約展示席位所需的額外費用刷入您的信用卡帳上。當您抵達時，我們將立即引領您至攤位，並發給您一張名牌，讓您在展場中的任何飲料及食物攤位都能享有折扣。

要提醒您活動報名費並不含住宿費。欲於鄰近地區訂房，請查看 www.parishotels.com。藉由出示參加本雜誌展的證明，您可以以定價 75 折的價格訂房。本信函可為適當證明，當您入住時只需向櫃檯人員出示本函即可。

隨信附上本次巴黎會區地圖，有助於您熟悉附近環境。地圖內容也包含了該區最受歡迎的餐廳與飯店。

再次感謝您，希望本次的國際雜誌展能成為您收穫滿載的一個經驗。

會展統籌
妮可‧德雅爾丹司 敬上

字彙
registration 報名，登記
bill 給……開帳單
admission 入場費；門票
arrival 抵達
beverage 飲料
vendor 攤販，小販
accommodation 住宿
rate 費用，價格
proof 證明
Enclosed, please find . . .
隨函附上……
acquaint 使熟悉
turn out to be
結果是，證明是
rewarding 有益的，值得的

為什麼會寄這封信？

(A) 提供部分退款
(B) 告知地址變更
(C) 說明流程
(D) 告知收到報名

字彙
**partial** 部分的
**refund** 退款
**acknowledge**
告知收到（信件等）

**158** Why was the letter sent?

(A) To offer a partial refund
(B) To inform of an address change
(C) To explain a procedure
(D) To acknowledge registration*

在文章的前半部，大多會出現與文章主旨有關的解題線索。第一句寄件人先向對方決定參與國際雜誌節表達感謝之意，之後表示已經收到了報名（We received your registration.），因此答案為 (D)。

---

史帝文森先生被建議事先檢閱什麼？

(A) 當地地圖
(B) 會議議程
(C) 合約條款
(D) 班機時間

字彙
**agenda** 議程
**contract** 合約
**term** 條款
**flight** 班機

**159** What is Mr. Stephenson advised to review ahead of time?

(A) A local map*
(B) A meeting agenda
(C) Contract terms
(D) Flight times

第三段中的「Enclosed, please find a map of this particular area of Paris.」，表示隨信附上了巴黎會區地圖，有助於對方熟悉當地環境，因此答案為 (A)。

---

下列句子最適合出現在[1]、[2]、[3]、[4]的哪個位置中？
「本信函可為適當證明，當您入住時只需向櫃檯人員出示本函即可。」

(A) [1]
(B) [2]
(C) [3]
(D) [4]

字彙
**suitable** 適當的，合適的
**verification** 證明

**160** In which of the positions marked [1], [2], [3], and [4] does the following sentence best belong?

"This letter is suitable verification so simply present it to the clerk when you check in."

(A) [1]
(B) [2]
(C) [3]*
(D) [4]

本題的解題線索為插入句中的 check in，表示「辦理入住飯店的手續」。可以推知插入句的前文會提到住宿的相關訊息。(C) 的位置最為適當，因為前方提及訂房時獲得優惠的方法，且 proof 對應到插入句中的 This letter is suitable verification，故 (C) 為正確答案。

Questions 161-164 refer to the following article.

## Unforeseeable Delays for the Hammer Electronics 8000 Series

By Sophia Miachi

Last week, [161] Hammer Electronics, the world's leading producer of smart phones, announced a delay in the launch of its new 8000 Series smart phone line. Industry professionals and customers alike were shocked by the news. Hammer Electronics enthusiasts took to social media to express their frustration with the cancellation of the much-anticipated 8000 Series.

According to Hammer representatives, the 8000 Series, which will consist of three individual models and various companion technologies, has been delayed due to unforeseeable problems with the company's new screen design. --[1]--. While the prototypes were initially approved, the first batch of devices were unable to pass safety tests. --[2]--. [162 (A), (B)] This may be due to a flaw in the glass used to construct the screens, which makes the internal components vulnerable to overheating.

In addition to not passing the inspections, [164] Hammer's new line has proven to be less durable than the company intended. [162 (D)] Because of the flawed materials, the 8000 Series has proven to be quite delicate. --[3]--.

[161, 163] Hammer Electronics is now looking at alternative materials and plans to release the 8000 Series next year. --[4]--. However, the company may have already lost many of its eager customers.

--------------------------------------------

### 漢默電子8000系列不可預期的延誤

蘇菲亞‧米亞琪 撰稿

上週，全世界主要智慧型手機製造商——漢默電子，宣布了新智慧型手機8000系列延後上市的消息。業界專家與顧客們對此消息同感震驚。漢默電子的擁護者在社群媒體上，對深受期待的8000系列手機取消一事，表達了失望之情。

根據漢默電子代表表示，由三種個別模型及各種伴生技術所組成的8000系列，由於公司新款螢幕設計上不可預期的問題而延誤了。雖然一開始原型被核准了，但第一批生產的裝置卻無法通過安全檢測。這可能是因為用來製作螢幕的玻璃有瑕疵，使得內部組件容易過熱。

除了無法通過檢測外，漢默的新系列已證實它並不如公司預期地持久。由於材質的瑕疵，8000型被證實是相當脆弱的。對於一家以生產耐用產品而自豪的公司來說，推出這系列的產品將會是非常難堪的一件事。

漢默電子正在探尋其他替代材料，計畫明年推出8000系列。但是，該公司或許已經流失許多渴望新產品的顧客了。

**字彙**

**unforeseeable**
不可預見的，無法預料的
**electronics** 電子（產品）
**launch** 上市，推出
**enthusiast**
愛好者，熱烈支持者
**take to . . .** 開始從事……
**frustration** 失望，挫敗
**much-anticipated**
深受期待的
**representative** 代表人員
**companion** 伴隨
**prototype** 原型
**initially** 最初地
**batch of** （一）批
**flaw** 瑕疵，缺陷
**internal** 內部的
**component** 零件，組件
**vulnerable to . . .**
易受……，易於……
**overheating** 過熱
**inspection** 檢驗，檢查
**prove to be . . .** 證明是……
**durable** 持久的，耐用的
**intend** 計劃，打算
**material** 材料
**delicate** 脆弱的
**alternative** 可供替代的
**release** 推出
**eager** 渴望的

下列何者與漢默電子有關？

**(A)** 是智慧型手機科技的頂尖製造商。

**(B)** 將以折扣價來銷售8000系列。

**(C)** 要把總部遷至另一個城市。

**(D)** 將持續生產有瑕疵的產品。

字彙
**headquarters**
總部，總公司

**161** What is indicated about Hammer Electronics?

(A) It is a top producer of smart phone technology.*

(B) It will sell the 8000 Series at a discount.

(C) It is moving its headquarters to another country.

(D) It will continue producing a flawed design.

由第一段的「Hammer Electronics, the world's leading producer of smart phones」，可以得知答案應為 (A)。(C) 沒有在文章中提及，而由末段的「Hammer Electronics is now looking at alternative materials and plans to release the 8000 Series next year.」，可知 (B)、(D) 錯誤。

* 答案改寫：**leading** → **top**

---

下列何者不是8000系列設計上的問題？

**(A)** 螢幕是有瑕疵的玻璃。

**(B)** 產品會過熱。

**(C)** 材料太貴。

**(D)** 裝置是脆弱的。

字彙
**overheat** 過熱
**fragile** 脆弱的；易損壞的

**162** What is NOT mentioned as a problem with the 8000 Series design?

(A) The screens have flawed glass.

(B) The devices may overheat.

(C) The materials are too expensive.*

(D) The devices are fragile.

解題時，請將各選項的內容對照對應段落，再刪除文中有提及的「產品問題」。(A) 和 (B) 出現在第二段當中「This may be due to a flaw in the glass used to construct the screens, which makes the internal components vulnerable to overheating.」由第三段的「Because of the flawed materials, the 8000 Series has proven to be quite delicate.」，可以確認 (D)，因此本題的答案應為 (C)。

---

漢默電子為什麼要到明年才會推出8000系列？

**(A)** 他們需要處理專利權的問題。

**(B)** 檢測已經重新安排時間。

**(C)** 有些工廠需要升級。

**(D)** 他們需要足夠的時間來找新原料。

字彙
**address** 處理，應付
**patent** 專利（權）
**issue** 問題

**163** Why will Hammer Electronics release the 8000 Series next year?

(A) They need to address a patent issue.

(B) Their inspections have been rescheduled.

(C) Some factories need to be upgraded.

(D) They need enough time to find new materials.*

閱讀文章時，請特別留意題目關鍵時間點 next year。在最後一段中的「Hammer Electronics is now looking at alternative materials and plans to release the 8000 Series next year.」，表示目前漢默電子正在找尋替代的材料，預計於明年上市，因此 (D) 為最適當的答案。

* 答案改寫：**alternative** → **new**

**164** In which of the positions marked [1], [2], [3], and [4] does the following sentence best belong?

"For a company that prides itself on durable products, releasing this line of devices would be an embarrassment."

(A) [1]
(B) [2]
(C) [3]*
(D) [4]

題目句的重點在於「產品的耐用度」，而關鍵字為 durable。第三段中提到新產品的耐用度不如公司預期（less durable than the company intended），題目句最適合放入此段落中，因此答案為 (C)。

下列句子最適合出現在 [1],[2],[3],[4]的哪個位置中？
「對於一家以生產耐用產品而自豪的公司來說，推出這系列的產品將會是非常難堪的一件事。」

(A) [1]
(B) [2]
(C) [3]
(D) [4]

字彙
embarrassment
令人尷尬的事，令人難堪的事

字彙
realize 意識到；明白
trim 門窗的邊框
at least 至少，起碼

---

**Questions 165-168 refer to the following text message chain.**

| Messages | | Edit |
|---|---|---|

**Lester Gibbs [9:00]**
Hi, Michelle. Are you at the office?

**Michelle Chong [9:01]**
Almost there. Why?

**Lester Gibbs [9:03]**
165, 166 I'm working on a house here on Kensington Avenue, and just realized that I don't have enough red exterior paint left for the trim around the doors and windows. Do we have any cans of it left in our store? If not, I will just drive over to a store in Anders Park and pick up a can.

**Michelle Chong [9:04]**
Justin is at the office now. I'm including him right now. How many cans do you need?

*Justin Whittaker has been added to the chat.*

**Lester Gibbs [9:05]**
167 I need two cans of red exterior paint. Can you please check the storage, Justin?

**Justin Whittaker [9:07]**
This must be your luck day.

**Lester Gibbs [9:10]**
Super! I have to finish painting the east side of the house and won't be starting the trim for at least an hour, so I will come by and pick them up after 10:00.

字彙
**back up** 倒（車）
**loading dock** 裝卸區
**drop off**
把……放下；
把……從車上卸下

**Michelle Chong [9:11]**
Actually, I just backed my truck up to the loading dock and will get everything I need for a job on the corner of Nelson Avenue and Bicks Street. [166] You're not far from that area so I can easily drop off the cans of red exterior first.

**Lester Gibbs [9:15]**
That would be great. Thanks a lot! [168] Justin, please add my name and the current time to the stock record sheet. I will be sure to come by after lunch and sign the form.

**Justin Whittaker [9:17]**
No problem.

-----------------------------------------------------------------------

| 訊息 | | 編輯 |
|---|---|---|

萊斯特·吉伯斯 **[9:00]**
嗨，蜜雪兒，妳在辦公室嗎？

蜜雪兒·鍾 **[9:01]**
快到了。怎麼了？

萊斯特·吉伯斯 **[9:03]**
我正在進行肯辛頓大道上一棟房子的工程，剛剛才發現我沒有足夠的紅色室外漆，來粉刷門窗邊框。我們店裡還有油漆嗎？沒有的話，我就要開車去安德斯公園的商店買一罐了。

蜜雪兒·鍾 **[9:04]**
賈斯汀現在在辦公室。我現在加他進來。你需要幾罐？

**賈斯汀·惠特克被加入對話。**

萊斯特·吉伯斯 **[9:05]**
我需要兩罐紅色室外漆。賈斯汀，你可以去倉庫查看一下嗎？

賈斯汀·惠特克 **[9:07]**
你今天運氣真好。

萊斯特·吉伯斯 **[9:10]**
太好了！我必須先塗完房子東側的油漆，至少要一個小時後才會開始粉刷邊框，所以我十點之後回來拿。

蜜雪兒·鍾 **[9:11]**
事實上，我才剛把我的卡車倒車到卸貨區，為了尼爾森大道和比克斯街轉角的工作，我要去拿所需要的東西。你離那一區不遠，所以我可以順便先把紅色室外漆拿給你。

萊斯特·吉伯斯 **[9:15]**
那太棒了！非常感謝！賈斯汀，麻煩在庫存記錄單上添上我的名字和現在的時間。午餐後，我一定會回去在表格上簽名。

賈斯汀·惠特克 **[9:17]**
沒問題。

**165** What type of business does Mr. Gibbs probably work for?

(A) A home improvement contractor*
(B) An Internet provider
(C) A plastics manufacturer
(D) A fast food restaurant

吉伯斯先生在 9 點 03 分的訊息中寫道:「I'm working on a house here on Kensington Avenue, and just realized that I don't have enough red exterior paint left for the trim around the doors and windows.」,由此可以得知 (A) 為最適當的答案。

---

**166** Where does Ms. Chong say she will go next?

(A) To Anders Park
(B) To Kensington Avenue*
(C) To Bicks Street
(D) To Nelson Avenue

請特別留意鍾女士的訊息,9 點 11 分的訊息中,她表示可以順道去吉伯斯先生那邊一趟(You're not far from that area so I can easily drop off the cans of red exterior first.),因此請找出吉伯斯先生所在的地點。由 9 點 03 分的訊息「I'm working on a house here on Kensington Avenue」,可以確認答案為 (B)。

---

**167** At 9:07 A.M. what does Mr. Whittaker most likely mean when he writes, "This must be your lucky day"?

(A) There is enough money for a new project.
(B) The directions to the house are easy to follow.
(C) The exact number of cans needed is in stock.*
(D) He will be able to help Mr. Gibbs in the evening.

請閱讀此訊息前後方的內容。前方吉伯斯先生表示需要兩罐油漆(I need two cans of red exterior paint.),並請惠特克先生確認,因此對方回覆「您真幸運」,意思就是倉庫裡剛好有兩罐紅色室外漆,故答案為 (C)。

---

**168** What does Mr. Gibbs ask Mr. Whittaker to do?

(A) Fill in the main details on a form*
(B) Place some items on a shelf
(C) Set up a consultation with a client
(D) Send an invoice to a local business

請特別找出吉伯斯先生傳送給惠特克先生的訊息。吉伯斯先生在 9 點 15 分的訊息中寫道:「Justin, please add my name and the current time to the stock record sheet.」,拜託惠特克先生幫忙在庫存記錄單上寫下他的姓名和現在時間,因此 (A) 為最適當的答案。

## 字彙

**affordable**
負擔得起，買得起
**land (v.)**
（輕而易舉或意外地）得到
**track** 追蹤
**trend** 潮流，趨勢
**up-to-date** 最新的
**in cooperation with . . .**
與……合作
**advanced** 進階的；先進的
**résumé ( = resume)** 履歷表
**extensive** 廣泛的；龐大的
**pair (v.)** 與……配對
**based on . . .** 依據，基於

Questions 169-171 refer to the following advertisement.

### BizNet
### Networking at the click of a mouse!

BizNet is the latest development in online networking services. Quick, affordable, and easy-to-use, [169] BizNet can connect you with industry professionals and help you land the job of your dreams. Our online services allow you to track trends in the job market as well as get up-to-date information on business conferences in your area.

In cooperation with [170] our sister network, StudyNet, you get numerous advanced features, such as:

- [171 (B)] A simple résumé builder that allows you to create a perfect résumé in minutes
- An extensive list of businesses and [171 (D)] search tools for finding the right job opening
- [171 (A)] A library of videos on everything from applying to interviewing for your dream job
- Weekly matching services that pair you up with new jobs based on your skills

For more information, visit www.biznet.com.

-------------------------------------------------------------------------

商業網絡
滑鼠一點就能建立關係網絡！

商業網絡是線上網絡服務的最新發展。快速，價格合理，又容易使用，商業網絡可以讓您與業界專業人士建立良好關係，幫助您找到夢想中的工作。本公司的線上服務可以讓您追蹤就業市場的潮流，同時也能獲得您領域中企業會議的最新資訊。

與本公司姊妹網絡——研讀網合作，您可以獲得許多進階功能，例如：
- 簡便履歷建立器，讓您可以在幾分鐘內就做出一份完美的履歷表
- 龐大的企業名單與搜尋工具，尋找適當職缺
- 應有盡有的影音圖書館，主題從申請到面試理想的工作應有盡有
- 每週配對服務，依據您的技能來媒合新工作

更多資訊，請至網站 www.biznet.com 查詢

**169** How would a customer most likely use BizNet?

(A) To shop for online services
(B) To find employment at a company*
(C) To complete tax documents
(D) To advertise the services of a company

本題要問的是商業網絡（BizNet）所提供的服務屬性。由第一段中
「BizNet can connect you with industry professionals and help you
land the job of your dreams.」，可得知它提供「就業」資訊，因此答案
為 (B)。

---

**170** What is suggested about the company that developed BizNet?

(A) Its representatives can be contacted by telephone.
(B) It has a reputation for helping home businesses.
(C) It was founded by a large sales corporation.
(D) It has more than one networking website.*

第二段中提到 our sister network, StudyNet，由此可以得知 (D) 為最
適當的答案。(A)、(B)、(C) 都未曾在文章中提及。

---

**171** What is NOT mentioned as a feature of BizNet?

(A) A library of videos
(B) A résumé generator
(C) Tickets to conferences*
(D) Employment search tools

解題時，請從文章中找出與商業網絡功能（feature）有關的段落（最後
一段），對照各選項的內容，並刪除文章中提及的選項。由功能第一項
A simple résumé builder 可以確認 (B)；功能第二項 search tools for
finding the right job opening 可以確認 (D)；功能第三項 A library of
videos 可以確認 (A)，因此本題的答案為 (C)。

客戶可以怎麼運用商業網絡？
(A) 購買線上服務
(B) 找到公司的職缺
(C) 完成稅務資料
(D) 宣傳公司服務項目

字彙
employment 就業，工作

下列何者與開發商業網絡的公
司有關？
(A) 可以去電和公司代表人員
    聯繫。
(B) 在幫助家庭事業上頗具聲
    譽。
(C) 是由一間大型的銷售企業
    所創立的。
(D) 擁有不只一個網絡網站。

字彙
reputation 聲譽；名望
corporation 大公司

下列何者不是商業網絡的特
色？
(A) 影音圖書館
(B) 履歷表產生器
(C) 會議門票
(D) 職缺搜尋工具

字彙
generator 產生器

Questions 172-175 refer to the following notice.

### Lake Porticole Beach and Campground (LPBC)

[172] Lake Porticole Beach and Campground will be open this spring & summer season beginning April 10 through September 1. Please note, however, LPBC reserves the right to impose additional restrictions on campers. [173] Due to the repeated occurrence of dry weather, campers may be prohibited from having open campfires at certain times. This does not apply to the use of camping stoves and barbecues for cooking, however. When fires are permitted, campers must purchase pre-cut wood from the park. Cutting down trees will not be permitted at any time.

Lake Porticole Beach may be accessed by non-campers for day visits for a small fee. Beach goers may arrive as early as 8 A.M. and stay until 5 P.M. [174] Group tickets may be booked in advance for a discount. Additionally, the park offers guided tours of the Lake Porticole Museum, a historical estate originally owned by Sir William Marks. Tickets for the museum can be purchased at the front gate on the day of the tour.

### Payment and Reservations

• For campsite reservations, call 888-341-0867. Campsites are $65.00 per night. [175] A non-refundable deposit of $30.00 must be made at the time of reservation. This deposit goes toward the cost of your stay.

• Beach day passes for non-campers can be purchased upon arrival for $8.00 per person. Groups of more than 15 can receive a 20% discount if reservations are made in advance.

• Lake Porticole Museum tickets are available for $7.00 per person. Tours are offered three times per day at 11 A.M., 1 P.M., and 3 P.M.

波帝歌湖海灘與營地（LPBC）

波帝歌湖海灘與營地於今年春夏兩季開放時間，為自 4 月 10 日起至 9 月 1 日。但請注意，LPBC 將保留對露營者施加其他限制的權力。由於連續的乾燥氣候，露營者將禁止在特定時間內使用露天營火。以野營爐和烤肉方式烹煮食物則不在此限。一旦開放用火，露營者必須向公園購買預先砍好的木柴。任何時間都不得砍伐樹木。

非露營者可於白天造訪波帝歌湖海灘，但需酌收費用。海灘遊客可於早上八點待到下午五點。團體票可事先預訂，以享優惠。另外，公園還提供波帝歌湖博物館導覽服務，是一座原由威廉·馬克斯爵士所擁有的歷史莊園。博物館門票可於導覽當天在前門購買。

**付款與預約**

• 預約營地，請撥打 888-341-0867。營地每晚 65 元。預約時，需繳納 30 元訂金，訂金恕不退還。訂金可抵露營費用。

• 非露營者的海灘一日卷可於抵達時購買，每人八元。15 人以上的團體事先預約可享八折優惠。

• 波帝哥湖博物館門票每人七元。每天三次導覽，分別為上午 11 點、下午 1 點及下午 3 點。

---

**172** What is announced in the notice?

(A) A new policy
(B) A business's closing
(C) An increase in fees
(D) An operation schedule*

由文章的第一句「Lake Porticole Beach and Campground will be open this spring & summer season beginning April 10 through September 1.」，可以得知為春、夏季開放時間的公告，因此 (D) 為最適當的答案。

這個公告的內容是什麼？

(A) 新規定
(B) 結束營業
(C) 費用調漲
(D) 營業時間表

字彙
**policy** 規定；政策
**operation** 營業

下列何者與到訪波帝歌湖營地有關？

**(A)** 露營者在森林亂丟垃圾會被罰。

**(B)** 露營者可能無法使用營火。

**(C)** 露營者必須加入團體才能參觀博物館，。

**(D)** 露營者需另外付費才能進入海灘。

**字彙**
**indicate** 指出，表明
**fine** 罰款
**litter** 亂丟垃圾

**173** What is indicated about visiting Lake Porticole's campground?

(A) Campers can be fined for littering in the forest.

(B) Campers might not be able to have campfires. *

(C) To see the museum, campers must be part of a group.

(D) To access the beach, campers need to pay another fee.

本題的解題關鍵為「露營地使用注意事項」。第一段中表示營地管理處對露營者增加了額外的規定，並說明在特定期間內禁止使用營火（Due to the repeated occurrence of dry weather, campers may be prohibited from having open campfires at certain times. ），因此答案為 (B)。

下列何者與波帝歌湖非露營服務有關？

**(A)** 可預約博物館門票。

**(B)** 海灘遊客在週末時可留下過夜。

**(C)** 海灘遊客可免費使用陽傘。

**(D)** 團體於造訪海灘時可享有折扣。

**字彙**
**overnight** 整夜，一晚上

**174** What is mentioned about the Lake Porticole's non-camping services?

(A) Museum tickets can be reserved.

(B) Beach visitors can stay overnight on weekends.

(C) Parasols are offered to beach visitors free of charge.

(D) Groups can get a discount when visiting the beach. *

針對「非露營遊客」的服務，在第二段的「Group tickets may be booked in advance for a discount.」，表示團體票可事先預訂，以享優惠，因此答案應為 (D)。

取消營區預約會發生什麼事？

**(A)** 損失訂金。

**(B)** 款項可退還。

**(C)** 會收到帳單。

**(D)** 會員資格會被降級。

**字彙**
**refund** 退還，退（款）
**bill** 帳單

**175** What happens when a campsite reservation is canceled?

(A) A reservation fee is lost. *

(B) A payment is refunded.

(C) A bill will be sent.

(D) A membership will be downgraded.

閱讀文章時，請特別留意「營地預約事項」。在 Payment and Reservations 的第一項中提到「訂金恕不退還（A non-refundable deposit of $30.00 must be made at the time of reservation.）」，因此 (A) 為最適當的答案。

**Questions 176-180 refer to following letter and e-mail.**

[180] 10 March

Ms. Kelly Norstram
Simpson Publishing
Human Resources Department
55 Center St.
Sydney, Australia

Dear Ms. Norstram,

I would like to take this opportunity to submit my application for the editorial director position at Simpson Publishing in its new Sydney office. [176] As you can see from my enclosed résumé, I have extensive experience in the editorial field, including five years as head editor at *Lush Magazine* and three years as an editorial assistant at the *Sydney Times* newspaper.

[176] Aside from this experience, I also have a Bachelor's degree in Journalism and a Master's degree in Publishing Studies. Furthermore, I believe I would add a new dimension to the editorial director position given that I am also a published author of seven children's books. I believe that my unique combination of experience will contribute greatly to the company.

Thank you very much for your time. I look forward to speaking with you.

Sincerely,

Adrian Perdu

-------------------------------------

3 月 10 日

凱莉‧諾斯翠女士
辛普森出版社
人力資源部
澳洲雪梨中心街 55 號

親愛的諾斯翠女士，

我想利用這個機會遞上我的求職函，以應徵辛普森出版社於雪梨新辦公室的編輯主任一職。正如您可從我所附上的履歷表看到的，我在編輯領域有相當豐富的經驗，包括五年在《樂序雜誌》擔任主編以及在《雪梨時代》報紙擔任三年的編輯助理。

除了這些經驗外，我還擁有新聞學士學位及出版研究碩士學位。此外，有鑑於我也是出版過七本童書的作家，我相信自己可以為主編一職增添新亮點。我相信我個人獨特的經歷將帶給公司極大的貢獻。

非常感謝您撥冗。期待能與您會談。

艾德利安‧柏杜 敬上

字彙

**propose** 提出
**commend** 讚揚，稱讚
**publication** 出版
**approach** 臨近，即將到來
**overall** 整體上的
**input** 投入
**guidance** 指引，引導
**collective** 共同的
**fruition** 實現，完成
**proofreader** 校對人員
**fall behind** 落後
**release** 出版，發行
**launch** 推出；發布
**biography**
個人簡介；個人傳記
**suffice** 足夠

---

**To:** Simpson Publishing Editorial Staff
**From:** Adrian Perdu
[180] **Date:** April 30
**Subject:** [178] Some Reminders

Editorial Staff Members,

[180] It has been nearly a year since we first proposed our new line of educational children's books. I'd like to commend you all on your hard work on this series. With our publication date fast approaching, [178] I'd just like to remind everyone of a few things.

First, please ensure you communicate with designers weekly regarding the overall design of our books. It is important that you give them your input and guidance in bringing our collective vision to fruition.

Second, some freelance proofreaders have fallen behind on their deadlines. Please make sure you contact them regularly and if need be, hire additional freelancers to complete the work.

Finally, [179] as the release of our series will include a website launch, I'd like everyone to submit a biography for the "about us" section. A simple biography of about 100 words will suffice.

Thank you all for your continued hard work, and I look forward to launch day!

Adrian

------------------------------------------------------------

**收件者：**辛普森出版社編輯同仁
**寄件者：**艾德利安‧柏杜
**日期：**4 月 30 日
**主旨：**提醒事項

編輯同仁：

從我們第一次提出兒童教育新系列書籍的企劃至今將近一年了。我要稱許大家在這一系列上的辛苦付出。隨著出版時間的逼近，我想要提醒大家幾件事。

首先，請務必每週和設計師討論書本的整體設計。在實現大家共同的願景中，讓設計師看到各位的投入，並提供指引是很重要的。

再者，部分自由校對人員的進度已經落後。請確實定期與他們保持聯繫，必要的話，增聘更多自由校對人員來完成工作。

最後，套書出版時將包括網站的發行。在「關於我們」的部分，希望大家都能繳交一份小篇的自我介紹。大約 100 字的簡單小傳就夠了。

感謝大家一直以來的努力，期待發行那一天的到來！

艾德利安

**176** What is one purpose of the letter?

(A) To inquire about a starting salary
(B) To list some professional qualifications*
(C) To provide an employment reference
(D) To ask about the location of a job

在信件（第一篇）的第一段和第二段中，柏杜先生在求職信中介紹了自己的學經歷，因此 (B) 為最適當的答案。

這封信的目的是什麼？
(A) 詢問起薪
(B) 列出一些專業能力
(C) 提供就業推薦函
(D) 詢問工作地點

字彙
**salary** 薪水，薪資
**qualification** 資格條件，能力

**177** In the letter, the word "dimension" in paragraph 2, line 2, is closest in meaning to

(A) demand
(B) precedent
(C) matter
(D) characteristic*

本句表達的意思為在編輯主任這個職位上，柏杜先生廣泛的經驗可以提供新的「層次，特點」，因此意思最為相似的單字為 characteristic，答案為 (D)。

在信件中，第二段、第二行的「dimension」與下列哪一個意思最接近？
(A) 要求
(B) 前例
(C) 問題
(D) 特點

字彙
**demand** 要求，需求
**precedent** 先例，前例
**matter** 問題
**characteristic** 特點

**178** Why did Mr. Perdu write the e-mail?

(A) To praise workers for getting tasks done
(B) To stress the importance of some duties*
(C) To motivate employees to take on extra work
(D) To inform new hires of special procedures

電郵（第二篇）的標題為 Some Reminders，由此可以得知郵件內容應和「提醒事項」有關。而主旨句（I'd just like to remind everyone of a few things）和後方三段的內容，為各類業務相關的要求，因此 (B) 為最適當的答案。(A) 選項內容雖然出現在第一段第二句，但卻不是柏杜先生寫這封電郵的主要目的，故 (A) 不能選。

柏杜先生為什麼會寫這封電子郵件？
(A) 稱讚員工完成工作
(B) 強調一些工作的重要性
(C) 激勵員工接受額外的工作
(D) 告知新進員工特別程序

字彙
**praise** 稱讚
**stress** 強調
**motivate** 激勵

ACTUAL TEST 5

PART 7

中譯＋解析

下列何者與辛普森出版社有關？

(A) 主要出版電子書。
(B) 在七個國家聘用編輯。
(C) 將停止出版部分書籍。
(D) 將於網站上介紹員工。

primarily 主要地
employ 聘雇
discontinue 停止，中斷

下列何者與柏杜先生有關？

(A) 之前擔任圖書設計師。
(B) 一年前受僱於辛普森出版社。
(C) 因為工作機會搬到雪梨。
(D) 他不再寫童書。

previously 以前，之前

**179** What is stated about Simpson Publishing?

(A) It publishes primarily e-books.
(B) It employs editors in seven countries.
(C) It will discontinue some publications.
(D) It will introduce its staff on its website.*

電郵（第二篇）寄送的對象為辛普森出版社的員工們，在第四段中提到「新的網站」，並要求每位員工繳交自我介紹（as the release of our series will include a website launch, I'd like everyone to submit a biography for the "about us" section），因此答案為 (D)。

**180** What is suggested about Mr. Perdu?

(A) He previously worked as a book designer.
(B) He was hired by Simpson Publishing one year ago.*
(C) He moved to the US for a job opportunity.
(D) He no longer writes books for children.

信件（第一篇）為柏杜先生應徵辛普森出版社分社編輯主管職缺的內容，該封郵件的日期為 3 月 10 日；而電郵（第二篇）為柏杜先生向辛普森出版社編輯部門下達指令的內容，寄出時間為 4 月 30。另外，在第二篇第一段中的「It has been nearly a year since we first proposed our new line of educational children's books.」，由此可以得知柏杜先生進公司後進行新業務至今，已經過了將近一年的時間，因此答案應為 (B)。

**Questions 181-185 refer to the following e-mail and business plan.**

**To:** Wanda Willis <willis@utcbankandloans.com>
**From:** Jeffrey Thomas <jthomas@mailmail.com>
**Date:** March 12
**Re:** Business Plan
[183] **Attachment:** Revised Plan

Dear Ms. Willis,

Thank you so much for your quick reply. I am very happy you are able to help me secure financial backing for my new business venture. [181] I have looked over all the feedback you sent and edited my business plan accordingly. **As you advised,** [183] I have included a section that details our potential customers and attached the revised version.

I think this is all I need to complete the application package for my business loan. However, if there's anything else I need to fill out, please contact me.

I look forward to hearing from you.

Sincerely,

Jeffrey Thomas

-------------------------------------------------------------------

收件者：汪達·威利斯 <willis@utcbankandloans.com>
寄件者：傑佛瑞·湯瑪斯 <jthomas@mailmail.com>
日期：3 月 12 日
回覆：經營企劃書
附件：修訂版企劃書

親愛的威利斯女士，

感謝您這麼快就回覆。很高興您能幫我取得新事業的資金支持。我已經看過您寄給我的所有回饋意見，也依其編寫我的經營企劃書。如您所建議的，我已經在企劃書內加上詳述潛在客戶的部分，隨信附上修改後的版本。

我想這是申請企業貸款所需完成的全部文件。但若還有其他需要填寫的文件，再請您與我聯繫。

期待您的消息。

傑佛瑞·湯瑪斯 敬上

字彙
**revised** 經過修訂的
**secure** 獲得
**financial** 財務的
**accordingly** 照著，相應地
**potential** 潛在的
**attach** 附加，附上
**loan** 貸款

**Revised Business Plan: The Brim**

### Section 1. Purpose

Downtown Portside has become a bustling business district, filled with numerous office buildings, banks, and department stores. My business, The Brim, will be located near the prestigious courthouse, a busy area of the downtown core. [184] We hope to offer a wide variety of international gourmet coffees at affordable prices, while also providing a relaxing atmosphere to enjoy our gourmet lunch items.

### [183] Section 2. Target Market

The Brim will serve business professionals working downtown. Because there are so many law offices and banks within walking distance, our customers are likely to visit our coffee house in the mornings, during break times, and at lunch. Furthermore, weekend customers will consist of shoppers who are visiting the nearby Portside Department Store.

### Section 3. Timeline

The Brim is scheduled to open on June 1. We expect the following preparations to be completed by:

| | |
|---|---|
| **March 28** | Sign the lease and apply for a business permit |
| **April 10** | Renovate the dining area and upgrade the kitchen |
| **April 20** | Hire staff and complete employee training |
| **May 15** | Finalize the menu, order inventory, and plan the grand opening |

### Section 4. Marketing Plan

[185] Please see the attached spread sheet for our detailed marketing plans prior to opening and after.

-------------------------------------------------

修訂後的經營企劃書：布理恩咖啡

**第一部份：目的**
市中心港口區已經成為活躍的商業區，到處都有許多辦公大樓、銀行和百貨公司。本店——布理恩咖啡鄰近著名法院，為市中心繁忙核心地帶。希望以合理價格提供各種國際精品咖啡，同時也提供一個可以享受美味午餐的輕鬆氛圍。

**第二部分：目標市場**
布理恩咖啡將為在市中心上班的商業專業人士提供服務。由於在步行距離內就有多家法律事務所與銀行，我們的顧客可能在早上、休息時間及午餐時到咖啡店來。另外，週末的顧客也包含到附近港區百貨公司的購物者。

**第三部分：時間表**
布理恩咖啡預定於 6 月 1 日開幕。希望以下前置作業能於這些日期前完成：

3 月 28 日　　簽訂租約與申請商業許可證
4 月 10 日　　整修用餐區與提升廚房設備
4 月 20 日　　聘用員工並完成員工訓練
5 月 15 日　　確定菜單、預訂存貨以及規劃開幕

**第四部分：行銷計畫**
開幕前與開幕後的詳細行銷計畫，請見附件試算表。

---

**181** What is the purpose of the e-mail?

(A) To review the guidelines of a permit
(B) To send feedback about some financial data
(C) To request advice on writing a business plan
(D) To respond to a requested revision*

由郵件（第一篇）第一段的「I have looked over all the feedback you sent and edited my business plan accordingly.」，可以得知 (D) 為最適當的答案。詢問文章目的的題型，在文章的前半部大多可以確認文章的目的。

這封電子郵件的目的是什麼？

(A) 審閱許可證的指導方針
(B) 送出有關財務資料的回饋意見
(C) 要求撰寫商業計畫的建議
(D) 回覆對方所要求的修訂版

字彙
**revision** 修正，修改

**182** In the e-mail, the word "secure" in paragraph 1, line 1, is closest in meaning to

(A) guard
(B) obtain*
(C) save
(D) fasten

請閱讀單字所在句子的內容，當中湯瑪斯先生表示感謝對方幫助自己「取得」新事業的資金支持，因此選項中可以替換的動詞為 obtain，故 (B) 正確。

在電子郵件中，第一段、第一行的「secure」與下列哪一個意思最接近？

(A) 護衛
(B) 取得
(C) 節省
(D) 繫牢

字彙
**guard** 護衛，看守
**obtain** 取得，獲得
**fasten** 繫牢，扣緊

經營企劃書新增了哪一個部分？

(A) 第一部分
(B) 第二部分
(C) 第三部分
(D) 第四部分

**183** What section of the business plan was added?

(A) Section 1
(B) Section 2*
(C) Section 3
(D) Section 4

湯瑪斯先生所撰寫的第一封電郵（第一篇）中，請特別留意「額外追加的內容」。先看到郵件（第一篇）中表示附件為「修訂版企劃書」，且在第一段的「I have included a section that details our potential customers and attached the revised version.」，湯瑪斯先生提到了他在修訂企劃書內加上「潛在客戶」有關的內容。再對照企劃書（第二篇）後，可以確認與客戶相關的內容在 Section 2. Target Market，故 (B) 正確。

湯瑪斯先生計劃要做什麼生意？

(A) 貸款公司
(B) 百貨公司
(C) 法律事務所
(D) 咖啡店

**184** What type of business does Mr. Thomas plan to start?

(A) A loan company
(B) A department store
(C) A law office
(D) A gourmet café*

本題要詢問的是湯瑪斯先生「創業的性質」，請把閱讀重點擺在商業企劃書（第二篇）上。由第二篇第一段的「We hope to offer a wide variety of international gourmet coffees at affordable prices, while also providing a relaxing atmosphere to enjoy our gourmet lunch items.」，可以得知答案為 (D)。gourmet 的意思為「美食家」，而當它接在食物或酒類前方時，則表示「優質的」。

根據經營企劃書，何種資料被另外提交？

(A) 預期獲利的詳細估算表
(B) 求職推薦人的聯絡資訊
(C) 公司的宣傳方式
(D) 整修公司的介紹

**185** According to the business plan, what information was submitted separately?

(A) A detailed estimate of expected profits
(B) Contact information for employment references
(C) A list of ways the business will advertise*
(D) Recommendations for renovation companies

請從商業計劃書（第二篇）中找出與「另外繳交的資料」有關的內容。最後一段中湯瑪斯先生提到請對方參考附件試算表（excel 檔案），為開幕前後的行銷企劃（Please see the attached spread sheet for our detailed marketing plans prior to opening and after.），因此答案為 (C)。

字彙

**separately** 各自地；分開地
**estimate** 估算，估價
**profit** 利潤，獲利
**recommendation** 介紹，推薦

http://www.partysuppliers.com

| PRODUCT GALLERY | HOME | PARTY TIPS | ORDER FORM | CONTACT US |

**Party Suppliers Online**

Welcome to our online shopping site. Have a look at our product gallery for over 1000 different party products. [186] Be sure to check out our party decorating tips in order to make your party a hit!

**Latest Promotional Deals:**

February through March: Buy One, Get One Half Off (applies to all in stock items)

[187] April through August: Free Delivery For Orders Over $30

--------------------------------------------------------------------------------

http://www.partysuppliers.com

| 產品陳列館 | 首頁 | 辦派對訣竅 | 訂購表 | 聯絡我們 |

**派對商品供應網**

歡迎來到本公司線上購物網站。瞧瞧我們的產品陳列館有 1,000 多種不同的派對產品。為了讓您的派對大受歡迎，一定要看看本公司的派對布置訣竅！

**最新促銷方案：**

2 月至 3 月：購買一件，即享第二件半價優惠（適用於所有現貨商品）

4 月至 8 月：訂購滿 30 元可享免運

---

**From:** Mathew Sparks [msparks@stantonautomotive.com]
**To:** June Baxtor [juneb@stantonautomotive.com]
[187] **Date:** April 27
**Subject:** Grand Opening Update

Hi June,

I've compared Party Suppliers Online with Cape Bernard Party Mart and chosen the former to get everything we need for the grand opening party on the 4th. They seem to provide a lot of great tips for setting up their products, so it shouldn't be much work to make the showroom look great.

I think we should order a custom banner for the showroom along with streamers and balloons. [189] We can also get a larger banner made, which will hang in front of the door outside.

If you agree with me, I'd like to get our order in quickly. The workspace is still pretty messy, but [188] the painters should finish up soon, which will give us just enough time to set up before the big day.

Let me know what you think when you get a chance.

Mathew

**字彙**
**order form** 訂購單
**supplier** 供應商，供貨商
**check out** 看看
**decorate** 佈置，裝飾
**hit** 非常受歡迎的人（事）
**promotional**
促銷的；廣告宣傳的
**deal** 交易
**in stock** 有現貨或存貨

**字彙**
**compare A with B**
將 A 與 B 比較
**the former** 前者
**streamer**（裝飾的）飾帶
**hang** 懸掛，吊
**messy** 凌亂的，雜亂的

寄件者：馬修・史帕克斯 <msparks@stantonautomotive.com>
收件者：裘恩・貝司特 <juneb@stantonautomotive.com>
日期：4 月 27 日
主旨：更新開幕活動

嗨，裘恩：

我比較了派對商品供應網與開普伯納派對商場兩家店，並選擇了前者，以添購我們在四號開幕派對當天所需要的東西。看起來他們提供了許多擺設自家產品的好方法，這樣應該不用花太多功夫就能讓展示間看起來很棒。

我想我們應該為展示間訂購客製旗幟，以及飾帶與氣球。我們還可以做一個掛在門前的大型旗幟。

若你也同意的話，我想要盡快下訂。工作區域還是一團亂，但是油漆工應該很快就可以完工，這讓我們在大日子來臨前，還有足夠的時間可以布置。

有空時，告訴我你的看法。

馬修

**Order Number:** 112233265
**Contact Info:** Mathew Sparks (444) 232-0916
**Delivery To:** Stanton Automotive Dealership, 14 Brooks Lane, Atlantic City
[187] **Delivery Window:** 01-02 May, 09:00-13:00

| Quantity | Product Code | Description |
|---|---|---|
| 1 | YZ0933 | Custom Banner (3 feet long) |
| 1 | YZ0955 | [189] Custom Banner (6 feet long) |
| 12 | GH3345 | Rainbow Balloons 12 per pack |
| 2 | BB3200 | Streamers (white) |
| | | [187] Total:  $104.50 |

**Note:** [190] All our custom banners are printed at our manufacturing headquarters in Baltimore. Those items will be shipped into Atlantic City from Baltimore instead of our Port Edward store, which means you will have two separate shipments. Should you have any questions, do not hesitate to call us immediately.

----------------------------------------

訂單編號：112233265

聯絡資訊：馬修‧史帕克斯 (444) 232-0916

寄送地址：史丹頓汽車經銷商，大西洋城布魯克斯巷 14 號

配送時段：5 月 1 日至 2 日，上午 9 點至下午 1 點

| 數量 | 產品編號 | 產品敘述 |
|------|----------|----------|
| 1 | YZ0933 | 訂製旗幟（3 呎長） |
| 1 | YZ0955 | 訂製旗幟（6 呎長） |
| 12 | GH3345 | 彩虹氣球每組 12 個 |
| 2 | BB2300 | 飾帶（白色） |
| | | 總計：104.50 元 |

備註：所有訂製旗幟皆於巴爾的摩生產總部印製。這些商品將直接從巴爾的摩寄送至大西洋城，而不是從艾德華港店寄出，這表示您將收到兩件不同的包裹。若有任何疑問，歡迎立即與我們聯絡。

---

**186** What is indicated about Party Suppliers Online?

(A) It provides complimentary product samples.

(B) It offers decorating advice to customers.*

(C) It recently opened up another store.

(D) It will expand its product line next year.

本題的關鍵字為 Party Suppliers Online，在他們網頁（第一篇）的第一段中「Be sure to check out our party decorating tips in order to make your party a hit！」，可以得知該網站為顧客提供布置訣竅，故答案為 (B)。

下列何者與派對商品供應網有關？

(A) 提供免費的產品樣本。

(B) 提供顧客布置建議。

(C) 最近開了另一間分店。

(D) 明年將擴展產品線。

字彙
complimentary 免費的
expand 擴大，增加

---

**187** What is probably true about Stanton Automotive Dealership's order?

(A) It will be delivered for free.*

(B) It includes foreign products.

(C) It includes half-price items.

(D) It will be refunded in May.

由第三篇的訂購明細，可以得知總金額為美金 104.50 元，另外由第二篇和第三篇的內容，可以得知訂購與配送的時間約在四月底至五月初之間。而派對商品供應網（第一篇）中的最後一段 April through August: Free Delivery For Orders Over $30，綜合以上內容，答案應為 (A)。

關於史丹頓汽車經銷商的訂單，下列何者為真？

(A) 將免費寄送。

(B) 包含外國商品。

(C) 包含半價商品。

(D) 五月將可退費。

字彙
refund 退款，退費

為何史帕克斯先生想要盡快
安排寄送？

(A) 需要時間購買更多東西。
(B) 想要利用促銷優惠的機會。
(C) 需要更多人手來幫忙清理。
(D) 想要有足夠的時間布置。

字彙
take advantage of 利用
promotion 促銷（活動）

**188** Why does Mr. Sparks probably prefer to schedule a delivery quickly?

(A) He needs time to purchase more items.
(B) He wants to take advantage of a promotion.
(C) He needs some workers to help clean up.
(D) He wants to have enough time to set up.*

史帕克斯先生所撰寫的電郵（第二篇）中，在第三段他表示想要盡快下單，因為油漆工快要完成粉刷作業，希望能有足夠的時間進行布置（the painters should finish up soon, which will give us just enough time to set up before the big day），因此答案應為 (D)。

---

史丹頓汽車經銷商大門外可
能擺放哪種產品？

(A) 3呎長的訂製旗幟
(B) 6呎長的訂製旗幟
(C) 彩虹氣球
(D) 飾帶

**189** What product will most likely be placed outside Stanton Automotive Dealership?

(A) Custom Banner 3ft
(B) Custom Banner 6ft*
(C) Rainbow Balloons
(D) Streamers

電郵（第二篇）的第二段中史帕克斯先生寫道：「We can also get a larger banner made, which will hang in front of the door outside.」，由此可以得知他將在戶外擺放更大的旗幟。而在表格（第三篇）中，較大尺寸的旗幟為 Custom Banner (6 feet long)，因此可以確認答案為 (B)。

---

根據表格內容，氣球很可能從
哪裡寄送出去？

(A) 巴爾的摩
(B) 大西洋城
(C) 開普伯納
(D) 艾德華港

**190** According to the form, where most likely will the balloons be shipped from?

(A) Baltimore
(B) Atlantic City
(C) Cape Bernard
(D) Port Edward*

請特別留意「汽球出貨地點」，並閱讀訂單（第三篇）的內容。在最後一段的備註（Note）中提到貨物配送會分成兩批，旗幟會由生產總部巴爾的摩（Baltimore）出貨，其餘品項則由艾德華港店（Port Edward）出貨（Those items ( = custom banners) will be shipped into Atlantic City from Baltimore instead of our Port Edward store, which means you will have two separate shipments.）。題目問的是氣球並非旗幟，因此會由艾德華港店出貨，(D) 為最適當的答案。

**Questions 191-195 refer to the following e-mail, menu and comment card.**

**From:** Jimmy Pertelli <jpertelli@jimmysitalianrestaurant.com>
**To:** Sue Hamilton <suehamilton@jimmysitalianrestaurant.com>
**Date:** Monday, January 10
**Subject:** Menu tasting event

Hello Sue,

It's hard to believe we're reopening in less than a month. 191 Since we've yet to finalize a menu, let's take some time to think about the best dishes for Jimmy's Italian Restaurant. I think it would be a good idea to host a private tasting event for our friends and families next week on Saturday.

I have some ideas about what we could serve at the tasting. What about making a hearty deep-dish vegetarian pizza? This would really highlight our new vegetarian menu options. 193 I think our baked lobster platter would be another great entrée choice. 195 I'd also love to serve some of our new dessert options, but that all depends on whether or not construction on the pastry station is completed. In the event that it's not, how about serving some of our new organic ice cream flavors topped with your amazing chocolate sauce? I will leave it all up to you, though. As head chef, you have complete freedom.

Finally, I'd love to offer our guests an ice-cream making demonstration after the tasting. Let me know if you think that would be possible.

Thanks,

Jimmy

----------------------------------------------------------------------

寄件者：吉米‧普特利 <jpertelli@jimmysitalianrestaurant.com>
收件者：蘇‧漢灡頓 <suehamilton@jimmysialiantrestaurant.com>
日期：1 月 10 日星期日
主旨：菜單測試活動

嗨，蘇，

很難相信離重新營業已經不到一個月了。既然我們還沒敲定最終菜單，就讓我們花點時間來為吉米義大利餐廳想些最棒的餐點吧。我覺得下週六舉辦一場專屬親朋好友的非公開試菜活動，會是個不錯的主意。

對於試菜會上可以提供哪些餐點，我有一些構想。來做一道豐盛的深盤素食披薩如何？這真的可以突顯我們新的素食菜單選擇。我認為烤龍蝦拼盤是另一道絕佳的主菜。我也想要提供一些新的甜點，但這全得取決於糕點區是否已經完工。如果還沒有的話，是不是就提供一些新口味的有機冰淇淋，再淋上你迷人的巧克力醬？不過，這讓你決定。身為主廚，你有絕對的自主權。

最後，試菜完後，我想要展示冰淇淋製作過程給賓客們看。告訴我你覺得這個想法是否可行。

謝謝
吉米

**字彙**
**hearty** 豐盛的，份量大的
**deep-dish** 用深盤烘烤的
**vegetarian** 素食的
**option** 選擇
**lobster** 龍蝦
**platter** 大淺盤
**entrée** 主菜
**construction** 建造
**pastry** 糕點，甜點
**in the event that . . .**
如果，萬一
**organic** 有機的
**flavor** 味道

479

## Jimmy's Italian Restaurant Tasting Menu
## Saturday, January 15

Caprese Salad with mozzarella cheese and fresh basil
Coconut Shrimp
Baked Garlic Bread
Vegetarian Pasta with tomato sauce
[193] Baked Lobster Platter smothered in melted butter
Rib eye Fire-Grilled Steak served with roasted potatoes
[195] Jimmy's Famous Puff Pastries

-----------------------------------------------------------------

吉米義大利餐廳試菜菜單
1月15日星期六

卡布里沙拉佐莫扎瑞拉起司與新鮮巴西里
椰汁蝦
烤大蒜麵包
紅醬素食義大利麵
奶油悶烤龍蝦拼盤
肋眼火烤牛排佐烤馬鈴薯
吉米著名泡芙甜點

## Tasting Comment Card

**Name:** Fran Humphrey

**Please comment on your tasting experience at Jimmy's Italian Restaurant.**

I enjoyed the appetizers very much. The salad, however, had too much balsamic dressing for my taste. The vegetarian pasta dish was quite good, but I found the noodles to be a bit overcooked. [194] The baked lobster, on the other hand, was the best I've ever tasted. I found the steak to be a bit rare, but the potatoes were seasoned very nicely. The dessert was perhaps too sweet for me, but I thought the pastry was cooked to perfection. I also enjoyed the ice cream making demonstration, though I wish we could've tasted some of the flavors.

-----------------------------------------------------------------

試菜意見卡

姓名：法蘭·漢普瑞

請針對您在吉米義大利餐廳的試菜經驗提供意見。

我非常喜歡開胃菜。但是，對我來說，沙拉淋了太多的義大利老醋醬。素食義大利麵相當不錯，但是我覺得麵條有點煮過頭了。另一方面，烤龍蝦是我吃過最好吃的。我覺得牛排有點生，但是馬鈴薯調味調得非常好。甜點對我來說可能太甜了點，但是糕點烘焙得很完美。我也喜歡冰淇淋製作示範，但我希望可以吃到當中的一些口味。

**191** What is the purpose of the menu tasting?

(A) To select dishes for a new menu*
(B) To prepare for a restaurant inspection
(C) To audition new cooking staff
(D) To decide who will be head chef

電郵（第一篇）的第一段中，普特利先生表示需要一些時間想出最佳的菜單（Since we've yet to finalize a menu, let's take some time to think about the best dishes for Jimmy's Italian Restaurant.），並建議邀請朋友和家人前來參加試菜活動，藉此定案新菜單，因此 (A) 為最適當的答案。

菜單測試的目的是什麼？
(A) 挑選新菜單的餐點
(B) 為餐廳查驗做準備
(C) 測試新廚師
(D) 決定誰是主廚

字彙
**select** 挑選，選擇
**inspection** 查驗，檢查
**audition**
對……進行面試；使測試
**head chef** 主廚

**192** In the e-mail, the word "hearty" in paragraph 2, line 1, is closest in meaning to

(A) sincere
(B) aromatic
(C) satisfying*
(D) original

本句的文意為普特利先生建議準備「豐盛的披薩」，而選項 (C) satisfying，表「使人滿足的、滿意的」，為選項當中意思最為接近的單字。

在電子郵件中，第二段、第一行的「**hearty**」與下列哪一個意思最接近？
(A) 誠摯的
(B) 芳香的
(C) 滿足的
(D) 原始的

字彙
**sincere** 誠摯的
**aromatic** 芳香的，有香氣的
**satisfying**
使人滿足的，令人滿意的
**original** 原先的

**193** What is true about the tasting menu?

(A) It showcases only old menu items.
(B) It lists several new ice cream flavors.
(C) It is only available to customers on weekends.
(D) It includes an entrée suggested by Mr. Pertelli.*

本題要綜合分析試菜菜單（第二篇）和電郵（第一篇）中的建議菜單，才能進行解題。普特利先生在第一篇的第二段寫道：「I think our baked lobster platter would be another great entrée choice.」，再由第二篇試菜單中的 Baked Lobster Platter，可以確認普特利先生的建議被納入試菜單中，故答案為 (D)。

下列何者與試菜單有關？
(A) 只展現舊菜單上的餐點。
(B) 列出幾個冰淇淋新口味。
(C) 只在週末供應給顧客。
(D) 包含了普特利先生建議的主菜。

字彙
**showcase** 展示，展現

漢普瑞女士最喜歡的餐點是哪一道？

(A) 沙拉
(B) 義大利麵
(C) 龍蝦
(D) 牛排

**194** Which menu item was most likely Ms. Humphrey's favorite?

(A) The salad
(B) The pasta
(C) The lobster*
(D) The steak

漢普瑞女士所寫的意見卡片（第三篇）中，在中間部分説道：「The baked lobster, on the other hand, was the best I've ever tasted.」，表示烤龍蝦是她吃過最棒的餐點，故答案為 (C)。

---

關於糕點區，文中暗指的是？

(A) 對廚房來說太大了。
(B) 搬到另一個位置。
(C) 在整修過程中損壞了。
(D) 準時完工了。

**字彙**
**damage (v.)** 損壞
**renovation** 整修，翻修

**195** What is suggested about the pastry station?

(A) It was too large for the kitchen.
(B) It was moved to another location.
(C) It was damaged in a renovation.
(D) It was completed on time.*

閱讀時，請特別留意關鍵字 pastry station。郵件（第一篇）的第二段中提到「I'd also love to serve some of our new dessert options, but that all depends on whether or not construction on the pastry station is completed.」，表示提供糕點與否取決於糕點區是否完工。而試菜單（第二篇）中的餐後甜點為 Jimmy's Famous Puff Pastries，可推測糕點區當時已經施工完畢，因此答案為 (D)。

**Questions 196-200 refer to the following advertisement, e-mail, and text message.**

**Hartford Opera House
45 Bellview Street
New York City**

www.hartfordoperahouse.com

The Hartford Opera House is pleased to announce an exciting schedule of events that will take place this summer. [196] We will be featuring everything from concerts to stage plays, so we are sure to have something for you. Tickets will be available on our website for each event, and seasonal passes may be purchased for a lump sum. [200] Seasonal pass holders will be able to attend as many events as they wish and bring up to three guests at a time free of charge.

## Schedule of Events:

June 23 — The Miller Brothers Classical Ensemble
July 3 — Stand-Up Comedy by Alan Brewer
[198] July 4 — *Into the Jungle*, an award-winning musical featuring songs by Catrina Belford
July 10 — *Women of Egypt*, a stage play directed by Tommy Wilson
For a complete summer schedule, please visit www.hartfordoperahouse.com.

--------------------------------------------------------------------------------

哈特佛德歌劇院
紐約市貝爾韋街 45 號
www.hartfordoperahouse.com

哈特佛德歌劇院很高興宣布，今年夏天本院將有精彩的活動時程表。我們將提供從演唱會到舞台劇的各項演出，所以我們相信一定有適合您的活動。所有活動門票皆可於本院網站購買，也可一次購買季票。持有季票者能依自己喜好參加各項活動，還可免費攜伴，每場以三位為限。

活動節目表：
6 月 23 日──米勒兄弟古典樂團
7 月 3 日──亞倫·布魯爾的單人喜劇脫口秀
7 月 4 日──《走入叢林》，由卡崔娜·貝爾芙德所寫的得獎音樂劇
7 月 10 日──《埃及女人》，由湯米·威爾森所執導的舞台劇

完整夏季節目表，請上 www.hartfordoperahouse.com 查詢。

字彙
**term** 條件；條款
**merger** 合併
**excursion** 遊覽，遠足
**entertainment** 娛樂活動

**To:** Lila Sampson
**From:** Roderick Kelly
**Cc:** June Varek
**Subject:** Your Trip to Meadworth Paper and Packaging
**Date:** June 2

Dear Ms. Sampson,

We at Meadworth Paper and Packaging are looking forward to your visit to our company headquarters from July 2 to [198] July 4. [197] We are very pleased that your company has agreed to discuss the terms of a possible merger between our two businesses.

In addition to providing you with a tour of our factory and offices, we have an exciting schedule planned for you, which will include a lunch with our CEO, a trip to Westflower Golf Club, and an excursion at the Harbor Yacht Club. [198] We have also scheduled an evening at our local opera house for some live entertainment on your last night. We hope you will enjoy your trip, and if you need anything else, please let me know.

Sincerely

Roderick Kelly
Meadworth Paper and Packaging

--------------------------------------------------------------

收件者：里拉‧山普森
寄件者：羅德里克‧凱利
副本：瓊恩‧凡瑞克
主旨：密德華斯紙業與包裝公司之行
日期：6月2日

親愛的山普森女士，

密德華斯紙業與包裝公司期待您於7月2日至7月4日至本公司總部參觀。很高興貴公司同意討論我們兩家企業可能合併的條件。

除了提供工廠和辦公室導覽外，我們還為您規劃了一個很棒的行程，包括與本公司執行長共進午餐、西花高爾夫球俱樂部之旅以及港口遊艇俱樂部之行。我們也在您行程的最後一晚，安排了本地歌劇院現場演出的娛樂活動。希望您會喜歡這趟旅程，若有任何需要，請告訴我。

密德華斯紙業與包裝公司
羅德利克‧凱利 敬上

字彙
**forecast** 預測，預報
**switch** 調換，交換

From: Varek

To: Kelly

The weather forecast predicts rain during our trip to the golf club with Ms. Sampson next week. [199] I think it would be best if you switched the golf club visit with the opera house event. This will change the opera house event we'll attend, but there's no need to buy new tickets. [200] I'm allowed to bring a few guests free of charge.

寄件者：凡瑞克
收件者：凱利

下週我們與山普森女士進行高爾夫球俱樂部之行時，天氣預報預測會下雨。我想若能對調高爾夫球俱樂部參訪行程與歌劇院活動會比較好。這會更動到我們參加的歌劇院活動，但不需重新購票。我可以免費攜帶數位賓客入場。

**196** What is suggested about the Hartford Opera House?

(A) It is merging with another company.
(B) It gives away free seasonal passes.
(C) It is located next to a golf club.
(D) It schedules a variety of events.*

本題的關鍵字為 the Hartford Opera House，由該劇院廣告中的第一段「We will be featuring everything from concerts to stage plays, so we are sure to have something for you.」，可以得知答案為 (D)。

下列何者與哈特佛德歌劇院有關？
(A) 要和另一間公司合併。
(B) 贈送免費季票。
(C) 位於高爾夫球俱樂部旁。
(D) 安排各式各樣的活動。

字彙
**merge with . . .** 與……合併

**197** What is Ms. Sampson scheduled to do during her visit?

(A) Discuss a new deal*
(B) Review a contract
(C) Consult a lawyer
(D) Present a product

請特別留意山普森女士「拜訪的目的」，並閱讀收件人為山普森女士的郵件（第二篇）。第一段中凱利先生提到感謝山普森女士願意討論關於合併的交易（We are very pleased that your company has agreed to discuss the terms of a possible merger between our two businesses.），因此 (A) 為最適當的答案。

山普森女士預計在參訪中做什麼？
(A) 討論新的交易
(B) 檢視合約
(C) 諮詢律師
(D) 展示產品

字彙
**deal** 交易

山普森女士原本預定出席哪
一個歌劇院活動？

(A) 古典樂表演
(B) 現場喜劇表演
(C) 受歡迎的音樂劇
(D) 有關埃及的舞台劇

字彙
performance
演出，演奏，表演

**198** What opera house event was Ms. Sampson originally scheduled to attend?

(A) A classical music performance
(B) A live comedy performance
(C) A popular musical*
(D) A stage play about Egypt

請綜合山普森女士收到的郵件（第二篇）和哈特佛德歌劇院的廣告（第一篇）的內容。第二篇的第二段中「We have also scheduled an evening at our local opera house for some live entertainment on your last night.」，再從第一段確認山普森女士最後一天的行程日期為 7 月 4 日，對照第一篇歌劇院的時間表：July 4 — *Into the Jungle*, an award-winning musical featuring songs by Catrina Belford，答案應為 (C)。

凱利先生需要重新安排什麼？

(A) 搭船之旅
(B) 高爾夫球賽
(C) 午餐會報
(D) 工廠導覽

**199** What does Mr. Kelly need to reschedule?

(A) A boat trip
(B) A game of golf*
(C) A lunch meeting
(D) A factory tour

請閱讀收件人為凱利先生的訊息（第三篇），並特別留意「活動的更動」。當中提到要將高爾夫俱樂部之行和歌劇院活動時間調換，由此可以確認答案為 (B)。

凡瑞克女士為什麼不需要購買
入場券？

(A) 他們要參加的活動是免費的。
(B) 山普森女士尚未同意行程表。
(C) 凡瑞克女士已經有歌劇院的季票。
(D) 凱利先生必須等票券退費。

**200** Why most likely does Ms. Varek not need to purchase tickets?

(A) The event they will attend is free for everyone.
(B) Ms. Sampson has not approved the schedule yet.
(C) Ms. Varek already has a seasonal pass for the opera house.*
(D) Mr. Kelly must wait for some tickets to be refunded.

請從凡瑞克女士所撰寫的訊息（第三篇）中，找出與購票相關的內容。在訊息後半段凡瑞克女士提到可以免費攜伴參加（I'm allowed to bring a few guests free of charge.）。再看到歌劇院關於「票券」的廣告（第一篇），在第一段中的「Seasonal pass holders will be able to attend as many events as they wish and bring up to three guests at a time free of charge.」，由此可推測出凡瑞克女士有季票，故答案為 (C)。

ACTUAL
TEST
中譯+解析

6

# PART 5

東側倉庫裡的架子一定塞滿了節慶季節的東西。

字彙
warehouse 倉庫
stock 把……填滿；
為……備貨

**101** The shelves in the east warehouse must be _____ stocked for the holiday season.

(A) full　　　　　　　(B) fully*
(C) fuller　　　　　　(D) fullest

空格位在 be 動詞與過去分詞 stocked 之間，是為被動語態句型，因此空格要填入副詞 fully 修飾有動詞性質的 stocked，故 (B) 正確。

- **full** 滿的，充滿的　**fully** 完全地，全部地

---

游泳池是保留給住在高級套房裡的賓客使用的。

字彙
reserve 保留，把……專門留給
deluxe 高級的，豪華的
suite 套房

**102** _____ to the swimming pool is reserved for guests staying in one of our deluxe suites.

(A) Access*　　　　　(B) Accessed
(C) Accessing　　　　(D) Accessible

空格為句子中的主詞，而後方的內容（to the swimming pool）則在空格後方進行後位修飾，因此空格中應填入名詞 access，故 (A) 正確。access 作為名詞時，會使用「access to ＋地點」的結構，但作為動詞時，則不連接 to，而是直接連接受詞「access ＋地點」。

- **access** 進入或使用的權利　**accessible** 可進入的；可得到的

\* 與介系詞 to 搭配使用的名詞：
**solution / exposure / response / trip / answer / visit / approach / access ＋ to ＋名詞**

---

隆先生承認他被期待能接下更多管理工作。

字彙
admit 坦承，承認
expect 期待；預料
managerial 管理的
duty 工作，職責

**103** Mr. Takashi admits that _____ is expected to take on more managerial duties.

(A) he*　　　　　　　(B) his
(C) him　　　　　　　(D) himself

本題要從人稱代名詞中找出適當的格。that 子句需要主詞，因此答案為主格 he，故 (A) 正確。

---

達維斯維爾企業將於月底更換網路供應商。

字彙
incorporated
組成（有限）公司的
provider 提供者，供應者

**104** At the end of the month, Davisville Incorporated is _____ its Internet provider.

(A) changing*　　　　(B) attending
(C) holding　　　　　(D) turning

受詞（Internet provider「網路供應商」）前方要填入適當的及物動詞於空格當中，根據文意 (A) 為最適當的答案。請特別熟記可以用現在進行式，表達未來將發生的事情。

- **attend** 參加，出席　**hold** 舉行　**turn** 轉動

**105** Better City Travel offers bicycle tours _____ Skiff Lake at very reasonable rates.

(A) between
(B) along*
(C) below
(D) apart

本題要找出適當的介系詞。本句應是「沿著」湖的自行車之旅，語意最為通順，故 (B) 為最適當的答案。

- **along** 沿著，順著　**apart**（空間或時間）相隔

尤佳城市旅行社以非常實惠的價格，提供史基夫湖環湖自行車之旅。

字彙
**reasonable**
（價錢）公道的；合理的
**rate** 費用，價格

**106** Of all snow tires, Marten's new MR-200 is, without a doubt, the most durable _____.

(A) that
(B) any
(C) one*
(D) either

定冠詞（the）＋最高級（most）＋形容詞（durable）＋空格，空格中要填入名詞，而前方已經出現名詞 Marten's new MR-200，所以要使用代名詞 one 指稱它，因此答案為 (C)。

馬頓新款 **MR-200** 型無疑地是所有的雪胎中最耐用的輪胎。

字彙
**without a doubt** 無疑地
**durable** 經久的，耐用的

**107** As the amount of orders increased significantly, Lawford's Coffee Shop was able to _____ new deals with its suppliers.

(A) negotiating
(B) negotiates
(C) negotiated
(D) negotiate*

be able to 和助動詞 can 的意思相似，表「能夠做……」，後方要連接原形動詞 negotiate，故 (D) 正確。

- **negotiate** 談判，協商

* 高頻率「形容詞＋ to ＋ V（不定詞）」慣用片語：
**be ready to . . .** 準備做某事　**be likely to** 可能
**be willing to** 願意，樂意　**be about to** 即將，正要
**be supposed to** 應該；被期望　**be liable to** 易於，很可能會發生的
**be eager to** 渴望的，急切的　**be sure to** 肯定，必定，必然會

隨著訂單量顯著地增加，勞福咖啡廳得以和供應商洽談新協議。

字彙
**increase** 增加
**significantly** 顯著地
**deal** 協議；交易
**supplier** 供應商，供貨商

**108** Pandora Hair Design offers employees _____ opportunities to advance their careers.

(A) plenty
(B) each
(C) very
(D) many*

空格後方為可數名詞的複數形，空格中應填入 (D)，表示「提供很多機會」，最符合文意。在此補充，(A) 可與可數名詞或是不可數名詞搭配使用，但需要連接介系詞 of。而在口語中，有時會忽略文法規則而省略 of，使用 plenty time。

- **plenty** 充足；大量

潘朵拉髮型設計提供員工許多提升職涯的機會。

字彙
**opportunity** 機會
**advance** 使提升，使進步

格林維爾和崔頓之間的56號高速公路，因為電線桿倒塌而封閉。

**字彙**

**block off**
封住（路），封鎖（出入口）
**power pole** 電線桿

---

**109** Highway 56 between Greenville and Trenton has been blocked off _____ fallen power poles.

(A) so that
(B) as a result
(C) in order to
(D) because of*

根據文意，空格後方應為高速公路被封閉的「原因」，因此答案為 (D)。在此補充，(A) 後方要連接「主詞＋動詞」的子句；(C) 後方必須連接原形動詞。(B) as a result 亦可表原因，但後方接受詞時要改成 as a result of。

* **so that . . .** 以便……　　**as a result** 結果，所以

\* 表示原因的介系詞片語：
**due to / thanks to / owing to / as a result of / because of**

---

沒有現任房客的轉介，是不可能在多切斯特大樓租到公寓的。

**字彙**

**rent** 承租，租用
**tenant** 房客，承租人

---

**110** It is impossible to rent an apartment in the Dorchester Building without a _____ from a current tenant.

(A) referring
(B) referred
(C) referral*
(D) refer

介系詞（without）＋不定冠詞（a）＋空格，空格中只能填入名詞 referral，故 (C) 正確。

* **refer** 提到，參考　　**referral** 轉介，介紹

\* 以 al 結尾的名詞（注意勿當成形容詞）：
**arrival** 抵達　　**proposal** 計畫；提案　　**denial** 否認；拒絕
**refusal** 拒絕　　**survival** 倖存，存活

---

只有在車輛檢查完成後，才會在擋風玻璃上貼上綠色貼紙。

**字彙**

**windshield**
（汽車的）擋風玻璃
**inspection** 檢驗，檢查
**vehicle** 車輛

---

**111** A green sticker will be placed on the windshield _____ after the inspection of the vehicle is complete.

(A) when
(B) only*
(C) still
(D) most

根據文意，空格後方應為「唯一」可以在車輛貼上貼紙的情況，因此 (B) 為最適當的答案。

---

由於兩位主管決定提早退休，必須在7月30日前找到替代人選。

**字彙**

**opt** 選擇
**retirement** 退休
**replacement**
接替者，代替的人

---

**112** Since two managers have opted for early retirement, it is _____ to find replacements by July 30.

(A) necessitating
(B) necessary*
(C) necessarily
(D) necessities

虛主詞（it）＋be 動詞（is）＋空格＋ to ＋ V（不定詞當真主詞），因此空格中可以填入 (B) 形容詞 necessary，或 (D) 名詞 necessities 作為主詞補語，但填入 (B) 較符合文意。It is important to . . . 和 It is impossible to . . . 也是經常使用的虛主詞句型。

* **necessitate** 使必需　　**necessary** 必要的，必需的
　**necessarily** 必定地，必然地　　**necessity** 需要；必需品

**113** The cargo elevator in the south end of the building will not be in operation _____ further notice.

(A) until*　　　　　　(B) onto
(C) since　　　　　　(D) all

本題只要知道 until further notice 的意思為「直到進一步通知」，就能輕鬆解題。

- onto 在……之上

要等到進一步的通知，大樓南側底部的載貨電梯才能使用。

字彙
cargo 貨物
in operation 在運作，在操作

---

**114** The weight indicated on the outside of this package is _____ accurate.

(A) fairness　　　　　(B) fairest
(C) fairly*　　　　　(D) fair

本句中的空格為主詞補語的一部分，同時用來修飾形容詞 accurate，因此空格要填入副詞 fairly，故 (C) 正確。

- fairness 公正，公平　　fairly 相當，頗為　　fair 公正的

這個包裹外面所標示的重量相當準確。

字彙
weight 重量
indicate 顯示，指出
accurate 精確的，準確的

---

**115** David sent a link to a website that has a _____ of information on engine repair.

(A) wealth*　　　　　(B) height
(C) labor　　　　　(D) fame

根據文意，本句應為網站上「大量的資訊」，語意上最為適當，因此空格中最適合填入名詞 wealth，故 (A) 正確。請注意，a wealth of = a lot of。

- wealth 大量，豐富　　height 高度　　labor 勞工；勞動　　fame 名聲

大衛傳了一個含有大量引擎維修資訊的網站連結。

---

**116** To find the easiest route to Simmons, Darthmouth, and nearby towns, be sure to look at an _____ map.

(A) update　　　　　(B) updated*
(C) updates　　　　(D) updating

不定冠詞（an）＋空格＋名詞（map），空格中可以填入 (B) 或 (D)，作為形容詞形容 map，但地圖應為「被更新」，要使用過去分詞表示被動，因此答案為 (B)。

- update 更新；為……提供最新資訊

為了找出到西門子、達思茅斯和附近城鎮最便捷的路線，一定要查看更新後的地圖。

字彙
route 路線
nearby 附近的

既然申請截止日期已過，招聘委員會將開始審視履歷表。

字彙
committee 委員會
résumé 履歷表
application 申請
deadline 最後期限，截止日期

---

**117** The hiring committee will start reviewing résumés _____ the application deadline has passed.

(A) how  
(C) now that*  
(B) nor  
(D) whether

空格後方應連接招聘委員會開始審視履歷表的「緣由、原因」，因此連接詞 now that 表示原因為最適當的答案，故 (C) 正確。

• **now that . . .** 既然

---

知名藝術評論家葛羅莉亞·汎·辛格爾在她的電視節目裡分析許多時期的畫作。

字彙
critic 評論家
a variety of
各種各樣，多種類型

---

**118** On her television show, Gloria Van Cingel, the well-known art critic, _____ paintings from a variety of periods.

(A) analysis  
(C) analyzes*  
(B) analyzer  
(D) analyzing

主詞（Gloria Van Cingel）＋主詞同位語（the well-known art critic）＋空格＋受詞（paintings），此句型結構中均已具備主詞與受詞，因此需要動詞 analyzes，故 (C) 正確。

• **analysis (n.)** 分析　　**analyzer** 分析器　　**analyze (v.)** 分析

---

瑞福超市安裝數座自助結帳機，預期將對員工數量造成異動。

字彙
installation 安裝，設置
self-checkout kiosk
自助結帳機

---

**119** The installation of several self-checkout kiosks in the Redford Supermarket is expected to create changes _____ the number of employees.

(A) in*  
(C) positions  
(B) again  
(D) ultimately

片語 changes in 或 changes to，用來表示「……的變化」，因此答案為 (A)。

• **position** 職位；職缺　　**ultimately** 最後，最終

\* 名詞 change 的其他用法：  
**a change of address** 變更地址　　**make/create changes** 做出改變  
**Don't forget your change.** 別忘了你的零錢 。

---

與其他人相比，唐諾準備房地產證照考試的時間短的驚人。

字彙
compared to . . .
與……相比
real estate 不動產

---

**120** Compared to everyone else, Donald prepared himself for the real estate license exam in a _____ short period of time.

(A) surprised  
(C) surprisingly*  
(B) surprise  
(D) surprising

本句的結構為「不定冠詞（a）＋空格＋形容詞（short）＋名詞（period）」。請根據文意，判斷空格中填入的單字，要用來修飾形容詞 short，還是用來修飾名詞 period。本句要表達的意思應為「時間短的驚人」，因此空格中要填入副詞 surprisingly，用來修飾形容詞 short，故答案為 (C)。

• **surprised** 令人驚訝的　　**surprise** 使驚訝  
**surprisingly** 驚人地，出乎意料地　　**surprising** 使人驚訝的事

**121** The production supervisor of Gleason Shoes is _____ of all the factory's operations.

(A) aware*　　　　　　(B) current
(C) serious　　　　　　(D) alert

本題只要知道片語 be aware of，表「知道的」，就能輕鬆解題。

• **aware** 知道的，察覺的　**alert** 警覺的，機敏的

萬利森鞋業的製造部主管，對於工廠所有的運作情況都很清楚。

字彙
**production** 製造，生產
**supervisor** 主管，管理者，監督者

---

**122** The tourism _____ of Cape Breton Island has dramatically improved ever since the harbor was reopened last year.

(A) economical　　　　(B) economic
(C) economize　　　　(D) economy*

定冠詞（the）＋空格＋介系詞（of），空格中只能填入名詞 economy，和 tourism 組成複合名詞，故 (D) 正確。

• **economical** 經濟的，節約的　**economic** 經濟上的
**economize** 節省，節約　**economy** 經濟

自從港口去年重新開放以來，布雷頓角島的觀光經濟明顯地改善了。

字彙
**dramatically** 明顯地，顯著地
**harbor** 港口

---

**123** Someone from Renforth Building Supplies asked us to _____ the type of lumber needed for the project.

(A) personify　　　　　(B) magnify
(C) specify*　　　　　(D) testify

空格與 to 形成不定詞，因此空格要填原形動詞，連接後方的受詞 the type of lumber . . . 。「具體說明」特定的木材種類，最符合文意，因此答案為 (C)。

• **personify** 擬人化　**magnify** 放大，擴大　**specify** 具體說明
**testify** 作證，證明

藍福建築供應商的人員要求我們具體說明工程所需的木材種類。

字彙
**supplies** 用品，供應品
**lumber** 木材，木料

---

**124** Fitzgerald Air offers flights to over 200 destinations _____ northern Canada.

(A) toward　　　　　　(B) throughout*
(C) regarding　　　　　(D) aboard

根據文意，比起兩百多架航班同樣飛往某個方向（toward），飛機飛行遍及（throughout）北加拿大各航班點，文意上更為適當，因此答案為 (B)。

• **toward** 向，朝　**throughout** 遍及，遍布　**regarding** 關於
**aboard** 上（公車、火車、飛機）

費茲傑羅航空提供200多個飛遍北加拿大各處的航班。

字彙
**flight** 航班，班機
**destination** 目的地，終點

賴斯特維爾學院的吉他初級班很快就額滿了，所以我們建議填寫線上報名表格。

**字彙**
fill up 填滿；充滿
recommend 建議

**125** The beginners' guitar class at the Lesterville Academy fills up quickly, so we recommend filling out an online _____ form.

(A) enrollment*　　　(B) inventory
(C) complaint　　　(D) solicitation

賴斯特爾學院人員建議填寫線上「報名」表格，較符合文意，所以 (A) 正確。

- enrollment 報名，註冊　　inventory 存貨　　complaint 抱怨，客訴
  solicitation 請求（幫助、金錢）

---

蘭卡斯特企業新任命的副總裁，將於週五向員工發表第一次的談話。

**字彙**
address 向……發表演說，向……致詞

**126** On Friday, Lancaster Incorporated's newly _____ vice president will address his staff for the first time.

(A) appoint　　　(B) appoints
(C) appointed*　　　(D) appointing

副詞（newly）＋空格＋名詞（vice president），因此空格中要填入形容詞，用來修飾名詞 vice president，而分詞也可以當作形容詞使用，因此要從 (C) 和 (D) 當中選出答案。根據文意，應為「被新任命的」副總裁較為適當，因此要使用過去分詞表示被動，答案為 (C)。

- appoint 任命，指派

---

公共關係部的主管必須不斷地與媒體聯絡，所以藍道夫企業正在尋找具優秀溝通技巧的人選。

**字彙**
head 領導人，負責人
public relations 公共關係
continually 不停地，連續地
be in contact with . . .
與……聯絡，保持聯絡
exceptional 優秀的，卓越的

**127** The head of public relations must be continually in contact with the media, so Randolph Industries _____ someone with exceptional communication skills.

(A) seeking　　　(B) is seeking*
(C) are sought　　　(D) have been sought

連接詞 so 連接的子句中，主詞為 Randolph Industries，因此空格中需要填入動詞。公司在尋找（seek）人才，要使用主動語態較為適當，因此答案為 (B)。請特別留意，若公司的名稱以 s 結尾，仍要視為單數（指一家公司）。

- seek 尋找

---

拉波特女士籌劃募款活動的方式明顯地與哈洛威女士不同。

**字彙**
approach 方法，方式
organize 籌劃，組織，安排
fundraising 募款

**128** Ms. Laporte's approach to organizing a fundraising event is _____ different from Ms. Halloway's.

(A) haltingly　　　(B) intimately
(C) permissibly　　　(D) markedly*

根據文意，應為拉波特女士籌劃募款活動的方式「明顯地」與另一位女士不同。副詞選項中，(D) 為最適當的答案。

- haltingly 斷斷續續地　　intimately 密切地　　permissibly 獲准地
  markedly 明顯地，顯著地

\* markedly 的用法：
differ markedly (= considerably, greatly, radically)：顯著地差異
markedly (= noticeably) improved：明顯地改善
markedly ＋比較級：更加明顯……

**129** Recently, Kingston has experienced a huge increase in the number of residents, _____ are international students.

(A) inasmuch as  (B) the reason being
(C) because of them  (D) most of whom*

空格位在逗點後方的子句，為主詞的位置，因此答案為 (D)，whom = and most of the residents。先行詞 residents 為人，應使用 who，但是關係代名詞在此作為 of 的受詞，則要使用 whom。

• **inasmuch as** 因為，由於，鑑於

最近金斯頓居民人數大幅增加，其中大多數是國際學生。

字彙
**increase (n.)** 增加
**resident** 居民

---

**130** To help the staff of the Carrington Inn make your stay more _____, please fill out a guest feedback form and leave it at the front desk.

(A) knowledgeable  (B) considerable
(C) enjoyable*  (D) available

根據文意，本句是飯店員工為了要讓賓客有「更愉快的住宿經驗」，因此 (C) 為最適當的答案。請特別留意，本句中的 stay 作為名詞使用。

• **knowledgeable** 博學多聞的  **considerable** 重要的，相當多的
  **enjoyable** 令人愉快的  **available** 可得到的；可用的

* make 的用法：
**make** ＋人＋原形動詞：使、讓某人做……
**make** ＋人＋形容詞或過去分詞：使人變得……
**make** ＋ A ＋ B：把 A 變成 B

為協助卡林頓旅社的員工讓您的住宿更愉快，請填寫賓客回饋表，並留置於櫃台。

# PART 6

**字彙**
expert 專業的
advance 發展
generation （能源等）產生
consumption 消耗
facility
設備；（特定用途的）場所
training 訓練，培訓
prompt 迅速的
response 答覆
so that . . . 以便

Questions 131-134 refer to the following e-mail.

**To:** sandrabae@gladstoneresearch.com.au

**From:** markjohnson@sydneyunienergy.au

**Date:** 15 May

**Subject:** Thank you!

Dear Dr. Bae,

Thank you very much for ___131.___ our main research center last Friday. Your expert advice, as always, ___132.___. Our entire engineering team benefited greatly from your presentation on the exciting new advances in energy generation and consumption systems for industrial facilities. This fall, our department plans to hire five more engineering researchers. Would ___133.___ mind leading a training session on the topic you spoke of last week? ___134.___. We will look forward to your prompt response so that details can be discussed.

Sincerely,

Mark Johnson

------------------------------------------------------------------

收件者：sandrabae@gladstoneresearch.com.au
寄件者：markjohnson@sydneyunienergy.au
日期：5 月 15 日
主旨：感謝您！

親愛的貝博士，

非常感謝您上週五造訪我們主要的研究中心。正如以往，我們非常感激您專業的建議。您的演說，關於工業設備能源生產與消耗系統的最新發展，讓我們全體工程團隊獲益良多。今年秋季，本部門打算增聘五位工程研究員。您是否願意主持一個與上週演講主題相關的訓練？如果您方便，那無疑地會對新員工大有幫助。我們期待您能盡快回覆，以便討論相關細節。

馬克・強生 敬上

**131**
(A) calling
(B) opening
(C) visiting*
(D) staffing

本文為向講者貝博士傳達感謝之意的電郵。由後方的 Our entire engineering team benefited greatly from your presentation，以及 the topic you spoke of last week，推知 visiting（拜訪）為最適合的答案，因此答案應為 (C)。

• **staff (v.)** 成為員工；（為機構）提供人員

**132**
(A) appreciates
(B) will be appreciated
(C) is appreciating
(D) was appreciated*

電郵開頭感謝貝博士「上週五的來訪（第一句提到 last Friday）」，因此答案應為過去式，故 (D) 正確。空格的句構為被動語態，故 (A) 與 (C) 亦不能選。

• **appreciate** 感謝，感激

**133**
(A) his
(B) yours
(C) you*
(D) he

空格位在以 Would 開頭的問句上，空格中應填入主詞。依照文法規則，空格可填入 (C) 或 (D)，但根據文意，本句應為向「對方」提出的請求，意即「請問您……」，因此 (C) 為最適當的答案。本題的句型 Would you mind . . . ?（您介意／願意……?），請務必熟記。

**134**
(A) All engineers must adhere to our center's strict regulations.
(B) A large number of candidates have impressive résumés.
(C) If you can, it would undoubtedly prove beneficial to the new staff.*
(D) With your feedback, we will be able to build it quickly.

前句提到研究中心打算增聘研究人員，請求對方協助主持訓練。根據文意，後方應連接 (C)「如果您方便（主持訓練），那無疑地會對新員工大有幫助」較為適當。

• **adhere to** 遵守　**strict** 嚴格的　**regulation** 規定，規則
**candidate** 求職者　**impressive** 給人留下深刻印象的
**undoubtedly** 毫無疑問地，肯定地　**beneficial** 有益的，有利的

(A) 所有工程師都必須遵守本中心嚴格的規定。
(B) 許多應徵者有令人印象深刻的履歷。
(C) 如果您方便，那無疑地會對新員工大有幫助。
(D) 有了您的回饋意見，我們將能很快建造起來。

Questions 135-138 refer to the following article.

GEARY (April 5) — This morning, the National Transportation Authority announced that a $41 million grant has been awarded to Weston Valley Air Travel Network. Thanks to this ‾‾135.‾‾, the dream of having two airports in Weston Valley will soon be realized. Many residents in the region welcome news of this expansion to the current air service. ‾‾136.‾‾. Business owners throughout the Weston Valley are truly delighted. Jennifer Rossignol, a local business owner, expressed her delight with the grant earlier today. "This is fantastic news for someone like myself ‾‾137.‾‾ has to travel to Toronto frequently on business," says Rossignol. "We have had no choice ‾‾138.‾‾ years but to endure a four-hour bus ride into the city, but soon, I will be able to board a plane and be there in under an hour."

---

基爾瑞（4 月 5 日）──今天上午，國家交通管理局宣布，將提供威斯頓谷航空網 4100 萬的補助金。有了這筆資金，威斯頓谷有兩座機場的夢想很快就可以實現了。該地區許多居民歡迎這個針對現有航空服務的增建消息。這次的開發預計將在兩座機場創造超過 500 個工作機會。整個威斯頓谷的企業主都非常開心。一位當地企業主，珍妮佛‧羅西尼奧今天稍早表達了她對這筆補助金的欣喜之情。「這對像我這樣必須頻繁出差到多倫多的人來說，是個非常棒的消息。」羅西尼奧表示，「多年來，我們毫無選擇，只能忍受四個小時的公車車程進城。但很快地，我就可以在一小時內搭上飛機到那裡了。

---

**135** (A) funding*
(B) policy
(C) design
(D) strategy

空格前方的句子中提到了資金（$41 million grant），因此答案為 (A)。在此補充，雖然 fund 與 funding 意思相近，但 fund 為可數名詞，funding 為不可數名詞，請務必熟記。

● **funding** 資金　**policy** 政策　**strategy** 策略

**136**
(A) Weston Valley Air Travel Network confirmed that the project must be delayed.
(B) Passengers will have access to more parking spaces at one of the airports.
(C) This development is expected to create over 500 jobs at both airports.*
(D) Air fares for most regional flights, however, will most likely be raised.

(A) 威斯頓谷航空網確認這個計畫必須延緩。
(B) 其中一個機場會有更多的停車位供旅客可使用。
(C) 這次的開發預計將在兩座機場創造超過500個工作機會。
(D) 但是，大多數的地區性航班票價有可能提高。

空格位在「當地居民歡迎機場增建消息」的後方，(C) 的 development 呼應前句的 expansion，因此為最適當的答案，表示「這開發創造了就業機會」。機場增建消息才剛宣布，因此 (A) 的「計畫延誤」不合適。文中也和航班票價無關，故 (D) 也不能選。

- **confirm** 確認，證實　**delay** 延誤　**passenger** 旅客，乘客　**access** 使用或進入的權利　**fare** 交通費用　**flight** 航班，班機　**raise** 提高，增加

---

**137**
(A) likewise
(B) another
(C) then
(D) who*

空格為關係子句的主詞，其後接動詞 has to travel，因此空格中只能填入表主格的關係代名詞 who，故 (D) 正確。

- **likewise** 同樣地

---

**138**
(A) for*
(B) with
(C) about
(D) on

本題要找出適當的介系詞。空格後方連接 years，表示時間，因此答案應為 (A)。for 表「達……時間」，雖然 for 的後方經常連接「數字＋表時間的名詞」，但表示「多年、數日、數個小時」時，後方可以不用加上數字，直接寫成 for years，for days，for hours。在此補充，during 的後方要連接表「有特定起始期間」的名詞，例如 the vacation，the winter 等。

字彙

**managerial** 管理的
**division** 部門
**positively** 肯定地
**sensational** 極好的，轟動的
**paycheck** 薪津，工資
**salary** 薪水
**effective** 生效的
**take over** 接任，接管
**triple (v.)** 增至三倍
**achieve** 達到
**outstanding**
卓越的，傑出的，優異的
**performance** 表現
**on behalf of** 代表
**dedication** 貢獻

Questions 139-142 refer to the following e-mail.

**To:** Arnold Mallory [amallory@channel6news.net]
**From:** Melinda Calhoun [mcalhoun@channel6news.net]
**Re:** Fantastic reviews

**Date:** March 21

Dear Arnold,

The managerial division here at Channel 6 News was positively excited to read sensational reviews of our program in both the *Moncton Gazette* and *Uptown Entertainment*. All of us agree that your work here has been nothing but ‾‾‾139.‾‾‾. For this reason, Channel 6 News is truly delighted ‾‾‾140.‾‾‾ you a yearly bonus that will be added to your next monthly paycheck on March 30. ‾‾‾141.‾‾‾, your current salary will be raised by 12% effective April 1. Since you took over as head news anchor last November, our number of regular viewers has tripled. ‾‾‾142.‾‾‾. We could not have achieved any of this without your outstanding performance. On behalf of everyone at Channel 6 News, thank you for your hard work and dedication.

Melinda

------------------------------------------------------------

收件者：阿諾‧馬洛里 <amallory@channel6news.net>
寄件者：米蘭達‧卡爾霍恩 <mcalhoun@channel6news.net>
回覆：超棒的評論
日期：3 月 21 日

親愛的阿諾，

第六頻道新聞管理部很高興看到《蒙克頓公報》與《上城娛樂》對本節目的精采評論。我們所有人都同意您在此的表現只能用傑出形容。為此，第六頻道新聞很樂意在您下個月 3 月 30 日的薪資中增發一筆年度獎金。此外，您目前的薪資也將自 4 月 1 日起增加百分之 12%。自去年 11 月您接掌頭條新聞主播以來，我們固定收看的觀眾量已經增加三倍。第六頻道也得到了全國各報紙的好評。沒有您卓越的表現，我們無法達到這個成就。謹代表第六頻道新聞的全體同仁，感謝您的辛勤工作與付出。

瑪琳達

**139**
(A) withdrawn
(B) matched
(C) affordable
(D) exceptional*

空格上一句提到「節目獲得了相當好的評價」，可以推測阿諾·馬洛里的工作表現是「傑出的」，因此 (D) 為最適當的答案。nothing . . . but . . . 表「只能（說）」，請特別熟記。

- **withdrawn** 孤僻的，沈默寡言的　　**matched** 相符的
  **affordable** 負擔得起的　　**exceptional** 傑出的，優秀的，傑出卓越的

---

**140**
(A) to award*
(B) an award
(C) it awarded
(D) that awards

award 為授與動詞，用法為「award ＋間接受詞＋直接受詞」，因此空格後方出現間接受詞 you 和直接受詞 a yearly bonus，表「給予您一筆年度獎金」。而空格前方為 be delighted，意思為「感到高興的」，用法為「be delighted to ＋ V」，因此空格中要填入原形動詞 award，故 (A) 正確。

- **award** 給予，授予

---

**141**
(A) For example
(B) In addition*
(C) Nevertheless
(D) On the other hand

根據文意，除了給予阿諾年度獎金之外，還「加上」調薪，因此空格中最適合填入的片語為 in addition，答案為 (B)。

- **for example** 例如，舉例來說　　**in addition** 此外
  **nevertheless** 然而，不過　　**on the other hand** 另一方面

---

**142**
(A) Channel 6 News has also received fabulous reviews in national newspapers.*
(B) An assistant news anchor will be hired sometime next month.
(C) Our team will meet next week to discuss changes to your show.
(D) You are one of two employees who are entitled to an annual bonus.

(A) 第六新聞頻道也得到了全國各報紙的好評。
(B) 下個月某一天將聘用一位助理新聞主播。
(C) 我們團隊將於下週開會討論為您的節目做些改變。
(D) 您是其中一位有資格獲得年度獎金的員工。

電郵開頭提到第六新聞頻道獲得兩家刊物的好評，而空格前方的內容為「觀眾量增加了三倍」，根據文意，要再補充「另外一項功績」語意較為通順，因此填入 (A) 最為適當。

- **fabulous** 極好的，絕佳的　　**entitle** 使符合資格，使享有權利
  **annual** 年度的

electronics 電子（產品）
trade 貿易
consecutive 連續的
represent 代表
organizer 主辦者，籌辦者
significantly 顯著地
noticeable
明顯的，顯而易見的
the majority of
大多數，大部分
showcase 展示
appliance 電器用品

Questions 143-146 refer to the following article.

**Electronics Trade Show**

(25 August) The annual Global Electronics Trade Show came to Tokyo on Saturday, 23 August for the fifth consecutive year. _____ 143. . As was the case last year, China was the most _____ 144. represented nation. _____ 145. , organizers reported that the number of South American companies was significantly higher than previous years. Another noticeable change at this year's _____ 146. was the fact that the majority of companies showcased kitchen appliances rather than the usual entertainment electronics.

----

電子產品貿易展

（8月25日）全球電子產品年度貿易展連續第五年來到東京，於8月23日星期六展開。這場盛會有來自全世界各地超過500家公司參與。跟去年一樣，中國是出席最踴躍的國家。再者，主辦單位報告說，參加的南美洲企業數量也較往年明顯提高。今年活動另一項明顯的變化是，大多數公司展示的是廚房電器，而非以往的電子娛樂產品。

(A) 活動志工不需付報名費。
(B) 產品展示將於三個不同的禮堂舉行。
(C) 這場盛會有來自全世界各地超過500家公司參與。
(D) 招聘人員收取與會的大學生履歷。

**143**

(A) Volunteers at the event were not required to pay the registration fee.
(B) Product demonstrations will be held in three different auditoriums.
(C) The event featured over 500 companies from every corner of the world.*
(D) Recruiters collected résumés from university students in attendance.

空格後方提到許多參展的國家，因此空格中應填入 (C)，說明「展覽整體參展狀況」，最符合文意。

• **require** 需要，要求　**fee** 費用
**recruiter** 招聘人員　**attendance** 出席，到場

**144**
(A) heavy
(B) heavily*
(C) heavier
(D) heaviness

本句的結構為「定冠詞（the）＋最高級（most）＋空格＋過去分詞
（represented）＋名詞（nation）」。請先確認空格要修飾過去分詞還
是名詞，才能找出答案。heavy nation（沉重的國家？），並沒有這樣的
說法，而 heavily represented（代表數量最多的→參展者最多的）最符
合文意，因此答案為 (B)。

• **heavy** 沉重的　　**heavily** 大量地；沉重地　　**heaviness** 沉重

---

**145**
(A) Moreover*
(B) Rather
(C) Instead
(D) Thus

文章逐一列出了參展國家的狀況，先陳述中國的參展狀況，再補充南美
洲企業的參展情況，因此最適合用來連接的單字為 moreover，故 (A)
正確。

---

**146**
(A) class
(B) demonstration
(C) event*
(D) ceremony

本文為針對貿易展（Trade Show）的報導，因此空格應填入 event，表
示為「今年的活動」，答案應為 (C)。

• **ceremony** 典禮

# PART 7

字彙
**announce** 宣布
**host** 主辦，主持
**talent** 才藝，才能
**set up** 設置，搭起
**participant** 參與者
**instrument** 樂器
**sign up for** 報名參加
**slot** 場次，時段
**duration** 持續期間

Questions 147-148 refer to the following notice.

[147] To our dear customers,

We are happy to announce that we will be hosting a weekly talent night starting in October. The event will be held every Wednesday from 6:00 P.M. until 8:00 P.M. and [147] the stage will be set up on the first floor of our café.

Participants may sing, play instruments, or read poetry. Make sure to arrive early to sign up for a twenty-minute slot. [148] All participants will be allowed free coffee or tea for the duration of the event.

For more information, please visit our website at www.cafémaria.com or call us at 777-4367.

--------------------------------------------------

致親愛的顧客，

我們很高興宣布，自十月起本店將舉辦每週才藝之夜。這個活動將於每週三晚間 6:00 至 8:00 舉行，舞台將設置於本餐館的一樓。

參加者可唱歌、彈奏樂器或朗誦詩歌。務必提早到場以便報名 20 分鐘的場次。所有參加者於活動期間可免費享用咖啡或茶。

更多資訊，請上本店網站 www.cafemaria.com 或來電 777-4367。

---

這則公告最有可能出現在哪裡？

(A) 地鐵站
(B) 音樂書籍
(C) 咖啡館
(D) 醫生診所

字彙
**appear** 出現

**147** Where would the notice most likely appear?

(A) In a subway station
(B) In a music book
(C) At a coffee house*
(D) At a doctor's office

To our dear customers 表示公告通知的對象，且由第一段的「the stage will be set up on the first floor of our café」當中提到咖啡廳地點，可以推測出答案應為 (C)。

---

根據公告，參加者可獲得什麼？

(A) 優惠折價券
(B) 小額款項
(C) 參賽證明
(D) 免費飲料

字彙
**payment** 支付的款項
**participation** 參加
**certificate** 證明，證書
**beverage** 飲料

**148** According to the notice, what will participants receive?

(A) Discount coupons
(B) A small payment
(C) A participation certificate
(D) Free beverages*

本題的解題重點為「參加者可以得到的東西」。由第二段中的「All participants will be allowed free coffee or tea for the duration of the event.」，表示活動期間將免費提供咖啡或茶飲，因此答案為 (D)。

\* 答案改寫：**coffee or tea → beverage**

**Eastview Convention Center**
**55 Lakeview Road**
**Seattle, Washington**

| | |
|---|---|
| **Date:** April 12<br>**Invoice number:** 9800032 | **Bill To:**<br>Trisha Baxter<br>Pure Motorcycles<br>90 Yamer Street<br>Orlando, Florida |

Invoice for the Eastview Convention Center's Annual Automotive Show from June 25 – June 27.

| Item: | Rate: | Total: |
|---|---|---|
| Convention Booth (30 square feet) | $100.00/day | $300.00 |
| 149 **Additional Services:** | | |
| 3 display tables | $10.00/unit | $30.00 |
| Storage | $30.00/unit | $120.00 |
| Computer rental | $20.00/unit | $20.00 |
| 55-inch television rental | $30.00/unit | $30.00 |
| Show passes | $20.00/person | $200.00 |
| | **Subtotal**<br>**Tax**<br>**Total** | $700.00<br>$45.50<br>$745.50* |

150 *Please visit your online account to arrange payment by April 20.

--------------------------------------------------------------------------------

**東景會議中心**
**華盛頓州西雅圖湖景路 55 號**

| | |
|---|---|
| 日期：4 月 12 日<br>發票編號：9800032 | **帳單收件者：**<br>特麗莎‧巴克斯特<br>道地機車<br>佛羅里達州奧蘭多亞莫街 90 號 |

6 月 25 日至 6 月 27 日東景會議中心年度汽車展發票

| 品項： | 單價： | 總計： |
|---|---|---|
| 會議展位（30 平方英尺） | 100.00 元／天 | 300 元 |
| 額外服務： | | |
| 3 張展示桌 | 10 元／張 | 30 元 |
| 倉儲 | 30 元／單位 | 120 元 |
| 電腦租用 | 20 元／台 | 20 元 |
| 55 吋電視租用 | 30 元／台 | 30 元 |
| 展場通行證 | 20 元／人 | 200 元 |
| | 小計：<br>稅：<br>總額： | 700 元<br>45.5 元<br>745.5 元* |

＊請於 4 月 20 日前至線上帳戶繳費

字彙
invoice 發票；費用清單
annual 年度的，一年一次的
automotive 汽車的
rate 費用，價格
display 展示
storage 倉儲
rental 出租；租借
pass (n.) 通行證
subtotal 小計
account 帳戶

下列何者未包含在本次活動
費用中？

**(A)** 展場的通行證
**(B)** 展示桌
**(C)** 電視租用
**(D)** 擺設與清理

**149** What is NOT included in the cost of the event?

(A) Passes to the show
(B) Display tables
(C) Television rental
(D) Setup and cleanup*

解題時，請先找出活動提供的出租項目，再對照各選項的內容，並刪除
文章中提及的選項。在額外的服務（Additional Services）欄中，可以
依序確認 (B)、(C) 和 (A)，因此本題的答案應為 (D)。

---

巴克斯特女士被要求做什麼？

**(A)** 登記會員
**(B)** 寄支票到會場
**(C)** 支付發票款項
**(D)** 確認參加者數量

字彙
**venue**
會場，發生場所，舉行地點
**settle** 支付，結算
**confirm** 確認，確定

**150** What is Ms. Baxter asked to do?

(A) Sign up for a membership
(B) Mail a check to the venue
(C) Settle an invoice*
(D) Confirm the number of participants

發票最後一行「Please visit your online account to arrange
payment by April 20.」，明確寫出結帳方式與繳費期限，因此答案為
(C)。答案經常出現在文中有標示＊、note 或是括號的內容中。

＊ 答案改寫：**arrange payment → settle an invoice**

---

字彙
**property** 房地產
**expand** 擴大；擴展
**on-site** 實地，現場的
**definitely** 肯定，一定
**portrait** 人像照片

**Questions 151-152 refer to the following text message chain.**

**Jennifer Porter [11:23 A.M.]**
Hi, Raphael. Were you able to stop by the Rickter Avenue property this weekend?

**Raphael Morez [11:25 A.M.]**
Yes, I went on Saturday. 151 Since most of our photographers will be working at events every day, are you sure we need such a big place?

**Jennifer Porter [11:27 A.M.]**
The rooms are large, but as we expand, we'll need the space.

**Raphael Morez [11:28 A.M.]**
That might not happen for a few years, though.

**Jennifer Porter [11:30 A.M.]**
Yes, but we should be thinking about our long-term goals for the company. 152 The Rickter Avenue property will give us a chance to finally develop 151 an on-site studio.

**Raphael Morez [11:32 A.M.]**
You're right. We'll definitely need the extra space once 151 we start offering portrait services.

珍妮佛・波特 [ 上午 11:23 ]

嗨,拉斐爾。你這週末有去瑞奇特大道的辦公場所嗎?

拉斐爾・莫雷茲 [ 上午 11:25 ]

有,我星期六去的。既然我們大多數的攝影師每天將忙於活動,妳確定我們需要這麼大的空間嗎?

珍妮佛・波特 [ 上午 11:27 ]

那些房間是很大,但如果我們擴大規模的話,就會需要那些空間了。

拉斐爾・莫雷茲 [ 上午 11:28 ]

但這件事應該近幾年都還不會發生吧。

珍妮佛・波特 [ 上午 11:30 ]

是沒錯,但我們還是應該為公司的長程目標著想。瑞奇特大道的空間讓我們我們最終有機會設置實地攝影棚。

拉斐爾・莫雷茲 [ 上午 11:32 ]

妳說的沒錯。一旦我們開始提供人像攝影服務,我們肯定需要額外的空間。

---

**151** At what kind of business do the people most likely work?

(A) A photography company*
(B) A fashion design house
(C) An event planning business
(D) An art gallery

這些人有可能從事何種行業?

(A) 攝影公司
(B) 時尚設計坊
(C) 活動規劃公司
(D) 藝廊

由上午 11 點 25 分訊息當中的 photographers、11 點 30 分訊息當中的 an on-site studio、以及 11 點 32 分訊息當中的 portrait services,可以確認答案為 (A)。

---

**152** At 11:32 A.M., what does Mr. Morez most likely mean when he writes, "You're right"?

(A) A location is too far from the city.
(B) The building will help the company meet its goals.*
(C) Much interior design work is needed in the building.
(D) The property has some significant flaws.

在上午11:32時,莫雷茲先生說的「妳說的沒錯。」是什麼意思?

(A) 那個地點離市區太遠。
(B) 那棟大樓將有助公司達成目標。
(C) 那棟大樓內需要進行大規模的室內設計工程。
(D) 那處所有一些明顯的缺陷。

波特小姐在「You're right.」的前方提到,選擇瑞奇特大道的工作空間,可以讓他們最終有機會設置實地攝影棚(The Rickter Avenue property will give us a chance to finally develop an on-site studio.),莫雷茲先生對此表示同意,因此 (B) 為最適當的答案。當題目詢問文中某句話的含義時,請務必掌握該句前後方的文意。

字彙
meet 達到,滿足
flaw 缺陷,瑕疵

Questions 153-155 refer to the following e-mail.

**To:** Tristan Starr
**From:** Emilia Simpson
**Date:** June 2
**Re:** Walton Shopping Center contract

Hi Tristan,

I just got an e-mail from Marcus Pine about the budget proposal you sent him yesterday. [153] Apparently, several of the figures are incorrect. It seems you included the initial figures we presented to him during our first advertising pitch on May 6 and [154] not the figures we later agreed on during negotiations on May 20.

Mr. Pine was hoping to present the advertising plan to his superiors on June 5. He mentioned that there are several other agencies that have sent him proposals, and he will select one of them instead if we cannot get this paperwork done by June 3. Since I'm just about to fly to our Chicago office, I'm hoping you can handle this right away. [155] Please send Mr. Pine the revised proposal and e-mail me when you get his response.

Sincerely,

Emilia

-------------------------------------------------------------

收件者：崔斯坦·斯塔爾
寄件者：艾蜜莉亞·辛普森
日期：6 月 2 日
回覆：沃爾頓購物中心合約

嗨，崔斯坦，

我剛收到馬克思·潘恩的電子郵件，提到你昨天寄給他的預算企劃案。很明顯地，有些數字是錯的。你沒有寫進我們後來在 5 月 20 號協商時所同意的數字，而是寫上我們在 5 月 6 號首次廣告比稿時跟他報告的原始數字。

潘恩先生希望在 6 月 5 日把這個廣告企畫向他的主管報告。他提到還有其他幾家公司也向他提出企劃案。如果我們無法在 6 月 3 號前處理好這份文件，他就會從它們當中挑選一家。因為我正要飛往芝加哥的辦公室，我希望你能立刻處理這件事。請把修訂後的企劃案寄給潘恩先生，並在收到他的回覆後寄電子郵件給我。

艾蜜莉亞 敬上

**153** Why was the e-mail written?

(A) To request a vacation
(B) To introduce an applicant
(C) To announce a policy change
(D) To point out some mistakes*

由電郵第一段中的「Apparently, several of the figures are incorrect.」，表示數據有誤，因此 (D) 為最適當的答案。在文章的前半部，大多可以找到與文章目的有關的重要線索。

為什麼會寫這封電子郵件？

(A) 要求休假
(B) 介紹一位應徵者
(C) 公告規定變動
(D) 指出一些錯誤

字彙
**request** 要求
**policy** 規定；政策

---

**154** When was the proposal modified?

(A) On May 6
(B) On May 20*
(C) On June 3
(D) On June 5

第一段中提到 5 月 6 日是預算企劃案首次發表的時間，之後又在 5 月 20 日協商出雙方所同意的數字（not the figures we later agreed on during negotiations on May 20），表示企劃案數據已被修改，因此答案應為 (B)。在此補充，(C) 為寄出修訂企劃案的最後期限；(D) 則為潘恩先生預計跟上司報告企劃案的日期。

企劃案是何時修改的？

(A) 5月6日
(B) 5月20日
(C) 6月3日
(D) 6月5日

字彙
**modify** 修改

---

**155** What would Ms. Simpson like Mr. Starr to do?

(A) Make a phone call
(B) Issue a refund
(C) Send a document*
(D) Speak with a manager

辛普森女士為此郵件的寄件人，而斯塔爾先生為收件人。寄件人的要求和建議事項，通常可以由郵件後半部的內容找到線索。由第二段中末的 Please send Mr. Pine the revised proposal，推知答案應為 (C)。

\* 答案改寫：the revised proposal → a document

辛普森女士要斯塔爾先生做什麼？

(A) 打電話
(B) 退一筆款項
(C) 寄送一份文件
(D) 和經理談話

字彙
**issue** 核發，發給
**refund** 退款

---

Questions 156-157 refer to the following article.

Restaurant sales are down in Plymouth County. According to a report in the *Plymouth Journal*, sales have dropped by more than 15 percent this winter. The drop has shocked many restaurant owners, especially since the winter holidays usually increase restaurant business. [156] Bob Fulton, owner of Little Italy Eatery, attributed the drop to an increase in wholesale prices as one factor of the drop. "With the prices of everything going up, we've had to increase our prices as well," Mr. Fulton said in an interview. "Most customers just don't want to pay that much for a meal." [157] To encourage more business, many local restaurants have joined forces to develop membership programs. These programs provide customers with discounts at numerous restaurants in the county.

字彙
**drop** （價格）下降
**attribute A to B**
把 A 歸因（咎）於 B
**wholesale** 批發
**factor** 因素
**encourage** 激發，促進
**join forces** 協力

普利茅斯縣的餐廳業績正在下滑。根據《普利茅斯日報》的報導,今年冬季業績已經下滑了超過 15%。這個下滑幅度已經讓許多餐廳老闆深感震撼,特別是冬季假期一般餐廳業績是提升的。小義大利餐館的老闆,鮑伯·富爾頓認為,這個衰退現象的因素之一就是批發價格的提高。「隨著所有東西價格提高,我們也必須提高自己的餐飲售價。」富爾頓先生在一場訪問中提到,「但大多數的客人不想為一頓飯付那麼多錢。」為了刺激更多營業額,許多當地餐廳已經協力研擬會員方案。這些方案將提供顧客在全縣許多餐廳的消費折扣。

---

根據這篇文章,餐廳業績為什麼會下滑?

(A) 天氣變得很不舒適。
(B) 成本上升得太高。
(C) 蓋了更新的餐廳。
(D) 許多當地工作機會消失。

字彙
unpleasant 不舒適的

**156** According to the article, why have restaurant sales dropped?

(A) The weather has become unpleasant.
(B) The costs have risen too high.*
(C) Newer restaurants have been built.
(D) Many local jobs have been lost.

由文章中間的「Bob Fulton, owner of Little Italy Eatery, attributed the drop to an increase in wholesale prices as one factor of the drop.」,表示所有東西的批發價格上升,導致餐廳成本上升反映在餐點價格,是餐廳業績下跌的原因之一,因此 (B) 為最適當的答案。

---

餐廳老闆如何回應這個趨勢?

(A) 改善食物品質
(B) 減少員工數量
(C) 與其他餐廳合作
(D) 推出電視廣告

字彙
respond to . . .
回應……
trend 趨勢
decrease 減少
launch 推出

**157** How are restaurant owners responding to the trend?

(A) By improving the quality of the food
(B) By decreasing the number of workers
(C) By working with other restaurants*
(D) By launching television advertisements

閱讀文章時,請掌握解題關鍵為「餐廳老闆們的因應策略」。文章後半部寫道:「To encourage more business, many local restaurants have joined forces to develop membership programs.」,由此可知餐廳老闆協力因應問題,答案為 (C)。

* 答案改寫:join → work with

---

字彙
assignment 工作,任務
be in charge of 負責
assign 分配,指派
human resources
人力資源(部)

Questions 158-161 refer to the following online chat discussion.

**Rita Frasier [2:23 P.M.]**
Ms. Norton, do you have a minute? Thomas and I are unclear about our assignments. Last year, I was in charge of developing the seasonal training program, but Thomas was assigned the exact same job this year.

**Patrina Norton [2:25 P.M.]**
Yes, [158] everyone needs a chance to work on developing their own programs for human resources.

**Rita Frasier [2:26 P.M.]**

So, we will no longer use the materials I developed last year?

**Patrina Norton [2:28 P.M.]**

That's right. Thomas is expected to develop new materials that will be used this year.

**Thomas Woods [2:30 P.M.]**

But [160] what if I would like to use some of Rita's ideas?

**Patrina Norton [2:33 P.M.]**

Program development is part of the job.

**Thomas Woods [2:35 P.M.]**

Yes, but [159] Rita's program was excellent last year.
[161] I would hate all her hard work to go to waste.

**Patrina Norton [2:39 P.M.]**

If Rita is OK with it, I think you could use some of her materials so long as you update them where appropriate. [161] Let me review last year's materials first and get back to you.

**Rita Frasier [2:41 P.M.]**

What if Thomas and I worked together on the project?

**Patrina Norton [2:44 P.M.]**

[158] don't think that will be necessary.

**Rita Frasier [2:45 P.M.]**

OK, I understand.

**Thomas Woods [2:46 P.M.]**

Let us know when you've decided. Thanks.

| 瑞塔・弗雷澤<br>[ 下午 2:23 ] | 諾頓女士，您有空嗎？湯瑪士和我不太清楚我們的工作。去年我負責開發每一季的訓練課程，但湯瑪士今年被分配了一模一樣的工作。 |
|---|---|
| 派翠琳娜・諾頓<br>[ 下午 2:25 ] | 是的，每個人都需要有為人資部開發他們自己課程的機會。 |
| 瑞塔・弗雷澤<br>[ 下午 2:26 ] | 所以公司不再使用我去年研製的資料了嗎？ |
| 派翠琳娜・諾頓<br>[ 下午 2:28 ] | 沒錯，湯瑪士應該要研製出今年使用的新資料。 |
| 湯瑪士・伍茲<br>[ 下午 2:30 ] | 但是如果我想使用瑞塔部分的構想呢？ |

| | |
|---|---|
| 派翠琳娜‧諾頓<br>[下午 2:33] | 課程研發是這個工作的一部分。 |
| 湯瑪士‧伍茲<br>[下午 2:35] | 是,但瑞塔去年的課程很棒。我不想她所有的心血都浪費了。 |
| 派翠琳娜‧諾頓<br>[下午 2:39] | 如果瑞塔同意的話,只要你把適用的部分更新,我想你是可以使用她部分的資料。先讓我審閱去年的資料後,再回覆你。 |
| 瑞塔‧弗雷澤<br>[下午 2:41] | 如果湯瑪士和我一起合作這個專案呢? |
| 派翠琳娜‧諾頓<br>[下午 2:44] | 我覺得沒這個必要。 |
| 瑞塔‧弗雷澤<br>[下午 2:45] | 好,我了解。 |
| 湯瑪士‧伍茲<br>[下午 2:46] | 當您決定後,請通知我們。謝謝。 |

諾頓女士有可能是誰?

(A) 財務規劃師
(B) 人力資源部主管
(C) 企業實習生
(D) 廣告顧問

字彙
**financial** 財務的,金融的

**158** Who most likely is Ms. Norton?

(A) A financial planner
(B) A human resources manager*
(C) A company intern
(D) An advertising consultant

由諾頓女士下午 2 點 25 分傳送的訊息「everyone needs a chance to work on developing their own programs for human resources」,以及她在下午 2 點 44 分對整體討論所做的決定「I don't think that will be necessary.」,可以推知她應該是人資部門的主管,因此答案應為 (B)。

下列何者與弗雷澤女士有關?

(A) 她去年開發一個很成功的訓練課程。
(B) 她通常和伍茲先生一起合作專案。
(C) 她對今年所分配的工作很滿意。
(D) 她明年將接管諾頓女士的工作。

字彙
**take over** 接管,接手

**159** What is suggested about Ms. Frasier?

(A) She developed a successful training program last year.*
(B) She usually works with Mr. Woods on projects.
(C) She is pleased with this year's assignment.
(D) She will take over Ms. Norton's job next year.

閱讀文章時,請特別留意關鍵人名弗雷澤女士 ( Rita Frasier )。在下午 2 點 35 分的訊息中,伍茲先生提到了「Rita's program was excellent last year.」,表示弗雷澤女士去年研發的訓練課程非常棒,因此 (A) 為最適當的答案。

* 答案改寫:excellent → successful

**160** At 2:33 P.M., what does Ms. Norton most likely mean when she writes, "Program development is part of the job"?

(A) Her job duties include program development.
(B) She believes Ms. Frasier is better suited for the job.
(C) She disagrees with Mr. Woods' suggestion.*
(D) Her contract with the company needs revising.

請先看一下問題句的前一個訊息的內容，伍茲先生詢問諾頓女士是否可以使用瑞塔·弗雷澤女士的點子（what if I would like to use some of Rita's ideas?），後方連接的回覆「課程研發是這個工作的一部分。」，暗示了伍茲先生要負責研發，不要使用瑞塔的課程構想，因此 (C) 為最適當的答案。

在下午2:33，當諾頓女士說：「課程研發是這個工作的一部分」時，她是什麼意思？

(A) 她的工作職責包括了課程開發。
(B) 她相信弗雷澤女士更適合這份工作。
(C) 她不認同伍茲先生的建議。
(D) 她與公司的合約需要修改。

字彙
suit 適合
revise 修改，修訂

---

**161** What will most likely happen next?

(A) Ms. Frasier will contact a supervisor.
(B) Mr. Woods will begin working on a project.
(C) Mr. Woods and Ms. Frasier will have a meeting.
(D) Ms. Norton will look at some old materials.*

當題目為以 next 結尾的問句時，通常可以從文章的後半部中，找到與題目相關的線索。2 點 35 分伍茲先生說直接丟掉瑞塔去年的資料，太可惜了（I would hate all her hard work to go to waste.），而諾頓女士於下午 2 點 39 分的訊息中回覆：「Let me review last year's materials first and get back to you.」，表示她會審閱去年的資料，因此答案為 (D)。

接下來很有可能發生什麼事？

(A) 弗雷澤女士將連絡主管。
(B) 伍茲先生將開始進行一項專案。
(C) 伍茲先生和弗雷澤女士將開會。
(D) 諾頓女士將檢視一些舊資料。

---

**Questions 162-165 refer to the following e-mail.**

**To:** Tamika Keynes
**From:** Marcel Ventrue
**Re:** Information
**Date:** April 22

[162] I'm writing in regard to the service quote you requested on our website. I'm delighted you're interested in Lawn and Garden Care's extensive range of services. --[1]--. I can assure you that we are the top landscaping company in the city. We service many local businesses, such as hotels and country clubs. --[2]--. We also maintain the extensive lawns at Memorial Stadium downtown.

I have attached the service quote you requested. --[3]--. [163] The quote is based on weekly lawn maintenance services for The Renolds Gallery. [165] In the event that you require additional services, such as garden planting or tree removal, you would be charged extra. --[4]--. Have a look at the quote and [164] I will be in touch early next week to answer any questions you might have.

Sincerely,

Marcel Ventrue

字彙
in regard to 關於
quote 報價
extensive 廣泛的，廣大的
range 範圍
assure 向……保證
landscaping 造景，景觀美化
maintain (v.) 維護，保養
memorial 紀念的
maintenance (n.) 維護，保養
in the event that 如果，萬一
removal 移除
charge 收費

ACTUAL TEST 6

PART 7

中譯＋解析

513

收件者：塔米卡·凱恩斯
寄件者：馬賽爾·凡卓
回覆：資料
日期：4 月 22 日

我來信是有關您在本公司網站所申請的服務項目報價。很高興您對草坪與庭園管理的多項服務有興趣。我可以向您保證，我們是本市最佳造景公司。我們為本地許多商家維護景觀，像是飯店與鄉村俱樂部。我們還負責維護市中心紀念體育場的大草坪。

我已經附上您所申請的服務項目報價單。這個報價是依據雷諾茲藝廊的每週草坪保養服務而訂的。但如果您要求額外服務，像是庭園植栽或是移除樹木，則將另行收費。但如果您與本公司簽訂兩年期的合約，那所有的額外服務將可享優惠折扣。請參考報價單，我將於下週初與您聯繫，回答您可能有的疑問。

馬賽爾·凡卓 敬上

---

這封電子郵件的目的是什麼？

(A) 更動時程表
(B) 回覆一項請求
(C) 寄設計圖
(D) 繳交申請書

**162** What is the purpose of the e-mail?

(A) To change a schedule
(B) To respond to a request*
(C) To send a blueprint
(D) To submit an application

由電郵第一句「I'm writing in regard to the service quote you requested on our website.」，可以確認答案為 (B)。若題目詢問文章的目的，線索通常會出現在文章的前半部。

---

凱恩斯女士可能從事何種行業？

(A) 藝廊工作
(B) 體育館事務
(C) 鄉村俱樂部
(D) 飯店業

**163** For what kind of business does Ms. Keynes most likely work?

(A) An art gallery*
(B) A stadium
(C) A country club
(D) A hotel

由第二段第二句的「The quote is based on weekly lawn maintenance services for The Renolds Gallery.」，可知凡卓先生報價的依據是雷諾茲藝廊（Renolds Gallery），進而推測凱恩斯女士的工作行業可能和藝廊相關，所以答案為 (A)。其餘的選項皆為曾接受草坪與庭園管理服務的公司。

**164** What is mentioned in the e-mail?

(A) Ms. Keynes is a new employee at Lawn and Garden Care.
(B) Lawn and Garden Care is a new business.
(C) Ms. Keynes will hear from Mr. Ventrue next week.*
(D) Mr. Ventrue visited Ms. Keynes' business.

請將各選項對照郵件內容，並從中找出答案。在郵件最後一段中的「I will be in touch early next week to answer any questions you might have.」，表示寄件人（Mr. Ventrue）下週會聯繫對方（凱恩斯女士），因此 (C) 為最適當的答案。

下列何者出現在電子郵件中？

(A) 凱恩斯女士是草坪與庭園管理的新職員。
(B) 草坪與庭園管理是新開的公司。
(C) 凱恩斯女士將於下週收到凡卓先生的聯繫。
(D) 凡卓先生參觀了凱恩斯女士的公司。

字彙
**new employee** 新員工
**hear from** 收到……的信；得到……的消息

**165** In which of the positions marked [1], [2], [3], and [4] does the following sentence best belong?

"However, all additional services will be discounted should you sign a two-year contract with us."

(A) [1]  (B) [2]
(C) [3]  (D) [4]*

題目句的重點為「額外服務將可享優惠折扣」，因此前方應與「額外服務」相關的內容，文意才連貫。因此適合放在第二段下列句子的後方「In the event that you require additional services, such as garden planting or tree removal, you would be charged extra.」，故答案為 (D)。

下列句子最適合出現在[1]、[2]、[3]、[4]的哪個位置中？
「但如果您與本公司簽訂兩年期的合約，那所有的額外服務將可享優惠折扣。」

(A) [1]  (B) [2]
(C) [3]  (D) [4]

字彙
**contract** 合約（書）

---

Questions 166-168 refer to the following article.

**Parker Wallace to Join Adventure Software**
[166] By Amy Swanson, *The Daily Chat*

NEW YORK (24 February) — Parker Wallace has announced he will join the new start-up Adventure Software. Wallace, who has been developing software applications for five years now, is best known as the creator of Marble FM, a music sharing application. Marble FM accumulated over three million downloads in just two years, leading Wallace to become one of the most sought-after developers in the industry.

Despite turning down jobs at Liquid Apps and T&B Developers, Wallace has made the surprising move and accepted an offer to join a company that is less than two years old. "When I met [166] Alan Pike of Adventure Software, I knew he and I shared the same goals," [167] Wallace recently said at the launch of his latest app. "He and I are both passionate about music, and he had some great ideas for future projects. I am extremely confident that we'll be putting out hot new products in the next year."

[167] Wallace's newest app, Marble Video, has already generated over 500,000 downloads in less than a month. The tech world will be expecting big things from the partnership between Wallace and Pike, starting with [168] the rerelease of an upgraded version of Pike's Smart Symphony on March 30.

字彙
**application (= app)** 應用軟體，應用程式
**accumulate** 累積
**sought-after** 廣受歡迎的
**industry** 業界，行業，產業
**despite** 儘管
**turn down** 拒絕
**launch** 發表會
**passionate** 熱衷於
**extremely** 非常
**put out** 生產，發行
**generate** 造成
**rerelease** 再發行

ACTUAL TEST 6

PART 7

中譯＋解析

----------------------------------------

**帕克‧華倫斯加入冒險軟體**

《每日漫談》艾咪‧史旺森撰稿

紐約(2月24日)——帕克‧華倫斯已經宣布他將加入新創公司「冒險軟體」。華倫斯先生至今已從事軟體應用程式開發五年。他最廣為人知的身分,便是音樂分享應用程式——大理石 FM 的創造者。大理石 FM 在兩年內就累積了超過三百萬的下載量,讓華倫斯成為業界最搶手的軟體程式開發者之一。

儘管拒絕了流體應用程式與 T&B 開發者兩間公司的工作,華倫斯卻跨出了驚人的一步,接受一家成立不到兩年的公司的工作機會。「當我見到冒險軟體的亞倫‧派克時,我就知道他和我有共同的目標。」華倫斯最近在他最新應用程式的發表會上說道,「他和我都熱愛音樂。他對未來的工作有一些很棒的點子。我非常有信心明年我們就會發行熱門新產品。」

華倫斯最新的應用軟體——大理石影片在不到一個月的時間,就造成了超過 500,000 次的下載量。科技世界正引領期盼,華倫斯與派克的合作會帶來大創舉, 打頭陣的便是兩人將於 3 月 30 日再次發表的更新版派克智慧交響樂。

---

派克先生有可能是誰?

(A) 影片導演
(B) 交響樂作曲家
(C) 音樂影片製作人
(D) 軟體公司老闆

**166** Who most likely is Mr. Pike?

(A) A film director
(B) A symphony composer
(C) A music video producer
(D) A software company owner*

閱讀文章時,請特別留意關鍵人名派克先生(Mr. Pike)。第二段中提到了軟體開發公司——冒險軟體(Adventure Software),由 Alan Pike of Adventure Software,可以推測出派克先生應為軟體公司的老闆,故答案為 (D)。

---

關於史旺森女士,下列何者為真?

(A) 她之前任職於流體應用程式。
(B) 她出席了大理石影片的發表會。
(C) 她購買了一份大理石 FM。
(D) 她在活動上與派克先生碰面。

**167** What most likely is true about Ms. Swanson?

(A) She was formerly employed at Liquid Apps.
(B) She attended the launch of Marble Video.*
(C) She purchased a copy of Marble FM.
(D) She met with Mr. Pike at an event.

關鍵人名史旺森女士(Ms. Swanson)為撰寫本篇報導的人。由第二段的採訪內容,可以發現她去過新產品大理石影片(Marble Video)的發表會現場(Wallace recently said at the launch of his latest app),又在第三段中第一句,可以確認新產品為 Wallance's newest app, Marble Video,因此答案為 (B)。

**168** What is indicated about Smart Symphony?

(A) It is an already existing app.*
(B) It was originally developed by T&B Developers.
(C) It will be limited to 500,000 copies.
(D) It will feature elements of Marble FM.

請找出關鍵字 Smart Symphony 所在的位置。文章最後一段中提到，將再次發表更新版本的智慧交響樂應用程式，因此可以得知它是已經存在的應用程式，(A) 為最適當的答案。

下列何者與智慧交響樂有關？
(A) 是一個已經存在的應用程式。
(B) 原本由T&B開發者所開發的。
(C) 下載量將限制在500,000次。
(D) 將展現出大理石FM的特點。

字彙
**existing** 存在的，現存的
**be limited to** 限制
**feature** 以……為特色
**element** 要素；(基本)成分

---

Questions 169-171 refer to the following brochure.

**Energy Savers**
Are you paying high utility bills during the summer or winter months?
[169] With Energy Savers, you can find the energy solutions that will save you money. Contact us for your free four-step consultation.

**1. Determine your energy needs**
Our qualified energy consultants will visit your home to determine what your energy needs are. [170 (A), (B)] You will be asked to complete a detailed survey regarding the number of hours you spend at home, your desired temperatures during each season, and your cooking and cleaning habits.

**2. Home inspection**
Once our consultants determine your needs, they will inspect the windows, walls, and doors of your home to ensure proper insulation. [170 (C)] They will also test your heating, cooling, and lighting systems for weaknesses. Unlike other companies, Energy Savers will prepare a detailed report of flaws and make suggestions for improvements.

**3. Choose your upgrades**
Our consultants will discuss the recommended upgrades for your home while keeping your budget in mind. We can help you choose and install everything from double-paned glass for your windows to solar panels on your roof.

**4. Installations**
Our team will work around your schedule to install your upgrades. [171] However, most installations take several days to complete. You will see instant savings on your utility bills and the best part is those savings never end. You will continue to save money for years to come. Should you have problems with your upgrades within the first year, Energy Savers will fix them free of charge.

---

節能戰士

您是在夏季還是冬季支付高額的水電帳單呢？有了節能戰士，您就可以找到幫您省錢的節能方法。聯絡我們，就提供您免費的四步驟諮詢。

**1. 判斷您的用電需求**
本公司合格的能源顧問將造訪貴府，以決定您的用電需求。您需要填寫一張詳

字彙
**utility bill** 水電煤氣帳單
**solution** 解決辦法
**consultation** 諮詢
**determine** 決定，確定
**qualified** 合格的
**survey** 調查(表)
**regarding** 關於
**temperature** 溫度
**inspection** 檢測，檢查
**inspect** 檢測，檢查
**ensure** 確保
**proper** 適當的，合適的
**insulation** 隔絕，隔熱
**weakness** 缺點，弱點
**flaw** 缺失，缺點，瑕疵
**make a suggestion** 提出建議
**improvement** 改善，改良
**budget** 預算
**install** 安裝
**double-paned** 雙層玻璃的
**instant** 立即的

細的調查表，表中會問您在家的時數，您在每個季節希望的室溫，以及您烹飪與打掃的習慣。

## 2. 居家檢測
一旦本公司的顧問決定您的用電需求後，他們將檢測貴府的窗戶、牆壁和門，以確保適當的隔絕效果。他們也會測試您的暖氣、冷卻與照明系統以找出它們的缺點。與其他公司不同的是，節能戰士將準備一份詳細的缺失報告，並提出改善建議。

## 3. 選擇您的升級方案
我們的顧問將以您的預算為考量，為您的住家討論出推薦的升級方案。我們將協助您選擇並安裝所有設備，從窗戶的雙層玻璃到屋頂的太陽能面板。

## 4. 安裝服務
我們的團隊會配合您的行程來安裝所有的升級配備。但大多數的安裝工作都需要花上數天才能完工。您會看到帳單上立即省下的錢，而且最棒的是這些錢會一直省下去。接下來幾年您可以不斷地省錢。若您在第一年間對升級的設備有任何使用上的問題，節能戰士都將免費為您維修。

---

**169**

這個手冊的目的是什麼？

(A) 公告一項新能源
(B) 比較兩家能源公司
(C) 宣傳公司服務
(D) 討論隔熱的好處

字彙
advertise 為……打廣告
benefit 好處

What is the purpose of the brochure?

(A) To announce a new type of energy
(B) To compare two energy companies
(C) To advertise a company's services*
(D) To discuss the benefits of insulation

第一段中提到面對高額的水電費用，節能戰士已有解決辦法（With Energy Savers, you can find the energy solutions that will save you money.），後方接著說明節能戰士所提供的免費諮詢服務，以吸引顧客，因此 (C) 為最適當的答案。本文在開頭使用自問自答的方式，呈現廣告業者解決問題、招攬生意的性質，這類文章十分常見。

---

**170**

在居家諮詢服務中，下列何者不會被檢測？

(A) 住家使用的時數
(B) 住家主人偏好的室溫
(C) 暖氣設備的效能
(D) 目前每月的水電費用

字彙
occupied 在使用的
efficiency 效能

What is NOT examined during the home consultation?

(A) The number of hours the home is occupied
(B) The home owner's preferred temperatures
(C) The efficiency of heating systems
(D) The current cost of monthly utilities*

解題時，請先找出與 home consultation 有關的段落，對照各選項的內容後，再刪除文章中提及的選項。由第二段的 You will be asked to complete a detailed survey regarding the number of hours you spend at home, your desired temperatures during each season，可以確認 (A) 和 (B) 曾在文章中提及；由第三段的「They will also test your heating, cooling, and lighting systems for weaknesses.」，可以確認 (C) 也出現在文章中，因此本題的答案應為 (D)。

\* 答案改寫：desired → preferred

**171** What does the brochure suggest is one disadvantage of the upgrades?

(A) The upgrades are costly to purchase.

(B) It takes time to install all the features.*

(C) Home owners must be present during the installations.

(D) Monthly bills will not decrease for a year.

閱讀文章時，請特別留意題目關鍵字 disadvantage。文章最後一段「However, most installations take several days to complete.」，表示安裝節能設備必須花上幾天的時間，因此 (B) 為最適當的答案。請注意，考題答案經常會出現在 however 的後方。

手冊中提到升級設備的什麼缺點？

(A) 購買升級設備要花不少錢。

(B) 安裝所有的設備要花一些時間。

(C) 安裝期間，住家主人必須在家。

(D) 有一年的時間，每月帳單都不會減少。

字彙
**disadvantage** 缺點
**decrease** 減少，降低

---

**Questions 172-175 refer to the following article.**

### Newmont Technology Convention to Launch World Tour

March 5 — The Newmont Technology Convention (NTC) is scheduled to make the first stop on its world tour next month. The convention is one of the world's largest technology exhibitions and features everything from medical technology to aerospace engineering demonstrations. [172] The NTC was founded in Sydney, Australia by Newmont Industries and its CEO, Barret Michaels. --[1]--. [173] Every year, over 30,000 people visit the Sydney convention to see some of the most innovative technologies that have not yet reached the market.

The NTC commonly hosts scientists from all over the world, but this is the first year it will become an international traveling exhibition. --[2]--. Mr. Michaels stated in an interview, "We're very excited about this expansion. When we started the convention 10 years ago, we had no idea it would grow to be the biggest technology event in the world. -- [3]--. [174] We're extremely happy to kick off our six-country tour in London, England next month. We're already expecting a huge crowd."

The U.S., Brazil, Japan, Germany, and South Africa will also host the NTC during its tour. Tickets to most of the tour dates are already sold out. --[4]--. [175] "Industry professionals in both Canada and France have already reached out to us with proposals," Mr. Michaels said. "We're optimistic that other countries will make similar proposals."

----------------------------------------------------------------

紐蒙特科技會議展開世界巡迴之旅

3月5日——紐蒙特科技會議（NTC）預定於下個月展開世界巡展的第一站。這個會議是世界最大科技展之一，展出涵蓋了醫療科技到航空工程展示。NTC 由紐蒙特企業及其執行長巴雷特·麥可斯於澳洲雪梨所創辦。每年有超過 30,000 名民眾到訪雪梨會場，參觀尚未上市的最新創新科技。

NTC 通常接待來自世界各地的科學家，而這是它第一年成為國際巡展。麥可斯先生在一場訪問中提到，「我們對擴辦感到非常興奮。當我們在十年前開辦

字彙
**exhibition** 展覽
**aerospace** 航空航太工業的
**found** 創辦，創建
**innovative** 創新的
**commonly** 通常地
**host** 接待（來賓），（作為主人）款待
**state** 陳述
**expansion** 擴展，擴張
**kick off** 開始
**optimistic** 樂觀的

這場會議時，絲毫沒有想到它會成為世界最大的科技盛會。我們真的很開心下個月就要在英國倫敦展開六國之旅。我們已經開始期待大批與會人潮了。」

美國、巴西、日本、德國和南非也將在這趟巡展中。巡展大多數日期的入場券已經銷售一空。如果 NTC 全球巡迴之旅成功的話，麥可斯先生打算在明年的巡展中增加更多展點。「加拿大和法國的專業人士已經向我們提出企劃書了，」麥可斯先生說。「我們很樂觀其他國家也將提出類似的企劃。」

---

有關紐蒙特企業，下列何者為真？

**(A)** 協助成立紐蒙特科技會議。

**(B)** 在英國、巴西和日本都有分公司。

**(C)** 是醫療科技業的主要開發商。

**(D)** 買賣航太工程設備。

字彙
**establish** 成立，建立
**leading** 主要的；尖端的
**equipment** 設備，器具

**172** What is true about Newmont Industries?

(A) It helped establish the Newmont Technology Convention.*
(B) It has offices in England, Brazil, and Japan.
(C) It is the leading developer of medical technology.
(D) It buys and sells aerospace engineering equipment.

閱讀文章時，請特別留意 Newmont Industries。第一段中寫道：「The NTC was founded in Sydney, Australia by Newmont Industries and its CEO, Barret Michaels.」，由此可以得知答案為 (A)。

* 答案改寫：**found → establish**

---

下列何者與雪梨的會議有關？

**(A)** 花了五年的時間才受到歡迎。

**(B)** 僱用超過30,000名員工。

**(C)** 展出還無法購買的科技技術。

**(D)** 是第二個展出地點。

**173** What is stated about the convention in Sydney?

(A) It took five years to become popular.
(B) It employs over 30,000 workers.
(C) It features technologies that cannot be purchased.*
(D) It was the second location for the exhibition.

閱讀時，請特別留意位於雪梨（Sydney）的 NTC 會議。由第一段中「Every year, over 30,000 people visit the Sydney convention to see some of the most innovative technologies that have not yet reached the market.」，可知許多人到訪雪梨會場，參觀尚未上市的最新創新科技，因此 (C) 為最適當的答案。

* 答案改寫：**have not yet reached the market → cannot be purchased**

---

下一場紐蒙特科技會議將於何處舉行？

**(A)** 法國

**(B)** 英國

**(C)** 巴西

**(D)** 日本

**174** Where will the next Newmont Technology Convention be held?

(A) In France
(B) In England*
(C) In Brazil
(D) In Japan

本題的重點在於紐蒙特科技會議「下次舉辦的地點」。由第二段末「We're extremely happy to kick off our six-country tour in London, England next month.」，可以推知該會議下次舉辦的地點在英格蘭，故答案為 (B)。

**175** In which of the positions marked [1], [2], [3], and [4] does the following sentence best belong?

"If the NTC tour is successful, Mr. Michaels plans to add additional locations to next year's tour."

(A) [1]　　　　　　(B) [2]
(C) [3]　　　　　　(D) [4]*

根據文意，題目句應接在與「NTC 全球巡迴之旅」相關的內容後方較為適當。另外，題目句的 additional locations 表示 NTC 明年的巡迴會議可能會新增其他的國家，而 (D) 的後方提到了加拿大和法國也提出申請企劃，文意連接順暢，故為正確答案。

---

**Questions 176-180 refer to the following letter and survey.**

Grand Palace Hotel
Koh Samui, Thailand

Bethanie Sparks
44 Brock Road,
Toronto, ON L1T 4W2

Dear Ms. Sparks,

Thank you for choosing the Grand Palace Hotel as your accommodation from October 12 to October 25. According to our records, [177] you purchased your stay as part of our Vacation in Thailand package, which celebrated our hotel's 50th anniversary. We are conducting a short survey regarding this package. [176] We would appreciate your completion of the enclosed survey and its return in the self-addressed envelope. [179] If you respond by January 2, you will receive a 10% discount on your next trip as our thanks. However, should you send it back after that deadline, we would still like to enter you into a draw for a free night's stay in any of our hotels.

Sincerely,

Rita Lao
Grand Palace Hotel

----------------------------------------------------------

大皇宮酒店
泰國蘇美島

貝戴妮·斯帕克斯
L1T 4W2 安大略省多倫多布洛克路 44 號

親愛的斯帕克斯女士，

感謝您選擇大皇宮酒店作為 10 月 12 日至 10 月 25 日的住宿地點。根據我們的紀錄，您的住宿含在本酒店泰國假期套裝行程中，以慶祝我們 50 周年紀念。我們正在進行該套裝行程的簡短問卷調查。如果您能填寫這份隨信附上的問卷，並以回郵信封寄回，我們將非常感激。如果您於 1 月 2 日前寄回，將可獲得

**字彙**

accommodation 住宿
anniversary 週年紀念
appreciate 感激，感謝
enclosed 隨函附上的
self-addressed 寫明回郵地址的
draw 抽獎；抽籤

ACTUAL TEST **6**

PART **7**

中譯＋解析

下次旅程的九折優惠折扣，作為本酒店的謝禮。但如果您在該截止日期後寄回，我們仍提供您抽獎機會，獎項為免費入住本酒店旗下任何一家飯店。

大皇宮酒店

瑞塔·劉 敬上

---

**Grand Palace Hotel, Thailand**
**By participating in this survey, you can assist us in providing the best possible services to all our guests.**

| **Name:** Bethanie Sparks | [179] **Date:** 28 November |
| --- | --- |

1. May we call you to discuss your answers further?
   • Yes, phone number_____  • NO

2. How would you rate the quality of our facilities and services?
   • Poor   • Fair   • Average   • Good   • Excellent

**Please explain your response:** I found my room to be luxurious and clean. The food in the restaurant was also excellent. However, when I ordered room service, the food was always delivered quite late.

3. How would you rate our amenities?
   • Poor   • Fair   • Average   • Good   • Excellent

**Please explain your response:** [180] I enjoyed the variety of the activities you had to offer. During my stay, I was able to go scuba diving, cave exploring, attend a dance lesson, and even take a tour of the local markets. There were so many exciting things to do!

---

**泰國大皇宮酒店**
**參加問卷活動，您就可以協助我們為所有賓客提供最佳服務**

| 姓名：貝戴妮·斯帕克斯 | 日期：11 月 28 日 |
| --- | --- |

1. 本酒店可否致電您，以進一步針對您的回答進行討論？
   • 可，電話號碼 _____  • 不方便

2. 您對本酒店的設備與服務品質的評價為何？
   • 很差   • 略差   • 普通   • 好   • 很好

請說明您的回答：我覺得我的房間十分舒適也很乾淨。餐廳的食物也很棒。但是當我點客房服務時，食物總是很晚才送到。

3. 您對本酒店的設施評價為何？
   • 很差   • 略差   • 普通   • 好   • 很好

請說明您的回答：我很喜歡貴酒店提供的各種活動。在住宿期間，我可以去潛水，參加洞穴探險，上舞蹈課，甚至還可以遊覽當地市場。有好多刺激的事可做！

**176** Why did Ms. Lao write to Ms. Sparks?

(A) To notify of a late payment
(B) To reschedule a hotel stay
(C) To request some customer feedback*
(D) To respond to a complaint

本題要詢問的是信件（第一篇）的目的。信件中感謝對方（斯帕克斯女士）入住自家的飯店，並請求對方協助填寫顧客意見表（We would appreciate you completing the enclosed survey and returning it in the self-addressed envelope.），根據文意 (C) 為最適當的答案。

* 答案改寫：**survey → feedback**

劉女士為什麼要寫信給斯帕克斯女士？

(A) 通知遲付的款項
(B) 重新安排飯店住宿時間
(C) 要求顧客回饋意見
(D) 回覆投訴

字彙
**notify** 通知
**complaint** 投訴，抱怨

---

**177** What is indicated about the Grand Palace Hotel?

(A) Its head office is located in Thailand.
(B) It plans to build a hotel in Toronto.
(C) It wants to expand its recreational activities.
(D) It launched a promotion to celebrate an anniversary.*

信件（第一篇）的前半部寫道：「. . . you purchased your stay as part of our Vacation in Thailand package, which celebrated our hotel's 50th anniversary」，由此可以確認答案為 (D)。

下列何者與大皇宮酒店有關？

(A) 它的總部位在泰國。
(B) 它打算在多倫多蓋飯店。
(C) 它想要拓展休閒娛樂活動。
(D) 它推出促銷活動以慶祝週年紀念。

字彙
**recreational** 休閒的，娛樂的
**promotion** 促銷（活動）

---

**178** In the letter, the word "conducting" in paragraph 1, line 3, is closest in meaning to

(A) administering*
(B) authorizing
(C) behaving
(D) transferring

單字所在句的文意為「進行，執行」意見調查，根據文意，最適合替換的同義字為 (A)。請特別注意，conduct a survey = administer a survey = carry out a survey

在信件中，第三行的「conducting」與下列哪一個意思最接近？

(A) 執行
(B) 授權
(C) 表現
(D) 轉調

字彙
**administer** 執行；管理
**authorize** 授權
**behave** 表現
**transfer** 轉調，調任

斯帕克斯女士最有可能收到
大皇宮酒店提供的什麼？

**(A)** 折價券
**(B)** 比賽入場許可
**(C)** 進入比賽現場
**(D)** 免費住宿一晚

**179** What will Ms. Sparks most likely receive from the Grand Palace Hotel?

(A) A discount coupon*
(B) Entry into a contest
(C) Free scuba diving lessons
(D) A free night's stay

請從大皇宮酒店（Grand Palace Hotel）所撰寫的信件（第一篇）中，找出與「優惠」有關的部分。當中提到只要在 1 月 2 日之前寄回問卷，就可以獲得下次旅程的九折的優惠（If you respond by January 2, you will receive a 10% discount on your next trip as our thanks.）。查看問卷（第二篇）中的日期為 11 月 28 日後，確定符合優惠的資格，因此答案為 (A)。

斯帕克斯女士提到了有關大皇
宮酒店的什麼？

**(A)** 它的員工沒有幫她解決
問題。
**(B)** 它提供賓客許多各種不同
的活動。
**(C)** 它的食物品質不佳。
**(D)** 它位於大都市的地點很棒。

**180** What does Ms. Sparks mention about the Grand Palace Hotel?

(A) Its staff did not help her solve a problem.
(B) It has a wide range of activities for guests.*
(C) Its food was of poor quality.
(D) It has a great location in a large city.

請把重點放在斯帕克斯女士所填寫的大皇宮酒店問卷（第二篇）。她在最後的回覆中寫道：「I enjoyed the variety of the activities you had to offer.」，表示她享受於酒店的各式活動，因此答案為 (B)。

\* 答案改寫：the variety of → a wide range of

字彙
**a wide range of**
許多各種不同的

Questions 181-185 refer to the following notice and form.

**To:** Employees of Tombes Financial Monthly
**From:** Tombes Publications Acquisition Board
**Re:** Tombes-Parker Business and Finance
**Date:** 6 March

As you have been made aware, *Tombes Financial Monthly* plans to officially merge with *Parker Business Magazine* on April 27. [181] This merger will be an exciting opportunity for both companies. [182] *Parker Business Magazine* is one of the top three business publications and specializes in reporting on international business issues and trends. This merger will allow us to create the first-ever business and finance magazine, which we're sure will boost our publication to the number 1 spot. In addition, with our larger staff, we'll now be able to put out biweekly editions and generate more sales.

[183] Department managers will meet during the week of April 2 to work out some of the details of the merger as well as the renovation of our brand-new office space downtown. [184] If you have any concerns you'd like to raise during the meetings, please send an e-mail to the relevant department manager in advance.

Tombes Publications Acquisitions Board

---

收件者:《圖姆斯金融月刊》全體員工
寄件者:圖姆斯出版收購委員會
回覆:圖姆斯——派克商業與金融
日期:3月6日

正如各位已經知道的,《圖姆斯金融月刊》計劃於4月27日正式與《派克商業雜誌》合併。這個合併案對兩家公司來說,都是很棒的機會。《派克商業雜誌》是前三大商業刊物之一,專門報導國際商業議題與趨勢。這次的合併將讓我們創造出史上第一本的商業與金融雜誌,相信絕對可以將我們的雜誌推向第一名的位置。此外,有了更大型的編制,我們就可以推出雙週刊號,創造出更高的銷售量。

部門主管將於4月2日那週會面,以處理合併及市中心全新辦公室翻修的部分細節。如果各位有任何想在會議中提出的疑問,請提早以電子郵件寄給相關部門主管。

圖姆斯出版收購委員會

**字彙**
financial 金融的,財務的
publication 出版物,刊物
acquisition 收購
board 委員會,董事會
merge 使(公司等)合併
merger 合併(案)
opportunity 機會
specialize in 專攻,專營
trend 趨勢
issue 議題,問題
boost 提高,推動
biweekly 每兩週一次的,每週二次的
edition 版,版本
raise 提出
relevant 相關的,有關的

| Department | Date / Time | Department Managers |
|---|---|---|
| Editorial | Monday, April 2<br>9:00 A.M. – 1:00 P.M. | Joanne Steele, Editorial Director<br>(*Tombes Financial Monthly*) /<br>Tommy Renaldo, Editor-in-Chief<br>(*Parker Business Magazine*) |
| Design | Tuesday, April 3<br>10:00 A.M. – 2:00 P.M. | [184] Samuel Westford, Lead Designer<br>(*Tombes Financial Monthly*) /<br>Wendy Skeller, Head of Design<br>(*Parker Business Magazine*) |
| Administrative | Wednesday, April 4<br>11:00 A.M. – 4:00 P.M. | Annabelle Cordel, Office Manager<br>(*Tombes Financial Monthly*) /<br>Steven Parinon, Office Manager<br>(*Parker Business Magazine*) |
| Public Relations | Thursday, April 5<br>9:30 A.M. – 12:00 P.M. | Laini Peterson, Lead Advertiser<br>(*Tombes Financial Monthly*) /<br>Sandy Baxter, Head of Advertising<br>(*Parker Business Magazine*) |

★ All meetings will take place at *Tombes Financial Monthly* in the relevant department.

★ Steven Parinon will retire prior to the merger. Annabelle Cordel has been selected to run the new office following the merger. [184, 185] All department managers are expected to attend the meeting on April 4, which will be in conference room A to accommodate the number of attendees.

---

| 部門 | 日期／時間 | 部門主管 |
|---|---|---|
| 編輯部 | 4 月 2 日星期一<br>上午 9:00 —下午 1:00 | 編輯部主任 瓊安・絲蒂爾<br>（《圖姆斯金融月刊》）／<br>總編輯 湯米・雷納多<br>（《派克商業雜誌》） |
| 設計部 | 4 月 3 日星期二<br>上午 10:00 —下午 2:00 | 首席設計師 山謬・韋斯特福德<br>（《圖姆斯金融月刊》）／<br>設計主管溫蒂・史凱勒<br>（《派克商業雜誌》） |
| 行政部 | 4 月 4 日星期三<br>上午 11:00 —下午 4:00 | 部門主管 安娜貝爾・科代爾<br>（《圖姆斯金融月刊》）／<br>部門主管 史蒂芬・貝里昂<br>（《派克商業雜誌》） |
| 公關部 | 4 月 5 日星期四<br>上午 9:30 —中午 12:00 | 首席廣告企劃 拉伊尼・彼得森<br>（《圖姆斯金融月刊》）／<br>廣告部主管 珊蒂・巴克斯特<br>（《派克商業雜誌》） |

★ 所有會議均於《圖姆斯金融月刊》相關部門舉行。

★ 史蒂芬·貝里昂將於合併前退休。安娜貝爾·科代爾已經獲選在合併後管理新部門。所有部門主管須出席 4 月 4 日的會議，該會議將於 A 會議室舉行，該會議室可容納所有出席者。

---

**181** What is one purpose of the memo?

(A) To remind of changes to a financial plan
(B) To explain why some employees were let go
(C) To announce the retirement of an office manager
(D) To note the benefits of an upcoming merger*

備忘錄第一段中告知了合併的計畫，並表示該合併案是有利於兩個公司的機會（This merger will be an exciting opportunity for both companies.），後方繼續詳細說明合併將帶來的益處，因此 (D) 為最適當的答案。

這個備忘錄的其中一個目的是什麼？

(A) 提醒一項財務計畫的變更
(B) 說明為什麼解僱部分員工
(C) 公告一位部門主管的退休
(D) 論及即將進行的合併案益處

字彙
retirement 退休
note 論及，提到

---

**182** According to the memo, what is *Parker Business Magazine*'s area of expertise?

(A) Local finance
(B) Company mergers
(C) Government policies
(D) International business*

備忘錄第一段中寫道：「Parker Business Magazine is one of the top three business publications and specializes in reporting on international business issues and trends.」，由此可以確認答案為 (D)。

根據備忘錄，《派克商業雜誌》專長的領域是什麼？

(A) 當地金融
(B) 公司合併
(C) 政府政策
(D) 國際商務

---

**183** What is suggested about the employees of Tombes-Parker Business and Finance?

(A) They have been asked to retire early.
(B) They will be able to apply for management positions.
(C) They will relocate to a new office building.*
(D) They all need to attend the meeting on April 6.

由備忘錄（第一篇）的第二段「Department managers will meet during the week of April 2 to work out some of the details of the merger as well as the renovation of our brand-new office space downtown.」，知道該出版公司將翻修全新的辦公空間，因此 (C) 為最適當的答案。

下列何者與圖姆斯派克商業與金融的員工有關？

(A) 他們被要求提早退休。
(B) 他們可以申請管理職。
(C) 他們將搬到新辦公大樓。
(D) 他們全都需要參加4月6日的會議。

字彙
management 管理
relocate 搬遷，遷移

下列何者與韋斯特福德先生
有關？

(A) 他計劃接管部門主管一職。
(B) 他將在會議中討論電子郵
件寄來的問題。
(C) 他安排了兩家雜誌的合
併案。
(D) 他為新公司總部挑選地點。

**184** What is indicated about Mr. Westford?

(A) He plans to take over the position of office manager.
(B) He will discuss some e-mailed questions at his meeting.*
(C) He organized the merger between the two magazines.
(D) He chose the location for the new company headquarters.

關鍵人名韋斯特福德先生（Mr. Westford）出現在會議日程表格（第二篇）當中，由 Samuel Westford, Lead Designer 可以得知他是首席設計師，且會參與高層會議（All department managers are expected to attend the meeting on April 4 . . .）。若要從選項中找出相關的內容，請一併參考備忘錄（第一篇）的部分。第二段中提及，如果有任何想在會議中提出的疑問，請提早以電子郵件寄給相關部門主管（If you have any concerns you'd like to raise during the meetings, please send an e-mail to the relevant department manager in advance.）。綜合上述兩者的內容，可知韋斯特福德先生作為部門主管會收到電郵寄來的問題，並在會議中討論，故答案應為 (B)。

---

4月4日的會議將發生什麼事？

(A) 將有更多的參加者出席。
(B) 貝里昂先生不會出席討論。
(C)《派克商業雜誌》的執行
長將發表演說。
(D) 員工會被告知新工作職務。

**185** What will happen at a meeting on April 4?

(A) A greater number of participants will be present.*
(B) Mr. Parinon will be absent from the discussion.
(C) The CEO of *Parker Business Magazine* will give a presentation.
(D) Employees will be informed of their new job assignments.

請從會議日程表（第二篇）中，找出與 April 4 有關的部分，得知當天為行政會議。由最後一段「All department managers are expected to attend the meeting on April 4, which will be in conference room A to accommodate the number of attendees.」，表示每個部門的經理都會出席，會議將安排在可以容納所有出席者的會議室，因此 (A) 為最適當的答案。

Questions 186-190 refer to the following announcement, instructions, and e-mail.

## Individuals Needed for Mini Focus Groups

Dressler Marketing, the biggest market research company in Edmonton, is recruiting people between the ages of 21 and 70 for a study focused on travel. The event will take place in the conference center of the Sanderson Hotel, 48 Emery Avenue, during the second week of June. The study begins by viewing a series of short travel-related videos followed by small group discussions that are facilitated by our moderators. The entire session will last three hours and [186 (A)] compensation will be provided for all who participate. Anyone interested can phone Dressler at 409-5321-8082. Be sure to mention study 73. [186 (B)] To determine if a caller is eligible to take part in this study, he or she will be asked to remain on the line and respond to a few screening questions.

------------------------------------------------------

迷你焦點團體誠徵人員

艾德蒙頓最大的市場研究公司，杜斯勒行銷公司正在招募 21 歲至 70 歲的民眾參加一場以旅遊為主題的研究。這個活動將於 6 月第二個禮拜，在艾麥里大道 48 號的桑德森飯店會議中心舉行。這個研究將以觀賞一連串旅遊相關短片開始，接著由我們的主持人協助進行小組討論。整場會議將持續三個小時。將提供所有參與者津貼。有興趣者，可致電杜斯勒行銷公司 409-5321-8082。請務必聲明是 73 號研究。為確定來電者是否符合參與本研究的資格，請勿掛斷電話，並回答一些篩選問題。

---

Roland,

Dressler Marketing really appreciates you taking time out from your busy work schedule to assist with our market research project for Pacific Adventures at the Sanderson Hotel. [188] You will be facilitating four mini focus groups composed of five people each. Since the focus is travelling along Canada's west coast, [186 (C)] our client insists that we locate individuals with extensive travel experience, either for business or leisure, in that region.

Schedule of Sessions from 3:00 to 6:00 P.M.
Age Range/Date
21-35 Tuesday, June 9
36-45 Wednesday, June 10
46-60 Thursday, June 11
61-70 Friday, June 12

Upon arrival, participants will be given yellow name tags. Make sure their name tags are clearly visible at all times during the study, especially when making the video recordings of the members' discussions. [189] This will allow Dressler to refer to individuals by their names when submitting our findings and recommendations to Pacific Adventures.

**字彙**
**center on**
以……為中心，圍繞著
**aspect** 面向，方面，層面

Each of the four video clips centers on a different aspect of Pacific Adventures:

Video Clip 1: Group Discussion of Whale-watching tours
Video Clip 2: One-Day Kayaking Adventures
[190] Video Clip 3: Popular Mountain Resorts
Video Clip 4: Hiking Adventures in Whistler Mountain

Nina Hernandez

------------------------------------------------------------

樂藍，

杜斯勒行銷公司真的很感謝您從忙碌的工作中，撥冗協助本公司於桑德森飯店為太平洋探險公司所進行的市場研究專案。您將協助四組迷你焦點團體的討論，每組會由五人所組成。由於這次主題是漫遊加拿大西海岸，我們的客戶堅持要求我們將對象設定於該地區中，具豐富旅遊經驗（不限於商旅或休閒為目的）的人選。

會議預定自下午 3:00 至 6:00

**年齡組／日期**
21-35，6 月 9 日星期二
36-45，6 月 10 日星期三
46-60，6 月 11 日星期四
61-70，6 月 12 日星期五

一抵達會場，參與者將發給黃色名牌。請確保研究進行期間，特別是在錄影成員們討論的影片時，名牌上的名字清晰可辨。這樣我們把研究結果與建議交給太平洋探險公司時，可方便杜斯勒公司以姓名來提及這些參與研究的人員。

以下這四部影片，每一部關注在太平洋探險公司不同的旅遊主題面向。
影片一：賞鯨之旅小組討論
影片二：單日獨木舟之旅
影片三：受歡迎的山區度假中心
影片四：惠斯勒山峰的健行之旅

妮娜・赫南德茲

字彙

notify 通知
specific 特定的
indicate 指出，顯示
represent 展現
overview 概述，概觀
ensure 確保，保證
lengthy 長的，長時間的

**To:** rothschild@pacificadventures.ca
**From:** nhernandez@dressler.ca
**Date:** 28 June
**Subject:** Study 73
**Attachment:** Study 73 findings

Dear Mr. Rothschild

I am contacting to notify you that the research you requested last month for a specific target market has been completed. As the attached report indicates, one theme was the favorite of all focus groups. [190] This theme represents an overview of the most popular places for travelers to stay. To ensure that we have covered all the key aspects in our findings, we would like to view the video with you and your representatives and have a lengthy discussion on it. Please inform us of a convenient time and date to meet.

Best regards,

Nina Hernandez
Head of Client Services, Dressler Marketing

-------------------------------------------------------------------

收件者：rothschild@pactificadverntures.ca
寄件者：nhernandez@dressler.ca
日期：6 月 28 日
主旨：73 號研究
附件：73 號研究結果

親愛的羅斯柴爾德先生，

我要通知您，您上個月要求針對特定目標市場的研究已經完成了。如附件報告指出，其中一個主題獲得所有焦點團體的喜愛。這個主題概述了旅行者最喜歡的住宿地點。為了確定我們的研究結果涵蓋了所有的重要項目，我們想與您以及貴公司代表一同觀看影片，並進行長談。請告知我們方便碰面的日期與時間。

杜勒斯行銷公司 客戶服務部主管
妮娜・赫南德茲 敬上

下列何者與迷你焦點團體參與者無關？

(A) 他們會收到付款。
(B) 他們在來電時需要回答一些問題。
(C) 他們必須是有經驗的旅行者。
(D) 他們是飯店員工。

字彙
payment 款項，付款
experienced 有經驗的

**186** What is NOT suggested about the participants of the mini focus groups?

(A) They will receive a payment.
(B) They need to answer questions when they call.
(C) They must be experienced travelers.
(D) They are hotel employees.*

閱讀文章時，請特別留意「參加迷你焦點團體的資格」。由公告（第一篇）後半部的 compensation will be provided for all who participate，以及「To determine if a caller is eligible to take part in this study, he or she will be asked to remain on the line and respond to a few screening questions.」，可以確認 (A) 和 (B) 曾在文中提及；由説明（第二篇）第一段的「our client insists that we locate individuals with extensive travel experience, either for business or leisure, in that region」，可以確認 (C)，因此本題的答案應為 (D)。

在說明中，第一段、第四行的「locate」與下列哪一個意思最接近？

(A) 評論
(B) 相信
(C) 找到
(D) 確認

字彙
remark 評論

**187** In the Instructions, paragraph 1, line 4, the word "locate" is the closest in meaning to

(A) remark
(B) believe
(C) find*
(D) check

請先找出單字所在的句子，掌握句子的重點後，再選出意思相似、最適合替換的單字。根據文意，本句應為太平洋探險公司希望參與研究者是經常旅行的人，也就是「找到」符合這項條件的人選，因此 (C) 為最適當的答案。

下列何者與73號研究有關？

(A) 將於杜勒斯總部舉行。
(B) 包含四個相同規模人數的小組。
(C) 只著重水上休閒活動。
(D) 將於兩天內完成。

字彙
solely 只，僅

**188** What is indicated about study 73?

(A) It will be held at Dressler's headquarters.
(B) It includes four groups of the same size.*
(C) It centers solely on water leisure.
(D) It will be completed in two days.

寄送給主持人的説明（第二篇）中，赫南德茲女士寫道：「You will be facilitating four mini focus groups composed of five people each.」，表示四組焦點團體人數都是五名成員，由此可以得知答案應為 (B)。

**189** According to the instructions, why were the participants provided with name tags?

(A) So that the marketing company can identify them easily.*
(B) So that each registration number matches with the correct name.
(C) So that they would be able to find their seats quickly.
(D) So that they would be permitted to enter the conference center.

閱讀相關說明（第二篇）時，請特別留意 name tags。第三段中杜斯勒行銷公司要求參加者配戴名牌時，名牌上的名字要清晰可辨，並說當他們把研究結果與建議交給太平洋探險公司時，才能用姓名來提及這些參與研究的人員（This will allow Dressler to refer to individuals by their names when submitting our findings and recommendations to Pacific Adventures.），因此「方便辨識出每一位參加者」是正確答案，因此 (A) 正確。

根據說明，參與者為什麼會配發名牌？

(A) 這樣行銷公司才能輕易地辨認參與者。
(B) 這樣每個登記號碼才能搭配正確的名字。
(C) 這樣他們才能快速找到自己的座位。
(D) 這樣他們才得以進入會議中心。

字彙
**identify** 辨認，識別
**registration** 登記
**permit** 允許，許可

---

**190** Based on the results of the study, what video clip was the most popular?

(A) Video Clip 1
(B) Video Clip 2
(C) Video Clip 3*
(D) Video Clip 4

本題必須綜合分析報告成果的電郵（第三篇）和針對影片的說明（第二篇）後，才能順利解題。第三篇中提到每個小組都很喜歡的一項主題，並說明：「This theme represents an overview of the most popular places for travelers to stay.」。請特別留意當中的 popular places for travelers to stay，並從第二篇錄影短片中找到「受歡迎的山區度假中心」，可以發現答案應為 (C)。

根據研究結果，那一個影片最受歡迎？

(A) 影片一
(B) 影片二
(C) 影片三
(D) 影片四

字彙
exhibition 展覽
brief 簡短的
description 敘述，說明
material 素材，物質
sculpture 雕刻品，雕像
scrap 廢鐵，廢物
transform
使徹底改觀，使大變樣
breathtaking 美得驚人的
athlete 運動員
remarkable
非凡的，引人注目的
Mediterranean 地中海的
mesmerize 迷住，迷惑
trace 追溯

Questions 191-195 refer to the following schedule and two e-mails.

## St. John Art Gallery
## Upcoming Exhibitions

| Dates | Title of Exhibition | Brief Description |
|---|---|---|
| 11 April – 20 August | Recycled Materials as Sculptures | People usually see recycled materials as mere scrap piles. However, as this exhibition featuring the works of 10 artists throughout [191] South America shows, any material can be transformed into breathtaking sculptures. |
| 28 April – 3 October | The Portraits of Athletes | This watercolor collection features beautiful paintings of professional athletes by [191] artists from every corner of the globe. |
| 5 June – 29 November | More than Just Trees | This remarkable collection of photographs and paintings by artists throughout [191] Africa and several Mediterranean nations captures the mesmerizing power of forests. |
| [193] 11 June – 14 July | The History of Food in Art | Through video recordings, sculptures, photographs, and paintings, this unique exhibition traces the history of food in Europe from the 15th to the 19th century. |

Tickets can be purchased through our website or by sending an e-mail to banderson@stjohnartgallery.org. To learn about our wonderful membership plans, simply go to our website and click on "Become a St. John Art Gallery Member!" [192] Members receive two free tickets to the exhibition of their choice.

--------------------------------------------------------------------

## 聖約翰美術館
## 即將展出的展覽

| 日期 | 展覽名稱 | 簡介 |
|---|---|---|
| 4 月 11 日— 8 月 20 日 | 回收物也可以是雕刻品 | 人們通常把回收物看成是破銅爛鐵。然而，正如這 10 位南美洲各地藝術家作品的展覽所呈現的，任何素材都可以改造成美得令人屏息的雕刻品。 |
| 4 月 28 日— 10 月 3 日 | 運動員百相 | 這場水彩畫展示了來自世界各地藝術家的作品，其畫作展現了專業運動員美麗的肖像。 |

| 6月5日—11月29日 | 不只是樹 | 這場來自非洲各地與地中海數國藝術家的非凡攝影與畫作展捕捉了森林迷人的力量。 |
|---|---|---|
| 6月11日—7月14日 | 藝術中的食物史 | 透過影像記錄、雕塑、攝影與繪畫，這個特別的展覽追溯了 15 世紀至 19 世紀歐洲的食物沿革。 |

購票可至本館網站或寄電子郵件至 banderson@stjohnartgallery.org。欲了解本館精彩的會員專案，只要上本館網站，點選「成為聖約翰美術館會員！」即可。會員可免費獲得兩張自選展覽的入場券。

---

**From:** Chevon Jabar <CJabar@rogerstalent.ca>
**To:** Belinda Anderson <banderson@stjohnartgallery.org>
**Subject:** thank you
**Date:** March 10

[192] I am e-mailing to say thank you for the two free tickets to "The History of Food in Art." I also need another ticket for this event for my division head, Helena Lafleur. I assume the gallery has a record of my credit card details, so please bill the same card and send the tickets to the same address.

I would like to thank your staff for providing such fantastic exhibitions.

Chevon Jabar

-------------------------------------------------------------------

寄件者：謝汶‧賈巴爾 <CJabar@rogerstalent.ca>
收件者：貝琳達‧安德森 <banderson@stjohnartgallery.org>
主旨：感謝您
日期：3 月 10 日

我來信的目的，是要謝謝您那兩張「藝術中的食物史」的免費門票。我還需要一張該展覽的門票給我的部門主管，海蓮娜‧拉弗勒。我想，美術館應該有我的信用卡記錄，因此請將款項刷入同一張信用卡帳上，將票寄到同一地址即可。

感謝您們的人員提供這麼棒的展覽。

謝汶‧賈巴爾

字彙
**patronage** 惠顧，光顧
**circumstance** 情況，形勢
**replacement** 代替

**From:** Belinda Anderson <banderson@stjohnartgallery.org>
**To:** Chevon Jabar <CJabar@rogerstalent.ca>
**Subject:** a cancelled exhibition
**Date:** March 14

Dear Mr. Jabar,

St. John Art Gallery would like to thank you for your patronage during the past seven years. We are truly sorry that the exhibition you and your colleague planned to see was cancelled due to circumstances beyond our control. However, we have already scheduled a replacement exhibition of black and white photographs. [193] It is scheduled to run during the exact same dates (11 June – 14 July) and is called "The Working Classes of Latin America." [195] I have already sent a new program guide in the mail to your office. Please let me know which exhibition you would like to see instead.

Thank you for your understanding in this matter.

Sincerely yours,

Belinda Anderson
St. John Art Gallery

--------------------------------------------------------------

寄件者：貝琳達·安德森 <banderson@stjohnartgallery.org>
收件者：謝汶·賈巴爾 <CJabar@rogerstalent.ca>
主旨：展覽取消
日期：3月14日

親愛的賈巴爾先生，

聖約翰美術館感謝您過去七年來的惠顧。我們深感抱歉，由於不可抗拒因素，您與貴同事打算參觀的展覽已經取消了。然而，本館已經安排了一場黑白攝影展代替展出。預定於相同日期(6月11日—7月14日)舉行，定名為「拉丁美洲的勞工階級」。我已經將新的展覽指南郵寄至貴公司。麻煩再告訴我，您想改看哪場展覽。

感謝您對此事的諒解。

聖約翰美術館
貝琳達·安德森 敬上

**191** According to the website, what do all of the exhibitions have in common?

(A) They showcase works from various nations.*
(B) They showcase paintings from Mediterranean countries.
(C) They include video presentations.
(D) They include sculptures.

聖約翰美術館即將展出的展覽中，有非常多的國家參展（South America, artists from every corner of the globe, Africa and several Mediterranean nations, Europe），因此答案應為 (A)。

根據網頁內容，所有展覽的共同點是什麼？

(A) 它們展出來自各國的作品。
(B) 它們展出來自地中海國家的作品。
(C) 都有影片播出。
(D) 都有雕刻品。

字彙
**common** 共同的，相同的

---

**192** What is indicated about Mr. Jabar?

(A) He donated a collection for an exhibition.
(B) He is currently employed as an art instructor.
(C) He has already seen three of the exhibits.
(D) He is a paid member of the art gallery.*

賈巴爾先生所撰寫的電郵（第二篇）中，第一段寫道：「I am e-mailing to say thank you for the two free tickets to "The History of Food in Art."」，由此可以得知他收到了兩張免費票券。而在展覽行程表（第一篇）的最後部分，提到只要加入會員，就可以獲得免費票券（Members receive two free tickets to the exhibition of their choice.），因此可知賈巴爾先生為會員，故 (D) 為最適當的答案。另外，由第三篇中館方提到感謝賈巴爾先生多年的贊助，亦可以得知他為付費會員。

下列何者和賈巴爾先生有關？

(A) 他捐了一組收藏品供展覽。
(B) 他目前擔任美術指導員。
(C) 他已經看過其中三場展出。
(D) 他是美術館的付費會員。

字彙
**donate** 捐贈
**employ** 僱用
**instructor** 指導員

---

**193** Which exhibition has been canceled?

(A) Recycled Materials as Sculptures
(B) The Portraits of Athletes
(C) More Than Just Trees
(D) The History of Food in Art*

請綜合主辦方美術館的展覽行程表（第一篇）和第二封郵件（第三篇），找到「展覽取消」的相關內容。第三篇中間提到展覽取消後，同樣的時間會改成展出其他展覽（It is scheduled to run during the exact same dates (11 June–14 July)。請再從第一篇中找出此日期對應的展覽名稱，可以得知答案為 (D)。

哪一場展覽已經被取消了？

(A) 回收物也可以是雕刻品
(B) 運動員百相
(C) 不只是樹
(D) 藝術中的食物史

---

**194** In the second e-mail, the word "run" in paragraph 1, line 4, is closest in meaning to

(A) direct
(B) remove
(C) be shown*
(D) be announced

單字所在句的重點應為「預定於相同日期展出展覽」，根據文意，(C) 為最適合用來替換的單字。

在第二封電子郵件中，第一段、第四行的「run」與下列哪一個意思最接近？

(A) 指揮
(B) 移除
(C) 被展示
(D) 被宣告

字彙
**remove** 移除

安德森女士為賈巴爾先生做了什麼？

**(A)** 將款項刷入他的信用卡帳上
**(B)** 郵寄更新後的節目手冊
**(C)** 升級他的會員資格
**(D)** 重新安排一場社交活動

字彙

**reschedule**
重新安排……的時間

字彙

**property** 房產，地產
**branch** 分公司
**construction** 營建，建設
**equipment**
設備，機具，器具
**rental** 租賃，租用
**eager** 熱切的，渴望的
**objective** 目的，目標
**appropriate**
適當的，恰當的
**budget** 預算
**criteria** 標準，準則
**compile** 編成，編製

---

**195** What did Ms. Anderson do for Mr. Jabar?

(A) Bill his credit card
(B) Mail an updated program guide*
(C) Upgrade his membership
(D) Reschedule a social event

由安德森女士所撰寫的郵件（第三篇），她在後半部寫道：「I have already sent a new program guide in the mail to your office.」，表示她已經寄出新的展覽指南，因此答案應為 (B)。

\* 答案改寫：send → mail
new → updated

---

**Questions 196-200 refer to the following e-mails and the attachment.**

**To:** Marcus Lount; Gabriella Sanchez; Daniel Wilkes
**From:** Shelly Dorcas
**Date:** July 16, 9:09 A.M.
**Subject:** business space
**Attachment:** available properties

Hi everyone,

198 I really enjoyed last Friday's lunch with you at the Davisville Grill. I am truly excited about opening our first Miami branch of Ebbet Construction Equipment Rentals. As Miami's housing market grows more and more each day, I am sure that we are all eager to attract our very first customers and start advising companies on the equipment that is most suitable for their projects and objectives.

I appreciate all the input you offered on the most appropriate business space. Using the budget and criteria you suggested, I searched for spaces at www.vanzylerealty.com. I found several possible spaces and compiled them into a list. That document is attached. Please have a look at it and get back to me with any comments you may have.

196 Shelly Dorcas, Ebbet Construction Equipment Rentals

- - - - - - - - - - - - - - - - - - - - - - - - - - - - - - - - - - - - - - - - -

**收件者：** 馬克思・朗恩，加布里埃拉・桑切斯，丹尼爾・威爾克斯
**寄件者：** 莎莉・多卡斯
**日期：** 7 月 16 日上午 9:09
**主旨：** 辦公空間
**附件：** 可用地產

大家好，

我真的很開心上週五和大家在戴維思微爾燒烤共進午餐。我對我們埃貝特營建機具租賃於邁阿密開設的第一家分公司深感興奮。由於邁阿密的住房市場日益成長，我相信我們都摩拳擦掌準備吸引第一批顧客，並開始推薦各公司最適合他們工程與目標的設備。

我很感謝各位對最合宜的辦公地點所投入的心力。利用各位所建議的預算與標準,我在 www.vanzylerealty.com. 上搜尋,找到了幾個可能的地點,並編成一張清單。我已附上該檔案。請大家查看,並提供意見。

埃貝特營建機具租賃
莎莉‧多卡斯

---

### 13990 Gifford Way

Suburban two-story rental facility. Second floor office suites. Parking lot can accommodate up to 100 automobiles. Located across from Devon City's main bus terminal and near a large number of hotels used by business travelers. Half an hour from downtown Miami.

Monthly lease: $975

### 1389 Singleton Highway

[200] Large retail space located in the heart of downtown Miami. Large sign on building makes it high visible to highway motorists. Building includes large storage facilities for parts and equipment. The newly installed air conditioning unit is guaranteed to keep you comfortable during the hot summers.

Monthly lease: $1,150

### 7643 Beckford Avenue

Third-floor retails and office space. Located uptown within Miami's main business district. Located on the same street as two major shopping centers. Facility includes state-of-the-art security alarm system. Printer/scanner/fax/color copier on-site for company use.

Monthly lease: $1,050

### 6094 Wilmot Drive

Single-story building. Comes with small office space. Land contract is also offered for property immediately behind facility. [197] Located on the city's east side in lovely Ryerson Park, a prime Miami development site for condominium towers.

Monthly lease: $825

---

基爾福特路 13990 號

郊區兩層樓出租房產。二樓辦公處室。停車場可容納 100 部汽車之多。位於丹蒙市公車總站對面,鄰近許多出差旅客投宿的商務飯店。距離邁阿密市中心半小時。

月租:975 元

蘇格登公路 1389 號

邁阿密市中心大型零售空間。大樓大型標示對公路上駕駛人而言清楚可識。大樓包括大型存放空間,可放置零件與機具。新安裝的空調設備保證讓您在炎夏中保持舒適。

月租:1150 元

貝克福德大道 7643 號

位於三樓的商業與辦公空間。坐落於邁阿密主要商業區的住宅地段。與兩座大型購物中心位於同一條街。設備包括最先進的保全警報系統。現場提供列表機、

掃描器、傳真機及彩色影印機,供公司行號使用。
月租:1050 元

### 威爾莫特路 6094 號

單層樓建築,附小型辦公空間。土地契約亦立即適用於建築後方的地產。坐落於城市東側,懷德遜公園中,為邁阿密公寓塔樓首要開發位置。
月租:825 元

**To:** Shelly Dorcas; Marcus Lount; Gabriella Sanchez
**From:** Daniel Wilkes
**Date:** July 20, 11:23 A.M.
**Re:** business space

Hi everyone,

Thank you very much, Shelly, for all your work in narrowing our search to the options in the list you provided. I'm certain the strategy meeting held last Friday was quite productive. [198] My apologies for not being there, but I was called to Boston all of a sudden on an urgent business matter. Also, I have to say thank all of you for being patient in waiting for my response to this important e-mail discussion.

Marcus, while I truly appreciate the need to save money on an inexpensive suburban facility, [200] our company should not ignore the significance of having a facility conveniently located downtown as more and more homes are being built in that area.

[199] I am also in agreement with Gabriella's idea that our company needs a booth at Miami's upcoming housing fair. Next week, I will be flying to Miami to visit relatives so I will look into the matter then. Also, while in Miami, I am scheduled to have lunch with a local realtor who worked for our company up until two years ago. Thank you, Shelly, for reminding me that Helen Richardson now resides in Miami. I'm sure she will have useful insights for us.

Daniel Wilkes, Ebbet Construction Equipment Rentals

--------------------------------------------------------------------

**收件者:**莎莉・多卡斯,馬克思・朗恩,加布里埃拉・桑切斯
**寄件者:**丹尼爾・威爾克斯
**日期:**7 月 20 日上午 11:23
**主旨:**回覆:辦公空間

大家好,

莎莉,非常感謝妳將搜尋結果縮小至所提供的清單範圍。我確信上週五所舉行的策略會議相當地有收穫。很抱歉,因為一個緊急的業務問題臨時被叫到波士頓,讓我無法到場。我同時也要謝謝各位,這麼有耐心地等候我回覆這封重要的電郵討論。

馬克思,雖然我也了解在便宜的郊區設置辦公場所,有其省錢的必要,但我們公司也不該忽略在市中心設置辦公室的重要性與便捷,畢竟那個區域的房子愈蓋愈多。

我也同意加布里埃拉的看法。我們公司需要在即將到來的邁阿密住房博覽會擺設攤位。下週我將飛往邁阿密探訪親人，屆時我會了解一下這事。同時，在邁阿密期間，我計劃與一位當地的房地產經紀人共進午餐，他一直在我們公司服務直到兩年前才離開。莎莉，謝謝妳提醒我，海倫·李察遜現在就住在邁阿密。我相信她一定可以為我們提供一些實用的見解。

埃貝特營建機具租賃 丹尼爾·威爾克斯

---

**196** Who most likely is Ms. Dorcas?

(A) A real estate expert
(B) An official in Miami Housing Bureau
(C) A construction equipment specialist*
(D) A cook at Davisville Grill

多卡斯女士為第一封郵件（第一篇）的寄件人，由郵件最後的 Shelly Dorcas, Ebbet Construction Equipment Rentals，可以確認她應為機具公司專業人員，故答案為 (C)。

---

**197** What is one property feature mentioned in the attachment?

(A) An energy-efficient heating system
(B) A newly-installed carpet in the office
(C) A large cafeteria for employees
(D) A location close to housing development*

請從附件（第二篇）中與房地產有關的說明中，找出選項中有提到的內容。最後一間的條件中寫道：「Located on the city's east side in lovely Ryerson Park, a prime Miami development site for condominium towers.」，表示該間房地產離住宅開發區很近，故 (D) 正確。

---

**198** What is suggested about Mr. Wilkes?

(A) He will fly to Miami tomorrow morning.
(B) He is renting some property in Boston.
(C) He did not make it to the Davisville Grill meeting.*
(D) He plans to apply for a managerial position.

請先閱讀威爾克斯先生所撰寫的郵件（第三篇）。當中的第一段提到「上週五」的會議非常有效率，接著則表示因為自己臨時有事，所以無法參加會議，對此感到很抱歉（My apologies for not being there, but I was called to Boston all of a sudden on an urgent business matter.）。請再從第一封郵件（第一篇）中，找出有關上週五的資訊，確認 there 所指的位置。由第一句「I really enjoyed last Friday's lunch with you at the Davisville Grill.」，綜合兩者內容，可知威爾克斯先生沒有出席戴維思微爾燒烤的午餐之約，故答案為 (C)。

下列何者與桑切斯女士有關？

(A) 她用電子郵件向同事提出一個點子。

(B) 她以前住在邁阿密市中心。

(C) 她將與前同事碰面。

(D) 她開設自己的機具租賃公司。

**colleague** 同事

---

威爾克斯先生最有可能中意哪一塊地產？

(A) 基爾福特路13990號

(B) 蘇格登公路1389號

(C) 貝克福德大道7643號

(D) 威爾莫特路6094號

---

**199** What is indicated about Ms. Sanchez?

(A) She suggested an idea to her colleagues by e-mail.*

(B) She used to live in downtown Miami.

(C) She will meet a former colleague.

(D) She started her own equipment rental business.

閱讀文章時，請特別留意與桑切斯女士（Gabriella Sanchez）有關的訊息。在第二封電郵（第三篇）的第三段，威爾克斯先生寫道：「I am also in agreement with Gabriella's idea that our company needs a booth at Miami's upcoming housing fair.」，可知桑切斯女士向威爾克斯先生提出參展的建議，因此 (A) 為最適當的答案。

---

**200** Which property does Mr. Wilkes most likely favor?

(A) 13990 Gifford Way

(B) 1389 Singleton Highway*

(C) 7643 Beckford Avenue

(D) 6094 Wilmot Drive

本題要綜合威爾克斯先生撰寫的郵件（第三篇）和第二篇的各間房地產簡介。他在第三篇的第二段中寫道：「. . . our company should not ignore the significance of having a facility conveniently located downtown as more and more homes are being built in that area.」，由此可知威爾克斯先生「強調鄰近市區的重要性與便利性」。請再從第二篇中找出相關的內容（Large retail space located in the heart of downtown Miami.），可以推測他會選擇位於市中心的房地產，因此答案為 (B)。

答案紙

**ACTUAL TEST 03**

## READING SECTION

| | | | | | | | | | | |
|---|---|---|---|---|---|---|---|---|---|---|
| 101 | Ⓐ Ⓑ Ⓒ Ⓓ | 111 | Ⓐ Ⓑ Ⓒ Ⓓ | 121 | Ⓐ Ⓑ Ⓒ Ⓓ | 131 | Ⓐ Ⓑ Ⓒ Ⓓ | 141 | Ⓐ Ⓑ Ⓒ Ⓓ |
| 102 | Ⓐ Ⓑ Ⓒ Ⓓ | 112 | Ⓐ Ⓑ Ⓒ Ⓓ | 122 | Ⓐ Ⓑ Ⓒ Ⓓ | 132 | Ⓐ Ⓑ Ⓒ Ⓓ | 142 | Ⓐ Ⓑ Ⓒ Ⓓ |
| 103 | Ⓐ Ⓑ Ⓒ Ⓓ | 113 | Ⓐ Ⓑ Ⓒ Ⓓ | 123 | Ⓐ Ⓑ Ⓒ Ⓓ | 133 | Ⓐ Ⓑ Ⓒ Ⓓ | 143 | Ⓐ Ⓑ Ⓒ Ⓓ |
| 104 | Ⓐ Ⓑ Ⓒ Ⓓ | 114 | Ⓐ Ⓑ Ⓒ Ⓓ | 124 | Ⓐ Ⓑ Ⓒ Ⓓ | 134 | Ⓐ Ⓑ Ⓒ Ⓓ | 144 | Ⓐ Ⓑ Ⓒ Ⓓ |
| 105 | Ⓐ Ⓑ Ⓒ Ⓓ | 115 | Ⓐ Ⓑ Ⓒ Ⓓ | 125 | Ⓐ Ⓑ Ⓒ Ⓓ | 135 | Ⓐ Ⓑ Ⓒ Ⓓ | 145 | Ⓐ Ⓑ Ⓒ Ⓓ |
| 106 | Ⓐ Ⓑ Ⓒ Ⓓ | 116 | Ⓐ Ⓑ Ⓒ Ⓓ | 126 | Ⓐ Ⓑ Ⓒ Ⓓ | 136 | Ⓐ Ⓑ Ⓒ Ⓓ | 146 | Ⓐ Ⓑ Ⓒ Ⓓ |
| 107 | Ⓐ Ⓑ Ⓒ Ⓓ | 117 | Ⓐ Ⓑ Ⓒ Ⓓ | 127 | Ⓐ Ⓑ Ⓒ Ⓓ | 137 | Ⓐ Ⓑ Ⓒ Ⓓ | 147 | Ⓐ Ⓑ Ⓒ Ⓓ |
| 108 | Ⓐ Ⓑ Ⓒ Ⓓ | 118 | Ⓐ Ⓑ Ⓒ Ⓓ | 128 | Ⓐ Ⓑ Ⓒ Ⓓ | 138 | Ⓐ Ⓑ Ⓒ Ⓓ | 148 | Ⓐ Ⓑ Ⓒ Ⓓ |
| 109 | Ⓐ Ⓑ Ⓒ Ⓓ | 119 | Ⓐ Ⓑ Ⓒ Ⓓ | 129 | Ⓐ Ⓑ Ⓒ Ⓓ | 139 | Ⓐ Ⓑ Ⓒ Ⓓ | 149 | Ⓐ Ⓑ Ⓒ Ⓓ |
| 110 | Ⓐ Ⓑ Ⓒ Ⓓ | 120 | Ⓐ Ⓑ Ⓒ Ⓓ | 130 | Ⓐ Ⓑ Ⓒ Ⓓ | 140 | Ⓐ Ⓑ Ⓒ Ⓓ | 150 | Ⓐ Ⓑ Ⓒ Ⓓ |
| 151 | Ⓐ Ⓑ Ⓒ Ⓓ | 161 | Ⓐ Ⓑ Ⓒ Ⓓ | 171 | Ⓐ Ⓑ Ⓒ Ⓓ | 181 | Ⓐ Ⓑ Ⓒ Ⓓ | 191 | Ⓐ Ⓑ Ⓒ Ⓓ |
| 152 | Ⓐ Ⓑ Ⓒ Ⓓ | 162 | Ⓐ Ⓑ Ⓒ Ⓓ | 172 | Ⓐ Ⓑ Ⓒ Ⓓ | 182 | Ⓐ Ⓑ Ⓒ Ⓓ | 192 | Ⓐ Ⓑ Ⓒ Ⓓ |
| 153 | Ⓐ Ⓑ Ⓒ Ⓓ | 163 | Ⓐ Ⓑ Ⓒ Ⓓ | 173 | Ⓐ Ⓑ Ⓒ Ⓓ | 183 | Ⓐ Ⓑ Ⓒ Ⓓ | 193 | Ⓐ Ⓑ Ⓒ Ⓓ |
| 154 | Ⓐ Ⓑ Ⓒ Ⓓ | 164 | Ⓐ Ⓑ Ⓒ Ⓓ | 174 | Ⓐ Ⓑ Ⓒ Ⓓ | 184 | Ⓐ Ⓑ Ⓒ Ⓓ | 194 | Ⓐ Ⓑ Ⓒ Ⓓ |
| 155 | Ⓐ Ⓑ Ⓒ Ⓓ | 165 | Ⓐ Ⓑ Ⓒ Ⓓ | 175 | Ⓐ Ⓑ Ⓒ Ⓓ | 185 | Ⓐ Ⓑ Ⓒ Ⓓ | 195 | Ⓐ Ⓑ Ⓒ Ⓓ |
| 156 | Ⓐ Ⓑ Ⓒ Ⓓ | 166 | Ⓐ Ⓑ Ⓒ Ⓓ | 176 | Ⓐ Ⓑ Ⓒ Ⓓ | 186 | Ⓐ Ⓑ Ⓒ Ⓓ | 196 | Ⓐ Ⓑ Ⓒ Ⓓ |
| 157 | Ⓐ Ⓑ Ⓒ Ⓓ | 167 | Ⓐ Ⓑ Ⓒ Ⓓ | 177 | Ⓐ Ⓑ Ⓒ Ⓓ | 187 | Ⓐ Ⓑ Ⓒ Ⓓ | 197 | Ⓐ Ⓑ Ⓒ Ⓓ |
| 158 | Ⓐ Ⓑ Ⓒ Ⓓ | 168 | Ⓐ Ⓑ Ⓒ Ⓓ | 178 | Ⓐ Ⓑ Ⓒ Ⓓ | 188 | Ⓐ Ⓑ Ⓒ Ⓓ | 198 | Ⓐ Ⓑ Ⓒ Ⓓ |
| 159 | Ⓐ Ⓑ Ⓒ Ⓓ | 169 | Ⓐ Ⓑ Ⓒ Ⓓ | 179 | Ⓐ Ⓑ Ⓒ Ⓓ | 189 | Ⓐ Ⓑ Ⓒ Ⓓ | 199 | Ⓐ Ⓑ Ⓒ Ⓓ |
| 160 | Ⓐ Ⓑ Ⓒ Ⓓ | 170 | Ⓐ Ⓑ Ⓒ Ⓓ | 180 | Ⓐ Ⓑ Ⓒ Ⓓ | 190 | Ⓐ Ⓑ Ⓒ Ⓓ | 200 | Ⓐ Ⓑ Ⓒ Ⓓ |

**ACTUAL TEST 04**

## READING SECTION

| | | | | | | | | | | |
|---|---|---|---|---|---|---|---|---|---|---|
| 101 | Ⓐ Ⓑ Ⓒ Ⓓ | 111 | Ⓐ Ⓑ Ⓒ Ⓓ | 121 | Ⓐ Ⓑ Ⓒ Ⓓ | 131 | Ⓐ Ⓑ Ⓒ Ⓓ | 141 | Ⓐ Ⓑ Ⓒ Ⓓ |
| 102 | Ⓐ Ⓑ Ⓒ Ⓓ | 112 | Ⓐ Ⓑ Ⓒ Ⓓ | 122 | Ⓐ Ⓑ Ⓒ Ⓓ | 132 | Ⓐ Ⓑ Ⓒ Ⓓ | 142 | Ⓐ Ⓑ Ⓒ Ⓓ |
| 103 | Ⓐ Ⓑ Ⓒ Ⓓ | 113 | Ⓐ Ⓑ Ⓒ Ⓓ | 123 | Ⓐ Ⓑ Ⓒ Ⓓ | 133 | Ⓐ Ⓑ Ⓒ Ⓓ | 143 | Ⓐ Ⓑ Ⓒ Ⓓ |
| 104 | Ⓐ Ⓑ Ⓒ Ⓓ | 114 | Ⓐ Ⓑ Ⓒ Ⓓ | 124 | Ⓐ Ⓑ Ⓒ Ⓓ | 134 | Ⓐ Ⓑ Ⓒ Ⓓ | 144 | Ⓐ Ⓑ Ⓒ Ⓓ |
| 105 | Ⓐ Ⓑ Ⓒ Ⓓ | 115 | Ⓐ Ⓑ Ⓒ Ⓓ | 125 | Ⓐ Ⓑ Ⓒ Ⓓ | 135 | Ⓐ Ⓑ Ⓒ Ⓓ | 145 | Ⓐ Ⓑ Ⓒ Ⓓ |
| 106 | Ⓐ Ⓑ Ⓒ Ⓓ | 116 | Ⓐ Ⓑ Ⓒ Ⓓ | 126 | Ⓐ Ⓑ Ⓒ Ⓓ | 136 | Ⓐ Ⓑ Ⓒ Ⓓ | 146 | Ⓐ Ⓑ Ⓒ Ⓓ |
| 107 | Ⓐ Ⓑ Ⓒ Ⓓ | 117 | Ⓐ Ⓑ Ⓒ Ⓓ | 127 | Ⓐ Ⓑ Ⓒ Ⓓ | 137 | Ⓐ Ⓑ Ⓒ Ⓓ | 147 | Ⓐ Ⓑ Ⓒ Ⓓ |
| 108 | Ⓐ Ⓑ Ⓒ Ⓓ | 118 | Ⓐ Ⓑ Ⓒ Ⓓ | 128 | Ⓐ Ⓑ Ⓒ Ⓓ | 138 | Ⓐ Ⓑ Ⓒ Ⓓ | 148 | Ⓐ Ⓑ Ⓒ Ⓓ |
| 109 | Ⓐ Ⓑ Ⓒ Ⓓ | 119 | Ⓐ Ⓑ Ⓒ Ⓓ | 129 | Ⓐ Ⓑ Ⓒ Ⓓ | 139 | Ⓐ Ⓑ Ⓒ Ⓓ | 149 | Ⓐ Ⓑ Ⓒ Ⓓ |
| 110 | Ⓐ Ⓑ Ⓒ Ⓓ | 120 | Ⓐ Ⓑ Ⓒ Ⓓ | 130 | Ⓐ Ⓑ Ⓒ Ⓓ | 140 | Ⓐ Ⓑ Ⓒ Ⓓ | 150 | Ⓐ Ⓑ Ⓒ Ⓓ |
| 151 | Ⓐ Ⓑ Ⓒ Ⓓ | 161 | Ⓐ Ⓑ Ⓒ Ⓓ | 171 | Ⓐ Ⓑ Ⓒ Ⓓ | 181 | Ⓐ Ⓑ Ⓒ Ⓓ | 191 | Ⓐ Ⓑ Ⓒ Ⓓ |
| 152 | Ⓐ Ⓑ Ⓒ Ⓓ | 162 | Ⓐ Ⓑ Ⓒ Ⓓ | 172 | Ⓐ Ⓑ Ⓒ Ⓓ | 182 | Ⓐ Ⓑ Ⓒ Ⓓ | 192 | Ⓐ Ⓑ Ⓒ Ⓓ |
| 153 | Ⓐ Ⓑ Ⓒ Ⓓ | 163 | Ⓐ Ⓑ Ⓒ Ⓓ | 173 | Ⓐ Ⓑ Ⓒ Ⓓ | 183 | Ⓐ Ⓑ Ⓒ Ⓓ | 193 | Ⓐ Ⓑ Ⓒ Ⓓ |
| 154 | Ⓐ Ⓑ Ⓒ Ⓓ | 164 | Ⓐ Ⓑ Ⓒ Ⓓ | 174 | Ⓐ Ⓑ Ⓒ Ⓓ | 184 | Ⓐ Ⓑ Ⓒ Ⓓ | 194 | Ⓐ Ⓑ Ⓒ Ⓓ |
| 155 | Ⓐ Ⓑ Ⓒ Ⓓ | 165 | Ⓐ Ⓑ Ⓒ Ⓓ | 175 | Ⓐ Ⓑ Ⓒ Ⓓ | 185 | Ⓐ Ⓑ Ⓒ Ⓓ | 195 | Ⓐ Ⓑ Ⓒ Ⓓ |
| 156 | Ⓐ Ⓑ Ⓒ Ⓓ | 166 | Ⓐ Ⓑ Ⓒ Ⓓ | 176 | Ⓐ Ⓑ Ⓒ Ⓓ | 186 | Ⓐ Ⓑ Ⓒ Ⓓ | 196 | Ⓐ Ⓑ Ⓒ Ⓓ |
| 157 | Ⓐ Ⓑ Ⓒ Ⓓ | 167 | Ⓐ Ⓑ Ⓒ Ⓓ | 177 | Ⓐ Ⓑ Ⓒ Ⓓ | 187 | Ⓐ Ⓑ Ⓒ Ⓓ | 197 | Ⓐ Ⓑ Ⓒ Ⓓ |
| 158 | Ⓐ Ⓑ Ⓒ Ⓓ | 168 | Ⓐ Ⓑ Ⓒ Ⓓ | 178 | Ⓐ Ⓑ Ⓒ Ⓓ | 188 | Ⓐ Ⓑ Ⓒ Ⓓ | 198 | Ⓐ Ⓑ Ⓒ Ⓓ |
| 159 | Ⓐ Ⓑ Ⓒ Ⓓ | 169 | Ⓐ Ⓑ Ⓒ Ⓓ | 179 | Ⓐ Ⓑ Ⓒ Ⓓ | 189 | Ⓐ Ⓑ Ⓒ Ⓓ | 199 | Ⓐ Ⓑ Ⓒ Ⓓ |
| 160 | Ⓐ Ⓑ Ⓒ Ⓓ | 170 | Ⓐ Ⓑ Ⓒ Ⓓ | 180 | Ⓐ Ⓑ Ⓒ Ⓓ | 190 | Ⓐ Ⓑ Ⓒ Ⓓ | 200 | Ⓐ Ⓑ Ⓒ Ⓓ |

答案紙

**ACTUAL TEST 05**

## READING SECTION

| | | | | | | | |
|---|---|---|---|---|---|---|---|
| 101 Ⓐ Ⓑ Ⓒ Ⓓ | 111 Ⓐ Ⓑ Ⓒ Ⓓ | 121 Ⓐ Ⓑ Ⓒ Ⓓ | 131 Ⓐ Ⓑ Ⓒ Ⓓ | 141 Ⓐ Ⓑ Ⓒ Ⓓ | 151 Ⓐ Ⓑ Ⓒ Ⓓ | 161 Ⓐ Ⓑ Ⓒ Ⓓ | 171 Ⓐ Ⓑ Ⓒ Ⓓ | 181 Ⓐ Ⓑ Ⓒ Ⓓ | 191 Ⓐ Ⓑ Ⓒ Ⓓ |
| 102 | 112 | 122 | 132 | 142 | 152 | 162 | 172 | 182 | 192 |
| 103 | 113 | 123 | 133 | 143 | 153 | 163 | 173 | 183 | 193 |
| 104 | 114 | 124 | 134 | 144 | 154 | 164 | 174 | 184 | 194 |
| 105 | 115 | 125 | 135 | 145 | 155 | 165 | 175 | 185 | 195 |
| 106 | 116 | 126 | 136 | 146 | 156 | 166 | 176 | 186 | 196 |
| 107 | 117 | 127 | 137 | 147 | 157 | 167 | 177 | 187 | 197 |
| 108 | 118 | 128 | 138 | 148 | 158 | 168 | 178 | 188 | 198 |
| 109 | 119 | 129 | 139 | 149 | 159 | 169 | 179 | 189 | 199 |
| 110 | 120 | 130 | 140 | 150 | 160 | 170 | 180 | 190 | 200 |

**ACTUAL TEST 06**

## READING SECTION

| | | | | | | | |
|---|---|---|---|---|---|---|---|
| 101 Ⓐ Ⓑ Ⓒ Ⓓ | 111 Ⓐ Ⓑ Ⓒ Ⓓ | 121 Ⓐ Ⓑ Ⓒ Ⓓ | 131 Ⓐ Ⓑ Ⓒ Ⓓ | 141 Ⓐ Ⓑ Ⓒ Ⓓ | 151 Ⓐ Ⓑ Ⓒ Ⓓ | 161 Ⓐ Ⓑ Ⓒ Ⓓ | 171 Ⓐ Ⓑ Ⓒ Ⓓ | 181 Ⓐ Ⓑ Ⓒ Ⓓ | 191 Ⓐ Ⓑ Ⓒ Ⓓ |
| 102 | 112 | 122 | 132 | 142 | 152 | 162 | 172 | 182 | 192 |
| 103 | 113 | 123 | 133 | 143 | 153 | 163 | 173 | 183 | 193 |
| 104 | 114 | 124 | 134 | 144 | 154 | 164 | 174 | 184 | 194 |
| 105 | 115 | 125 | 135 | 145 | 155 | 165 | 175 | 185 | 195 |
| 106 | 116 | 126 | 136 | 146 | 156 | 166 | 176 | 186 | 196 |
| 107 | 117 | 127 | 137 | 147 | 157 | 167 | 177 | 187 | 197 |
| 108 | 118 | 128 | 138 | 148 | 158 | 168 | 178 | 188 | 198 |
| 109 | 119 | 129 | 139 | 149 | 159 | 169 | 179 | 189 | 199 |
| 110 | 120 | 130 | 140 | 150 | 160 | 170 | 180 | 190 | 200 |

# 決勝
# 新制多益

## 閱讀6回模擬試題 解析版

| | |
|---|---|
| 作　者 | Kim dae Kyun |
| 譯　者 | 林育珊／關亭薇 |
| 編　輯 | 林晨禾 |
| 校　對 | 陳妍希 |
| 主　編 | 丁宥暄 |
| 內文排版 | 林書玉 |
| 封面設計 | 林書玉 |
| 製程管理 | 洪巧玲 |
| 發行人 | 黃朝萍 |
| 出 版 者 | 寂天文化事業股份有限公司 |
| 電　話 | +886-(0)2-2365-9739 |
| 傳　真 | +886-(0)2-2365-9835 |
| 網　址 | www.icosmos.com.tw |
| 讀者服務 | onlineservice@icosmos.com.tw |
| 出版日期 | 2024 年 5月 二版一刷（寂天雲隨身聽APP版） |

決勝新制多益：閱讀6回模擬試題
（解析版）/Kim dae Kyun著；蔡裴驊, 關亭
薇,林玉珊 譯.
-- 初版. --
[臺北市]：寂天文化, 2024.05
　　面；　公分
ISBN 978-626-300-253-1 (16K平裝)

1. 多益測驗

805.1895　　　　　　113005642